Praise for Shelly Laurenston and her novels

"No one beats Laurenston when it comes to combining the weirdly wacky with humorous and over-the-top violence."—*RT Book Reviews on The Unleashing,* 4.5 Stars Top Pick

"Laurenston's trademark blend of action, earthy humor, and romance is on full display. Her characters enjoy profane language, screwball comedy, and lusty bedroom antics at every opportunity, while advancing a fast-paced, satisfying, and often deadly serious story."—*Publishers Weekly*

"*The Unleashing* is everything you could wish for in a paranormal romance and more. If you enjoy outrageous scenarios, witty banter, and hilariously over the top characters then look no further than Shelly Laurenston's Call of the Crows series."—SmexyBooks, Best Books of the Year

"Filled with crass yet clever banter, tons of action and romance, and a pit bull with wings . . . fast-paced, funny and profane—and it's surprisingly sweet given the considerable amount of violence in the story."—*BookPage*

"When it comes to combining offbeat humor and mayhem, it is tough to beat Laurenston—or her alter ego G.A. Aiken."—*RT Book Reviews*, 4 Stars

"Laurenston has a gift with words and humor."—*USA Today.com*

"Shelly Laurenston's shifter books are full of oddball characters, strong females with attitude and dialogue that can have you laughing out loud."—*The Philadelphia Inquirer*

Everlasting
Bad Boys

More Dragon Kin novels from G.A. Aiken, who also
writes as Shelly Laurenston

Dragon Actually
About a Dragon
What a Dragon Should Know
Last Dragon Standing
The Dragon Who Loved Me
How to Drive a Dragon Crazy
Light My Fire
Feel the Burn
A Tale of Two Dragons (ebook novella)

More from Cynthia Eden

Playing With Fire
Once Bitten, Twice Burned
Burn For Me

Angel of Darkness
Angel Betrayed
Angel in Chains
Avenging Angel

Everlasting Bad Boys

SHELLY LAURENSTON
CYNTHIA EDEN
NOELLE MACK

KENSINGTON PUBLISHING CORP.
http://www.kensingtonbooks.com

KENSINGTON BOOKS are published by

Kensington Publishing Corp.
119 West 40th Street
New York, NY 10018

All Kensington Titles, Imprints, and Distributed Lines are available at special quantity discounts for bulk purchases for sales promotions, premiums, fund-raising, educational, or institutional use. Special book excerpts or customized printings can also be created to fit specific needs. For details, write or phone the office of the Kensington special sales manager: Kensington Publishing Corp., 119 West 40th Street, New York, NY 10018, attn: Special Sales Department, Phone: 1-800-221-2647.

Kensington and the K logo Reg. U.S. Pat. & TM Off.

ISBN-13: 978-1-4967-0614-0
ISBN-10: 1-4967-0614-5
First Kensington Trade Edition: September 2008
First Kensington Mass Market Edition: September 2017

eISBN-13: 978-0-7582-3583-1
eISBN-10: 0-7582-3583-6

10 9 8 7 6 5 4 3 2 1

Printed in the United States of America

CONTENTS

CAN'T GET ENOUGH

Shelly Laurenston

1

"*You whore!*"

Ailean the Wicked, veteran Battle Dragon of the Dragon Queen's Armies, third-born son of Afton the Hermit, and one of the many from the Cadwaladr Clan, leapt naked and wet from the tub and made a mad dash for the door. Unfortunately, town guards and one blindingly angry father waited for him right outside that door, so he quickly turned and charged hard for the open window.

"Stop him!"

He heard the guards coming into the room, but he didn't waste time looking over his shoulder to see how close they were or bid good-bye to the damsel he'd had his full of the night before. He'd done this enough times in his life to know you never stop and you never look back. Even if you feel their breath on your neck, you never look back.

Several floors up, Ailean dived right through the window, bracing his human body for impact and rolling when he felt the ground beneath him. By the time he pulled himself back to his feet, the soldiers were on the first floor, barreling through the door.

Ailean took off running through the city of Kyffin, an ancient city many leagues away from Dark Plains and Devanallt Mountain, the seat of power for the dragons of Dark Plains. Winding and congested with people, it was easy to disappear in Kyffin.

Unless, of course, you were a completely naked male with dark blue hair. Humans had a tendency to notice that sort of thing.

But he wouldn't be caught. He should have known the woman wanted more from him than a simple tumble for the night. It had happened before. He goes to bed with a woman who promises no commitments and wakes up to a lass whose father wants Ailean dead for "deflowering" his daughter. A daughter the man had planned to sell off to the wealthiest lord looking for a wife.

After all these years there were still some things about humans Ailean would never understand.

And, clearly, they'd never understand him. For Ailean lived life on his own terms. He answered to no one. Not the human lords of this land, nor the dragon lords of his own. He lived as he wanted, fucked who he wanted, and never had a moment of regret about it.

As the years had passed, he'd collected many names. Ailean the Beautiful. Ailean the Killer. Ailean the Bold. Ailean the Wicked, which was still his personal favorite. And, over the last thirty years specifically, Ailean the Whore. Brutal but honest, depending on who you spoke to.

What he didn't plan to take on for a name anytime this millennium was Ailean the Captured by Some Female Who'll Try and Tie Me Down.

No, that name would have to wait for another four or five hundred years. With so many females to taste and enjoy, he had no desire to lock himself in. Why waste all his talents on just one?

Ailean felt the soldiers move closer. He could shift to his true form and destroy them where they stood, but what fun would that be? Besides, he'd kill other humans who happened to be standing around. He had no desire to do that. Not when he enjoyed humans so thoroughly. They had their many flaws, but that was to be expected of any lower creature.

Picking up his pace, Ailean lost the soldiers, at least for a time, when he dashed down a busy street filled with sellers and buyers. He kept moving, charging up a set of steps and inside a building. He immediately recognized it as a school. Perhaps a training ground for sorcerers or those who simply enjoyed learning. He considered himself a "learner," but what he learned he never got out of a simple book. The world taught him all he needed to know.

His dragon hearing picked up the sound of the soldiers heading down the street, so Ailean went up many flights of stairs until he ended in an enormous room filled with books. They were everywhere. On bookshelves, piled on the floor, and on the tables. Students kept their heads down, not even noticing him. Perfect. Nothing had become more tedious than explaining his blue hair. After so many years, simply telling people his poor mother had been cursed while he slept in the womb seemed to quickly end the conversation and had many women going out of their way to prove it didn't matter—which he never minded.

Moving among the stacks, Ailean slid to a stop in the very back, near an exit and another window—in case he needed that as well. Then he caught a scent. It was deliciously familiar. He sniffed the air again. A dragoness. He grinned. Oh . . . he knew that scent quite well.

After more than three decades, he'd never forgotten the owner of that scent. How could he? She'd thrown his own battle ax at his head. Among his kin, that was merely a declaration of never-ending love.

No longer thinking of the soldiers searching for him, he let his nose lead him. The library went deeper than he realized, the scent luring him into near darkness among old, dusty tomes he'd never give up a second of his life reading. When he finally stopped, he stared at the human form sitting on the floor. She had her back against the bookshelf and wore the robes of a human acolyte, the brownish-red tint of the cloth suggesting alchemy as the area of study.

Ailean stared at the top of her head, the hood of the robe slipping off a bit to reveal golden hair.

He'd never expected to see her *living* as human. Fascinated, he crouched down in front of her and stared, waiting for her to lift her head up. He wanted to see her face again.

It took her a bit to pull herself out of her book, but eventually she looked up at him. Ailean took in a sharp breath at the sight of her.

Gods of hellfire . . . she really is gorgeous.

She had a pretty enough face and those always-intense gold eyes. But it was those spots splattered across the bridge of her pug nose and onto her cheeks that fascinated him most. Freckles, the humans called them.

And below that . . . he almost sighed. Those lips. They were ridiculously full and the softest pink. He could spend hours enjoying those lips. *Hours.*

Breaking into a wide grin, knowing he was the last being on the planet she'd ever wanted to see again, Ailean said with glee, "By all the gods of blood and death—if it isn't Shalin the Innocent! Did you miss me?"

Oh, gods. Not him!

Anyone *but* him.

The one dragon she'd give anything to have in her cave, in her bed—anywhere she could get him.

But even now, just having him here in the library put her at risk. Especially with him naked.

Ahh, but what a beautiful naked he was.

No. No. She couldn't think like that. Ever. First off, what exactly would she do with him? She'd had lovers before. Well . . . she'd had two. But two nice, quiet, well-schooled ones. But Ailean the Slag . . . well, he was the stuff fantasies were made of. So very tall and wide, all of it sturdy strength and powerful muscle. Whether as dragon or human, he stood much taller than those around him. Then there was that hair. A silky mass of midnight blue she could easily imagine sliding through her fingers, draping over her body. It was long and luxurious and simply . . . och! She was doing it again.

But how could she not? Especially with those bright silver eyes watching her and that adorable grin on those decadently full lips. Even his nose, which clearly had taken considerable abuse as human, made her think all sorts of distracting, I'll-never-be-an-Elder-if-I-keep-this-up thoughts.

Fool, Shalin!

And she was a fool. The one dragon she could never again go near, the one dragon she could never even think of talking to, was Ailean the Wicked. Also known as Ailean the Whore, Ailean the Slag, and a host of other names, depending on who you talked to.

Why? Why did she have to deny herself the one thing every other dragoness and human female seemed able to enjoy since Ailean had been no more than twenty winters?

Because of that night. That one damn night when he'd become the absolute obsession of Princess Adienna. The dragoness spoke of him constantly. Obsessed over every move she'd heard he'd made. Although she'd never demean herself by tracking him down herself, Adienna still waited for him to return. And every female who had graced his bed before or since—and there had been so very many—became the enemy of this one irrational female.

Adienna said she loved him, but Shalin had a hard time believing love and obsession were the same thing. Would the princess be so "in love" with Ailean if he'd come back to her begging for more time in her bed? If he'd crawled to her on his belly, professing a never-ending love? Or would she have tossed him aside like quite a few others?

But Ailean had done none of those things. He'd run from her bed as though the gods of despair and loathing chased him, and he never came back. In fact, he never came back to Devenallt Mountain again. And every day Shalin prayed to any god who would listen that this would be the day when Adienna would stop talking about him, thinking about him, living for him. But, invariably, at some point, Adienna would find something that would bring her back to that point. Back to Ailean.

Even worse, Adienna blamed Shalin. Especially once

the rumors spread that Ailean had left Adienna's bed specifically to search out Shalin.

Shalin almost snorted. If only *that* were true. But she knew better. That night, when Ailean had found her alone in the royal archives deep in the bowels of Devenallt Mountain, that had been nothing more than pure luck. He'd been looking for a quiet escape from Adienna and Shalin had been looking for much needed time alone.

If Adienna hadn't come looking for him, who knows where things would have led. But the bitch *had* come looking for him. Shalin scented her before Ailean, who'd been quite intent on convincing Shalin to come with him to a human town to find a pub and a meal. "We can spend a bit of time together," he'd said. "Get to know one another."

Looking into those silver eyes, all Shalin had wanted to do was push him to the ground and have her way with him. But that couldn't happen, not with Adienna coming ever closer. Yet Ailean wouldn't listen to her when she tried to explain. He kept cutting Shalin off, trying to convince her he was worth her time. And the more he cut her off, the more frustrated she became.

Her temper was a rarely seen thing. But when she'd heard the flap of Adienna's wings and knew Ailean wouldn't stop talking, proving once again how everyone had a tendency to ignore her, she let a bit of that temper take control and she did the only thing she could think of . . .

She threw his battle ax at him.

In retrospect, perhaps she could have thought of something better. She felt especially bad when it grazed his temple and the blood began to spurt.

Then the rumors took hold.

At first, Adienna paid little attention to them, although her teasing toward Shalin became a little crueler, her venomous tongue a little more pointed. The more time that passed, however, the more Adienna began to turn on her. "*You* are the reason he has not returned," she'd finally accused. "*You* are the reason he stays away from me." Soon the situation had gotten so unstable, Shalin's father met with the Elders and the decision was made to send Shalin out among the humans sooner rather than later. She'd been studying in Kyffin for five years now and not once had she missed the hallowed stone halls of Devenallt Mountain.

Now, nearly thirty winters later, she had the one dragon she could never stop thinking about, dreaming about, or lusting over standing right in front of her—naked.

Of course, he was also the one dragon who could get her killed.

"Ailean," she somehow managed to squeak out. "Good morn to you."

"And to you, Shalin. You look awfully beautiful today."

The fact he could say that and sound like he meant it was probably why so many females fell under his spell. Yet Shalin couldn't be fooled. She had mirrors, did she not?

"Thank you. So why are you—"

"Och!" he cut in as he always did. The dragon rarely took a breath, it seemed. "You won't believe my morning, Shalin. You truly won't. Mind if I sit?"

"Uh—"

"Good. Thanks." He dropped down beside her. All that dragon as naked human male. It took every ounce of her strength not to reach out and touch him. Like that solid thigh brushing against her robe-covered leg, to see how it felt under her human hands. She'd never been with a male as human. She'd heard it could be . . . entertaining.

"So there I am, taking a bath, as she said I could, when suddenly her father comes in."

"Oh, that must have been—"

"Horrible, right. Because she told me that we were alone in that house. But apparently not. I think she wanted me to Claim her or marry her or whatever they call it."

"Even though you're—"

"A dragon, right. She doesn't know that bit, you see. Best to keep her in the dark about that, don't you think?"

"Well—"

"Especially for just a night of entertainment. Why she'd want me as a mate, I have no idea. So what are you reading?"

It took her a moment to realize he'd asked her a question he expected her to answer. *"Alchemic Formulas from the Nolwenn Witches of Alsandair."*

"Is it interesting?"

"A—"

"I don't know how you can read so many books. I get bored after a few pages."

"So," Shalin found the courage to ask, "you've never read the books about yourself?"

Ailean groaned, rested his elbows on his raised knees, and dropped his head in his hands. "Tell me you haven't read those."

Read them? She'd devoured them.

"Well—"

"Because I didn't authorize those to be written."

The books had begun to show up among humans and dragons nearly ten years before. She'd only just finished reading volume three the previous night and word of volume four being available soon had her nearly breathless. Each volume had two editions. One for humans and one for dragons written in the ancient language of their people. A language the humans of this world could never hope to learn with their much weaker minds, ensuring the fact that dragons roamed among them freely remained a well-kept secret.

"The books aren't true, then?"

Based on his wince, she knew they were as true as they could be.

"I never said those things didn't happen. I just said I never authorized them being written about." He turned his head and looked at her, those silver eyes hot on her face. "I don't want you to think I run around telling tales about my relationships, Shalin. I can keep a secret quite well."

And how tempted she was to take him up on his unspoken offer, but that would be cutting her own throat. She'd officially be an enemy of Adienna then, and she simply wouldn't risk her life for any male.

"I—"

"Perhaps I could tempt you away from your interesting book with promise of a delicious meal at one of the nearby taverns?"

Shocked, Shalin gripped the book in her lap tightly. He wanted to take her out? In public?

What should she say? *I'd love to? How about dinner in my room? Forget that, let's go for it right here, right now?*

Instead what she heard herself stuttering was, "I . . . I can't."

"Can't or won't?"

"Both." She shot to her feet, the book still in her hands. "I have to go."

He stood and towered over her as no human could. "Don't go, Shalin. Spend the night with me."

She should be insulted. He'd just left another female's bed and now, still naked and wet from the woman's bath, he'd asked Shalin to warm his bed. But this was Ailean the Whore. He wasn't doing anything out of character. She actually felt kind of proud he'd asked her at all. Although she knew that to be pathetic. And she'd never admit it out loud.

Shalin focused on the book in her hands. "That's very kind of you, but . . . but I . . . I—"

Big fingers lightly gripped her chin and tilted her face up to his.

"Gods, Shalin. You do so tempt me."

She nearly melted at his words. Melted right into a big puddle at his feet.

"Ailean, I—"

Shalin stopped talking when she realized guards stood behind him.

"There you are," one of them said, slapping his hand down on Ailean's shoulder.

Ailean gave a short snort. "And such a good job finding me, since I've been standing here for the last twenty minutes."

With a snarl, the guard motioned to the others and large steel manacles were locked onto Ailean's wrists.

"Don't look so, Shalin." Ailean grinned. "I have every intention of coming back for you."

Shalin opened her mouth to say something, but no words would come out. He'd rendered her completely speechless. But since he really didn't let her get a word in edgewise, this wasn't exactly an incredible feat. Holding the book close to her chest and pulling the hood of her acolyte robe down over her face, she nodded, turned, and fled.

* * *

The city guards handed Ailean the pair of leggings he'd left behind. Ailean pulled them on, the steel manacles on his wrists clanking against the chains as he did so, while the guards asked him questions about his intentions toward the lady. He'd had none except for what they'd done the evening before. But when they demanded to know if he was aware he'd bedded a virgin, Ailean had laughed outright.

At that point, they led him downstairs to the great front doors of the school. As he walked out into the bright morning, he saw Shalin standing on the front steps talking to an aged human male who wore the robes of a master.

Although she nodded and made noises as if she paid attention, Ailean knew Shalin was fully aware of his presence.

"Shalin."

Shalin stopped talking to her teacher and, with a nod, faced Ailean. "Yes?"

He glanced at the guards who grudgingly allowed him to step closer.

"I am sorry."

Shalin frowned. "Sorry? Sorry about—what are you doing?"

"Doing what I've been dying to do since I saw you in the royal archives."

Before she could even think to ask what that might have been, Ailean's manacled hands gripped the front of her robe and yanked her close, forcing her to rise on her toes. She gasped and then his mouth was on hers. Startled, she automatically slammed her fists on his shoulders and, if he were actually human, she might have crushed him where he stood. But with a Battle Dragon it was like hitting a mountain. His head tipped to the side and she felt his tongue slip between her lips and into her mouth. She drew her tongue back but his only followed until it had the poor thing cornered. Then it stroked and stroked and Shalin's human body heated, everything beginning to ache, demanding the dragon finish what he'd just started.

But as she reached for him, Ailean abruptly pulled away. He stared down at her, his eyes wide in shock.

"I never thought . . ." Ailean shook his head, looking confused. Finally, he said, "I promise, Shalin, I will be back for you."

Not sure she understood, she asked, "Back for me?"

"It might be a bit, though." He took several steps back, holding up the chains and manacles that had been clamped to his wrists, only now he held them in his hands. "And, uh . . . sorry. Think of it as retribution for that bloody ax."

Ailean dropped the chains and gave her a wicked smile and wink seconds before he took off running.

Watching him bolt down the street, that big grin on his handsome face and the town guards right behind him, Shalin could do nothing more than laugh. Even as the school masters took her back inside the school to calm her "hysteria" after her brutal "assault," she continued to laugh and laugh as she never had before.

2

"Wake up, brother."

Ailean felt the bed lift when his brother's big foot kicked it. His big, cold, lonely bed.

It had been nearly a full moon since he'd had a female in his bed. The father of the woman whose name he could no longer remember still searched for him, so Ailean had taken up residence in his home. A castle buried in a valley between the Taaffe Mountains of Kerezik. He knew he could find a female—many females—to share his bed, but he didn't want that. He wanted to go back and get Shalin. He knew from that kiss alone the name "Innocent" had been wrongly given. Until things calmed down a bit, however, he'd have to wait to go back to Kyffin. But not much longer. He didn't think he could wait much longer.

"Go away, Arranz," he grumbled, turning his face away to bury it deeper into his pillow.

"You did this," his brother replied in that calm way he had that barely hid a veneer of ruthlessness Ailean appreciated during a time of war. "You need to fix it."

"I did what?"

"Shalin the Innocent."

Realizing his brother wouldn't leave, Ailean rolled to his back but still did not leave his bed. "What about her?"

"You've caused her much trouble, brother. And you have little time left to go and protect her."

"What are you talking about?" No one believed she'd helped him, did they? He would have taken her with him that day if he thought for a second she'd be in any danger. "Are you telling me the city guards are planning to punish her for what happened?"

His brother, a silver dragon nearly three decades his senior, dropped into a chair across from him. "City guards? This has nothing to do with them. It's your princess I speak of."

Cringing at the mere mention of her, Ailean snapped, "That viper is not *my* anything."

"Someone told her you two have been together. You were seen kissing the little gold outside that human school she attends. The princess seems to think you love Shalin."

"Love her?" With a laugh, Ailean shook his head. "I don't know where that fool Adienna got that idea but—"

"She's sold her, brother."

Ailean's grin slowly faded. "I'm . . . I'm sorry. What?"

Violet eyes stared at him. "She's sold her. To old Tinig."

Sitting up, Ailean growled, "The Lightning dragons? She's sold her to the Lightning dragons?" Their greatest enemies and some of the most dangerous warriors.

"Tinig has nineteen sons." Like the humans of that desolate place, dragons the Northlands bred few females. Instead they stole them from wherever they could find them. "Adienna sent word she had a female to sell. He was reluctant when he heard she was no great beauty, but when he found out Shalin could read and write, he doubled his offer, and they settled on a price."

"And you're telling me Shalin is all right with this?" If so, then he needed to speak with her. He wouldn't allow her to leave her people over this ridiculous situation.

But Arranz shook his head. "Shalin does not know, brother. But I have a lover in the court. She told me all this. She's always liked Shalin and thinks this is unfair."

"Of course this is unfair!"

"Then you best get up. The Lightnings are coming for her. I've heard they near Kyffin as we speak."

Ailean tossed off his bedcovers, rage singing through his veins. "How could Adienna do this? Shalin is her friend."

"That beast has no friends. I warned you, brother. I warned you not to involve yourself with her."

"I know. I know. Don't you think I know?" he said, yet again, as he temporarily dragged on leather leggings so he wouldn't walk through his castle naked. The humans always seemed so flustered by that. "It was barely one night. And trust me, it was not up to my usual standards, because I couldn't wait to get out of there."

"You bruised that mighty ego of hers. If you'd crawled back to her on your knees, this wouldn't be a problem. But you ignored her like you do all the rest."

"I don't ignore the rest. I ignore her because she makes my skin crawl."

Together the brothers strode from Ailean's bed-chamber and down the hall. As they made it to the top of the stairs, the second oldest of the brothers rushed up. "There you are. Have you heard?"

"Aye."

Bideven shook his head. "What did you do to that poor dragoness?"

"Nothing."

Bideven had always been the meddlesome worrier of the three, which was why they sometimes called him "Biddy"—which he hated.

"I don't understand all this," Ailean continued. "It was a kiss."

"A kiss in front of everybody in Kyffin, including one of Adienna's spies. Seems she's had Shalin watched for years. She's been sure you two were lovers, but she'd had no proof—until you kissed her."

"And, brother," Bideven added, "you seem to forget that rumors have swirled around you and Shalin since the morning after you lay with the princess."

"Rumors? What rumors?"

Arranz shook his head. "How do you remain so oblivious to all that is around you?"

"Skill."

"The rumor," Bedevin continued, "that you left the princess's bed to track down Shalin."

"I didn't track her down. I stumbled upon her when I was making my escape."

"And that she threw an ax at your head to protect her innocence."

"That's not what happened. Although I must admit, the rumors are much more interesting."

As was their custom since they were young, Ailean grabbed hold of one brother, Bideven, in this instance, while the other deftly turned and opened one of the windows carved into the stone wall.

"Ailean! Don't you—"

Using both hands, Ailean chucked his older brother out the window.

Bideven didn't hit the ground below—for once—and instead shifted midair. "Bastard!" he snarled while hovering outside the window they'd chucked him through.

"You need to learn to be prepared at all times," Ailean stated simply before Arranz closed the window.

"Whatever the truth, Ailean, your princess believes much differently."

The brothers quickly walked down the stairs, heading toward the Great Hall and the courtyard.

"She's not *my* anything, so I wish you'd both stop saying it."

They made it out into the front courtyard. The two suns hung low and bright as the wintertime inched toward them.

"You know if you interfere, Ailean, you risk the wrath of the royals."

Ailean shrugged as he easily stepped out of the way of Bideven's swinging tail. "I don't care. It's like father used to say: it's one thing to fuck up your own life—"

And with a smile the brothers finished the words together, "—but shit all to fuck up another."

Shalin, sitting in a field no more than several hundred paces outside Kyffin with her back comfortably resting against a large tree, studied closely the parchments she'd brought with her. Deciphering ancient text remained one of her top skills and one she was woefully behind on. Lately she'd found herself easily distracted with thoughts of a kiss so blindingly intense, she often couldn't focus for hours.

Now, however, she'd begun to get back into the swing of things. She had no choice. Ailean had not returned for her and that was best. Time with him would only get her killed. So she threw herself into her work, hoping she'd eventually forget all about him.

So completely lost in the moment, she didn't know she wasn't alone until she heard a low voice say, "You read?"

She looked up and saw three males in front of her. They all wore black capes, the hoods pulled over their heads. Shalin's nose twitched. They were dragons in human form. Fully dressed.

Her nose twitched again—but not dragons of Dark Plains.

She forced a smile, trying to remain calm. "Aye."

"That is a skill we value, dragoness." The tallest of the three crouched in front of her. She could now see his face and he was . . . beautiful. She'd always heard the Northland dragons were anything but. They lived in a hard, brutal land and their faces, their bodies, showed that clearly. This dragon bore scars, but nothing that detracted from the natural beauty his body possessed.

But Shalin was no fool. Although the tenuous treaty had been agreed upon at the end of the last war, the North dragons were still considered dangerous enemies of Shalin's people and had been for hundreds of centuries. They had no overall ruling body and instead lived in kin-related fiefdoms. Again, just like the Northland humans. And, like the land they came from, they were a brutal lot. Cruel—many said heartless—and Shalin would concur, based on what she'd read.

"Sweet dragoness, how would you like to come to a land where you'd be appreciated for your intelligence as much as your beauty?"

She had to admit, that sounded wonderful. Although her "beauty" had never been much revered in Dark Plains, education was hard to come by in the Northlands and they searched for females who could help with that. Just being a beauty meant nothing to the North dragons.

"That's very kind, but I don't want to leave my home."

"We waste our time, brother," one of them snarled. "Let us just—"

The dragon's words were cut off when his brother stood and spun so quickly, all the other could do was stumble away.

"We discussed this, brother. It is my rule you follow on this trip."

While the brothers argued, Shalin slowly stood. She knew something was wrong here, she simply didn't yet know what.

But she knew no Northland dragon would be this far south without a reason.

The hairs on the back of her neck began to stand, and Shalin quickly called up spells she could use if necessary.

The brothers seemed to come to some sort of silent agreement, and the one she'd been speaking to all along faced her again.

"Sorry for that, Shalin. My brother knows not when to keep silent."

Shalin gave herself a moment of calm. She felt the bark of the tree against her back. She could hear crows over her head, talking to each other as they did. She smelled the earth beneath her bare human feet and the warm suns over her head.

When she knew her voice was steady, she asked, "How do you know my name?"

Sharp blue eyes watched her closely. "We've come for you, Shalin the Innocent. To take you to your new home." He said it kindly, but Shalin knew if she ran they'd simply drag her back to their lands in chains.

"Let us show you what we can offer someone like you." He took a step closer and she had to lean her head back to look at him. "I'll do all in my power to make sure you never regret coming with us."

Shalin swallowed hard, her gaze trapped by his.

"Brother," one of his kin said with a chastising tone, "you know the rules. We all get a chance to prove ourselves to the dragoness."

"I have not forgotten," he murmured while staring at her mouth. "I forget nothing."

He stepped back from her and held out his hand. "Come, Shalin."

Still staring into his eyes, she realized she had reached for him. Her hand slipping into his firm, dry grasp . . .

And like that, he was gone.

She watched the dragon knocked across the field by a blast of flame so hot it almost singed off the front of her dress.

"Battle Dragons!" one of the brothers warned too late and then they began shifting to their dragon form.

Shalin escaped into the woods, knowing if she didn't move fast, she could easily be crushed before she could shift. She burst through the trees into another clearing. With a thought, she shifted from human to dragon and took to the air. She'd barely gotten off the ground when another set of strong dragon arms wrapped around her from behind, blocking her wings from fully extending.

"Got you!"

She went to spit out a spell until she saw midnight-blue scales on the arms that held her. Shalin looked over her shoulder and started in surprise. "Ailean?"

"I can explain everything."

What kind of greeting is—

Her eyes widened. "This is your fault, isn't it?"

"Why assign blame here?"

"Wait. What?"

"No time for answers, dragoness. We have bigger problems at the moment."

Northland dragons bursting from the clearing and heading straight for them proved him right.

Ailean pushed her away. "Fly, Shalin! Toward Kerezik. Go! *Now!*"

Shalin did as ordered, turning away from Ailean—barely noticing that the dragon had on his battle armor—and heading toward the land of Kerezik. Although what waited for her in Kerezik, she had no idea.

The first blast of lightning hit him dead in the chest, knocking Ailean back a hundred feet. Thank the gods for his battle armor. The breastplate protected him from the power of their attack. At least until they went for his head.

They sent out another blast and Ailean spun to his left. As the purple bastards took in breaths to assault him again, he unleashed a line of flame, hitting the one in the front. The dragon flew back right into the range of Arranz, who hit him with a breath of flame that shoved him into one of his kinsmen. Bideven swooped up from underneath and took aim at the weakest spot on any dragon, the underbelly. While Ailean's armor protected him from that, the Lightning dragons wore no armor. Probably because they'd felt safe coming into Dark Plains territory at the behest of the princess.

Too bad Ailean had never been known for following the dictates of anyone but himself. Hence why his time in active duty in the Dragon Queen's Army had been short-lived. He was too good a fighter for them to take his rank completely, but he was only called to battle when they needed him. Otherwise Ailean had been too much trouble to tolerate among the general rank and file.

The Lightning dragons screamed in agony as Arranz circled around them, his battle sword drawn. "Go, little brother. We'll follow."

"Are you sure?"

"Go!" Arranz ordered before unleashing another blast of flame.

Ailean turned and followed Shalin.

Not far from Kerezik, Shalin waited until the blue dragon passed beneath her. Ailean hadn't told her everything, and waiting until he'd come up with a satisfactory excuse didn't sit well with her. Besides, she was angry and felt the need to take it out on someone.

Eyes narrowing, she dived into Ailean, crash-landing on his back.

"What the—"

"What did you do?" she demanded, grabbing handfuls of his hair and yanking.

"Ow! *Have you lost your mind?*" Ailean bellowed, angering her more for some reason.

"What did you do? I know this is your fault!"

She yanked again, knowing how much Ailean the

Wicked prided himself on his hair. True, it was shinier and more beautiful than most, but that only made Shalin want to rip every hair from his head!

Ailean headed toward the land below them but, tricky bastard dragon that he was, he waited until the last moment before flipping onto his back. Shalin slammed hard into the soft lakeside dirt, the weight and speed they'd been going pushing her until she slammed into ancient trees half-circling the lake.

Yet even after all that, Shalin still refused to release his hair.

Ailean scrambled off her, not wanting to crush her. She was small for a dragoness and he was bigger than many dragons. Add in his armor, and he could easily crush her.

But still . . . *his hair!*

Yet when he went to stand, he realized she still held on to his hair with both claws and kept yanking. Not only did it hurt, but he could feel hair ripping from his head.

Mad cow!

"Release me, Shalin!"

"Not until you tell me what you did! I'll rip every hair from your enormous head if I have to!"

To prove it, she did just that, strands of hair tearing right from his scalp.

Snarling, Ailean slapped at her claws. When that didn't work, he grabbed hold of her wrists and slammed her forearms to the ground, using his weight to pin her into place. Startled, she released him, but he knew she might go for his hair again if he didn't calm her.

"Shalin, stop this. Now!"

"Tell me what you did, Ailean the Whore!" she spat into his face. "Tell me!"

Sitting back on his haunches, he released her, holding up his claws. A placating gesture. Seemed the little innocent had quite a temper. "Just . . . calm down."

"I won't calm down," she promised, scrambling back to her feet and away from him. "Just tell me."

"Someone told Adienna about the kiss I gave you outside the school. She seems to believe you've betrayed her."

The rage went out of her, replaced with confusion.

"I don't understand. What do the North dragons have to do with Adienna? Or with me for that matter?"

"We can talk about this later." He wanted to get her back to his home, where he knew she'd be safe.

"No. You'll tell me now."

Gods, where was the mouse he was used to? The shadow who silently followed Adienna? The female calmly ordering him around was far from the Shalin the Innocent he'd heard about all these years.

"Fine. Adienna sold you to the Lightnings."

"She . . ." Shalin sat back on her haunches and stared at him. "She sold me?"

"Aye. To old Tinig. I've fought him in battle. I took his eye. It just made him look crazier."

Taking in a deep breath, Shalin nodded. "She sold me."

"Shalin—"

Shalin held up a claw to silence him. "And you," she looked directly at him. "You took me from the Northerners."

Ailean nodded solemnly, completely comfortable with his role as hero and rescuer. "I couldn't let this happen to you, now could I?"

Years later he'd admit—he never saw that tail coming.

Covering his jaw where the sharp tip of her tail had slashed him, Ailean glowered. "Is there a reason you did that?"

"You brought war to our people and you stand there looking *smug*?"

"*I* brought war?"

"Yes. You." She shook her head, turning as she did. Ailean took a step back to avoid that tail. He wasn't frightened, but he wasn't stupid, either. "I have to go back," she finally said and looked as if she were seconds from taking flight.

Ailean grabbed hold her arm. "What are you talking about?"

"I have to go back, Ailean. It hasn't been that long." She glanced up at the sky to confirm. "And if your brothers haven't killed them yet, I can fix this."

He knew from her words and her expression what she planned to do. Sacrifice herself for the greater good of her people.

"You'll fix nothing, Shalin."

She tried to walk away from him. "Ailean—"

Ailean yanked her back, harshly, making sure he had her attention. He did.

"You'll. Fix. Nothing."

"Get your claws—"

He gave her a hard shake. "Listen well, Shalin. I've created this, but I'll fix it. But I'll be damned if I let you sacrifice yourself because of that mad bitch."

"She's not mad, Ailean. She's mean. Meaner than you or I."

"I don't care."

"You have to know she won't stop. She won't stop until I'm gone or dead. I think gone is better."

"So you'll . . . run?" The word was foreign on his tongue. Male or female, young or old, his Clan never ran.

"Why not? I'm quite speedy. And I have this odd love of having my neck attached to my body."

With a growl, Ailean turned, dragging her behind him.

"What are you doing?"

"We're going to my home, if I have to drag your pretty ass there myself."

"But won't your family be there?"

Finally, his full anger snapped and he turned on her. "*You think you're not safe with my family?*"

Now Shalin held her claws up in a placating gesture. "That's not what I mean at all."

"Then what do you mean?" he demanded.

He watched her gather her courage before saying, "You'll be putting them at risk, too. Adienna will stop at noth—"

Amazed she seemed more concerned with everyone but herself, Ailean calmly cut in, "If Adienna crosses my family, she'll soon learn how little her royal title means."

"Ailean—"

"We're not discussing this any more. You'll come with me."

Her mind turned. He could see it, see her trying to figure anyway out of this. Her gold eyes furtively glanced around, desperate, but he only had to flash a fang to make it clear how far he'd go.

"Fine," she said with an absurdly tragic sigh. "I'll come with you. But . . . my father. He's *not* safe."

"I've already sent two of my cousins' mates to protect your father."

"Only two?"

"Trust me. These two . . . your father will be fine."

"Knowing my father, he'll want to go to the queen. To see if he can fix this."

"And they'll go with him when he's ready. His own personal guards. No one will get near him."

Shalin sighed again, and Ailean knew he'd won. At least he'd won this particular argument. He sensed other fights wouldn't be so easy.

"I'll go with you."

Ailean forced himself not to grin. He sensed she wouldn't appreciate it and his scalp still stung. "Thank you." With that, he took several steps back from her and extended his wings in preparation to take flight, but stopped a moment, compelled to make something very clear.

"Shalin?"

She'd just unfurled her wings, ready to follow, when she looked up at him.

"There's something you should know."

She merely tilted her head, waiting for him to continue.

"I am sorry this happened, and I'll do what I can to fix it—but I'm not sorry I kissed you." He winked as her eyes widened in surprise. "She'll not make me regret that."

3

Shalin had so many things that annoyed her at the moment, she wasn't sure what topped her list.

Perhaps the dress she had to wear? A brazen dark red that was much too big for her, since it belonged to one of Ailean's cousins. Big enough that she constantly tripped over the hem and couldn't seem to keep both sleeves on her shoulders at the same time. Every time she adjusted one side, the other slid off and every male eye in the house seemed to focus right on her.

Or perhaps the fact she wasn't in a lovely cave. No, she was in a . . . a . . .

Shalin glanced around and barely contained her annoyed growl.

She was in a castle. A bloody castle. What dragon willingly lived in a castle? A nice enough castle, to be sure, but a *castle*. If she shifted and spread her wings here, she'd take out a good portion of the Great Hall.

Or perhaps that, because she was in this castle, she had to remain human—all the time. When they'd first arrived, Ailean had actually shown her to a bedroom . . . with a bed in it! A bed he expected her to sleep on!

Now, true enough, she'd been living among humans for quite some time, but that had been different. A necessity. The sacrifice she'd been willing to make to further her knowledge. But to live this way on purpose irritated her.

And although all those things annoyed Shalin to the point of distraction, she'd begun to realize that what annoyed her most of all, what had her teeth grinding, her hands tightly clenched in her lap so she wouldn't unleash her claws, and kept her gaze focused on the floor to stop herself from showing the growing rage and annoyance in her eyes . . .

What annoyed her—was *them*.

Not just Ailean's brothers. Or an uncle or two. But *all* of them. The entire Cadwaladr Clan from within a league. And, even worse, they never shut up. She'd never heard anything like it. Like a tree full of hungry crows, but with much more rough language and abrupt changes of topic. Now Shalin understood why Ailean cut her off so often . . . they all did it to each other constantly. If one wanted to be heard among this brood, one literally had to scream.

Since Shalin didn't scream, she merely kept her hands in her lap, her head bowed, her eyes on the floor, and her mind as far away from this place as she could imagine. While they all shouted at each other, Shalin flew in the bright bronze skies of Alsaindair. She'd only gone once to the desert lands with her father, but she'd never forgotten. And the desert dragons themselves had fascinated her. The same colors as the dragons of Dark Plains but there was a shiny bronze overlay to their scales she absolutely adored. They'd looked like jewels to her, and she'd been fascinated by their history and language and lifestyles.

So focused on her own thoughts, it wasn't until

someone gently tapped her shoulder that she realized they'd all finally gone silent. Yet she sensed that was only because they were waiting on her to say something. What exactly, Shalin had no idea.

Clearing her throat, she looked up and found them all watching her. Good gods, what exactly had they asked her?

"I'm sorry, I—"

"Now, no need to apologize, lass," one of Ailean's aunts told her while patting her hand. "This isn't your doing, now, is it?"

Before Shalin could respond, the entire room erupted into angry shouts about Adienna, and Shalin lost the thread of conversation yet again.

Frustrated, Shalin pulled her right dress sleeve onto her shoulder. Of course, that only meant the left fell off the other side, hanging low on her arm. Knowing he watched her, Shalin glanced over and, as she suspected, Ailean stared at her from behind several rows of his kin. He smirked and raised an eyebrow. If she could have reached him, she would have slapped his face.

She wished she'd aimed her tail lower. Perhaps cutting his vocal chords would have eased her growing resentment.

Enjoying that vision more than she should, Shalin let her gaze slide back to the floor and back to the images of her flying.

Flying anywhere but here.

"You'll need to leave her be, Ailean."

Surprised, Ailean glanced at his aunt. One of his mother's bloodline. When his mother had died, his Aunt Briaga had done what she could for Ailean and his brothers, when not dealing with her own offspring or in battle.

"What are you talking about?"

"You and the innocent. Stay away from her."

"Why?"

His aunt gave him that look she used to when he'd bang his head into walls to see how long before he could actually break through. "Look at her. Poor, shy little thing."

"Shy? Her?" He watched Shalin for a moment and saw how his aunt could make that mistake. Sitting there with her back straight, the dress she wore slipping off all the best places, but still managing to look innocent and untouched, hands in her lap, eyes downcast. But Ailean was no longer fooled by Shalin the Innocent. "She's not shy."

"Och! Deniela, tell him." One of his father's many sisters, Deniela had two things to her name. Her lethal way with a battle ax and that she was the mother of the Cadwaladr Twins.

"Tell him what?" Deniela asked, chewing on what better be dried cow. Ailean forbid the eating of humans on his territory. He'd already had to clear up a few things for Shalin when she'd casually asked, "Is she dinner?" as one of his servants had walked by with two water buckets from the kitchens. The buckets hit the floor, and water went everywhere.

And then there had been the hysterical screaming . . .

That was when Shalin realized the humans in his territory knew exactly who and, more importantly, *what* he was. That had confused her, which he had to admit, he enjoyed doing. The look on her face was comical and adorable all at the same time.

Briaga leaned across Ailean and said to Deniela, "Tell

him he can't be bothering the little dragoness. Look at her up there."

"Och. I know. Isn't she a sad little thing."

"What are you two looking at?" Because all he could see was the viper who ripped the hairs from his head. And the discovery of some bald spots did nothing but make him want to return the favor to the little royal.

Deniela pinched Ailean's arm lightly and it took all his strength not to scream out in agony. "You stay away from her, Ailean the Blue. Look at her. Poor wee thing."

"Oh, come on! She attacked me, you know?"

"Aye," Briaga agreed. "Threw that ax at you to protect her innocence."

"That is not what happened, and that's not what I'm talking about. Just today she attacked me. Pulled hair from my head."

"Why do you lie to me?" Deniela laughed. "We both know I'm smarter than you. That wee thing would never attack you, so stop making up stories. Don't you feel bad for her?"

"No!"

"Ailean! I expected more from you." She leaned in closer and whispered louder, "Look at her face. That deformity."

"What?" Ailean looked at Shalin. "What are you talking about?"

"Those horrible things on her face."

"Oh, no, no," Briaga explained, incorrectly, "that's just mud. She needs a bath."

"It's neither. It's freckles."

"Then I was right. Deformity."

"And you know," Briaga whispered, "she's probably a virgin. And you, Ailean the *Slag,* are not the dragon for virgins."

"What does *that* mean?" And was Shalin a virgin? Ailean shuddered a bit. He didn't entertain virgins. Much too much responsibility for his liking.

"She must be. How else would she get such a name?"

"Especially living at court," Deniela muttered, pulling more dried beef out of the little carry bag she kept tied to her sword belt. "All the fucking that goes on there."

"So you just keep your claws and your cock to yourself, Ailean the *Whore*," Briaga warned him, "or I'll be pulling your father out of his cave to deal with you and he'll be none too happy."

He definitely wouldn't be happy. For other dragons—a normally unsocial group—to call Ailean's father Afton the Hermit said a lot. Still, it was better than his earlier name. Afton the Murderer. But there had been a reason for that. A very good reason.

"Fine. I'll stay away from her." At least while she was at his home, under his protection, since that could easily be misunderstood. And how hard could it be? Once this had all been straightened out and Shalin went back to her school and Kyffin, he could finish what had been started that night in the royal archives. "But you two hags leave me be."

He covered his head with his arms as soon as he said the words, laughing while both his aunts slammed fists into his head. He didn't appreciate the kidney shot from Deniela, though.

Sneaking away had been a lot easier than Shalin thought it would be. No sneaking really involved; she simply stood up and walked out. So engrossed in their own disturbing conversations, none of the others even noticed her leaving.

Thank the gods.

She really didn't know how much more she could take. Her first thirty winters it had been only her, her father, and mother. Thirty winters of reading, quiet contemplation, and soft-spoken discussion on any topic from politics to religion. Her parents had taught her how to think, how to reason. They'd taught her how to survive without lifting a weapon. Good thing, since she was as hopeless with a weapon as Ailean was with a book. That thrown battle ax being nothing more than a lucky shot.

But the Cadwaladr Clan didn't really have quiet contemplation or soft-spoken discussions. There was nothing soft or quiet about these dragons.

Now, all Shalin wanted was some time to herself. Blissful silence. But would she ever find it?

"Need some help, m'lady?"

Shalin looked at the sturdy woman before her. One of Ailean's servants but, Shalin had quickly noticed, none of them looked downtrodden. She'd never seen servants who seemed happy and comfortable with their lot in life. Simply going about their day without misery.

"Yes . . . uh . . ."

"Madenn, m'lady."

"Shalin. Just Shalin."

"As you wish."

"I know this may be a tall order, but is there anywhere that I can . . . some place I can . . ."

"Get some quiet?"

Shalin almost dropped from gratitude that the woman so immediately understood her. "Yes."

"Just the place." She held one finger up and quickly went into the kitchens—with a clan this large, Shalin wasn't surprised Ailean needed more than one. When Madenn returned, she had a basket of warm scones, a chalice, and a wine-filled pitcher. "This way."

Madenn silently led Shalin down a winding path of hallways. The castle was enormous and Shalin wondered how Ailean could afford it. The Cadwaladr Clan was not born of wealth or title and had no inherited riches the way most of the royals and nobles did. Anything they had, they stole from humans. But Shalin couldn't imagine Ailean attacking some unsuspecting caravan.

"Here you are, luv," Madenn said while she pushed a door open with her foot. She'd gotten comfortable quickly and Shalin didn't mind. "Will this do you?"

Shalin sighed in absolute pleasure as she stepped into the well-lit and dust-covered library. "Aye. Very much."

"Thought it might. Ailean's kin—well, they're not much for reading, are they?"

Grinning, Shalin said, "So they won't be down here, is your point?"

"Luv, I don't think they know the castle has one, much less where this room is. You should be fine here for quite a bit. Especially when they make battle plans. They can do that sort of thing for hours."

Madenn placed the scones and drink on a long wooden table. "I don't have any cooked meat for you yet, but I'm guessing the scones will hold you for a while."

Slowly walking down one row of shelves, looking at each title, Shalin said, "You know what I am. What we all are."

"Aye. I do. We all do."

"But you've never told."

"We never have, we never will. But it's a long story and not one I'm much in the way of telling at the moment. Besides, it's more Ailean's story to tell than my own. I wasn't there, ya see."

Shalin grabbed a book she'd never read and pulled it off the shelf. "I understand."

Madenn walked toward the door, but before she left, she added, "We protect Ailean and his kin as he's protected us and ours. Our loyalty is deeper than any you'll find and well-earned."

Sensing some kind of warning, Shalin turned to look at Madenn, but she'd already walked out the door, silently closing it behind her.

The chant for food started when the suns set. It turned to catcalls and loud screaming until the servants began bringing out the platters of hot food and placing them on the tables.

"Where's Shalin?" Ailean asked Arranz, who only stared at him. Blankly.

"You lost her?"

"We didn't lose her. She's around somewhere. We'll look after we eat." Of course Arranz said that around a mouthful of food.

Afraid she might have gone off to handle all this on her own, Ailean searched the castle for her.

He went to her room first but found it empty. He went down to the small dining hall in the back of his home, thinking she might have gone there in search of food. But he found that empty as well, except for a few of the dogs playing on the floor.

Ailean walked into the kitchen, getting more desperate by the second.

"Something we can help you with, Ailean?" asked Madenn. An older human, she'd worked for him since she'd been a young girl, as had her mother and her mother's mother. He liked Madenn very much. She made him laugh.

"The lady I brought home today? Have you seen her?"

"Last I saw her, she was in the library."

Ailean tilted his head to the side and stared at Madenn. After a long moment's pause, "I have a library?"

Madenn snorted. "Aye, m'Lord," she replied, not bothering to hide her laughter. "With books and everything!"

"Truly?" He grinned now that he knew Shalin was safe and not sacrificing herself for the dragon nation. "I never knew."

"As I'd guessed."

"Fascinating." He started to walk away, then gestured to the door. "Uh . . . can you point me . . ."

With a good-natured shake of her head, Madenn walked with Ailean out to the hall, giving him quick directions. "Once you're in that part of the castle," she finished, "go down the hall, all the way to the end, turn left, and the very last door on the right."

"Thank you."

"Welcome."

Ailean followed Madenn's directions and, as she suggested, he found Shalin in the library. Still wearing that dark red dress and barefoot, she sat on the floor, completely engrossed in a book. She probably had no idea how late the time had grown.

Even more fascinating, she had one of the new batch of black-furred puppies asleep in her lap. When Ailean had taken over this land, he'd begun to breed the animals to create bigger, more battle-ready dogs. They were wonderful pets and companions but could easily tear the limbs off a good-sized man. And had when the situation called for it.

"Shalin?"

"Mhhm?"

He couldn't help but grin. "Shalin?" he called again.

She finally lifted her head. "Yes?"

"It's time for evening meal."

"Evening . . ." She turned her head toward the window. "Oh. It is dark."

"Aye. It is. And I'm starving." He held his hand out for her. "So let's go feed, then."

"No." She waved him away. "I'll be fine until later."

"You will?"

"Aye."

"If you're sure . . ."

"Of course." She ran a hand down the puppy's back while staring at her book. "This little one will tide me over until I—oiy!" she barked when Ailean reached down and grabbed the puppy from her lap. "He's mine!"

"Not if you're planning to eat him."

"What else would I do with him?"

"He's a pet, Shalin. A companion animal. If you wish, you can keep him as such. But if you're planning to eat him—no."

"That's unfair."

"On my territory we don't eat dogs."

"You have the most ridiculous rules. You do know you're not human, yes?"

"I'm well aware of that, Shalin."

The puppy, now awake, yawned and tried to scramble out of Ailean's arms and back to Shalin. When Ailean held him tight, he began to cry and paw at his hands.

"You're hurting him," Shalin accused, quickly getting to her feet.

"You were going to eat him."

"Give him back to me," she ordered as only a royal could.

Ailean moved away from her grasping hands. "Only if you give me your word you'll not eat him."

"Fine. I give you my word."

"Good." Ailean shoved the puppy back at her and Shalin snuggled him close. "He seems to like you. I'd hate for that affection to be betrayed."

"It won't be." She giggled when the puppy licked her face and nipped her nose.

"Then he's my gift to you."

Shalin looked at him in surprise. "A gift? For me?"

"Of course." He reached over and stroked the puppy's head, smiling when the little bastard tried to bite his finger off. "While you're here, I'll show you how to care for him."

"No one but my father and mother has ever given me a gift before." She smiled, and Ailean wondered if he'd ever seen anything so beautiful. "Thank you."

He cleared his throat and stepped back from her, wondering why he had this sudden, almost overwhelming desire to give her everything he owned and fuck her beyond reason. He'd never felt both tenderness and lust at the same time for anyone and he didn't much like those feelings now.

"Let's go in and eat. You can bring the puppy."

With the puppy and the book she'd never released still in her hands, she peered up at him. "I don't spend much time with others, Ailean. I mostly keep to myself."

That surprised him a bit. "But all that time in Devenallt Mountain with Adienna . . . ?"

"I just followed. No one ever expected me to do or say anything." She gave a devious little smirk. "Very few at court find me very interesting. And I've found if I stay unbearably boring long enough, they wander away and stop talking to me altogether. I like when they don't talk to me. Before I went to school in Kyffin, I could sometimes clear a chamber simply by entering it."

Ailean laughed, tugging her forward until her bare feet touched his boot-covered ones. "Tragically for you, I haven't been bored yet. So I know how fascinating you truly are."

"And you'd know that how? You never let me finish a sentence."

His own smile fell at the innocent barb. "Are you saying I talk too much?"

"Well—"

"Because I don't. I don't talk too much."

"All—"

"I have things to say, sure. But it's not like I can't shut up if I have to. Because I can."

"O—"

"And do! When I have to."

Shalin stared up at him once again, her mouth closed.

"Well?" he demanded. "Answer me."

"You're right. You don't talk too—"

"Exactly! Now come on. You can even bring your book if you like and read at the table. This lot will never even notice."

It was like watching wild animals feed with much snarling, growling, and food stealing. But to make it uniquely theirs, there was also much laughing, taunting, and yelling. Shalin said nothing because she really didn't have to. With Ailean on one side of her having either a running argument or an animated conversation with his brothers—she didn't know which—and his infamous twin cousins on the other side, yelling at different family members across the room, Shalin didn't have to say a word. Instead, she devoured her delicious food, hand-fed the puppy comfortably ensconced in her lap and, much to her delight, read her book. That she would have never done at court. Ever. She'd have been forced to keep up some boring patter to entertain whatever noble sat beside her or she would have had to listen to Adienna softly mock everyone in the room.

Truth be told, Shalin hadn't had a meal this lovely since she'd lived with her father. He'd always brought work or books with him to their evening meal of a freshly butchered cow or two. They'd eat, read, and barely speak and were both quite comfortable doing so.

The hour had grown late and she'd devoured half a cow's worth of ribs before she finally lifted her gaze from her book.

"What you reading, then?" one of the twins asked.

"It's a book on the Northland pirates. The ones who come down along the coast and raid the small towns there."

"I heard about them. Oh, I'm Kyna by the way. This is Kennis."

Kennis greeted Shalin with a grunt, since she had a mouthful of food. Shalin had never met the twins before, but like every other dragon in Dark Plains, she'd heard of them, the pair having cut a bloody swath through the enemy during the last battle against the North dragons. They were feared as much by their own people as by their enemies.

"So go on," Kyna insisted, "tell us about the pirates."

Shalin glanced at the book and shrugged. "Well, there was this one story that was kind of interesting about how one of the raids went horribly wrong." Shalin leaned in a bit and proceeded to tell the cousins what she'd read, adding in some additional details about the town and the Northland pirates that she'd read in other books. Since the twins never looked bored the way most others did when she spoke for longer than a minute or two, she kept talking.

"He knew, then," she said.

"Knew what?" Kyna all but demanded.

"He knew he either had to cut her throat or watch his men die."

It was the silence Shalin noticed first. Neither Ailean nor Ailean's kin were ever quiet. Yet for a brief moment she thought that only she and the twins remained. But when she glanced around, she gave a little start of surprise. They were all watching her. If she hadn't known she had Ailean's protection, she'd have feared for her very life, the way they all watched her.

Then, finally, from the back of the room someone snarled, "Well . . . go on, then!"

"Aye," one of his many—*many*—aunts demanded. "Finish the story."

A chorus of "ayes" followed and Shalin briefly debated making a run for it.

"You best finish," Ailean murmured near her ear. "They'll tear this castle down around us until they get what they want. Besides," and the smile he gave her nearly had her melting in her chair, "I'm dying to hear the end as well."

Realizing she really did have their undivided attention and that she didn't much mind, Shalin continued. "But for the captain neither of those options worked for him. But if he was going to save them all, he'd have to move fast . . ."

The dinner ended and his family went off on their own, heading out to check Ailean's territory or simply enjoy the quiet night before the storms came. Storms were blowing in from the east, but it was the rainy winter season in Kerezik, so no one was particularly surprised or worried.

Ailean silently watched Shalin head up the stairs to her room, the puppy in her arms.

"Don't even think about it."

Ailean turned away from the tantalizing sight of Shalin walking away to that of his twin cousins, Kyna and Kennis.

"Don't think about what?"

"Now that is an innocent face, isn't it, Kyna?"

"That it is, Kennis. That it is. You'd never think he has nefarious plans for Shalin the Innocent."

Ailean rolled his eyes and laughed. "I do not have any plans for anyone."

"Not sure I believe that, cousin. Who can resist a female with the moniker 'the Innocent'?"

"Your lack of faith in me, Kyna, hurts." He held his hand to his chest. "Deep inside."

His cousins, two of the greatest Battle Dragons he'd ever known, laughed and each punched one of his arms. He gritted his teeth, trying to ignore the pain.

"They have a point, though, brother."

Forcing himself not to rub where the twins had hit him, he focused on Bideven, who stood over him. "What are you talking about?"

"You with a fresh, untried female under your roof. I'm concerned."

Ailean pushed away from the table he'd been leaning against and stood tall. "Concerned?"

"Aye, brother. Concerned. Shalin the Innocent is not like your other—"

"Whores?" Kyna added helpfully.

"Aye. She's not."

Ailean felt his rarely used anger growing. "I never said she was."

"But I saw how you looked at her."

"I have eyes. I was looking. It doesn't mean that I'll—"

"Take advantage?"

"I don't take advantage. I've never had to before."

"She's naive, Ailean. Sheltered. She's never been away from her library and her books before."

"And?"

Kyna stepped between the two brothers who were now toe to toe. "And she might misunderstand or expect more. More than you're willing to give. No one wants her hurt. Least of all you, I'm guessing." She rested her hand on his chest. "You have the biggest heart of us all, Ailean. But sometimes you make the mistake that everyone thinks like you. Or us. She's not like us. She's cultured and that, isn't she, Kennis?"

"Aye. Cultured and soft."

Kyna brushed her hand against Ailean's jaw. "Breakable, Ailean. So be careful what you do."

He took his cousin's hand, kissed the back of her knuckles. "You've a good heart yourself, little cousin."

She smiled, seconds before she slammed him hard across the face with her free hand. "Don't try and sweet-talk me, you wily bastard." But she grinned just the same.

"We're off, then," Kennis informed them all, heading toward the door. "We'll go up north a bit, make sure there's no other surprises from the Lightnings. We'll be back later tonight."

"And if you find more of them?" Ailean asked. "More of the Lightnings? What will you do then?"

Kyna grinned as she followed after her twin. "Then we'll have more horns to add to the ones already on our den walls, won't we?"

Ailean turned back to Bideven, but his brother did no more than sniff in disgust before storming off.

"What is wrong with him?" Ailean snapped, knowing Arranz stood behind him.

"Don't know. He's been strange all day. So are you going to fuck her?"

Ailean sighed and walked off.

"It was just a question."

4

It really galled him that his own kin thought so little of him. Thought he'd take advantage of Shalin or any female merely to sate his lust without a care for the female. He didn't need to take advantage of anyone and it insulted him anyone thought he would.

Passing Shalin's door, Ailean heard her cooing to her new puppy. Her scent had him pausing a moment. She always smelled so . . . delightful. Enticing.

His knuckles almost struck the door before he stopped himself.

Gods, I am weak.

Before he did something foolish, Ailean went to his bedroom, stripped, and got into bed. He ignored his desire to crawl back down the hall and scratch on Shalin's door like that puppy. He'd leave her alone. He would.

An hour into that chant, and the knock on his door came.

He ignored it, hoping she'd believe him asleep.

"Ailean," Shalin whispered urgently through the door. "I need you!"

When he still didn't answer, she began banging on the door.

"Hold on," he snapped, getting out of bed and wrapping a fur around his waist. He snatched the door open, ready to order her back to her own bed when he saw tears streaming down her face. "Gods, Shalin. What is it?"

She grabbed his hand. "I think he's dying!" Then she dragged Ailean toward her room. Once she got him inside, she dragged him around her bed where her puppy was hunched over.

"Do something!" she demanded, her panic tugging at his heart.

Ailean crouched next to the pup and said, "Well, luv, there's not much we can do."

Shalin looked at him with something close to abject horror. "You're just going to let him die?"

"No. I'm going to let him bring back up whatever he's been eating."

And that's what the little bastard did.

They both moved back, disgusted.

"Oh, that's vile!" Shalin gasped, covering her nose and mouth.

"That it is." Ailean glanced around until he found a few rags piled in a corner. He grabbed them and quickly cleaned up the mess while the puppy whined softly and crawled into Shalin's lap.

"He's still sick."

"His stomach ails him, is all." He took the rags out into the hall and dumped them where the servants could find them in the morning. When he came back in, closing the door behind him, he found Shalin staring down at the pup like she feared he might gasp his last breath at any moment. "Shalin, he'll be fine. You just have to watch what he eats."

Ailean washed his hands in the wash bowl before walking back to her side.

"Why don't you get some sleep?" he asked her, sitting beside her on the bed.

"What if he dies while I sleep? I'll never forgive myself."

It took all Ailean's strength not to roll his eyes. He knew she meant every word. "He won't die while you sleep, Shalin. He merely ate something that didn't sit well with him. You've no need to fret so."

"He's mine. My responsibility. I'll sit with him until he's better."

"No. You'll get some sleep." Ailean took the pup from her lap. "I'll stay up with him so you can rest."

"That isn't fair." She smiled and stood, taking back the puppy. "We'll stay up together."

"Uh . . ."

But he didn't have much choice, since she crawled into the center of the bed and sat down, her legs crossed so her ailing puppy could rest right in the middle. She patted the space across from her and Ailean reluctantly moved there, desperately clutching the fur covering against him.

They sat silently for several minutes, until Shalin said, "I enjoyed dinner tonight."

"Good. You, uh, blended in quite nicely."

"Did I?"

"Aye. They all like you. Oh, and I got word from the ones protecting your father. He's fine and safe."

Shalin briefly closed her eyes. "Thank you. I worry about him so."

"Why? I've never met him, but I've always heard he's well-respected."

"He is. Very well-respected, especially among our scholars. But, he can be a little . . . a little . . . " She suddenly smiled. The softest, warmest smile Ailean had ever seen. "He can be a bit befuddled at times."

"Is that why he's not an Elder?"

"He and the Elders don't see eye to eye on much. He never understands why anyone has disputes if they're not related to something scholarly. He'll argue for hours over some tiny historical fact or another, trying to prove his point, but he won't fight for his territory. And without much prompting he'll just give you his gold. He doesn't understand why our people can be, as he likes to put it, 'so bloody violent all the time.' Eventually even he had to admit that being an Elder was not for him."

Ailean began to relax, realizing he wouldn't leave her this night. She seemed to need him, although her puppy was just fine. Besides, he enjoyed her company more than he could say. "And what about you?"

"What about me?"

"I've heard it told you intend to be an Elder one day."

"Intend and will are two different things. I've a far way to go before I hope even to be considered."

"But it's not what you want, is it?"

And the way her entire body jerked at his question, causing her puppy to whine in annoyance before snuggling back to sleep, he knew he was right.

"Why would you ever think that?"

"Because I see no excitement in your eyes when you talk about it."

Excitement? In her eyes? Was that even physically possible? "What?"

With a yawn, Ailean leaned back on the bed and

Shalin felt a little guilty for not letting him go back to his room. But between her sick puppy and the fact she liked having Ailean around—especially when all he had on was that fur covering around his hips, giving her a delicious view of that chest—she had no intention of sending him away.

Could she do it, she wondered. Could she lure Ailean to her bed? True, she had him in her bed, but could she make him want her? Even she had to admit she'd never been known for her seduction tactics. And she couldn't bring up the courage to simply pounce.

"When you talk about a library or being alone, your eyes light up. Or when you were telling that story to everyone downstairs. There was excitement in your face and your voice that wasn't quite there when you discussed becoming an Elder one day. Looked more like you were going to the gallows."

"That's not true. I . . . I'm just tired. I'm not very enthusiastic about anything when I'm tired."

Although Ailean was a bit correct. The thought of becoming an Elder almost made her queasy. All the politics. All the centaur shit. She'd rather bury herself in a library than face that life on a daily basis. But she'd promised.

Because she didn't want to think of it any more, Shalin asked, "And what about *your* father?"

Ailean stared at her while he put one arm behind his head and Shalin immediately became fascinated with the way his muscles bulged from the action. *Gods, he makes a beautiful human.* "You know my father, Shalin."

"I know *of* your father. Can't say as I met him. Afton the Hermit."

"He's had other names. In the past."

If a dragon lived past his first hundred winters, he or she would start to gather many names over time. It was nothing to be ashamed of, yet Ailean appeared . . . troubled. "Like?" she prompted.

"Afton the Cruel. Afton the Murderer."

"Oh." Shalin pushed her hair behind her ear and she briefly noticed Ailean's eyes followed her hand while she did it. "Your father is *that* Afton? I always thought the Hermit and the . . . uh . . . Cruel were two different dragons."

"No. Just one." Ailean's gaze moved to the ceiling. "He wasn't always like that, you know. He didn't earn either of those names until after my mother died."

Now, that she understood. More than most, she was sure. "My father was lost after my mother died. Inconsolable for a while, and completely lost. She was equally brilliant, you see, and understood him so well, but much less befuddled. She kept everything organized and logical. Now when I go to visit, I find him under desks, behind desks, searching through piles of gold that turn out to be nothing more than brass coins merely painted gold." She shrugged at Ailean's smirk. "He can never tell the real from the fake. And I don't think he bothers to try."

"How did she die?"

"As only one of *my* parents can. She went out for a snack and picked up a bull instead of a cow. Its horn lodged in the roof of her mouth, piercing it. Nothing any healer did could fix it, and eventually she caught a brutal fever and died."

"How old were you?"

Shalin thought a moment. "Barely thirty winters. Young." With the puppy asleep, she rested her elbows on her knees and her chin on her fists, focusing on Ailean. "And you?"

"Eleven winters."

"Och. You were a babe, Ailean. I'm so sorry."

Ailean stared hard at the ceiling. "It was my fault, you know."

"Your fault? How could it be?"

"Because I didn't stay put. My father took my brothers hunting and I wanted to go with them. So I followed."

"At eleven winters? Could you even fly?"

"Barely. So of course my father told me to go back home. I did, but I was so low to the ground—unable to get any real height—soldiers spotted me and they thought I'd be fun to hunt." He suddenly closed his eyes. "They had me, too. Cornered. About half a battalion's worth."

"For a hatchling?" Sometimes humans truly disgusted her.

"And then she came. A battle dragon like all the other females of her line. She decimated them, but one of them . . . one of them had good aim. He wounded her, and though she saved me and destroyed them all, she couldn't save herself."

"And your father went on to become Afton the Cruel."

"Aye."

"Did any humans survive?"

To her surprise, Ailean opened his eyes and smiled. Truly, the most beautiful thing about him had to be that smile. "Some. You see, my father was gone for days, but three human females found me. All sisters. One a healer, one a barmaid, and the other a servant in the duke's castle. For three days they stayed with me. The healer, a witch, she tried to help my mother, but there was nothing to be done. So they made sure I ate and soothed me when I cried. Then my father came home. When he didn't find us in the cave, he tracked us down.

He almost killed the women until I stopped him, told him what happened. He left the villagers alone after that. They'd suffered enough, you see. The Duke, his men, they took the villagers' food and used their women, sometimes even the young ones barely old enough to breed themselves. They left untold numbers of babes of their own lying around but they never claimed them. But that duke and his soldiers—they didn't survive my father's wrath."

"So that's how your father got his name."

"Actually . . . no. No one thought he was cruel then—just angry. Then word spread that the duke was dead and others came to claim the land as their own. But my father always met them first, and he'd kill them all. He was still angry, you see. If it moved, he killed it. Eventually they all stopped coming and my father went into his cave and rarely came out. My uncles, my aunts, they all taught me and my brothers how to fight, how to survive." He glanced at her and shook his head. "No, Shalin. No one among my kin ever blamed me. At least not as much as I blamed myself."

"You were a babe," she reminded him fiercely, annoyed he'd even think otherwise.

"I should have stayed put. I didn't. And she died, all because I couldn't fight for myself."

"Fight for yourself? Ailean you were too—"

"Don't say I was too young. A dragon can never be too young to learn to protect himself. Not in this world. My sons and daughters will be able to fight from hatching."

"Ailean, isn't that a bit of a tall order?"

"No. My brothers and I came up with a training method that will get them started early. My hatchlings will be prepared for *anything*."

Shalin felt for the future hatchlings of Ailean the Wicked. They wouldn't have easy lives. Then she frowned for a moment when she wondered who exactly he'd fall so in love with he'd settle down and have hatchlings with. But she quickly pushed the feeling away when she realized it was none of her business.

"Did all this happen here?" she asked, trying to distract herself.

"Aye. Madenn's kin were the ones who stayed with me. Her great-great-grandmother and aunts. My father wanted nothing to do with any of them. Although he spared them, he still felt nothing for them. My brothers could go either way, but I knew these people needed protection. Human males can't stay away from unclaimed territory for long. It's like this overwhelming need they all have to conquer anything they've even heard about."

"So you stayed."

"Seemed natural, really. I'd already spent so much time with them and they never told my secret. Eventually the entire village knew about me and no one said a word."

"But didn't you hate them? The humans?"

"For the actions of a few? No. Doesn't seem fair to do that."

He had to be the first dragon Shalin had ever heard say something like that.

"You look tired," he suddenly told her.

"No. I'm fine." And to prove it, she yawned.

Smiling, Ailean turned on his side and picked up the puppy from her lap, laying the little fur ball lengthwise on the bed. Then Ailean patted the mattress. "Come on now. Stretch out here."

"But, the puppy . . . " Yet she was already stretching out on her side, facing Ailean, the puppy between them, her eyes rapidly closing. The day had caught up with her so quickly.

"He'll be fine," Ailean murmured, and she felt him take her hand. "And tomorrow, Mistress Shalin, we'll discuss his diet."

5

Ailean didn't know what woke him up first. The two suns shining in his eyes—or the paw repeatedly slapping at his head.

Yawning, he glared at the little monster trying to claw him to death. "Oh, now you're feeling fine, aren't you?"

He yipped in answer and that's when Shalin murmured in her sleep.

That's also when Ailean realized Shalin was asleep on his chest.

Slightly terrified, Ailean desperately tried to remember if they'd done anything the night before. He didn't think so and, when he looked down at her, she still wore the red gown from yesterday and the fur covering he'd brought with him still lay between them.

He let out a breath, but still didn't know what had come over him. He might not have touched her, but all the things they'd discussed . . .

Ailean never talked about his father with anyone but his brothers, and those two never mentioned the old dragon unless necessary. Ailean definitely never discussed his mother and what happened that awful day. His own kin knew never to mention it. Nearly a century ago, one cousin drunkenly brought it up after a family hunting party and lost both his horns when Ailean snapped them off.

But Ailean had told Shalin pretty much everything. Gods . . . why?

The puppy yipped again and Shalin's head snapped up from his chest. "Wha—where—?"

"You're safe, Shalin," he told her, seeing the confusion and panic on her face. When she looked at him, her panic seemed to pass and she smiled at him with real warmth.

"Good morn, Ailean."

"Good morn to you."

She turned a bit to look at the puppy, but she seemed more than comfortable cuddled up to his chest. "And look at you, Lord Terrify Me."

The dog yipped again and Ailean said, "You best let him out, Shalin. Or there'll be more mess to clean up."

"Let him out?"

"Just open the door. He'll find the rest of the dogs."

"All right."

He thought she'd roll away from him, but instead, she moved across him to get to the edge of the bed. Ailean gritted his teeth and willed his body not to react. It had to be one of the hardest things he'd ever done and he'd gotten in a fight once with a giant octopus.

"Will he come back?"

"I'm sure. He's bonded to you, Shalin." And he knew how the little bastard felt. Ailean knew if he left this moment, he'd probably come back, too.

"Come on, then, you little terror." Shalin picked the dog up and walked to the door. Ailean heard it open and then Shalin's strangled, "Uh . . ."

"What's wrong?" He rolled to his side, raising himself up on one elbow, and looked toward the door. "Shit," he barely had a chance to mutter before Bideven pushed past Shalin and stalked in, Arranz and the twins right behind him.

"You dirty bastard. Couldn't keep your hands off her, could ya?"

Ailean slid off the bed and stood in front of his kin, the only thing holding up that fur covering his hand.

"I'm not quite sure what it has to do with you, brother."

Bideven moved toward him but Shalin calmly stepped between them. "He never touched me."

Arranz sighed. "Shalin, love, could you move? You're in the way of some lovely violence."

Giving no more than an annoyed sniff, she didn't respond to Arranz and instead said again, "He never touched me, Bideven."

"Then why was he here?"

"I needed help with my puppy."

Arranz and the twins started laughing and didn't seem inclined to stop while Bideven's accusing gaze shot daggers at Ailean.

"You bastard!"

Shalin rested her hand against Bideven's chest. "Stop this now."

"Shalin, you're an innocent about this sort of thing—"

Ailean didn't realize he'd snorted out loud until they all looked at him.

He glanced at Shalin and shrugged. "Sorry."

"—and his intent," Bideven finished. "We're just trying to protect you."

Shalin folded her arms over her chest. "Do you think so little of your own brother?"

The confusion on their faces would be something Ailean remembered for ages.

"What?"

"Do you think so little of him? That he'd take advantage of me. Force me."

"I never said—"

"Is that truly what you expect of your own kin? I thought the Cadwaladr Clan loyal to each other."

"We are."

"I haven't seen it. Not when you barge in here and accuse your own brother of being all manner of lizard."

"I never meant to—"

"Then you should apologize."

"Apologize?"

"Yes."

"You can't be—"

Shalin's foot began to tap and Bideven growled. "Fine. I apologize."

Patting his shoulder, Shalin ushered Bideven and the rest out. "Now don't you feel better?"

"Not really," Bideven shot back, but Shalin had already closed the door in his face.

Ailean stared at Shalin. "That was . . . *brilliant*!"

Shalin held her finger to her lips while she bent over silently laughing. "He'll hear."

"Good!" Ailean watched her walk across the room. "How did you do that?"

She shrugged before falling back on the bed, her grin wide and happy. "Years of court life, my dear dragon."

*   *   *

It happened so fast, Shalin thought a wizard must be involved. But no. It was simply rainy season in Kerezik and that meant sudden darkness and sudden storms.

Well, she thought, *that might at least keep the beasts from the door for a little while*. Lightning dragons, from what she'd read, didn't much like traveling in this sort of weather. Not only did they possess lightning within them as her people possessed flame, but they attracted lightning. Which could make for painful, if not lethal, travels during storm seasons in the different regions.

Running a comb through her freshly washed hair, she looked at the courtyard beneath her window. Not surprisingly, very few of the human servants were about and the few that were quickly scurried toward one of the many buildings so they were out of the rain. Then she saw him, marching through the rain, not caring that his clothes were getting soaked.

Ailean stopped and spoke to a large, burly human. She'd guess the woman was the local blacksmith, based on her dress and the size of her arms. Laughing at some joke of his, the female placed her hand on his forearm, and Shalin's eyes narrowed dangerously.

With a quick hug, the blacksmith walked away and Ailean continued on to his destination. She watched until he walked into the stables.

Stables?

"Yum . . . horse."

Ailean gently brushed his favorite mare's coat and softly hummed. Black Heart liked when he hummed.

He loved doing this. It was one of those things he could do and still focus on something else completely. Like why his family had suddenly lost their collective minds. Never before, in his nearly hundred and fifty years, had they ever cared about what he did or who he did it with. But now, suddenly, he had the lot of them trying to push him away from Shalin as if they thought he'd purposely hurt her.

Could involving himself with Shalin only lead to hurting her more than anyone else because she truly was innocent? He hated the thought of hurting her and hated the thought of never lying with her even more.

So focused on his thoughts and feelings—something Ailean rarely paid attention to for more than three seconds at a time—he didn't notice Black Heart's growing nervousness until she bucked suddenly. Ailean placed his hand on her flank, felt the tensing muscles. He crooned to her softly while he slowly, carefully stood. It wasn't like Black Heart to be so jumpy around him. He'd ridden her and many from her line into local battles when he'd fought as human. She'd never balked before, although she could smell what he was.

"What is it, girl?" he asked softly. "What has you so nervous?"

"Is she for tonight's meal?" that sweet, innocent voice asked.

And Black Heart kicked at the stall door, forcing Shalin to back up.

"Hmm. She may be tough of hide, Ailean," Shalin said in all seriousness. "She'll be hard to chew."

Ailean quickly stepped in front of Black Heart before she could knock down the stall door. "Ssssh," he sang softly. "It's all right."

Once he had her relatively calm, he glanced over his shoulder at Shalin, forcing himself to ignore how beautiful she looked in another one of his cousin's gowns, this time a deep blue. Like before, it was too big for her and kept falling off her shoulder, giving just enough to tantalize and tease but still hold everything back. "She's not dinner, Shalin."

"She's not?"

"No."

"Then what are you doing with her?" she asked, honestly confused.

"Grooming her."

"For what, if we're not going to eat her?"

"Because I like to."

"Oh." Shalin looked down the long rows of stalls. "What about that one?" She pointed at Dragon's Gold. "She looks like she'd be tasty and enough for two."

Dragon's Gold, only a few feet away, jerked back and kicked her stall door.

"Shalin!" he snapped, startling her attention back to him. "We don't eat horses here."

"You don't?"

"No. These are working animals. Just like the dogs."

"Aren't you running out of food options?"

He couldn't help but chuckle. "We make do."

"I see."

She wandered off, glancing into each stall.

Ailean took a moment to brush his hand over Black Heart's snout. "It's all right, girl. It's all right."

Black Heart clicked her teeth together and motioned with her head. Ailean looked up in time to see Shalin open one of the stalls and step in.

"Gods, Shalin! Not that one!"

Ailean shot over the stall gate, not able to take the time to open it, and charged after the dragoness. He stumbled to a stop when he found her petting the enormous pitch-black horse inside.

"I can see why you enjoy this," she murmured. "It's quite soothing." She looked up at him. "What's his name?"

"Nightmare."

"Hmmm." She ran her hands through the horse's long mane of hair. "He's not as clean as the others and his mane's a mess. Why?"

Ailean smiled at the accusation in Shalin's voice and crossed his arms over his chest. "That's because no one else has ever been able to get near him except to give him a little food and water. He's known for having broken more ribs, arms, legs, and heads than any other horse in my province. He's mean, cranky, and foul-tempered. No one trusts him and we think he enjoys hurting people. Hence the name Nightmare."

At his words, Shalin shrugged. "He seems to like me well enough."

"That he does."

"I'll clean him myself, then."

"Shalin, wait—"

"It's not fair. All the others tended to and not him." Shalin grabbed a bucket and headed out to get water. "I know what it's like to feel like an outsider among your own," she said so softly he almost didn't hear her.

"I'll take care of him," she said again before disappearing out the stable door.

Ailean watched her go. It still astounded him Shalin was born a royal. She never acted like it.

And perhaps Nightmare wasn't as big a bastard as they'd all originally thought if Shalin found some good in him. Ailean almost believed that too, until Nightmare reared up on his hind legs and brought his forelegs down on Ailean's chest, sending him flying back into an empty stall. A human might have been killed, but—like Black

Heart—Nightmare knew exactly what Ailean was and how much he could take.

As Ailean tried to get his breath back, Shalin reappeared with a bucketful of water and one of the stable boys to assist her. She glanced down at him.

"What are you doing?"

When he didn't answer, mostly because he still couldn't, she shook her head. "So lazy, Ailean the Wicked."

6

It took her several hours to groom the horse to her particular standards. In the time it took her to do one, Ailean and the stable hands had done all the others. And while she groomed the horse, her puppy ran around and around until he'd drop wherever and sleep. Only to snap awake a little while later and do it all over again.

In all honesty, Shalin had never been so entertained before while doing absolutely nothing. She and Ailean never really spoke unless they asked each other specific questions, and yet she thoroughly enjoyed his company.

"You doing all right over here?"

She smiled as she ran the brush through Nightmare's mane, yet again. It took her hours to get all the brambles and things out of it, but it was worth it. "Aye."

"It shines."

She patted the horse's neck. "As it should."

Ailean pulled open the stall door. "You missed dinner."

Surprised, Shalin looked up. "I missed dinner?"

He nodded. "You've been out here hours. Didn't you notice you're the only one left in here?"

"I guess I missed that." Her fingers slid easily through the horse's mane. "Such a simple task and yet so . . . soothing."

"Are you hungry, Shalin?"

"I am."

"Then come. Madenn has food for you."

Shalin stroked Nightmare's forelock, which fell across his forehead. "He's a fine horse, Ailean."

"He's your horse now." When Shalin only stared at him, Ailean shrugged. "No one else can handle him, Shalin. No one else wants him. I tried to sell him once and he nearly bit the man's hand off. You are the only being who has ever been able to get this close to him. He's chosen you, so you might as well accept it."

"I can't take your horse."

"He's not my horse. He hates me. He's always hated me. And to be honest, I hate him, too. It's a mutual hate."

"I don't understand you."

"You sound like my kin. They never know what to make of me, either." He held his hand out. "Come on, then. He'll still be here in the morning."

Shalin nodded and patted the horse's neck. As she walked out, the puppy charged past her and out of the stables.

"Where does he disappear to?"

"To play with his brothers and sisters. He'll return when there's food."

Ailean locked the stall door, and together they walked out of the stables.

"The rains stopped," she said, feeling the need to say something.

"Hours ago. You really do get lost in what you're doing, don't you?"

He didn't sound mocking, merely curious. "There's always noise and such at Devenallt. In order to get any work done, I've had to teach myself to shut it all out. To focus only on what's important."

"That's a fine skill. No wonder you handle my family so well. You simply ignore them."

Shalin laughed. "If it works. But I'm sure you have the skill. When you're in battle."

"In battle I become aware of everything. I can't afford to shut anything out except my own fear."

"You don't seem afraid of anything, Ailean."

"I have fear. Anyone with sense has fear. You simply have to focus it where it'll do the most good."

"That first night we were here, your kin talked of going to Devenallt Mountain."

"They did."

"To—if I remember correctly—raid it."

"Aye. That was what we in the family call a Twin Battle Plan." At Shalin's frown, Ailean elaborated. "Anything that requires us to go into the most impenetrable fortresses in the land and kill everyone not friend is called a Twin Battle Plan. Because the twins are usually the ones who suggest it."

"There's a reason they've never been invited to Devenallt Mountain, isn't there?"

They paused at the steps leading into the Great Hall. "The Twins make the royals nervous. They're short on temper and long on bloodlust. The royals want them to fight their battles but they live in fear of having them around. Since my cousins care nothing for politics, they stay away. It makes no difference to them."

"Does anyone among your kin care about politics?"

"Only Bideven. But only enough to help when any of us get into trouble."

"And you?" she asked, smiling up at him. "Do you care about politics?"

"Not even a little." Big fingers brushed across her cheek. "Dirt," he explained.

With a nod, Shalin walked into the Great Hall, desperately trying to ignore the way her skin tingled where Ailean had touched her.

Ailean paced the length of his room again. Since he'd knocked the wall out of three rooms to create it, this was no short trip.

For two hours he'd tried to sleep. For two hours he'd tossed and turned and masturbated until he feared his hand would fall off. Yet nothing could alleviate the burning, clawing need he had at the moment.

And Ailean wished with all his heart that this need was merely sexual. That all he wanted from Shalin lay between her thighs. But he wanted more than that. He wanted to sit and talk to her again. He'd never been so at ease with anyone not blood, and he never had to yell over her to be heard. She listened to him and that meant more than anyone could realize.

"This is ridiculous," he told the air. "I'm a grown dragon. I can do as I like." And they would only talk. Like they had the night before.

Confident in his intent, Ailean stormed to the door, snatching it open—and froze.

"Good evening, brother," Arranz said calmly. He sat in a chair just outside Ailean's room, cleaning his weapons.

"What are you doing?"

"Just . . . keeping watch."

"Keeping watch outside my room?"

"This hallway, brother. Danger is everywhere. Even you. You're in danger, too, Ailean. We have to be ever vigilant with you as well as Shalin." Arranz looked at his brother, all innocence and naïveté, which Ailean knew for a fact was nothing more than centaur shit. "But Ailean, where are you off to so late? Is there something you need, brother? Something I can get you?"

Ailean's eyes narrowed and Arranz grinned.

"You have money on this, don't you?"

Arranz went back to wiping his weapon down. "How you think of me, brother. As if I'd bet hard-earned gold on something like this."

Snarling, Ailean stepped back into his room and slammed the door shut. He hated his kin.

Hated. Them.

Shalin jumped when a door slammed. Biting her lip, she charged across the room, sliding to a stop in front of her own door and placing her ear against it. She listened but could hear nothing that would lead her to believe Ailean made his way to her room.

Damn the gods! Why were they torturing her so? Putting her in arm's length of her greatest desire but keeping it just out of reach.

And the gods did not give her the kind of bravery that would allow her to march out of her room, down that hall, and to Ailean's chamber. To demand he take what she offered.

Instead she waited in her room like a frightened mouse, hoping someone would put the cheese before her.

Gritting her teeth, Shalin paced back to the window, the puppy stumbling behind her.

Would her life always be this unfair? This brutally cruel? Would she *ever* get what she truly wanted or would she always yearn for what she could never have?

"Do the gods have some vendetta against me, little one?" she asked as she picked up her puppy and held him close. "Some vendetta against my ancestors that I'm un-aware of? Or do they simply enjoy toying with me?"

Since Shalin came from a most boring line of dragons, she felt quite confident that the gods merely toyed with her.

"Bastards," she muttered before heading to her bed.

7

Shalin had not slept well. She'd pretty much done everything but sleep. She'd read. She'd tossed and turned. She'd played with the puppy until he fell asleep. Now all she wanted to do was spend some time with her horse.

She walked down the stairs and into the Great Hall.

"We need to get you a dress that fits," Arranz said in lieu of a proper greeting. "And some boots."

"Are you done?" And her clipped words had Arranz staring at her.

"Is there a problem?" he asked.

"No. Not at all. Feel free to comment on anything. My hair all right with you? My face? Anything else I can fix to your satisfaction?" When he didn't answer, Shalin looked at the rest of the Cadwaladr Clan. "Truly. Feel free while I'm standing here to comment on anything you like. No?"

Unable to stop sneering, Shalin grabbed a loaf of bread and walked out to the courtyard.

* * *

Ailean walked into the Great Hall. He passed by his kin, the lot of them nearly filling the room, grabbing a loaf of bread from the table. Before he went outside, he stopped and asked, turning back to his kin as he did so, "I need to train. Anyone up for—"

In the ten seconds since he'd started to ask his question, all but three of his kin remained. The twins stood.

"We'll—"

"Sit down," their mother ordered. And they both obeyed. She remained the only being on the planet who had full control over them. "What's going on with you two?" Deniela asked Ailean.

"What are you talking about?"

"That sweet, innocent dragoness—"

At Ailean's snort, Deniela's eyes narrowed, and he held his hands up, indicating she should continue.

"She was in a foul mood and I'm blaming you."

"How is it my fault?" Although deep in his soul, he prayed it was his fault. He shouldn't be the only one not sleeping.

"She's an innocent, Ailean. Don't play with her."

"I haven't. And she's not an innocent."

"She's probably a virgin."

"Don't be daft."

"Have you asked her?" Deniela demanded. "Maybe you should before you set your sights on dirtying her up."

"I have to say, *Aunt* Deniela, that I don't appreciate you suggesting her being with me would *dirty* her up."

When the old cow only stared at him, he walked out.

Shalin glanced up and that's when she saw Ailean staring at her—again. She'd found him doing it several times since he'd walked in to groom the horses a few hours before. Finally, unable to stand it anymore, she asked, "Is something wrong?"

"No. Why do you ask?"

"Because," she said, focusing back on Nightmare, "you keep staring at me."

"Sorry." But he didn't stop staring.

"Ailean," she finally said, "you haven't done anything wrong." In fact, he hadn't done a damn thing and she'd gotten tired of waiting for him to.

"I know that."

"Then why do you look like you've ravished me and left me pregnant like some human?"

"No, I don't." He finally grinned. "There'd be much more running away involved."

She petted Nightmare's neck. "I appreciate your family's desire to protect me, but I don't need them to protect me from you." She forced a smile. "I'm sure when this is all over we'll be the best of friends."

"Friends?"

Shalin's lip curled. "Is there a reason you snarled that?"

"Are you a virgin?"

Rearing back a little, Shalin wondered at the abrupt change of conversation. Her anger sliding away from her in seconds. "Sorry?"

"You heard me."

"I . . . uh . . ."

"Yes or no."

"No. But I'm not sure it's—"

"You sure?"

"Am I sure? Am I sure I'm a virgin or not?" She stepped away from Nightmare. "Is there something wrong with you? Mentally?"

"Yes. Or. No."

"Yes. I'm sure that I'm not a virgin. I haven't been one for quite some time although it's none of your damn business."

"No reason to get snappy. It was a simple enough question."

"I don't get snappy. Now if you'll—"

"Ever been with anyone while human?"

Shalin let out a long breath. "Why is this conversation getting stranger?"

"Answer me."

"You want me to answer you? Fine." Placing her feet in between the slats of the stall gate, Shalin rose up so she could look him right in the eye. "Here's my answer. No. I've never been with anyone while human. But after reading those books about you, I've always thought if there was anyone who could show me how good it could supposedly be, it would be you. Little did I know at the time that you were *insane!*"

Ailean carefully wiped off the bit of spit that hit his eye when she'd hissed that last part at him. "Good, because—"

"Ailean?" the human female said from the front of the stables.

Shalin realized it was the blacksmith from earlier and she growled, causing the woman to step back.

"Uh . . ." the blacksmith stammered, ". . . you said you wanted to see the blade as soon as it was done." She held up something long and wrapped in soft cloth. "I have it here if you'd—"

"Yes, yes. I'll look at it now."

"You're leaving?" But he hadn't finished what he'd been saying! *Good because what? Good because what? Dammit!*

"I'm not flying to the suns, dragoness. I'll be back."

And he thought she'd still be here?

He walked away, heading toward the blacksmith and Shalin jumped down from the stall door. She looked at the horse. "Would you like to teach me how to ride?"

In answer, Nightmare slowly lowered himself enough for her to easily mount him.

"Oh," she sighed, "if only they were all like you."

Once he'd approved the blade, Ailean walked back to the stables. His body almost vibrated with the thought of getting inside Shalin. Teaching her exactly how enjoyable a human body could be. To be the first to do so.

Still, that little voice of doubt wouldn't shut the hell up. Constantly asking him if he should do this with someone he'd sworn to protect. Would that turn him from Ailean the Whore to Ailean the Right Bastard?

Ailean stepped in front of Nightmare's stall and stared blindly inside.

When one of the stable boys walked past, Ailean asked, "Where's Mistress Shalin?"

"She took Nightmare out a few minutes ago."

He turned on the boy and yelled, "*And you let her?*"

"Well . . . she didn't actually ask my permission."

Ailean snarled and went to Dragon's Gold, his fastest mount. It wasn't that Shalin had walked away from their conversation. It was that she'd rode away with that demon horse. It was one thing for her to feed him and groom him, but riding that big bastard was another matter altogether. If he threw her and she landed the wrong way, her human neck could snap.

He saddled and mounted his horse quickly and took off after Shalin, using her scent to guide him. It didn't take him long to find her. Typical dragon. She'd gone to the lake. To water. Something his kind were elementally drawn to.

"Have you gone mad?" he demanded, dismounting before the horse had even stopped.

She'd already dismounted and stood staring out over the lake at the next coming storm. He, too, could see the dark thunder clouds approaching, which fit his mood quite nicely.

"He could have killed you."

"Well, you know us virgins. We just run off half-crazed."

"I can't believe you're still upset about that."

"Upset that you were discussing my intactness with your kin?"

"It wasn't like that, Shalin." Well . . . not *much* like that.

She waved him off. "At the moment, I really don't care."

Ailean gently swiped a hand down her back. "Are you all right?"

"I'm fine. I've just . . . " She let her hands fall at her side. "I've just never seen that before."

He followed her line of sight before returning his gaze to her face. "You've never seen storm clouds?"

"Of course I've seen storm clouds. I've just never *seen* storm clouds."

"Perhaps we should get you inside, Shalin."

"Don't be dull," she said before walking away from him.

"I beg your pardon?"

"You heard me. I don't want to go inside. Nothing is wrong with me."

Ailean entertained the idea she might be right until she took off running and did a somersault—for no apparent reason.

"In fact," she announced, "I feel *amazing*. At least a hundred years younger."

"Shalin, you're not old."

"No. I just feel like it most days." She suddenly did a handstand and Ailean briefly closed his eyes and groaned. He couldn't help himself once he realized she was completely naked under that dress.

"Shalin—"

"You know," she flipped forward and landed on her feet, "I don't *do* anything. I go where they tell me. Do what they tell me." She put her hands on her hips and said, "I almost handed myself over to the Northland dragons because I thought it was the right thing to do. I'm tired of living for others."

"Then don't."

"Don't?"

"Don't. Gods know, I don't."

"It's easy for you. No one expects anything from you."

"Thank you."

"I mean . . ." Again she waved her hand like she was waving away a fly. "Why lie? I meant what I said. All they expect from you, from your kin, is to kill on command. That's your skill. Your gift to our people. When you're not killing, they really don't care what you do."

"But you . . ."

She laughed, but there was no humor in it. "From me, they expect much."

"Your life is your own, Shalin. That's the true beauty of being dragon. Even our gods know not to demand much of us."

"It's not the gods I care about disappointing."

"Your father?"

She nodded. "I love him too much to ever want to hurt him. Failure—*my* failure—would hurt him."

"But, Shalin—your father's not here. And, based on those clouds, he won't be here for quite a bit. So, perhaps you can allow yourself a chance to just be. For once." He grinned. "Who knows what you'll discover about yourself?"

She frowned a bit. "I guess I can do that."

"You guess?"

She snorted. "I don't know how to throw all caution to the wind like you do, Ailean."

"Then isn't it time you learned?"

"How do you—"

"You just do it. You simply see what you want and you go after it. That's what I do. Trust me, Shalin, there's no one here who will hold you back."

"Truly?" And she looked afraid to hope.

"Truly. You may not always get what you want. But I've found it never hurts to at least have tried."

Shalin nodded. "All right, then."

Then she took off running—right at him. He barely had a chance to stumble back before she slammed right into his chest. If he hadn't been hit with so many other unexpected things over the years, he'd never have been able to stay on his feet.

Shalin wrapped her arms around his neck and her legs around his waist. She stared into his eyes for a long moment before she said in no uncertain terms, "I want you to fuck me, Ailean."

She couldn't tell if he looked horrified, appalled, or merely stunned.

Shalin swallowed and gave him a way out. "You can say no, of course. I don't want you to do anything you don't want to—"

"Shut up, Shalin."

Ailean closed his eyes, and she could hear him gritting his teeth. He looked as if he was in physical pain.

"What do you want from me, Shalin?"

That seemed like an odd question, and he seemed so angry, she decided retreat might be her best option. "Nothing, Ailean. Nothing." She tried to pull out of his arms and he yanked her back. That's when she felt his erection pushing against her sex.

"You don't understand me. What do you want from me, Shalin?" She shook her head, still unclear what he meant. "Are you a romantic, Shalin? Do you need the soft light of candles and the gentle touch of your lover?"

"Uh—"

"Normally, I could give you anything you'd want. I'm known for my versatile skills. But I can't promise that right now." He pushed a wind blown lock of her hair behind her ear. "I've wanted you too long to be much of a sensitive lover. All I can promise you at the moment is a rough ride right here in the dirt. If you don't want that, then walk away from—"

"Put me down, Ailean."

He looked so disappointed, she almost felt guilty for how happy that made her.

With a curt nod, he carefully placed her on the ground and she stepped back. "Give us your shirt."

"What?"

"Your shirt." She motioned to the linen shirt that fit him perfectly but would hang on her like one of his cousin's dresses. "Give it to me."

Not sure why she wanted it, he still reached back and grabbed up the shirt with both hands, dragging it over his head. He handed it to her and she took it but stopped a moment to simply stare at him. Gods, he had a nice body. And he wasn't even naked yet.

Clearing her throat, she shook the linen shirt out and placed it on the ground. "Until you've actually had dirt up your bum, you really can't appreciate how uncomfortable that could get."

She stood, brushing off her hands. "Now make sure to get me there." She pointed at the shirt. "You know, when we actually get to that point."

He seemed to struggle between wanting to glare at her and smile. "Did you hear a word I said to you?"

"Quite clearly. I have excellent hearing." She moved closer to him and Ailean's body tensed. "I appreciate the warning, though. It was very sweet of you to give me the option to run away . . ."

Ailean's hands were fisted at his side while he eyed her. She had the feeling he would not make the first move. He needed her to prove that she wanted this.

Wanted this? Gods, she *needed* this. Perhaps her only chance at getting something she really, truly wanted that had nothing to do with anyone or anything else. No matter how temporary, she needed this.

Now Shalin stood so close to him their bodies nearly touched. She raised her hand and let her fingers skim along a jagged scar across his upper chest. Ailean's big body trembled beneath her exploring fingers, and she felt a surge of confidence and lust she'd never known before.

She moved her fingers to another scar, this one on his shoulder. And while her fingers toyed with that, Shalin leaned in close and licked Ailean's nipple. His entire body jerked so she did it again. The fists at his side relaxed.

Shalin laid her hands flat against his chest while she

licked his other nipple. Ailean groaned and it reverberated through Shalin's body, making her feel hot all over, her skin itchy. She wanted to strip and rub herself all over him.

Big, strong fingers speared through her hair, and Ailean pulled her head back. His eyes roamed over her face and she tried hard not to shrink back from his examination. She was used to shadows. She liked shadows, liked blending into walls. But Ailean and his kin wouldn't let her. She tried to hide and they only pulled her back out again, but not out of cruelty. Not as a way to hurt her.

And that was why she kept her eyes on his. Because she wasn't afraid to meet his gaze, to challenge him as he was challenging her. He looked for fear, and she'd show him none. Not now, not ever.

Ailean groaned once, and then he kissed her. And Shalin knew she'd made the right decision.

She wanted him. And not in some shy, innocent way, begging him to lead. When he kissed her, she met him with as much passion as he felt. Her tongue met his, bold and demanding. Her hands slid up to his shoulders and around his neck. She raised herself on her toes, tipping her head to the side to get a better angle. For a dragoness who'd never been with a male as human, she seemed to know her way around. He truly thought she'd be lost without her tail.

Shalin's small hands reached for his leather leggings, tearing at them, trying to get them off. Her passion for him making her as rough as he'd threatened to be. Ailean pushed her hands away, so he could deal with her dress, doing his best not to rip it in the process. It was so large, it took no effort to push it off her shoulders and down her body. Once the dress cleared her arms, Shalin went right back to removing his leggings, sliding them over his hips. As she lowered them, she went along, crouching in front of him, her lips leaving a delicious trail down his naked hip and thigh.

His cock sprang free of his clothing, clearly begging for her mouth. And when she licked her lips, Ailean knew he had to get control of this situation or come before it even truly started.

"No," he said simply before digging his hands back in her hair and yanking her to her feet. He pulled her tight against his body and took her mouth again. Only now it was flesh against flesh and nothing had ever felt so wonderful to him. Gods, there had been so many others, but none like Shalin.

He didn't understand it. Maybe it was that innocent honesty. No lies or deceits. No seduction. Simply knowing what she wanted and making it clear. Now it was his turn to know what he wanted and to make it clear.

Ailean released her hair and slid his hands under her ass. Lifting Shalin up, he dropped to his knees and placed her on the shirt she'd laid out, careful not to slam her head into the ground.

Moving down her body, he kissed and licked her flesh, pinning her to the ground with his hands against her waist. Sliding between her thighs, Ailean pushed her legs apart and nuzzled her sex until she growled and grabbed hold of his hair.

"Don't pull," he warned.

"I'll pull every hair from your head if you don't—if you don't—"

"If I don't what?" He gently ran his finger along the already wet slit, her body jerking from the light touch. "If I don't what? Tell me."

He grinned, waiting to see her struggle with the words. But his little innocent grabbed his hair as firmly as any soldier during battle, yanked his head up, and snarled, "Fuck me with that tongue, Ailean the Whore, or I swear by all the dark gods you'll be bald before nightfall."

Ailean pulled back a bit and for one horrible second she feared he'd walk away, leaving her to teeter on this precipice. Her fear almost had her begging until Ailean smiled. His hands slid under her backside and lifted, her legs going over his shoulders. She watched his face disappear between her thighs. His tongue slid inside her and Shalin's eyes crossed.

To say this dragon had talent would be a gross understatement. This wasn't a talent. This was a gift from the gods.

Blindly, she dug her hands into the soft soil around her, panting as Ailean's tongue stroked and flicked and teased her beyond anything she'd ever felt before. While his tongue played there, his nose helped out in other areas until Shalin shook beneath him. She could feel the explosion coming, her breathing harsh and uncontrolled. Then, while keeping her legs on his shoulders, Ailean's arms slid under her hips and around her waist to her chest. His fingers took firm hold of her nipples, pulling and rolling until Shalin's climax crashed into her. Her screams of release echoing around the lake, the horses nearby restlessly pawing the ground.

Shalin's hands dug into Ailean's hair and held his head in place, her back lifting from the ground as another wave cut through her, ferociously stronger than the first, her screams turning to pitiful cries.

After several moments, her grip on him weakened,

and Shalin dropped back to the ground. Before she even had a chance to get her breath, Ailean was there, on top of her, his hands now in her hair, his lips against her neck.

"Shalin . . . I'm sorry . . . I can't . . ."

Shalin knew what he needed. It was what she needed. She opened herself to him and said, "Don't wait, Ailean. Please."

He didn't. He entered her with one brutally hard thrust. Shalin gasped seconds before his mouth covered hers and he drove into her again and again, giving her the rough ride he'd promised. She didn't care. She loved every second of it, holding him tight as he took her.

His lips moved from her mouth and down her jaw to her neck. She felt his teeth press against the skin and then he bit down, sending her flying over the edge again as he climaxed with her, his body pinning her to the ground as he emptied himself inside her.

Ailean couldn't move. *Wouldn't.* Why should he when he'd never been so comfortable before in his life?

Cool hands stroked his back, his hair; her soft voice sighed in his ear.

"Are you all right?"

Ailean laughed in surprise. No one had ever asked *him* that before. "I'm fine." He lifted up a bit so he could look into her face. "And you?"

She tried to hide her smile but she snorted, which started her laughing with him.

"I'm doing quite well, thank you," she finally managed.

"Good." He kissed her neck and felt the first drops of rain on his back. "Damn."

She ran her hand down his cheek. "We better get in. I got ill once while human—" her eyes rolled, "—took me days to recover."

Ailean chuckled. "Well, we can't have that, now, can we?"

Slowly, he pulled out of her, both of them groaning when he did. Unfortunately, once Ailean was out, all he wanted to do was get back in. Steeling his resolve, Ailean stood on shaky legs and reached down to help Shalin to her feet. She gripped his forearms and he sensed her legs were as shaky as his.

Making sure she could stand without him, Ailean then grabbed Shalin's dress and carefully pulled it over her head. "Will you be all right to ride?"

"Of course. Nightmare takes very good care of me."

Ailean grunted, suddenly feeling jealous over a bloody horse.

"He should still have a saddle," he said while pulling her arms through the armholes of the dress.

"I'll not put a saddle on him, Ailean."

"But, Shalin—"

"Is he mine or not?"

Ailean raised an eyebrow. "I certainly don't want him," he informed her before pulling on his clothes.

"Then he's mine to manage as I see fit."

" 'Then he's mine to manage as I see fit,' " he mimicked back to her in a high-pitched voice that had her slapping at his shoulders in a pitiful attempt at an assault.

Laughing, Ailean grabbed her around the waist and pulled her close again. "You have quite the temper, don't you?"

"Don't sound so mocking. I do have quite the temper. Few, though, make me angry enough to show it."

"I'll have to work on that. I'd like to see you truly angry."

Shalin's face fell and she looked a little . . . terrified. "No, Ailean. No you wouldn't."

Before he could ask her more questions, the skies opened up and rain poured down on them. Quickly setting the dragoness aside, Ailean pulled on the rest of his clothes and boots.

While he did, he watched Shalin merely crook her finger to get Nightmare to trot over to her side. Without any further prompting, he lowered himself so Shalin could mount him easily.

"Meet you back at the castle?" she asked, using Nightmare's hair for reins.

"We'll be right behind you." He whistled for Dragon's Gold. "Stay on the path and head straight home, Shalin. I don't desire searching for you in this downpour." Ailean placed his hand on her thigh. "Oiy."

"Yes?"

"No kiss?"

Leaning down a bit, she kissed him and Ailean felt no cold blowing in from the storm. He only felt warmth and desire, his hands reaching for her automatically.

"No, no," she laughed. "We have to go." Shalin sat up straight, her hand stroking his cheek. "Thank you for today."

He grinned at her, completely unaware that his clothes were already soaked through. "And are you leaving this afternoon?"

Shalin looked up at the sky. "In this storm? Of course—"

"Then we're not done. We can thank each other another day. For now . . ."

"For now . . . what?"

"For now we'll need to find a way to avoid my family's involvement. Unless you're hoping what we do every day turns into a nightly topic of discussion at dinner."

"Gods no!"

"Between us then?"

She surprised him by looking impossibly relieved and he didn't understand the bit of resentment that caused. Usually he adored the ones who wanted to keep their involvement between the two of them rather than spreading so many rumors it turned into another edition of those damn books.

"Yes. Between us."

"Then ride and I'll see you back at the castle."

Smiling, she pushed her soaking golden hair off her face and said to Nightmare, "Go."

And to Ailean's shock, the beast did just as she'd asked.

What power did this female possess over wild animals?

"Well, she has no control over me, Dragon's Gold." When the horse snorted at him, he glared until she looked away.

8

A meal had never been so delightful for Shalin. Especially with so many others around. But none of Ailean's kin bothered to note or question the two of them putting their horses up together or quickly going off their separate ways. Instead they were too busy arguing, because apparently that's what they did when trapped in close quarters for any length of time. Any length of time being about five minutes, because it really hadn't been raining that long.

So Shalin spent the rest of the afternoon in the library. The entire time she had a book open, but she never actually read it. She couldn't focus. Not when she kept thinking about Ailean and what they'd done that afternoon. And the fact that he wasn't done with her. Perhaps they could meet again at the lake tomorrow. Or someplace else on his territory out of his kin's line of sight. On her ride earlier in the day she'd noticed a nice little cave built into a small mountain. A perfect place to spend some time alone.

But that would be tomorrow and she still had to get

through the night. Still, not too hard when it involved the Cadwaladr Clan. What she never expected, though, was for the twins—who sat on either side of her so they could keep her laughing through the entire meal—to turn to her and say in unison, "So tell us another story."

The room immediately fell silent at their request and all eyes were on her.

"Me?"

"You told us one before. Didn't she, Kennis?"

"Aye. That she did, Kyna."

"It can't be hard, then, to tell us another."

Without even thinking about it, her eyes focused on Ailean at the other end of the enormous table. She knew he could see the panic in her face, but instead of rushing to her rescue, he simply gave her a warm smile and winked at her.

And like that . . . her panic melted away.

Swallowing, she asked, "Humans or dragons?"

"Och," Kyna said with a wave of her hand. "We know all the dragon stories. Give us some human ones."

"Uh . . . all right." She thought a moment. "There's the story of the blind warrior who challenged an entire army to get back the woman he loved."

His family sat enthralled by Shalin's softly spun tale. Yet he felt like a right bastard because he couldn't stop thinking about her naked. And coming. Naked and coming. He had to see her like that again.

Ailean had never known himself to be so enthralled by anyone. He'd lusted, panted even, but never been enthralled. He wasn't exactly sure how to handle enthralled. Although he knew what he *wanted* to do, but he felt pretty confident Shalin would tear his balls off should he simply grab her up and take her to his bedroom to finish what they'd only just begun by the lake.

The room erupted into laughter from something she said and Ailean tried again to focus on her words and not the way the green dress she'd put on before dinner draped over her curves, or the way her body loosened up the more comfortable she became while telling the story, or the way her breasts rose each time she took a deep breath. He really had to stop focusing on her breasts.

Knowing he had to do something or risk everyone in the room noticing his lust, Ailean tried focusing on his breathing and thinking about the new cattle he'd recently purchased and the weapons he'd ordered. He tried thinking of *anything*, but nothing worked. His gaze kept moving back to Shalin, sitting there in front of his kin, appearing so innocent and shy—he knew better now.

Gods! How much more could he take?

He forced himself to see where in the story she might be, perhaps she neared the end . . . but he quickly realized the blind warrior of this story had not yet gone blind! Since Shalin's audience seemed more than happy to let her ramble incessantly about some not-even-blind-yet bastard, Ailean had no choice but to sit and wait until the evening ended.

Oh, but then he'd get what he so desperately needed.

"No, no. Books are not for chewing." Shalin dragged her tenacious little puppy off one of the books she'd found carefully stacked in a corner of her room. The books hadn't been there when she'd changed before dinner, so she could only guess Ailean had them sent up for her. The gesture made her smile. "We need to get you something else to chew on."

She glanced around the room. "Here. Use this chair." She crouched down and unleashed him on Ailean's furniture. It had seemed like a good idea until she watched the puppy go after that chair leg like she went after grazing cows. She reached for the hungry little demon again when she heard a soft tap at her window.

Looking carefully through the thick glass, Shalin didn't see anything. But the soft tap came again. This time she put her hands against the glass to keep out the glare from the torches and pitfire and leaned in close.

"Are you going to open the window—" a voice snarled at her, making her jump back several feet "—or just keep staring at me?"

She took a deep breath before she snatched the lock back and pulled the window open. "You scared the life from me!"

"I couldn't figure out what you were doing."

"Trying to see you." She blinked. "I still can't see you." She leaned out the window only to bump into Ailean's snout. "Oh!" It took her a moment and then she exclaimed, "You're a chameleon!" Which meant he'd been able to blend into the night and the building perfectly. Unless one was right on top of him, they'd never know until it was too late. It was a rare gift among the dragons of Dark Plains.

"Must you shout that?" he whispered. "My kin don't know."

"Why?"

"Because it irritates them when they don't know how I get past their defenses. And their irritation brings me such good humor. Now, are you going to let me in or make me stay out here in the cold?"

Shalin placed her hands where she knew his head to

be and leaned forward, trying to see the rest of his body. "Ailean, this is simply fascinating—and stop sniffing me!"

"I can't help it." His snout pushed through the window and nudged her groin. "You smell so good."

His moaned words had her stumbling back into the room and, after a moment, Shalin watched the dragon shift from nearly invisible to clearly visible and human. He flipped himself into her room and she quickly looked away from the sight of all that lovely nakedness. Drooling would do nothing but embarrass her.

"What is that vicious animal of yours doing to my furniture?" Shalin turned in time to see the chair tip forward because the puppy had eaten through one of the legs.

"Oh!" She picked up the puppy and turned the chair around so it leaned against the wall. "Bad puppy!" she chastised, but he seemed much too happy to care about her harsh tone. "Your teeth seem unnaturally strong for someone so young."

"I bred them that way."

"I see. I'm sorry, Ailean," she said, turning to face him. "I'll get you a new—oh!" He stood right behind her, all naked and warm and sinfully delicious. "Chair! I meant to say, I'll get you a new chair."

"Later." He took the puppy from her hands and set him down. As soon as those little paws touched the floor, the puppy ran right back to the chair and, Shalin thought with some despair, the remaining legs.

Ailean's hands slid into her hair, massaging her scalp while his firm lips skimmed across her cheek, her jaw, down to her throat. Teeth nipped at flesh while hands began to purposely move. Pushing her dress off while brushing here, touching there.

Shalin groaned when teeth nipped a bit of flesh hard enough to bruise.

"They lied, you know," he muttered, walking her back to the bed and going down with her on it.

"Lied?" She found it hard to concentrate when he kept nipping at her with his teeth before laving the same area with his tongue. "Who lied?"

"Whoever named you 'Innocent.' They lied." He rose over her, his hips between her thighs. As if he belonged there, he slid inside her and Shalin let out a gasp of pure pleasure.

"Trust me," she panted, her hands gripping his shoulders, "it was better than my other options."

His first stroke was slow. The second equally so, only he'd moved a bit. The same with the third and fourth, moving a bit each time.

Frustrated, she demanded, "What are you doing?"

"Figuring out what you like."

She frowned. "Figuring out what I—oh, oh, *gods!*" Shalin's torso arched, and she barely had time to bury her face against his shoulder and moan desperately into his neck.

"Aye. That's the one."

He didn't have to sound so smug. Until he did it again a few more times and Shalin realized he could sound any damn way he wanted to.

Ailean kissed her, his mouth slowly moving over hers, his tongue exploring. Lazy was the word for it. Lazy and wonderful.

"I can make you come like this," he murmured. And she knew he wasn't boasting. Any moment, she'd come all over him. "But I'm not going to."

His rhythm changed and Shalin's eyes opened wide in panic. "What—wait—*why?*"

"That would be boring, wouldn't it? Making you come the same way every time."

She desperately grasped his face between her hands. "Please. Feel free to bore me. At least this time. Or, if you're so inclined, the rest of the night. I *like* being bored."

Ailean grinned. "You're funny."

"Ailean—"

"Sssh." He took her hands in his own, pushing them to the bed, one on either side of her head. He nuzzled her cheek. "Trust me, luv." Now he nuzzled her jaw. "I'll get you there," he whispered before nipping her earlobe, hard. "When I'm ready."

Ailean gritted his teeth and stared up at the ceiling. He tried counting to ten. Thought about the weather and tried to focus on the storm that had come back to life outside this room.

But nothing, absolutely *nothing*, could distract him from Shalin's mouth on his cock.

She lifted her head, releasing him with a "pop" sound that made him shudder.

"Is everything all right?"

Ailean fisted his hands in the fur coverings beneath him. "Yes, Shalin, everything is fine."

"Are you sure?"

He glared down the length of his body at her. She'd been doing this to him for the last hour. Keeping him on edge, torturing him, really. And she knew exactly what she was doing. She kept that innocent expression on her face but Ailean knew all that innocence for the lie it truly was.

"Yes. I'm quite sure."

"Well . . . if you're sure." But she rested back on her heels. "Although I'd hate to disappoint you."

Ailean closed his eyes, tried the counting thing again. It still didn't work.

"Shalin."

"Ailean."

"Everything you're doing is perfect."

"Perfect? Really?"

His eye twitched. "Yes. However—"

"However?"

"However, you must keep going in order for it to remain perfect."

"Ohhhh. I didn't realize that."

"I think you did realize that." And slowly, he sat up, going on his knees. "I think you know *exactly* what you're doing to me, Shalin the Not Really Innocent."

Laughing, she backed away from him. "I don't know what you're talking about."

"Yes, you do." He reached out, snatching her around the waist and yanking her close. "You're a cruel, vicious vixen." He kissed her hard. "Admit it."

Her arms went around his neck and she relaxed against him. Nothing had ever felt better. "You're right." She kissed his jaw, his throat. "But I can make it up to you."

"Think you can, do you?" But she was already making his eyes cross simply from kissing a line across his shoulders.

"Well, Ailean," she said in his ear after she'd kissed her way back up, "I think I can definitely try."

And who was *he* to stop someone from at least making the effort?

*   *   *

They'd fallen asleep with Ailean cuddled up behind her, his arms tight around her waist. And he was still like that when Shalin felt the first thrust as he took her from behind.

Gods. Insatiable. This dragon was insatiable. And she absolutely loved it.

"It's almost dawn," he murmured in her ear while he used one hand to pull her hair off her neck. "I'll have to go soon."

"I understand."

"Unless you want me to stay."

She did want him to stay. But she didn't want to end up in one of his books. Another Ailean the Wicked conquest for the annals. No thank you.

"No. Go." She gripped his thigh, digging her small nails into the ungiving, hard muscle. "But come back. Tonight."

One hand slid down to her sex, his fingers stroking her, while his other hand roughly grabbed her hair. Holding her, he took her harder, his cock hitting that wonderful spot inside her that he had found earlier. This time he didn't stop, this time he didn't change his rhythm. Instead he kept up the pressure, the harshness of it until Shalin's entire body shook in his arms.

"I'll be back, Shalin," he growled against her neck. "You won't be able to keep me away. Understand?"

She couldn't answer, not with that climax ripping through her.

"Understand?" he pushed.

Shalin nodded and buried her face into her pillow so she could muffle her cries. Then Ailean pulled out of her and flipped her onto her back. He drove into her again, another climax washing over her.

"I love looking at you when I fuck you," he told her

plainly, each harsh thrust extending the life of her climax until she feared the intensity of it would tear her apart.

Ailean kissed her as he came inside her, his shout of pleasure lost in her mouth.

When he finally pulled away from her, he covered her sweat-soaked body with furs and kissed her cheek.

"I'll see you tonight, my little innocent."

She tried to say something meaningful to him but all she could manage was a rather undignified grunt.

9

Ailean had barely stumbled into his own bed when his brothers knocked on his door and walked in without actually waiting for him to tell them to.

"What?" he barked, his forearm covering his eyes from the now-invading light of the two suns blasting through his window.

"The old dragon is on the move," Arranz informed him, dropping down on the foot of the bed.

"Where?"

"Devenallt Mountain. He's arranged for a meeting with the queen."

"And he's still protected?"

"Of course."

"Don't give me that look. If anything happens to Shalin's father, she'll never forgive herself and I'll never forgive myself for making her unhappy. And we all know I hate when I'm miserable."

"What's wrong with you?" Bideven asked, his eyes watching Ailean closely.

"Nothing. I'm tired."

"The twins will take her to their home if you don't want her any more."

As much as Ailean wanted to simply respond, "Hell, no!" he knew that would be a mistake. Instead he gave a long suffering sigh. "No, no. She's my responsibility."

"If you're sure," Arranz told him, and Ailean could hear the smirk in his voice. Later, he'd toss him out the closest window for it.

"Aye. I'm sure."

"So . . . are you a witch?"

Shalin swallowed the porridge she'd spooned into her mouth. "No. I mean . . ." She sat back and thought a moment, trying to answer Kyna's question. Questions she'd had to ask herself a long time ago. "I know spells. Many. But I wouldn't call myself a witch. I don't have that kind of elemental power."

"What are you studying, then?"

"Alchemy."

"That's turning brass to gold, yes?"

Shalin laughed. Everyone wanted to change things to gold. "I don't think of alchemy that way. Changing one thing to a complete other thing doesn't make sense to me. I think of it more like taking a branch and making it a tree. Expanding on what it already is."

"That's boring."

Shalin nodded. "It is. But you could also make a dagger a sword. A sword a lance."

"Imagine that, Kennis," Kyna said before diving back into her porridge. "Imagine how deadly we'd be in battle."

"I've heard you already are deadly. They talk about you at Devenallt Mountain."

The twins shrugged and continued to eat.

"What makes you such good warriors?" Shalin asked casually, enjoying a conversation that had nothing to do with scholarly endeavors or throne politics.

"We like to kill," Kyna replied simply.

Shalin choked up her porridge, barely covering her mouth in time to stop it from flying across the table.

"You all right?"

She nodded.

"And we hate to lose," Kennis elaborated.

"I see." Shalin cleared her throat. "Don't think I've heard any other warriors put it quite that way."

"I doubt they enjoy the killing as much as we do. Our mates, they say we have the bloodlust. Can't really argue with them, can we, Kennis?"

"No. We really can't."

It amazed Shalin there were two dragons out there brave enough to be mates of the twins.

"You take Ailean. He loves a good battle and he'll kill when he has to, but I don't think he enjoys it."

"Unless someone pissed him off, eh, Kyna?"

"Exactly, Kennis. Then he enjoys it as much as we do. But when the war ended, we found other wars to join and he came back here. To his horses and his . . . uh . . ."

Shalin smirked. "His women?"

Kyna gave a little wave of her hand, clearly deciding not to go down that road. "Only we fight as human in these wars."

"So you spend most of your time as human, too?"

"Not as much as Ailean. 'Course, don't think anyone does."

"That's true," Kennis agreed.

"We do like it. Doubt we could live this way forever, though."

Kennis made a face. "Och! Never."

"Is it true you plan to be an Elder?"

Shalin tensed at the sudden change of topic. "Aye."

"You don't seem like an Elder."

"Well, I'm too young at the moment. Another three or four hundred years at least."

"Even then." Kyna pushed her empty bowl away, as did her sister. Always the same, those two. They moved the same. Talked the same. Nearly everything synchronized. It was . . . strange. Especially because Shalin felt the twins did it all on purpose.

"Even then what?"

"Even then you don't seem like an Elder. Is that what you really want?"

For one hundred and forty-nine years, no one had asked her that before. Now she'd been asked twice. She looked down at her half-empty bowl of porridge, suddenly feeling no hunger at all.

"They say I'll make a good Elder. Fair."

"That's not what I asked you, luv."

Shalin pushed her bowl away. "I promised her."

"Promised who?"

"My mother. I promised my mother I'd become an Elder."

"The dead one?"

Two pairs of eyes locked on Kennis and she winced. "Sorry. That came out wrong."

"How does that come out right?"

"What my sister means, Shalin, is how can you base your future on something you promised someone who has long left this world for another?"

"Honor. That's how. I promised her."

"What about what you want?"

"I didn't say I didn't want to be an Elder."

Kyna shook her head. "That's not what we mean, Shalin. And you know it." But before Shalin could press them on what they did mean, the twins abruptly pushed back their chairs, and stood. "We have to train."

"Something wrong?"

"Not at all." Kyna patted Shalin's head and Shalin realized she'd have a lovely headache from that "gentle" touch. "We just realized how late the day is and more storms coming."

Shalin didn't like the twins' abrupt ending of their conversation, but she decided to ignore it, since they were too frightening a pair to push about anything.

She slipped out the book she'd stowed away under her chair and flipped it open. She didn't know how long she was reading before she sensed someone had sat next to her. Glancing up, she smiled. "Good morn to you, Arranz."

"And to you, mistress. Everything all right?"

"Fine."

He leaned in a bit and whispered, "I was wondering, Shalin, if you could help me with something."

Other than reading, she had absolutely nothing to do. "Of course."

Ailean stomped down the hallway toward the kitchens. He needed a new rag and Madenn's skills to stop the bleeding on his arm. But he abruptly stopped in the middle of the hallway and took several slow steps back.

He looked into the room that held all the maps and documents necessary for when they made battle plans. He glared.

Arranz sat at one of the tables, his feet up on the thick wood, his hands laced behind his head. Shalin stood before him in a dress Ailean had never seen. Even more annoying—she'd been posing when he walked in.

"What in all the hells is going on?"

Shalin gave him a quick, shy smile that had his entire body burning. "Arranz wanted to see this dress on me to see if it would look nice on his lady friend."

"Lady friend?"

"Aye," his brother answered, smugness personified. "She's a tall human. About Shalin's size and I wanted to make sure the dress would look good before I gave it to her. Since it looks divine on Shalin, I'm sure it will do wonders for my friend."

Shalin blushed and nervously combed her hair behind her ears with her fingers. "Stop it, Arranz."

"Aye," Ailean growled. "Stop it, Arranz."

"I only speak the truth, sweet Shalin." It annoyed Ailean even more that his brother ignored him. "But now that I look at you, I don't have the heart to take that frock back."

Frock? Ailean had seen and purchased enough dresses over the decades to know a casual frock and a dress made for a woman. And this dress, off-white with gold thread weaved through, had been made for Shalin.

"I can't keep it, Arranz. It's too fine."

"It's perfect for you."

Too perfect.

"Arranz, if this is about the other morn . . ."

The other morn? What about it?

"No reason to bring that up, Shalin. You'll keep the dress and tonight we'll pull the tables back and dance."

Shalin's eyes widened and she stepped back. "I don't know how to dance."

"I'll teach you."

Over my dead carcass . . .

"Arranz, students of the Magickal arts don't dance. Instead we walk around giving disapproving looks at such activities."

"Really? Can you show me?"

Shalin leaned forward a bit and drew her brows down.

Arranz laughed. "I've seen that look."

"I believe you and all your kin have seen this look."

"You're not with some stodgy acolytes, Shalin. You're with the Cadwaladr Clan, and you'll dance."

Arranz swung his long legs off the table and stood. "Brother," he said as he passed Ailean.

"Bastard," Ailean muttered back.

Once he knew his brother had walked a good bit away, Ailean stepped farther into the room and closed the door with his foot.

"You don't like this dress on me, do you?"

"What?"

"The dress. You don't like it." Shalin smoothed the front down, and Ailean knew she loved the dress.

"You look beautiful in that dress."

"Then why are you—what happened to your arm?" She rushed over to him, and he turned from her. "Ailean?"

"You'll get blood on your dress."

"Don't be foolish." She rushed around him and latched on to his arm.

"Shalin—"

"Let me see." She lifted the cloth and frowned. "Gods, Ailean, what happened?"

"That demon beast you call a horse did this."

"Nightmare?"

"Who else?"

"Why? What did you do?"

"What did I—" Ailean pulled his arm away from her grasp and took a few steps back. "This is *your* fault, wench."

"I beg your pardon?"

"Beg all you want. This is your fault. You've bewitched the males here and now they've all gone mad." Him included, because all he could think about was tearing her lovely new dress from her body and burying himself inside her until the two suns burned from the sky.

"You're insane, all right. But it has nothing to do with me."

Slapping the bloody rag back on his still bleeding wound, Ailean snarled, "Stay away from my brothers, Shalin." He stormed to the door and yanked it open. "That is *not* a request," he informed her before marching out in search of Madenn—and Arranz.

Shalin must have sat on that table with all the detailed maps for an hour, her mind blissfully blank for once. But she didn't understand . . . was Ailean jealous? Of his own kin? *About her?*

It didn't make sense. None of this made sense. She looked down at the gown she still wore. She'd never had anything so fine. Before her time in Kyffin, Shalin had spent little time as a human, so there'd been no need for dresses. And as an acolyte at the school, she wore the requisite robes. So a dress this beautiful and regal was something she never thought to have.

And why had Arranz given it to her? It would have made sense coming from Ailean because of their . . . uh . . . tryst? No, that word didn't seem quite right. Not any more. Liaison? No. Too fancy for the way she and Ailean . . . uh . . . fucked, as Ailean loved to say.

Perhaps this was simply some sibling rivalry that had nothing to do with her. And she refused to see anything beyond that. She knew her heart to be a fragile thing and she'd encased it in ice long ago. She'd not thaw it now.

No. She'd simply enjoy this . . . this . . . *thing* for what it was.

Resolved, she stood and turned in time to see Arranz fall by the window, landing hard on the ground. Convinced that his seemingly hard head could handle such a drop, she went out to check on her horse. But she still chuckled when she heard Arranz yell, "*You blue-haired bastard!*"

10

"What exactly did you do to my horse?" Shalin accused him lightly as she dropped into a chair next to Ailean and watched his family and many of the humans who lived on the territory dance. What had sounded like a simple little get-together after their evening meal had turned into a large party. Not that Shalin minded. She liked parties, although she never really participated before. She usually sat in a corner and watched. It seemed, however, that sort of thing wasn't allowed among Ailean's kin.

"Me? That evil bastard bit me."

"You must have done something. It took me ages to calm him down and I had to feed him by hand."

"Och!"

"What?"

"You are so easy, Shalin. He's trained you like you've trained that puppy. Only he's done a better job of it."

"What does that mean?"

"Nothing."

He'd seemed miserable all night and she didn't understand why.

She turned in her chair, her knees grazing his leg. "You should dance."

"I don't want to dance."

"Dance, Ailean. I'm sure any of these ladies would love to dance with you." The glare he gave her had her rearing back. "What was *that* look for?"

"For someone so smart you can be so . . ." He bit off his next words and growled, looking away.

"If you're going to be like this, I'll go." She went to stand up but Ailean's hand clamped onto her arm.

"You want me to dance? I'll dance."

Then he stood and dragged her with him.

"Wait! Ailean!" She'd danced with both his brothers and several of his male cousins, but she'd been horrible at it. In fact, she'd been quite grateful for their jovial attitude regarding her lack of skill. "I can't—"

He turned and yanked her in close. "*You can dance with my kin, but not with me?*"

Her eyes widened at his growled words. His family, dancing around them, seemed quite oblivious.

"I'm not good at it."

"That didn't stop you before."

"Because I don't care if I make a fool of myself with them."

And like that, Ailean's anger seemed to evaporate. He grinned, placing one of her hands on his waist and gripping her other hand tight. Pulling her close against his body, he said, "Trust me, Shalin. I'll teach you."

"You won't laugh?"

"At you? Never."

Even though a fast jig played, Ailean started off slow, taking her carefully through each step. He kept her spirits up and when she was moments from quitting, and before she even realized it, they'd danced around the floor as if they'd been dancing together forever. Fast music or slow, Shalin handled all of it as long as she stayed in Ailean's arms.

She'd lost track of how long they'd been dancing when Kyna patted her shoulder. "We're going up, luv. Care to come with us?"

Shalin looked around and realized they were one of the few couples left. Others were enjoying late-night meals or had already left.

Shalin pulled out of Ailean's arms, hoping to control her human body's weakness of blushing.

"Of course. I didn't realize it was so late." She smiled up at Ailean. "Thank you for the lessons."

"My pleasure, Shalin."

Hoping he'd still come to her room later, Shalin followed the twins up the stairs.

Ailean went to Shalin's window as he had the night before. As dragon, but using his camouflage skills to hide his presence from anyone, even another dragon, who might be watching. She'd left the window open for him this time and when he pulled himself through, she stood with her back to him, a fur covering wrapped around her.

"Shalin?"

She didn't face him when he called to her, but instead asked with horror in her voice, "Ailean, I found chains and a metal neck collar in the small closet back here. Why are they there?"

Ailean winced and gritted his teeth. He'd forgotten to clean out this room before Shalin took it and Arranz had unusual . . . tastes.

He took a deep breath and prayed she'd believe the truth—although he couldn't promise he would have if the roles were reversed. "Shalin, you need to believe me when I say that Arranz—"

"Because I took them out of the closet and stupidly tried them on." She finally turned to face him, her head bowed, completely naked under the fur that she parted just enough to tease. Naked, that is, except for the metal collar locked around her throat and the chain hanging from it. "And now I can't get them off."

Slowly, so slowly he thought he'd explode right there, she raised her eyes to look at him. "Do you think, Ailean the Wicked, you can help me with this?"

Ailean let out a breath and walked toward her, watching as she dropped the fur covering to the floor.

"Aye, Shalin the Innocent," he growled, reaching out and taking firm hold of the chain hanging from the metal collar. "I do believe I can help you."

Winding the chain around his hand, he tugged her close. "But first, I need your help."

Looking shyly up at him through her lashes, she said softly, "Anything you want, m'lord. I am yours until the chain comes off. Until then, until you release me, I am yours to do with as you will."

"Then I need your help with this intense ache I have." He tugged down on the chain and, with a small smile, Shalin slowly went on her knees in front of him. "I need you to give me relief, Shalin."

Shalin gently ran her hand down the length of him, her small smile growing until she fairly leered at him. "Oh, it'll be my great pleasure, m'lord," she said, before she took him into her mouth with one deep swallow.

*   *   *

"You have to tell me," he said softly.

Shalin, who'd found a comfortable position with her head on Ailean's flat abdomen while his fingers combed through her hair, glanced away from the window and at him.

"Tell you what?"

"Who, Shalin?" And he smiled in disbelief. "Who in all the bloody hells named you Innocent?"

With a chuckle, Shalin kissed his stomach, loving the way the defined muscles jumped at the touch of her lips. "Adienna." She chuckled at the surprised expression on his face. "Adienna named me Innocent."

"Why?"

Shalin repositioned herself a bit so her chin rested high on his stomach by his ribs and her right arm wrapped tight around his waist. "Because I kept rejecting her cast-offs. She kept tossing these dragons at me with these little comments as to how they were as lovers and why I should try them out. As if she were giving them a go first for my benefit. When I rejected one of Ceanag's sons—I forget which one—she started calling me 'innocent.' And I decided not to argue the point."

Ailean ran both his hands through her hair as he so often did and gazed into her face. "But you didn't see me as a cast-off?"

Her eyes narrowed and she saw the look of concern on his face. "I won't say she didn't want you from the beginning, Ailean. But I can assure you that her knowing I wanted you so badly made it extra special for her."

When he only stared at her blankly, she admitted, "She knew I wanted you. And she made it her mission to get you. And afterward, every time she obsessed about you or talked about the night you shared, she did it to make sure she hurt me. Adienna likes to see others in pain."

Ailean took a deep breath, let it out, and said, "I'm sorry."

Shalin shook her head. "I don't need you to be. I'm completely aware of how enticing she is. Of how much others desire—"

"No," he said softly, cutting her off. "I wish I could tell you I wanted her because I had to have her. Because I desired her so much. But it was really because I couldn't believe a princess could want me, the lowborn."

"I hate that term. It's cruel."

"But how we're viewed. I went to her bed that night for every wrong reason there is and as soon as I got there I regretted it more than I thought possible. I always felt like these past years with her obsessing over me was some sort of punishment for not doing what I normally do."

"Which is?"

"Fuck the ones I want." He laughed, but it was bitter. "I didn't even fuck her. I brought her pleasure but that night I found none myself. I pushed her until she passed out, and then I ran like some startled kitten."

"You wouldn't be the first who ran," Shalin said. "Although you may be the only one who didn't come back out of fear. I do think you may finally be free, though. I'd heard a bit before the North dragons arrived that the queen has chosen a mate for Adienna. And Adienna is none too happy about it."

"I feel sorry for the poor dragon sharing his life with her for the next six hundred years. I'd rather swallow glass."

Before Shalin could respond to that, Ailean gripped her shoulders and pulled her up until they were face to face. "I'm sorry, Shalin."

"Stop it. There's nothing to—"

"I should have done what I'd planned to do that night, but I was stupid." His hands went from her shoulders until they cupped her face. "It was you I was going to see that night. You I was walking toward. Then someone stopped me, I don't remember who, and asked me some questions. When I turned back around, you were gone."

Shalin stared at Ailean as that night came back to her with stunning clarity. Finally, she gave a soft laugh and shook her head. "That bitch." She stroked his chest with the tips of her fingers. "She came to me that night, telling me to track down one of her personal guards. I searched everywhere. Every cavern, every chamber. After more than an hour I returned and found her guard already there. But the two of you were long gone. That explains why her friends were snickering at me the rest of the night, but I didn't pay it much mind. They did that a lot, anyway."

Ailean pulled her head down a bit and kissed her forehead. "I should never have listened to her. She told me you ran from me. That me, my reputation, scared you. And, like a fool, I believed her."

"She's very good at making a body believe whatever she tells them. Trust me when I say I won't hold it against you. However," she kissed his jaw, his throat, "that doesn't mean you shouldn't make it up to me."

Ailean roughly grabbed her rear and pushed her up his body until her breast hung over his face. His tongue flicked against the nipple, making Shalin gasp until he took it into his mouth and she groaned.

He sucked and teased until Shalin gripped his head and held him tightly to her. That's when he flipped her onto her back, him on top.

"I promise, Shalin," he said, his mouth already moving to the other breast. "I'll make it up to you all night long."

Ailean looked down at Shalin again. Asleep, she had her head resting against his chest, one arm around his waist, the other fisted against his shoulder. Her legs were intertwined with his and she slept peacefully, positive she was safe in his arms. She trusted him when she trusted no one else but her own blood kin.

How did he let this happen? How did he let her dig her way into his heart and became mistress of it all? But she had, hadn't she? His little dragoness.

Yet, what now? Once this all got straightened out—and he was sure the queen would do what was right—Shalin had her life to return to. Her school. Her future as an Elder. Although it didn't seem like she truly wanted any of that. Did she really want to sit through painful, dead boring council meetings over fights for territory between dragons? Did she want to live her life in Devenallt Mountain? As an Elder, she'd be required to live there at least part of the year.

Yet after spending all this time with her, it looked to Ailean as though Shalin wanted nothing more than to be left alone to read.

If she promised her nights to him, he could give her that time alone and so much more. Gods, there was so much he *wanted* to give her if only she'd let him.

The little dragoness brought him so much joy. And not merely in his bed. While he knew he made her feel physically safe, she had yet to realize that she made him feel safe too. Safe talking to her, being with her. She made him laugh one minute and lust for her the next. And sometimes she broke his heart because she felt so alone. He could see it on her face, the way she watched his family. Her expression torn between envy and annoyance.

Yet Shalin still hadn't realized what had become so clear to Ailean. She fit into his life, among his kin, perfectly.

She was the one he'd been waiting for all this time and neither of them had known it.

Ailean stroked her hair and smiled when she growled softly in her sleep.

"Who knew?" he asked the puppy staring at him from the end of the bed, the giant bone Shalin had given him slobbered over but uneaten and resting by his tiny paws. "Who knew I'd fall in love with Shalin the Innocent?"

11

"How long are you going to pretend we don't already know?" Kyna demanded, dropping into a chair next to him.

Ailean didn't bother looking up from the hot porridge and bread he shoveled into his mouth. Shalin had already gone out to the stables and he wanted to meet her out there before he got in some training later that day.

"Already know what?"

"About you and Shalin. We guessed it before, but the party last night only confirmed it."

"It's no one's business until we decide it is. Stay out of it." He reached for another loaf of warm bread, tore it in half and gave a piece to each sister. Kennis thanked him with a grunt as she dived into her own porridge, but Kyna wasn't so easily distracted.

"Come, Ailean. Really. Do you think it's fair to toy with her?"

"I'm not toying with her."

Kyna snorted. "Then what are you doing? Planning to have hatchlings with her?"

Ailean finished his porridge, grabbed another loaf of bread, and stood. He smiled down at his cousin. "That's exactly what I'm planning."

Enjoying the way the twins froze in shock, Ailean went out to the stables.

Shalin ran the brush through Nightmare's mane again and stepped back. "How about some braids today?"

"Because you're a big *mare* of a stallion, aren't you?"

Glaring at Ailean over the stall door, she corrected, "*Warrior* braids."

"For him? He's never been in battle."

"How do you know? You only found him a few months ago." She stalked up to Ailean and shook the brush at him. "And if I want to give *my* horse warrior braids, I'll damn well do it. Understand?"

Turning away from him before she got an answer—because she knew she wouldn't get an answer she'd like—she still heard the sudden grunt of pain and spun back around.

Ailean rubbed his head—and the lovely hoof print in the middle of it—and glared daggers at Nightmare.

"Oh, Ailean." But even as she went to him to comfort him, she still couldn't stop the laughter. "Are you all right?"

"As if you care."

"I care." She placed her feet on the slats of the gate and stood until they were eye to eye. She kissed his forehead and did her best not to laugh in his face. "I'm sorry. He's very sensitive."

"He's mad, Shalin."

"He's mine," she reminded him. "You promised him to me, did you not?"

"Yes. But I might be willing to temporarily change my rule on eating horse in Kerezik."

Nightmare moved forward but Shalin held up her hand. She knew she was the only thing standing between these two beasts getting into an ugly fight.

"Stop it. Both of you. Honestly, it's like dealing with two young ones."

"He started it."

Disagreeing, Nightmare slammed his front hoof down.

"I said stop this." She motioned to the partially eaten loaf of bread in Ailean's hand. "Give me some of that, would you? I'm taking Nightmare for a ride."

"Alone?"

"Yes. Alone."

"I'll go—"

"You said you have training and I'm only going to the lake. Besides, Nightmare will take care of me."

"That does not bring me ease."

"Bread," she ordered, holding out her hand. He tore what remained in half and gave it to her. "Thank you." Shalin kissed him, her tongue slipping between his lips to tangle with his own. They both groaned and Shalin realized she'd have to pull away or Ailean would take her right here in the stables. Not that she would have minded, but still—it seemed a tad inappropriate.

"We won't be long."

"Meet me in your library later."

Shalin blinked. *Her library?* "Yes. All . . . all right," she stammered, stepping down from the gate and unlocking it. She walked out and Nightmare followed.

"Be careful, Shalin."

"I will." She smiled before she took Nightmare out the less used exit at the back of the stables. She took him that way since he had a tendency to bite and kick anyone he passed.

"You like that horse better than me, don't you?" Ailean called after her.

"Sometimes . . . yes!" she replied and got a little nuzzle for her trouble. "And take care of the puppy!" Although her puppy seemed more than happy to spend his time during the day with the pack of dogs who had free rein of the castle grounds and surrounding forests, only to appear suddenly at her feet during mealtimes, clearly expecting to spend that time in her lap with food at his disposal.

Once she'd awkwardly mounted Nightmare—she really would have to learn to do that a bit better—he immediately took off at a full gallop. She didn't mind; she liked how it felt. Together they made a quick turn around the grounds right outside the castle before heading out to the lake. Once there, Shalin dismounted just as awkwardly and fed him apples from the leather pouch she'd tied around her waist. While she did, she chatted with him and petted his head and neck.

Eventually she held up the last apple and said, "I'll give you this apple . . . if you promise to stop hitting Ailean in the head with your hooves."

The horse snorted and turned his head away.

"Oh, come on!" she laughed, until he startled her by charging back a few feet before turning around.

Standing in front of her, Nightmare rose up on his hind legs and Shalin prepared herself to shift.

She stepped beside Nightmare and the twin males examined her from head to toe. They were fire dragons, but she didn't recognize them.

"He's protective," said one.

"Aye. That's good," said the other.

She placed her hand on Nightmare's neck to calm him. "Who—"

"Is Ailean about?" one of them asked abruptly.

"Castle."

They nodded and walked off. One decided to push the other, so the other pushed him back. Then there were headlocks and fists thrown—all while they kept walking.

"They're like that—*constantly*."

Shalin turned at the new voice and grinned.

"Daddy!"

Ailean dived for his blade, but Kennis slammed her lance down in front of it and raised an eyebrow. "You'll need to be faster than that, cousin."

He hated training with the twins. They were brutal and fierce and bloody mean. But he and his brothers knew—if they could hold their own with the twins, they could defeat anyone else. Kennis and Kyna were, by far, the greatest warriors of their clan and the most deadly of the Battle Dragons of Dark Plains.

Still, training with them was never fun.

He sensed but never heard Kyna as she moved up behind him and brought her lance toward his head. Kennis went for the legs.

Before the twins could even fly, they'd taught themselves how to fight in tandem. With fourteen older brothers, they really had no choice. They could use almost any weapon, but favored the lances they'd designed and helped forge themselves, which could adjust to their smaller human size or extend when they were in dragon form.

Ailean maneuvered back, reaching for the lances

but below the always-sharpened steel tips. Yet, like him, they sensed it and quickly adjusted, Kennis now going for his head and Kyna going for the legs.

He ducked the blow aimed for his head, but Kyna took him out at the legs, dumping him on his back.

Each slammed a foot against his chest and grinned down at him. "Sloppy, sloppy," Kennis chastised.

"Perhaps he has something—"

"Or someone."

"—on his mind, eh, sister?"

"I say we put him out of his misery."

"Good idea."

Together they raised their battle lances and Ailean cringed. They'd never kill him, but one never knew what damage they would decide to do.

"Oiy! Female!"

Kennis lowered her weapon and turned. When she saw her mate, she squealed, dropped her lance, and charged toward him, throwing herself in his arms.

"Don't make me come get you," Kyna's mate warned.

She snorted at Ailean. "Lucky for you." Then, like her sister, she dropped her weapon and charged her mate, landing in his arms.

Ailean raised himself on his elbows and stared at the quartet. How Kyna and Kennis had found their true mates with another set of twins, he had no answer. Especially when sets of twins were as rare among his people as white dragons.

"Oiy," he said to the males. "What are you two doing here? You're supposed to be watching old Baudwin."

"We did and we are. We left him by the lake with his daughter."

Ailean stood, and Arranz, still bleeding from the head wound Kennis gave him, and Bideven, still limping from one of Kyna's blows, walked over to him. "What about that?"

"What about what?"

"Her father. Here." Arranz gave a little smirk. "You going to tell him what you've been doing with his daughter the last few nights?"

"I find it amusing you didn't think we'd know," Bideven sardonically sneered.

"That old dragon may be weak, but a father is a father. He won't like what you and Shalin have been up to."

"I'm not too worried." Ailean wiped blood from the wound over his eye.

Arranz snorted. "Oh. You're not?"

"No. Once he finds out I love her and we're going to be together forever, he'll be fine."

Ignoring the shocked expressions on his brothers' faces, Ailean headed over to the well for fresh water.

"Ailean," Bideven rushed up behind him and asked, "have you actually mentioned any of this to Shalin?"

"No." He shrugged. "Why should I?"

Shalin hugged her father again before stepping back. She really saw his age when he was in human form and it hurt her heart. She knew she only had another hundred years with her father. Maybe two, if lucky, but no more. Her parents had waited until very late in their lives to have Shalin and although it never really bothered her, she also knew it made her different from all the other dragons who grew up with parents young enough to take them on long flights and teach them the proper way of hunting and fighting.

But Baudwin the Wise only hunted up that which stood right outside his cave. And although he could give detailed histories on every war that had taken place among the dragons *and* humans, he was a worthless fighter himself.

None of that mattered to Shalin, though. Her father meant everything to her. Always had.

"I'm so glad you're all right, Father."

"And I you." He pulled back, examining her carefully. "You don't look any the worse for wear."

She smiled. "No. I'm just fine."

And that's when her father's sharp brown eyes narrowed. "Are you?"

Clearing her throat, she said, "Oh. Yes. Just fine. We should go." She walked around him to get to the clearing.

"Go where, Shalin?" he asked in that calm way of his. "Do what? And shouldn't we have those two oversized beasts with us?"

Turning around, Shalin chewed on her lip. "I guess." She nodded. "You're right, of course."

"And aren't you interested in what the queen has to say?"

It took Shalin a moment to remember she hadn't been on Ailean's territory merely for sexual satisfaction. And if she hoped to conceal what happened between her and Ailean from her father, she'd better act more like she cared.

"Oh! Of course. Yes. What was the decision?"

"No decision. Not until the council meeting."

"A . . . a council meeting?"

"Calm yourself, Shalin. I see the panic in your eyes." He rubbed a soothing hand against Shalin's back. "The queen and Elders wish to have the case presented in front of all the court. And to everyone's surprise, the Northern dragons have put in a demand for the deal struck with Princess Adienna to go through as planned."

Shalin crossed her arms in front of her chest. "To everyone's surprise because who would want me?"

Her father shook his head in confusion. "What are you talking about? I mean surprising because we all assumed the Northerners would simply try to take you rather than follow the usual rules of etiquette. That's usually how they do things." Baudwin sniffed. "Barbarians. The lot of them." He nodded at his daughter. "That oldest one seemed much more civilized than his brethren. I assume it was his decision to put in the claim. I believe he truly likes you."

"Well, I can read," she said on a chuckle.

"Of course you can. You're my daughter." Her father glanced around impatiently. "Where do you think those two bickering ninnies went?"

"Drive you mad, did they?"

"Don't misunderstand me, daughter. I will appreciate until my dying day their protection. Truth be told, I knew with all certainty they would kill anyone or anything that moved within a dragon's tail of me. But the constant chatter—" He shuddered. "—it drove me to distraction." Which was her father's quiet way of saying if he could have killed them both . . .

"I should take Nightmare back anyway. I'll get them and bring them back here."

"Nightmare?"

She motioned to the horse. "Nightmare. My horse."

Her father frowned. "You named your midmeal? Shalin, you know better than to—"

"No, no. He's not . . ." she cleared her throat. "They don't eat horses or dogs here, Daddy. They're considered pets and working animals."

Her father made a small gesture with his hands. "I can't . . . they're just . . . the entire Cadwaladr Clan simply confuses . . ."

Shalin kissed her father's cheek. "I completely understand. And for that reason I won't mention the puppy Ailean gave me."

"Puppy?"

Shalin laughed. "I won't be long."

She walked off and Nightmare dutifully followed behind her. She led him back to the stables and to his stall. She made sure he had ample food and water. She rubbed her hand down his muzzle. "Now listen to me. I want you to let them feed you. Please. I have to go away and—" she swallowed "—and I won't be back. So I need you to take care of yourself and to let them take care of you. I've already had a word with that stablemaster."

Leaning forward, she kissed his muzzle and stepped back. "I'll miss you."

Then, before she did something horrifyingly human—like cry—she walked out the back door.

And right into Ailean.

Legs braced apart, arms folded over his chest, he stared down at her with one brow raised.

"They warned me you would simply try and leave and I didn't believe them. But you were, weren't you?"

Shalin sighed. "Don't you think that's for the best?"

"No, Shalin. I don't."

"I fear if my father sees us together, he'll know. And we both agreed this would be kept between—where are you going?"

But she knew exactly where Ailean was going and what he most certainly planned to do.

Ailean could hear her charging up behind him, demanding he stop and talk to her. But he had nothing to say to her. He knew exactly what she'd been planning to do and it made him blindingly angry even to think about it.

So he marched on until he arrived at the clearing by the lake. The old brown dragon stood as human, staring up at one of the trees. He seemed to be studying the birds. Why anyone would do that was lost on Ailean, but at the moment he really didn't care.

"Lord Baudwin?"

The older dragon turned, looked up at him, and took a hasty step back. "Ailean the Wicked? Gods. Did your mother perform spells before your hatching to get you that size?"

Ailean blinked. "Not that I know of."

"You are simply gargantuan! I thought those twins you sent were big, but you . . . simply frightening."

"Well—"

"How do you get around as human? Does no one question someone of your size lumbering around?"

"I don't lumb—"

Shalin pushed her way between the two males. "Father, we have to go."

"Where are those large fellows? Aren't they coming?"

"No. We'll go without them."

"Like hell you will," Ailean snapped.

"Don't," Shalin warned, "get in my way, Ailean."

The old dragon glanced between the two. "Is there something I should know?"

"No!"

"Yes!"

Baudwin sighed. "Somehow I sense I won't like this, will I?"

* * *

"I need to speak with you," Shalin said softly before walking away from her father.

Ailean followed and when she felt they stood far enough away, she said, "What are you doing?"

"Don't you know?"

"You have to know this is over. You must."

"That unhappy with me?"

"Of course not." She'd never been happier. But she had to be realistic as well. Passion and multiple climaxes did not a future make. And she had to think of her future. She had to stay on this path. "We both know I had a wonderful time here, but we also knew it would end."

"Why does it have to end, Shalin?"

"You're mad if you think I'll become one of your regular trysts."

"That's not what I—"

"I go to see the queen and the Elders today to get their ruling," she cut in. It horrified her when the thought of having *any* time with Ailean sounded better than none. The fact she'd sunk so low as to even consider spending her life as one of the females he regularly dropped in on when in certain towns made her stomach turn. She deserved better than that. "What happens from now on is no longer your concern. I appreciate everything you've done, and it will never be forgotten, but we both knew it couldn't go any further. So please, don't make this any harder than it has to be."

She'd kept it direct and calm, never once raising her voice or losing her temper. Considering how angry she was, she felt extremely proud of herself.

Suddenly, Ailean asked, "Do you love me?"

Startled, Shalin took a quick step back. "What?"

"You heard me. Do you love me or not?"

"What kind of question is that?"

"A simple one. Yes or no, Shalin. Do you love me or not?"

She forced herself to remain perfectly calm, perfectly in control. "No."

Ailean snorted. "You lying cow."

"I beg your—"

"Fine. I'll tell your father the truth myself."

Shalin grabbed Ailean's arm. "Don't you dare!"

"I'll make it quick," he said casually. "I promise."

He started walking, heading over to her unsuspecting father as well as the two males who'd been protecting him, Ailean's brothers, and the twins who'd just arrived. A veritable audience!

"Ailean, I'm not joking!"

"Nor am I. I understand why you're nervous. So I'll handle it."

It was his calm, casual tone. His relaxed nature. As if telling her father they'd been sharing a bed for days was something of no real concern.

Shalin jumped in front of him, slamming her hands against his chest. "You're not understanding me, Ailean. You're not to tell my father anything."

He leaned forward a bit and whispered loudly, "Don't you think he'll notice?"

"Notice what?"

"That I've Claimed you as my own. He'll definitely notice after the first hatchling."

Somehow, she still managed to control her temper— but it was definitely getting harder to do so. "You won't be Claiming me. Not you."

"Why not me?"

"Do you really need me to give you a list?"

"*A list?*"

"Don't yell, Ailean. Simply accept it."

"Like hell I will. You love me, why won't you just admit it?"

"And why won't you admit I only wanted one thing from you, I got it, and now I'm done?"

She saw it for only a moment, a flash deep in his eyes, the grim set of his mouth. She'd hurt him. But the part that wanted to soothe him, to see him smile again, she ruthlessly battered into submission. She'd shake this dragon from her tail even if she had to make him cry.

But Ailean didn't cry. He didn't argue. He did slightly flinch, but it was so small only she would have noticed it.

Without another word said between them, Ailean gently gripped her by the shoulders and moved her out of his way.

Shalin watched him walk over to her father and knew he'd ignore her wishes. Like everyone else, he assumed she'd be compliant. Adienna certainly thought so. She thought Shalin would quietly go off with enemy dragons to live in the North until she became ancient. And what made Shalin wince was the truth of it. Before Ailean and his brothers showed up, she had been taking the Northerner's hand. Without a fuss, she would have gone with them even as her heart screamed for her to fight, to flee. To at least try to stop them.

So, perhaps it was no great surprise Ailean thought the same of her. Like everyone else, he thought she'd comply. Bend to his will for her "own good."

To get what he wanted, he was willing to embarrass her in front of her father while his kin stood and watched. Then years later they could joke about weak little Shalin and how her futile protests were ignored. The pain of it ripped through her, leaving her shaken and angry. So angry, she could barely see or hear.

In that instant, something inside her snapped—and there'd be no going back now.

Ailean stood only a few feet away from the old dragon when Shalin suddenly stepped in front of him. The cold expression on her face surprised him. Wait. Not cold. Icy. An icy rage.

The instincts he'd honed in battle and war screamed at him to step away from her, but he didn't understand why. This was his sweet Shalin. And she'd simply have to understand this would be better in the long run. They were meant to be together and there was no use in fighting it any longer. Besides, Ailean had no patience to wait for her to realize it.

Ailean reached for her to again move her out of his way and, hundreds of years later, he'd refer to this as "one of the stupidest things I'd ever done."

In one fluid moment, as her father and his kin quickly scrambled out of the way, Shalin turned and her human body shifted to dragon. As she did, the razor-sharp tip of her tail lashed out and ripped across his human throat, slicing it from ear to ear.

Ailean's hands wrapped around his neck and he dropped to his knees. Blood flowed between his fingers and dripped onto the forest floor.

"Shift, you fool!" Shalin's father shouted. "Shift now!"

Ailean did, calling up the ancient spell and shifting right where he kneeled. His scales quickly covered his body, preventing him from bleeding to death right there.

As his body changed and tried to right itself, he watched Shalin motion to her father and take off from the clearing. Confusion on his face, the old dragon followed.

"Gods, Ailean!" His brothers stood on either side of him now in dragon form, trying to figure out the best way to help him while the twins tried to go after Shalin and most likely kill her in the air. But their mates held them back until Ailean, shaky from the loss of blood, stood.

He couldn't speak, not with his vocal chords sliced in half and still trying to mend, so he motioned to the twins' mates to follow Shalin and her father. To keep them safe. They understood and did as he bade. While his cousins continued to rant and swear blood oaths to Shalin's death, Ailean placed his blood-covered claws on each of his brothers' shoulders.

They'd grown up together. Fought together. Killed together. He didn't need words for them. Never had.

They knew they'd be going after Shalin themselves.

And then, Ailean would settle all of this.

12

Shalin waited outside the queen's meeting chamber. Soon she would have to enter and plead her case. Unfortunately, she really didn't care.

"I'll speak for you, Shalin."

She shrugged. "As you wish."

His claw brushed her cheek. "Look at me, daughter."

She did, but she quickly tried to turn away, unable to bear his gaze. But her father's other claw came up and gripped her other cheek.

"Do not turn from me."

"I'm so sorry, Father." Tears began to flow and she couldn't stop them. "I know I've disappointed you."

"Och! What is this? How have you disappointed me?"

"Ailean," she said simply.

"Because you tried to kill him?"

"No." Her tail nervously swished across the stone floor. "Because he and I . . . um . . ."

"You and he what?"

"I'd prefer not to spell it out, Father." Although she

had no doubts their story would become known throughout Dark Plains before the next full moon.

"Spell it . . . oh. Oh!" He absently patted her head before brushing nonexistent crumbs off his chest. "Yes. Of course you did, dear. You're not made of stone and he is quite a virile specimen."

Only her father could make it all sound so . . . medicinal. "And you're not ashamed of me?"

"Ashamed of what?" He quickly combed his claws through his gray and brown hair. "What were we talking about again?" he asked. It wasn't that he was confused, merely not interested. But when this was all over and settled, then he'd want to discuss it in complete detail and she didn't look forward to it. Nothing was worse than her father turning to her after a day, a decade, or even a century, after something she'd thought had long gone away and suddenly demanding, "Wait. What just happened?"

Stepping back, he motioned to her eyes. "Dry those tears, little one. This queen detests weakness. And when you are called, come in with your head high. Understand?"

She nodded. "Yes, sir."

"Good."

"Baudwin the Brown," one of the heralds called out.

Her father patted her cheek and gave her a quick smile before entering the meeting chamber.

Once his tail disappeared after him, Shalin took several soothing, calming breaths and wiped the tears from her eyes and cheeks with the backs of her claws.

Her father was right. She needed to get her emotions under control, but it would not be easy after that rage she'd let loose on Ailean. Unlike many of her brethren, Shalin kept her temper under control with a will of iron. In her mind, to show rage was the same as show-ing sadness, which meant showing weakness. She'd learned during her time at court that to show emotion of any kind merely gave Adienna what she needed to destroy those who crossed her.

Then Ailean came along and he had this uncanny ability to get all sorts of emotions out of her—irrita-tion, affection, rage. Even worse—love.

"As lovely as I remember," a voice said near her. She turned and blinked. It took her a moment to recog-nize him in dragon form, though the purple hair and scales were clear enough. But it was the eyes. Such a startling blue. Simply beautiful.

"Are you here to drag me away while I scream and cry?"

He laughed. "No, no, dragoness. That had been my father's idea. He still follows the old ways. I have, however, come here today in the hopes of convincing you to come with me of your own free will."

Now Shalin laughed. "I barely know you and you expect me to become your mate?"

"No. But I would love for you to come with me so I can show you my home. It's a rugged land, but you'll find more beauty there than any other place that you've seen."

Shalin looked away. "And if I don't come? There will be war amongst our people?"

The herald called to the dragon and, with a sigh, he headed toward the meeting chamber. "That I do not know. My brothers have different ways of dealing with females." He glanced at her over his shoulder. "They may not stop until there is war."

He entered the chamber, and she watched his tail disappear inside. For the first time, she noticed that the tip wasn't purple like the rest of him, but more like burnished silver. She sensed he sharpened it. Smooth and charming he might be, but a predator just the same.

Many long minutes passed until the herald returned. The green dragon stared at her. "Shalin the Gold. You have been summoned."

Ahh, yes. The Gold. When you entered the royal meeting chamber, the name you had earned over time was stripped so no one was above another.

Knowing she'd have to face Adienna, Shalin briefly closed her eyes, refusing to panic. Then, she raised her head proudly and walked into the meeting chamber where they all waited.

Ailean and his brothers landed at the entrance of Devenallt Mountain. He allowed Bideven to lead the way, knowing his brother knew the world of politics better than he or Arranz. All three brothers were dressed in their battle armor, but that was for show and rank rather than actual fighting. Although he'd do whatever necessary to get what he wanted.

"This is the meeting chamber," Bideven whispered.

With a nod, Ailean headed toward it.

"Ailean, wait. You can't just go in there!"

A large green dragon, a herald most likely, stepped in front of the chamber's entrance. Ailean grabbed him by the snout, yanked him away, and entered. As he'd been trained to do, he quickly took in everything around him so he could act accordingly.

The Elders sat on a dais built out of solid rock. The queen sat on a separate rock protrusion but hers was neither higher nor lower than the Elders. Although she was queen, the Elders still held great powers among the dragons of Dark Plains. Only during a time of war did the queen's decisions outrank the Elders', simply because they didn't have the time to vote and debate when lives were in jeopardy.

On the far side of the chamber he saw one of the purple dragons who'd originally come for Shalin. A good, solid fighter and strong, he'd be a worthy opponent. But when it came to Shalin, Ailean would tear the purple beast apart scale by scale to keep her.

The bastard sat with an audience made up mostly of royals . . . and Adienna. The smugness on her face made Ailean want to rip off her head himself. But his main concern was Shalin.

She stood alone, in the middle of the chamber in the center of a rune design etched into the cave floor. She held her head high and stared at each Elder without flinching. He felt unbridled pride watching her. She'd give him hatchlings to be proud of.

"Shalin the Gold," said Elder Cilydd—he had to be nine hundred years old if a day and, last Ailean heard, very nearly blind—"we've made our decision on this matter."

The herald strode up behind Ailean with his brothers right behind him. Ailean reached back and batted the green dragon out of his way and grabbed Bideven's shoulder and dragged him forward.

He motioned to his brother and Bideven only stared, so Ailean slammed his fist into his shoulder, hard enough to break something.

"All right. All right. Don't hit me."

Bideven stepped forward. "Elders. My Queen. I must interrupt these proceedings in the name of Ailean the Blue."

Ailean slammed his brother with his claw and Bideven hissed at him. "In this chamber all monikers are stripped save for the one given to you at birth. Now would you shut up and let me handle this?"

Forcing a smile, Bideven turned back to face the Elders and the queen.

The queen looked over at the brothers. "I've known Ailean the Blue many years, Bideven the Black. Can he not speak for himself?"

Bideven cleared his throat and glanced at Ailean. All Ailean could do was shrug and Arranz agreed with a shrug of his own.

"Actually, my Queen, he cannot. At this time." Another throat clear, and this time a furtive glance at Shalin, who refused to look at any of them. "His throat was cut while human and it still heals. It will be a few more hours or even days before he'll be able to speak without pain."

The queen's body went rigid and her eyes lashed across the hall to the Lightning dragon.

"Is this down to you, Theodoric?"

"Not I, Queen. Nor my kin—that I'm aware of. I sent them back to the Northlands yesterday."

"Then who did this to Ailean?" She looked around the chamber and finally settled her clear blue eyes back on Bideven. "Who, Bideven?"

Bideven scratched the back of his neck with his tail and stared down at his claws. "Uh . . . well, my Queen . . . uh—"

"I cut his throat," Shalin suddenly piped in, grabbing everyone's attention. But it was Ailean she now stared at and, with a viciousness he never heard from her before, she added, "And I'd do it again at the asking."

The room fell deathly silent and Ailean raised an eyebrow. Something Shalin took as challenge. Gasping, she stormed toward him but Arranz stepped between the pair.

"Now, now, hatchlings," his brother chided with obvious amusement, "let's be calm here."

"This is your fault," Shalin snarled over Arranz's shoulder. "*Your* fault. I wouldn't be here if it weren't for you."

Frustrated that he couldn't speak, Ailean grabbed Bideven by his hair and dragged him forward.

"Ow!"

He hit the black dragon on the shoulder and gestured at Shalin. Looking between the pair, Bideven shrugged. "What do you want me to say?"

Gritting his teeth, Ailean pointed at Shalin, pointed at himself, made circles in the air with his claw, and slammed his fist into the palm of the other.

Bideven's eyes grew wide. "Am I supposed to understand any of that?" he demanded.

But Shalin gasped and stepped back. "*I'm* being unreasonable. How can you say that? I'd told you to leave my father to me, but you wouldn't listen. *Like always!*"

Ailean slapped his claw against his chest, pointed at the ground with it, and then slashed both arms across each other, accidentally hitting Bideven in the snout.

"Ow!"

"Ho, ho!" Shalin barked. "Do you actually expect me to believe that? Or to base my whole future on that load of centaur shit?"

Ailean flashed his fangs and smoke curled from his snout.

"Don't you dare threaten me, Ailean the Slag!"

Resting his fists on his hips, Ailean slammed down his back claw, accidentally crushing Bideven's claw in the process.

"*Ow!*"

"No," Shalin answered with a haughtiness he'd never noticed before. Damn royals. "Absolutely not."

He brought his tail forward to make his point, accidentally slapping Bideven in the back of the head and shoving his kin forward.

"*Owww!*"

"That's enough." And then the queen was there, gently lifting Bideven's massive head, examining his wounds. "Much more of this conversation and your brother will be dead before the two suns set."

She gestured Bideven and Arranz away and stood between the pair. Enormous, and one of the rare white dragons, Queen Ganieda towered over Shalin while meeting Ailean eye to eye. "I have to tell you two that all of this complicates things. When your father came to me, Shalin, this was all very simple. Simple because what happened to you was and is unacceptable. Dragons don't sell dragons. I don't care if you're a lower-born, a royal, or future heir to the throne." Glittering blue eyes cut across the room to a glaring princess. "It was something that was understood, but now the Elders and I have been forced to put that down in writing so there is no mistake ever again." The queen sighed. "And once that decision was made, well, all need be done was track you down and let you know you could safely return to your life among the humans. Return home to your father. Or, if you so wished, and as Theodoric of the North so humbly offered, go with him into the Northlands and see if you could find your mate there. The choice, of course, was yours."

She took several steps away from the pair before turning back to face them. "Now, however, things have changed, haven't they, Ailean the Blue?"

He nodded, his eyes locked with Shalin's. Without a word, without moving, the greatest battle took place between them. The greatest and the most important.

"You wish to Claim her as your own, do you not?"

Ailean gave one determined nod in agreement.

"No!" The word rang out over the chamber, but it wasn't Shalin who spoke. She'd only shaken her head to let him know she'd rather eat stone than be his mate. It was from the princess.

She pushed past the other royals into the middle of the chamber. "I demand to speak," she snarled.

Her mother chuckled. "Denied. Your mate has already been chosen for you."

"I have not agreed—"

"You'll do as I say or regret that I ever gave you life," the queen hissed. "Your future mate waits for you. Go to him. Now. And on the next full moon, he'll make you his own."

"You can't make me—"

Ailean grabbed Shalin by the arm and yanked her against him as a line of flame lashed by, hitting the princess in the chest and sending her flying back across the chamber. Then Queen Ganieda, in a rarely seen full rage, stormed forward. She grabbed the heir to her throne by the neck and lifted her from the floor.

"You dare tell *me* what I can and can't make you do? You betray your friend, break our laws, and bring the potential of war down on our heads, and you think you have rights to tell me *anything*?"

Adienna gasped and slapped at her mother's claw, but the dragoness was simply too powerful. Even Ailean would have thought twice of challenging Ganieda. But he would have—for Shalin. For Shalin he'd take on an entire army of Lightnings and even his own kin.

"And you do all this," the queen continued, "for a male. A male who never loved you and never will. Now," she threw her daughter across the chamber to the exit, "go to your chosen mate before I can no longer control my temper."

Palpable rage radiating from her, Adienna dragged herself to her feet. The onetime friends locked eyes, but Shalin never backed down. She never looked away.

Then Adienna's gaze moved to Ailean and although he expected to see the same rage, he saw nothing but an obsessive longing that unnerved him more than the rage could have.

Without another word, the princess left, and the queen let out a disgusted sigh and shook her head. "Honestly. These hatchlings today."

She turned back to face Ailean and Shalin. "And as for you two—"

"My queen," one of the Elders gestured to her and she went to him. The queen and the council whispered amongst themselves while Shalin snatched her arm out of Ailean's grip and stepped away. She glared at him and didn't seem to appreciate when he blew her a kiss and winked at her.

"I agree," the queen finally said and turned to face them all. "I have one question for you, Shalin the Gold. Did you give yourself willingly to Ailean or did he have to seduce you into his bed?"

"What does that have to—"

"Answer me, dragoness." Shalin gritted her teeth and the queen smiled, showing many rows of bright, white fangs. "You've already seen how I handle my daughter's impudence. Do you really want to test me as well?"

Shalin glanced once at her father before looking away and answering, "Willingly."

"I see. Then yes, we have no choice but to follow the law regarding this. Ailean the Blue has until the next full moon to mark you as his own. Shalin the Gold will stay on his territory until that time. If she is not marked by the full moon, Ailean, you must leave her be. Is that understood?"

Ailean nodded and he could see it in Shalin's eyes. She had no intention of letting him mark her . . . ever.

"That being said, Shalin the Gold, Ailean can use anything in his, shall we say, *arsenal* to convince you to remain with him forever. Except, of course, violence or the threat of violence against you or your kin." Suddenly Shalin's father moved up behind the queen and whispered to her. She frowned in confusion and added, "Or against your . . . dog?" Shalin's father whispered something else, "Or against your . . . horse?" The queen blinked and shook her head. "You have a dog and horse?"

Shalin nodded, her head down to hide the rage Ailean could feel like he could feel the cold wind whipping through a hole in the cave wall.

"As pets?" Shalin nodded again. "How . . . fascinating." Although the queen sounded more disturbed by it than fascinated. "That is the decision of this council," she walked back to her dais. "We wish you both good luck." She smiled again, her rows of fangs twinkling from the light of the pitfire nearby. "I sense you'll both need it."

Livid beyond all reason, Shalin stormed to an exit that would take her from Devenallt Mountain. That's where Ailean caught up with her, grabbing her arm and pulling her around.

She slammed her two front claws against his chest and pushed. Of course, she might as well have pushed the mountain instead, for all the good it did.

"I hate you, Ailean the Slag. I'll always hate you and I'll never be your mate!"

She tried to pull away, but he held fast. He swallowed and she saw him wince from the pain. She ignored the pang in her heart that ordered her to soothe him. To take him to a healer and help control the pain. She ruthlessly tamped that desire down as ruthlessly as she'd cut his throat in the first place.

"Shalin, wait." His voice, always low, sounded like the hardest gravel and she knew each word caused him immeasurable pain. "Please."

"No. I'll come back to Kerezik as I've been ordered, but I'll not stay in your bed or even in that blasted castle. But I'll be on your territory until the full moon. Then I'll be heading back to school, and I never want to see you again."

She yanked her arm away and walked to the edge of the exit, ready to take flight.

"I'll come for you, Shalin. I don't care if you're on my property or living in a desert cave in Alsandair. I'll not give you up. You're mine. I am yours. Face it."

Shalin didn't even turn around. "The only thing I have to face is that I'll be paying for the foolishness of leaping into your well-used bed for decades to come." With a sigh, she glanced at him over her shoulder and the look in his eyes nearly tore her heart from her chest. She ignored it. "Leave me be, Ailean," she forced herself to say. "I'm sure there are thousands of females who'll happily warm your bed. Someone more suited to you and your life—for it is not me."

Shalin let her wings stretch out, but before she

took off, she felt compelled to add, "And I wouldn't shift to human anytime soon. You'll only bleed to death if you do."

Without another word or another glance back, she pushed off from the edge and headed back to Kerezik.

Ailean stood at the edge until his brothers arrived. Without bothering to look at them, he managed to ground out, "We need to find a healer."

"I know," Bideven answered. "My snout is still bleeding."

Rolling his eyes, Ailean snapped, "Not for you, you big baby."

"You really do love her, don't you, brother?" Arranz asked, awe in his voice.

Ailean nodded rather than answering. With every spoken word, pain ripped through him.

Arranz grinned. "Then we'll help you, Ailean. We'll get you your dragoness." Abruptly looking off, Arranz stroked his chin. "In fact . . . I think we should round up the entire clan." When his brothers only stared at him, he shrugged. "Trust me, Ailean. We may be low-born Battle Dragons, but we'll do whatever necessary to help one of our own. If you want that royal . . . you'll get her."

Ailean smiled, loving his brother more than he ever thought possible. He placed his hand on Arranz's shoulder and Arranz did the same to him.

"If you two are done having this moment of brotherly bonding, I am possibly bleeding to death here."

Ailean gave a small shrug at Arranz before using his tail to ram Bideven in the back, shoving the poor bleeding—and now screaming—bastard out of the cave.

He hit the side of Devenallt Mountain three times before he could catch flight.

"He's going to get you for that," Arranz warned.

"Perhaps," Ailean said, ignoring the pain so he could get this out. "But it was so worth it."

13

It started the first morning she woke up in that cave she found on Ailean's territory. Big and roomy, she'd nearly crashed into it, immediately falling asleep in the first chamber she found. She'd been more exhausted than she realized and slept a good twenty hours. She awoke when something indescribably small and adorable nipped at her snout and climbed up onto her head.

He'd brought her the puppy.

A few hours later she found Nightmare in one of the caverns with lots of hay and water.

The next day books began to appear. All sorts of books. Many she'd read. Quite a few she hadn't. She'd find piles of them in chambers, lined up against walls. Everywhere.

Then his kin came to visit. His aunts first, in teams of two or three.

"Just talk to him," they'd say.

"You know you love him," they'd accuse. "Why are you fighting this?"

Her favorite comment of the day? "I heard you were smart. You couldn't be that smart."

After the aunts, the uncles and male cousins arrived the following day. But they said very little and mostly brought flowers or cows before hastily leaving.

If only the same could be said of the female cousins. They came back and stayed for hours. They talked. They cajoled. They outright threatened. Except the twins. They never spoke to her and instead sat on the edge of the cave entrance sharpening their weapons. Every once in a while, they glared out over the land. Their silence hurt the most because Shalin had grown so fond of them. But unlike the rest of Ailean's kin, they clearly had "not forgiven you for the whole slashing throat incident," as Ailean's Aunt Briaga put it.

By the fourth day, and as the full moon neared, they all stopped coming. Leaving her alone to fully realize exactly how much she missed Ailean. Gods, and she did miss him. With her very soul she missed him.

Determined not to focus on the acute ache in her heart, Shalin shifted to human later in the day and put on one of the dresses the aunts had left for her, since the cave could get quite chilly for human flesh. She groomed and fed Nightmare, appreciating the way he kept nuzzling her, trying to cheer her up.

Once done, she didn't bother to shift back and instead walked to the cave entrance and sat down, her legs hanging over the edge. She stared out over the land. It was quiet. Not like the busy streets of Kyffin, where it was never quiet unless it was a religious holiday or a public execution was taking place.

Shalin didn't know exactly when Ailean sat down beside her but she wasn't really shocked.

"I'm surprised to find you as human, Shalin."

She gave a little shrug. "It's easier to tend Nightmare."

Glancing at him, she saw that his wound had healed but it had left a nasty scar behind. Would take a decade or two for that one to fade.

"Are you all right out here? Need anything?"

Shalin couldn't help but smile. "Hardly. I've had quite the influx of your kin stopping by with gifts."

"Good. Madenn sent up some food for you as well. It's cooked, though."

"That's fine," she said casually, although she'd already scented the food and her mouth had begun to water. Nothing like fresh meat she'd torn open herself, but she'd learned to enjoy the herbs and seasonings the humans used to enhance their cooked meats and fish. She'd definitely begun to miss it.

Not that she'd ever admit that out loud.

"Thank you for bringing my puppy and Nightmare."

"I had to." He chuckled. "Big bastard wouldn't eat and nearly stomped one of the stableboys when he tried to groom him. And the puppy whined incessantly when he couldn't find you at evening meal."

As if sensing they spoke of him, the puppy yipped and charged forward, but Ailean easily caught him before he slid right out of the cave. "You ever going to name this little one?" he asked as he placed him back on the floor and patted him back inside.

"Name him?"

"You have to name him, Shalin. We can't keep calling him 'puppy.' Especially once he gets to be about two or three hundred pounds."

Ailean slid his hand under hers, big fingers intertwining with her smaller ones.

"I've missed you, Shalin. I've missed you so very much."

She closed her eyes, trying to block out the sound of his voice and the words. But she didn't have the heart to shake his hand off. She liked how it felt against hers.

Ailean leaned in close and nuzzled her neck. "Let me stay the night, Shalin."

"I—"

"I promise I won't Claim you until you want me to."

She snorted. "So sure I'll want you to?"

"Not sure. Hopeful."

He kissed a trail down her neck to her shoulder, tugging the dress down a bit so he could toy with the flesh beneath.

"If I let you stay," she whispered, already losing the battle, "you know it won't mean anything."

Ailean reached around, sliding his hand into her hair and gripping the back of her head. He forced her to look at him. "We both know that's a lie. But if it makes you feel better this night, I won't argue." His gaze traveled to her mouth. "Gods," he moaned, "I've missed you, Shalin."

Shalin opened her mouth to speak, to tell him to go before she lost any more of her heart to him, but before she could get the words out, he kissed her. And, as always, her human body nearly burst into flames from the passion of it.

She couldn't fight him. Not when she'd missed him so much. So she released herself into that kiss. At least for the moment, she let go the anger and stubbornness and simply unleashed the desire she'd been bottling up for days.

*   *   *

Gods, he truly had missed her. Just the feel of her mouth on his or the way she pressed her body into his. Whether human or dragon, she always fit him perfectly. For days he'd been longing for her, following his kin's dictate that the time wasn't right. His aunts were insistent. "When a dragon pushes a dragoness, he ends up very lonely . . . and very bloody."

Without prompting, Shalin straddled his waist, her knees on either side of him. She dug her hands into his hair and kissed him with as much need as his own.

Desperate and unable to wait, Ailean pulled the skirt of her simple peasant dress out of his way and entered her in one powerful thrust. He found her wet and hot, more than ready for him.

Shalin wrapped her arms around his shoulders, buried her nose in his neck, and it all felt so perfect. Ailean didn't move. They simply held still like that.

When Shalin began to shyly kiss his neck and jaw, Ailean pulled back a bit to look at her. "Tell me what I did wrong." When she only stared at him, he said again, "Tell me what I did wrong and I'll do whatever necessary to make it right."

Her gaze lowered until she seemed firmly focused on his neck and she admitted, "You didn't listen to me. I'm ignored by everyone. I never thought I'd be ignored by you as well."

"I didn't ignore you."

She gave an adorable little snort and looked away from him completely.

"I didn't ignore you," he said again. "But I was fighting for my life. For our future. I knew if I'd let you go, you wouldn't come back."

Those bright golden eyes suddenly locked on him and he could see the bitter anger in them. "Isn't that my right? To choose my own lovers, my own mate? Or do you wish to control that, as Adienna does?"

"Don't throw her at me, Shalin. That's not fair and you know it. Don't you see or are you so blind? I would have broken any law, destroyed any army, done *anything* to keep you as my own."

"Why?"

"Why what?"

"Why are you so determined to 'keep me'? Is it because I'm sweet and innocent like the puppy? Or solid and reliable like Dragon's Gold? A good work horse to breed you sons?"

And it was at that very moment, before he could stop himself, that he laughed at her.

Snarling in outrage, Shalin tried to scramble out of his arms, but he grabbed her around the waist and kept her right on his lap and his cock.

"Oh, no, you don't. You'll not run away from me again until we're done here. Until you hear everything I have to say."

"Then say it and let me go."

"Fine, then. You're not sweet, Shalin. Oh, I know you fool everyone else into thinking you are, but I know better. And you? Like Dragon's Gold? More like that beast you love sitting in his chamber plotting his next attack."

She gasped in anger, but his grip merely tightened on her waist, holding her still.

"You're just like him, you know. Just like Nightmare. Exactly. He, too, stands by appearing placid and mild. Then, when you get close enough to touch him, he proves how dangerous he truly is. Just like you. Nor can I call you a reliable work horse since I never see you actually working, lazy sow."

"Ailean!"

"Anytime I look for you, I always find you in the library reading. I'm relatively certain three hundred years from now that's exactly where I'll find you still." He chuckled again. "You're the most dangerous kind of dragon, Shalin. Like the sand dragons, you blend into your environment and you wait. You wait until the very last second, until there's no hope for escape or mercy, and then you strike."

Shalin shook her head, confused. "If I'm so horrible—"

"I never said you were horrible. I said you were dangerous."

"And a lazy sow!"

"You are a lazy sow," he taunted back. "A spoiled royal, expecting everyone to serve *you*." And he punctuated that "you" by slapping her ass . . . rather hard.

Startled into action, she reached for his face with fingers bent into human claws but Ailean easily caught her hands and forced them behind her back, laughing the entire time.

"You're a bastard!" she hissed.

"A mad bastard, according to my kin." He blinked and with false shock said, "Why, Shalin? You're getting even wetter! Enjoy that slap, did you?"

She screamed and fought to pull her arms away.

"Gods," he gasped. "Like a vice. You like a bit of a struggle too, I see. And," he added before kissing her throat, "you like when I won't let you go."

"Lies," she moaned, melting against him. "These are all lies."

He moved up her throat, across her chin and cheek. He held her arms crossed behind her back but his fingers continued to stroke her skin, teasing her.

Ailean rocked up into her while he pulled her body down. Shalin threw her head back, the feel of him inside her nearly more than she could bear.

"Kiss me, Shalin," Ailean panted. "Kiss me now."

She looked at him then, but didn't understand what she saw. What she knew he was trying to tell her with his expression alone. Yet even though she didn't understand, she was still drawn to him as she'd never been drawn to another. And, she feared, as she never would be again.

Shalin kissed him and the power of it tore through them both. Holding her arms tighter, Ailean slammed her down as he pushed up, the rhythm of it bringing her to climax within seconds, her surprised screams disappearing into Ailean's mouth. He groaned in absolute pleasure and kept going, kept taking her. She exploded a second time, reduced to nothing more than whimpers and soft mewling.

Finally, when she didn't think she could take much more from him, he brought her down hard and held her in place as he climaxed inside her. His face buried against her neck, he groaned and gasped as his pleasure seemed to roll on and on, yanking her over the edge a final time. She nearly passed out from the intensity of it and could do nothing more than let her body go limp against his.

Ailean released his grip on her arms and Shalin brought them forward, too weak to do much of anything but drop them around his shoulders.

"Oiy," he said softly. "Lazy sow."

She knew she should be insulted but she was simply too tired to argue with him at the moment. "What?"

"There's another reason I like to keep you around."

"And that is?"

"I love you."

Shalin tensed at the words, but Ailean's hands rubbed her back, soothing her. "Sssh. No need to panic. I just wanted you to know everything for when you make your decision.

"I'll stay the night," he added.

Arms around him, Shalin laid her head against his shoulder and nodded.

14

Shalin awoke early to the puppy scratching at her head. She dragged herself up and gave him water and food. She checked on Nightmare, who seemed to be enjoying his solitary life quite well. She gave him some fresh water and hay before pulling on another little frock left by Ailean's kin. Once dressed, she set off to find Ailean.

It had been a long and delightful night with the dragon. He hadn't let her get much sleep but she didn't really feel the need to complain about it. Besides, after their night, she'd come to a decision. But there was one thing she had to do first, and she wanted to let Ailean know.

Eventually she tracked him down by the cave entrance. Still human as well, he stood naked at the very edge, staring out over the land. She walked up to him and immediately knew something was wrong.

"What is it?"

Ailean nodded toward the east.

She looked and immediately her heart fell. "I see lightning."

"And not a cloud in the sky."

Shalin let out a little sigh. "I guess Theodoric's kin didn't abide by his decision."

"I had a feeling they wouldn't."

She nodded. "As did I." Shalin began to pull off the dress, preparing to change and not wanting to ruin it, but Ailean stopped her.

"No."

"Why not?"

"If you shift, and they catch up to you, they'll take at least one of your wings. Stay human as long as you can." He took her hand and dragged her back inside. "Take Nightmare back to the castle."

"No." She stopped, and he turned to face her. "If I go there, they'll only follow."

"They'll go there anyway. I need you to protect the castle and my people."

"Me? How can I protect them?"

"Think of something," he said plainly, again dragging her toward where they'd bedded for the night and where Nightmare was standing. "You've read enough books. You must have some ideas."

He stopped long enough to open the gate built into the cavern walls and let Nightmare out. Shalin quickly grabbed the puppy, but Ailean shook his head.

"He'll be safer here."

She nodded and placed him back on the ground. Ailean again grabbed her hand and pulled her out of the chamber and down deep into the catacombs, Nightmare right behind them. It took some time, but eventually she saw a shaft of light and she finally knew how he and his kin had been getting in and out of this cave. Which quickly brought her to another realization.

"This was your mother's cave, wasn't it?"

"Aye. I was born here." And close to where his mother had died.

Once outside, he released her hand and she mounted Nightmare's back and took firm hold of his mane.

"You know your way back?"

"Aye."

"Then go. Protect our people, Shalin."

Ailean slapped Nightmare's rump, forcing her horse to sprint off into the forest.

Ailean waited until they were far enough away, then he shifted and grabbed hold of the outside cave wall. He easily climbed it until he reached the top. Then he lay flat against it, using his gods-given skill to change his coloring to blend into the rock face.

He waited, and it wasn't long before four of them came into sight. Ailean closed his eyes, his other senses taking over. Their scent moved closer, but Ailean waited until he heard their wings and felt the air around him move. When he knew they'd passed him, Ailean rose up into the air and grabbed one, his arm wrapping around the Lightning's throat. The outsider roared and his comrades turned to face them. That's when Ailean unleashed a ball of flame that forced them back. While he had the moment, Ailean flipped the smaller dragon in his arms upside down and used his talons to rip apart his soft underbelly.

Ailean had only just reached inside the screaming dragon and yanked out his intestines when a harsh bolt of lightning hit him in the shoulder. He dropped his prey and slammed into a tree, the leaves surrounding him, momentarily confusing him. Once he'd pulled himself out, another Lightning waited for him.

Before Ailean could react, the bastard unleashed a bolt of lightning aimed right at his head. Ailean began to move out of its way when a glint of metal momentarily blinded him. He jerked to the side and his vision cleared. One of his aunts hovered in front of him, her large shield up. The lightning hit it and bounced off, slamming back into the sender.

"Go!" his aunt yelled. "I've got them. Go!"

Nightmare tore through the forest while Shalin held on to his mane and kept low. She did know the way back, but she didn't need to.

The horse kept close to the trees, using them as cover, and kept away from the clearings. But no matter what they did, unless they wanted to go days out of their way, they'd have to cross the clearing near the lake.

And, as Shalin had predicted, as soon as Nightmare made it out of the forest, he had to scramble to an abrupt halt. They dropped from the sky, stretching out in a line from the lake, and across a good portion of the clearing. They didn't attack. They didn't want her hurt.

They wanted her to shift, hoping she'd panic and try to go over them. The glint of their sharpened weapons told her exactly what they'd do. With one wing, she wouldn't be going anywhere and then they could carry her wherever they'd like. She'd read that's how they kept dragonesses they stole, but Shalin had always hoped those were merely lies told by their enemies. Now she saw there was truth to it. And although Theodoric obviously had hoped for more from his kin, some of the old ways were simply too hard to give up

when desperate. For although they could sate their lust
with a human, they could never breed with one.

"Dragoness," one said, and the voice sounded familiar. She remembered him.

"You're Theodoric's brother."

"Aye. Erdmann. Twelfth oldest."

Shalin didn't even want to know how many they
had in total to warrant that answer.

"Theodoric won't be happy with what you've done
here today," she told him.

"Not at first. But once we battle for the right to be
your mate, he'll understand."

"Ailean will come for me." And she knew it to be
true. She knew it with all her heart. "He'll destroy all
of you to get me back."

"We smell him on you," one of the others remarked. "But I'd bet gold he hasn't marked you. So
how attached could he be?"

A few of them moved in a bit closer, slowly trying
to surround her. Nightmare stood perfectly still but
Shalin could tell by his tense muscles he knew what
was happening; he was just waiting for the right moment.

"It doesn't matter, Shalin the Innocent, if he comes
for you," Erdmann told her softly. "The queen of this
land will never send an army out to bring back one
dragoness. And if he comes alone, he'll die alone."

Slowly, Shalin smiled. She'd heard nothing, she'd
always remember that, but still somehow she knew.
"Ailean the Wicked needs no army to bring me back—
and he *never* fights alone." Her smile grew wide. "He
has his kin."

Moving as silently as the smallest mouse, Kyna
landed on Erdmann's back, bringing her tall steel shield
down with her. She slammed it into his neck, slamming

him to the ground. The sharp end of her shield rammed into the purple scales with such force it ripped through them and into the flesh until it was buried in the dirt and Erdmann's head thudded to the ground.

Kennis landed on the back of another dragon and buried her lance in his spine.

Kyna looked over at Shalin and Shalin no longer saw anger. At least, not toward her. "Go!" Kyna ordered, jumping off Erdmann's still flailing body as the blood from his neck continued to spay across the clearing.

Nightmare must have understood Kyna because he took off with no prompting, running under and around the battling dragons as more of Ailean's kin dropped from the skies, weapons in hand, and ready to kill.

They tore back to the castle and burst through the courtyard gates as bells rang in warning, and Ailean's human soldiers prepared for battle, the servants scrambling for someplace safe to hide.

Nightmare slid to a halt right in front of Madenn.

She let out a breath when she saw Shalin on the horse's back. "I feared—"

"I know." Shalin reached down and grabbed a soldier trying to dart by. "Get the gates closed—now."

With a nod, he took off running as Shalin slid off Nightmare's back.

"What good will that do?" Madenn demanded. "They'll simply fly over it."

"Leave that to me. Get everyone—" Shalin cut herself off as she grabbed Madenn around the waist and yanked her out of the way, the bolt of lightning hitting where the woman had been standing.

Shalin pushed her away, staring up at the sky. "Go. Now."

Moving quickly to the center of the courtyard, Shalin finally shifted. Going on memory alone, she drew a circle of ancient symbols in the dirt. Once done, she looked around desperately until she spotted another soldier.

"Your shield," she shouted at him. "Give it to me." He tossed the metal shield at her, and Shalin caught it easily, placing it carefully on the ground inside the circle.

Lightning danced around her, but she knew none would hit her directly since they couldn't afford for her to be hurt. She kept her wings tucked in close to her body and focused all her energy into the shield. As it pulsed to life, she slammed her claw down on it and the metal flattened, turning to liquid. She chanted a recently learned spell and the liquid disappeared inside her hand. It tore through her. Through her organs and veins, tearing up through her lungs.

Shalin raised her other claw, palm up, and liquid burst out and up, heading toward the sky. It exploded over the castle and the courtyard, creating a solid metal bubble over all she visualized. A shield now for the entire structure.

She heard roars of anger, then screams as unleashed lightning bolts slammed back into those who sent them.

"By the gods," she heard Madenn whisper.

For some reason that made Shalin chuckle—just before everything went black and her head took out the front of the castle where she landed.

Ailean held the head while Arranz held the back claws and Kennis happily chopped away at the neck. Once they separated head from body, they let it drop.

It hadn't taken long, wiping out a small army of

Lightning dragons. Well, it would have if he'd been fighting with the queen's army. There were rules to follow and those who gave orders to listen to.

But a family free-for-all, as his father liked to call it, usually ended pretty quickly. Although it was quite enjoyable while it lasted.

Glancing around, he saw that his kin had it under control, so he motioned to Arranz and Bideven. "Back to the castle. We need to—"

Ailean abruptly stopped talking. His head tilted to the side as he stared out over the trees toward his home.

"What's that?" he asked his brothers, pointing at the silver thing glinting from the early afternoon sun.

"I . . . I have no idea," Bideven responded. And since he was the smartest of them all, if he didn't know, none of them knew.

Panic flooded through him and Ailean charged forward, heading toward the castle. As he neared, he saw several Lightning dragons lay on the ground. They weren't dead, but they were unconscious.

His brothers were on either side of him, Kyna and Kennis hovering behind him.

Slowly, he moved around the foreign thing above his castle. It fit snuggly against the gate surrounding his castle. A perfect fit. Eventually, not knowing what else to do, Ailean leaned forward a bit and rapped on it with his fist. It was metal. Solid metal.

"What in all the hells is this?"

Arranz tapped his shoulder and pointed to the middle of it. "Brother . . . isn't that your crest?"

It was. The crest his human soldiers wore on their shields and surcoats.

Ailean laid his claw flat against it, and the solid metal suddenly wobbled a bit before dropping away completely. Stunned, he watched the metal shrink and change back into the small human shield it once was, landing with a loud clatter at the clawed feet of Shalin.

"Oh, gods!"

He quickly landed beside her, his brothers and the twins right by his side, Nightmare anxiously pawing the ground near her left shoulder.

"Shalin?" He pushed her hair from her face, leaned in close and said loudly, "*Shalin! Can you hear me?*"

She winced. "Don't scream."

Ailean let out a breath and glanced back at his kin. "She lives."

In answer to that, Shalin coughed and a piece of metal flew out of her mouth, landing near the shield. Arranz picked it up and held it next to a small open hole toward the base.

"Look at that . . . it fits."

"That's it." Kyna stood. "I'm going out beyond the castle gates to kill the rest of the Lightnings. That I understand. This—" she motioned to the shield Arranz held "—I don't." She took flight, her sister right behind her.

"Shalin . . . what did you do?"

"Did what you told me to. I protected our people."

Ailean gave a small smile. "Yes, luv, you certainly did."

But she didn't answer. She'd passed out again.

15

Shalin woke when she heard arguing. She rolled her eyes. *Can they never get along?*

Glancing around, she realized they had her back in the cave. She lay on a huge pile of furs, a large pitfire nearby, and the disgusting taste of metal still in the back of her throat.

She pushed herself up until she could sit back on her haunches. The cave shook as the arguing between kin became more . . . insistent.

Shalin didn't know what they were arguing about and she didn't care. Instead she focused on finding a bit of parchment and a quill.

Shaking blood out of his eyes, Ailean slammed his fist into one brother's face and used his tail to toss the other across the cave floor.

Bideven jumped up and charged and Ailean lowered himself, waiting for the hit.

But Kyna stepped between them, grabbing both

brothers by the hair and shaking. Ailean would have to admit—it hurt.

"Stop it. Both of you." She shoved them apart while Kennis helped Arranz to his feet. "Is this about Shalin?"

Ailean frowned, confused by the question. "No."

"Then what are you three up to?"

The brothers all shrugged. "We were bored," they said at the same time.

Disgusted, Kyna paced away from them. "That's brilliant."

"What's wrong?"

"She's gone," Kennis informed them.

"What do you mean she's—" Ailean pushed past them and walked into the chamber they'd put her in. All that was left—a piece of parchment.

"I'll be back," Bideven read over Ailean's shoulder.

"Is that a promise or a threat?" Arranz asked.

Ailean crumpled the parchment in his hand at the same time he expanded his wings, sending both of his brothers flying across the chamber.

Shalin walked into her father's work chamber and smiled. How could she not when she found the old dragon on his knees and under the enormous wood desk he used to work on? His tail lazily swung back and forth while he dug through books and muttered to himself. Her heart swelled at the sight of him. Even *that* sight. Gods, she loved him so much.

"Father," she said softly, as not to startle him. But he jumped anyway, slamming his head into the desk.

He moved out from under it and smiled at his daughter. "Shalin!"

"Hello, Father."

"What are you doing here? Is everything all right?" He walked closer to her. "You look tired?"

"North dragons came for me."

"Oh, dear." He leaned in a bit, his face solemnly sincere. "I feared as much. Do you need me to protect you?"

Shalin snorted, and her father smirked. "Thank you very much, Daughter."

Covering her snout, Shalin shook her head. "Forgive me, Father. I didn't mean—"

He waved her words away. "We both know I'm no warrior."

"But you'd die to protect me."

"Of course." He hugged Shalin. "You mean everything to me." He kissed her brow. "Sit and you'll tell me why you're here."

Her father motioned to a spot closer to the pitfire.

"Now I have some delicious wine here somewhere. If I could just remember where I put it."

Shalin smiled. Her father misplaced everything. It used to drive her poor mother insane.

"Ahh. Here." He grabbed two goblets and what looked to be a very old bottle of wine before he sat down across from his daughter.

"Are you hungry?"

"Not really."

"Like your mother with that. Won't eat when something worries you." He pushed the filled goblet closer to her with the tip of his claw. "Drink then talk."

She sipped the wine. "It's very good."

"I found it just the other day. I think I put it away three or four hundred years ago." He shrugged. "Or maybe it was last week. I never remember."

Her father sipped his wine and said, "So what is it, Shalin?"

"I've made a decision."

"About Ailean?"

She nodded. "He told me he loves me."

"And do you love him?"

"I do."

"Then why the hesitation to admit you want him as your mate?"

"Father, they call him Ailean the Whore."

"Aye. They do. They also call him Ailean the Deadly. Ailean the Powerful. Ailean the Decimator, which is my personal favorite. He has many names you can be proud of." Her father thought for a moment. "If you're a dragon," he added for good measure.

"But there are so many of them, father. There's Ailean, his two brothers, an untold number of aunts and uncles. Cousins. And the twins. I'm not used to so many around me."

"It's time you had kin of your own, Shalin. You've never been like your mother and me."

That surprised her more than she could say. "I haven't?"

"No. Don't you think a father knows? You were lonely. And bored. When the queen asked for a companion for her daughter, I sent you there thinking it would be good for you to get out and meet others. I had no idea the princess was a vindictive little bitch, though."

Shalin almost spit up the wine she just drank. "Father!"

"It's true. If I'd known how bad she was, royalty be damned."

"It was a good experience. I've had access to books and knowledge I never would have, had I not been part of the court."

Her father smiled at her attempts to soothe him. "And you've become quite the diplomat as well."

Shalin laughed. "I guess I have."

"The Cadwaladr Clan needs that, Shalin. They need *you*. Ailean needs you."

"He does?"

"Gods, lass. Are you that oblivious?" She couldn't believe her father, of all dragons, had the nerve to actually say that. "He's lost his heart to you, Shalin. Make no mistake."

"And I've lost my heart to him, Father. That's why I've decided to stay with him." She placed the glass down and ran her claws through her hair. "But—"

"But what, Shalin? What has you so worried?"

"I promised her. Promised I'd become an Elder and I doubt I can do that if I'm the mate of Ailean the Whore. His reputation alone will—"

"Promised who?"

"Mother. Before she died. I promised her."

Her father stared at her for several long moments, then said, "She's dead, Shalin."

"Father!"

"She is. I miss her every day, but she's dead. And I will be soon enough. Will you go on living for me as well? Long after I've gone?"

"I don't want to disappoint her."

"It's impossible to disappoint the dead. You made promises to a dying dragoness when you were barely fifty winters." Actually thirty, but why argue with him now? "Still a hatchling, in my estimation."

"And you, Father?" she asked the question that bothered her more than anything. "Will I disappoint you?"

"Disappoint me? If you don't become an Elder? I'll

be more disappointed if you don't allow yourself some happiness."

Annoyed that her father saw some things so clearly, she muttered, "I never said Ailean made me happy."

Her father laughed, his old voice cracking. She remembered when it was strong and clear, ringing out through the cave chambers.

"If he didn't make you happy, you wouldn't be worried about staying or going. You would have already left. Sweet the world may see you as, Daughter, but I know better. And so does that frighteningly large dragon you love, I'd wager. You always get what you want in the end. Not only that—" Her father took her goblet and poured what was left of her wine into his glass. "—you bring out the best in each other. There are some who bring out the worst, but you and Ailean . . ." He nodded. "A good, solid match."

Shalin threw up her claws in exasperation. "I've tried to kill him. And I've tried to pull the hair out of his head. Actually, I've tried to kill him twice—although that first time was a necessity."

"And both times, I daresay he most likely deserved it. But you're dealing with the Cadwaladr Clan now, my love. They don't want the weak in their bloodline. Every time you fight him, challenge him, you make him yours. And, if I thought for a minute he meant nothing to you or he was a bad match, I'd tell you to send him a very stern letter and get back to your studies. But he means everything to you, Shalin, and we both know it."

She sighed in resignation. "True."

"And think of it this way—among that family, you'll always be the smartest."

"*Father!*"

"Yes, dear?"

* * *

"So you're just going to sit here? And wait?"

"Yes," Ailean stated to Bideven—yet again. "I'm just going to sit here and wait."

He thought when he began sharpening his swords and spears, his brothers and cousins would leave him be. No such luck.

"And what if she doesn't come? What if she stays in her school?"

"Then she'll have made her decision."

One of his cousins angrily tapped a finger against the Great Hall's worn wood table. "I say we tear the school down stone by stone until she agrees to come back to you."

Ailean held his blade close to his face and studied the edge, examining it for any nicks or jagged edges. "And why would I do that, cousin?"

"So she'd understand her place belongs with you."

"Should I cut off one of her wings too, so she can't escape? Then we can be just like the Lightnings."

"I never said—"

"No. You didn't. But you might as well have."

"The full moon is tonight, brother," Bideven pointed out—yet again.

"Yes. I'm well aware of that fact."

"And if she doesn't come tonight, Ailean? Or any night? Then what will you do? Find another?"

"There is no other, Arranz. We both know that."

"Then perhaps our cousin is right. Perhaps—"

"No. This is her decision to make. I ignored her wishes once before and she cut my throat. And that I'd happily risk again, but I won't risk losing her."

As one, all of the kin cluttering his Great Hall began shouting at him, telling him what they thought he ought to do. Most of it involving violence against anyone who would possibly step between him and Shalin.

But Ailean's patience waned, and in one movement, he stood and brought the blade of his favorite broadsword down on the thick oak table, splitting it into two.

Not surprisingly, that brought immediate silence.

"Now," he said calmly, "I'll ask again. Does anyone else have anything to say?"

"No," they all said as one.

16

It took Shalin a bit longer to get back to Kerezik, since her father decided to drink a bit more than was good for him and she had to stay to ensure he didn't pass out. But she had a few hours before the moon would rise. Enough time for something to eat and some time to talk to Ailean before tonight. Before he made her his.

She landed outside the castle gates and shifted. A guard standing outside immediately handed her a robe. What she found fascinating was that he wouldn't look at her.

"Something wrong?"

"No, ma'am."

"All right." She pulled the robe on and tied it at the waist. The gates immediately opened and she walked inside. It took her only moments to realize that, although they all nodded to her in greeting, no one looked her in the eyes.

Madenn met her on the stairs, a basket of warm bread in her hands. "Don't worry. They'll get over it."

"I scared them."

"A bit. But they're grateful. Give them time. Our ancestors were scared of Ailean in the beginning as well."

Wincing at the state of the front of Ailean's castle where her head had crashed into it, she asked, "Is Ailean in his room?"

"No," Kyna told her from inside the castle walls where a makeshift door had been erected. "He's not here."

Patting Madenn on the shoulder, Shalin walked into the Great Hall. "Where is he, then?"

"Out with his brothers. He should be back soon."

"You just left," Kennis accused.

"That's between me and Ailean."

"Fair enough."

Shalin nodded at the two and walked toward the stairs. She had her foot on the first step when she was propelled forward. She never hit the stairs, though, as hands gripped her tight and pinned her arms behind her back.

Looking over her shoulder at the twins, "What do you think you're doing?"

"Handling this."

The pair forced her up the stairs as Shalin tried to shake them loose. "You can't do this!"

"We can," Kyna told her.

"We are," Kennis confirmed.

"We know you two. You'll talk and talk and the full moon will pass. That won't work for us."

"*Work for you?*"

"Aye. And don't screech so. Makes me head ache. Don't it, Kennis?"

"That it does, Kyna."

"I'll shift," she threatened. "I'll shift and take this whole blasted building with me."

The twins stopped walking. Kyna moved right up next to her and said against her ear, "And kill all these lovely humans? Would you really do that, Shalin the Innocent?"

"From protector to murderer in the beat of a heart," Kennis said with a smirk.

Shalin glared at them. "I hate you both."

"Hate us today. Love us tomorrow," Kyna laughed while she and her sister shoved Shalin through Ailean's bedroom door.

Ailean walked out of the stables and into Madenn, who was about to walk in.

"What?" he grumbled.

"Still in a bad mood, I see?"

"And it's getting worse. What is it?"

Madenn gave a small smile. "She's back and—oh!"

Ailean kissed her forehead and ran off toward the castle. He was up the stairs and heading toward his room when the twins stumbled out, laughing hysterically. But when they saw him, they immediately stopped, which had his eyes narrowing in suspicion.

"What have you done?"

Kyna and Kennis passed him, both patting his shoulders.

"Just helping," Kyna said on a giggle.

"But you better get in there," Kennis added.

"Before she tears the walls down around us."

Then they took off running.

Ailean walked to the door and opened it. His first thought was, *When did I get a headboard?*

Shalin heard the door open again, but when she looked over her shoulder, it wasn't the twins.

"Oh, gods," she groaned, then again desperately tried to get loose of the leather bonds the twins had tied around her wrists and to the headboard that, according to the twins, had only been put up that afternoon while Ailean was away.

And she thought the North dragons had laid in wait for her.

"Well, well, well," Ailean said jovially, closing the door behind him. "Look what we have here. A gift for Ailean!"

"I'm going to kill *all of you*. It will be my mission in life."

Bad enough they'd tied her up at all, but they'd bound her wrists so close to the wood headboard that she faced the wall. And although they'd tossed a fur over her, she still had her ass sticking out to the world—and to Ailean!

"Now, now, my sweet, *innocent* Shalin. No need to get so testy."

Shalin closed her eyes as Ailean slowly pulled the fur off her body.

"I do have the *best* family," he groaned.

"Ailean—"

"Do you know why the ancestors began marking each other while human?"

"I—I never really thought . . ." Ailean's hand brushed down her back to her thigh. "I have no bloody idea," she laughed, reveling in his touch. The way his fingers stroked her.

"Damn." And he laughed with her. "I was hoping one of us would know."

The bed dipped as Ailean moved in behind her. He brushed his head against her back, his hair trailing along her skin like the finest silk, his lips against her spine.

"Where should I mark you, Shalin?"

He'd already stripped and the heat from his naked body nearly seared hers. His hands landed on either side of her own, his big body braced over hers.

Ailean pressed his hips forward and Shalin groaned at the contact.

"Tell me."

"I don't care," she finally admitted.

"The breast?" One rough fingertip circled her nipple, toying with it. "Or perhaps the neck." He kissed her on the back of her neck while his hand moved lower. "Perhaps your belly or something lower . . ."

Shalin pushed back against him. "I don't care where, Ailean," she panted out. "Just make me yours."

Ailean briefly buried his face between Shalin's shoulder blades and let what she'd said wash over him. She wanted him as her own. She wanted him until their ancestors called them home.

"And Ailean?" she said softly. "I do love you."

That was more than he could stand. More than he could ever hope to handle.

Rising up, he dug his hand into her hair, turning her head so he could kiss her, plundering her mouth with his own. Their tongues tangled and stroked until Shalin pulled back.

"Don't make me wait. Not a second longer."

He didn't. Kissing his way down her back, Ailean gripped her breasts with both hands. He massaged them and toyed with the nipples, loving how hard they were against his fingers.

Ailean kissed her lower back where her hips met her ass. He released one breast and used that hand to stroke her pussy, already wet and hot and all his.

Then, when he had her writhing, had her begging, he dragged his tongue across her lower back. Shalin gasped and groaned in pain even as her body shook under his, even as her pussy gripped his fingers. He stroked her clit while his tongue continued its journey across her lower back.

"Gods," she moaned desperately, her body shaking. "Ailean . . ."

"I love you, Shalin," he told her as he pushed her over the edge, the mark of his Claiming burned into her flesh. "I'll always love you."

"I know," she sobbed before she came all over his hand.

Then Shalin was his.

Reaching up, he untied her bonds, determined to keep the leather thongs for later. Ailean grabbed Shalin's hips and flipped her over while pulling her down on the bed and under him. He kissed her and pushed his cock inside her, gasping at how hot and tight she was.

He wiped the tears from her cheeks with his thumbs and rested his forehead against hers. "I love you."

She smiled, her hands cupping his face. "Finish it, Ailean."

Ailean started off slow, taking his time so he could enjoy every second. He kissed her as he drove into her, wanting to touch every part of her. Shalin's legs wrapped around his waist, her grip on him near-painful.

"Gods, Shalin," he told her, "you feel so good."

He took her harder, deeper, until Shalin climaxed again. He came with her, his head thrown back, his own body shaking in release.

Gasping, exhausted, Ailean collapsed on top of her. He grinned when he heard her grunt, laughed when she started hitting him.

He rolled onto his back, bringing her with him. "I only needed a moment to relax."

"You're as big as an ox," she growled at him.

"I was recovering," he said before he pulled her close and started kissing her throat.

Shalin giggled and pushed at his shoulders. "I thought you were recovering!" she squealed desperately.

Grinning, Ailean pushed her to her back, "I recover quickly."

"I don't."

"Guess we'll have to work on that," he sighed as he sunk into her again.

Shalin stared up at the ceiling in the dark bedroom and wondered how late it was. She'd lost track of time hours ago. Ailean simply didn't give her time to think about anything but him.

"Ravenous beast," she whispered softly, smiling.

"You called?" Ailean asked, reaching for her again.

"No!" she squealed, slapping at his hands. "Rest! I need rest!"

He snuggled in close. "Fine. Another ten minutes."

"Very generous."

"Keep that tone and it goes to five."

Ailean's arms were wrapped tight around her, keeping her warm and safe.

"Where did you go this morning?" he asked, one hand stroking her forearm.

"To see my father." She turned her head and looked at Ailean. "He means too much to me not to have talked to him before—"

"There is nothing to explain to me, Shalin. I understand." And he did. She could see that in his eyes. "You know, Shalin, there's this nice little cave not far from here, close to my mother's. If we fixed it up nice, think he'd mind living there?"

"It—it depends," she stuttered in surprise. "Knowing my father, we could probably move him and all his things without him ever complaining as long as we don't disturb his current work."

"We'll do that, then. I worry about him. He's older and alone. I know you'd feel better with him closer."

Letting out a shaky breath, Shalin said, "That would mean much to me, Ailean. Thank you."

"Nothing to thank." He kissed her temple, her cheek. "Family is family, luv."

He stared at her intently and said, "Rest is over, Shalin."

"That was not ten minutes."

"Too bad."

She batted at his hands and slipped out from under him. "Wait. Wait. I want to see."

She scrambled off the bed and went to the tall mirror in the corner of the room. She had to wipe off all the dust first since it seemed never to have been used and probably belonged to the humans who'd once lived there.

Turning so her back faced the mirror, she looked over her shoulder at what Ailean had burned into her flesh. "Huh," she said in surprise.

"What's wrong?"

"It's so small." It truly was. A lounging dragon burned into her lower back. The point of its tail aimed right above the cheeks. Over the years she'd seen and heard of some very elaborate Claimings. Brands covering an entire arm or leg, sometimes an entire back or chest. One day, she'd mark Ailean as her own as well, but not right away. It was a male thing and she didn't bother trying to understand it.

"You don't like it?" He stood in front of her, his hands on her waist and leaning over her shoulder to take a better look.

"No, no. I do like it. Very much. It's just so . . . so . . ."

"So . . . what?"

"Subtle."

He glared down at her. "Your point being?"

"Nothing."

"You don't think I'm subtle?"

"I didn't say that." But the laughing wasn't helping, either.

"Your rest is over, dragoness."

"I'm not done—"

"Later," Ailean told her, walking her back to the bed until he could push her on it.

But as Ailean moved over her, they both stopped and stared at the window.

"What is that?" she asked.

"You don't want to know."

Slipping out from under him again, Shalin walked to the window and pushed out the thick glass encased in a metal frame. In shock, she stared down into the courtyard.

"Told you," Ailean said, now standing behind her, again looking over her shoulder.

They all stood out there, all the Cadwaladr kin, cousins, aunts, uncles, and brothers of Ailean. Now her kin. Ale in hand, they all stood outside the window—singing.

For the life of her, she'd never be able to tell a soul what they'd been singing—it was unintelligible—but she knew it came from their drunken hearts. And gods, they were so very drunk.

"Congratulations, you two," Kyna called up.

"We're so happy," Kennis added, sobbing for no apparent reason.

"Does this mean we're royals too?" another cousin asked.

"Let's fly to Devenallt Mountain and ask the queen!" cried his aunt Briaga. "Who's with me?" She didn't get far, though. She fell backward seconds later. Out cold.

Shalin grinned, trying not to laugh instead, until one of Ailean's uncles called out, "The royal there . . . she's got nice tits, eh?"

Ailean kissed Shalin's cheek and let out a sigh. "Welcome to the family, luv."

She looked down at her chest and back up into his beautiful face. "Thank you?"

Epilogue

"Oiy, brother!" The bed went up and crashed back down. "It's time."

Shaking his head and yawning, Ailean dragged himself out of bed. "Good. I want my mate back where she belongs." Under him. Over him. As long as he was in her, all was right.

"So selfish," Arranz chided.

"I'm not the one been complaining about no stories at mealtime, you whiny bastard."

Ailean tugged on a pair of leather leggings and walked past his brother and out into the hall. At midday, the house was its usual busy self. Servants and young ones under foot, along with kin who'd dropped by for whatever reason. He walked past one of the bedrooms and saw one of his younger sons in human form leaning out the window, flirting with one of the local girls.

Arranz smiled and stepped back as Ailean snuck up behind the young dragon. He stood behind him a good five seconds and the little fool, so busy trying to seduce the blacksmith's daughter, didn't even realize he was behind him.

Grinning, he slammed his hands against his son's back, sending him flipping out the window. So stunned, the little bastard didn't even shift to dragon and instead landed on the hard, unforgiving ground. Although the girl moved fast enough out of the way. Not too bad for a human.

"You need to learn to pay attention, boy!" Ailean yelled down, earning a snarl and a curse that would have his mate yanking someone's tail in reprimand.

Brushing his hands together, he walked back into the hallway and to his brother.

"I'm surprised your children haven't tried to kill you in your sleep, Ailean."

"They hate me now, but they'll learn to appreciate me when they go into battle."

The brothers went down the stairs and across the hall. Ailean took flight as soon as he made it outside, and he arrived at his destination in minutes. He walked into the brightly lit cave, now decorated with torches and tapestries along the walls. Shalin had made the space her own and he was happy to have life in it again as it had when his mother breathed.

And this time, the cave was always protected. Shalin and their offspring were always protected, even when he was leagues away. He never worried for their safety because his kin made sure he never had to.

Ailean walked past a new batch of puppies, direct descendants of Shalin's first dog—whom she never did get around to naming. A few more steps brought him past the cavern where she kept her favorite horse. Right now that meant a direct descendant of Nightmare, whom Shalin called Dragon's Heart, but whom everyone else called Insane Bastard.

Ailean found Shalin in the hatching chamber. With gentle flame, she blew on the egg and brushed it with her claw while holding a book with the other. After eight sons and daughters already, the whole process seemed to have lost most of its allure for his Shalin.

"Well?" he asked, walking in.

"Give it time," she said without raising her head from her book. "You're too impatient."

"I miss you," he growled and Shalin smiled, finally looking up at him.

"And I miss you, you old bear. But only a dragoness can protect her egg properly."

"What does that mean?"

"It means yelling at your own that they need to get a move on because you're bored is not how the life-giving process works, my love."

"That was one time."

"You're much better once they're out of the egg than while they're in it. But barely."

The shell cracked and Shalin grinned, motioning him forward. He'd missed the last three because he'd been off in battle against the Northland dragons. But he'd been very glad to be here for this one.

He stood over the egg and watched as a small black fist punched through the shell. He went to remove more of it but Shalin slapped at his claws.

"Leave it be, Ailean. They must do this on their own."

He sighed impatiently and stared. A few more punches. Several long pauses. And then the top of the shell broke off. Ailean leaned over even farther and looked in. Pitch-black eyes nearly covered by pitch-black hair glared up at him.

"Is he supposed to frown like that?"

Shalin leaned over like her mate. "He's serious, is

all." She leaned in a bit closer. "And I'm not sure he likes you."

Ailean smirked. "Thank you."

The hatchling finally looked away from him and at his mother. The glare faded to a much more neutral frown and Shalin reached for him.

"Let's see you, little one." She lifted him up and said, "A male."

"Another one? We need more daughters."

"Must you complain? I've given you nine all together. Four of them daughters. You're lucky you got any hatchlings at all."

His son wrapped around Shalin's neck, his long black tail looping around her arm.

"Maybe this one will be a scholar, eh?" Ailean said hopefully.

"I don't think we should hold our breath for that anymore."

Ailean leaned in close to get a better look at his son. "What will we call him?"

"I don't know."

The dragon turned and glared at his father and then unleashed a puff of smoke that, when he was older, would be a deadly ball of flame.

Coughing, Ailean stepped back. "Little bastard."

Shalin laughed out loud, no longer remotely shy after so many years around his kin. "Ailean," she chastised. "Be nice. You're probably scaring him."

"This one doesn't look scared of a damn thing." A good warrior he'd make with his horns already growing in. Although Ailean did hold out hope that at least one of their offspring would be more reader than born killer. At least for Shalin's sake.

"I know what we can name him," he finally said, once he brushed the soot off his snout.

"It better not be 'little bastard.' "

"No. No. That name your father always liked. What was it?"

Nearly a decade ago, Shalin had lost her father and it had devastated her. And although she'd gotten through it as they all knew she would, Ailean still knew she missed the old brown dragon every day.

Shalin looked at her son. "Bercelak. He always liked the name Bercelak."

"Aye. That's the one." They'd already named their oldest Baudwin, so Ailean thought they could use one her father had liked. "What do you think, little bastard? Bercelak the Black fit you well enough?"

"Stop calling him little bastard."

"He is a little bastard."

Glaring at her mate, she pulled her son off her neck and into her arms. "Would you like that, my son? To be Bercelak the Black?"

Still too young to answer, the small dragon instead studied his mother intently. Small black claws petting her cheeks, down her snout. She nuzzled him and Bercelak nuzzled her back.

"Aye," she finally said. "I think that name fits him well." She hefted Bercelak in her arms. "He needs to sleep now and, later, he'll feed."

She turned to walk toward the pitfire and that's when the little demon lashed at Ailean with his tail, almost taking out an eye. The glare he gave his father over his mother's shoulder told Ailean all he needed to know about this one.

"You'll stay?" Shalin asked as she stretched out by the fire, her son tucked tight into her arms.

"Aye. I will." Ailean settled in behind her and kissed her neck. "Now tell me what's wrong. You're worried. I hear it in your voice."

"With Adienna on the throne now? Of course I'm worried." But she still tangled her tail with his own—gods, he loved when she did that. Whether as dragon or human, Shalin made every moment they shared perfect.

"Don't be. They'll all be ready when the time comes. Especially this one. Look at that angry face, Shalin. He'll take care of himself just fine."

"Aye, Ailean," Shalin teased, rubbing the frown lines on her son's forehead, "but besides us, who will ever love him with such an angry frown?"

"Who says I love him?"

She slammed her elbow into his stomach so hard he could only gasp. And, for the first time, the little bastard grinned.

"I'll find him someone," Ailean vowed through gritted teeth, watching as his newest son fell asleep against his mother's shoulder.

"Think he'll ever find what we have?" she whispered, her voice sounding drowsy, her body relaxing against his.

Holding his family close to his heart, Ailean whispered back, "We can only hope he'll be that lucky."

SPELLBOUND

Cynthia Eden

1

She summoned him at midnight. The witching hour. Power swept through every inch of Serena Tyme's body, pulsing, growing, and the words of the spell poured from her lips, faster, *faster*.

Her arms shot above her head, and the air crackled with magic. Thunder roared and lightning flashed across the cloudless night sky.

Her eyes squeezed shut, just for one fearful moment, and when her lashes lifted, *he* was there.

The relief that rushed through her body had her trembling.

Then he spoke. "Nice body, sweetheart." Voice deep and rumbling like the thunder. Golden eyes drifted over her skyclad form. Heat flared in those depths, then, voice slightly rougher, he snarled, "Now why don't you tell me who the hell you are and *where the fuck I am*."

Serena drew in a deep breath and watched the man's eyes dart to her chest. Jeez. Men. All alike—mortal or immortal—they always got distracted by a pair of breasts.

But she hadn't called him across space to ogle her. She crept forward, keeping an anxious eye on him. She knew how much power he possessed, far more than a mere hereditary witch could hope to control. The sooner she explained things to him, the better.

After all, it wasn't an easy task to summon the devil.

The fire she'd built flared higher. Not her magic, *his*. Serena reached for her black robe, belted it quickly.

"You didn't have to dress," he muttered, and his powerful legs were braced apart, arms resting easily at his sides. "But I am *waiting* on my answers."

His tone implied that he wasn't a happy waiting camper. She really hadn't expected him to be, though. She licked her lips, cleared a throat gone dry from chanting and the flames and said, "M-my name's Serena Tyme. I'm a witch and—"

He grabbed her then. Moved far too fast for her to follow, even with her slightly enhanced senses.

The circle she'd drawn should have held him in place, at least for a few minutes.

But it had failed.

Oh, damn.

His hands locked around her upper arms. A hold too tight to break, but not fierce enough to hurt, not yet. But the threat was in his steely grip, and in the eyes that blazed down at her.

"I know you're a witch." The flames were reflected in his golden stare. A stare that burned brighter every moment. "No one else could have forced me here. Dammit, tell me—"

Her chin lifted. "Look, I'm *answering* your questions, OK?" He'd wanted to know who she was, and well, question one was now answered. As for the second question . . . "You're in Atlanta, Georgia." When those eyes of his narrowed, she added, in a questioning tone, "The U.S.?" The guy spoke with no accent, and she had no idea where he had been when her spell had grabbed him. Although the where didn't really matter to her. All that mattered was that he stood before her now.

She saw a muscle flex along the hard, square line of his jaw. Black brows fell low. The brows were a perfect match to the slightly too long, night-black hair that brushed the collar of his shirt. "*Why* am I here, witch?"

Ah, this was the tricky part. She took a moment, letting her gaze dart down his body. He was dressed as any man would have been. Loosely buttoned black shirt. Jeans. Ragged boots. Oh, yeah. He looked normal. Could have been the guy next door.

If the guy next door happened to be the most powerful paranormal being known in the *Other* world.

For, despite what most folks thought, paranormals *did* exist. They lived right alongside the humans. Demons, vampires, and witches like her—they were everywhere. But the humans, well, sometimes they had a hard time seeing what was right in front of them.

But she could see exactly who, or rather *what*, was in front of her.

The man before her had many names. After all, if the legends were true, he'd been roaming the earth for centuries, and he'd continue to roam and fight and raise hell long after she was dust.

Cazador del alma. Soul-hunter. Destroyer.

The rarest of the paranormals, *cazadores* were produced from the mating of witches and all-powerful, level-ten demons—the terrors of the demon world.

Cazadores were gifted with the full powers of a hereditary witch, the full powers of a demon, *and* the soul-hunters, well, they could live forever.

All the better to hunt.

She stared at him, unable to stop the nervous tremble that shook her body.

Hell, when she'd been a kid, her parents had told her that he was the boogeyman.

The immortal who came after the *Other* when they crossed that fine line between right and wrong. Because a *cazador* had more than just witch and demon powers. He was the immortal who could also steal a life away, with but a simple touch.

"Always be good, Serena." Her mother's husky voice echoed in her mind. *"Because the cazador, he comes after witches when they're bad."*

Oh, yeah, the threat of the big, eternal badass had kept her on the straight and narrow for years.

His fingers tightened around her arms. "Are you trying to piss me off?"

Serena blinked. "Uh, no. Really—I—" Oh, hell, what had he wanted to know? Damn, but she was tired. And scared. And so weak.

The first binding had hurt her more than she realized. She'd barely managed to focus enough power for the summoning spell.

When his fingers moved, just a bit higher on her right arm, and he brushed the still tender flesh, she winced.

"Why. Did. You. Summon. Me." Gritted from between his clenched teeth.

Ah, yes. Simple enough answer for that one. "Because I need you."

He glared down at her and she realized his features *could* have been handsome but weren't—no, they were far too hard. As if they'd been carved from ancient stone. Too-sharp cheekbones, nose too long, high brow. Thin lips. Skin a darkened gold—made only more so by the flickering light of the flames.

As she stared at him, that hard mask slackened—just for a moment—and disbelief flashed across his face as he said, "You know what I am."

Of course. Would she have gone to the trouble of bartering for a dark spell if she hadn't?

"You know what I am, and you still summoned me." He shook his head as if he couldn't believe she'd actually called for him. "I bring death." He freed her. Stepped back. Clenched his hands into fists. "I'm not some kind of idiot demon that you can screw around with, sweetheart. I'm—"

"A soul-hunter." Soul-eater. OK, that was the less-than-respectful term. Her voice was soft but firm as she continued, "I *know.* I also know that you're exactly what I need." The others in her coven had said that she was crazy. That she was courting the devil.

Summoning him didn't mean that she could control him, and the *cazadores*, well, they were damn unpredictable.

In fact, until the menacing guy before her had appeared, she'd actually wondered if *cazadores* were just myths. She'd never actually met anyone who'd known a *cazador*, and certain paranormals had sure been crossing that good/evil line at will lately.

Which brought up just why she needed her hunter.

"What is it that you need from me?" The words were a rumble of sound that seemed to shake through her body.

"I need you . . . to save me." The mark on her arm burned with remembered pain. "And to do your damn job and kill the bastard who is after me." Not just her, but her entire coven.

If the *cazador* didn't help her, well, they'd all be dead before Halloween, just a few terribly short days away.

Serena was *not* ready to die. Not without putting up one hell of a fight, anyway.

Because she was one witch who wasn't about to burn easily.

Luis D'Amil shook his head and stared in disbelief at the shapely witch before him.

Dammit. One moment, he'd been sitting in his favorite bar in Cozumel, and the next, he was in the middle of a forest, facing a naked woman.

A woman with a lot of power.

A woman who'd dressed far too quickly.

The witch had ripped him across time and space— hell, the least she could have done was let him look at those pink-tipped breasts a while longer.

The witch had *gorgeous* breasts. It'd been far too long since he'd seen breasts that—

"Are you going to help me?" she demanded, and her voice held a tight, hard edge.

Luis sighed and gave up the tempting image of her bare flesh. "No." He crossed his arms over his chest. "Now do your magic, and get me the hell out of here!" He had a bottle of tequila waiting on him.

Her mouth dropped open. Good lips, he couldn't help but notice. Sexy. Red and full. Just the way he liked 'em. Nice little heart-shaped face. Pretty. Cute nose, even if it did turn up a bit. High cheeks. Wide eyes. Green eyes. *Cat eyes.* Those eyes seemed to glow at him. And her hair . . .

Wild. A thick, curling black mass that skimmed her shoulders. The firelight burned brightly around them, making the red highlights lurking in the darkness of her hair flare to life.

But even if the flames hadn't burned, he would have been able to see perfectly. It was the *cazador's* way.

Made the hunting easier.

His witch was all curves and soft skin. Not too thin— good, he'd never been attracted to a woman he couldn't hold tight. Lush breasts and hips and legs that—

"Didn't you hear me?" she nearly shrieked at him and Luis winced. "I said I need your help. Someone's after me—"

"Then go to the cops. The *Other* are everywhere these days. You'll be able to find a paranormal to help you."

"I don't trust cops."

"No, you don't trust *human* cops."

"I don't trust *any* of them." Said with absolute certainly. Ah, so his witch had experienced a bad run-in with the law, eh? "I've seen cops on the take," she muttered, "humans, *Other*—they can all be bought if the price is right." She exhaled, shaking her head. "Besides, no crime has been committed yet. Even if I went to them—and I'm *not*—what would I say? Someone's trying to bind me? Like they'd care!"

Someone's trying to bind me. Luis stiffened.

Witches were bound all the time. Some willingly because their powers were too much for them to handle. And some, well, *not* so willingly.

Long ago, the binding spell had only been used for protection. To bind those who would do harm. To stop the negative forces and to bind them safely. But the spell had been perverted by many over time, and the old ways were long gone.

"The cops can't help me." She glared at him. "Shit, isn't your job to catch the *Others* who go bad? To stop them from killing?"

Sometimes it was. Sometimes his job was just to clean up the blood left behind and make the humans forget the chaos they'd seen.

"Please." Her voice dropped, and for an instant, Luis swore he saw a flash of tears in her eyes. "I *need* you. My coven—someone's trying to destroy us."

He swallowed, memories flooding through his mind. No, no, this couldn't be—

Serena pulled aside the top of her robe, baring her upper chest, the tempting swell of her breasts. Then she twisted, bringing her right shoulder forward and he saw . . .

The first binding mark.

A long, angry red slash cut across the top of her arm. A slash that could have been made with a red-hot knife.

But had really been made by magic.

"It takes three to bind," she said, but he already knew that. His mother had been a damn strong witch, and she'd taught him all the magic she knew, both light and dark. "Some sick bastard is out there. I don't know who he is or how he's doing this, but he's binding the members of my coven, one at a time."

A bound witch was a weak one. Perfect prey.

So very easy to kill.

Almost as easy as a human.

"Half of the coven fled when the first mark appeared on their flesh. I don't know how long the others will stay. They're scared, *I'm* scared, and I don't know what the hell to do."

She fixed her robe, tightened the belt, then closed the space he'd put between them. Serena reached for his arm. Her fingers felt so soft against his flesh.

Her scent teased his nostrils. Roses. Lavender. A

sweet, light blend. One that reminded him of innocence. Youth. A time long past for him.

Poor little witch. She thought the danger was hiding out there in the night, stalking her.

She didn't realize that the real threat was standing right in front of her.

One touch, just one. If he focused his power, he could drain her dry in an instant.

By the time she gathered the breath to scream, it would be too late.

Soul-eater. Yes, he knew that was what many called him. Because he didn't just hunt. He took. Drained his prey dry until nothing was left but the shell of the body.

No soul. No power. No life.

Because he took everything.

"Three years ago, this same thing happened in LA." Her nails were long and sharp. Red. The hand that clasped him shook. "I wasn't in the coven that was marked, but my aunt—she was." Pain echoed in her voice and he saw the faintest quiver in her lips. "My aunt raised me, *cazador.* Took me in when my parents died." She shook her head. "I was eleven, she was seventeen—*and she raised me,* all those years, all by herself."

The pain was deeper now.

"Then she got marked. I couldn't help her." Rage with the pain. A hard fury. "I couldn't help any of them. The witches in her coven were bound by a force they couldn't fight. Then one by one, they were killed."

His gut clenched. Hell, yeah, he knew about that case. He'd been fighting his ass off in Brazil at the time, because a pack of panther shifters had laid a trap for him and he'd been forced to eliminate them.

One shifter's soul after another.

"Some of the coven tried to run, but it didn't do them any good. They all still *died*." She drew in a ragged breath. "When the rest of the witches in LA found out, they were scared as hell. Most of the unbound ones cut out of the city—"

"Like you did?" Why else would his little witch be all the way on the other side of the country?

"I couldn't stay in LA without Jayme. I couldn't live in her house, day after day, when she was gone." Serena shook her head, and a twisted smile curved her lips. "Besides, I thought I'd be safe here," she muttered. "And for a while, I was." Her lips, the ones that he really wanted to touch, firmed as her smile disappeared. "Then the asshole showed up here and started marking *my* coven—the only damn family I have any more."

Ah, the coven. To hereditary witches, a coven tie was deeper than blood. The coven was power, security, trust. Life.

"You have to stop him." Serena's pointed little chin lifted into the air. "If you don't, then I'm dead."

He stirred at that, as a wave of tension rolled through him. Why should he care if one more witch— or even a dozen—passed to the next realm? There were others who would take her place.

And yet . . .

Her eyes. There was just something about them. So deep. Greener than the fields near his mother's old home.

Those eyes . . . *innocence.*

No. There was no way the witch was an innocent. Too much knowledge filled her voice, and she'd used the darkest of spells to rip him away from his promised drink.

And the promised fuck that had been waiting for him.

"I will do anything," the witch said, and the desperation on her face and in her words was undeniable. "*Anything,* if you help me and my coven."

Ah, the pleading. He'd heard it before. Too many times to count. Normally, that shit didn't do a thing for him.

Her eyes. What was it about them? The woman was no virgin, not with that ripe body. He could smell her power in the air, and the lush scent of her body.

Sex.

No, not innocence in her eyes, Luis realized.

Hope.

How long had it been since he'd seen that?

"There are thousands of others in this world who could use me," he told her, keeping his voice hard. His hands were fisted because damn if he didn't have the urge to draw her close. To press her tight against him and feel those breasts against his chest. "But I'm not a savior." He'd tried that route once, and fucked up admirably. No, saving wasn't really his bit.

Seeking vengeance, sending monsters to hell, yeah, that was more his deal.

"Help me!" Her nails dug into his skin. For an instant, he imagined the two of them together. A dark room. Rumpled sheets. Her nails digging deeply into his flesh. "I have power, I can give you *anything—*"

Again with that magic word. *Anything.*

A dark, hungry temptation flickered through him. *Because I am my father's son.*

It had been far too long since he'd lain with a witch and tasted the magic on her tongue and sipped the power from her body.

Anything.

Those green eyes . . .

He lowered his head toward hers. She was so small, her head barely came to his shoulders. She didn't back away when he closed that distance. Her eyes widened, but she held his stare.

A fire there. Burning inside her.

He'd always liked to play with fire.

"Are you trying to put me under a spell, witch?" A possibility. Her magic was more focused, even with the first binding mark, than any other witch he'd ever met. The hunger he was feeling, the stirring in his groin, it could be a trick.

Sure, a succubus was far better at laying a sensual trap than a witch, but with the right spell, Serena would still manage to turn him on.

Had managed to turn him on.

He'd been aroused from the first glimpse of her pale skin. As soon as the fog cleared and he'd seen her, he'd wanted to fuck her.

Not a usual response for him.

Killing, yes, that was normal.

But wanting to fuck on first sight, not so typical.

Unless a spell was involved.

Serena licked her lips and the sight of that pink tongue nearly made him groan. "I-I only had enough power left to summon you. I c-can't hold a lust spell now."

He stared into her eyes and let his own power out. *Truth.*

One of his handy talents. A soul-hunter held the

power of truth. He could hear lies—the words twisted, grated in his ears. He could discern truth with but a light push of power.

Before he killed, he liked to make certain he was executing the right monster.

He inhaled softly and caught her breath. Tasted her fear and her need.

The witch would do anything to save herself and her coven.

Luis realized he should probably admire that.

But he didn't.

Because the hunger he felt for her was growing too strong. His decision was made in that instant. A choice that came fast and wild—just like the need he felt for the curvy little witch. "I'll find the one after you." It wouldn't be easy. The hunts never were. The psychotics were always smarter than they appeared, twisting and turning and leaving a tangled mess for him to sort out. "But it *will* cost you."

That hope flared even brighter in her gaze and her whole face seemed to light up. Not pretty, *beautiful*. "My coven will—"

"Not your coven, sweetheart." He wasn't interested in the others. No, he only cared about the witch who'd drained her powers to summon him.

And then offered the man feared by all *anything*.

"What do you want?" No fear. Good, because he'd never wanted fear in his women.

"You."

She shook her head. "I don't understand." But the dawning realization was in her eyes and her voice pitched too high in his mind. *Lie*.

Luis didn't call her on the falsehood. There would be time for that, later. Just as there would be time for much, much more. "You will, witch. *You will.*" Because he wasn't just talking about sex. A few hours of mindless pleasure.

He wanted all of her. Body and soul.

The hunt was on.

2

Exhaustion flooded Serena's body, but she walked doggedly forward, putting one foot in front of the other and focusing as hard as she could on not falling face-first onto the ground. She'd barely managed to cleanse the earth and break the remnants of her spell before the last of her power deserted her.

"Uh, is walking around naked out here a real good idea?" The *cazador* spoke from behind her.

She didn't stop. Couldn't, or she just might do that face-first routine. "Look, hunter—"

"Luis." Soft. "Luis D'Amil."

Now she did pause, glancing over her shoulder. This was almost worth a fall. "Where are you from, Luis?" Luis—that was a Spanish name, and it fit with the Spanish designation the hunters had long ago been given. But D'Amil—

"Once upon a time, I grew up in the area you know as Spain." His lips twisted into the faintest of smiles. "As the legends say, many of my kind hailed from that rich land."

Rich in magic. Always had been, but . . . "You don't

sound Spanish." His voice was deep and dark, and completely devoid of any accent.

A shrug. "Witch, I've been everywhere on this earth. Languages, accents—after a few hundred years, they all blur."

"But you have to . . . live . . . somewhere now. I mean, you do have a house, or an apartment or *something,* right?"

A shrug. "I travel. There are safe places for me to stay."

I travel. OK, big euphemism for stalking prey. She swallowed. "I didn't . . . ah . . . take you away from your family or anything, did I?" Serena hadn't even thought of that. Oh, damn, but what if he had a wife who was frantic because her hubby had up and vanished? But the guy had just propositioned her. Well, she was ninety percent sure he'd propositioned her, and the jerk had better not have a wife at home who—

His smile died. "I have no family left." Cold. No, *arctic.* Then, "My mother died in the Burning Times."

Oh, shit. *The Burning Times.* Those horror-filled years when witches had been hunted and hundreds, no *thousands* had been put to the flames. She shouldn't ask, really shouldn't, but . . . "Your father?" A level-ten demon was the only sire for a *cazador*, and level tens were all but immortal themselves.

In the demon world, there were several levels of power. The weaker demons were generally considered levels one through three—they barely had powers above a human's inherent psychic gifts. But the big, dangerous bastards who were ranked as level tens— well, those were the guys who could bring true meaning to the old phrase, "Hell on earth." Get them angry enough, and folks around the level tens would literally fry.

"My father died after her. He trusted me to save her. I didn't, and he couldn't live without her," he bit off the words. "See, witch, I'm not a savior—I couldn't spare my mother from the flames."

Her lips parted. *What do I say?* "I-I'm sorry, Luis." And she was. She knew just how much it hurt to lose a loved one to the fire.

He kept talking, as if he hadn't heard her—and maybe he hadn't. "I tried to save her. When I learned what the villagers had planned, I tried to help her. But I was too far away and couldn't get to her fast enough." His eyes narrowed. "And we all know just how fast witches burn, don't we?"

The image of her aunt's charred body flashed through her mind.

Serena swallowed back the bile that wanted to rise in her throat.

"Still sure you want my help, witch?"

Taunting, but she could hear the echo of pain in his voice. *Pain for the family he'd lost.* Perhaps the *cazador* wasn't so very different from her after all. "Absolutely."

He was her best bet.

Her only chance. "I'm sorry about your family, Luis, and you may not believe me—but I *do* understand."

The wind blew against her cheek. He stared into her eyes, and after a moment, his shoulders seemed to relax, just a bit. "I do believe you."

Well, that was something.

"But don't waste your time feeling sorry for me. I don't need your pity."

Her brows shot up. "Sympathy isn't the same thing as pity." *Jerk.*

"I need neither from you."

"And just what is it that you need?" she demanded, but she knew, dammit, deep down she knew—

The smile that curved his lips had her heart slamming into her chest—and her nipples tightening beneath the robe.

Dangerous.

"I'll show you exactly what I need. Very soon." A darkly sensual promise.

She just bet he would. Serena cleared her throat. *Enough.* Keeping her shoulders straight, she turned and resumed her march.

She felt his stare upon her with every step that she took. Heavy, hard and—

"You didn't answer me, little witch." Answer him? What had the question been? She paused, and then, when the rest of his words sank in, she almost snorted. Little, her ass. Her abiding love for chocolate and all things dessert meant that she generally stayed out of the "little" category.

He snagged the back of her robe, and Serena stumbled, barely catching herself. "Wait! Stop!"

"Aren't you concerned about wandering around naked?" He grated, and there was a different note in his voice. Anger?

Shoving a lock of hair out of her eye, she muttered, "Not really. This is coven land. No one but us should be out here." If any human intruders tried to cross the protected land, well, they'd find themselves turning and inexplicably walking the other way—fast.

Oh, the power of a good spell.

His hold on her loosened. "And we'll return to your house . . . with you unclothed?"

The guy was obsessed with her nudity. "I've got clothes in the car, OK?" She wasn't a flasher. Just a really desperate woman.

"Good." He *finally* released her.

"Glad you approve." Arrogant ass. But an arrogant ass that she needed.

They trudged the rest of the distance in blessed silence and Serena soon saw the glorious sight of her beat-up Chevy and—

Luis grabbed her, locking his fingers around her wrist and moving in a whirl to stand before her.

"What—"

"We're not alone." The shoulders before her were tight with tension.

As his response sank in, her eyes widened. But she hadn't sensed any danger. Even weakened, she should have felt a premonition of warning.

Rising to stand on her toes, Serena peered over his shoulder. Then she saw them.

Robed figures. Four. No, five of them. Walking from the woods near her car. Black hoods drawn over their heads.

"Don't get in my way," Luis ordered. "I'll take them down, stay back and—"

"*No!*" OK, maybe her scream came too loudly.

But the hunter didn't even flinch.

She pushed against his back. "Luis, they're my coven!" What was left of the coven, anyway.

The women walked toward them. Serena scrambled to Luis's side, a nervous knot tightening in her stomach. One by one, the women drew back their hoods. First, Susan, the stylish matriarch who didn't look a day over fifty, but who Serena knew was actually pushing seventy. Patricia was next, her cloak falling away to reveal her long, straight black hair and her perfect, dark cream skin. Patricia's twin sister, Pamela, tossed back her hood almost in unison, exposing her delicate features and her close-cropped hair. Then Sasha, the youngest member of the coven, shoved back her covering. Sasha was barely nineteen, but, like Serena, she had grown up hard in a big city. The girl was tough as nails.

The last face to be revealed was that of Vanessa Donnelley, a fiery redhead Serena had met shortly after moving to Atlanta. Vanessa worked for Dr. Emily Drake—or, as the paranormals in the city called her, the Monster Doctor. The psychologist only treated the *Other,* and Serena was pretty certain that by the time this whole mess was finished, she'd have to pay the good doctor a visit.

Susan didn't look at Luis. Her horrified stare went straight to Serena. "What have you done, sister?"

Condemnation. She should have expected it but, "I'm trying to save this coven." They were all marked. They knew that death was coming.

No sense running. *Why couldn't they see that?* Serena wondered, as her hand rose to brush against the always wild locks of her hair.

"I-is this him?" Sasha asked, eyes wide as she stared up at Luis.

Serena glanced to the left. Saw Luis smile. "What do you think, witch?" he murmured.

The women flinched.

"You've destroyed us," Susan whispered, but the words carried easily on the wind. "The *cazadores* aren't to be trusted. You know that—you know the stories. They turned against the council years ago, slaughtered innocents—"

"Careful, lady, you're about to piss me off." His words were easy, but the power suddenly pulsing in the air was hard.

Susan fell back a step. Hmm. Fell back, or was pushed? Before Serena could decide, the elder witch stiffened her shoulders and said, "He'll demand a price from you, from *all* of us."

Luis laughed. "Serena already knows my price, and she's agreed to pay." A shrug. "I have no interest in the rest of you."

Pity flashed across Susan's face. "What did you do, Serena?"

The only thing she could.

"I'm hunting now." From Luis. "I won't stop until I find the one after your coven."

"And then?" Vanessa's voice trembled. Normally so tough, but now, she was afraid. As were they all.

"Then I'll make him disappear. Permanently."

Soul-eater.

"We're leaving," Patricia muttered quickly. "Getting out of town until—"

"Won't do you any good." Luis crossed his arms over his chest and stared down at her. "He's got your power trail, that's how he's binding you, *all* of you. He has something personal, and he can track you now, no matter where you go."

Yeah, Serena had been telling them all the *same damn thing.* But when the *cazador* said it, well, the witches gulped and whispered. And their plans changed.

"Tell us when you find the bastard." Susan lifted her silvery mane proudly. "We will help you." The glow of magic lit her body.

Luis shook his head. "I don't need you to help me." He waved a mocking hand toward them. The witches were standing between them and Serena's car. "I just need you to get out of my way . . ."

The witches moved, fast.

As Serena hurried toward her car, she was given one last warning.

"Be careful, Serena, once you use the dark magic,

there's no going back." Susan's eyes flickered with power. She knew that the summoning spell Serena had used wasn't on the light spectrum. No, it tipped the scales sliding into the darkness—as did any spell that utilized force on the unwilling.

Dammit, she hadn't wanted to use the summoning spell—it had been her only option. Dark magic scared the shit out of her. When she'd been performing her spell, she'd heard the whispers of temptation from the damned. The lure of the ancient power.

But she'd resisted the whispers.

Done her job—and gotten her *cazador.*

There had been no choice. She lifted her chin. Squared her shoulders and heard her mother's voice whispering through her mind, *"The cazador, he comes after witches when they're bad."*

Well, it looked like he was already after her.

But just what he planned to *do* with her . . . she was a bit afraid to find out.

His little witch needed more clothes. The black T-shirt and too-tight jeans barely covered her body, and he kept getting a teasing glimpse of the smooth flesh of her stomach.

The *tattooed* flesh of her stomach. A five-pointed star enclosed her navel, and a glittering gold hoop flashed from the center of her belly button.

Luis didn't even bother acting as if he weren't staring at her flesh. He'd been so busy admiring his witch's breasts earlier that he'd missed the tat and the piercing.

A pity, because the gold was damn sexy on her body.

Was she holding any more secrets on her flesh? He would discover them all—very soon.

She braked in front of a small ranch house. One on a perfectly normal-looking street. One that had small, blooming purple flowers along the sidewalk.

Her fingers clenched around the steering wheel. "I'm not going to just wait around while you hunt."

Her words had his brows rising.

She turned to him, jaw locked. "You're not gonna shut me out of this, do you hear me? I *summoned* you, and that means I have some control over you. You're not gonna shove me in some corner while you go off and hunt alone."

Ah. He almost smiled at her fierce words. Almost. Instead, he moved fast, catching her shoulders and pulling her against him. "Time for the rules here, witch." Her lips were parted in surprise. It always amazed him that even the *Other* were surprised by the speed of his movements.

"R-rules?" Her eyes were wide and so damn green. He could stare into those eyes for hours.

He drew in a deep breath and caught her scent. "Yeah, rules." Although, really, there weren't many. "First rule, no one controls me." *Ever.*

Her mouth opened ever more. "But—"

He kissed her. Took her mouth with his tongue and his lips like he'd been fantasizing about for the last half hour. And, damn, but the witch tasted good. Sweet, hot. Fucking incredible. Her tongue moved against his, tentatively at first, as if she were almost afraid to respond.

He didn't want her fear.

His arms wrapped around her, his embrace becoming more like that of a lover. Her breasts pushed against him and the feel of her nipples pressing into his chest made his cock swell. He stroked her with his tongue, holding on to his control, courting her, *not* demanding . . . but he needed her response.

Her willing response.

A moan built in the back of her throat. The sound shot straight to his erection, made the lust double. Then her fingers were on his flesh, digging into his shoulders.

Those nails. Hell, yes. Pushing into the skin as she held on tight.

And she kissed him with the same ravenous hunger that he felt.

Their mouths became rougher. Hands more demanding. The heat in the car ratcheted up about twenty degrees.

His fingers slipped down her arms. He wanted to touch those fucking perfect breasts. Feel the nipples. They'd more than fill his hands. He'd caress her, squeeze her, then get those gorgeous nipples in his mouth so that he could suck and lick and make her moan again.

But Serena flinched and he froze.

Not pain. From her, he didn't want pain or fear.

Only pleasure.

Slowly, he pulled back. Realized that he'd touched her binding mark. His finger stroked the flesh just under the jagged line, silently soothing her.

Her breathing panted out, and so did his.

More.

His gaze darted to the dark house behind her.

"You . . . didn't have to do that."

Luis blinked. "Trust me, sweetheart, I did." He would do a hell of a lot more once he had her safe and beneath him in a bed.

"What do you want from me?" she whispered, and

the sound of her husky voice was like a silken stroke right over his throbbing arousal.

Everything—and that was what he would take.

"The summoning spell didn't give you any control over me." The minute he'd stepped out of her circle, her control had vanished. If she thought she'd be able to manipulate him, well, the lady was dead wrong. Best to get that cleared up right now.

Long ago, a council of *Other* elders had been created to keep the paranormal peace. They'd made the mistake of thinking they could control the *cazadores*, too.

As far as Luis knew, no members of that illustrious council still lived.

Not that he was particularly concerned with what had become of them all. Once he'd learned that the majority of those assholes had ignored their own so-called peace rules and slaughtered humans—he'd stopped caring about their lives then.

And begun focusing more on their deaths. He'd hunted down several of the killers, despite their pretense of authority.

"The summoning spell brought you here." A satisfied smile curved her lips and drew him from the past. "That was what I wanted and—"

"No, what you wanted was to live." His words had her smile vanishing. "And I'll do my damned best to see that you do."

For a price. He didn't say the words this time, because his witch already knew.

Before she could speak, there was a loud screech of sound, and something pounded against the windshield of her car.

Something small. Black. With claws.

Fuck.

He turned his head and glared out the windshield, meeting a pair of shining yellow eyes. "That damn well better not be your familiar."

The sensual spell between them had shattered. Serena turned away, fumbled with the lock on the door. "He's not," she said. "Just a stray who wandered up a few days ago." She climbed hurriedly from the car and didn't bother glancing back at him.

His nostrils flared. The scent of her arousal carried easily to him. Like a shape-shifter, he had very advanced senses. Smell, taste, sight, sound, and touch—they were all substantially heightened for him.

He could smell the rich cream from his witch's sex. She wanted him.

Good. That would make things easier.

When he got out of the car, Serena stood waiting near her small porch, one delicate foot tapping, and the cat, a too-skinny, long-haired beast, had his tail wrapped around her legs.

She lifted her keys. "The poor thing looks like he's starving. I'm going to let him inside and find some milk or something for him."

The cat let out a satisfied purr.

Luis frowned.

His magic didn't work with animals. He wasn't a charmer and in all of his years, he'd never taken the soul of an animal-talker. Charmers generally weren't on the lists of fatal badasses who needed to be put out of their misery. Since he'd never taken one's power, that meant Luis couldn't communicate with beasts, but . . .

But he *felt* a whisper of dark power hanging around the cat.

Serena opened her door and the cat ran in front of

her, tail up, darting down the darkened hall as if he owned the place.

Serena stepped forward.

"Wait."

Her curls bobbed as she glanced back at him and he could see the shadows of exhaustion under her eyes. His witch had been fighting a dark foe on her own for too many nights.

But not any longer.

"I don't want you anywhere near that cat," he said.

A surprised laugh burst from her lips. "You can't be serious!"

But he was.

Brushing by her, and greedily inhaling her scent, he headed after the feline.

Behind him, Serena tapped a button, and the overhead lights flickered on.

The living room was to the left. Oversized couch. Cozy fireplace. Candles. Spell books.

And paint. Brushes. Easels. The heavy scent of the paint filled the air.

So his witch was an artist. Interesting. And, judging by the paintings that sat on the two easels, she was very, very good.

A castle filled one canvas. Heavy grays. Dark blues. A fortress under siege, battling the wind and rain and the night.

The second painting was of a woman. A portrait. A beauty with hair as black and curly as Serena's, but with green eyes that shone with light and happiness.

He hadn't seen happiness in his witch's eyes.

The cat nosed around the easel positioned near the window. Brushed its fur against a brush that lay all but forgotten on the floor.

A personal item would be needed for the binding

spell. Something Serena had touched. Something from her home.

He growled. The sound was a perfect match for a wolf, not a man.

The cat jerked his head up, arched his back and hissed.

Luis bared his teeth.

The furball took off, running straight toward him, and Luis was ready. He grabbed the beast by the scruff of his neck and lifted him high into the air.

Yellow eyes blazed at him.

"Uh, what are you doing to the cat?"

He didn't answer Serena. All of his attention was on the beast.

Usually humans were the only ones who mistakenly thought animals were harmless.

A witch should have known better.

"Tell your master I'm coming for him," Luis snarled, "and that he'd better start fucking running."

The cat's whiskers shivered. Then the feline twisted and fell from Luis's hands. He landed on all fours with a soft whisper of sound. The front door was still open, and he ran toward it, hissing.

Luis didn't bother chasing the animal. He had the creature's scent. The cat wouldn't get away from him.

Serena slammed the door shut, locked it. "I-I don't understand. I didn't sense evil from him—"

"He's linked with a charmer, sweetheart." Had to be. "The cat's been visiting you, probably all the coven, and providing the charmer with the link he needed to *know* you." A string, a piece of hair—the cat could have taken anything small back to his master. In order for a binding spell to work, a personal possession was needed. The cat had been a perfect thief.

She shook her head. "But charmers can't bind witches. They don't have that kind of power."

On that note, she was dead right. "The guy's not working alone." It was the conclusion he'd reached as soon as he recognized the taint of power lingering around the cat. Which meant . . . "There's not just one asshole out there trying to take down your coven." No, not just one.

A smile lifted his lips. Ah, damn but he loved a challenge.

"We've got to go after them! Let's go follow that cat and—"

"No."

Her mouth tightened. "I thought you were *helping* me."

"I am." He strode toward her. "You're dead on your feet. I'm getting you in bed."

Her breath jerked. "You're—no, you're just trying to go off on your own—"

He shook his head and touched her cheek. Such soft skin. So smooth. "I'm not going to leave you."

"I don't trust you."

Good. "You're tired. If you're going to hunt with me, you'll need your strength." It would take some time for her to recover from the summoning spell.

Her lips tilted. "Y-you're going to let me hunt with you?"

He'd never let another accompany him, but in the past, he'd gone to seek vengeance. Not to stop the crime.

Since it was her life, it was the least Serena deserved.

So he nodded.

A relieved laugh burst from her lips, the sound high and sweet.

Nice.

"I thought you'd be pissed as hell at me for forcing you here, but you're—"

"I am." *Pissed as hell.* Yes, a fairly apt description.

The smile faded from her lips.

"Don't forget who I am, not for a moment," he told her. She needed the warning, and he wouldn't give her another. "I agreed to help you, but I am most definitely *pissed as hell* at being yanked thousands of miles across the globe. You didn't have my consent, witch, and I don't take lightly to those who would seek to control me."

I summoned you, that means I have some control over you.

Her words lay between them.

Her throat moved as she swallowed. "Can you—can you really kill with just a touch?"

His hand was on her cheek, because he wanted to keep stroking that flesh. Slowly, he trailed his fingers down the side of her face. Down the elegant column of her throat. His fingers wrapped around her neck. "Yes." One simple touch.

But he didn't have to give just pain and death. He could also give pleasure. He'd give that to her, when the time was right.

"Are you afraid of me, Serena?"

Her eyes held his. So steady. So deep. "No."

Lie.

The one whispered word grated in his mind.

"Pity." He meant it. His hand rose slowly, cupping her cheek, and his head lowered toward hers. Her lips were parted. "Do you want me to kiss you again, witch?"

"Yes."

Truth.

His mouth took hers. Claimed it. Tasted the sweetness on her tongue and greedily took everything that her tender mouth had to offer.

He'd have her naked soon. Beneath him in bed. Taking him deep inside of her.

Her body was supple against his. Her thighs shifted and he fought to control the impulse demanding that he reach down and search out all her secrets.

Such tempting female flesh. Waiting for him.

He wanted her breasts. In his mouth.

His tongue brushed over hers. Thrust into her mouth. So good.

Her hands seemed to scorch his flesh. Even through the thin fabric of his shirt, he could feel the heat of her touch.

If only they were naked, he'd feel her, *everywhere*.

Not now.

Dammit.

Luis forced his head to lift. Serena's cheeks were flushed, her eyes sparkling, her lips red and swollen from his mouth.

"You want me." Luis said the words because he wanted no pretense between them. When he was between her thighs, thrusting as hard and deep as he could, he didn't want her pretending the sex was just some sort of sacrifice for the safety of her coven.

The price for the coven's protection would be met later.

The sex—that was just between them. A need he hadn't expected, certainly never imagined that he would feel for a witch who'd tried to control him.

He could smell her arousal, the lush perfume of woman filling his nostrils and making his cock twitch.

He waited for her denial. None came.

The witch wasn't going to give him the speech about how she was a good girl, one who didn't sleep with strangers.

Because good girls didn't use dark magic.

"That's what you want from me, then? My body?" Still so calm. Too calm.

"I'm gonna be taking a lot more than just your sexy flesh, Serena." She'd learn what he wanted, soon enough. "Besides, don't you want my body?" If there was anything he'd learned about witches, it was that they were sensual creatures. It was partly due to the magic that constantly streamed through their bodies. All of that glorious, rich power.

Sex was necessary for witches. Not as necessary as it was for sex demons, but witches mated often.

With Serena's power running low, she'd need the brief boost she'd get from a hard climax of pleasure.

And the thing about witches . . . they had a reputation for always leaving their lovers well satisfied.

The succubi usually only cared about their own pleasure.

Not so for a witch.

"You know I want you." Her words came slowly. *Truth.*

"I shouldn't," she said, and her breath feathered over his face. "It's the wrong damn time and you're sure as hell the wrong man."

His brows shot up.

"If I wanted to play with a devil, there are any number of demons I could find in this town for a fix."

A growl worked in his throat. He didn't want to think of the witch with another. Not when he hadn't even come close to possessing her yet.

"No other," he ordered, and meant it. The lust between them was unexpected as hell, but Luis had never been the sharing type. He'd have Serena, and no being—human or *Other*—would touch her while he was near.

"And no other for you," she said, her words holding the same edge of possession that his had.

"Agreed." The response was instantaneous. He wanted no other.

His right hand still held her chin. He squeezed gently then slid his hand down and let his fingers curve around her neck once more. Beneath his touch, he felt her pulse beating far too fast.

Serena's hunger matched his, but her strength didn't. *Not now.*

"I won't hunt without you," he told her again. Then, "Don't be afraid . . ."

Her eyes widened. "What? Why are you—"

"I'll be here when you wake."

Understanding dawned too late in her gaze.

Exhaling slowly, he blew a stream of magic right at her.

She sagged against him, her body limp as sleep claimed her. He pulled her close.

And thought about the magnificent twists of fate.

And how very, very easy it was to kill a witch.

After all, his mother had burned so quickly . . .

"*Anubis.*"

The black cat hissed and arched his back as Julian Kathers crouched before him. Julian listened intently, a frown forming along his brow, then, "*Dammit.*"

The warlock who sat on the other side of the room arched a brow. "Trouble, charmer?"

Julian stroked the cat's back, trying his best to calm Anubis. The cat was shaking, scared to death.

With damn good reason. "A soul-hunter's in town."

For the first time in the fifteen years that Julian had

known the warlock, fear flickered over Michael Deveaux's face. "Bullshit."

Anubis hissed again.

"He's with one of the witches." Fucking bad news. The witches—they were easy enough to pick off one at a time, after they'd been bound, anyway. And he sure did enjoy the sight of a witch bitch burning, but—

But the *cazadores* were a different game.

He'd never gone up against one of them. Didn't have the power to face one.

Did the warlock? Julian's heart pumped fast at the thought. Maybe. *Maybe.* A wild laugh sprang to his lips, but he bit it back.

I'd love to see a cazador die.

Maybe the bastard would beg. Plead. He loved it when prey pleaded.

Made the death so much sweeter.

Fuck, but he should have been born stronger! Not as a damn worthless charmer who could only talk to strays. Those fucking witch bitches in his old neighborhood had taunted him, using their magic to make every day of his life so damn miserable, one spell after another.

But he'd shown them. *He'd shown them all.*

A witch's screams were so sweet, and the flesh of a witch smelled so very good when it burned.

The laugh he couldn't hold back any longer broke from his lips.

The warlock had swiped a hell of a lot of energy from the witches over the years. *Yes,* maybe he could do it—

Another laugh. The cat shook beneath his petting hand.

The warlock rose, the light of a nearby lamp reflecting for a moment in his golden hair. "The hunter saw the cat?" His voice was calm, even.

No fear—of course not. *Because he knew that he could take the cazador bastard.*

Excitement had Julian's heart drumming even faster. Anubis arched his back again and his whiskers twitched.

"The hunter was with the witch—the black-haired one, Serena—at her house. He followed the cat inside."

Anubis *meowed.* A high, plaintive sound.

"What did the damn feline just say?" The warlock demanded, voice snapping as he stalked toward them.

"The *cazador*—he said he'd be coming." *And that I'd better start fucking running.*

But Julian hadn't run from anyone, not since he was sixteen and those witch bitches at his school had thought it would be funny to chase him after class with one of the stone gargoyles that *should* have forever stayed resting on the roof of the old building next to his high school.

They'd known he was *Other,* so they'd felt confident in playing with him. The bitches never would have worked tricks like that on humans.

For the longest time, he'd heard their laughter when he closed his eyes at night.

Then, after he'd hooked up with the warlock, he'd been able to hear only their screams.

"He'll have the cat's scent." The momentary heat that had flared in the man's voice was gone. He walked around Julian, keeping a careful distance from Anubis.

The warlock had never liked his cat, Julian knew that.

But he'd sure used Anubis every chance he got.

Such a perfect pet. So good at sneaking into the homes of witches.

Witches always had a soft spot for black cats.

Fools.

"We can be ready for him," Julian said, confidence and the thrill of the kill filling him. "Let the hunter come, we'll gut him and—"

Snap. Julian's words ended. His hand stopped stroking the cat.

Anubis jerked back, tiny teeth bared.

Slowly, the warlock lifted his hands from Julian's neck.

So easy to kill charmers, Michael thought. *Almost as easy as killing humans.*

The best part? He hadn't even needed to waste a drop of his magic.

"One problem down," he muttered, and smiled at the cat. The soul-hunter could trace the cat's scent all he liked now—he'd just find death waiting for him.

Lifting his hand, he motioned for the cat. "Here, little kitty . . . come to me . . . so I can send you to hell with your master . . ."

The cat turned and ran, jumping up onto the window ledge and then diving into the night.

Michael laughed.

The cat had been smarter than the charmer.

Not really surprising.

So, the witch, Serena, had summoned a soul-hunter. Interesting.

Resourceful.

Usually the witches just ran and hid when the first binding mark appeared on their flesh.

Hmm. The witch had to be strong. Most couldn't use a summoning spell even at full power, much less initially bound.

Good. It had been far too long since he'd taken a strong witch's magic.

He stepped over the body. Headed for the door. He'd face the *cazador* on his own time . . . and at a place of his choosing.

But first, first he had to finish the witches.

Because he'd need every last drop of their power to kill the soul-hunter on his trail.

Fortunately, he knew just which of the coven members he would mark for first death.

The lovely Serena.

3

She woke to find him standing at the foot of her bed. Dawn had yet to creep across the sky, so he stood, clothed in the shadows and darkness. His golden eyes glittered at her, lit with a heat that reflected his dark hunger.

Lust.

Serena sat up slowly. She was still dressed, just missing shoes, and a sheet had been pulled over her body.

She licked her lips, staring up at him. The silence in the room was thick and heavy and she waited . . .

Luis crept around the bed, and the carpet muffled the sounds of his footsteps. Closer, *closer* . . .

Her heart hitched faster, but she didn't speak, not yet.

He neared the side of her bed. Stopped and gazed down at her with those burning eyes.

So much need.

Was the same desire reflected in her own stare?

It had been so long since she'd been with a lover. So long since she'd let down the wall around her and trusted another to be close to her.

You can't trust him, a soft, niggling voice warned.

No, she couldn't.

She *shouldn't*.

But she did want him.

Her last lover had left over a year ago. Gotten tired of her secrets. Human, he'd sensed she was holding back on him, but Serena had never felt ready to tell James the truth about herself. She'd been afraid he would run.

Then, one day, she'd come home to find a note waiting for her.

And no James.

After a few days, she'd stopped missing him.

Would the same thing happen when her hunter left? When his job was done, would she be able to write him off as easily?

When Luis's hand brushed over her cheek, she jumped.

"I want you." His voice, so deep, almost guttural, growled from the darkness.

Just the sound of his voice, hardened with hunger, had her breasts tightening, nipples pebbling.

She'd never been with a man as strong as he was. Her lovers had generally been mortals, except for the bear charmer and the fox shifter, and—

"Don't think about anything right now . . . but me." His fingers slid over her flesh. Caught her chin. Tipped back her head and—

He kissed her. Pushed his tongue past her lips and took her mouth just as he'd done before.

And, just as before, her blood began to heat, desire to uncoil, hard and fast, within her. Her hands caught his shoulders, held on tight.

Magic.

Passion.

Power.

It was all there in his kiss, and she wanted it—
wanted him.

For the first time in twenty-nine years, dammit, she
decided to take what she wanted.

Serena's lips widened, and she met him, tongue to
tongue, mouth to mouth, kissing greedily, rising to
hold him tighter.

Fuck being the pristine one. Holding out for love—
well, that had never worked so well for her.

Going for the wild, mad ride of pleasure—she'd just
see how that worked out.

Besides, death was on her trail, and she wanted to
make certain she lived as much as she could.

Every. Single. Moment.

"I want you." He gritted the words against her
mouth. Her lashes lifted and she found Luis staring
down at her.

A rush of sensual power flooded through her veins
and Serena heard herself respond, in a voice gone husky
with matching desire, "Then why don't you take me?"

In the next second, she was flat on her back in the
bed. Luis was over her. Her hands were pinned in the
bedding. His legs tangled with hers. The thick length
of his arousal pushed against her.

Yes.

This was what she wanted. Wild. Fast. Hot. Hard.

His mouth blazed a path down her neck. Lips brand-
ing. Tongue licking. And his teeth . . .

Serena shuddered when the edge of his teeth grazed
her flesh.

Her sex tightened and cream flooded between her
folds.

She twisted beneath him, wanting to feel his naked

skin against hers. "Dammit, too many clothes—" The words tumbled from her lips as she drew in ragged breaths.

He freed her hands as he reared back. His long, strong fingers caught the edge of her shirt. Jerked it over her head. The garment disappeared, tossed somewhere in the room—she had no idea where and didn't care.

She'd put on a bra when she'd dressed. Now his fingers went to it, fumbling quickly with the front clasp. Then he was touching her, pushing the lacy cups aside and running those rough fingers over her flesh.

A moan fell from her lips. Her fingers found his shirt front, jerked it open and sent buttons flying across the bed.

His hands cupped her breasts. Teased. Fingertips caught her nipples, caressed, then his dark head lowered.

The warm, wet lap of his tongue sent a shock wave through her.

"Luis!" Her nails skated down his chest. Power was in the air around them. Energy vibrating against her skin.

There was magic for a witch in sex. The renewing power of life, the blissful wonder of pleasure.

Just what she needed.

No, *he* was what she needed.

He pulled her breast into his mouth, laved her with his tongue. Suckled.

Her sex contracted and she arched her hips, rubbing against the bulging length of his arousal.

Flesh to flesh. That was how she wanted him—and how she would have him.

Her hands gripped his upper arms. Tested the muscles, then caressed the hot flesh of his chest as her hands began to trail down his body. His strong abs rippled beneath her fingertips. Damn, but the man was like some kind of perfect freaking statue.

Not a man.

More.

He freed her breast, lifted his head. "Serena . . ."

Such hunger. Raw lust.

She loved the way he said her name.

Her fingers caught the top of his jeans. Unhooked the button, eased down the zipper with fingers that shook with eagerness.

"Are you afraid?" He asked the question, his voice as demanding as the hands that were now stroking her flesh.

"No." Right then, she couldn't get close enough to him. Afraid? *Only that he'd stop.*

Her vision wasn't shifter strong, but she caught a glimpse of his smile. The flash of his teeth.

"Good answer."

His hand slipped down her stomach, hesitated over her belly button. "I want to kiss you."

Hadn't he already? What—

He shifted his body, pulling back and bringing a cry of protest to her lips.

Then his mouth pressed against her stomach. His fingers eased open the top of her jeans, and he licked her. A long, slow lick right along her belly—and along the piercing she'd gotten as a birthday present just last year.

Her heels dug into the mattress and her thighs clenched around him.

"I can smell you," he whispered, the words merging with the darkness. "So damn sweet."

Her arousal. She knew instantly what he meant,

and the knowledge that he knew of her hunger only made her sex cream more.

"Get rid of the jeans," she ordered, and meant hers, his. She'd never been one for too much foreplay—she loved the act of sex too much. The slide of bodies. The hard thrusts. The joining.

She wanted to join with Luis. To mate.

A growl shook his body and an answering moan rose in her throat. When his fingers pushed the denim completely off her hips and his breath fanned over the front of her panties, she arched toward him, ready—

White hot pain lanced her, burning, cutting into her upper arm, the agony so intense that she contorted, tears trickling down her cheeks.

"Sonofabitch!"

Luis stilled at once. "Serena?"

She clenched her teeth, trying to choke down the pain. It felt as if someone were cutting her arm. Driving a knife all the way to the bone and carving her flesh.

Not again. Goddess, no, not the second mark.

"Fuck!" The cry was Luis's. He jerked away from her and shot from the bed. Chanted a spell of protection.

A spell that would do no good.

The lights flashed on in her room. Burning far too brightly. A burst of air tousled her hair.

The pain began to recede. Throbbing now, in time with the rapid beats of her heart.

She squeezed her eyes shut, needing to block out the light, and not wanting to look at her arm.

Because she knew exactly what she'd see.

A second mark meant her powers would be even more limited, dammit.

Who was doing this to her?

A feather-light touch upon her shoulder had her screaming, her eyes flashing open.

Luis stared at her, his face tense. Looking so fierce— as fierce and deadly as he'd appeared when she first summoned him.

"Are you all right?"

No. She was most damn definitely not *all right.* Her life was spiraling out of her control. Some sick bastards were screwing with her and her coven, and a second binding mark meant her time was running far too low.

"When did the first mark appear?" Luis demanded.

Serena pulled in a slow breath. The passion she'd felt so deeply moments before was gone, erased by a tide of pain.

And rage.

"When the Blood Moon took the night." Had it really been just a few nights before when the full moon had risen so powerfully into the sky?

And the first mark had appeared.

Steeling herself, Serena finally dropped her gaze to stare at the flesh of her upper arm. Already, the binding cut looked like a scar. Four inches long. The flesh raised, angry red.

Only one more mark to go, then the spell would be complete.

She would be as helpless as a human.

Luis's fingers hovered over the mark, as if he wanted to touch her, but was afraid.

"It's a warlock, you know." He said the words softly.

Serena's gaze was on her arm. "I know." The throbbing continued. The aching flesh pulsed as she stared at the skin. *A warlock.*

In the *Other* world, those who practiced their power in good faith—following the rule of *to harm none,* were termed witches or wizards.

But a witch who crossed that line, or a wizard who harmed innocents, well, then that person was given a new designation.

Warlock.

Shunned by the coven. Expelled from the magical community.

Alone to work the dark magic.

She'd known, of course, for only another witch would be able to work a binding spell. Demons didn't have the power. Djinn couldn't strip a witch of her magic.

No, it took one of her own to work spells like this.

A fact that made the betrayal all the harder to bear.

His fingers brushed over the marks. She sucked in a sharp breath, expecting the burning pain to flare to life again but—

But she felt a cool balm on her skin. The throbbing eased. The redness lightened.

Her eyes widened.

His head bent toward her and he pressed a kiss to the second wound, then the first.

The pain vanished.

Serena stared at him, stunned. He was the bringer of death, not a healer. "How the hell did you do that?"

He looked up at her through his lashes, his mouth poised over her arm.

A spark of remembered need had her shifting and realizing that she was mostly nude and that if she'd had but a few minutes more before that bastard had struck—

Well, she wouldn't have been thinking about pain.

"I don't just bring fear and terror, you know." Another kiss, then he eased away. "I can also ease pain or . . ." His gaze dropped to her bared breasts. "Give pleasure."

Oh, yeah, she'd gotten a firsthand sample of that *pleasure.* And she wanted more. Serena swallowed and jerked on her bra. She'd sure as hell like to just lie back with Luis and get a few more samples, but . . . "W-we've got to go after them." The warlock and his charmer. "If the warlock marked me, he could be trying to mark the others—we have to go!"

Luis gave a grim nod but asked, "Are you certain you're up to facing him?"

Like she was going to back down. "This is my life he's fucking with so, hell, yeah, I'm ready."

"Then we'll fight now." Again, a dark heat flashed in his eyes, "And later . . ."

We'll fuck.

Yes, they both knew exactly what would happen later.

Damn. Damn. Damn. He was going to make the bastard pay. He'd hunt him down, no, hunt *them* down, and make them beg for mercy.

Then he'd kill them.

Luis knew he was after a team of killers. Had to be a charmer working with a warlock. No way the charmer who controlled the black cat would be able to bind the witches on his own.

The memory of Serena's pain-filled cry echoed in his mind. His hands clenched and magic snapped in the air around him.

Oh, yeah, those bastards would pay in blood.

He'd been seconds away from tasting the sweet cream between her thighs, then some assholes had fucked up his plans *and* hurt his witch.

Luis couldn't wait for the fighting to begin. He was definitely in the mood to kick ass and send a few deserving paranormals straight to the next world.

"Stop!" He gave the order when Serena's car turned the corner of Ruthers Lane.

The window on his side of the car was down. He'd been following the trail of the black cat—using his enhanced sense of smell to catch the feline's scent. He'd also been tracking the taint of the dark magic that had hung heavily on the cat—a taint that, to his eyes, appeared as a fine mist in the air. A mist that led him straight to the small shop at the end of Ruthers Lane.

"Turn off the car," he said.

Serena obeyed instantly. "Is this—is the warlock here?"

He wasn't sure, but the cat had been there. The cat had gone inside the antique shop that boasted the sign, HIDDEN TREASURES.

Dawn had come, the sun rising and chasing away the shadows. They were on a small business street, one lined with curiosity shops and galleries. One that would soon be teeming with humans.

They'd have to move fast.

Luis turned to Serena, "Let's—"

She shoved open her door and hopped outside.

He blinked. OK, so his witch was ready to kick ass, too.

She'd changed her clothes before they left. Slipped on a long blouse that covered her arms and that stomach he loved to see. She was wearing jeans—jeans that hugged the rounded curves of her hips and thighs. Her small feet were encased in snug, black leather boots.

Serena had even managed to find him a shirt, a fact that pissed him off. Why the hell would his witch have men's clothes handy? And she hadn't conjured them—

they'd been hanging in the back of her closet. She'd muttered something about her ex leaving the items behind.

The bastard had better not be coming back to claim the clothes—or Serena.

Luis climbed from the car and glanced around to make certain no human was nearby. The last thing he needed was a nosy mortal catching sight of his battle.

Or of him.

Satisfied that the humans hadn't yet come to play, his hand lifted, and he pointed toward HIDDEN TREASURES. The shop's windows were dark, and a CLOSED sign hung haphazardly against the front door.

His nostrils twitched as he caught a darker, pungent smell on the wind.

Hell.

"Luis?" Serena called his name softly.

"Death's waiting, sweetheart." No mistaking that dank scent. "Stay on your guard."

She gave a grim nod.

And he led the way toward the scent he knew too well.

4

The door was locked, but one quick jerk of his hand made the cheap lock shatter. He yanked open the door and heard the squeal of an alarm. His gaze darted around the room, locked on the small black box with the blinking red dot.

Luis grabbed a nearby candlestick, one that was a perfect polished silver to his eyes, and threw it, sending the candlestick hurtling end over end toward the alarm.

When it smashed into the box, blessed silence filled the air.

So much for going in quietly, but, then, he'd never really been the quiet type.

Besides, for one of the bastards he was chasing, the noise wouldn't matter. Not much could wake the dead.

"The cops will be coming," Serena said, her voice carrying just to his ears. Cautious witch. "The alarm will have been connected, the security service will alert them—"

"Then we'd better move, fast."

A *hiss* sounded from the back of the store. An all too familiar sound.

Damn cat.

He hurried forward, saw the small beast pacing in front of an old, scarred door.

The cat arched his back at Luis's approach and bared his teeth.

"Out of the way, pussy." Not in the mood to deal with the feline, Luis flashed his own teeth.

The cat turned and ran back toward the entrance of the shop.

"Luis . . ."

Serena stood behind him. So close he could feel the warmth of her body.

He lifted his hand, touched the door. Then sent the wood crashing to the ground with one hard punch.

Sometimes enhanced strength could be a real bonus.

His gaze fell on the body. The still man with bright red hair. The fellow whose neck was twisted and whose eyes were wide open.

Never saw death coming.

Because he'd trusted his killer.

Serena sucked in a sharp breath. "Oh, goddess, is he a human?"

"No." A quick scan showed that no one else was in the small room. Luis crouched beside the body, reached out his hand—

"Meow." The black cat ran back into the room and pressed against the dead man's side.

Luis exhaled. "It's the charmer." The asshole who'd been working with the warlock. Dammit. *The kill should have been mine.*

"I don't understand." He glanced up at her. Serena's face had gone pale and her eyes were staring fixedly at the body. No, at the bastard's twisted neck. "W-why is he dead? If he was working with the warlock—"

The cat's head prodded the charmer's side as he tried to get his master to wake.

"Not gonna happen," Luis muttered to the small creature and rose to his feet. "The warlock knew I could trace the cat back to his master."

Her gaze jerked away from the body. Understanding dawned on her face. "Then, once you had the charmer, you could have tracked the warlock."

As easy as connecting the dots.

Or, it should have been.

But the warlock had decided to cover his ass and throw a dead body in their path.

Serena swallowed and lifted her hand to her throat.

Ah, hell. "Is this your first body, witch?" How many corpses had he seen in his time? Hundreds? Thousands? The sight of the dead no longer fazed him.

But Serena was another matter. "Not my first." Her brows pulled low. "My aunt—I found what was left of her."

The urge to go to her, to hold her, rocked through him—and what the hell was up with that?

He was *not* the comforting type. The killing type. The fucking type.

Not comforting.

The witch was screwing with his head.

Luis found himself taking a step forward, blocking the dead body. "Nothing can be done for the bastard now."

In the distance, a siren wailed.

Serena shook her head, and some of the color seemed to return to her cheeks. Her gaze darted around the room. "We've got to get out of here," she muttered. "We've got to—" She broke off. Her eyes widened and then she was nearly running across the small room, her hip thumping against the side of a desk as she skidded to a halt.

"Serena?"

"This is Vanessa's." She lifted a long, blue hair ribbon. "She had it in her hair last week." Her fingers reached for a swatch of fabric. "And Susan was working on a quilt just like this—*dammit!*" She dropped the fabric. "The bastard has us all right here!"

Actually, he had to have even more of their belongings stashed somewhere else. In order to continue the spell, he had to hold one personal article from each witch. No way would the guy have left all his treasures behind.

The wails of the sirens were getting closer.

Serena swore, then started to frantically grab all the witches' possessions.

"What are you doing? We don't have time—"

"And if the cops connect any of this stuff to the coven? We'll be screwed!"

She was right. So he started helping her, fast. Their hands were overflowing when they ran from the store.

Fate was on his side, for once, because the street was still deserted. Good. He wouldn't have to waste any magic on the humans.

They hurried to the waiting car, tossed the materials inside and—

A police cruiser hurtled around the corner. Brakes screeched and the lights above the vehicle flashed in a blur. Two officers jumped out, guns drawn. "Freeze!" The command came in unison.

Serena stilled near the driver's side door of her car. "Shit," she muttered and glared at the cops. "This isn't what you think—"

"We're not here," Luis said, walking toward them, pitching his voice low and calling on the powers he'd been given by his father.

A level ten, the strongest of the demons—and those who could most easily control the minds of humans.

The guns lifted higher. The cops' hands shook. "D-don't m-move." The shaky order came from the guy on the right, the one who looked like he was barely twenty-one.

"*Luis.*" Serena's horrified voice.

Horrified—because she was used to living in her safe coven world, a world where the good rules said not to hurt humans.

Well, he wasn't going to hurt these two, unless that option became absolutely necessary.

He really did try to spare the innocents when he could.

It was those who deserved his fury that he unleashed his power upon. And let the fire rage.

But he would make the humans forget, with a quick compulsion sure to drive the memory of him and Serena forever from their minds.

"You didn't see us," Luis told the men softly, as Serena swore behind him. "When you arrived on the scene, there were no other cars in the vicinity."

The young kid's eyes bulged. He swallowed, once, twice, then his gaze shot to Serena, and the gun moved to aim straight at her chest.

"*Drop the weapons!*" Luis snarled, heart lurching as something he'd not felt in centuries reared its head.

Fear.

Fuck.

The weapons hit the ground with a clatter.

Luis turned his head and glared at Serena.

She blinked. "What?" Then she looked over her shoulder, as if expecting to see some kind of threat.

She was the threat, to him.

Dammit. The danger his mother had warned him of. A weakness.

He ground his back teeth together. This wouldn't do. Not at damn all.

With an effort, Luis turned his attention back to the cops. "You didn't see us," he repeated, forcing the compulsion deeper. The kid was stronger than the slightly balding guy behind him. Could be the rookie even had a touch of psychic power.

But there was no way either of the humans were strong enough to resist him.

Another paranormal, yeah, because the *Other* could resist his compulsion. Serena would be able to because of her witch blood.

But the humans before him didn't stand a chance of fighting him.

"Get in the car," he told Serena, not wanting to push his luck. He didn't want to risk a shifter or charmer cop pulling up on the scene.

She didn't move.

By the grave of—

"The cat," she said, and bit her lip. "We can't just . . . leave him alone with that dead body."

His eyes closed for a moment. Witches and their damn soft spots for animals. Had to be a leftover trait from the heavy familiar days. "Fine!"

Luis jabbed his index finger in the rookie's direction. "There's a cat inside. A furry, skinny-as-hell stray."

The officer waited.

"*He's yours now.*"

A nod.

"Satisfied?" He threw the question at Serena as he ran around the car. More sirens were sounding, probably because he'd heard someone from the station trying to contact the officers on their radio during his compulsion, and the men hadn't responded as requested.

"For now," Serena agreed as she climbed into the car. She revved the engine. Then Serena threw the car into reverse, shot backward, narrowly avoiding a hard slam into the side of the cruiser. She shifted gears, twisted the car into a tight turn, and floored the gas as she roared down the road.

A touch of admiration filled Luis as she got them out of the about-to-be-swarmed neighborhood in less than thirty seconds.

Nice.

His witch had secret talents.

"Are you, Luis?" Her voice floated to him.

His gaze jerked to her face, locked on her profile.

"Are you satisfied?" she asked.

The flash of fear he'd felt moments before returned.

She was too vulnerable.

And he'd just found her.

"Fuck, no," he snapped, and her gaze flew to his.

He leaned closer to her, wrapped his fingers around the supple flesh of her thigh. Damn but she felt good.

She'd feel even better naked.

"Drive faster, Serena."

A shiver worked over her body, then her gaze darted to the rearview mirror. "Are the cops behind—"

"No one's behind us." His fingers inched up her leg. Paused near the juncture of her thighs. He swore he could feel the heat from her sex burning through the fabric.

Her breath jerked in. "Then w-why?"

He pushed his fingers between her legs. Stroked the crotch of her jeans and shoved the bitter memory of fear from his mind. "Because it's time for us both to be satisfied." His fingers strummed against her, and a red flush brightened her cheeks.

The engine rumbled as her foot pressed down even harder on the accelerator.

She'd been too close to death. His witch had felt the icy breath of the specter when she entered the dusty storage room. She needed to fight the fear and the anger that churned in her.

And passion, lust—well, for him, they'd always been perfect weapons.

Time for him to take his witch.

When her car screeched to a stop in front of her house, Serena wasn't thinking about dead bodies any more. She wasn't thinking that a dead man's eyes could hold such shock, and she wasn't thinking that death felt cold . . . far too cold. She'd thought of all that before. Back in that horrible storage room.

No, as she jumped from the car and she and Luis hurried up her steps, she wasn't thinking about death any more.

She thought of *him*.

Luis's touch. His body. The pleasure he'd give her.

The pleasure that would block the fear of the waiting cold.

The door slammed closed behind them.

His hands settled on her hips. "How fast can you get naked?"

Ah, now wasn't that a question she'd never heard

before? Excitement had her blood pumping, and Serena pulled away, turning to face him as she cocked her head and asked, "How fast can you?"

In a blink, he was naked, his clothes having vanished with but a wave of his hand.

Gotta love that magic.

Her gaze dropped to his chest. She loved his chest. So strong, with all those rippling muscles. His stomach was flat, the abs damn perfect.

His hand lifted, and his fingers grazed over his erection.

Oh, *yes*. The man was *built*. His cock bobbed up from a thatch of dark, curling hair. Long and thick.

Moisture gleamed on the broad head.

He was ready for her.

Good, because her panties were soaking wet for him and her nipples were so tight they ached.

Her magic might be limited by the binding, but she still had a few tricks of her own. She waved her hands over her body, and her clothes and shoes disappeared.

Yeah, sometimes, it was good to be a witch.

When the devil wasn't after you.

She pushed the thought away as quickly as it rose. For just a few minutes, she wanted pleasure.

Not fear.

His eyes heated as he looked at her. The gold gleamed so brightly. His cock swelled even more.

They didn't have to worry about birth control, a nice little *Other* perk. Witches completely controlled their cycles, and as for *cazadores* . . .

Immortals never caught illnesses of any sort.

He was the safest partner she'd ever had.

And the most dangerous.

He reached for her.

Shaking her head, she caught his hand in hers. "I want a bed." She wanted cool sheets, soft mattresses, and him. Thrusting as hard and deep as he could between her thighs, until the hungry ache in her sex had been assuaged.

"What my witch wants . . ."

She expected more magic. Wondered just what he was truly capable of doing. Could he move them by spell alone to her room or would he—

His arms wrapped around her and he pulled her up against his warm chest. His mouth crushed down on hers, tongue thrusting deep and she tightened her lips around him, sucking lightly. She loved the man's taste. Dark and rich and—

She was on the bed.

He sprawled over her, mouth still locked to hers, and he pushed her deep into the mattress. His legs— *the man had thick, muscled thighs that she'd love to ride*—angled between hers so that Serena was spread wide for him. Her sex was open and wet and so ready that she knew he had to catch the scent of her arousal.

He tore his mouth from hers. Lifted up to gaze at her body. "Fucking gorgeous," he growled. Then took her breast with his mouth. Licked. Bit. Sucked.

Made her moan.

His fingers—she *loved* those clever fingers—parted the folds between her legs. His thumb pressed over her clit, and Serena nearly came off the bed.

"Easy . . ." A dark rumble.

But she didn't want it easy. Not with him. Hard, fast, *wild*—that was how she wanted it.

And how she would take it.

Her nails dug into his back. Her thighs lifted and wrapped around his hips. "Hard." The demand snapped from her mouth.

His head jerked up. His mouth was wet, glistening, his lips parted.

She scored her nails down his back. Pressed her hands into Luis's taut ass. "*Wild.*"

His face hardened. "Then that's what I'll give you . . ."

The fingers that had caressed her sex stilled.

A wave of anticipation had her trembling.

Luis pulled back, dislodging her legs, and he brought his left hand up and curled the fingers over her thigh. When his gaze dropped to her sex, she knew what he was going to do.

And she couldn't wait.

His shoulders pushed between her legs. His breath fanned over the dark curls that shielded her feminine core.

Then he drove two fingers deep into her creamy opening.

Every muscle in her body stiffened.

She opened her mouth to cry out, but the sound broke on her lips when Luis pressed his mouth against her. He locked his open lips over her clit. His tongue teased, tasted.

Drove her *wild.*

His fingers thrust, moving in a fast rhythm. First just the two, then a third large finger lodged inside of her.

He licked her, swirling his tongue over the straining button of her desire, then lapping up the moisture that pooled between her legs as the lust grew and grew.

Serena felt the edge of his teeth, a light graze that had her freezing, then all but whimpering with pleasure when his tongue licked between her folds.

Her heart thudded in her ears and sweat slickened her body. The sunlight trickled through her blinds, and

she watched Luis, unable to look away from the sight
of his dark head between her thighs.

Her sex squeezed around him, clenching tight with
every thrust of his hand. Her nipples stabbed into the
air, her thighs trembled, and the promise of release
beckoned, just seconds away.

"*Luis.*" He was driving her crazy. And damn him,
he was holding the control. Every single bit of control.

Time to break that control, time to—

His fingers withdrew—shit, just when she was close—
then he drove his tongue inside of her.

The mounting tension erupted. Serena squeezed her
eyes shut and her head jerked back as the powerful
spasms shook her.

Pleasure was power.

A secret every succubus and incubus knew.

And one that the witches used for their own gain.

Her eyes flashed open, and her lips parted on a sigh
of satisfaction.

The magic of the release filled her body and as her
sex clenched in powerful contractions, Luis moved.
Rose above her. Pushed the head of his cock against
her opening.

"Time to get wild, witch."

He slammed into her, the force of his thrust strong
enough to send the bed sliding back against the wall.

More than ready for him, Serena arched her hips
and whispered his name.

His cock filled every inch of her sex and stretched
muscles gone sensitive from her climax. He was big,
thicker than she'd thought, and he felt *amazing*.

Once again, her legs clamped around his hips. As
he began to move, rocking harder, driving deeper, she
held on as fiercely as she could.

And enjoyed the ride.

Their mouths met. Tongues thrust as hips jerked. Breaths panted. Their hearts raced. The spiral of lust built, *built.*

His hands fondled her breasts. Teased the nipples and had her squirming beneath him.

When he rose, pulling that delicious cock nearly out of her, her head lifted. Her fingers traced his nipples, then she licked him, loving the slightly salty taste of his skin.

They rolled, twisting and turning as they fought for release. For a pleasure that was just out of their grasp.

Serena settled on top of him, legs on either side of his hips, sex clamped around his cock, feeling every inch of his arousal pulse inside of her.

His hands were on her hips. Holding too tightly, but she didn't care.

She squeezed him, clamping down hard on his erection. Then releasing her muscles with a hiss of pleasure.

His teeth ground together.

Another slow squeeze.

Now she had the control.

"Witch." Gritted. An accusation.

One she'd never deny.

Bending over him, she licked his nipples, drawing out the slow movements of her tongue, then glancing up at Luis from beneath her lashes.

His eyes glittered.

In the next second, she was on her back again. Her legs splayed over his shoulders and he thrust fast, hard, and she was—

Exploding. A white-hot pulse of release ripped through her as Serena climaxed. Her whole body shuddered beneath him and the cry that burst from her lips seemed to echo in the room.

Lights danced before her eyes. Magic.

Pleasure.

Still, he thrust. Deeper.

The bed was a mess. Sweat coated their bodies.

Flesh to flesh. Sex to sex.

He swelled within her. Another wild inch, so thick now that the friction of his thrusts sent a stab of pleasure through her with each move of his body as aftershocks reverberated in her core.

"*Serena.*" He drove deep. Froze. His gaze caught hers. For an instant, the molten gold of his eyes faded to pitch black.

Demon eyes.

The hot jet of his release filled her.

The air in the room heated, brushed against her skin.

Pleasure is power. For the hunter, as well as the witch.

He shuddered against her, held tight in the grip of his own climax. Her arms wrapped around him, and she clung to his stiffened muscles.

When the pleasure finally eased for them and their heartbeats began to slow, Serena stayed just where she was.

Right before she drifted to sleep, she could have sworn that their hearts were beating in perfect tune.

As if they were one.

Her aunt was in the middle of the circle of protection.

But the circle hadn't protected her.

Jayme Michaels lay on the ground, her long, curling black hair cascading around her face.

Serena ran to her, fear shaking her from the inside out.

No, no, not Aunt Jay. She was the strongest witch Serena had ever met. No one could harm her, not human, not Other.

Whoever was after Aunt Jay's coven, they wouldn't get to her, they couldn't have—

Her aunt's head was twisted. Her neck broken.

Her eyes were open. Her lips parted in surprise.

Serena skidded to a stop just outside of the sacred circle.

No, no, this wasn't right.

Not her aunt, not—

Serena awoke, jerking straight up in bed. Sunlight hit her hard in the face, and she turned away—

Only to have her gaze land on Luis's sleeping face.

The sight of him wiped away the fog from her dream.

No, not a dream. *Nightmare.*

She sucked in a deep breath. Her aunt hadn't looked like a broken doll when Serena had found her body.

The fire had already gotten to her and destroyed her beauty by then.

Another deep breath.

The dream had come because of the body they'd found—she knew it. Pleasure had only been able to push aside the darkness for so long.

Her hand reached for Luis. Hesitated.

His task was to stop the one after her. He would kill the warlock.

But she would not be useless in this battle.

As she'd been in the fight to save Aunt Jay.

Her fingers curled into a fist.

Her powers wouldn't return full force until the binding was removed, and that blessed event wouldn't happen until the warlock drew his last breath. Death— either the bound victim's or the spell caster's—was the only way to remove a dark binding.

Fortunately, she wasn't completely without magic— thanks in part to the furious pleasure she'd taken from Luis.

She would not be helpless.

Luis would destroy the warlock.

It would be up to *her* to find him.

Serena eased from the bed. Grabbed a light silk robe and belted it across her waist. The day was vanishing; already the clock told her it was long past noon.

Night would hold dangers, perhaps another binding.

The dark ones were always stronger at night.

Time for her to hunt *now*.

Carefully, she crept across the room, not wanting to risk waking Luis. He wouldn't like what she planned to do with the vestiges of her magic, but that was just too bad.

Her power, her life.

The door closed behind her with a soft click.

Luis waited a moment. Listened to the faint footfalls as Serena disappeared down the hallway.

Then his eyes opened.

He drew in the scent of woman and sex.

His cock was already erect. Just from the lingering traces of her sweet fragrance in the air.

What mischief was his dangerous little witch up to now?

He'd give her a few minutes, then he'd find out exactly what spells she was crafting so secretly.

Serena should have realized that after their mating, there would be no more secrets.

The soul-hunter had found the perfect soul that he wanted to take.

And she was just down the hallway.

5

Serena placed the items she and Luis had taken from the antique store in the middle of her living room. She'd pushed the furniture back moments before, the better to work.

Her fingers were steady as she positioned the candles around the witches' possessions. North. East. South. West. She lit them with a wave of her hand.

She'd sat her scrying mirror down near the sofa. She picked it up, aware, as always, of the icy feel of the mirror in her hands.

Serena walked back toward the candles. Put the mirror at her feet. She drew in a deep breath, raised her hands high above her head in the goddess position, and began her spell.

"Show me the one who used his spell,
To bind the witches I know too well.
Show me the man—show me the one
Whose magic I seek to have undone.
As I will,
So mote it be."

A simple spell. One that she wasn't certain would work. But the warlock had made a mistake. He'd worked magic on the items before her, and the dark magic left a faint taint. A touch of darkness.

A touch that would reflect him, *if her spell worked.*

The candles flickered around her.

Serena's glance fell to the mirror. She watched as the surface darkened, as if black clouds were sweeping over the face of the mirror. Then moving faster, faster as the wind blew.

Air brushed over her face. Sent the edges of her robe flapping back.

Her body trembled as she poured her magic into the spell, forcing the image to sharpen.

She wouldn't be able to last much longer.

Show me the one I seek.

The clouds thickened in the mirror. Pressed closer. Slowly began to form the face of a man.

Blue eyes stared up at her. Clear and sparkling. Dimples winked at her from the sides of his curving mouth. His blond hair blew, as if he, too, felt the breeze stirring in the closed room.

Dammit. Why did evil always seem to hide behind a pretty face these days?

"Got you, bastard." Luis's voice growled from right behind her.

"Not yet," Serena muttered, memorizing that face. She'd never forget him. "But we will."

The candle flames died. Serena's arms dropped to her sides. Her gaze was still on the mirror and on the man who laughed up at her.

Luis's hands wrapped around her waist and he pulled her tightly against him.

The grinning warlock slowly vanished.

Asshole, we're coming for you.

"He has more, you know." Luis picked up the tattered cloth that Serena had assured him several times was actually a swatch of Susan's quilt. "He wouldn't have left everything behind. If he had—"

"He wouldn't have been able to put the second bind on any more of the coven, I know." Serena ran an agitated hand through her curling locks. Damn, but he loved her hair. The wild curls. The soft, silky feel of the tresses under his fingers.

"Vanessa and Susan were both hit by the jerk this morning. So he *has* to have more of a stash." She jerked on her shoes. She'd dressed moments before, though he rather wished she'd just stayed in that silky blue robe. He liked the way it exposed the tempting swell of her breasts.

Serena had been practically pulsing with rage since her spell. "The bastard's out there. You saw him—he's out there, *laughing* at us."

Because he mistakenly thought he held the power. *Fool.* "We're just waiting for the night, Serena."

She slanted him a frowning stare. "Why? Isn't that supposed to be *his* time?"

Her shirt had lifted when she started running her fingers through the hair that *he* wanted to touch, and Luis had to fight to hold her stare and not let his gaze drop to that glittering belly of hers.

"Luis? Are we just going to be some kind of damn sitting ducks for this psycho?"

"No." He crossed his arms over his chest. Hell, who did the lady think she was dealing with here? An amateur? "The night is *my* time, Serena. Mine more than any other being you'll ever meet." Vampires might have mistakenly thought they ruled. Demons could skulk in the shadows all they wanted, but *he* was the one who drew power with the setting of the sun.

Soon it would be time to use that power.

Her eyes sharpened with interest and her hand dropped. "What's our plan?"

Our. Well, she had summoned him, and he'd given his word that she could hunt.

But that had been before he'd learned what pain sounded like on her lips.

"We have two options, sweetheart."

Her foot tapped.

"As soon as night falls and the demons and vamps crawl out to stalk the city, *we* stalk them." It would be easy enough to catch the stench of the vampires—most of 'em smelled like decay and rot. As for the demons, well, being part demon meant he could stare right through the veil of glamour that cloaked the majority of his kind. And he'd be able to smell 'em, too.

"And, uh, when we catch them?" She looked *and* sounded hesitant.

Probably because, unlike him, she didn't spend the better part of her nights stalking the psychotic demons most wanted to pretend didn't exist.

But it never seemed to matter how many of the assholes he stopped. There were always more out there.

And Serena—she was proof of just how damn little good he could really do in this shit screwed world. If she hadn't summoned him, he would have stayed in Mexico, finished his drink, had his fuck, then gone off to hunt the level-nine demon who'd been spotted in the area—the one who'd made a recent habit of hurting humans.

While he was hunting that bastard, Serena would have died. *Serena would have died.*

There just weren't enough hunters in the world any more. Too few to begin with. Too few left after the strongest, sickest paranormals had targeted his kind decades ago.

Maybe it was time for new blood.

His gaze caught Serena's.

"What do we do when we find the vamps?" Her nose wrinkled. "I hate the way those bloodsuckers are always staring at my neck."

Yeah, he could understand that. Luis made a mental note to give serious pain to any vamps unlucky enough to be caught ogling Serena's gorgeous neck.

He cleared his throat. "When we find 'em, we make 'em talk. A warlock strong enough to bind an entire coven—he'll be known by someone." *Something.*

They just had to look in the right place.

Or, in this case, the wrong one.

The wrong side of town. The dangerous side. The side most humans inherently knew to stay away from when the sun set.

A deer could sometimes sense a hunter.

Luis had learned in his lifetime that humans could all too often sense the *Other* that would prey on them.

Not that the sensing usually did much good for them.

"Make 'em talk," she repeated slowly. Her head tilted, the curls danced. "Are we going to have hurt someone?" Not particularly concerned.

Because she'd been hurt.

"Maybe a little," he allowed. *A lot.* But he'd be the

one doing the hurting. Serena would keep her lily-white hands clean.

She nibbled on her lips. Fuck. Did the woman not understand just how badly he *still* wanted her?

Her tongue swiped out.

His cock jerked.

Business.

Well, business *should* come first. But there were several more hours until dusk . . .

"What's our second option?" Serena asked.

The lust cleared a bit. He didn't like option two. Not a damn bit. "We wait for the third bind. Let the bastard think that he's broken your coven, and when he comes . . ." He shrugged, tried to look careless when he was starting to care too much, too quickly. *The way my father had fallen.* "I'll be waiting for him."

She backed up a step, and her shoulders hit the wall. "You—you mean you'd use me as bait."

Not the choice he wanted, but, if they couldn't track down that blond warlock, it might be their only option. "I wouldn't let him get to you, Serena." A promise.

"I'd be a sitting duck!" She shook her head frantically. "One more bind on me, and I'm—I'm—"

"Human." Or as close as a woman like her would ever come to that fate.

"Yes, dammit! And we both know that if a bound witch dies while her powers are locked up inside of her—"

The witch's killer took her powers at the moment of passing. "I wouldn't let him get to you," he repeated.

Serena didn't look particularly convinced and her doubt—it pissed him off.

Luis stalked toward her. She was already trapped against the wall. She'd trapped herself, so it wasn't like there was room for the witch to run. He crowded her deliberately, though, brushing his body close against hers. His arms rose, caged her, as his hands pressed against the white wall behind her head. "Do you trust me, witch?"

She'd let him into that tempting body of hers just hours before. Let him take her with the hot passion that still burned him.

And made him ache for her.

Serena hesitated.

A ball of anger unfurled in his gut. It was the answer he should have expected, but—

He wanted her trust.

As much as he wanted her.

His head lowered over hers. "Do you trust me?" he repeated as he caught her scent, inhaling deeply.

"I-I don't know." *Truth.*

The anger flared brighter. "So you trust me enough to fuck, huh, sweetheart? But you don't trust me with your life—is that the way this game works?" Damn, was it because of his mother? Because he'd failed before, did Serena not think that he could keep her safe? "I'm not gonna leave your side, witch—I won't leave you like I left her." He'd been on a hunt. Going after a djinn who'd slaughtered half a village. He hadn't realized his mother was in any danger. He'd thought she was safe and—

"Luis, no, I didn't mean—"

"Forget it, sweetheart." He shoved the memories of his past away and focused only on her. "Know this—I *will* keep you safe, whether you trust me or not. I'll protect you *and* do my damn job of eliminating the warlock."

"Luis, *I'm* the one who summoned you, remember? That means—"

"Jackshit."

Green eyes narrowed and tension tightened her body.

"You summoned me because you wanted a guard dog, and that's what you got, Serena. A fucking killer dog who would take anyone and everyone down before they had a chance to hurt you." He meant it. No one was going to sacrifice his witch.

No one.

Her lips parted and, hell, a man could only take so much temptation.

His mouth crushed hers, taking her. *Good enough to fuck.* Well, if that was the case, then he'd just go ahead and take his pleasure with her.

She was wearing a skirt now. A short, black skirt that teased the tops of her thighs and made his cock pulse with arousal.

Luis drove his tongue into her mouth and pushed his left hand between her spread thighs.

Her gasp was swallowed by his mouth.

She twisted, pushing against him, and her tight nipples stabbed into his chest.

The witch wanted him. He'd caught the scent of her arousal even when she'd glared at him with sparks of anger in her green eyes.

When he touched the crotch of her soft cotton panties, his fingers felt her wet heat.

No preliminaries this time.

He was pissed with her for doubting him. With the blond asshole who was hunting her.

And he was hungry—for her. Her body. Her damn soul.

It was his nature to hunt. To take.

He wanted to take her more than he'd ever wanted anything in all of his centuries.

Serena's hands were on his shoulders. Not pushing away, pulling him closer, and her mouth was wide and hungry on his.

Trust me enough to fuck.

The growl in his throat sounded just as he ripped her panties away.

"Luis!" She jerked her head back, gazed up at him with eyes gone dark with need.

Her folds were slick and swollen, heavy with the same lust that hardened his cock. He pushed his finger into her tight opening, loving the feel of her clenching sex around him.

She'd feel even better around his cock.

"Not here, we can—"

"*Here.*" They were in the middle of her kitchen, and her blinds were up, windows wide open.

He didn't really care.

His fingers retreated, drove deep once more, and her head tipped back against the wall on a hard sigh.

Then she started to ride his hand.

A flush rose up in the open vee of her shirt. Darkened her neck. Stained those glass-sharp cheeks.

Gorgeous.

Her breath quickened as he watched her. Her movements jerked faster.

Sexy witch. Sensual as a succubus.

His.

He drew his fingers away from her, and had to bite back a fierce smile of pleasure when she shook her head in protest.

Her eyes were on him as he lifted his fingers to his lips and tasted her. A long, slow lick.

She swallowed.

"Later, I'm gonna have more of you, sweetheart." *Later,* she'd be spread beneath him again and he'd lick her until he'd had his fill of her rich cream.

But for now . . .

His hand dropped to the front of his jeans. He popped open the button, eased down the zipper, and pulled out the cock that was twitching for the feel of her hot, tight sex.

"Put your hands on me," he ordered and his voice came out like a snarl. No help for that. He was living in a red haze of hunger right then.

All for her.

Her hands slid down his body, soft as a butterfly. Slowly, she wrapped her fingers around his arousal.

Serena squeezed him, then pumped his straining flesh with a long stroke, from root to head.

Again.

Again.

It took all of his control not to come in her hands.

He grabbed her hips, aware that his hold was too tight, too rough, but not able to ease his grip.

No damn way.

Luis lifted her, pinning her back even harder against the wall. Her legs were up, her sex open, and her hands still pumped him.

Fuck.

"Guide me in," he growled. "Take me deep inside, Serena. Let me watch you . . ."

Her skirt was bunched at her waist. The folds of her sex were flushed pink and glistening.

Damn, but he wanted another taste.

Her fingers tightened around him.

His hips thrust forward helplessly as sweat slid down his back.

Serena guided the head of his cock toward her body, straight toward the tight opening that quivered for him. When he felt the first brush of that creamy, hot flesh along his erection, Luis clenched his back teeth.

Control wasn't going to be lasting much longer.

Every instinct he possessed screamed for him to thrust forward—as hard and deep as he could go.

But he wanted to watch her. Wanted to watch as his cock slid slowly into her straining core.

"Luis . . ." His name came on a breath.

Ah, hell—

He slammed balls deep into her.

And immediately felt Serena's sex begin to spasm around him as she came.

His spine prickled. Her contractions were silky, strong, squeezing him even better than her hand. He pulled back, drove deep.

Retreated. *Her creamy grasp was so strong and—*

He plunged deep.

Heard her strangled cry of pleasure.

Felt the bite of her nails on his skin.

He wanted her to come again. With him.

Her legs locked around his hips and he pumped into her, driving as fiercely as he could for the rush of release that he knew was waiting.

The ripples of her sex continued. She moaned and shuddered against him. "Luis. Luis. *Luis!*"

He felt the second climax hit her because the pleasure hit him, too.

Semen jetted from him, spilling deep into her body as he came, pumping and thrusting and holding on to her with all of his strength.

The power of his release had his knees trembling, his breath rasping out, and the room shaking around them as his magic and power surged through the kitchen.

The release went on, the pleasure filling every pore in his body. He emptied into her, hungrily drinking in the ragged sounds that tore from her lips.

Pleasure is power.

Power for his witch.

Power for him.

His gaze met hers as the spasms began to ease. Her lips were blood red. A tear tracked down her cheek.

Then her mouth curved and her hand released its fierce grip on his shoulder to slide down his chest, stopping right over the heart that raced for her.

"Again."

And the already swelling cock inside of her was only too happy to oblige.

After all, only a fool would deny a witch's demand.

She yanked off his shirt. Her mouth locked on his nipple, and he thrust deep into her wet heat.

Luis had never thought of himself as a fool.

Night found them on the streets. Walking in the darkness on the side of town that most didn't even realize existed.

Buildings stood as battered shells. Boards lined the windows of the closed shops. A few burning garbage cans spit flames into the sky and chased a bit of the darkness away.

In the distance, a drum pounded in a furious, driving beat.

There were clubs in the city. Places that the *Other* frequented. They were close—close enough for Luis to smell the blood in the air.

The blood that would lure the vampires.

They weren't heading to the clubs. No, their prey wouldn't be inside.

The monsters they sought were *on* the streets. Waiting. Planning. Hunting.

Just as he was.

"Dammit, didn't we have this whole talk already about using me as bait?" Serena muttered, slanting him a simmering glance.

She stood just under one of the few street lights that actually worked. Her arms were crossed over her chest, her booted feet spread apart.

He stood a few feet behind her, body pressed tight to the cold brick wall and completely hidden by the shadows.

"We both agreed you weren't going to be bait for the warlock." She wouldn't be, unless that dark choice became absolutely necessary.

But he would protect her.

He wouldn't fail again.

"Then why the hell am I the one standing out here all defenseless with come-and-get-me written on my forehead?"

Simple. Because the woman looked like perfect prey in the dark sweater that cupped her gorgeous breasts and in the jeans that clung all too well to her great ass and legs.

"It's easier to get the *Other* to come to us this way." Or, rather, to her. The ones he was hunting, they'd love to get their hands on a morsel like her.

Deceptively innocent, with her wide eyes and nervous hands, she'd bring the bastards right to her.

"Aren't they gonna sense you?" she asked. "Demons *can* sense each other, you said it yourself—"

"No one will sense me." Not even a level-ten demon

would be able to pick up his power trail. "Don't forget, sweetheart, I'm not a full-blood demon."

He thought he saw her shiver. "So everything I've ever heard about you—it's true, isn't it? Your kind—*cazadores*, born of witch and demon, you're immortal."

"Yes." A blessing and a curse.

Everyone else died. It was so hard to watch the people he loved slip away.

Easy to watch the assholes he stalked pass from this earth, but when it was the others, like his mother—

"How many of your kind are there, Luis?"

Too few. "Less than there were a hundred years ago." Luis realized he hadn't seen another of his kind in what—five, ten years?

Too busy killing.

And fighting to stay alive.

Just because a being had been graced with the ability to live forever, well, that didn't mean some smart bastard couldn't come along and figure out the secret to his death.

Everyone and everything could die, but the real trick in this world was figuring out just *how* to kill the monsters.

"Is it true that you can't be hurt by mortal weapons?"

He coughed. "That rule's for level-ten demons." And, since he was part demon, yeah, weapons forged by man couldn't hurt him—but he didn't make a habit of revealing that fact to anyone.

"So, what? You have to have your heart cut out? Get beheaded?"

The old immortal-killing standbys. Luis sighed. "It's complicated—and I'm not going to explain it now. Wrong part of town for this talk, sweetheart."

But his witch was on the right track. *If* his head was severed and *if* his heart was cut from his chest—*while it still beat*—and *if* his head and heart were burned to ashes, then, yeah, he'd finally die.

"Has anyone ever almost . . . killed you?" The question was softer than the others. Her gaze wasn't on him. It was on the shadows on the opposite end of the street.

No monsters were there.

He'd sensed no threats on the street, *yet*, so he'd let Serena keep up her questions because he knew that she was afraid.

And he'd discovered that when she was nervous or afraid, his witch liked to talk.

A rather cute trait, and one that he'd allow for a few more moments.

Just until the demons came out.

"Yeah, sweetheart, I've almost been killed a few times." Those panthers in South America had actually come pretty close to taking him out of this world. One had swiped at his chest with those razor sharp panther claws and another had gone for his neck, slicing right at his jugular.

He'd bled *too much,* gotten *too* weak, but still managed to rip through the pack.

Then he'd healed, as was his nature. And lived to fight and kill another day.

Or night.

Like tonight.

"Have you ever been afraid?" Her voice was even softer now, and, still, she didn't glance his way. He was angled diagonally behind her, so he could just make out the faintest movement of her lips.

"Once or twice." With her.

And that long ago day when he'd rushed to save his mother, only to arrive far too late.

Her head jerked toward him, "Luis, I—"

"*Quiet.*"

Power was in the air, flickering.

They weren't alone any longer.

His eyes narrowed as he watched Serena take in a deep breath. Her attention turned back to the dark street.

She wouldn't see the one coming for her . . .

But Luis already had the demon in his sights.

6

Damn, damn, *damn,* but this was a bad idea, one no smart witch should *ever* have agreed to go along with in the first place.

Serena hunched in front of the light post, because, yeah, standing underneath that freaking *beacon* was such a fine plan.

Every psycho in the area would be after her.

Just what Luis wanted.

The warmth had seeped from the city with the fall of night, the temperatures taking a serious nosedive from the warmer weather of previous days, and Serena shifted, rubbing her arms together as she tried to stave off the growing chill in the air.

A week ago, she wouldn't have been afraid. She would have used her power to blast any idiot stupid enough to confront her all the way across the street and into that busted building that looked like an old pawnshop.

A week ago.

Now, she had to rely on Luis, and relying on someone else wasn't exactly her strong suit.

But that's why I summoned him—because I knew he could help me.

She just hadn't realized he'd be doing the whole "bait" routine with her.

Immortal jerk.

And just *where* was the paranormal he'd sensed? She couldn't see anyone, didn't hear anything but the crackle of flames—and who had lit those fires anyway? No one was around but—

"Lost, witch?"

The voice came from her left. Whispered into her ear.

Blood of the goddess.

Serena swallowed. Straightened her shoulders. *The boogeyman's got my back.* He'd better.

"I'm not the least bit lost," she answered slowly, proud that her voice didn't shake even a little. She turned her head toward him, lifted one brow. "Are you?"

One glance was more than enough to tell her that this guy—yeah, he was most definitely *lost.*

His eyes were coal black. Every single bit of his eyes—a demon stare. Usually, demons cloaked their eyes with a glamour and made the color appear like a human's. The true black color only appeared when their emotions and passions were high—like when Luis's gaze had flashed black on her during their wild mating.

But this guy—he wasn't bothering with glamour. No, he was letting his gleaming black eyes show to the world.

His face was long and angular. Too pale. Bloodless. His teeth were sharp, when they shouldn't have been. *What the hell?* The guy's teeth were all narrowed to points, like a vamp's fangs.

Serena realized the demon before her had deliberately filed his teeth.

The better to kill?

She balled the hands that wanted to shake into even tighter fists.

Where's my power when I need it?

The answer, of course, was *tied up in a warlock's web*.

"Seems I've just found the thing I was looking for tonight." He smiled at her, showing off those wicked teeth. Then his gaze raked over her body.

Hell.

"I would have preferred a human. They scream so very loudly, you know."

She wanted to scream right then. Scream for the demon to get the hell away from her.

No, not just away. Out. Out of the city. Out of the damn country.

Her skin crawled as she stared at him. He wore a long black coat, dark pants. His hair was slicked straight back from his forehead, and his fingers . . . bony, with long nails no man should have possessed.

Nails that, even in the bad light, she could see were stained red.

"You—you're not from around here, are you?" She hated that the faintest tremble had entered her voice. OK, so every time the guy opened his mouth, she smelled death. No need to freak out about that fact.

Her bodyguard was just a few feet away.

And Luis had been right—the demon didn't sense him, *at all*.

Perhaps the guy was too focused on her to even see the danger that waited.

The demon laughed. "No, this is my first . . . trip . . . to your city." He lifted a hand toward her, and Serena steeled herself. "I think I'm going to have so much fun here . . ."

At the last second, Serena stepped back so that she missed the touch of his gnarled fingers. "What makes you think I'm a witch?" she asked, her mind jumping back to the first words he'd spoken to her. Demons didn't normally have the ability to recognize her kind and—

" 'Cause you're bound," he muttered, and his nostrils flared. "I can smell the marks on you. Every demon and shifter in the city can." Another chilling smile. "Poor witch. No magic, and all alone."

"Not exactly," she snapped and lifted her chin. If that guy tried to touch her again—

"Oh, *exactly.* You're *exactly* what I want." Not a smile any more. "Let's hear you scream—" His claws came at her.

Serena jumped away.

Luis bounded from the shadows. "Let's here *you* scream, demon." He grabbed the demon, spun the asshole around.

"What the—*fuck!*"

"Hello, Jack."

Jack?

Serena stumbled back a few more feet. If Luis knew the guy, the demon had to be trouble. The kind she didn't want.

"What are you doin' here?" the demon snapped. "Last I heard you were huntin' in Mexico—"

"And that's why you thought it was safe to come out of hiding, huh?" He moved then, in one of his too-fast-to-see whirls. When Serena blinked, she found him holding the demon up against the light post. Luis's fingers were locked around the guy's throat. "Mistake, Jack. Big mistake. It's *never* safe for you to be on the streets. Not safe for the humans, the paranormals, and damn sure not safe for *you*."

The demon's eyes began to bulge.

"Luis . . ."

He didn't glance her way. Not that she blamed him. Luis was dangling a bastard demon two feet up in the air and slowly choking the life from him. Kinda busy . . . but they had come out on these streets for a reason.

The terrorizing of this jerk needed to pause a bit.

"You're weak, Jack. Only a level four." Luis made a clicking sound with his tongue. "Is that why you go after the humans? Cause you feel powerful with them?"

Jack tried to gasp out a reply, but the wheezing wasn't much of a response.

When his face started to purple, Serena stepped forward. "Luis, we're not here for this. The warlock—"

Those bulging black eyes slanted toward her.

"Don't fucking look at her!" His roar shook the street.

The demon's eyes flew back to Luis.

Serena reached out, touched Luis's back. Felt the rock-hard, battle-ready tension in him. "The warlock," she repeated. She didn't know what Luis's past was with this guy, and, yeah, the demon creeped the shit out of her, but they had to find out about the bastard after her.

A shudder passed over Luis's body. "You want to keep breathing," he snarled at the demon, "you answer my questions—and you tell me the *truth*." He rammed the guy's head back into the light pole. Metal groaned. "Got it?"

The demon's lips formed "Yes," but no sound escaped him.

"Stay behind me, Serena," Luis ordered.

Fine with her. She wasn't interested in getting any

closer to the demon. He knew that she was bound. Well, partially bound. Easy prey.

Slowly, Luis lowered the demon to the ground. Jack's feet touched down with a soft sigh. Luis eased his hold, but didn't completely move his fingers away from the demon's throat. "I'm looking for a warlock."

"L-lot of 'em h-here . . ." the demon said, voice hoarse.

"Blond. Blue-eyed. One that makes a habit of hanging out with charmers."

Jack blinked. "D-don't k-know h-him. J-just got in-into t-town . . ."

Luis laughed and the sound chilled Serena. She was glad that she couldn't see his face.

But over Luis's shoulder, she could see the demon's face—and the fear that flashed over it.

Luis lifted his hand, and Serena saw claws spring from his fingertips— *What the hell? He wasn't a shifter.*

He slashed the demon's face. Left side. Right. Long, jagged marks dripped blood as the demon howled.

"Wrong answer," Luis murmured.

Jack whimpered.

"Now, let's try again, Jack, and, remember, I can tell when you lie to me . . ."

He could tell when the demon lied—oh, shit! The guy was a detector!

The demon started talking then, fast. "H-he's in one of th-those big, white houses, w-with columns, f-fancy, in R-Roswell—"

The name clicked instantly in Serena's mind. *Roswell.* The antebellum homes. Historic district.

"G-got a b-big, bl-black gate, iron. N-name's Michael . . . something. D-didn't know y-you . . . were af-after him—"

"But you knew he liked to hunt witches."

"Y-yes . . ."

Luis shook his head. "You knew, but you didn't care, did you, Jack? Because you had hunting of your own to do."

Jack didn't reply to that.

Serena figured that was probably answer enough.

"Turn away, Serena," Luis said, and his voice was ice cold.

Jack's lips trembled. "N-no, witch, d-don't, he'll—"

"*Turn away, Serena.*"

Her shoulders stiffened. "I'm not your pet bitch, Luis. Remember that when you talk to me."

He finally shifted to stare at her, glancing back over his shoulder. His eyes were as black as Jack's. "Please, Serena, don't watch me do this."

Voice low, but hard.

She spun on her heel.

The fast and desperate cries of the demon rang in her ears.

Almost helplessly, Serena glanced back—

Luis had freed the demon's neck. Jack was shrinking back against the post. Luis lifted his hands, palms up. The flesh of his hands—it glowed and—

She jerked her gaze away when his fingers landed on the demon's shoulders.

The scream that she heard had her choking back her own cry.

Don't look. The order was her own this time.

But she looked anyway. A witch's curiosity was a dangerous thing, and a weakness most of her kind shared. So her eyes flickered back and she saw the darkness of the demon's eyes fade to a stark white. Heard the last rasp of his breath leave his body. Then watched as Luis lifted his hands. The demon dropped to the ground.

"I told you not to watch." Emotionless.

Her gaze jerked to him. "Luis . . ." His eyes were still black and a faint glow seemed to light his flesh from the inside out.

"Witches . . . always curious, just like the damn cats you all used to be so sickeningly fond of." He spared a glance for the demon on the ground. "I hope you're burning somewhere now, asshole."

Then he turned his back on the demon and fully faced her.

Her heart hammered in her chest and Serena realized her palms were slick with sweat. Not cold any longer, she was burning hot.

Fear could do that to a woman.

He lifted his right hand and Serena jerked back.

His mouth tightened. "You knew what I was when you summoned me, Serena."

Yes, yes, she'd known.

"And when you fucked me."

It was hard not to flinch at that one.

His hand was still in the air between them. Regular nails now, thank the goddess, but . . . "I don't understand." She stopped. Cleared her throat because her voice sounded too weak—and she didn't want to be weak. "How—how did your hands change? *Cazadores* don't come from shifters and—"

His fingers balled into a fist. "I've killed shifters. Dozens of them. Demons. Djinn. The ones who stalked the earth, determined to torture and murder, *I* stopped them." Slowly, he uncurled his fist and his fingers, as they extended, had what looked to be about four-inch long claws sprouting from their tips. "Most don't understand. They think all I do is kill, but I'm a *soul-hunter.* I hunt, and I take the powers that lurk in the souls of the *Other*, so that when they leave this world, they go out as helplessly as humans."

I take the powers that lurk in the souls. Oh, shit. *Shit.* "You mean—all the beings you kill—"

"I get their power." A shrug. The claws vanished in a blink. "Think of my touch as a binding spell, sweetheart. Instead of the three marks, it just takes the grasp of my hand, and any *Other* becomes helpless. When the powers drain away, the body dies." His lips twisted. "And my job is done."

No regret. No guilt. "You just . . . kill." No, he drained powers first, *then* he killed. Her gaze darted to the fallen demon. She shuddered.

He killed.

Just like the warlock who was after her.

Her arms wrapped around her stomach. "Why did you kill him?" OK, yeah, the guy had scared the hell out of her, but other than making her heart jump into her throat, he hadn't actually *done* anything to her and—

"Jack fancied himself a modern-day copy of the original."

Serena shook her head and forced her gaze back to him. *Stop looking at the dead guy.* "I don't know what you're—"

"Jack the Ripper."

She blinked.

"He liked to slash his victims apart just like the original Ripper, except he didn't go after prostitutes—he went after humans, or weak paranormals. Then he had a good old time making them scream and slicing up their flesh."

Let's hear you scream.

Serena rocked back. "You-you knew who he was the moment you first sensed him, didn't you?" He'd

known, and he'd let her stand there and talk to a fucking sadistic killer.

One who wanted to make her scream.

A grim nod. "You were never in any danger. I
would not have—"

"Asshole!" Maybe it was a *good* thing she didn't
have her full power right then—she would have tried
to fry the jerk. "How many times do I have to tell you,
I'm not bait?" Her hands were at her sides now, fisted,
because she really, really wanted to slug him.

All powerful *cazador* or not.

"Serena—" He stepped forward, reaching for her.

She threw out a spell. Sent the air to swirling around
her as a force field sealed her away from his touch.

His fingers slammed into the invisible wall. His
eyes slit. "*Serena.*"

Her brow furrowed as she fought to hold the field. It
was weak as hell, but she was making a point! "Don't
use me, *cazador*!"

His fist punched against the field. "I'm trying to
save your life!"

"You could have warned me about Jack, you could
have—"

"I didn't know that asshole would be hunting here.
By the time I realized it was him, it was too late, and he
hunts by sensing *fear*. If I'd told you what was happening and how easily I could take him down, your emotions would have changed and he would have sensed it."

Her temples began to throb. The wall was getting
even weaker. "I don't want to be bait," she repeated,
but this time, she was talking about the warlock. Or
maybe she'd been talking about him all along. Her hand
rubbed her right temple. "I don't want to be bound."

"*I* am with you, Serena. No one is going to hurt you.
No one."

"I want to protect myself." She always had. "I don't want to be weak." As weak as the pitiful spell that wasn't really holding him off. He could have broken through her force field with one push of magic.

But he hadn't.

"You're not going to be weak," he promised and his hand flattened on the field. "We're going to get the bastard, you're going to be safe, and I promise, I'll return you to full power."

Her hand lifted, hovered over his. "Why did you agree to help me, Luis?" She'd summoned him, but he could have left. Could have vanished in a blink.

"Because I wanted you. From the first glimpse through the fog, *I wanted you.*" Power filled his words.

And she'd wanted him.

"Trust me, Serena. Trust me to save you. Trust me to—" He broke off, shaking his head.

For a moment, her gaze again dropped to the body of the dead demon. Goose bumps rose on her flesh.

Luis had spent lifetimes battling demons like Jack. Fighting to keep the world safe.

Fighting alone. Always alone.

"Why do you do it?" she whispered. "The council is long gone. It's not your duty to keep fighting these bastards." Though she'd screamed that it was his *job* the first time they'd met. But it wasn't. He was entitled to live a life just like any other. So *why* did he do it? Why keep fighting the darkness?

"Because someone has to," he said simply. "And I'm one of the only beings strong enough to face those in the dark."

Her heart pounded so hard that her chest hurt. Was it truly that simple for him? And, goddess, but what must his life be like? So many battles. So much evil.

"Serena . . ." A plea was in his voice now, with even a touch of . . . desperation? "*Trust me.*"

She jerked her gaze away from the demon. Met Luis's stare. Her lover with the golden eyes and the touch of death. The man who fought evil, when others would have run.

Trust him? Oh, yes, she did. With her life.

And with her soul.

As her spell faded with a whisper of air, her fingers curled over his. "I do trust you."

He got her off that street and away from the body as fast as he could. Luis didn't worry about disposing of the demon. The cops would find the body, or, if they didn't, well, the other demons who frequented the area would make certain that *no one* found Jack.

Another bastard off his list.

Damn. When he'd caught the demon's scent and realized who was out stalking, he'd nearly lost it. Almost let his power rip out full force.

He hadn't wanted Serena close to that bastard. Hadn't wanted Jack to so much as *look* at her.

But he'd known that if any *Other* in the city knew about the warlock, well, it would have been a piece of shit like Jack. So he'd held on to his control as long as he could. Let Serena lure the guy in, and when Jack had made the mistake of reaching for Serena, he'd attacked.

He hadn't wanted Serena to see him make the kill.

When she looked at him, sometimes, *sometimes,* he'd catch a hint of fear or worry in her eyes.

But she often just looked at him as if he were . . . a man.

He wanted her to keep looking at him that way. Wanted her to *always* look at him as if he were just her lover.

And not the killer she'd summoned.

His body was bursting with energy. The power of the touch ran through him, pulsing in his veins. The demon's energy blended with his own, sending the currents of magic pumping through him.

Usually after a touch of death, he found a woman. Got between her legs and rode hard and fast for the rest of the night.

He felt the same wild need now, the same lust.

But he didn't just want *any* woman.

He wanted the woman who sat so stiffly beside him as she drove her car, streaking down the streets and racing through the darkness.

The woman who had touched him after a kill and said she trusted him.

Truth.

"Luis . . ." Her voice was husky.

He glanced over at her.

"Something's . . . wrong."

He tried to unclench his fingers from their white-knuckled grip on the door handle.

"Are you all right?"

She hadn't lied to him. He wasn't about to lie to her. "I will be." Once the edge of tension wore off.

In about eight or nine hours.

Fuck.

She braked at a red light. Turned to face him. "Tell me what's happening. You're stiff as a board over there. You're sweating, and you haven't moved in fifteen minutes. Are you sick? Are you—"

"It's aftereffects, sweetheart." The only weakness his kind had. The energy from the kill pumped through his body too hard, too fast. The result was a furious tension and a ravenous sexual hunger.

But then, his hunger for Serena was always pretty ravenous.

The light changed to green, but Serena didn't take her foot off the brake. "What does that mean? Do you need to rest? To eat, to—"

"Fuck."

She blinked.

No lies. Not between them. *Not to her.* "To get back to being one hundred percent, I need to fuck. I need to get you, naked, and plunge into that pretty pink sex until the power shock fades and I'm close to normal," *normal for him*, "and I can stop breathing without my cock twitching for you."

Her lips parted. "Ah . . . I . . . see."

Probably not. She didn't understand that he was literally drowning in her scent then, that talking was hard, and that every breath he drew, he tasted her.

And wanted to fuck her so bad he ached.

She glanced around the darkened streets. Gave a nod, then punched the gas and spun the wheel to the left.

"Serena!"

Tires squealed.

She didn't glance his way. "You want me."

Hell, yes.

"You need to have sex to . . . work through this tension."

He needed to have sex because he wanted inside her. But, yeah, getting past the power surge was necessary, too.

"My art studio is a few blocks away. I-I had to get a place to meet with my clients. It's not real big, but if you don't mind the paint and the lack of a bed—"

If he could have her, he wouldn't mind a damn thing.

"Then we can be there in two minutes." She glanced at him, and Luis was caught by the desire he saw in her emerald stare. One that was almost a match for his own ferocious need. "And you can have me in three."

Hell, yes.

7

The scent of paint hit him the moment Serena unlocked the door to the small loft.

"I-I rented here because the light is so good. The
clients like the studio and I like to have a separate
place for doing their work." She flipped on the lights.

Luis tried to bite down on his hunger. Her art was on
the wall. Same dark colors. Same proud passion.
"You're damn good, Serena."

Her lips parted in surprise.

He had to kiss those lips. Feel that tongue he could
see peeking behind her teeth.

"Ah, thanks. Painting—it's almost like magic to me."

She smiled at him, a sweet, real smile.

His heart lurched.

Ah, hell . . . No way was he going to be able to wait.

Luis dragged her into his arms. Kicked the door
closed and took her mouth.

He kissed her with a fury and a hungry need. Started
stripping off her clothes. Heard the thud of her boots as
she kicked them to the floor.

He wasn't going to take the time to strip. He un-buckled his pants, shoved them out of the way, caught his straining erection and—

"Let me." She breathed the words against his mouth.

Then she pulled back and dropped to her knees be-fore him.

"*Serena.*" A few drops of liquid pulsed from the tip of his cock.

Her fingers closed around him. Squeezing. Strok-ing. She seemed to know exactly how to touch him and make the hunger grow even more.

His knees trembled as his cock jerked eagerly in her grasp.

Her lips curved. Parted.

Then she bent her head toward him, that luscious red mouth open, and took him inside.

His teeth clenched as a ragged groan burst from his lips.

She moved her head, sucked, her cheeks hollowing as she drew on him.

Stars danced before his eyes. His fingers sank into the riotous mass of her curls. So damn soft.

And her mouth was so hot.

She drew him in deep, then pulled back to lick the head of his arousal. Swirled her tongue over his flesh. Another long, deep suck.

Then she swallowed.

His fingers tightened as his control snapped. He started moving her, faster, harder, thrusting his cock, trying to go deeper.

She swallowed again.

Luis came, roaring her name and shuddering help-lessly as she drank in his essence.

When she'd wrung every drop from his body, she pulled away from him. Rocked back on her haunches.

Luis stared down at her.

His cock began to swell again.

What looked like white sheets were draped across the floor behind her. Paint spotted the material.

The sheets would be better than the floor.

"Take off the rest of your clothes, witch." The strongest witch he'd ever met.

She'd bewitched him with nothing more than a touch that first night. Enslaved him with a smile.

He knew the truth now. He would never, *ever* get enough of her.

She laughed as she pushed off her panties. "But I wanted more." Her eyes danced with hunger and sensual power.

Because she'd just broken a *cazador's* control.

He dropped to his knees before her. Kissed the delicate inside of her ankle. One, then the other. Licked his way up the silky smooth skin of her leg. "My turn to taste." He wanted to hear Serena scream *his* name.

And what a cazador wanted . . .

He parted her legs. Touched the warm, creamy flesh that had already plumped with arousal. Her clit was waiting for him, and when he touched the button of her desire, Serena's back arched off the floor.

A good start.

He put his mouth on her and *took.*

Her moan was so sweet.

But he wanted more.

His tongue stroked over her. Licked. Fast, hard licks. Then short, slow swipes.

She began to call his name.

But not to scream for him. Not yet.

He pushed two fingers inside her. Felt the delicate muscles of her sex clamp greedily around him. He thrust, driving knuckle deep, then retreating.

Licking.

Her hips rocked against his hand, jerking faster with each move of his fingers.

Luis wanted more.

He pulled his fingers free. Lowered his mouth. Touched her trembling flesh with the tip of his tongue.

Then drove his tongue inside of her.

The scream she gave was pure music to his ears.

Luis thrust his cock into her just as the last tremors of her climax faded.

Serena stared up at him. Lines of tension and need were etched onto his face.

A dark power drove him. She could feel the magic in the air. But there was more.

The hunger she felt for him, the stark lust she'd experienced nearly from the beginning, was reflected in his eyes.

Power to power.

Lover to lover.

Sex to sex.

She locked her legs around him. Held on tight as he slammed into her, driving that thick cock deep into her. Her muscles clamped around him. Clutched tight, and a flash of pleasure had her undulating beneath him.

Then he thrust harder. Curled his hands around her hips and lifted her into his strokes.

His eyes began to darken as he gazed down at her.

The pleasure built again.

She didn't look away from him. Couldn't.

Serena tightened around him and rode his cock as wildly as she could.

When the next climax hit her, she didn't even try to muffle her cry of release.

But then, neither did he.

She slept at some point. After she rode him, breasts bouncing as she took his cock inside. After he flipped her onto her stomach and took her with her hands digging into the paint-stained sheets.

She slept, and he watched her.

His fingers traced the star on her belly. Such a beautiful, simple design. One witches had long used.

I don't want to be weak. Her words played through his mind.

His little witch didn't understand, even without her magic, she wouldn't be powerless. She was smart, resourceful, and brave. Not many would have stood beneath that streetlight and waited for a lost demon to walk from the darkness.

And not many would have risked using dark magic to summon him.

He brushed his face against her curls. Inhaled her scent.

I don't want to be weak.

His head lifted. His mother had been weak, at the end.

Life was too short for so many.

He put his hand back over Serena's stomach. Power and a dark need still filled him.

But his control was back, and it *would* hold. No matter how much his witch tempted him.

Because he had a promise to keep and a warlock to kill.

She shifted against him, and her lashes blinked open. "Luis?"

Bending, he pressed a kiss to her sleep-softened lips. "We have to go, sweetheart." There were only about two more hours of darkness left.

Enough time to finish this battle.

Understanding filled her eyes as the mist of dreams faded. "We're going after him."

"You won't worry another night about the warlock." He pulled away from her, found his clothes scattered on the floor, and began to dress.

Serena sat up slowly. "And then you'll go away. Back to—wherever the hell you were before, huh?" A touch of anger had entered her voice.

Yeah, he'd go back to Mexico. He had a level-nine demon with a death wish to track.

There was always someone to track.

He picked up Serena's clothes, handed them to her. "Our deal will be over."

Her eyes narrowed. "You'll just walk away." The words were bitten out from between her teeth.

Luis frowned. "What do you want of me, witch?" He'd fight with his last breath for her, *kill* for her.

"More than you can give, *dammit*." She swiped at her eyes.

Oh, hell, was Serena crying?

"This wasn't supposed to happen!" She jumped up, jerked on her clothes. Didn't look at him. "You were supposed to come here, help me, leave and not—" Her words tumbled to a halt, and she shook her head. "Forget it. Let's go get the warlock and end this."

End this. The words echoed in his mind.

Not yet. "What wasn't I supposed to do, Serena?" The question was important. He didn't want to have failed her.

Not when she'd given him a glimpse of life. Passion. Warmth.

Things he hadn't felt or seen in centuries.

Her hands balled onto her hips. "*Care*. OK, asshole? You weren't supposed to make me *care*."

He stilled.

"This is stupid!" Another hard swipe with her hand. "Look, just forget it. I'm scared, I'm tired, I'm trapped in some weird lust-land with you and I don't know what the hell I'm saying." She tugged on her boots, hopping. "Just forget—"

His hands caught her and held her steady. "I'm not ever going to forget you."

For a moment, her lips trembled. Then she pressed them together and shook her head.

He freed her, then stepped back.

"You will," she said, voice steady, eyes wide. "When years pass and I'm nothing more than ashes on this earth and you're still living, you'll forget me. Just like you've probably forgotten so many others and—"

"*I've never forgotten.*" The snarl burst from him and the room trembled. "Not a soul I've taken, not a loved one I've lost."

Her breath hitched. "Luis . . ."

"You're wrong if you think immortality is easy, sweetheart. It's not. It's not fun, and it's sure as hell not pretty. It's dark and it's cold. It's finding villages torn to the ground by fucking killers—and seeing the bodies of innocents left in their wake. It's tracking murdering bastards—and burying the dead they leave behind. It's—"

"Stop." Her fingers pressed against his mouth. "Don't tell me any more."

This life, it hadn't been *his* choice. To walk alone, no, he'd never wanted that.

To kill forever.

And live in the darkness.

Torture. Hell, for him.

"I'm sorry," she whispered, and her fingers slid down to cup his jaw. Serena rose on tiptoe. She pressed her mouth against his.

His arms locked around her, pulled her tightly against him.

The kiss wasn't wild this time. Not desperate.

Softer. Sweeter.

Tender.

He tasted her slowly. Savored the flavor of her on his tongue. He brushed his lips over hers, so lightly.

After a time, Luis forced his head to lift.

She hadn't expected to care. Well, in such a short time, he sure as hell hadn't, either.

But he cared for her. He exhaled heavily. Why lie to himself? The feelings were a lot more than just *caring*.

Lust. Need. Want. Yeah, he felt all of those things.

He also wanted just to hold her. To watch her paint in the sunlight. To see her smile.

That wouldn't happen. It wasn't what fate had planned.

At the beginning, he'd thought he'd try to take her. To force her into his world so that he could have a bit of the burning light that he saw shining so brightly within her.

But he couldn't do that. He couldn't force Serena to come into his world.

Not when she didn't belong in his life of violence and death.

She needed life and passion.

She didn't need him. Even if she had started to . . . *care* for him.

His mother had warned him of this. Warned that the

men in his family fell too quickly, could need and want too much.

His father, for all his power, had died of a broken heart. After all, no mortal weapons could kill one such as he.

But the death of his wife, yeah, that had done it.

Luis gazed down at his witch. "Tomorrow is Halloween." A day normally celebrated by witches. All Hallow's Eve.

A nod.

"We have to stop him before midnight. He'll bind you today if he can, and then he'll try to kill you—"

"On Halloween," she finished, voice quiet. "That's what he did to the witches in LA. Binding, then death."

Because the magic was always stronger on All Hallow's Eve. He stroked her cheek. Brushed back a stray curl. "I'm not going to let that happen."

That pert chin of hers lifted. "Neither am I."

It would be the end for them, though. Serena couldn't go with him where he had to travel. She couldn't, *wouldn't* want to spend the years of her life battling the dregs of the *Other* world.

The foolish plan he'd hatched in the heat of his hunger and selfish lust felt hollow now.

He'd just been alone for so long, and Serena . . . she made him feel so alive.

Yet she deserved peace. Happiness. A happy ending, those endings that princesses got in stories, and witches never did.

He'd always hated those stories.

"Are you ready?" He wasn't.

Serena nodded again.

Then it was time. "Let's go take us down a warlock."

*   *   *

Serena drove to Roswell, knowing the area in the northern section of Atlanta well. There was no traffic on the streets—it was far too early for most folks. She and Luis didn't talk as they drove. Luis was tense and silent, and after her stupid confession fiasco, she wasn't about to open her mouth.

Once they reached Roswell, there were several houses that sported the white columns Jack had mentioned, but only one concealed behind a huge, wrought-iron gate.

"He's going to sense us," she warned, but knew Luis must have already realized that fact. She braked a distance from the house. She didn't feel the pull of the warlock's power, not yet, but if she got much closer . . .

"Won't do him any good. A thirty-second warning isn't going to save his ass."

No, it wouldn't. Not from Luis. And not from her.

"You . . . don't have to come inside, Serena. Let me finish this. There's no need for you to see—"

Me kill. He didn't finish the sentence, but Serena knew exactly what Luis meant.

"I'm coming."

His lips parted as if he would speak, but then he merely gave a grim nod.

"Luis . . ." She touched his arm. "I'm not afraid to see you kill. The idea that psychotic bastards are out there and that they might get to keep hurting and killing others—just like this prick has done—that *frightens* me."

His head cocked to the left side.

"When I saw you kill, yes, for a moment, I was scared—but I was sure as hell terrified more when I realized just what old Jack was capable of doing—*and* what he'd already done."

His eyes were so very golden. She loved those eyes, even when they flooded black with his demon power. "Someone has to stop the darkness, and I think we're all lucky that someone is you."

"I-I can't stop it all. I never can."

Of course not, he was one being. And the world was so very big. And so very bad. "You make a difference, Luis. To me, to others, you make a *huge* difference. I-I want you to know that, and to know that I won't be forgetting you, either."

He bent his head. Crushed his lips to hers. "You damn well better not, sweetheart, or I might just have to come back and remind you of exactly who I am."

Then he was gone. Climbing from the car. Shutting the door.

Serena inhaled slowly, then turned to shove open her own door. As she stood, she realized that she wanted him to come back to her.

Hell, she didn't want him to leave at all.

Not enough time.

She began stalking toward the house. She felt the stir in the air that told her one of her kind was close.

One of her kind—one that had chosen the dark magic. So tempting, that magic. Offering untold power and, according to some, eternal life.

"I've got him," she whispered.

Luis gave a slight inclination of his head. "So do I."

Almost in unison, they began running forward. If they sensed the warlock, then he would have to sense them. *His warning.*

They bounded up the wooden steps of the porch. Luis blasted open the door with a wave of his hand. Serena darted after him, ready to face the bastard who had tormented her. She wanted to find him and—

A sudden, fiery pain knocked her off her feet. She

fell onto the gleaming floor of the foyer, a sharp cry on her lips.

The burning cut into her muscles, dug down to the bone, and she didn't need to jerk away the sleeve of her sweater to know what had happened.

The third binding mark branded her upper arm.

Bastard.

Oh, yeah, she had him.

But the asshole sure had her, too.

8

Serena's cry iced his veins. Luis glanced back, saw her stumble to the floor. He reached for her—

"No!" Her face snapped up toward him. Tears slid down her cheeks. "It's the bind—*go!* Stop him!"

He didn't want to leave her on the floor, crying in pain, but there was no choice. With a last glance, he spun on his heel and stormed through the house.

He could feel the magical pull of the warlock's power. There, up ahead, to the right—

A wave of his fingers sent the door flying inward.

It smashed into the wall, missing the warlock's blond head by about a foot.

Lucky bastard.

Well, not for long.

The warlock spun around, a small cloth and a black-hilted athame clutched in his hands.

He looked at Luis for a moment, then he smiled.

Luis hesitated. *Not the usual way death was greeted.*

"Where's the little witch?" the warlock drawled, and the knife slashed across the cloth, cutting the fabric into two pieces that fluttered to the floor.

Serena's shirt. It looked just like one he'd glimpsed in her closet. "You're not going to get her power."

The warlock's smile widened. "I've already gotten the witch's power—it's all tied up and waiting for me."

Bound.

Luis stepped forward and tried to block the image of Serena crying out in pain. His legs were braced apart, and he lifted his hands, letting his claws out. "You're going to die here, warlock."

"Michael. Michael Deveaux." The warlock shook his head. "Really, if you're going to hunt, you should at least know the name of the one you seek."

The name was familiar. A Deveaux had attacked a coven of witches back in the 1900s in South Carolina, but word had passed that he'd died in the fire that consumed the coven house and—

The warlock laughed. "Trying to figure it all out, are you, *cazador*?" He shook his head. "Come now, surely you didn't think that one of my kind wouldn't find the secret to immortality, too? Why let the vampires and your sick lot have all the fun?"

Hell.

"Most witches and wizards—those fucking idiots—think the dark path just brings pain, terror. Death. But they're wrong. The dark—it can bring life, and the secret to living forever, it's so simple, really." He tossed the knife in his hand. The blade glinted. "All you have to do is steal a bit of magic . . ." His hand moved in a deceptively slow twist—and then the blade was spinning, tumbling end over end as it flew toward Luis.

He knocked the knife away with a toss of his right hand. The blade clattered to the floor. "I'm not one of your bound witches, asshole. It'll take a hell of a lot more than you've got to stop me." He didn't care how old the guy was.

Or how powerful the idiot thought he was.

Deveaux would die soon.

"I'm stronger than you think," the warlock growled. "And I know what makes *you* weak."

A scream echoed through the house.

Serena's scream.

Deveaux lifted his hand—

Serena flew into the room, fighting, thrashing, struggling against an invisible force that pulled her through the air.

Luis lunged across the room. Caught the warlock in a fierce grip and threw him against the wall.

Serena's body dropped to the floor. She scrambled across the hard wood and—

The warlock slammed his fist into Luis's chest, the full wrath of his magic behind the blow. This time, Luis was the one who rocked back, stumbling and slamming into the side of a chair.

OK, so the bastard was strong.

He wasn't strong *enough*.

"To me, witch!" the warlock screamed, lifting his hands as power whipped through the room. Wind howled inside the house.

Serena seemed to rocket to the bastard. The warlock smiled that sick, twisted grin as she screamed and shot toward him.

Luis lunged to his feet and—

Serena whipped the warlock's knife from behind her back. "Here I am, asshole!" She plunged the blade into his chest.

The warlock shrieked, an earsplitting cry of rage and fury.

Luis grabbed Serena's wrist and yanked her behind him. As fast as he could, Luis threw up a spell to shield her. The warlock wouldn't touch her again—not with magic or hands.

Deveaux pulled the knife from his chest. "You've desecrated my athame, bitch!"

Serena gave a ragged laugh behind him. "Like I give a damn! You've desecrated all of *our* kind!"

Enough talk. Luis grabbed the warlock. Lifted him into the air. "Tell me, Deveaux, have you killed witches? Bound them, stolen their powers and their lives?"

The question of guilt or innocence was always asked before death. Though he *knew* what answer he'd get from the warlock straining in his grasp.

"Yes, yes, *cazador*, I have, and I'll do it again. I'll kill those bitches and—"

Truth.

"Get ready to burn," Luis whispered and the hot breath of his power flowed through him. His hands heated, the magic boiling beneath his touch and—

"You get ready," Deveaux snarled and slammed his forehead into Luis's.

Luis growled at the snap of pain, but never released his hold on the warlock.

The fire of his magic burned brighter. His hands began to glow.

"I'm not some weak demon, *cazador!* I'm the strongest warlock who has ever walked this earth! You won't kill me, you can't—"

A gust of wind sent the pictures flying from the walls and slid the furniture across the room.

Then the warlock managed to snatch his right hand free of Luis's grasp. His fingers went for Luis's eyes.

"Let's see what you fear, *cazador*!"

The dark spell came at him, hard, fast, and too powerful to block.

His mother. Burning. Screaming his name.

His father, lost, dying.

Serena. Three raised slashes near her shoulder. She lay curled on the floor. Fire raced toward her.

"Luis! Help me! Luis!"

"Dream to reality . . ." The warlock whispered as his fingers fell away. With a snap of sound, fire sparked near the curtains behind them.

Then greedily swept across the room.

"Witches burn so quickly. They're so weak . . ."

"No!" Serena's voice. But not afraid. Furious. "Don't let him trick you!" Her fingers dug into his arms. The nails he loved bit into his flesh. "Forget the flames—fight him!"

But the fire burned so hot.

I don't want to be weak.

She would never be.

"Luis, forget about me. He can't be allowed to hurt the coven. We have to stop him!"

Never weak.

The fire was too close.

He gathered his magic, and let the soul-eater loose.

His hands burned through the warlock's clothes. Deveaux whimpered. Denial. Fear.

His eyes widened when his magic was bound.

The fire around them faded into weak tendrils of smoke.

Deveaux's mouth opened in a scream when death whispered in his ear.

Luis pressed all the harder onto him. He felt the surge of all the dark power trapped within the warlock's body.

Power that would be his.

Every last bloodstained drop.

Deveaux began to shudder against him. Spittle flew from his mouth and the warlock choked, gasping for breath.

His death was too easy. For the crimes he'd committed, he should have suffered, writhed in agony.

But that wasn't the way of the *cazador*.

No, it was for another far stronger than he to give final punishment.

His job was just to deliver the souls.

Luis lifted his hands.

Deveaux fell to the floor, body hard as a rock, breath gone.

Heart forever still.

Luis spun to face Serena then. She was staring, lips parted, at the warlock. He grabbed the sleeve of her sweater. Yanked—

"What—"

The seams snapped free and the sleeve fell to the floor. The three slashes lined her upper arm. Red, angry and—

Fading.

As he watched, the binding marks lightened. The raised skin lowered.

"You did it," she whispered.

He touched her soft skin, smoothed his fingers over her flesh.

The marks vanished.

Her smile was so beautiful it broke the heart he'd long forgotten.

"You're safe, Serena, and your coven's safe."

She had her magic, her sisters of the blood.

Her life would be just fine.

As for his . . .

It would never be the same.

He wasn't the type for good-byes. Especially not with her.

They went back to her home, crossed the threshold just as the first rays of the dawn light trickled across the sky.

He knew that he should leave her. Just walk away.

But he couldn't, not without having her just one more time.

A final time.

Luis carried Serena to her bedroom. He didn't bother turning on any of the lights. He undressed her slowly, tenderly. Kissed the hollow of her throat. Tasted the sweetness of her nipples.

His tongue laved the soft curve of her belly, teased the piercing that drove him wild.

His fingers caressed her hips. Parted her thighs. Touched the warm cream that waited for him.

Before, he'd known heat and wild passion with her.

This time, it was different.

When he sank into her, the first thrust was slow. Her sex took him eagerly, squeezing his cock and coating his flesh with her slick heat.

Her eyes were open and locked with his as he withdrew, then thrust. The rhythm was slow, but the hunger burned just as fiercely as before in his blood.

Their lips met in a kiss. Mouths open, tongues tangling. His fingers caressed the center of her arousal even as he drove into her.

The bed squeaked beneath them. The scent of sex filled the air, and her taste flowed onto his tongue.

His head lifted. He raised his body, bracing his weight on his arms, and watched as his cock plunged past her plump nether lips.

Her pale thighs trembled.

He withdrew. Drove back into her snug sex.

Felt the creamy clasp of her body from his cock's root to tip.

She came, clenching around him, breathing out his name.

Another thrust. Another slow, deep drive into her body.

It would never be this good again.

When he climaxed, he didn't speak her name.

But his soul did.

He was gone.

Serena knew that Luis had left her even before she opened her eyes. There was a coldness, an emptiness, in the room. In the bed.

Steeling herself, she opened her eyes. The bright light of the afternoon sun filled the room.

The imprint of Luis's head was still on her pillow, but her *cazador* was gone.

A long-stemmed red rose lay in his place.

She reached for the flower and lifted it to her nose. The soft petals brushed against her skin.

Such a sweet smell.

Such a fucking painful good-bye.

He did his job. He saved you. The coven. He had to go back to his life.

Her fingers clenched around the rose. A thorn pierced her thumb, drawing blood.

He hadn't even said good-bye. Hadn't even asked if she might want him to stay . . . or if she might want to go with him.

"Because he's a damn *cazador*," she muttered, dropping the rose and glaring at the flower. It was either glare or cry, and she was *not* going to cry. "He has to fight the world. He doesn't have time to spend his days with a witch."

But she would have liked to have spent her days *and* nights with him.

Dammit. She hadn't bargained on falling for him.

Not for a second.

He wasn't supposed to be a man that she could love. He was supposed to have been the worst kind of monster.

Not the perfect mate.

She inhaled, catching the scent of the rose, sex, and . . . him.

"No." Serena shook her head. No, she'd just been through hell. She wasn't going to skulk away now and let her dreams die.

Because she'd realized when that third binding mark bit into her skin that she *did* have dreams. Dreams of a home, of a man who loved her.

Dreams of Luis.

Too late. She should have told him how she felt, not that crap about caring, but how she *really* felt.

There had to be a way. Something she could do.

She'd fought the warlock.

She was sure as hell going to fight for love.

What could she do—

Her mother's voice whispered in her ear, *"The cazador, he comes after witches when they're bad."*

A smile twisted her lips as inspiration filled her. "Time to get bad."

Midnight on All Hallow's Eve. The witching hour, as some called it.

The perfect time for her.

Serena pulled out her athame and carefully cast a circle in the dirt. A small tremble shook her hand as she gripped the knife, remembering the last time she'd held such a weapon.

But the athame—it *shouldn't* have been a weapon. It was meant for magic, not pain and death.

There had been no choice.

Serena exhaled and then bent to light her candles. The wind was still this night. No leaves fluttered in the breeze. As if the air itself were waiting . . .

Just as she had waited. *Too many hours.*

The circle was cast. The words of the spell poured from her. Magic blazed in her heart.

"I summoned you once," she whispered, "and I'll do it again."

Luis gazed down into his tequila and realized that if he tried hard enough, he could see Serena's reflection in the gleaming liquid.

His beautiful witch.

He'd kissed her before he left. Pressed a soft kiss to her cheek and conjured her a rose.

Leaving without a word had seemed to be the right choice. Because if he'd stayed and seen her when she woke, he would have broken down . . . and begged her to stay with him. Not for a few days. Forever.

Forever was a very, *very* long time for him.

Behind him, two coyote shifters snarled over a pool

table. He didn't spare them a glance. He was far too focused on memories of his witch.

Would she have considered staying with him? Tying her soul to his so that she could share his life?

No.

Shit. Had he really been arrogant enough to think that he could force her into his life? Back at the beginning, for a wild moment, *he had.* He'd taken one look at her, fallen as hard and fast as his father had for his mother all those centuries before, and he'd thought, simply—

Mine.

But no matter how much he craved her, he couldn't force her into his world.

He brought the glass to his lips. Drained the fiery liquid in one swallow.

A soul bond with someone like him—that was no easy undertaking. Serena would have been forced to give up her home. Her coven. His witch deserved happiness, and she wouldn't find that battling demons every day of her life.

She deserved more. So much more.

So he'd given her the only gift that he could.

He'd walked away to let her live a real life with someone else.

Some utterly lucky asshole who would never, *ever* deserve her and—

The air began to swirl around him. A small tornado that separated him from the others.

Luis stilled. This had happened before. Actually, just seconds before Serena had—

He disappeared and his empty glass fell to the floor, shattering.

* * *

He didn't look pissed.

Serena slowly lowered her arms and gazed at Luis's face. Such a handsome face, really. Not hard at all. Strong. Determined.

Perfect.

His eyes narrowed. He stepped out of her circle. "You can't keep playing with dark magic."

"I'm not playing." The whispers in her mind as she'd performed the spell had been louder this time—but she hadn't been the least bit tempted by their lures.

She'd done the spell for one reason. *Love.* The dark powers in this world—and the next—couldn't touch that.

"Why, Serena?" Stark. "Why risk the danger?"

"Why did you leave me without a good-bye?" The rose was on the ground near his left foot. Another part of her spell.

"To spare you." He lifted his right hand, and she saw his claws. His left, and she saw a ball of flames. "Tell me, witch, did you really want to wake to this in your bed every day?"

No hesitation. Besides, she now understood that he'd know when she lied. "Yes."

His nostrils flared.

"That was a truth, wasn't it, *cazador?*"

His head jerked.

"Want to hear a few more?"

He didn't move.

"I didn't expect you—oh, I knew I was getting the big, bad, *cazador*—but I didn't expect *you.* You touched me, and I hungered. Pleasured me, and I wanted more. You held me—" By the blood, she was stripping her pride bare before him, but she wasn't letting him go without a fight! "And I wanted to stay in your arms forever."

Truth. She saw the knowledge in his eyes.

"I told you I cared, and that was a lie."

So easy to see the lies now. Waking up alone with hope gone had a tendency to make things crystal clear for a witch.

Or any woman.

"My body aches for you and so does ... *shit*! So does my heart, Luis. I feel like I've been waiting for you to come into my life for years, and I didn't even know it until I woke up without you." She sounded sappy, and she wasn't the sappy type.

She was the desperate type. "If you don't want me, tell *me*. I'm a big girl. I can take it." Yeah, it would hurt like hell, and she'd miss him for the rest of her days, but she wouldn't stop him from leaving her. "But do *not* just walk away, without telling me good-bye. Give me that much and—"

And Luis had her in his arms, his hold too tight. "I can't walk away again. *I won't.*"

Truth, even she could sense that.

"I need you, witch. More than I need the night. More than breath. More than magic."

Oh, hell, her knees went weak.

"I left you once, because I didn't want to force you into my world." He drew in a ragged breath. "Because if I think you're mine, if I claim you and cross that line, I'll never let you go and—"

"I am yours." Her mother had told her once that souls recognized their mates. Luis was the mate of her soul. "I've been from the beginning." Understanding had just taken some time.

"If I bind us," he whispered, "there will be no going back, don't you see that? I'll lock you to me, forever. Chain your soul to mine—"

"*Cazador*, it already is." That wrenching emptiness she'd felt upon waking—her soul had missed his.

No more. The binding he spoke of—it wasn't something she feared. No loss of powers, only a joining of spirits.

"Tell me, Luis, tell me how you feel—"

"I feel like you're my world. *My damn world*."

She didn't try to stop the smile that stretched across her face. "Then I think you're going to be stuck with me."

"Sweetheart, forever is a very long time for me—for *us*—if I bind our souls—"

"Good." She'd never sought immortality and, had forever not promised her life with Luis, well, she probably never would have chosen it. But as long as she had him . . . "Then I'll fight by your side. Love by your side. My magic's back and I can help you. We can make this world better—"

"You already have." He kissed her, the touch of his lips so sweet that she nearly cried out. "You already have."

Air swirled around them. Magic warmed the night.

"Luis?"

"Hold onto me, witch. This ride might get rough . . ."

She laughed and held on tighter. "Just the kind of ride that I like."

He kissed her again and the power bloomed between them.

Serena realized that her mother had been right, about so many things. *If only she'd gotten the chance to tell her so.*

Souls did touch others in this world. They looked for their mates.

The big, bad monsters that waited in the dark—they *did* come after the bad witches.

And sometimes, well, sometimes, it was just good to be a little bit bad . . .

And under love's sweet and sexy spell.

TURN ME ON

Noelle Mack

1

"SpectraSign," the receptionist said automatically, continuing to type as she talked into the microphone of a headset. "Our creative concepts light up your—whoops, I have to put you on hold for a sec, okay?"

Beth Danforth, who was waiting to be interviewed, watched as the receptionist corrected something on the computer screen, saved it with a tap on the keyboard, and punched the flashing hold button on the phone console, multitasking for all she was worth.

"Sorry about that," the receptionist was saying. "Of course you don't want your whoops to light up. Yes, sir. I can hear how upset you are." She listened to whoever was screaming at her for another minute. Beth, who was sitting on a padded bench not far away from the reception desk, heard a threat to have the receptionist fired come through loud and clear, peppered with curse words.

It was a weird world and getting weirder every day. Nobody could wait five seconds anymore without tempers being lost and rank being pulled.

"Of course, sir," the receptionist said politely. "Yes. Let me transfer your call." She punched a glowing button on a brushed-aluminum console and the faint yelling stopped. "You are now in voicemail hell, sir," she said to the air and took off her headset.

Then she swiveled in her chair, away from the console and her monitor, to face Beth Danforth. "Justin's expecting you," the receptionist said. "Go on in. First door you come to."

Beth stood up and looked into the corridor that led away from the reception area, seeing only seamless walls. She opened her mouth to ask where the door was, but the other woman seemed to have read her mind.

The receptionist winked. "Trust me, there is a door, but it's closed. Right that way." She pointed with a candy-striped pen that she took out of the straggly but pretty arrangement of cobalt-blue hair piled high on her head. Beth would not go so far as to call the arrangement a bun. There were several other items stuck into the blue hair: a painted butterfly trembling on a spring, a striped feather, and what seemed to be a pair of chopsticks.

"Okay. Thanks very much." Beth picked up the laptop, her presentation for the interview safely snuggled inside its hard drive, and headed right that way, wondering a little.

The CEO was referred to as just . . . Justin? Not Mr. Watts? Looked like SpectraSign was a really laid-back place, even by the freewheeling standards of ad agencies and graphic design companies.

She'd already gotten out of the elevator and gotten lost on the floor below before she made her way up here for her interview. The company was bigger than she'd thought. Judging by the drop-dead funky decor and buzz of activity, it was on the cutting edge of its very competitive field. The receptionist returned to whatever she'd been doing again. In back of her, Beth could hear fingertips clicking lightly on the keyboard. The receptionist answered an internal ring on the phone console and Beth heard her talk to someone she assumed was Justin Watts. "She should be at your door in a second. Uh-huh. Yes, the Times Square pedestrian pattern report's almost done."

There was a door with a recessed latch at the end of the long, white, sun-filled corridor, but it was invisible until you stood in front of it. Beth reached out a finger and traced a few inches of the infinitesimally thin crack that separated the door from the wall. Even with that light pressure, she could feel a hum coming from inside, an electronic kind of hum.

Computers, probably. Lots of them.

She wondered what Justin Watts looked like, mentally running through the possibilities at warp speed. Tall or short? Lean or chunky? Cute or not? Cool cat or dirty dawg?

Beth took a calming breath, told herself she could ace this, added a silent rah-rah and threw in a couple of Hail Marys as a nod to her Catholic grandmother. For good measure, she summoned up her comic-book alter ego, Graphic Design Girl, who could rock a website and simplify a layout in a single bound. She was good at what she did, even if she was starting from scratch all over again, beginning with this interview.

Visionary, her former employer, had closed up shop two months ago, leaving nothing behind in their downtown loft but crumpled sandwich bags and broadband wiring sprouting from a lot of holes in the drywall.

She had brushed up her resumé, posted it every place she could, and hit the hiring trail immediately. So far, no takers. Unfortunately, no one, whether they were in corporate HR or an independent client, seemed to care one way or another about the way her creativity had been praised to the skies. By her friends. On their arty blogs. There were not enough adjectives to describe her talent, according to them. Her marketing concepts had been touted as unique, outstanding, and fantastic.

It was just too bad that Visionary, the video game company whose national advertising she'd created, had tanked so fast. The two geek gods who'd founded the company, college pals whose entire wardrobe consisted of sweatpants and funny, funny T-shirts, had burned through a million dollars of start-up capital and gone back to live with their parents.

Shortly after her search for meaningful employment began, Beth had hustled up a few freelance jobs—one for table lamps, one for pickled beets, one for kitty litter—and given each her all, but the money, at least for the first two, was almost gone. Number three, the kitty litter account, had gone up in smoke when the Whizzy Whizkers king ran off to Boca Raton with his mistress and cleaned out the company account. So the company check had bounced, boing boing, and her bank had socked her with a $35 fee just for letting her know. Nice of them.

No, freelancing wasn't going to cut it. She needed a steady job and she needed health insurance and she needed to pay the exorbitant rent on her dreary little studio apartment in lower Manhattan.

So far, there hadn't been one response to her posts, except from SpectraSign. Would she fit in here? The voice who'd called her cell and made the appointment for today belonged to the receptionist she'd just met, who seemed nice enough, but not like the kind of person who was easily wowed. Beth had no idea what anyone at SpectraSign thought of her credentials and she hadn't been able to find out too much about the company or its CEO. Justin Watts didn't even have a picture on Google Images.

She looked around again, stalling just a little bit longer. For a media-biz company, it definitely seemed to be prospering. The corridor—unlike those at the Visionary—did not bear the sneaker marks of postgrad dudes playing foam-football and colliding bodily with the walls. There was no eviction notice posted on a dartboard, either. No, this space was spectacular in an austere way. Every surface was pure white or brushed aluminum; every piece of furniture was high-end modern design.

She put her hand on the recessed latch to turn it, letting it stay there for a second or two. The latch was pleasantly warm and Beth didn't want to give Justin Watts a chilly-fingered handshake.

"C'mon in," a friendly voice said. A nice, deep, male voice.

Beth took a deep breath. She wanted to make a favorable impression from the second she walked in. Confidence was key. Her ex-boyfriends had always told her she was pretty and the reflection in the mirror this morning hadn't been too scary. Eyeliner and lipgloss and a touch of blush had done the trick today. Her skin had cooperated, for once, not presenting her with an evil little surprise on her nose the way it sometimes did when she was stressed. So she looked okay. There was nothing to distract him from her creative genius and her portfolio. And then there were . . . she searched her mind for irresistible physical attributes and drew a blank.

She did have nice knees, she thought desperately and a little irrationally, and the skirt she had on showed them. Above the knees things got a little plump, below the knees were legs that were okay but not great. Work the knees, she told herself. Beth felt like she was picking up a mysterious charge from this place. Her skirt clung to her thighs, even edged up slightly. She tugged it down. In the store the skirt had been just right. Not demure and not too revealing, either. It didn't wrinkle. That was why she'd worn it. But material that didn't wrinkle had a slithery side, betraying its origin in Satan's Little Tailor Shop, she thought.

"Anyone out there?" The voice from inside sounded even deeper and more male.

Rah rah rah. He was waiting for her. She turned the latch and went in.

"Hello." Beth took a look at the man working away on one of two monitors and her poor, unemployed heart beat faster.

"Hey . . . be right with you. Hold on a sec," he murmured.

The glow from the screen made his face look faintly luminous, which was an interesting effect. His features were on the rugged side, and there was a dimple involved on the left side of his mouth. Melt me fucking down, she thought. Justin Watts was hot.

"Sorry," he said without looking up just yet. "I don't want to lose this thought and I don't mean to be rude but—"

"You're not," she said. "I understand." How many seconds had she dawdled on the other side of the closed door? *Way to go on making a good first impression,* she scolded herself. He continued to study the screen, and she continued to study him.

"Thanks. Okay. That'll do it. Let me just input these changes—" he tapped at the keyboard— "and I'll be right with you."

"No problem. Take your time."

She took the opportunity to flat-out stare at what she could see of him while he concentrated on finishing what he was doing. Justin Watts had thick, dark hair that was the opposite of styled. It stuck up every which way and looked like he had been running his hands through it while he pondered layouts on the drafting table he sat at.

"Done." He tapped another couple of keys and glanced up at her at last. The glance turned into a look that turned into a stare. His gaze was intense, but for some reason Beth didn't feel intimidated. Probably because he had nice, really nice, eyes. Supersexy. And beach-glass blue, shadowed by lashes that were as thick and dark as his hair. His smile made his eyes crinkle at the corners.

Save me, she thought weakly. He rose from the drafting table and walked around it to meet her, giving her a warm, strong, almost electrifying handshake that chased away her nervousness. Mmm. On second thought, she didn't want to be saved.

"Okay," he said. "So you're Beth. I'm Justin." He laughed a little self-consciously. "That's obvious, I guess."

She was charmed. Justin Watts might be a big deal, but he didn't act like one. For one thing, he wasn't sitting behind a typical, CEO-style fortress of a desk made of bleached titanium or whatever, but at a real, old-style, honey-pine drafting table with a state-of-the-art double monitor setup, plus scrap paper and layouts and art stuff all over it. He was clearly a hands-on kind of guy.

"It's really nice to meet you," he was saying. She returned her gaze to his face. "I checked out some of your work on your website—I was impressed."

"Oh. Ah, thanks." Now that he had let go of her

hand, her nervousness returned. She clutched the handles of her laptop case like it was her third-grade lunchbox and she was guarding the cupcakes in it from the Table Five death squad, then told herself not to be so twitchy. "Which ones?"

"You can set the laptop right here," Justin said, pointing to the drafting table. "Um, the lamp ads were great. And that animated campaign you did with the dancing beets? Even better—genius, in fact."

She gave him what she hoped was a cool, totally professional nod of acknowledgment. "Thanks," she said, thrilled inside that he'd looked at more than just her resume. "I worked really hard on those."

The lamp assignment had involved nothing more than a good layout using the company's photos, but the stop-motion process of putting tap shoes on pickled beets and making them shuffle off to Buffalo had been a bitch. But she wasn't going to say that. Let him chalk it up to pure genius if he wanted to. And she wasn't going to mention the kitty litter gig at all. He hadn't. Anyway, it didn't count, since she hadn't been paid, the way guys said a date didn't count if they hadn't been laid.

She suspected Justin Watts would never say anything so crude. But no doubt there were women waiting in line just to do him.

She imagined him beckoning and her going to the head of that line and smiled inwardly. No, no, no. She needed this job more than she needed sex right now.

Justin leaned over the drafting table and pushed the layouts to one side. She couldn't help looking. One atmospheric, faux Depression-era photo showed a half-naked guy in faded jeans leaning on a 1930s pickup truck out in a field somewhere. Waving wheat. Hay fork propped on the truck. And the faux farmboy was to die for—it was classic prairie porn, all the way.

The model had quite a manly bulge, she noted. Almost as big as the bale of hay his battered workboot was resting on. Then she looked at the model's face. Oh, yeah. He was famous, even if she couldn't remember his name at the moment. Who he was didn't matter, because a well-known logo was splashed across the bottom of the photo. Blue Blaze Jeans. That was a huge company. She breathed an inward sigh of relief. So SpectraSign had at least one major client to pay their bills. Her paycheck wouldn't bounce.

You're not hired yet, she told herself, setting down her laptop case. Quit ogling manly bulges and get back to convincing Justin Watts that he needs you and only you, on staff, with benefits, as a designer.

Beth unzipped the case and took out the laptop, bending down a little to raise the screen and angle it up while she went through the beep-and-boop ritual of starting it.

"Sorry. You need something to sit down in." He brought over a chair that matched his own—gleaming curves of aluminum formed the legs and seat and back.

Beth settled herself into it and put on her best interview smile as she looked up at him. It made her face feel stretched.

"Did you bring a portfolio?"

She shook her head. "Everything's on my laptop. It just seemed like an easier way of giving you a comprehensive overview."

True and not true. Her ancient cat, who did not take kindly to sudden awakenings, had been sleeping on her actual portfolio. Moving him meant a revenge hairball on the bathmat sooner or later. Usually sooner.

She hadn't been willing to risk it when she'd been rushing to get here as it was. Besides that, the contents of the portfolio were disorganized and she had a lot of personal stuff—letters and photos and old comic books—mixed in with her project layouts. It needed winnowing and she hadn't had time.

"Fine." He sat back down and scooted his chair over to the end of the table. "Let's see what you've got."

"Okay." Fumbling a little, Beth pulled up the files she wanted. His being so near was a little disconcerting. Justin wasn't trying to lean in or lech or anything remotely like that, and his long legs were tucked back under his aluminum chair, but even so. He radiated warm sexuality. He couldn't help it, she decided.

"Beth, since I've already seen the final versions of the lamps and the beets, could you give me an idea of how you got there? Second thoughts, mistakes, and all."

"Sure." She tapped the touchpad to open a file.

"I'm interested in your creative process."

Beth laughed. "If you could call it that. Sometimes I think what I do is like trying to catch light in midair. Sometimes I can hold on to it. Not often, though."

His face grew thoughtful. "Funny you should say that."

She looked up at him before she turned the laptop his way. "What do you mean?"

"Ah—geez, it's hard to explain." He searched for the right words while she waited politely. "Basically, I guess I feel that way sometimes myself."

"Oh."

"I just bought SpectraSign," he explained. "I have a lot of ideas to grow the company, but I'm not sure where to start. That's why I decided to bring in a really original designer. And by that I mean someone who hasn't hit the big time yet."

That would be her. But not from want of trying. "Interesting. I didn't know that." She made a vague gesture at the door she'd come through. "I understood the company's been around for several years. I just assumed you were the founder."

He shook his head. "The new owner."

"I see."

"And the CEO, of course. SpectraSign seemed like a worthwhile investment and a good fit for my area of expertise."

"And what's that? If you don't mind my asking," she added hastily.

"Electrical engineering. Quantum mechanics and physics."

Mega-smart and super-sexy. Beth sighed inwardly. She was not remotely in his league. With her luck, he'd turn out to have a spandex suit and the ability to fly.

"I won't bore you with the technical details," he was saying. "Because they don't have much to do with SpectraSign. Long story short, I specialized in the study of photons, angstroms, wave energy, things like that."

Spacey things. Even though she'd been tagged as a space cadet for her comic-book habit, Beth wouldn't know what a photon was if one bit her, and she suspected one had in Science 101 back in high school.

"Anyway, I was curious to see what would happen if I could combine that knowledge with a creative approach," he went on, "and right now I want to build the most dazzling sign Times Square has ever seen."

"Is there a contest going on or something?" Beth searched her brain. He must have just made half a billion by selling a tech company she'd never heard of and was looking for something else to do. Maybe he had money to burn. Hmmm. She couldn't very well ask if he did in so many words.

"No."

"Then why—"

"I have a lot of energy, Beth. Running a world-class sign company ought to be fun, don't you think?"

"World-class? Really? I didn't know SpectraSign was at that level." She flinched the second the words were out of her mouth. "Gah. Sorry. I guess I should have known, huh?" *Good going, you bigmouth bass,* she told herself bitterly. *And after he did his homework on you.*

Justin only shrugged. "They started out in Las Vegas, made a fortune on the strip. Then the company founder moved to Japan for some reason. They did most of the Ginza signs in Tokyo, you know."

"Awesome place. That's very cool."

"Anyway, he retired, and I bought the company just for the hell of it. First I hired the best software programmers in the business, and then got them started developing multiscreen vid displays, light-emitting diode designs, and other new signage concepts."

"Aha. That explains the humming in the air—the worker bees are busy."

"What humming?" he asked blandly. "I'm not following you."

"I felt it when I touched the door."

He rested his big hands, fingers splayed out, on the drafting table. "You know, I think you're right. The IT department is below my office. I stay out of there, but you pegged the hum. Not surprising. It's a rat's nest of cables and computers and guardian geeks."

"I know the type," Beth said, grinning. She had just

noticed, with joy, that he wore no wedding ring, and, furthermore, that there was no telltale trace of a former wedding ring indenting his fourth finger, left hand.

He was single. He radiated sexual energy. He was brilliant. A girl couldn't ask for anything more, besides a job offer.

"Let's get back to Beth Danforth. Tell me more," he was saying. "I want to know everything about you."

An executive who didn't just brag about himself and his company? Now that was unusual. She looked down at her skirt. The knees must be working. She looked back up. All he seemed fixated on was her face, as if he thought she was really pretty. Good going. It was almost time to trot out her talent, but if he wanted her life story, he could have it, judiciously edited to podcast length.

"Oh, I grew up on Long Island," Beth began. "Wait a minute. You don't want to hear that."

"Yes, I do."

"You do? Really?"

"Yeah." He looked totally enthusiastic. In fact, he had a born-yesterday quality that she really liked and his interest in her seemed totally unfaked.

Ahh. She felt even warmer all over. Attention, the ultimate aphrodisiac.

She took a deep breath. "I'll make it mercifully short. My father was a comic book artist. He raised me on his own after my mother died of cancer."

"I'm sorry."

"I was really little," she said matter-of-factly. "I didn't know her, but I wish I had. No, it was just me and the Ink Man."

She was not going to tell Justin Watts that she was Graphic Design Girl.

"Anyway, my aunt—his sister—made sure I ate my

vegetables and brushed my hair and did my homework and applied to college."

"In that order?"

"Pretty much. Eventually I majored in marketing, but I always cherished the hope that I could make a living doing what I loved."

Justin looked at her thoughtfully. "You can do better than make a living."

"Huh?"

Out of the blue, he named a salary for the job she was interviewing for that made tears come into her eyes. One rogue tear even trickled into her ear. Great. Her ears were crying. But she had heard him correctly.

"Are you kidding? That much?"

He only nodded. "I have a feeling you're exactly what this company needs."

"But I didn't even finish my presentation. You're not offering me the job, are you?"

"Not if you don't want me to." Justin grinned as he leaned back in his chair and crossed his arms in back of his head. "Go ahead and finish."

"Ah—okay." Beth shook her head, a little nonplussed, and got back to her laptop, opening file after file before he could change his mind. She lost track of time as they brainstormed ideas for a sign to end all signs, she was having so much fun. They eventually agreed to disagree on what he called the dazzle factor.

Justin was for it, she was against.

"It doesn't matter how dazzling an ad is," she informed him, "The second it goes up in Times Square, another company will try to out-dazzle you."

Justin grinned. "Bring 'em on. We'll make another one that's brighter and bigger."

Beth shook her head. "Good marketing doesn't

work like that. You have to reach people on an emotional level, not just blow their minds with special effects."

"Really. Tell me more." He sat back up, propped his chin on his hand and gave her an encouraging look.

She reached down to pick up the photo of the male model in jeans, which had slipped out of the paper clip holding it to the layout. "All right. Take him, for example—"

"Why?" Justin gave the faux farmboy a bored look. "He has better abs than I do. So I wouldn't buy the jeans," he said.

Beth waved the photo at him. "You're missing the point. He's designed to appeal to a female customer in a subtle way."

"I wouldn't call that pose subtle."

"But he's not all lit up. This looks like an old photograph of the bad boy she, meaning our hypothetical customer, used to love. Who she still wants."

"Whoa." Justin held up both hands. "Isn't he selling men's jeans?"

"Women buy jeans for their guys. Or they make their guys buy the right jeans. You know, the nuances of how jeans should hang on a male body and what jeans should do for a male butt are lost on most straight guys, who will go out and buy the cheapest pair they can find unless—"

He was smiling. Beth realized she had gotten off-topic. Way off-topic. And this was a job interview.

"Um, I talk too much. Sorry."

"Not at all," he laughed. "This is great. You just lay it out there. And I obviously have a lot to learn."

"Really." She covered her flustered feeling by talking fast. "About what? I mean, you have a major client already—Blue Blazes Jeans is huge—" She stopped, telling herself not to babble.

He looked . . . eager. If that was the right word. At least his face still had that luminous glow she'd noticed when she came into his office, even though both monitors on the drafting table were off and he wasn't looking at her laptop at the moment.

"Yeah, well, they are. Anyway, Blue Blazes sent over those mock-ups and some others but I'm not sure the concept will work when the model is forty feet tall, in motion, and lit up."

She nodded in agreement, although she wouldn't have minded seeing that particular male model strutting his stuff at any size. Come to think of it, that went for Justin Watts too. She doubted that the model had better abs than Justin. She would guess that they were about even when it came to world-class male abs.

"Your company has at least one sign in Times Square right now, right?"

"We do." He named the brand and the global food conglomerate that owned it. "It's a great big bag of holographic potato chips. The bag rotates and the potato chips float out. The idea is that they're lighter than other potato chips."

"Got it."

"Of course, we don't show the calorie count or fat grams. Both would give a cardiologist a heart attack."

"I understand," Beth said, laughing. "But that's a great account to have."

"But visually not exciting. There's a limit to what you can do with potato chips. Seen one, seen 'em all. That's why I was so interested in what you did with the tap-dancing beets. They had personality."

She smiled. "That wasn't easy."

"I can imagine."

"So . . ." She was curious, and he had asked all the questions. "You really do have the Blue Blazes account?"

"Yup."

She nodded in understanding. "And you want to do a jeans ad that will have everyone talking and stopping to look."

"That's right," Justin said. "But I don't think their approach is going to do it." He flicked the photograph of the male model to one side.

"Hmm." Beth clicked through older folders in her documents. "Let me show you the first sign I ever did—here it is. I scanned in these drawings."

Justin peered at the image on the screen. "What is that?"

"A fried clam. Sammy the Clam, to be exact."

"You've improved."

Beth laughed. "Well, I was only seventeen when I did those. I worked at the Olde Clamme Shacke as a waitress and the owner needed a new sign. So I came up with Sammy. The orders went up right away."

"Why?"

"We printed Sammy on the menus and the place-mats, too. He was a goofy little character that stuck in people's heads, I guess. Different from what I usually drew."

Justin shot her an interested look. "Which was?"

"Superheroes. If you grow up reading comic books, it comes kinda naturally."

"I see. Doesn't seem like a girl thing to do, but why not?"

"Hey, I put plastic dinosaur heads on my Barbies. I wasn't ever a girly girl—basically, I was just a weird kid."

"Weird kids usually grow up to be some of the most interesting people, Beth."

Awww. She beamed at him, momentarily forgetting that she was supposed to be in interview mode. "Sometimes I was shy and sometimes I couldn't stop talking."

"I'm not sure that's changed." Justin chuckled in a very nice way. "So keep talking."

Encouraged by his wink, Beth took a breath and continued. "Um, I never really felt like I belonged in suburban Long Island. When I was old enough, I took the train into New York every chance I got. It always seemed like a perfect place for superheroes and it felt like home to me. Lots of comics are set in, quote-unquote, Gotham. Anyway, blah blah, I went looking for the settings I'd seen in my dad's portfolio and I actually found a few."

"I'd like to see them."

Beth gave him a curious look. "They're still there. Maybe not for long. The city's getting ripped up and torn down."

"I know what you mean. An entire YMCA can disappear overnight."

"Yeah. At least in comics, an intergalactic rec center would pop up in its place."

"Sign me up," Justin said with a huge, guy-type grin.

Beth grinned back. They just looked at each other for a minute that didn't feel at all uncomfortable or weird.

"So," he said at last, "how would you define your approach to a campaign like this?"

Beth thought it over. "You have to make people believe that wonderful, impossible things are real. It's all about that."

"Which makes you perfect for advertising work."

Beth smiled. "I hope so." Perfect for this job would be just fine. Had he decided? Evidently not.

"Show me more," he said.

Beth clicked open a few more files with drawings and concepts for all kinds of things. Then she came to one with a title she didn't recognize and opened it without thinking.

The image appeared. It showed a canopy bed with four posts made of neon tubes. Hot pink neon tubes.

"What's that?" Justin seemed more than curious. He leaned in for a really good look.

Holy cow. She never should've clicked on that one. Beth wanted to close it out, but she couldn't quite bring herself to. It would be like slamming a door right in Justin's face.

"Ah—not my work. An ex-boyfriend of mine designed that. Not exactly practical."

Justin was reading the fine print next to the image of the bed. "Says here that it lights up at the moment of orgasm."

Uh-oh. She'd forgotten about that part. Beth gave him a sheepish smile. "He never did build it."

"Great concept, though."

Beth cleared her throat. "Never was more than that. Okay, moving right along—"

She finished her presentation and Justin's attention never strayed. If she had to describe his reaction, she would say that he seemed really excited by her ideas. Maybe even by her.

His energy was definitely contagious. Her initial nervousness had completely vanished by the time the interview was over.

He got up while she shut down her laptop and wandered around his office, looking out the floor-to-ceiling windows.

"You never did mention where you're from," she said, by way of making conversation. She closed the cover with a snick. "New York?"

"Yeah." He waved at the skyline outside. Or the sky. Whatever. She didn't need to pry.

"Still live in the city?" she asked lightly.

Justin turned around. His energy almost seemed to crackle around him, but then he'd said he'd just bought the company, so maybe the carpets were new and full of static.

Beth tugged at her skirt to keep it down, just in case it got electrified and started clinging. The interview had been all about her talent and not her knees. *Good sign,* she thought.

"Yes, I do. How about you?"

She nodded. "I have a studio just off Hudson Street."

"Oh, then you're not far from me. I live in the Bolt Building."

Beth thought a minute. "The Art Deco skyscraper that's way downtown? The one with all the lightning bolts on the façade?"

"That's right. Built in 1935 by Jasper Bolt, the world's craziest billionaire."

"How did he make his money?"

"No one really knows. But the building is great, full of freaky architectural details."

He didn't say anything tacky like *come on up and play in my penthouse.* But given a few weeks of working with him, assuming she had been hired, she wouldn't mind if he did. Was she, then? He had quoted a salary. He just hadn't said the most wonderful three little words in the world. *You have job.*

I love you would've been okay with her too, but that was definitely rushing things.

"I bet it is," Beth said politely.

"Okay," he said suddenly. "Let's get back to business. You do have the job, if you want it."

She inhaled, and tried desperately not to squeak on the exhale. "I do? This job?"

"Yes." He waited for a beat. "Now you say yes."

Beth willed herself to remain completely calm and forced her voice to reflect some self-control. "Exactly what will my responsibilities entail?"

He shrugged. "We'll figure that out as we go along, Beth. You know the salary."

She nodded, rigid with the effort of not jumping around the room. "I think it's commensurate with my abilities."

He stuck his hands in his pockets. "Talk corporate to me. I love it. Is that a yes or a no?"

That damned dimple of his was flashing like a go-for-it sign. "Full benefits, by the way. Dental. Disability. And 401K matching, the whole nine."

Beth fought the urge to throw her arms around him and give him an exuberant kiss on the cheek. But she couldn't resist the excellent offer a second longer.

"I accept. Thank you." She wanted to scream a yes. She hoped her measured voice communicated some enthusiasm. She knew her eyes were sparkling, because her nose was itching. She couldn't scratch it, just couldn't.

Justin nodded, and gave her a huge grin. "All right. See you Monday. Bright and early."

"Okay." She couldn't think of anything else intelligent to say. "Wow. This is so incredible. Thanks again. This is going to be great."

"I agree."

He stayed where he was. She backed out, trying not to trip on his new carpet. Beth clutched her laptop under one arm and gave him a fingery wave. Then she skittered down the long, white hallway, flashed a huge smile at the receptionist, and went out the door. She did dance in the elevator. There was no one in it but her.

Out on the sidewalk, she felt like she was walking on air. She had a job. She wasn't going to be broke. She was ready, really ready to sell blue jeans. Life was good again.

She blew her last bucks on a work-appropriate wardrobe for SpectraSign, shopping until early evening. You deserve it, you need it, you will be able to pay for it in another week, she told herself, lugging the bags home, along Hudson Street, trying to keep the strap of her laptop case from sliding off her shoulder.

It was twilight and the streetlamps were just coming on. A strong westerly breeze was blowing from the river, making a few pieces of litter fly around through the side streets, including hers. Beth went up the stoop of her five-story building, the bags rattling and bouncing against her legs. Her short skirt was a lost cause, flipping wildly.

It was a relief to edge inside the main door. She set everything down except the laptop and peered into the brass grille of her mailbox. There was something white in there. Probably another bill.

Ha ha. She could pay them all now. She could even afford senior-care cat food for old Freddy, and maybe cut down on the hairball count. Beth found her key ring and looked for the tiny brass one that opened the mailbox, pulling out a letter from her father.

She knew it was from him without even looking at the return address. He always drew on his envelopes and letters, something he couldn't do with e-mail. She saved each missive—since she'd moved out of his house on Long Island, there had been one every week for years. She slipped the decorated envelope into one of the shopping bags and continued upstairs.

Four locks later, she was inside her studio apartment. Still struggling with the bags, Beth bumped into the antique dressmaker's dummy that she called Miss Boom Bah and used as a coatrack. The full-figured dummy tipped forward, then stood upright again when she gave it a shove back. It took a lot to upset Miss Boom Bah.

Beth slung her light jacket over the coat on the dummy's shoulders and looked down at the old gingerbread-colored cat rubbing her ankle. "Guess what, Freddy?"

The cat gave a wheezing, very faint meow. She bent down to give him a chin rub just the way he liked it.

"We're in the money. I have a job."

Freddy wheezed, and she sat down and stroked him for a while. He got bored with it, wandered off, and stuck his nose into one of the shopping bags.

"Stay away from my fabulous new wardrobe," she told him sternly. Freddy glared at her as she got up, gathered all the bags, and hung them on an inside hook in her tiny closet. Then she went into the kitchenette to call her dad.

2

"So this is the famous Bolt Building."

Justin was waiting for her, a bulging plastic shopping bag in his hand. He was wearing jeans with a few for-real rips, and a linen shirt, and disreputable-looking sneakers. He looked fabulous. "Yup. And this is just the lobby."

"Wow," she said. The riotous Art Deco ornamentation didn't stop. Every surface she could see was covered with stylized motifs, quite a few of them representing lightning, as far as she could tell.

The concierge, an unassuming older guy, sat at a console, if that was the right word, which would have been a great altar for a pagan god. Huge, freestanding bolts of lightning bolts framed it, done in chrome polished to a high shine. The console itself was also metal, with a huge bronze sun emitting spiky rays adorning the front.

When Beth got done looking at it, she studied the vaulted ceiling, shot through with more bronze rays and zigzagging lines. No matter where her gaze settled, something about the restless design made it move on. She got the dizzying feeling she'd walked into an alternate galaxy and glanced down again, at the floor, hoping it would ground her.

No such luck.

Even the floor was decorated with fanciful planets and stars and comets, done in flat metal and imbedded at random in each of the tiles.

"Welcome to my world," Justin said laughing. "It's a bit much, isn't it?"

"It's spectacular," she said, "but I guess you get used to it after a while, like anything else."

"Yeah, I am by now." He walked toward the bank of elevators, and Beth followed.

"How long have you been living here?"

"I bought my apartment when I bought Spectra-Sign," he said. He punched the up button, which was in the shape of a very small lightning bolt, and waited with her. "Glad you could come."

"I wouldn't have missed this for anything," she said. And she didn't mean the lobby. He'd taken her out for dinner several times since he'd hired her, and it was clear that his interest in her wasn't all about work.

Though they had been doing plenty of that. The design team, a bunch of thirtyish men and women with eyeglasses so narrow she wondered how they saw out of them, had slaved away on the Blue Blazes account and the software geeks had actually been able to turn their ideas into something that worked.

The resulting sign concept was accepted by Blue Blaze top management and was now being built in Times Square. It would be fifty feet high, thirty feet wide. Beth couldn't wait to see it. They were celebrating the go-ahead tonight.

She'd coordinated the project from her first day on the job, simply because she worked so closely with Justin. At first Beth had wondered if that was wise, but it wasn't like she exactly had a choice. That was how he wanted it.

And it was really clear that he wanted her. Likewise, as far as she was concerned. Which was why she'd bought killer lingerie from Agent Provocateur for tonight. It did wonderful things for her, um, things. If he got that far.

From the way he was looking at her right now, she suspected he would.

An elevator arrived, the door whooshed open, and they went inside. She looked around, wondering why it had glass walls, then figured it was to let the passengers look at the decorated inside of the shaft. Yep, more lightning.

"This Bolt guy was crazy," she said.

"Certifiable." Justin put a keycard in a slot next to the PH button and up they went.

A penthouse. Ooh. She really wanted to see what life was like that high up in the air.

"Do you get vertigo?" he asked.

"Not usually, why?"

"We'll be in the glass part of the elevator shaft in another few floors. It was added much later, about ten years ago—here it comes."

Beth gasped. "Oh my God, what a view!" All of lower Manhattan suddenly appeared. The buildings thrust upward, almost appearing to move along with them, their lit windows turning into streaks of light here and there. She glimpsed details that were impossible to see from the street—on the older buildings, gargoyles and lion's heads and decorative pediments and, on the new buildings, raked angles of glass that glowed strangely in the twilight and even neon outlining the tops.

What a view, she thought. She wasn't going to crow it out loud again, because it was a corny thing to say and he was probably just as used to the spectacular scene as he was to everything else about the Bolt Building.

"Yeah, it's incredible."

There was a note of awe in his voice, which pleased her. She'd picked up on his natural enthusiasm from the first day they'd met and in the eight weeks that she'd been on the job, observed how it inspired the company clients and his employees, her, most of all.

Beth looked at him instead of the cityscape for a moment, observing the way the otherworldly glow of the city at night brought out something that was indescribably wonderful in his face. The color of his eyes seemed to intensify and become a different blue. Call it blue times two.

Justin sighed with pleasure as the elevator came to a stop and he held the button for her to exit ahead of him.

"Hold on. I just want one last look," Beth said. She turned around to take in the panoramic view of New York's harbor. Even in the semidarkness, she could make out the giant orange ferries coming and going from Staten Island, trailing long white wakes, and innumerable small boats out on the water. The vast shapes of tankers moved slowly, guided by the tugs she'd loved to watch as a kid, heading toward the graceful, gigantic bridge that soared over the narrows before the open sea.

"You can see that from my living room," Justin said, keeping his finger on the open button and letting her look her fill. "And the Statue of Liberty, too. My big green girlfriend."

She thought of Miss Boom Bah and smiled.

"We can drink a toast to her," Justin added. "I have champagne on ice."

"Sounds glamorous."

He chuckled. "It's good champagne. And I made great cheese dip to go with it."

"Is that the gourmet meal you promised me?"

"In the bag." He held it up so she could see it. "The delivery dude got to the lobby just before you did."

"And I thought you came down to meet me."

"I'm willing to take the credit for it."

Beth shook her head. "Nope. And I thought that you were going to do the cooking."

"I made no promises to that effect. Hey, you said you didn't feel like going out to another restaurant tonight. Anyway, we've gone to all my favorites and yours."

She nodded, understanding his unspoken message: I want to get you alone. He probably assumed she had a roommate, although he had never asked. Nothing doing. She wasn't about to invite him over to her place for an intimate dinner with wheezing Freddy and Miss Boom Bah.

The kitchenette wasn't really big enough to cook in, anyway. She could just imagine Justin perched on her rump-sprung sofa with a plate on his lap and a Chinese takeout bag between them, rolling up shredded moo shu cabbage inside those thin pancakes and trying to make small talk while the gooey sauce squirted out the other end.

Too suggestive. Nothing doing. He'd finally asked her over and she'd said yes at once.

He led the way down a hall lined with . . . that couldn't be lapis lazuli. She looked closer and touched a hand to the smooth, floor-to-ceiling panel. Maybe it was. The deep blue stone was speckled with tiny fragments of gold. How rich was he?

Okay, she admonished herself, his apartment, which he owned, was on this floor, but that didn't mean he owned the whole floor and had paneled the hallways in semiprecious stone. Justin Watts didn't seem like the kind of guy who had to show off to that degree. He didn't really show off at all, despite his engaging, boyish enthusiasm. And as far as she knew, he wasn't a billionaire, which would have been fairly weird. No, he was down-to-earth, even if he lived up in the clouds. She couldn't wait to see his place.

"So you didn't do the cooking. Hmm. Any other secrets to reveal, Justin?"

"Not just yet," he said.

Watching his broad shoulders under the linen shirt he hadn't bothered to tuck into his jeans, Beth was willing to bet that all would be revealed—meaning her fabulous new underwear—before midnight.

He used the same keycard to unlock his door and in they went.

Beth looked around. Huge windows gave an even better view of lower Manhattan by night. She almost ran to them. There were the massive gothic arches of the Brooklyn Bridge, joined by the delicate tracery of lights on the supporting cables. She could see for miles, over all of Brooklyn, low but lit up, and out into the harbor and beyond. Beth looked right and there was the Statue of Liberty, looking small and stalwart, her torch raised.

"Oh my God," she breathed. "This is amazing. Just amazing."

"Glad you like it. Haven't been here long enough to decorate much. Walk around, make yourself at home."

He got busy in the kitchen, unloading the bag as she

did what he suggested. There wasn't much furniture and it wasn't too different from what any young, successful guy in Manhattan had. Leather sofa, nine feet long. Monster plasma TV. Squooshy leather armchairs with ottomans. In a bedroom she peeked into, a really big bed. There were a lot of rooms but some doors were closed and she wasn't going to snoop.

She realized she was going in a circle, though, and that the apartment was a floor-through. My, my, my.

Beth ended up in the kitchen again, determined to sound casual. What could she possibly say that wouldn't make her sound like a gold-digger or a hick from the sticks?

She was going to keep right on relating to him like he was just this incredibly cute, nice guy she worked with, that was all.

"So what's for dinner?"

"Steak. Salad. Baked potatoes." He ripped off the menu stapled to the bag and read aloud. "From Peter O'Grady's legendary steakhouse, home of the hundred-dollar sirloin."

"How bad can it be?"

He gestured at the foil containers lined up neatly on his kitchen counter, which she was relieved to see was made of mere granite. "Let's eat."

She picked up a fork and speared a piece of salad. "Can't go wrong with the tried and true."

"Is it? I guess food like that is still kinda new to me," he laughed.

Beth didn't really hear him say it. The lettuce she was chewing was very fresh and very crunchy.

He stuck a fork into a piece of sliced steak and ate it. "Fantastic," he said. "Have some. Want a plate?"

"Not really," she laughed, "I'm starving."

He nodded. "Me too. What about the champagne?"

Beth slid the foil container of sliced steak in front of her. "Let's have it with dessert."

"Good idea."

They were both starving and the movable feast disappeared pretty quickly. Satisfied, feeling pleasantly absentminded, Beth licked the tines of her fork when she was done. Justin noticed. Boy, did he notice. What she was doing made him stop eating.

"Are you trying to turn me on?"

She snorted and put the fork down. "No. Does that do it for you?"

"Your pretty pink tongue? Licking? Yeah," he answered boldly. "It really does."

Well, all right. They had gone from zero to sixty in less a second.

"That was fast," she said.

He sighed. "No sense fighting it, then, is there? I really care about you, Beth. And you turn me on like no one else."

She squirmed in her seat. Not as if she hadn't imagined herself in his arms a thousand times already. But being here, alone with him, was different.

"What's for dessert?" she asked.

"You are." He smiled a slow, slow smile that was scorchingly sexy. It melted whatever was left of her resistance.

As it turned out, he knew how to take his time. He'd suggested a move to the sofa and a look at the ever-changing view, and eventually he'd opened the champagne.

Giddy from it, and her own excitement, she was lying on his bed in nothing but stockings attached to a gartered thong and a demi-cup bra.

"Wow," was all he said as he stroked her legs. "You are incredible."

Beth blushed, a head-to-foot feeling of warmth.

"Would you mind rolling over? I want to see what this pretty stuff looks like from the back," he murmured.

"There's not much of it." She smiled, though, and rolled over on her tummy, supporting her head on her folded arms.

Justin's big hands moved in sweeping caresses over her back and shoulders. He took a minute just to play with her hair, running his fingers through it and letting the long locks slide away from her neck.

With gentle pressure, using mostly his thumb, he rubbed her neck and went on down her spine from there.

Slow, small circles. Circles that seemed interconnected in some way, as if he was joining together parts of her that needed to get to know each other again. Beth felt a whole-body sense of profound relaxation. And trust.

"Mmm."

He kept on rubbing. "Moan away. I want this to feel as good as possible."

When his fingers reached the back part of her bra, he unhooked it and pushed the two parts away. Then he continued to massage her spine all the way down to her tailbone and up again to her neck.

Beth sighed with delight. He stopped and she could tell from the sounds of zippers and buttons that he was shedding his clothes.

She wanted to look and almost turned around . . . and then it occurred to her how wonderful it would be to experience him first just through his touch. The feel of his bare skin against hers.

And Justin didn't disappoint her.

She felt him clamber onto the bed, pleasurably aware of the muscular hardness of the thighs that suddenly straddled her bare ass. The prickle of the fine hair on them was stimulating. Little shivers of arousal coursed through her.

Staying up, he continued his luxurious massage of her back and shoulders. Every so often she felt his balls brush against her behind, and she smiled into the tumbling hair that covered the side of her face.

They felt soft but heavy, and tighter each time they touched down. His gentleness held an unmistakable strength, and she relaxed even more as the caressing pressure of his hands grew more intense.

He moved her hair away so that he could come down and kiss her neck and the one ear he could get at.

Then she felt it. His huge, silky-stiff cock rested between the cheeks of her bare ass. Not doing anything, not thrusting, just there.

He was down on his elbows now, his legs folded up, his whole body covering hers.

Justin kissed her neck and treated her to tiny bites on the nape. The sensation traveled down every nerve she had and ended up between her legs. In another few minutes, he licked and nipped at her ear, suckling on the lobe, and had her dripping wet. The soft front panel of the thong was soaked.

Usually she would never get that hot without nipple play and it was incredible to even imagine how good that was going to be.

Beth began to rock under him, savoring the feel of that big, hard body covering her but not weighing her down. He slid down a hand under her, moving it over the front of her hips, until he could slip a probing finger into her wet thong panties.

Her clit just about jumped when he touched it. He

sighed with warm satisfaction into her ear. "There it is. You're as hard as I am."

"Yeah?" she murmured, giving a sensual, almost inaudible laugh. "But you've got a good nine inches on me. That feels like quite a cock."

"Like it?"

"Yes," she said.

"Want it?"

"You know I do," she whispered.

"It's almost in you," he whispered back. He continued to kiss and nip her neck while he pressed down a little more and played with her clit through the panties. The sheer size of his rod kept her ass cheeks apart.

Justin withdrew his finger and touched it to her lips. "Taste yourself. I want to see that pretty pink tongue again."

She darted it out and licked his finger daintily.

"You're delicious," he said.

"If you say so," she murmured. She turned her head a little more so she could open her mouth and suck on his finger, letting him slide it in and out.

His breathing got faster and his cock got stiffer.

"I can't wait to taste you myself," was the last thing he said before he rose up again. But he stayed essentially where he was, still straddling her, only lower down.

This time it was her ass that got the royal treatment.

Justin placed a big, warm hand on each cheek and began to alternate strokes and squeezes.

Not quite aware she was doing it, Beth began to moan.

"You like that, don't you?"

"Uh-huh. Oh . . . . ohhhh. Don't stop . . . ohhh."

Now he was pushing her hips down into the soft, ultracomfortable bed but doing it lightly. Still, the repeated press-and-release motion was incredibly exciting.

He stopped and she held her breath.

Staying on his knees, Justin moved out of the straddle and to the side. Then he got off the bed and she heard him walk around.

She stayed motionless. Whatever he wanted to do was fine with her.

Beth smiled a hidden smile when she felt his hands encircle her ankles and spread her legs with a swift, strong motion that left no doubt in her mind that he was staring at her juicy pussy. The thong front had been pulled between her labia, which were freshly shaved and exquisitely sensitive.

The powder-puff of springy curls she left at the top couldn't be seen in this position. Just plump, utterly feminine flesh split in two, begging to take cock.

He sighed as he looked his fill, holding her ankles more tightly than before.

"I wish you could see yourself like this," he said at last.

Beth raised her head but she didn't turn around. "I masturbate with a hand mirror sometimes, but I can't get this view. Glad you like it."

"Oh, I do." He didn't speak for just a beat. "Tell me about that. Tell me how you do it with a mirror."

He let go of her ankles and kneeled between them, rubbing her ass again, taking a voluptuous pleasure in doing it extra slowly.

"I use a dildo," she murmured. "I hold the mirror in the other hand. It's an antique dildo, made of sterling silver."

He chuckled in a very soft, very male voice.

"And where'd you get that?"

"In London, of all places. In one of those goddess shops."

"Sterling silver, huh? I'd love to see that penetrating your beautiful, slippery, pink pussy."

"It feels really good. And it gets warm quickly, almost hot. It's different from the plastic ones. It's not that big. Nowhere near as big as you."

"Just right for starters, hmm?"

She nodded.

"Go on."

Beth sighed with pleasure. He had begun to push her down into the bed again. She wasn't sure of how much more she could take before she flipped over and begged him to fuck her if he had to shred the thong to do it.

"Where was I?"

"The mirror."

"Right. I hold it so I can see all of my pussy and I get the silver dildo nice and slick on the outside. Then I put it most of the way in."

"Mmm," he said. "I can see you doing that."

"Then I tease my clit. If my pussy gets too excited, the dildo begins to rise and I push it back in. The base is kind of swollen and kind of flat so it can't go all the way in."

"Unlike me. Because I will. When you're ready."

Beth stretched luxuriously, enjoying the absolute best ass massage she'd ever had for as long as he was willing to do it.

"Then I put the mirror aside," she said after a while.

"Yes. And?" He knew better than to quit.

"I hold the base of the dildo and thrust it in and out while I pinch my clit. I try—" She faltered for a moment. Thinking about what she had done for solo pleasure combined with what he was doing to her right now was about to make her have an orgasm. And this was only the foreplay, she thought with wonder.

"Yes?"

"I try to make my fingers feel like tight lips on my clit. Sucking me and sucking me until I come—I want to come—oh!"

Several playful but pleasurably strong slaps on the ass from Justin put that thought out of her mind.

In another second, he had her turned over. And then she saw him naked.

He was much better than her imagination. The solid muscles of his torso were beautifully cut and sprinkled with fine, dark hair that twirled into a narrow trail down past his bellybutton, a sexy innie.

That pointed straight to his gorgeous, thick cock, which he was holding.

He let out a ragged breath. "I'm trying to get a grip. You make it hard, Beth."

He looked down, drinking her in. The bra had fallen off the bed when she turned and her breasts were still bouncing.

Justin let go of his cock and bent over her on all fours, sucking one nipple and caressing the other under his circling palm. He reversed his attentions until both breasts were wildly stimulated. She cupped them in her hands and squeezed to intensify the pleasure he was giving her, squeezed so that her fingernails dug into her own soft flesh, leaving little scratches.

Justin rose onto one hand and stopped her, kissing each mark lovingly and soothingly.

"Your tits are hotter than your ass, if that's possible," he murmured, stroking them next. "All of you is round and gorgeous. You're made for sex, do you know that?"

Beth shook her head. Her hair was tangled, hot underneath her. She was frustrated as hell, but enjoying this to the max.

"What do you want me to do next?"

Beth reached down and ran a finger over the front of his cock, down the part like a seam and up into the split part of the plumlike head, all the way down and then up again, over and over.

Her subtle stroking obviously excited him. He held still, but finally trembled when a pearly drop of pre-cum welled from the head and stayed there on the heated, swollen skin. She swiped it off with a fingertip and popped it into her mouth, savoring the thick saltiness taste while she looked into his mesmerized eyes.

"Get over my mouth," she whispered.

Justin did—the bed was huge and there was plenty of room for them to try a hundred different positions.

She looked up, her eyes half-closed with pure pleasure at the sight of everything he had between his legs but much closer now: heavy, big balls and that unbelievable cock.

She reached for a pillow, rolled it under her head, and began to lick him exactly as she guessed he wanted to be licked—thoroughly and sensually. She gave him long strokes along the shaft, teasing ones over the head, wet, eager laps over and around his balls until he began to moan, gripping his thighs until the veins on his hands stood out just to keep upright in the precise position for her to pleasure him orally like this.

He tasted so good. His smell was a combination of plain clean and pure man. She nuzzled between his legs, breathing it in. Then Beth stopped and encircled her fingers around his cock, pushing him back a little with one hand on his groin.

"I want this," she said. "Get ready."

Never had she seen a man get up, find a condom, and sheathe himself that fast. She got rid of the thong and the stockings in record time herself. Just watching him roll the nearly transparent latex on as his huge rod strained against his hand turned her on. A lot.

In another second Justin was over her on all fours, lifting one of her legs over his bent arm. She could just reach to help him position the head, but her hand was almost caught between their bodies when he suddenly rammed into her with a rough cry.

Oh, God. His eyes widened as he looked into hers, the sensation of that first, deep penetration thrilling them both.

"More," she begged. "Give it to me hard. I want it hard. I want you—"

His thrusts were charged with erotic energy, his body vibrating with it. Bucking under him, taking all nine very hot inches deep inside her pussy again and again, Beth wanted to scream with pleasure, but bit her lip instead.

His hand went around her chin and he gave her a deeply passionate kiss while he fucked her, capturing her moans.

"Go ahead," he growled when he stopped kissing her to take a breath. He didn't stop fucking her, though. He was rolling and rocking now, stimulating her clit with the pressure of his body in between thrusts. "We're on top of the world, girl. Make all the noise you want to."

Lost in the extreme pleasure of what he was doing. Beth let go completely. She brought her hips up to meet every downward thrust of his, clawing at his fine, hard ass, and begging for more.

She got it. She got everything she ever dreamed of

from a man who seemed to have come out of her wildest dreams. She screamed his name when he made her
come and he shouted hers.

   Slowly, slowly, the glorious feeling ebbed away. He
pulled out, did what he had to with the condom, turned
her on her side and curled completely around her, her
bare ass tucked against his groin and her breasts lifted
by one of his mighty arms. The other was stretched
over the long curve of her hip, heavy with his weariness.
From the very male and beginning-to-be-scratchy chin
that rested on her head to her toes, which rested on the
tops of his big warm feet, she felt protected and utterly
satisfied.

   On top of the world? Not quite, she thought. She
felt more like she was on top of the universe as she
drifted off, half in love, blissed out. Somewhere around
midnight, they woke up and did it again. Only better.

   The long moan of a ship's horn startled her out of a
very deep sleep. Beth eased out of Justin's cocooning
embrace—he was in back of her, which made it easy—
and wriggled to look at the clock. Five-oh-five a.m.
Just before daybreak. There was no light coming from
the windows to speak of—they were uncurtained, it
was too high up for anyone to see in. But there was a
light in the room that puzzled her, an ambient glow
that was a deep, indefinable blue. It didn't seem to be
coming from anywhere in particular. But what if it
woke Justin? They would both have to get up in time to
shower and she would have to dash home to change
her clothes, she thought drowsily.

   Gee. She felt kind of proud. She hadn't had to do the
Stayed-Out-All-Night-Wearing-The-Clothes-I-Slept-

In Walk of Shame in front of coworkers for a long time.

Beth rubbed her eyes, thinking about it. Maybe it would be best if she left first, got a taxi before the early-rising traders got down to the Wall Street area, even before the coffee vendors arrived in their rattling, quilted-steel carts.

Yeah. Good idea.

She rolled over to look at Justin. He had flopped back into the pillows, still naked, a hand on his balls and one big arm over his head. He was still asleep but . . .

What the hell was going on?

The odd light in the room was coming from him. She stared in wonder. Patterns of shimmering color, moving in waves like the aurora borealis, moved over his skin as if he were lit from deep inside. As if he was hollow. As if he was made of light.

What the hell?

Beth's mouth opened, but no words came out. His eyes opened slowly as if he felt hers on him. Eyes that had been blue times two were now blue times ten.

She looked at him a few seconds longer, fainted, and fell right off the bed.

Dawn was breaking when she came to. She was nestled into the pillows, on her back with the covers drawn up and tucked in. He was sitting beside her, stroking her thoughtfully, a troubled look on his face.

He looked exactly like himself again, wearing a cotton robe.

"Justin!" She struggled to sit up.

"I'm here, baby," he soothed her. "Right here." He took her in his arms and she clung to him.

"I had the weirdest dream," she said. "I woke up in the middle of the night and I turned around and you—you were lit up from inside. The colors of the light kept changing."

"Shhh," he said, stroking her hair.

Beth looked up at him. "Do you have a dream book or something? I know they're ridiculous, but I'd love a little insight on that one."

"I can understand why you would."

"It seemed so real." She searched his face. His eyes were the same as when she'd first seen them: beach-glass blue. Not blue times two or ten. Just normal blue eyes, really beautiful blue eyes. Everything about him was beautiful. His body, naked or clothed. His very male charm. His unpretentiousness. His skill at love-making. She was never, ever, going to forget the sex they'd had last night. It must have unhinged her mind a little and triggered that crazy dream.

Justin sighed and let her go. "It was real."

"Come on," she said. "It was not. Just tell me I'm not going crazy. That's all I need to hear."

"No, you're not going crazy."

"Well, then. I guess you fucked my brains out."

He shook his head. "Ugly phrase. Never liked it. Didn't do it."

"Okay, I know when I'm being humored." She pushed the covers aside. "What's for breakfast? I gotta get out of here, get home, and get changed."

Justin rose so she could get up. "No rush. I told the receptionist we were going out early to scout a sign site, and that we would be in late. Let her do the explaining."

"We can't come in at the same time, Justin. People will know."

He studied her for a long moment. "You may be right. Go look in the mirror."

"Tell me what I'm going to see. Pouty, kissed-up lips? Rosy cheeks?"

He nodded.

Beth rose and dragged a sheet from the bed to serve as a robe. Uninhibited as the sex had been, the light of day still demanded a little modesty. She let a couple of yards of sheet trail after her like the train on a wedding dress, and it wound around the doorjamb when she went into the bathroom.

She peered into the mirror. Sure enough, she looked like she'd been kissed, good and hard and often. No surprise there. Her eyelashes were glumpy with left-over mascara and her lids were puffy. Her hair was a hopeless snarl. It was kind of funny, though, that she also looked happy and satisfied and womanly. Beth gave herself a scrunched-up, screwy little smile.

"See it yet?" Justin called.

She stretched her chin out, looking for a hickey on her neck. The skin was smooth and unmarred. "See what?"

A flash of moving light on her face caught her eye. She tried to focus on it, but it was small and kept moving. To her cheek. To her forehead. Shimmering. The colors in it kept changing.

Beth saw Justin standing behind her in the mirror. He nodded. "Full disclosure," he said. "I'm made of light. It seems to be catching."

Beth whirled around and the train of sheet caught on the doorjamb tightened all the rest of it and made her lose her balance. She fell into his arms.

Justin held her, looked at her ruefully and dropped a kiss on her nose. "It wasn't a dream, Beth." Right before her eyes he started turning colors again. Glowing. He felt just the same. Big and warm and strong. But he wasn't the same. She pummeled his chest. It didn't echo and he wasn't hollow. She stopped and looked up into his eyes. They were turning an otherworldly shade of blue, little by little.

"Explain!" she shrieked.

"Like I said, I'm made of light."

She was willing to believe it by now. He had stood stoically in the bathroom while she did her damnedest to beat him up, changing colors on her again and again. When she'd scratched at him, trying to draw blood, he'd glowed red and his eyes had flashed.

Beth had bagged it at that point. She'd run into the living room, collapsed into the sofa and curled up into a ball of misery. His gentle and very real caresses had made her uncurl eventually.

"I wanted to come to Earth. The stratosphere was kind of boring. Nothing to do but wave at Swedes and Inuit walrus-hunters and a couple of Canadians now and then."

"How did you end up in New York?"

Justin shrugged. "It's pretty fucking bright. Easy to blend in."

"So's Vegas."

"Yeah, but who wants to go to Vegas? The whole city smells like an ashtray. And I don't like to gamble."

"Gotcha." It did make sense. She hated gambling herself.

"So, I zoomed around in the skyscrapers for a while. This was a few years ago. Lit up a few new ones that hadn't been turned on yet, just for fun."

Beth looked at him curiously. "Is that you?"

"What?"

"When the spire of the Chrysler Building switches on or the Empire State Building turns different colors, is that you?"

Justin smiled. "I wish. No, lighting designers do those buildings. And I guess one of the building crew gets to flip the switch. No, that's not me."

Beth had a point to make but it was kind of escaping her. What he did do was enough to boggle anyone's mind. Oh, yeah. It came back to her. "But that's not me. I may have caught a little piece of your rainbow but I'm still only human. While you're zooming around in the sky, I'm on the sidewalk, just being ordinary. Walking around with the pigeons."

Justin looked interested. "Hey, why is it that New York pigeons hardly ever fly?"

"Because they can't get off the ground with a whole bagel in their beak," she snapped.

He laughed. "Good one."

Beth didn't know whether to cry or howl or what. "I wish I could fly," she said all of a sudden. "I'd be outa here in a heartbeat."

He gave her a sad look. "Don't say that. It's not that big a deal. By my standards, you're the lucky one. I wanted to be inside a real body. I was doing too much zooming around the universe, if you really want to know."

"Doing what, exactly?"

"Causing trouble and raising hell. Joyriding on comets. Kinda got old after a while. I didn't have anyone to do it with."

"Oh."

Justin slumped down on the sofa, looking unhappy, and didn't say anything more for a little while.

What a trip. Even a man with superpowers who

traveled at the speed of light—who was light—was just a great big baby when he didn't get his way. "Sulk if you want to." Beth got up, grabbing at the sheet. "I'm going to take a shower."

She went back into the bathroom and looked very, very hard at herself, naked, all over. The moving spot of light seemed to have vanished. Good riddance.

She turned the shower on full blast and stood under the hot, pulsing jets of water, hoping it would wash away all trace of her contact with him.

Then she began to cry. The shower washed away the tears. She didn't want that, not at all. His touch, his lovemaking, his born-yesterday eagerness—born yesterday. From what he'd just told her when they sat on the sofa, it was literally true. And she had to go and practically fall in love with him. She bawled like a baby. From what she remembered of the properties of light, he could be born yesterday and live forever. It was everlasting. He was everlasting.

She was not.

But there was something about him that she had to have. They'd worked together, and been pals; they'd slept together, and now they were lovers. No matter the circumstances, she felt different around him. Brighter. Her heart felt genuinely happy for the first time in a long while. It wasn't just thudding along, it was really beating.

Well, she resolved, as she toweled off, she was going to enjoy this as long it lasted. When she came out of the bedroom to find him, she was dressed in a shirt of his that went down to her knees.

Justin had gotten dressed while she was in the shower and was pottering around the kitchen. He looked at her and ventured a smile.

"Not mad at me anymore?"

She shook her head. "I want some coffee. And more explanations."

"You want milk and sugar with your explanations?"

"No, I take mine straight up." Beth eased on a high stool and leaned on the counter. "First of all, where'd you get the body?"

He poured two cups of black coffee and pushed one over to her.

"Friend of mine at MIT. Brilliant guy but a serious wacko. I used to hang out with him when I was in a photon state. But I'll explain that later."

Beth narrowed her eyes. "Why?"

"I just want to begin at the beginning."

"Okay."

"Beth, you have to understand that light takes a lot of forms. And humans can only see a small fraction of it. Being in a body and having a brain is really new to me. A whole different set of rules applies."

"Uh-huh. I think I understand."

"It's not like I only wanted to roam around the galaxies, you know."

She shot him a not entirely sympathetic look. "Poor you. No comets and UFOs and asteroids to play with."

Justin sighed. "You know, when you said you loved comic books and superheroes, I thought you'd get what I was all about, if it ever came to that."

"I do. In my book, you're not a hero."

He drank half his coffee in one go. "Maybe I'm not. But I felt like I needed to be contained. To be pure light is just so—so amorphous."

"Explain."

"Sometimes I'm wave energy that no one on earth can see—no one human, anyway. I'm not so sure about cats."

Beth thought of old Freddy and how he stared at

nothing for a long, long time. "You could be right about cats."

"Who knows? Anyway, getting back to what you were asking about, sometimes I was a sunspot or rays of sunlight that hit the earth."

"Which did you prefer?"

Justin thought it over. "It was kind of cool being sunlight. Every woman who turned her face to me got a kiss and didn't know it. The office chicks grabbing a few rays before they had to get back to their cubicles. The nice old grandmas who just dug being warm and outside. The teenagers with all that glossy hair I could shine on. Swinging, bouncing. And I helped out on a lot of modeling shoots, of course."

"Did you like the models?" Beth asked, disliking the jealous edge in her voice.

Justin shook his head. "They don't do anything for me. Too skinny. They complained that the lights made them sweat."

"Was that you?

He gave her a sheepish look. "I got into big lights sometimes. On photo shoots and movie sets. Not table lamps or anything."

"I see."

"Could we rewind this discussion?"

"Sure. Let the sun shine in."

Justin gave her a bad-boy grin. "Let me explain. I could shine on beautiful girls on the beach, get them to roll over. Glistening butts. Lotioned-up boobs. The more I shone, the creamier they got. It was making me insanely horny. But that was as far as I could go."

"Right. Got it. You know," she hesitated, looking at him with a little more respect, "sometimes when I was sunning myself I could swear the warmth felt like an invisible hand moving over me."

"Yeah," he said with satisfaction. "That's what I'm talking about."

"And when the clouds got in between it used to make me really annoyed," Beth added.

"Then it would have been time for a cloud smack-down. I always tried to dissolve them. Or ask my best friend, Wind, if he wanted to move them along."

"And did he want to?"

Justin lifted up both hands in a who-knows gesture. "Wind does what he wants. If what you want coincides with that, then count yourself lucky. Know what I mean?"

"I don't know him. So, no."

"Depended on what he was up to. You know, if he was playing with summer skirts in Chicago or making a sarong blow open in Tahiti, then he wouldn't bother."

"The two of you are double trouble for woman-kind."

Justin eased onto a stool next to her. "Maybe. You're cute. Come here often?"

"Once might be enough." She looked into his eyes, which were plain blue again. He slipped a hand under the part of the shirt that covered her thigh and caressed her there, moving up but not too far up.

He came close enough to nuzzle her neck, and she let him. When he raised her head, she'd turned her face to catch a kiss. He gave her one, slow and deep and easy and lightly flavored with coffee. Then they bumped noses and he smiled at her, the dimple flickering in his cheek like he wasn't sure she was going to smack it off him or not.

The smile stayed where it was, though.

God, she could love a guy who was sunny in the

morning, instead of grumpy and foul-breathed—oh, fuck me, she thought. How ironic that she'd found him at last.

"Could I have more coffee? And a croissant, if you have one."

"Blackberry jam, or strawberry? How about honey? You look good in my shirt."

"Thanks," she said, fluffing out her nearly dry hair. "I'll try not to get jam on it. I'll take strawberry."

"I don't care if you do mess up my shirt. I want you to be happy and I'm an easygoing guy."

"You and Wind both," she said. "Let me guess. He, like you, fell to earth once upon a time. What name does he go by?" She was beginning to enjoy this. It beat reality, at least for a while.

Justin went about making her breakfast, getting out butter and the jam, and putting a pat of one and a spoonful of the other on a plate. He took out a croissant from a bakery bag—it looked like a real one, with multiple buttery layers and fragile flakes—and put it in the microwave on a paper towel to warm up for a few seconds. Then he leaned across the counter to kiss her again.

"You're so pretty in the morning, with no makeup and your hair off your face. I can't help myself. So . . . where was I? Oh yeah, he decided to go by Windham Devane—" He stopped talking when the microwave beeped.

He took out the croissant and slid it onto the plate, handing it to her. "Don't get me wrong. It wasn't always about chasing women for Wind. Sometimes he was at Birdland with old J.T. Carten when J.T. was playing the saxophone, giving him the extra breath for cool grooves. Sure worked for him. Women just have to hear good music that makes their bodies move and they're, like, all over a guy. Music gets them way down deep, in a secret place. So Wind was getting something I couldn't."

"What do you mean?"

"You ever see the sun in a jazz club? They're like caverns. Most of those guys don't even get out of bed until nightfall."

"You have a point."

"So I could hang with Wind during the day but I was pretty much limited to the great outdoors."

"Hard to believe that a good-time guy—" she stopped in midsentence—"or a good-time being or whatever the hell it is you are, didn't go out at night," Beth said.

"I just didn't. No chick was going to throw her leg over a lamp, if you know what I mean. And I didn't have a body then."

Beth giggled.

"Anyway, when J.T. sat out a set, Wind could make his sax moan and whisper and cry just like he did—it was emotional, not just physical."

"Got it. The women went wild for him. You were frustrated."

Justin stole a bite of her croissant and dipped it in the jam, then ate it thoughtfully.

"He and I discussed getting our own bodies, but that wasn't easy. I hadn't met up with the MIT guy yet, so we figured we had to wait for the right ones. And they had to be unoccupied but not dead."

Beth almost finished her croissant before he swiped the rest, just in case he didn't have another one. It was really good. "You should have tried a frat house. It's full of brainless bodies in reasonably good condition."

"We didn't think of that."

"So what happened?" She looked at Justin as the last bite went into her mouth.

"Wind got to know this dancer, a great guy, a real wild man who performed at Birdland sometimes. One night he jumped so high he didn't come back down, mentally speaking. But his body was there and Wind slipped in."

Beth nodded. "Wow. How'd that work out?"

Justin put the dishes and cups into the sink. "Eventually the dancer did come back and Wind got evicted. He did a deal with a basketball player from the West Fourth Street team next. Sometimes he has the body, sometimes the basketball player does. I understand that Wind likes being really tall."

"I bet," Beth said. "So how'd you find yours?"

"The MIT guy wanted a challenge. He called in a few favors, found someone at Harvard, a young guy who was a professor of Eastern religions. He transcended physical reality on his way to nirvana and he didn't want to be saddled with this body or reincarnated so I got it."

"Permanently?"

"Yup. Works really well. Added some custom-built improvements, though."

"So I noticed," Beth said wryly.

"It felt good right from the start. I had to figure out how not to burn it up. I scorched a few shirts when I started, burned holes in my boxers, that kind of thing."

"I'm not sure I want to know how," Beth said.

"What can I say? I'm a man on fire."

She shook her head, but she smiled anyway.

"Are we done with the questions? I actually would like to get some work done today." He slid off the stool.

"Excuse me?" Beth said. "You just announce you're

made of light and you used to not even have a body and I don't get to ask questions? You plant your butt right back on that stool."

"Yes, ma'am." He did as she asked.

"Where does all the money come from? You seem to have an awful lot of it."

"Energy futures. I played the market. Did really well, got out while I was ahead."

"That explanation is way too short."

He smirked. "It happens to be totally true. I paid cash for this place."

"Wait until you see mine," she said with a groan.

"I'd love to."

"It's just me and Freddy and—"

"Who's Freddy?"

"My ancient cat. And Miss Boom Bah. She's my coatrack. I'm not bringing you home."

"Have it your way," he said reluctantly. "But it still doesn't seem fair."

"You know what, Justin? Life isn't fair. You being an everlasting being really isn't fair to me. I can't get a new body like you can. If you're mortal, it's one to a customer."

He looked at her worriedly. "You sure about that?"

"Yes!' she said with instant exasperation. "Enjoy me while it lasts."

"Does that work in reverse? Are you going to enjoy me?"

"Yes," she said a lot more slowly. "I had a good cry in the shower about it and that—that's pretty much what I decided. I mean, it's crazy, but I've been crazy before about guys who didn't hold a candle to—who couldn't outshine—I give up," she cried out, "they weren't you. And I want you. For as long as I can have you. I may wake up in Bellevue with a team of shrinks at my side when it's all over, but for right now, I want you."

"That's a start," Justin said.

"When I'm with you, my heart feels . . . light. That's the only way I can explain it."

"Works for me."

Beth patted his cheek. "But please try not to turn colors and glow in public."

"I never have," he said. "That happened after you and I had sex. I don't know why, though. Want me to ask the MIT guy?"

"No way." She looked at him, aghast. A strange man with a pocket protector finding out all the fascinating details of what she liked to do in bed? Absolutely no freaking way. "This is strictly between you and me. No one else is going to know about this."

"Okay," Justin said. "I promise. No one will."

3

"Let's get going. I want to take you to Times Square. Part of the installation is up."

He was done explaining, evidently.

Beth looked down at what she was wearing. "I guess I'd better change."

"Why? You look great."

"Will there be other SpectraSign people there?"

"Maybe." He narrowed his eyes at her. "So?"

"I could just embroider *I'm fucking the boss* over the pocket of your shirt in case they can't figure it out."

"You worry too much."

She leaned in close to make sure he understood. "Listen, Mr. Born Yesterday, you have never owned a real live company before. Gossip travels faster than the speed of light."

"Really?" he said, genuinely curious. "Can I look up the physics on that? I don't think Einstein covered the subject."

Beth shook her head dismissively. "What else can I borrow of yours? Got something that doesn't look so morning-after?"

"Sweats?"

"Okay." He gestured for her to follow him and they headed back to his bedroom, where he pulled open a dresser drawer filled with neatly folded sweatshirts and pants. "I'll find something."

"Have at." Justin sat on the bed, looking around the room but mostly at her. Suddenly he leaned forward and came up with a scrap of feminine lingerie. Her bra, thong, and stockings fit right into his hand, all crumpled up. "Do I have to give these back?"

Beth held up one of the smaller sweatshirts in a nondescript gray. It would do.

"I need the bra right now. You can wash the rest and then give them back."

He grinned wolfishly. "I would be honored to see these dripping from my shower rack. Just seeing that thong on you was enough to blow my mind forever."

"Yeah," she said, unbuttoning the shirt. "That's nice." She put it on the bed and extracted the bra from his unwilling hand.

Justin stared, fascinated, as she clasped it, spun it around her waist, and flipped it up over her boobs. "Mind if I drool?"

"Aren't you the one who wanted to get going?"

He sighed. "Yeah."

She slipped on the sweatshirt and looked in the drawer for black pants that wouldn't look too weird with the dress shoes she'd worn last night. The sweatshirt would fit under her jacket and she could buy a bright scarf from a street vendor on the way. Something in neon green, perhaps. No one would look at anything but a neon green scarf, especially if it had long fringe. And it might be windy up on the roof where the installation was in progress, so she had a reason to be wearing it.

Done rationalizing, nearly dressed, she looked around for her shoes, wiggling her bare feet in his plush bedroom carpet.

He looked at them fondly. "Want your toes sucked?"

"Not right now." She rumpled his hair and he turned his head to give her a love bite on the meaty part of her thumb. Look at us, she marveled silently. Acting like honeymooners. Even after just one night, it felt like that to be with him.

But there was a part of having sex with Justin that was troublesome. What had he said? *It seems to be catching.*

She'd assumed she'd been able to wash off the dash of moving light on her face, but that was a pretty big assumption. True, the dash had seemed more superficial than his full-body light show, but she didn't know enough about the nature of the phenomenon to be totally sure. Versed in useless comic-book lore, she knew it wouldn't come in handy now—hey, it never had, except for online arguments with fanboys and other maniacs. And her marketing degree from Hofstra hadn't required physics.

In a word, she might be fucked if they ever fucked again. So they weren't going to until she got that aspect of the connection between them figured out.

Justin was still sitting there, giving her adoring looks, her dirty underwear and stockings forgotten in his hand. Why oh why did she have to fall for a cute guy from the wrong side of the asteroid belt? It really, really wasn't fair.

Beth bent down to plant an absentminded kiss on his forehead. "Let's get going," she said when she straightened up. Then she spotted her shoes under the nightstand and slipped them on. "Sweatpants and high heels," she said. "It's a look."

"I love it on you," Justin said loyally.

It was breezy up on the rooftop. Beth pulled a mouthful of long, neon-green fringe out of her mouth and tucked the ends of the scarf into her jacket. Justin was checking the installation with two guys from the SpectraSign tech department, so she was free to walk around. A New York City roof was an interesting place to be when you had nothing else important to do.

She went near the edge of the rooftop, looking out over a low wall rounded with asphalt tiles and decades' worth of slapped-on tar. There were pigeons perched on it, cooing and bobbing their heads, stepping to keep their balance in the breeze. One wrinkly, pink bird foot stepped on another and they all flapped in an irritated way. But basically, they were just like most New Yorkers. They got along somehow.

Times Square was teeming with people, tourists, office workers, oddballs. It was like watching a very colorful river that twisted around and doubled back. A river that had yellow taxis bobbing in the middle of the current.

Justin called her name softly as he came up behind her, and she turned around. "Hey. Didn't want to startle you so near the edge of the roof."

"Thanks," she said.

He leaned in a little closer like he was going to give her a kiss, but she glared at him and shook her head.

"Right," he said, glancing at the tech guys, who hadn't seen a thing. "Almost forgot. Sorry." A sign rigger had joined the two men and was helping them set up panels that would eventually become part of the main sign.

He got closer to the roof edge and looked over. "There's our pedestrian survey person." He waved and Beth looked into the surging crowds. A young woman in a baseball cap holding a clipboard was waving back, a clicker in her hand.

"What does she do again?"

"She counts people passing by and divides them by gender. That way we have an idea who sees the sign."

"Eyeballs are everything," Beth said wryly.

He unrolled the layouts he'd kept under his arm. It flapped wildly in the breeze and he set it down on the curved rooftop wall, pinning it with spread-out fingers. Beth got close enough to help him so he could have a hand free.

She held down a corner and he pointed to the first panel. "The model enters here, in the first video panel, walking from the background. Then," he pointed to the second panel, "he comes in closer and he gets bigger and bigger and starts to fill all the panels."

"Oh, boy."

"Then he towers over Times Square, throbbing with manliness," Justin said. "You can let go. What do you think?"

"It's okay." She raised her hand and the layout rolled itself back up into his hand. "Oughta sell plenty of jeans."

"That's the idea." One of the tech guys called him and he looked over that way. "Gotta go. You good over here?"

"Yeah. I'm having fun. Don't worry about me."

Justin winked at her and turned around.

Beth resumed her absentminded viewing of the panorama of Times Square. This would have to be one hell of a sign to compete with what was already up.

Her personal favorite—the giant, steaming Cup O' Noodles—was gone, replaced by an extravaganza of rippling colors that was eye-popping even in daylight. Half-naked women in high heels seemed to stalk over rooftops, eyed disdainfully or ignored by male underwear models on different billboards.

Giant cell phones revolved like objects of worship; gazed at by the happy customers of online dating sites. Music, candy, Broadway shows, movie posters, an endless digital ribbon of repeating headlines—it all moved, shouted, tickled the eye. If the Blue Blaze sign managed to stand out, it would be a marketing miracle.

Several hours later, they were seated at a table for two at Capsouto Frères. Beth looked around the serene space. Linen tablecloths, pale cream walls that glowed softly, classic menu—this place was posh and nothing like the Cowgirl Hall of Fame on Hudson Street, where she usually ate out if she was going to splurge.

No margaritas in mason jars here. No lethal chili. No vanilla-ice-cream fake potatoes dusted with cocoa for a nice brown skin and topped with whipped cream and peppermint chives.

She slipped a spoon into her onion soup, lifting up the bread and cheese crust to get at the oniony broth underneath, sipping it daintily. Then she looked up at him. "Why are you smiling like that?"

"I didn't know you could eat with utensils," he laughed.

"Oh. Well, I can. And a fork makes an excellent catapult for a roll." She took one out of the breadbasket and positioned it on the curving tines. "Don't tempt me."

"Okay, fair enough."

They polished off their soup and just sat there looking at each other for several awkward moments. Hot soup, good wine, unqualified adoration—a triple threat to her sanity.

"So." Justin set an elbow on the table and rested his chin in one hand. "What do you want to do tonight?"

"I should go home," she said primly.

"And where's that again?"

"Near Hudson Street. Not all that far from here."

He looked really happy about that. In fact, his eyes started to glow.

"Don't do that," she said hastily.

"I'm just sitting here looking at you."

Beth looked around the restaurant. "No, you're glowing at me. Any minute now you're going to look like a sign in Times Square."

The intensity in his eyes faded. "Do you honestly think anyone in New York would notice if I did?"

"They might."

He straightened up. "And is that, like, a bad reflection on you?"

"No, Justin." She fussed with her silverware and took the roll off the fork, tossing it back in the breadbasket. "It's just that—I don't know."

"Beth," he said. "You're not exactly making yourself clear."

She took a nice, deep, calming breath. "The light thing just makes me nervous, that's all. We have to talk about it."

Justin grinned and looked very pleased. "Hey, this

is my first we-have-to-talk moment. I guess I'm a real guy after all."

"That's exactly my point," she said, a little more crisply than she'd intended. "You're not."

Justin blew out his breath. "Last night you seemed happy enough. Maybe I don't have a whole hell of a lot of experience, but that seemed like great sex to me."

Another burning question that hadn't occurred to her until then. How had he learned everything he knew? He hadn't been in that gorgeous body all that long, even if it was permanently his. Beth surveyed him. He sure did look real. Big chest, broad shoulders, ribbed sweater. Tousled dark hair, crinkly eyes, dimple. All the damn details added up perfectly. She'd seen several women check him out, cast a disapproving eye at the black sweatpants accessorized with the neon-green scarf that she still had on, and go right back to poking at their collapsed soufflés.

There was one at the very next table. Beth smiled thinly at her and the watching woman returned it, giving her a very small smile that was even thinner than hers—a trimmed fingernail of a smile. The woman, who had been eating alone, got up and sauntered to the coat check area while the maitre d' fussed over her and took care of the bill.

Beth turned her full attention to Justin. "How and where did you learn to make love like that?"

"Um, the look and learn method."

"You perv."

He held up his hands in a whaddya-want-from-me gesture. "Hey, I was sunlight. Even moonlight, sometimes. That's just a reflection, really. I was everywhere, all the time. But invisible. You see a lot, you pick up a few pointers."

Beth frowned.

"You weren't objecting to anything I did," he said slyly.

"Okay, granted." She had to concede the point. "It was great. And you are who you are. I can't argue with that."

"So what's bothering you?"

Beth leaned back as the waiter silently set down their entrées. She wasn't hungry at all. Justin picked up his fork and knife and went to work "The light that was on me—or in me—for a little while. You said it seemed to be catching."

He nodded and chewed.

"Is it?"

She watched him swallow and cut another bite. "Dunno," he said before his mouth was filled with food again.

"So is it theoretically possible that I could somehow leave my body the way you entered yours, and become pure light?"

He thought that over, then pushed his food away. "Guess we'd better get this wrapped up to go."

"Fine with me." She hadn't even touched hers.

He motioned the waiter over and made some excuse about having to leave. Then he turned his attention back to her. "Anything's theoretically possible. Whether it would actually happen is hard to say. The sexual connection did seem to trigger it."

Beth nodded, fixing him with a meaningful look.

Justin reached for his wallet and pulled out a credit card. "I think I know where this is going."

"Good."

"You don't want to have sex again. You're afraid you'll dissolve or something. What's that called, having boundary issues?"

"Something like that. Justin, I've never been outside my body and I don't think I want to be. What if I can't get back in?"

He folded his arms across his chest. "Out-of-body experiences are great. We can take an extended vacation in the galaxy while you get used to it. You know, fly to the moon, cruise a nebula or two. Just you and me."

"I don't want to see a nebula. Not up close, anyway."

His eyes got dreamy. "You sure? They're really something. Very female. Pulsing, mysterious, beautiful—"

"No!"

"Okay, okay."

The waiter came back with two containers in a plastic bag and Justin settled the bill. They got their coats and left.

"Can I walk you home, Beth?"

She still didn't want him to see where she lived. Sure, he could Mapquest her address from her resume and find out for himself, but inviting him in was something else again. It was too intimate, somehow.

You let him inside your body, said a little voice in her head. *It doesn't get any more intimate than that.* She decided to ignore the little voice.

"Let's walk along the river," she suggested. "I need to clear my head."

In a few short blocks they were by the Hudson. The usual ships and boats drifted by and there was even a kayaker, paddling in a steady rhythm that made her wish she was out on the water too, bobbing along.

They kept to the pedestrian part of the path, letting the bicyclists and rollerbladers whiz past. Justin shortened his long stride to match her pace, swinging the bag and looking her way. "So where do we go from here?" he said after a while.

"I have to fold laundry and feed Freddy and play

with him a little. You can keep the food. I probably wouldn't eat it."

He frowned, not looking too thrilled at playing second fiddle to laundry and a geriatric cat. "Okay, Beth. If that's how you want it."

He seemed to be waiting for an invitation, which she couldn't bring herself to give. "I guess that means I'm going home to the Bolt Building," he finally said. "Alone."

Beth nodded.

He stopped and looked directly into her eyes. She drew in her breath with a gasp. They were a fiery blue, fueled with emotion. "You don't want to make that connection again, do you?"

"Not just yet," she said after a beat. "Not until I know more. I have to be sure that I'm in control of what happens to me. Mortal or not, it's the only body I have and I don't want to lose it."

The fire in his eyes died down some. "I think I understand. You mean no sex for right now. But you don't mean never again."

Beth breathed out a great big sigh of relief. "That's right."

"And we're still going to work together and pal around and talk until one in the morning and stuff like that."

"Well, yeah," she said cautiously. "Unless that gets the light show going again."

"It's fine with me if you want to chill for a while. Although we could try just oral sex. Me doing you."

"Do we have to have this conversation right here? Right now?"

"Let me know the second you want to have any kind of sex again." Justin swung the bag dangerously high, looking really happy. "Then you have a deal."

"Careful," she said. "Your entrée is going to end up in the Hudson."

He turned around in joyful circles, his arms outstretched, whirling and whirling. "I don't care! It's fish!"

"Yeah, but it's filleted. It'll never swim again," Beth said and smiled awkwardly at a little old lady passing by on an honest-to-God giant tricycle. "He's nice but he's nuts," she said to her.

"Enjoy it while you're young, dear." The old lady pedaled away, heading north.

"Stop it," Beth hissed at Justin. "You're so impulsive. Why are you so goddamned happy?"

He stopped whirling and enfolded her in his arms, giving her a huge hug. "Because you gave me a second chance. It may be a snowball's chance in hell, but I'm taking it."

Beth opened her mouth to argue and got herself a sensual kiss instead. She gave into it, half enjoying it and half wondering whether she was shimmering. The sensations racing through her one after another sure made it feel that way.

"Shtop it," she said around his tongue.

He shook his head and kissed her harder, and she gave in. Justin was a fabulous kisser. She could always do a light check on herself afterward with a pocket mirror, just in case. They could probably still do this even if they didn't have sex for a while.

His tenderness and his skill and his being so damn hot for her added up to a kiss that was just too good to stop.

A bicyclist whizzed by, bent way over his handlebars and so close they could hear his chain clicking, and Justin pulled her out of harm's way, right up against him. He lifted his head, about to shout after the jerk when Beth spotted the old lady on the giant tricycle coming back.

"Don't curse," she said.

He heard Beth just in time to yell, "Eff you, you effing eff!" after the cyclist, who was long gone.

The old lady beamed at Justin as she approached, picking up speed. "That crazy asshole almost sideswiped me!" she shouted. "I'm going to run over his skinny butt if I can catch up with him!"

They watched her head south, pedaling madly, bent on vengeance.

"Go, granny, go," Beth murmured. She looked up at Justin again. "Where were we?"

He bent his head to hers and got right back to kissing her.

"Ahhh." Justin eventually came up for air but he wasn't letting her get much. He was holding her very close. "I'm blissing out on you—your smell, your nearness, everything. I can't get enough."

"This *is* a public place," she reminded him.

"But no one stops long enough to see anything."

Beth laughed and pushed him away. "Let's do something else. Walk. Jog. I don't care."

Justin thought for a minute. "Tell you what. How about we watch a basketball game that makes the Knicks look like ninety-eight-pound weaklings? And it's free."

"Okay. You're on. Where?"

"West Fourth Street over in the Village. Not that much of a walk from here."

"Fine." She took the hand that wasn't holding their bagged entrées and they headed that way. Then she stopped. "Hey, wait a minute. Is that where your friend Windham Devane plays basketball?"

"That's right."

"I remember you saying he was on the West Fourth Street team."

Justin squeezed her hand in his. "He's amazing. All the guys are."

"Of course, Wind is the one who's a little bit more than human," she reminded him.

"He only uses his powers for good," Justin said seriously.

Beth snorted. "What, have you been reading comic books out there in the stratosphere?"

"No. But I read some over a few shoulders when I was just pure light. It's fun. I pick up stuff quickly."

"Guess so."

"Ask my genius buddy at MIT. The man knows how to mind-meld. I acquired the equivalent of a college education because of him in one night. It was a long night, but that's all it took."

"Uh-huh." She looked up at Justin, who was humming under his breath. "I sense there's more."

"There is. It involved a bong and Wikipedia. He got high and figured out how to download the whole damn website into my brain."

"Holy cow. No wonder you're such a know-it-all, Justin."

"I am not. I learn something new every day," he said with a little-boy grin.

On his rugged face, it was heart-meltingly effective. Beth didn't feel like arguing the point. It was just too peaceful to do anything but be together and be happy. The streets of the Village were relatively quiet, the old glassed-in restaurant fronts radiating a warm, golden glow onto the cobblestone parts.

She stopped to pet a dog sitting outside one, tied to

the tree while he looked inside anxiously at his master, who was paying for an order of takeout.

"Be right there, Beau," the man inside called to the dog.

Beau's tail thumped in anticipation. She gave his ears a final fondle and strolled on with Justin. There were a few other couples out, hand in hand, just like them.

They went down Bleecker Street and walked past the guitar store, stopping to admire what was in the window. A steel guitar was front and center, hand-engraved with a wild profusion of vines and flowers.

"Look at that," she breathed. "I've never seen a guitar like that in my life."

"Want it?"

She leaned on his arm, looking at the glittering beauty of the instrument and laughing. "I can't play a note. But thanks."

"You could learn."

"Not well enough to justify what that probably costs."

Justin bent down, looking for a price tag. "Uh . . . twenty thousand dollars."

"Yeah. Not for me." She sighed appreciatively, gave it one more look, and tugged at his hand to get him to move on.

Bleecker Street still had the small shops that made New York so great, she thought wistfully. The big chains hadn't taken over every single storefront. There were still grocers with fruit piled in neat pyramids on bright green racks, and still a couple of mom-and-pop stores. Okay, so what if mom and pop were selling flavored condoms? Small businesses had to do what they could.

Aglow with nostalgia, she got him to the intersection of Sixth and they dodged the onrushing taxis to cross the wide avenue, ignoring the blaring horns. A block or so up to the left were the West Fourth Street courts and she could hear a raucous game in progress even from here.

A crowd milled around the high chain-link fence, shouting and encouraging the players.

"There's Wind," Justin said.

Beth saw a tall, lanky black guy spring into the air and seem to hover there, the ball spinning on the tips of his fingers. He threw and the basketball went through the hoop in almost the same second.

Below it a bunch of shoving, screaming players tried to take control of it as the crowd roared. Someone she couldn't see passed it to Wind, and he handled it as deftly as before, scoring another point.

They were close enough now to see the game. Great-looking but sweaty guys in headbands, baggy shorts, and loose tanks, all different heights and different colors, slammed into each other, playing with a fierce passion that their audience shared.

Eventually Wind detached himself from the crowd and went over to the corner of the fence to grab a Gatorade, exchanging high fives and more complicated handshakes along the way.

He uncapped it and literally poured a full bottle of liquid down his throat in one go, swallowing smoothly and evenly. Beth was fascinated. She had never actually gotten this close to an athlete, pro or amateur.

Wind licked his lips and looked straight at Justin for almost a minute without saying anything.

Justin didn't look away. Beth realized that the blue of Justin's eyes was intensifying, but it wasn't because he was angry, just in challenge. A guy thing. A stare-down.

Which Justin won. Wind burst out in a huge laugh that made her jump.

"A'most had you," he said to Justin. The two of them exchanged a handshake of unbelievable complexity. She couldn't follow the ins and outs of which hand was where. "Justin, Justin. My man. How ya been?"

"Better than ever."

"Uh-huh. I can guess why. And who is this pretty lady?"

"This is Beth." He looked down at her proudly and then back up at Windham. "Beth Danforth."

"Nice to meet you, Beth. Is he—and I do mean Sunny Boy—treating you right?"

"Yeah, he really is," she said with a grin. "He's a great guy." So was Wind, whom she liked instantly. He had the same enthusiasm that Justin did, but it was more like a cool breeze.

"A'ight." Wind capped the bottle and slam-dunked it into a recycling bin. "Gotta get back in the game. See you two around."

"If you're lucky," Justin joked.

"Nice to meet you," Beth said, getting another uproarious laugh from Windham. She threw a what-did-I-do look at Justin, who only shrugged.

"Now that girl has good manners, Justin," Wind said. "Unlike you. Me and the boys and I are taking up a collection to send you to charm school. Take off them rough edges you got."

"Hey, just because I held on to the ball last time I played," Justin began.

"Naw, you didn't just hold on to it. Your hands were velcro'd on to that ball," Wind said. "That's not *po*-lite and you know it."

"Okay, okay," Justin laughed. "Next time I'm down here, we'll play a rematch. I'll be good."

"We'll see about that." Wind gave Beth a smile and jumped back in the game. They watched for a while and then wandered down a side street looking for a coffee shop.

Two decaf flufferinos later, he walked her all the way back to the street off Hudson, waiting on the sidewalk while she climbed the stoop, looking for her keys.

"I'm not going to ask to come up," he said.

Beth shot him a glance from where she was, feeling just a little disappointed. He could, though. They could talk and not have sex. Yeah, right, she told herself, letting her keys jingle on her finger while she looked at him more thoughtfully.

"Why not?" she asked him.

"Because I'll want to make love. And you don't want to."

"It's not that I don't want to, Justin. Oh, geez—I just need to figure all this out. How many times do I have to say it?"

"As many times as you like," he said affably.

A guy walking by looked at her and Beth realized that she was swinging the key ring even harder. "It's not what you think," she said to him.

The guy caught Justin's glare and mumbled, "I wasn't thinking anything," and hurried away.

Justin stayed down on the sidewalk and blew her a kiss.

"Where are you going?" she asked. "Not that it's any of my business."

He stuck his big hands in his pockets and shrugged. "I haven't decided. I might shoot some pool. Go to a bookstore. Maybe I'll check out that charm school that Wind has in mind."

"Is he for real?"

Justin laughed in a low voice. "He's about as real as I am. Will that do?"

"I guess it'll have to," she said. "Okay. Well, good night, then. I had a really good time."

"Me too."

"See ya at SpectraSign." She put the key in the down-stairs lock and pushed the door open, her back to him.

"Wow," she heard him say. "You have a great ass."

Beth got inside and ducked her head out. "You keep working on that charm, Justin. Good night."

He gave her a jaunty wave and headed off down the street, whistling. Beth watched him move from one pool of light under a streetlamp to another, until he came to a dark part of the street and stood still for a second. Then she thought he'd moved on . . . but she suddenly realized he'd made his own pool of light and was tying his shoe in it.

He really was one of a kind. Beth turned away and looked in the mailbox, seeing her weekly letter from her father behind the pierced brass grille.

4

Beth was the proud possessor of a vintage drafting table as beat-up as Justin's. It was the same honey-colored pine but a little smaller.

He'd given her a state-of-the-art computer setup to translate her sketches into a multimedia presentation for the Blue Blaze people. She still wasn't happy with the campaign. She uploaded a few images into Illustrator and fooled around with the male model, grafting a goat's head onto his neck and then a kitten's. The goat's head looked pretty good, actually.

Beth was idly rotating the image when Justin walked in. "How's it coming?"

"Not great."

He looked over his shoulder to make sure no one was behind him before he planted a kiss on her cheek. "That's allowed, right? Just have to make sure I don't forget how."

"Ha ha," she said glumly.

"Why, if I didn't know better, I'd say you needed to get laid or something."

"Oh, shut up." He was right and that only made it worse.

"Okay. Let's talk about—" he looked at the image of the male model on her screen—"him. Why is he upside down and where did the goat's head come from?"

"Clip art," she said absently. "He's upside down because I just don't like him."

Justin nodded. "Me neither."

"I know, I know. His abs are nicer than yours."

Justin slapped his belly. "Not for long, though. I've been working out with Windham at the gym."

"Yeah?" She gave him a wistful once-over. "You two are real men. This model is like a Ken doll. I hate the way he just stands there and stares into space."

"Maybe he needs a swift kick in his Blue Blazes jeans," Justin suggested. "He might not react, though."

"That's it." She clicked on her mouse to rotate him the right way and removed the goat's head.

"I seem to be missing the eureka moment. What are you talking about?"

"The model needs something to react to. Or someone."

Justin nodded sagely, coming to stand beside her. "He isn't the only one."

"Justin, please. Not now. Soon, though," she amended. "Do you think we can reshoot this?"

He gave a nonchalant wave. "And go $500,000 over budget? Sure. What the hell. Let's go for broke. The client will scream, but who cares, right?"

"Be serious."

"I could bring it up at the next storyboard meeting, I guess. But give me something visual to go on. Blue Blazes isn't going to pay for a reshoot unless we make it crystal-clear that our new direction is a big improvement."

Beth fiddled with various images, shrinking the model and bringing in a few sultry females from an image-bank folder. She did a quick-and-dirty collage and Justin nodded, concentrating on the screen.

"See what I mean? Even though I'm just slapping this together, he looks a lot more alive now."

"You're right."

Beth felt excited about this campaign. "If you put the right woman in there, you'll have a sign that will make everybody stop and stare. Men and women."

"I see what you're saying, but go on."

"It'd be like a romantic movie. A hot romantic movie. And you could make it a little different every day, so people don't know what to expect."

"Got it. That's great. We could post clips on You-Tube and try to get it to go viral."

"And we could track who was watching it online with Adzilla or Phorm. But the original sign in the Times Square location is key. You'd get repeat views. Traffic would come to a standstill."

"Yeah. This is really good, Beth. I think our client is going to eat this up."

Two days later, they were in the middle of a studio photo shoot that involved a rusty old pickup, a bale of hay, and amber waves of fake wheat, lightly stirred by a plastic fan.

The models actually did seem hot for each other, at least at first. They acted like there wasn't even a camera on them. In fact, there were fourteen cameras in all, still and movie. He was really into her and their chemistry came across.

Hours and hours of footage were shot the first day, and hours more were shot on the second day. The models pouted and posed and panted at each other until they got sick of it.

"So much for their chemistry," Justin whispered in Beth's ear when a playful tussle turned into a vicious slapping match.

"Great stuff!" the director shouted. The female model burst into unphotogenic tears and stormed off, refusing to return. The director finally called it a day after a few more close-ups of the male model tensing his abs and unbuttoning his fly until he couldn't take it any more and stormed off too.

"That's a wrap," the director said, like he'd planned it that way all along. The production assistants ran around, frantically breaking down the set and issuing orders to each other.

"Now what?" Beth said. She was exhausted. Her whole body was stiff and her mind echoed with the endlessly repeated dialogue. Making a movie, even a three-minute-long movie, was utterly unglamorous. All she wanted to do was to get out of there.

"Gil and the film editor shut themselves up in a dark room and make movie magic on a digital console. We're not going to see them for days."

"Thank God. I'm sick of looking at them. And everybody else on this set. Moviemaking is boring," she said crossly.

"You're just tired. Come on. I'll take you out for a burger."

"You're on," Beth said. "Fries and ketchup."

"That's my girl."

"Maybe I am at that," she said.

Justin looked at her curiously. "Would you mind telling me what's gotten into you?"

She blew out an exasperated breath. "All this fake lust. It worked in reverse. At first I couldn't take my eyes off them. And then I started watching you. And I wanted the real thing, even though you're not really real. And then they started fighting and I thought about the way you make me feel—"

"Which is?"

She scowled at him. "Lighthearted. Happy."

"So why are you making that face at me?"

"Because I really, really need to blow off steam. I want to get physical. Does that make sense?"

"No, but I can work with it."

He looked around for someone from SpectraSign and realized they were the last two from his company there. He didn't even have to make an excuse. They could just *go*. Then he hustled her out the door of the studio, into her coat and down to the street, where he hailed a cab.

"Where to?" the driver said as they got in.

"Just drive through Central Park, please. We're still trying to figure that out."

"Okay, boss. Whatever you say." The driver started the meter and the red numbers started running.

"So you want to fool around," Justin whispered. "You're tired and frantic and you need release. That definitely calls for oral. Hmm. May I put my hand on your leg while I think about it?"

"Are you going to ask permission for every little thing?"

"No."

"Good." Beth wrapped her arms around his neck and kissed him, rumpling his hair and half-crawling into his lap.

"Mrmmf. Yeah," he said thickly. "More of that. I suggest we check into a hotel. Before you change your mind."

She didn't.

They got checked in and headed for the elevator, eyeing each other heatedly. Once inside the suite, he got her naked in record time and had her spread out on the squooshiest, most luxurious bed ever. But he didn't take his clothes off. He didn't waste a second. That long tongue of his got to work, licking her clit and gently pushing between her labia.

Holy . . . wow. She had never been tongue-fucked. The sensation was amazing. Tender and lingering. She could concentrate just on what she was feeling. Her nervous tension was eased away as he sexed her down like a pro. She could go with this flow forever. Oh yessss . . . yesyesyes.

Justin Watts was a master of this, too. She surrendered to his expertise, running her fingers through his hair, pushing his head down between her legs so he could make her come . . . and come . . . and come . . .

"That was unbelievably excellent," she said when he had her cuddled up. She was still naked and he was still wearing every stitch of clothing he'd had on, but not shoes. "I can't believe you're still dressed."

"Had no choice. I would have rammed up inside

you right away," he said. "No, this is fine for a while. It's probably good for my character."

"Oh, please." She reached down and unzipped him. "Allow me to return the favor."

And she did.

5

A month later . . .

Beth was awfully glad she'd given in. He was right about the oral sex not causing her to turn different colors. His magic tongue could practically dissolve her and vice versa, but that was okay. The glow they experienced was no different from a standard-issue post-coital glow.

She'd been just fine afterward, thank you. And she was still fine. Humming as she walked down the street, a relaxed bounce in her walk, she was pretty much walking on air these days. In contrast to everyone else at SpectraSign, now that they were rushing through the last phases of completing the massive sign.

It was being installed under wraps, on top of the building where she'd had the panoramic view of Times Square. Justin spent most of his time there.

He was—the thought made her hesitate—not doing so great. His inexhaustible energy was being drained by his insistence on attending to every detail personally.

Late at night, wrapped in his arms, she would whisper the sweet word, "Delegate," in his ear, hoping he would hear it subliminally while he slept. It didn't seem to help.

His sleep was restless and he usually woke up in a bad mood. Not like him. Not like him at all.

Justin had finally offered an explanation.

"It's the sunspot cycle," he explained. "Every twelve years, there are suddenly a lot more of them and it changes everything. My energy level goes haywire. Up. Down." He seesawed a hand through the air. "I get a little manic and I don't sleep well."

"Is it just you? I thought that happened to everyone in New York."

He'd shrugged. "Could explain a lot of things. It's not all bad, you know. Way up north, the aurora borealis goes crazy—it's much more intense. Turbocharged ions howling in from outer space, woo hoo, and all that. The colors are stronger and the patterns get wilder and it just doesn't stop."

He was talking faster and faster, not seeing her worried look.

"We could go up to Alaska. Or Sweden. Hang out and watch the northern lights and forget all about this crazy sign for a while. Something about it is getting to me. Maybe I wasn't born to sell blue jeans. What do you think? I really want to know."

But he hadn't even listened to her answer. She'd vetoed the all-expenses-paid trip to the tundra he'd proposed and pointed out that she didn't think it was the sign that was making him crazy. He had a whole company full of dedicated geeks and visual freaks to help make that happen.

No, he had to be right about the sunspots. And he was more than a little manic. Beth wasn't happy about that. She was having second thoughts. Even third, fourth, and fifth thoughts. She really couldn't imagine introducing him to her father while he was in this state, although Dave Danforth, mild-mannered cartoonist, probably would be thrilled to have a son-in-law who could harness all the energy in the known universe when he wanted to.

Son-in-law?

Where the hell had that ominous phrase come from?

The great day came. The wraps came off. He didn't want her to see it before it was dark and he insisted on being the one to put it through its paces. The project team from SpectraSign had left him to it, at his insistence.

He stood at a high table in front of the sign, looking a lot like a conductor at a podium. The laptop that controlled the special effects of the enormous sign was on the table and he rested his hands by it, a minute away from switching on the sign. The fact that he hadn't combed his hair for a few days added to the messy air of genius.

"It's finished. My magnum opus," he sighed. "What do you think?"

"I haven't seen it yet."

He started typing on the laptop. The screen lit up and she saw that it was a miniature of the giant sign. Whatever he did on the laptop would be instantly replicated above him.

He summoned up colors first, in shifting, swirling patterns. Then random things. Flying taxis. Sharks in sunglasses. Motifs appeared and disappeared with dizzying speed.

"Fun, huh?" he murmured. His eyes were glowing.

A breeze whipped her hair up around her face and she pushed it away. "Wow," was all she said, looking up at the sign.

In its final, complete stage, it was forty feet high, composed of hundreds of vid screens that fit together like a mosaic. Justin pushed a button. "Enough of that." The sign went dark. "Here comes the Blue Blaze man."

The multiple vid screens shimmered to life again, each showing a piece of the jeans-clad male model for the ad campaign, as if someone had taken scissors and cut up an old photo, then blown it up to building size.

The pieces of the photo came together as the male model strode slowly across the field of waving wheat toward the battered 1930s pickup.

Tinged with sepia, the familiar scene they'd seen being shot in bits and pieces came to coherent life. Edited, it was compelling. It seemed to have come from an authentic old movie, rich with atmosphere and poignant longing.

"What is he supposed to be doing again?" Beth asked Justin. The theme music swelled and reached a crescendo when the male model stopped and looked toward the horizon.

"I forget. Searching for America. Or true love."

"Here she comes now."

The long-legged female model walked toward him, her jeans a more feminine version of his. The camera came in tight on his crotch, then hers.

The models caressed each other's bodies with lingering strokes that the final edit made the most of by repeating endlessly. The result was actually quite erotic.

Beth ran to the edge of the roof and looked down at Times Square to see if anyone was watching.

It was working. There was a knot of people craning their necks and commenting.

She ran back to Justin, who was entering keyboard commands into the laptop that controlled the gigantic array of screens. He played with the color, with the movement of the models, freeze-framing moments and wiping others away in an instant.

There was a rhythm to his improvising that was very sensual and he worked fast. Then faster, intensifying it. Beth went back to the roof's edge. The crowd below had grown much larger in just a few minutes and was oohing and aahing appreciatively.

The images of the Blue Blaze jeans campaign changed constantly, but the concept—a man, a woman, a truck—was so simple to begin with that the effect of the rapid changes was hypnotic. At least Justin seemed to be a little hypnotized. His fingers stayed on the keyboard while he looked up at the sign, as if he was creating music only he could hear out of thin air. He was riveted to what he was doing, his glittering eyes reflecting the brilliance of the display.

Beth tugged at his sleeve. "I think you should stop."

"No," he said without looking at her, "this is a blast."

"But Justin—"

"No," he said again and shrugged her off.

Beth studied his profile, alarmed now by his degree of absorption. It was like she wasn't there at all. It was like he was drunk. On light. On color. The sunspots, millions of miles away, were most definitely getting to him.

"Let's take a trip," he said again without looking at her. He reached a hand sideways, fumbling for hers and missing. "This is great. Yowza. Shazam." He jabbed a button. "Look what I can do. I'm on a sunspot high and I don't want to come down. Everything's moving. I want to move with it. I want to jump right in there. C'mon."

"Nothing doing. I'm staying right here."

"Okay, I'll go in alone." He put both hands on the keyboard and keyed in commands so fast she couldn't tell what he was doing.

And then, in less than a second, he was sucked into the laptop screen . . . and suddenly reappeared in the sign, forty feet high.

"Justin, come back!" she screamed.

He looked down at her, oddly flattened out but very much himself. The models in the movie had vanished. Justin strode through the waving wheat and propped his foot on the bale of hay, having a great time in his own personal movie.

"How do I look?" he asked her, laughing hugely.

"Way too big! Come back here!"

He frowned. "I don't want to." He unbuttoned his shirt and whipped it off. "Women of the world, check me out!" He grinned down at Beth. "Feels good to be gorgeous."

"Don't you think you're getting a little carried away with yourself?"

"I like getting carried away. Being forty feet tall is great. Hey, guess how long my dick is—"

"Be quiet, Justin!" She hoped the crowd hadn't heard that. SpectraSign could kiss the Blue Blazes account good-bye forever if she couldn't shut him up and get him out and calm him the fuck down. "I don't really want to know!"

He stayed inside the sign while she looked at the laptop and tried a few keys. She tapped one, not familiar with the keyboard commands he used to control the enormous sign. Nothing happened.

She tapped another and the sign went completely

black. She gasped in horror. What the hell had just happened?

"Beth?" It was just his voice. Disembodied. She looked around wildly but he was nowhere on the roof.

"Beth?" he said again. He sounded kind of nervous. "Where are you? Where am I?"

Oh no. He had to be trapped in that goddamn sign. She had to get him out.

The breeze carried the voices of the crowd below, dispersing. "Show's over." "That was cool." "Who was that guy at the end?"

If you only knew, she thought despairingly. Beth looked up at the black mosaic of screens and wondered if there was a way in.

Suddenly she realized it wasn't just the Blue Blazes sign that had gone black. All around her the signs of Times Square were fading out one by one, some popping off, some fading away.

The streetlights faded out. The ever-present rumble of New York City died away, because the subway trains had stopped on the tracks. The lights in all the buildings winked out.

Somehow, his fooling around with the laptop had started a chain reaction in the city's electrical grid. Justin had caused a blackout. A big one.

The mutters she could hear from the street below confirmed it. All five boroughs involved. No power. Nothing. People stuck in elevators, trains. Traffic lights gone dark. No red, no green, no yellow. Just nothing. Times Square could have been a dark canyon in the middle of nowhere.

Except for the tiny, lit-up screens of thousands of cell phones bobbing in the crowd below, the greatest intersection in the world was plunged into blackness.

"Beth?" Justin said quietly. "You there?"

She looked up. His voice *was* coming from the screen above her. "Yeah," she said. "I'm still here."

"I'm sorry."

"You oughta be, Justin Watts. And when I get you out of there, you're going to be even sorrier."

"Call Wind," his disembodied voice said.

"How?" she snapped. "I don't have a cell phone. And every line out of New York is already jammed. Can't you hear what people on the street are saying?"

She held up a hand to hush him just in case he could see her from inside the screen. "Then listen."

Apparently he was calm enough to obey. They both heard the complaints of no service and the occasional jubilant shout when someone got a call through.

"That's not what I meant," Justin whispered. "Just call him. He'll come, I swear."

Beth shook her head. "You call him."

Justin's voice echoed softly through the air above her, saying his friend's name as if he were breathing it. *Wind. Wind.*

And in another second Windham Devane was standing next to Beth.

"Hey," he said. "Got the word. Is that fool trapped in there?"

Beth just gaped at him. "How'd you know? How'd you get up here?"

"He called, I came. Not the first time I did a favor for him. But this is going to be a big one." He smiled at her, untroubled. Beth couldn't help but smile back, worried as she was.

"We have to get him out." She looked up at the black mosaic. "Fair warning. He's out of control."

"Guess so. You don't sound like you want to get him out, girl."

"He's been acting so crazy!"

Windham nodded. "It's the sunspots. They do it to him every time."

"I don't even want to know. This may not be the time to bring it up, but this superpower crap is getting to me. I want a real man."

"Justin's as real as you want him to be," Wind said.

"Hey, spare me the freaky little metaphysical asides, okay?" She sighed. "I don't know what to think any more. But I guess we'd better get him out of there."

What if he stayed huge? What if he stayed flat? Was it possible to slither through a laptop and blow yourself up to gigantic size and still remain human?

Beth reminded herself that strictly speaking, he wasn't human.

"Step aside, please." Wind took over the laptop from her. "Walk me through this, Sunny Boy," he called up to Justin inside the sign. "And brace yourself on re-entry. It ain't going to be easy."

"Whatever it takes."

"When you come on back through the circuits we can deal with this blackout."

"You mean Justin can fix it?" Beth asked him.

"Maybe. We won't know for sure until we can get him out, though."

Justin's voice issued the keyboard commands and one by one, Wind carried them out. "Is that it?"

"That should do it," Justin said.

Nothing happened. Beth and Windham stood there looking at each other.

"Shit," Windham said. "Okay, one more time. With feeling."

He tapped in the commands again and the huge sign above them rattled. Justin stepped out of it at one corner.

"I created a desktop shortcut," Wind explained

calmly. "That's why he didn't come out through the laptop screen. I was afraid he would bust it."

Justin shook his head like he was trying to clear it. He'd left his shirt back in the movie and was still bare-chested, Beth saw.

He looked around, a little dazed, spotted the two of them and ran over. "What happened? All the signs are black!"

"You done triggered a blackout, fool," Windham scolded him.

"Oh my God." He looked searchingly at Beth. "I got a little out of control, didn't I?"

"No, a lot."

"Guess it's time I turned into a hero."

"Beats being a fool," Wind said. "Let's go where we can do the most good."

Justin nodded. "The subway."

"I have a feeling the folks down there could use a cool breeze."

"And some light."

They were right across the street from the entrance to the labyrinth that ran for blocks under Times Square, where twelve subway lines converged. Beth shuddered. She'd gotten lost in the maze of corridors and connections when it was all lit up—it was hard to imagine what it was like in there now.

"Beth, you ever flown without a plane?" Wind was asking.

She backed away. "No. N-no. And I don't want to." Her hands stretched out toward them. What she meant as refusal they took as opportunity.

Wind grabbed one of her hands, Justin grabbed the other, and she was flying between them, soaring over the mass of humanity in Times Square, between the buildings—they scared a few pigeons—and then down to earth by the entrance to the subway station.

The three of them felt their way down, squeezing past the people who were struggling to get up.

They seemed surprisingly calm. Some exchanged tales of the last blackout. Justin worked up the energy to light their way and Wind began to blow subtly, not so anyone would notice.

But it was enough to alleviate the stale air.

"You gotta find a hot connection," he murmured between puffs to Justin. "Use your powers for good."

"So that's where you got that line," Beth said to Justin, who hadn't let go of her hand.

"Yeah. We both read comic books. I'm not much of a hero."

She shook her head. "No. Let's hook you up, light up this place, and help people get out of here."

He glowed more brightly. "There's a transformer around here. Anyone see a Con Ed sign?"

"Shine on, man," Wind said. "We'll find it."

The throng of people moved slowly but surely through the corridor they were in, and Justin got through them to a panel in the tiled wall.

"This is it." He lifted it off.

"You guys from Con Ed?"

"No," said Wind, who was dressed in his basketball clothes, Beth noticed.

"Yes," said Justin, who was bare-chested.

"Whatever," said the man who'd asked.

Justin reached into the wires and fuses, connecting this to that, and ultimately attaching a cord as thick as a finger to his own finger.

"Stand back," he shouted.

No one in the crowd paid any attention. Wind began

to blow in their direction, pushing people away without them knowing why.

Justin glowed a brilliant, pulsing yellow.

A lady with two babies in a stroller and an older boy clinging to its handle stopped and stared.

The air was filled with a crackling that made everyone's hair stand on end.

"Justin, be careful!" Beth whispered. She was fascinated, horrified, and totally pissed off at him all at once.

The air hummed and crackled. Justin radiated a light so strong she couldn't look at him. He was turning a thousand different colors in succession.

One guy stopped and dug in his pockets for money to give him. "That's a hell of an act, pal." He smoothed out a paper bag and put a handful of coins on it in front of the three of them.

Justin laughed and the connection broke. The corridor was plunged into blackness again.

"Man, pay attention," Windham said peevishly. "That's chump change. What have I told you about keeping focus?"

"Eyes on the ball," Justin said. "Got it. Okay, here I go." Beth watched as Justin slowly lit up again. He seemed to have less energy than before but for a good reason. One by one the lights that illuminated the labyrinth flickered on. And they stayed on.

People could see their way and streamed toward the staircases.

She heard the subways rumble to life and the doors whoosh open. For the most part, the passengers got off, not wanting to risk getting stuck.

A blackout, in a weird way, was just part of living in New York. Something to dine out on and talk about for years. And this had been a mercifully brief one, thanks to Justin.

But eight million people had been stopped in their tracks, also thanks to Justin. Who'd stopped turning colors and was looking at her sheepishly. "I screwed up, didn't I?"

"Yeah. You did."

"Can we go back to my place?"

"Not on the subway."

"We can take a cab."

"Your wallet's in your shirt pocket. You left it in the movie."

Justin thrust his hands into his pockets and looked at Windham. "Can I borrow twenty bucks, man?"

"Don't look at me," Wind said severely. "You got me off the courts. I wasn't carrying no wallet."

Justin looked back at Beth. "Guess you'll have to pay. I'll make it up to you."

"No!" Beth yelled. All the tension of the last several weeks and the sheer, mind-blowing weirdness of the last hour exploded out of her. "This will never, ever work! I can't be with a guy who can shut down the whole city of New York and hit me up for cab fare home!"

She turned and bolted, looking for the staircase that would bring her out in the heart of Times Square. Justin wasn't far behind her. She could hear his pounding footsteps as she reached the top, panting frantically.

He put a gentle hand on her arm. "Hey, I really am sorry. Whatever was going on with me is over. Turning everything on again took care of it."

She looked away from him, up at the lurid, immense signs that pulsed and glowed and sparkled. It was like the blackout had never even happened.

"Marry me, Beth," he said suddenly. "I love you."

"Hah! The answer is no. Not if you're going to go crazy on me every twelve years."

"I might," he admitted. "Just a little. Lock me in the back bedroom and tell the kids that daddy's watching TV."

"Tell the who? What?"

He reached out his arms and enfolded her in his strength. He was warm . . . so warm. Her temper dissolved in his embrace.

"The kids. Our kids. Someday, when you're ready, I mean. Freddy needs somebody to play with."

"Freddy hates kids."

"So we'll get him a feline friend to perk him up. I'm totally serious. Let's do it. We'll be happy."

She snuffled into his bare, hot chest. It was very satisfying. Her arms slipped around his waist. "How do you know?"

Justin dropped a kiss on her hair. "I just do," he whispered. "I really do love you."

"Will that be enough?" Classic girl-type question, but she couldn't help it.

"You won't have any in-laws."

Beth grinned against him. "You will. Wait til you meet the Ink Man. You'll like him, I think."

"Is that a yes?" He held her away from him and looked at her soulfully. She saw a blue, blue fire deep in his eyes that was close to heavenly. He was radiating pure love.

"Not yet," she said calmly.

*A whole year and a lot of couples counseling
later . . .*

They were sprawled on the enormous sofa in his
Bolt Building apartment. He was behind the sports section and she was brushing her hair. Beth looked over at
the big feet in clean white socks, which was about all
that she could see of him. She patted one fondly.

"Honey, how many superheroes does it take to
change a lightbulb?"

"I don't know," he said absently. "How many?"

"One," she replied. "But he has to ask his wife where
the lightbulbs are."

Justin rattled the paper. "Ha ha."

Just another peaceful Sunday in their aerie. She was
utterly content. She hadn't minded moving in and old
wheezy Freddy loved the Bolt Building. He'd laid
claim to the sunniest corner and pretty much stayed
there all day.

She pulled the sports section out of Justin's hands
and threw herself on him to steal a kiss.

He didn't protest. They kept on going from there.
Afterward, Beth lay in his arms and thought about how
incredibly happy they were, just as he'd said.

No surprise there. The man was the light of her life.

Hooked on the arrogant and sexy dragons of Shelly Laurenston, AKA G.A. Aiken? You won't want to miss the newest Dragon Kin novel, BRING THE HEAT!

HE SAYS . . .

I, Aidan the Divine, am, well, *divine.* My name was given to me by the Dragon Queen herself! I'm a delight! Cheerful. Charming. And a mighty warrior who is extremely handsome, with a very large and well-hidden hoard of gold. I am also royal born, despite the fact that most in my family are horrendous beings that don't deserve to live. And yet, Branwen the Awful—a low-born, no less—either tells me to shut up or, worse, ignores me completely.

SHE SAYS . . .

I'll admit, I ignore Aidan the Divine because it annoys him. A lot. But, we have so much to do right now, I can't worry about why he keeps staring at me, or why he always sits so close, or why he keeps looking at me like he's thinking about kissing me. We have our nations to save and no time for such bloody foolishness…no matter how good Aidan looks or how long his spiked tail is. Because if we're going to win this war before it destroys everything we love, we'll have to face our enemies together, side by side and without distractions. But if we make it out alive, who knows what the future will hold . . .

Read on for a teaser from Chapter One.

The broken spear caught her on her right side, knocking her off her stallion. She landed hard on the blood-soaked ground but allowed herself no time to get her breath back. Instead, she forced herself to her feet and quickly blocked the damaged spear with her armor-covered forearm.

She swung at her attacker with her free hand, her fist slamming into his chest, sending him flying back into the wave of soldiers coming toward her.

She reached over her shoulder and grabbed her halberd. A long poleaxe that she liked using because the head was made up of an axe, a spear, and a steel point. To her it was like three weapons in one.

Impaling the first man she saw, she jerked her weapon to the side, tossing her victim off and readying herself for the next attack.

They surrounded her and she took a quick moment to size them all up. She crouched a little lower, adjusted her stance a bit more...then she struck.

She slashed the tip of her weapon across several throats, lowered it, turned it slightly, and then thrust the tip into the sockets where some of the Zealots had eyes, but she pushed in far enough to tear through skull and brain.

The remaining soldiers moved in, and she dragged her weapon closer, lengthened her stance, and anchored the end of the staff against the inseam of her foot. Turning it, she thrust up with the axe head and into the groin of one soldier, sending his bowels pouring onto the ground. She yanked the weapon out and used the axe head to cut legs off at the knees.

She felt a breeze, a change of energy around her, and quickly lifted the staff while lowering the head. She blocked the oncoming blade attack and twisted her weapon to disarm her attacker before slamming the staff end against his head and knocking him out.

She then swung the weapon up and over, letting the momentum turn her around to face those behind her.

She moved in time to avoid a blade aimed for her head and thrust her weapon at her attacker's inner thigh, piercing flesh and tearing open an artery. With a twist of her hands, she brought the weapon over her left forearm, jabbed it forward and impaled the man next to her before he could strike. Did the same in the opposite direction and impaled a soldier on her right.

She blocked another attack from the front and brought the man down to the ground, holding him there with her foot against his throat while she used her halberd to dispatch the last two of those who'd attacked. Once they were dead, she impaled the man under her foot and finished off the one who'd just started to come around from his bash on the head.

Letting out a breath, Branwen the Awful, Captain of the First and Fifteenth Companies of the Dragon Queen's Armies and Colonel of the Ninety-Eighth Regiment of the Southland Armies, slammed the end of her halberd against the blood-soaked ground and took a moment to look over the carnage she'd caused on this mountain-side.

Her troops were in the valley below fighting the ones they now just called the Zealots. Those who were loyal unto death to the eyeless god, Chramnesind.

As she stood there, staring, she instinctively knew someone was coming up behind her. Turning only at the waist, Brannie brought the weapon up and through the head of the blood-soaked priest who stood behind her. As her weapon tore through the top of the priest's head, she had to jerk her body slightly to the left to avoid the spear that came through the back of the priest's head, almost skewering her in the process.

"Sorry!" Aidan the Divine called out. The gold dragon wincing a bit when he realized how close his spear had come to impaling her. "Just trying to help."

That's what he always said. "Just trying to help!" He should have that branded on his bloody forehead.

"Yes, I know," Brannie replied. "But I didn't need your help."

"Everyone needs a little help now and again."

"Not me."

Yanking her weapon from the priest's head, Brannie secretly enjoyed the way blood splattered across that pretty face and right into those bright gold eyes.

He said nothing as he attempted to wipe the blood away, but then he gave her that wide smile again, showing Brannie those annoying dimples. Or, as her Uncle Addolgar called them, "Pits in the face."

Turning away, she took a step, but then heard, "Aren't you going to thank me?"

"No."

"Not even a thank you kiss?"

She faced the gold dragon. Like her, he was in his

human form, shoulder-length gold hair perpetually falling in front of his gold eyes and nearly blocking the
sight of those sharp cheekbones. Brannie stepped close
to him, and put her fist under his nose. She didn't hit
him, just held her chainmail-covered fist there and
asked, "What about a thank you punch to the face?"

PENGUIN BOOKS

MR MIDSHIPMAN HORNBLOWER

C. S. Forester was born in Cairo in 1899, where his father was stationed as a government official. He studied medicine at Guy's Hospital, and after leaving Guy's without a degree he turned to writing as a career. His first success was *Payment Deferred*, a novel written at the age of twenty-four and later dramatized and filmed with Charles Laughton in the leading role. In 1932 Forester was offered a Hollywood contract, and from then until 1939 he spent thirteen weeks of every year in America. On the outbreak of war he entered the Ministry of Information and later he sailed with the Royal Navy to collect the material for *The Ship*. He made a voyage to the Bering Sea to gather material for a similar book on the United States Navy, and it was during this trip that he was stricken with arteriosclerosis, a disease which left him crippled. However, he continued to write and in the *Hornblower* novels created the most renowned sailor in contemporary fiction. He died in 1966.

C. S. FORESTER

MR MIDSHIPMAN
HORNBLOWER

PENGUIN BOOKS

Penguin Books Ltd, Harmondsworth, Middlesex, England
Penguin Books, 625 Madison Avenue, New York, New York 10022, U.S.A.
Penguin Books Australia Ltd, Ringwood, Victoria, Australia
Penguin Books Canada Ltd, 2801 John Street, Markham, Ontario,
Canada L3R 1B4
Penguin Books (N.Z.) Ltd, 182–190 Wairau Road, Auckland 10, New Zealand

—

First published 1950
Published in Penguin Books 1956
Reprinted 1958, 1959, 1965, 1967, 1969, 1970, 1971, 1972, 1973, 1975, 1977

—

—

Made and printed in Great Britain by
Cox & Wyman Ltd,
London, Reading and Fakenham
Set in Monotype Garamond

CONTENTS

CHAPTER ONE

THE EVEN CHANCE

A JANUARY gale was roaring up the Channel, blustering loudly, and bearing in its bosom rain squalls whose big drops rattled loudly on the tarpaulin clothing of those among the officers and men whose duties kept them on deck. So hard and so long had the gale blown that even in the sheltered waters of Spithead the battleship moved uneasily at her anchors, pitching a little in the choppy seas, and snubbing herself against the tautened cables with unexpected jerks. A shore boat was on its way out to her, propelled by oars in the hands of two sturdy women; it danced madly on the steep little waves, now and then putting its nose into one and sending a sheet of spray flying aft. The oarswoman in the bow knew her business, and with rapid glances over her shoulder not only kept the boat on its course but turned the bows into the worst of the waves to keep from capsizing. It slowly drew up along the starboard side of the *Justinian*, and as it approached the mainchains the midshipman of the watch hailed it.

'Aye aye' came back the answering hail from the lusty lungs of the woman at the stroke oar; by the curious and ages-old convention of the Navy the reply meant that the boat had an officer on board – presumably the huddled figure in the stern-sheets looking more like a heap of trash with a boat-cloak thrown over it.

That was as much as Mr Masters, the lieutenant of the watch, could see; he was sheltering as best he could in the lee of the mizzen-mast bitts, and in obedience to the order of the midshipman of the watch the boat drew up towards the mainchains and passed out of his sight. There was a long delay; apparently the officer had some difficulty in getting up the ship's side. At last the boat reappeared in Masters' field of vision; the women had shoved off and were setting a scrap of lugsail, under which the boat, now without its passenger, went swooping back towards Portsmouth, leaping on the waves like a steeplechaser. As it departed Mr Masters became aware of the near approach of someone along the quarterdeck; it was the new arrival under the escort of the midshipman of the watch, who, after pointing Masters out, retired to the mainchains again. Mr Masters had served in the Navy until his hair was white; he was lucky to have received his commission as lieutenant, and he had long known that he would never receive one as captain, but the knowledge had not greatly embittered him, and he diverted his mind by the study of his fellow men.

So he looked with attention at the approaching figure. It was that of a skinny young man only just leaving boyhood behind, something above middle height, with feet whose adolescent proportions to his size were accentuated by the thinness of his legs and his big half-boots. His gawkiness called attention to his hands and elbows. The newcomer was dressed in a badly fitting uniform which was soaked right through by the spray; a skinny neck stuck out of the high stock, and above the neck was a white bony face. A white face was a rarity on the deck of a ship of war, whose crew soon tanned to a deep mahogany, but this face was not merely white; in the hollow cheeks there was a faint shade of green – clearly the newcomer had experienced seasickness in his passage out in the shore boat. Set in the white face were a pair of dark eyes which by contrast looked like holes cut in a sheet of paper; Masters noted with a slight stirring of interest that the eyes, despite their owner's seasickness, were looking about keenly, taking in what were obviously new sights; there was a curiosity and interest there which could not be repressed and which continued to function notwithstanding either seasickness or shyness, and Mr Masters surmised in his far-fetched fashion that this boy had a vein of caution or foresight in his temperament and was already studying his new surroundings with a view to being prepared for his next experiences. So might Daniel have looked about him at the lions when he first entered their den.

The dark eyes met Masters', and the gawky figure came to a halt, raising a hand selfconsciously to the brim of his dripping hat. His mouth opened and tried to say something, but closed again without achieving its object as shyness overcame him, but then the newcomer nerved himself afresh and forced himself to say the formal words he had been coached to utter.

'Come aboard, sir.'

'Your name?' asked Masters, after waiting for it for a moment.

'H-Horatio Hornblower, sir. Midshipman,' stuttered the boy.

'Very good, Mr Hornblower,' said Masters, with the equally formal response. 'Did you bring your dunnage aboard with you?'

Hornblower had never heard that word before, but he still had enough of his wits about him to deduce what it meant.

'My sea chest, sir. It's – it's forrard, at the entry port.'

Hornblower said these things with the barest hesitation; he knew that at sea they said them, that they pronounced the word 'forward' like that, and that he had come on board through the 'entry port', but it called for a slight effort to utter them himself.

'I'll see that it's sent below,' said Masters. 'And that's where you'd better go, too. The captain's ashore, and the first lieutenant's orders were that he's not to be called on any account before eight bells, so I advise you, Mr Hornblower, to get out of those wet clothes while you can.'

'Yes, sir,' said Hornblower; his senses told him, the moment he said it, that he had used an improper expression – the look on Masters' face told him, and he corrected himself (hardly believing that men really said these things off the

9

boards of the stage) before Masters had time to correct him.

'Aye aye, sir,' said Hornblower, and as a second after-thought he put his hand to the brim of his hat again.

Masters returned the compliment and turned to one of the shivering messengers cowering in the inadequate shelter of the bulwark. 'Boy! Take Mr Hornblower down to the mid-shipmen's berth.'

'Aye aye, sir.'

Hornblower accompanied the boy forward to the main hatchway. Seasickness alone would have made him unsteady on his feet, but twice on the short journey he stumbled like a man tripping over a rope as a sharp gust brought the *Justinian* up against her cables with a jerk. At the hatchway the boy slid down the ladder like an eel over a rock; Horn-blower had to brace himself and descend far more gingerly and uncertainly into the dim light of the lower gundeck and then into the twilight of the 'tweendecks. The smells that entered his nostrils were as strange and as assorted as the noises that assailed his ears. At the foot of each ladder the boy waited for him with a patience whose tolerance was just obvious. After the last descent, a few steps – Hornblower had already lost his sense of direction and did not know whether it was aft or forward – took them to a gloomy recess whose shadows were accentuated rather than lightened by a tallow dip spiked onto a bit of copper plate on a table round which were seated half a dozen shirt-sleeved men. The boy vanished and left Hornblower standing there, and it was a second or two before the whiskered man at the head of the table looked up at him.

'Speak, thou apparition,' said he.

Hornblower felt a wave of nausea overcoming him – the after effects of his trip in the shore boat were being accentuated by the incredible stuffiness and smelliness of the 'tweendecks. It was very hard to speak, and the fact that he did not know how to phrase what he wanted to say made it harder still.

'My name is Hornblower,' he quavered at length.

'What an infernal piece of bad luck for you,' said a second man at the table, with a complete absence of sympathy.

At that moment in the roaring world outside the ship the wind veered sharply, heeling the *Justinian* a trifle and swinging her round to snub at her cables again. To Hornblower it seemed more as if the world had come loose from its fastenings. He reeled where he stood, and although he was shuddering with cold he felt sweat on his face.

'I suppose you have come,' said the whiskered man at the head of the table, 'to thrust yourself among your betters. Another soft-headed ignoramus come to be a nuisance to those who have to try to teach you your duties. Look at him' — the speaker with a gesture demanded the attention of everyone at the table — 'look at him, I say! The King's latest bad bargain. How old are you?'

'S-seventeen, sir,' stuttered Hornblower.

'Seventeen!' the disgust in the speaker's voice was only too evident. 'You must start at twelve if you ever wish to be a seaman. Seventeen! Do you know the difference between a head and a halliard?'

That drew a laugh from the group, and the quality of the laugh was just noticeable to Hornblower's whirling brain, so that he guessed that whether he said 'yes' or 'no' he would be equally exposed to ridicule. He groped for a neutral reply.

'That's the first thing I'll look up in Norie's *Seamanship*,' he said.

The ship lurched again at that moment, and he clung on to the table.

'Gentlemen,' he began pathetically, wondering how to say what he had in mind.

'My God!' exclaimed somebody at the table. 'He's seasick!'

'Seasick in Spithead!' said somebody else, in a tone in which amazement had as much place as disgust.

But Hornblower ceased to care; he was not really conscious of what was going on round him for some time after that. The nervous excitement of the last few days was as much to blame, perhaps, as the journey in the shore boat and the erratic behaviour of the *Justinian* at her anchors, but it meant for him that he was labelled at once as the midshipman who was seasick in Spithead, and it was only natural that the label added to the natural misery of the loneliness and homesickness which oppressed him during those days when that part of the Channel Fleet which had not succeeded in completing its crews lay at anchor in the lee of the Isle of Wight. An hour in the hammock into which the messman hoisted him enabled him to recover sufficiently to be able to report himself to the first lieutenant; after a few days on board he was able to find his way round the ship without (as happened at first) losing his sense of direction below decks, so that he did not know whether he was facing forward or aft. During that period his brother officers ceased to have faces which were mere blurs and came to take on personalities; he came painfully to learn the stations allotted him when the ship was at quarters, when he was on watch, and when hands were summoned for setting or taking in sail. He even came to have an acute enough understanding of his new life to realize that it could have been worse – that destiny might have put him on board a ship ordered immediately to sea instead of one lying at anchor. But it was a poor enough compensation; he was a lonely and unhappy boy. Shyness alone would long have delayed his making friends, but as it happened the midshipmen's berth in the *Justinian* was occupied by men all a good deal older than he; elderly master's mates recruited from the merchant service, and midshipmen in their twenties who through lack of patronage or inability to pass the necessary examination had never succeeded in gaining for themselves commissions as lieutenants. They were inclined, after the first moments of amused interest, to ignore him, and he was glad of it, delighted to shrink into his shell and attract no notice to himself.

For the *Justinian* was not a happy ship during those gloomy January days. Captain Keene – it was when he came aboard

that Hornblower first saw the pomp and ceremony that sur-
rounds the captain of a ship of the line – was a sick man, of a
melancholy disposition. He had not the fame which enabled
some captains to fill their ships with enthusiastic volunteers,
and he was devoid of the personality which might have made
enthusiasts out of the sullen pressed men whom the press
gangs were bringing in from day to day to complete the ship's
complement. His officers saw little of him, and did not love
what they saw. Hornblower, summoned to his cabin for his
first interview, was not impressed – a middle-aged man at a
table covered with papers, with the hollow and yellow cheeks
of prolonged illness.

'Mr Hornblower,' he said formally, 'I am glad to have this
opportunity of welcoming you on board my ship.'

'Yes, sir,' said Hornblower – that seemed more appropriate
to the occasion than 'Aye aye, sir', and a junior midshipman
seemed to be expected to say one or the other on all occasions.

'You are – let me see – seventeen?' Captain Keene picked up
the paper which apparently covered Hornblower's brief
official career.

'Yes, sir.'

'July 4th, 1776,' mused Keene, reading Hornblower's date
of birth to himself. 'Five years to the day before I was posted as
captain. I had been six years as lieutenant before you were
born.'

'Yes, sir,' agreed Hornblower – it did not seem the occasion
for any further comment.

'A doctor's son – you should have chosen a lord for your
father if you wanted to make a career for yourself.'

'Yes, sir.'

'How far did your education go?'

'I was a Grecian at school, sir.'

'So you can construe Xenophon as well as Cicero?'

'Yes, sir. But not very well, sir.'

'Better if you knew something about sines and cosines.

Better if you could foresee a squall in time to get t'gallants in. We have no use for ablative absolutes in the Navy.'

'Yes, sir,' said Hornblower.

He had only just learned what a topgallant was, but he could have told his captain that his mathematical studies were far advanced. He refrained nevertheless; his instincts combined with his recent experiences urged him not to volunteer unsolicited information.

'Well, obey orders, learn your duties, and no harm can come to you. That will do.'

'Thank you, sir,' said Hornblower, retiring.

But the captain's last words to him seemed to be contradicted immediately. Harm began to come to Hornblower from that day forth, despite his obedience to orders and diligent study of his duties, and it stemmed from the arrival in the midshipmen's berth of John Simpson as senior warrant officer. Hornblower was sitting at mess with his colleagues when he first saw him – a brawny good-looking man in his thirties, who came in and stood looking at them just as Hornblower had stood a few days before.

'Hullo!' said somebody, not very cordially.

'Cleveland, my bold friend,' said the newcomer, 'come out from that seat. I am going to resume my place at the head of the table.'

'But –'

'Come out, I said,' snapped Simpson.

Cleveland moved along with some show of reluctance, and Simpson took his place, and glowered round the table in reply to the curious glances with which everyone regarded him.

'Yes, my sweet brother officers,' he said, 'I am back in the bosom of the family. And I am not surprised that nobody is pleased. You will all be less pleased by the time I am done with you, I may add.'

'But your commission –?' asked somebody, greatly daring.

'My commission?' Simpson leaned forward and tapped the

table, staring down the inquisitive people on either side of it. 'I'll answer that question this once, and the man who asks it again will wish he had never been born. A board of turnip-headed captains has refused me my commission. It decided that my mathematical knowledge was insufficient to make me a reliable navigator. And so Acting-Lieutenant Simpson is once again Mr Midshipman Simpson, at your service. At your service. And may the Lord have mercy on your souls.'

It did not seem, as the days went by, that the Lord had any mercy at all, for with Simpson's return life in the midshipmen's berth ceased to be one of passive unhappiness and became one of active misery. Simpson had apparently always been an ingenious tyrant, but now, embittered and humiliated by his failure to pass his examination for his commission, he was a worse tyrant, and his ingenuity had multiplied itself. He may have been weak in mathematics, but he was diabolically clever at making other people's lives a burden to them. As senior officer in the mess he had wide official powers; as a man with a blistering tongue and a morbid sense of mischief he would have been powerful anyway, even if the *Justinian* had possessed an alert and masterful first lieutenant to keep him in check, while Mr Clay was neither. Twice midshipmen rebelled against Simpson's arbitrary authority, and each time Simpson thrashed the rebel, pounding him into insensibility with his huge fists, for Simpson would have made a successful prize-fighter. Each time Simpson was left unmarked; each time his opponent's blackened eyes and swollen lips called down the penalty of mast heading and extra duty from the indignant first lieutenant. The mess seethed with impotent rage. Even the toadies and lickspittles among the midshipmen – and naturally there were several – hated the tyrant.

Significantly, it was not his ordinary exactions which roused the greatest resentment – his levying toll upon their sea chests for clean shirts for himself, his appropriation of the best cuts of the meat served, nor even his taking their coveted issues of spirits. These things could be excused as understandable, the sort of thing they would do themselves if they had the power. But he displayed a whimsical arbitrariness which reminded Hornblower, with his classical education, of the freaks of the Roman emperors. He forced Cleveland to shave the whiskers which were his inordinate pride; he imposed upon Hether the duty of waking up Mackenzie every half hour, day and night, so that neither of them was able to sleep – and there were toadies ready to tell him if Hether ever failed in his task. Early enough he had discovered Hornblower's most vulnerable points, as he had with everyone else. He knew of Hornblower's shyness; at first it was amusing to compel Hornblower to recite verses from Gray's 'Elegy in a Country Churchyard' to the assembled mess. The toadies could compel Hornblower to do it; Simpson would lay his dirk-scabbard on the table in front of him with a significant glance, and the toadies would close round Hornblower, who knew that any hesitation on his part would mean that he would be stretched across the table and the dirk-scabbard applied; the flat of the scabbard was painful, the edge of it was agonizing, but the pain was nothing to the utter humiliation of it all. And the torment grew worse when Simpson instituted what he aptly called 'The Proceedings of the Inquisition' when Hornblower was submitted to a slow and methodical questioning regarding his homelife and his boyhood. Every question had to be answered, on pain of the dirk-scabbard; Hornblower could fence and prevaricate, but he had to answer and sooner or later the relentless questioning would draw from him some simple admission which would rouse a peal of laughter from his audience. Heaven knows that in Hornblower's lonely childhood there was nothing to be ashamed of, but boys are odd creatures, especially reticent ones like Hornblower, and are ashamed of things no one else would think twice about. The ordeal would leave him weak and sick; someone less solemn might have clowned his way out of his difficulties and even into popular favour, but Hornblower at seventeen was too ponderous a person to clown. He had to endure the persecution, experiencing all the black misery which only a seventeen-year-old can experience; he never wept in public, but at night more than once he shed the bitter tears of seventeen. He often thought about death; he often even thought about desertion, but he realized that desertion would lead to something worse than death, and then his mind would revert to death, savouring the thought of suicide. He came to long for death, friendless as he was, and brutally ill-treated, and lonely as only a boy among men – and a very reserved boy – can be. More and more he thought about ending it all the easiest way, hugging the secret thought of it to his friendless bosom.

If the ship had only been at sea everyone would have been kept busy enough to be out of mischief; even at anchor an energetic captain and first lieutenant would have kept all hands hard enough at work to obviate abuses, but it was Hornblower's hard luck that the *Justinian* lay at anchor all through that fatal January of 1794 under a sick captain and an inefficient first lieutenant. Even the activities which were at times enforced often worked to Hornblower's disadvantage. There was an occasion when Mr Bowles, the master, was holding a class in navigation for his mates and for the midshipmen, and the captain by bad luck happened by and glanced through the results of the problem the class had individually been set to solve. His illness made Keene a man of bitter tongue, and he cherished no liking for Simpson. He took a single glance at Simpson's paper, and chuckled sarcastically.

'Now let us all rejoice,' he said, 'the sources of the Nile have been discovered at last.'

'Pardon, sir?' said Simpson.

'Your ship,' said Keene, 'as far as I can make out from your illiterate scrawl, Mr Simpson, is in Central Africa. Let us now see what other *terrae incognitae* have been opened up by the remaining intrepid explorers of this class.'

It must have been Fate – it was dramatic enough to be art and not an occurrence in real life; Hornblower knew what was going to happen even as Keene picked up the other papers, including his. The result he had obtained was the only one which was correct; everybody else had added the correction for refraction instead of subtracting it, or had worked out the multiplication wrongly, or had, like Simpson, botched the whole problem.

'Congratulations, Mr Hornblower,' said Keene. 'You must be proud to be alone successful among this crowd of intellectual giants. You are half Mr Simpson's age, I fancy. If you double your attainments while you double your years, you will leave the rest of us far behind. Mr Bowles, you will be so good as to see that Mr Simpson pays even further attention to his mathematical studies.'

With that he went off along the 'tweendecks with the halting step resulting from his mortal disease, and Hornblower sat with his eyes cast down, unable to meet the glances he knew were being darted at him, and knowing full well what they portended. He longed for death at that moment; he even prayed for it that night.

Within two days Hornblower found himself on shore, and under Simpson's command. The two midshipmen were in charge of a party of seamen, landed to act along with parties from the other ships of the squadron as a press gang. The West India convoy was due to arrive soon; most of the hands would be pressed as soon as the convoy reached the Channel, and the remainder, left to work the ships to an anchorage, would sneak ashore, using every device to conceal themselves and find a safe hiding-place. It was the business of the landing parties to cut off this retreat, to lay a cordon along the waterfront which would sweep them all up. But the convoy was not yet signalled, and all arrangements were completed.

'All is well with the world,' said Simpson.

It was an unusual speech for him, but he was in unusual circumstances. He was sitting in the back room of the Lamb Inn, comfortable in one armchair with his legs on another, in front of a roaring fire and with a pot of beer with gin in it at his elbow.

'Here's to the West India convoy,' said Simpson, taking a pull at his beer. 'Long may it be delayed.'

Simpson was actually genial, activity and beer and a warm fire thawing him into a good humour; it was not time yet for the liquor to make him quarrelsome; Hornblower sat on the other side of the fire and sipped beer without gin in it and studied him, marvelling that for the first time since he had boarded the *Justinian* his unhappiness should have ceased to be active but should have subsided into a dull misery like the dying away of the pain of a throbbing tooth.

'Give us a toast, boy,' said Simpson.

'Confusion to Robespierre,' said Hornblower lamely.

The door opened and two more officers came in, one a midshipman while the other wore the single epaulette of a lieutenant – it was Chalk of the *Goliath*, the officer in general charge of the press gangs sent ashore. Even Simpson made room for his superior rank before the fire.

'The convoy is still not signalled,' announced Chalk. And then he eyed Hornblower keenly. 'I don't think I have the pleasure of your acquaintance.'

'Mr Hornblower – Lieutenant Chalk,' introduced Simpson. 'Mr Hornblower is distinguished as the midshipman who was seasick in Spithead.'

Hornblower tried not to writhe as Simpson tied that label on him. He imagined that Chalk was merely being polite when he changed the subject.

'Hey, potman! Will you gentlemen join me in a glass? We have a long wait before us, I fear. Your men are all properly posted, Mr Simpson?'

'Yes, sir.'

Chalk was an active man. He paced about the room, stared out of the window at the rain, presented his midshipman – Caldwell – to the other two when the drinks arrived, and obviously fretted at his enforced inactivity.

'A game of cards to pass the time?' he suggested. 'Excellent! Hey, potman! Cards and a table and another light.'

The table was set before the fire, the chairs arranged, the cards brought in.

'What game shall it be?' asked Chalk, looking round.

He was a lieutenant among three midshipmen, and any suggestion of his was likely to carry a good deal of weight; the other three naturally waited to hear what he had to say.

'Vingt-et-un? That is a game for the half-witted. Loo? That is a game for the wealthier half-witted. But whist, now? That would give us all scope for the exercise of our poor talents. Caldwell, there, is acquainted with the rudiments of the game, I know. Mr Simpson?'

A man like Simpson, with a blind mathematical spot, was not likely to be a good whist player, but he was not likely to know he was a bad one.

'As you wish, sir,' said Simpson. He enjoyed gambling, and one game was as good as another for that purpose to his mind.

'Mr Hornblower?'

'With pleasure, sir.'

That was more nearly true than most conventional replies. Hornblower had learned his whist in a good school; ever since the death of his mother he had made a fourth with his father and the parson and the parson's wife. The game was already something of a passion with him. He revelled in the nice calculation of chances, in the varying demands it made upon his boldness or caution. There was even enough warmth in his acceptance to attract a second glance from Chalk, who – a good card player himself – at once detected a fellow spirit.

'Excellent!' he said again. 'Then we may as well cut at once for places and partners. What shall be the stakes, gentlemen? A shilling a trick and a guinea on the rub, or is that too great? No? Then we are agreed.'

For some time the game proceeded quietly. Hornblower cut first Simpson and then Caldwell as his partner. Only a couple of hands were necessary to show up Simpson as a hopeless whist player, the kind who would always lead an ace when he had one, or a singleton when he had four trumps, but he and Hornblower won the first rubber thanks to overwhelming card strength. But Simpson lost the next in partnership with Chalk, cut Chalk again as partner, and lost again. He gloated over good hands and sighed over poor ones; clearly he was one of those unenlightened people who looked upon whist as a social function, or as a mere crude means, like throwing dice, of arbitrarily transferring money. He never thought of the game either as a sacred rite or as an intellectual exercise. Moreover, as his losses grew, and as the potman came and went with liquor, he grew restless, and his face was flushed with more than the heat of the fire. He was both a bad loser and a bad drinker, and even Chalk's punctilious good manners were sufficiently strained so that he displayed a hint of relief when the next cut gave him Hornblower as a partner. They won the rubber easily, and another guinea and several shillings were transferred to Hornblower's lean purse; he was now the only winner, and Simpson was the heaviest loser. Hornblower was lost in the pleasure of playing the game again; the only attention he paid to Simpson's writhings and muttered objurgations was to regard them as a distracting nuisance; he even forgot to think of them as danger signals. Momentarily he was oblivious to the fact that he might pay for his present success by future torment.

Once more they cut, and he found himself Chalk's partner again. Two good hands gave them the first game. Then twice, to Simpson's unconcealed triumph, Simpson and Caldwell made a small score, approaching game, and in the next hand an overbold finesse by Hornblower left him and Chalk with the odd trick when their score should have been two tricks greater – Simpson laid his knave on Hornblower's ten with a grin of delight which turned to dismay when he found that he and Caldwell had still only made six tricks; he counted them a second time with annoyance. Hornblower dealt and turned the trump, and Simpson led – an ace as usual, assuring Hornblower of his re-entry. He had a string of trumps and a good suit of clubs which a single lead might establish. Simpson glanced muttering at his hand; it was extraordinary that he still had not realized the simple truth that the lead of an ace involved leading a second time with the problem no clearer. He made up his mind at last and led again; Hornblower's king took the trick and he instantly led his knave of trumps. To his delight it took the trick; he led again and Chalk's queen gave them another trick. Chalk laid down the ace of trumps and Simpson with a curse played the king. Chalk led clubs of which Hornblower had five to the king queen – it was significant that Chalk should lead them, as it could not be a singleton lead when Hornblower held the remaining trumps. Hornblower's queen took the trick; Caldwell must hold the ace, unless Chalk did. Hornblower led a small one; everyone followed suit, Chalk playing the knave, and Caldwell played the ace. Eight clubs had been played, and Hornblower had three more headed by the king and ten – three certain tricks, with the last trumps as re-entries. Caldwell played the queen of diamonds, Hornblower played his singleton, and Chalk produced the ace.

'The rest are mine,' said Hornblower, laying down his cards.

'What do you mean?' said Simpson, with the king of diamonds in his hand.

'Five tricks,' said Chalk briskly. 'Game and rubber.'

'But don't I take another?' persisted Simpson.

'I trump a lead of diamonds or hearts and make three more clubs,' explained Hornblower. To him the situation was as simple as two and two, a most ordinary finish to a hand; it was hard for him to realize that foggy-minded players like Simpson could find difficulty in keeping tally of fifty-two cards. Simpson flung down his hand.

'You know too much about the game,' he said. 'You know the backs of the cards as well as the fronts.'

Hornblower gulped. He recognized that this could be a decisive moment if he chose. A second before he had merely been playing cards, and enjoying himself. Now he was faced with an issue of life or death. A torrent of thought streamed through his mind. Despite the comfort of his present surroundings he remembered acutely the hideous misery of the life in the *Justinian* to which he must return. This was an opportunity to end that misery one way or the other. He remembered how he had contemplated killing himself, and into the back of his mind stole the germ of the plan upon which he was going to act. His decision crystallized.

'That is an insulting remark, Mr Simpson,' he said. He looked round and met the eyes of Chalk and Caldwell, who were suddenly grave; Simpson was still merely stupid. 'For that I shall have to ask satisfaction.'

'Satisfaction?' said Chalk hastily. 'Come, come. Mr Simpson had a momentary loss of temper. I am sure he will explain.'

'I have been accused of cheating at cards,' said Hornblower. 'That is a hard thing to explain away.'

He was trying to behave like a grown man; more than that, he was trying to act like a man consumed with indignation, while actually there was no indignation within him over the point in dispute, for he understood too well the muddled state of mind which had led Simpson to say what he did. But the opportunity had presented itself, he had determined to avail himself of it, and now what he had to do was to play the part convincingly of the man who has received a mortal insult.

'The wine was in and the wit was out,' said Chalk, still determined on keeping the peace. 'Mr Simpson was speaking in jest, I am sure. Let's call for another bottle and drink it in friendship.'

'With pleasure,' said Hornblower, fumbling for the words which would set the dispute beyond reconciliation. 'If Mr Simpson will beg my pardon at once before you two gentlemen, and admit that he spoke without justification and in a manner no gentleman would employ.'

He turned and met Simpson's eye with defiance as he

spoke, metaphorically waving a red rag before the bull, who charged with gratifying fury.

'Apologize to *you*, you little whippersnapper!' exploded Simpson, alcohol and outraged dignity speaking simultaneously. 'Never this side of Hell.'

'You hear that, gentlemen?' said Hornblower. 'I have been insulted and Mr Simpson refuses to apologize while insulting me further. There is only one way now in which satisfaction can be given.'

For the next two days, until the West India convoy came in, Hornblower and Simpson, under Chalk's orders, lived the curious life of two duellists forced into each other's society before the affair of honour. Hornblower was careful – as he would have been in any case – to obey every order given him, and Simpson gave them with a certain amount of self-consciousness and awkwardness. It was during those two days that Hornblower elaborated on his original idea. Pacing through the dockyards with his patrol of seamen at his heels he had plenty of time to think the matter over. Viewed coldly – and a boy of seventeen in a mood of black despair can be objective enough on occasions – it was as simple as the calculations of the chances in a problem at whist. Nothing could be worse than his life in the *Justinian*, not even (as he had thought already) death itself. Here was an easy death open to him, with the additional attraction that there was a chance of Simpson dying instead. It was at that moment that Hornblower advanced his idea one step further – a new development, startling even to him, bringing him to a halt so that the patrol behind him bumped into him before they could stop.

'Beg your pardon, sir,' said the petty officer.

'No matter,' said Hornblower, deep in his thoughts.

He first brought forward his suggestion in conversation with Preston and Danvers, the two master's mates whom he asked to be his seconds as soon as he returned to the *Justinian*.

'We'll act for you, of course,' said Preston, looking dubiously at the weedy youth when he made his request.

'How do you want to fight him? As the aggrieved party you have the choice of weapons.'

'I've been thinking about it ever since he insulted me,' said Hornblower temporizing. It was not easy to come out with his idea in bald words, after all.

'Have you any skill with the small-sword?' asked Danvers.

'No,' said Hornblower. Truth to tell, he had never even handled one.

'Then it had better be pistols,' said Preston.

'Simpson is probably a good shot,' said Danvers. 'I wouldn't care to stand up before him myself.'

'Easy now,' said Preston hastily. 'Don't dishearten the man.'

'I'm not disheartened,' said Hornblower, 'I was thinking the same thing myself.'

'You're cool enough about it, then,' marvelled Danvers.

Hornblower shrugged.

'Maybe I am. I hardly care. But I've thought that we might make the chances more even.'

'How?'

'We could make them exactly even,' said Hornblower, taking the plunge. 'Have two pistols, one loaded and the other empty. Simpson and I would take our choice without knowing which was which. Then we stand within a yard of each other, and at the word we fire.'

'My God!' said Danvers.

'I don't think that would be legal,' said Preston. 'It would mean one of you would be killed for certain.'

'Killing is the object of duelling,' said Hornblower. 'If the conditions aren't unfair I don't think any objection can be raised.'

'But would you carry it out to the end?' marvelled Danvers.

'Mr Danvers –' began Hornblower; but Preston interfered.

'We don't want another duel on our hands,' he said. 'Danvers only meant he wouldn't care to do it himself. We'll discuss it with Cleveland and Hether, and see what they say.'

Within an hour the proposed conditions of the duel were known to everyone in the ship. Perhaps it was to Simpson's disadvantage that he had no real friend in the ship, for Cleveland and Hether, his seconds, were not disposed to take too firm a stand regarding the conditions of the duel, and agreed to the terms with only a show of reluctance. The tyrant of the midshipmen's berth was paying the penalty for his tyranny. There was some cynical amusement shown by some of the officers; some of both officers and men eyed Hornblower and Simpson with the curiosity that the prospect of death excites in some minds, as if the two destined opponents were men condemned to the gallows. At noon Lieutenant Masters sent for Hornblower.

'The captain has ordered me to make inquiry into this duel, Mr Hornblower,' he said. 'I am instructed to use my best endeavours to compose the quarrel.'

'Yes, sir.'

'Why insist on this satisfaction, Mr Hornblower? I understand there were a few hasty words over wine and cards.'

'Mr Simpson accused me of cheating, sir, before witnesses who were not officers of this ship.'

That was the point. The witnesses were not members of the ship's company. If Hornblower had chosen to disregard Simpson's words as the ramblings of a drunken ill-tempered man, they might have passed unnoticed. But as he had taken the stand he did, there could be no hushing it up now, and Hornblower knew it.

'Even so, there can be satisfaction without a duel, Mr Hornblower.'

'If Mr Simpson will make me a full apology before the same gentlemen, I would be satisfied, sir.'

Simpson was no coward. He would die rather than submit to such a formal humiliation.

'I see. Now I understand you are insisting on rather unusual conditions for the duel?'

'There are precedents for it, sir. As the insulted party I can choose any conditions which are not unfair.'

'You sound like a sea lawyer to me, Mr Hornblower.'

The hint was sufficient to tell Hornblower that he had verged upon being too glib, and he resolved in future to bridle his tongue. He stood silent and waited for Masters to resume the conversation.

'You are determined, then, Mr Hornblower, to continue with this murderous business?'

'Yes, sir.'

'The captain has given me further orders to attend the duel in person, because of the strange conditions on which you insist. I must inform you that I shall request the seconds to arrange for that.'

'Yes, sir.'

'Very good, then, Mr Hornblower.'

Masters looked at Hornblower as he dismissed him even more keenly than he had done when Hornblower first came on board. He was looking for signs of weakness or wavering – indeed, he was looking for any signs of human feeling at all – but he could detect none. Hornblower had reached a decision, he had weighed all the pros and cons, and his logical mind told him that having decided in cold blood upon a course of action it would be folly to allow himself to be influenced subsequently by untrustworthy emotions. The conditions of the duel on which he was insisting were mathematically advantageous. If he had once considered with favour escaping from Simpson's persecution by a voluntary death it was surely a gain to take an even chance of escaping from it without dying. Similarly, if Simpson were (as he almost certainly was) a better swordsman and a better pistol shot than him, the even chance was again mathematically advantageous. There was nothing to regret about his recent actions.

All very well; mathematically the conclusions were irrefutable, but Hornblower was surprised to find that mathematics were not everything. Repeatedly during that dreary afternoon and evening Hornblower found himself suddenly gulping with anxiety as the realization came to him afresh that to-morrow morning he would be risking his life on the spin of a coin. One chance out of two and he would be dead, his consciousness at an end, his flesh cold, and the world, almost unbelievably, would be going on without him. The thought sent a shiver through him despite himself. And he had plenty of time for these reflections, for the convention that forbade him from encountering his destined opponent before the moment of the duel kept him necessarily in isolation, as far as isolation could be found on the crowded decks of the *Justinian*. He slung his hammock that night in a depressed mood, feeling unnaturally tired; and he undressed in the clammy, stuffy dampness of the 'tweendecks feeling more than usually cold. He hugged the blankets round himself, yearning to relax in their warmth, but relaxation would not come. Time after time as he began to drift off to sleep he woke again tense and anxious, full of thoughts of the morrow. He turned over wearily a dozen times, hearing the ship's bell ring out each half hour, feeling a growing contempt at his cowardice. He told himself in the end that it was as well that his fate to-morrow depended upon pure chance, for if he had to rely upon steadiness of hand and eye he would be dead for certain after a night like this.

That conclusion presumably helped him to go to sleep for the last hour or two of the night, for he awoke with a start to find Danvers shaking him.

'Five bells,' said Danvers. 'Dawn in an hour. Rise and shine!'

Hornblower slid out of his hammock and stood in his shirt; the 'tweendecks was nearly dark and Danvers was almost invisible.

'Number One's letting us have the second cutter,' said Danvers. 'Masters and Simpson and that lot are going first in the launch. Here's Preston.'

Another shadowy figure loomed up in the darkness.

'Hellish cold,' said Preston. 'The devil of a morning to turn out. Nelson, where's that tea?'

The mess attendant came with it as Hornblower was hauling on his trousers. It maddened Hornblower that he shivered enough in the cold for the cup to clatter in the saucer as he took it. But the tea was grateful, and Hornblower drank it eagerly.

'Give me another cup,' he said, and was proud of himself that he could think about tea at that moment.

It was still dark as they went down into the cutter.

'Shove off,' said the coxswain, and the boat pushed off from the ship's side. There was a keen cold wind blowing which filled the dipping lug as the cutter headed for the twin lights that marked the jetty.

'I ordered a hackney coach at the George to be waiting for us,' said Danvers. 'Let's hope it is.'

It was there, with the driver sufficiently sober to control his horse moderately well despite his overnight potations. Danvers produced a pocket flask as they settled themselves in with their feet in the straw.

'Take a sip, Hornblower?' he asked, proffering it. 'There's no special need for a steady hand this morning.'

'No thank you,' said Hornblower. His empty stomach revolted at the idea of pouring spirits into it.

'The others will be there before us,' commented Preston. 'I saw the quarter boat heading back just before we reached the jetty.'

The etiquette of the duel demanded that the two opponents should reach the ground separately; but only one boat would be necessary for the return.

'The sawbones is with them,' said Danvers. 'Though God knows what use he thinks he'll be to-day.'

He sniggered, and with overlate politeness tried to cut his snigger off short.

'How are you feeling, Hornblower?' asked Preston.

'Well enough,' said Hornblower, forbearing to add that he only felt well enough while this kind of conversation was not being carried on.

The hackney coach levelled itself off as it came over the crest of the hill, and stopped beside the common. Another coach stood there waiting, its single candle-lamp burning yellow in the growing dawn.

'There they are,' said Preston; the faint light revealed a shadowy group standing on frosty turf among the gorse bushes.

Hornblower, as they approached, caught a glimpse of Simpson's face as he stood a little detached from the others. It was pale, and Hornblower noticed that at that moment he swallowed nervously, just as he himself was doing. Masters came towards them, shooting his usual keen inquisitive look at Hornblower as they came together.

'This is the moment,' he said, 'for this quarrel to be composed. This country is at war. I hope, Mr Hornblower, that you can be persuaded to save a life for the King's service by not pressing this matter.'

Hornblower looked across at Simpson, while Danvers answered for him.

'Has Mr Simpson offered the proper redress?' asked Danvers.

'Mr Simpson is willing to acknowledge that he wishes the incident had never taken place.'

'That is an unsatisfactory form,' said Danvers. 'It does not include an apology, and you must agree that an apology is necessary, sir.'

'What does your principal say?' persisted Masters.

'It is not for any principal to speak in these circumstances,' said Danvers, with a glance at Hornblower, who nodded. All this was as inevitable as the ride in the hangman's cart, and as hideous. There could be no going back now; Hornblower had never thought for one moment that Simpson would apologize, and without an apology the affair must be carried to a bloody conclusion. An even chance that he did not have five minutes longer to live.

'You are determined, then, gentlemen,' said Masters. 'I shall have to state that fact in my report.'

'We are determined,' said Preston.

'Then there is nothing for it but to allow this deplorable affair to proceed. I left the pistols in the charge of Doctor Hepplewhite.'

He turned and led them towards the other group – Simpson with Hether and Cleveland, and Doctor Hepplewhite standing with a pistol held by the muzzle in each hand. He was a bulky man with the red face of a persistent drinker; he was actually grinning a spirituous grin at that moment, rocking a little on his feet.

'Are the young fools set in their folly?' he asked; but everyone very properly ignored him as having no business to ask such a question at such a moment.

'Now,' said Masters. 'Here are the pistols, both primed, as you see, but one loaded and the other unloaded, in accordance with the conditions. I have here a guinea which I propose to spin to decide the allocation of the weapons. Now, gentlemen, shall the spin give your principals one pistol each irrevocably – for instance, if the coin shows heads shall Mr Simpson have this one – or shall the winner of the spin have choice of weapons? It is my design to eliminate all possibility of collusion as far as possible.'

Hether and Cleveland and Danvers and Preston exchanged dubious glances.

'Let the winner of the spin choose,' said Preston at length.

'Very well, gentlemen. Please call, Mr Hornblower.'

'Tails!' said Hornblower as the gold piece spun in the air. Masters caught it and clapped a hand over it.

'Tails it is,' said Masters, lifting his hand and revealing the coin to the grouped seconds. 'Please make your choice.'

Hepplewhite held out the two pistols to him, death in one hand and life in the other. It was a grim moment. There was only pure chance to direct him; it called for a little effort to force his hand out.

'I'll have this one,' he said; as he touched it the weapon seemed icy cold.

'Then now I have done what was required of me,' said Masters. 'The rest is for you gentlemen to carry out.'

'Take this one, Simpson,' said Hepplewhite. 'And be careful how you handle yours, Mr Hornblower. You're a public danger.'

The man was still grinning, gloating over the fact that someone else was in mortal danger while he himself was in none. Simpson took the pistol Hepplewhite offered him and settled it into his hand; once more his eyes met Hornblower's, but there was neither recognition nor expression in them.

'There are no distances to step out,' Danvers was saying. 'One spot's as good as another. It's level enough here.'

'Very good,' said Hether. 'Will you stand here, Mr Simpson?'

Preston beckoned to Hornblower, who walked over. It was not easy to appear brisk and unconcerned. Preston took him by the arm and stood him up in front of Simpson, almost breast to breast – close enough to smell the alcohol on his breath.

'For the last time, gentlemen,' said Masters loudly. 'Cannot you be reconciled?'

There was no answer from anybody, only deep silence, during which it seemed to Hornblower that the frantic beating of his heart must be clearly audible. The silence was broken by an exclamation from Hether.

'We haven't settled who's to give the word!' he said. 'Who's going to?'

'Let's ask Mr Masters to give it,' said Danvers.

Hornblower did not look round. He was looking stead-fastly at the grey sky past Simpson's right ear – somehow he could not look him in the face, and he had no idea where Simpson was looking. The end of the world as he knew it was close to him – soon there might be a bullet through his heart.

'I will do it if you are agreed, gentlemen,' he heard Masters say.

The grey sky was featureless; for this last look on the world he might as well have been blindfolded. Masters raised his voice again.

'I will say "one, two, three, fire",' he announced, 'with those intervals. At the last word, gentlemen, you can fire as you will. Are you ready?'

'Yes,' came Simpson's voice, almost in Hornblower's ear, it seemed.

'Yes,' said Hornblower. He could hear the strain in his own voice.

'One,' said Masters, and Hornblower felt at that moment the muzzle of Simpson's pistol against his left ribs, and he raised his own.

It was in that second that he decided he could not kill Simpson even if it were in his power, and he went on lifting his pistol, forcing himself to look to see that it was pressed against the point of Simpson's shoulder. A slight wound would suffice.

'Two,' said Masters. 'Three. Fire!'

Hornblower pulled his trigger. There was a click and a spurt of smoke from the lock of his pistol. The priming had gone off but no more – his was the unloaded weapon, and he knew what it was to die. A tenth of a second later there was a click and spurt of smoke from Simpson's pistol against his heart. Stiff and still they both stood, slow to realize what had happened.

'A miss-fire, by God!' said Danvers.

The seconds crowded round them.

'Give me those pistols!' said Masters, taking them from the weak hands that held them. 'The loaded one might be hanging fire, and we don't want it to go off now.'

'Which was the loaded one?' asked Hether, consumed with curiosity.

'That is something it is better not to know,' answered Masters, changing the two pistols rapidly from hand to hand so as to confuse everyone.

'What about a second shot?' asked Danvers, and Masters looked up straight and inflexibly at him.

'There will be no second shot,' he said. 'Honour is completely satisfied. These two gentlemen have come through this ordeal extremely well. No one can now think little of Mr Simpson if he expresses his regret for the occurrence, and no one can think little of Mr Hornblower if he accepts that statement in reparation.'

Hepplewhite burst into a roar of laughter.

'Your faces!' he boomed, slapping his thigh. 'You ought to see how you all look! Solemn as cows!'

'Mr Hepplewhite,' said Masters, 'your behaviour is indecorous. Gentlemen, our coaches are waiting on the road, the cutter is at the jetty. And I think all of us would be the better for some breakfast; including Mr Hepplewhite.

That should have been the end of the incident. The excited talk which had gone round the anchored squadron about the unusual duel died away in time, although everyone knew Hornblower's name now, and not as the midshipman who was seasick in Spithead but as the man who was willing to take an even chance in cold blood. But in the *Justinian* herself there was other talk; whispers which were circulated forward and aft.

'Mr Hornblower has requested permission to speak to you, sir,' said Mr Clay, the first lieutenant, one morning while making his report to the captain.

'Oh, send him in when you go out,' said Keene, and sighed.

Ten minutes later a knock on his cabin door ushered in a very angry young man.

'Sir!' began Hornblower.

'I can guess what you're going to say,' said Keene.

'Those pistols in the duel I fought with Simpson were not loaded!'

34

'Hepplewhite blabbed, I suppose,' said Keene.

'And it was by your orders, I understand, sir.'

'You are quite correct. I gave those orders to Mr Masters.'

'It was an unwarrantable liberty, sir!'

That was what Hornblower meant to say, but he stumbled without dignity over the polysyllables.

'Possibly it was,' said Keene patiently, rearranging, as always, the papers on his desk.

The calmness of the admission disconcerted Hornblower, who could only splutter for the next few moments.

'I saved a life for the King's service,' went on Keene, when the spluttering died away. 'A young life. No one has suffered any harm. On the other hand, both you and Simpson have had your courage amply proved. You both know you can stand fire now, and so does every one else.'

'You have touched my personal honour, sir,' said Hornblower, bringing out one of his rehearsed speeches, 'for that there can only be one remedy.'

'Restrain yourself, please, Mr Hornblower.' Keene shifted himself in his chair with a wince of pain as he prepared to make a speech. 'I must remind you of one salutary regulation of the Navy, to the effect that no junior officer can challenge his superior to a duel. The reasons for it are obvious – otherwise promotion would be too easy. The mere issuing of a challenge by a junior to a senior is a court-martial offence, Mr Hornblower.'

'Oh!' said Hornblower feebly.

'Now here is some gratuitous advice,' went on Keene. 'You have fought one duel and emerged with honour. That is good. Never fight another – that is better. Some people, oddly enough, acquire a taste for duelling, as a tiger acquires a taste for blood. They are never good officers, and never popular ones either.'

It was then that Hornblower realized that a great part of the keen excitement with which he had entered the captain's cabin was due to anticipation of the giving of the challenge.

There could be a morbid desire for danger – and a morbid desire to occupy momentarily the centre of the stage. Keene was waiting for him to speak, and it was hard to say anything.

'I understand, sir,' he said at last.

Keene shifted in his chair again.

'There is another matter I wanted to take up with you, Mr Hornblower. Captain Pellew of the *Indefatigable* has room for another midshipman. Captain Pellew is partial to a game of whist, and has no good fourth on board. He and I have agreed to consider favourably your application for a transfer should you care to make one. I don't have to point out that any ambitious young officer would jump at the chance of serving in a frigate.'

'A frigate!' said Hornblower.

Everybody knew of Pellew's reputation and success. Distinction, promotion, prize money – an officer under Pellew's command could hope for all these. Competition for nomination to the *Indefatigable* must be intense, and this was the chance of a lifetime. Hornblower was on the point of making a glad acceptance, when further considerations restrained him.

'That is very good of you, sir,' he said 'I do not know how to thank you. But you accepted me as a midshipman here, and of course I must stay with you.'

The drawn, apprehensive face relaxed into a smile.

'Not many men would have said that,' said Keene. 'But I am going to insist on your accepting the offer. I shall not live very much longer to appreciate your loyalty. And this ship is not the place for you – this ship with her useless captain – don't interrupt me – and her worn-out first lieutenant and her old midshipmen. You should be where there may be speedy opportunities of advancement. I have the good of the service in mind, Mr Hornblower, when I suggest you accept Captain Pellew's invitation – and it might be less disturbing for me if you did.'

'Aye aye, sir,' said Hornblower.

CHAPTER TWO

THE CARGO OF RICE

THE wolf was in among the sheep. The tossing grey water of the Bay of Biscay was dotted with white sails as far as the eye could see, and although a strong breeze was blowing every vessel was under perilously heavy canvas. Every ship but one was trying to escape; the exception was His Majesty's frigate *Indefatigable*, Captain Sir Edward Pellew. Farther out in the Atlantic, hundreds of miles away, a great battle was being fought, where the ships of the line were thrashing out the question as to whether England or France should wield the weapon of sea power; here in the Bay the convoy which the French ships were intended to escort was exposed to the attack of a ship of prey at liberty to capture any ship she could overhaul. She had come surging up from leeward, cutting off all chance of escape in that direction, and the clumsy merchant ships were forced to beat to windward; they were all filled with the food which revolutionary France (her economy disordered by the convulsion through which she was passing) was awaiting so anxiously, and their crews were all anxious to escape confinement in an English prison. Ship after ship was overhauled; a shot or two, and the newfangled tricolour came fluttering down from the gaff, and a prize-crew was hurriedly sent on board to conduct the captive to an English port while the frigate dashed after fresh prey.

On the quarterdeck of the *Indefatigable* Pellew fumed over each necessary delay. The convoy, each ship as close to the wind as she would lie, and under all the sail she could carry, was slowly scattering, spreading farther and farther with the passing minutes, and some of these would find safety in mere dispersion if any time was wasted. Pellew did not wait to pick up his boat; at each surrender he merely ordered away an officer and an armed guard, and the moment the prize-crew was on its way he filled his main-topsail again and hurried off after the next victim. The brig they were pursuing at the moment was slow to surrender. The long nine-pounders in the *Indefatigable*'s bows bellowed out more than once; on that heaving sea it was not so easy to aim accurately and the brig continued on her course hoping for some miracle to save her.

'Very well,' snapped Pellew. 'He has asked for it. Let him have it.'

The gunlayers at the bow chasers changed their point of aim, firing at the ship instead of across her bows.

'Not into the hull, damn it,' shouted Pellew – one shot had struck the brig perilously close to her waterline. 'Cripple her.'

The next shot by luck or by judgement was given better elevation. The slings of the foretopsail yard were shot away, the reefed sail came down, the yard hanging lopsidedly, and the brig came up into the wind for the *Indefatigable* to heave to close beside her, her broadside ready to fire into her. Under that threat her flag came down.

'What brig's that?' shouted Pellew through his megaphone.

'*Marie Galante* of Bordeaux,' translated the officer beside Pellew as the French captain made reply. 'Twenty-four days out from New Orleans with rice.'

'Rice!' said Pellew. 'That'll sell for a pretty penny when we get her home. Two hundred tons, I should say. Twelve of a crew at most. She'll need a prize-crew of four, a midshipman's command.'

He looked round him as though for inspiration before giving his next order.

'Mr Hornblower!'

'Sir!'

'Take four men of the cutter's crew and board that brig. Mr Soames will give you our position. Take her into any English port you can make, and report there for orders.'

'Aye aye, sir.'

Hornblower was at his station at the starboard quarter-deck carronades – which was perhaps how he had caught

Pellew's eye – his dirk at his side and a pistol in his belt. It was a moment for fast thinking, for anyone could see Pellew's impatience. With the *Indefatigable* cleared for action, his sea chest would be part of the surgeon's operating table down below, so that there was no chance of getting anything out of it. He would have to leave just as he was. The cutter was even now clawing up to a position on the *Indefatigable*'s quarter, so he ran to the ship's side and hailed her, trying to make his voice sound as big and as manly as he could, and at the word of the lieutenant in command she turned her bows in towards the frigate.

'Here's our latitude and longitude, Mr Hornblower,' said Soames, the master, handing a scrap of paper to him.

'Thank you,' said Hornblower, shoving it into his pocket.

He scrambled awkwardly into the mizzen-chains and looked down into the cutter. Ship and boat were pitching together, almost bows on to the sea, and the distance between them looked appallingly great; the bearded seaman standing in the bows could only just reach up to the chains with his long boat-hook. Hornblower hesitated for a long second; he knew he was ungainly and awkward – book learning was of no use when it came to jumping into a boat – but he had to make the leap, for Pellew was fuming behind him and the eyes of the boat's crew and of the whole ship's company were on him. Better to jump and hurt himself, better to jump and make an exhibition of himself, than to delay the ship. Waiting was certain failure, while he still had a choice if he jumped. Perhaps at a word from Pellew the *Indefatigable*'s helmsman allowed the ship's head to fall off from the sea a little. A somewhat diagonal wave lifted the *Indefatigable*'s stern and then passed on, so that the cutter's bows rose as the ship's stern sank a trifle. Hornblower braced himself and leaped. His feet reached the gunwale and he tottered there for one indescribable second. A seaman grabbed the breast of his jacket and he fell forward rather than backward. Not even the stout arm of the seaman, fully extended, could hold him up, and he pitched headforemost, legs in the air, upon the hands on the second thwart. He cannoned onto their bodies, knocking the breath out of his own against their muscular shoulders, and finally struggled into an upright position.

'I'm sorry,' he gasped to the men who had broken his fall.

'Never you mind, sir,' said the nearest one, a real tarry sailor, tattooed and pigtailed. 'You're only a featherweight.'

The lieutenant in command was looking at him from the sternsheets.

'Would you go to the brig, please, sir?' he asked, and the lieutenant bawled an order and the cutter swung round as Hornblower made his way aft.

It was a pleasant surprise not to be received with the broad grins of tolerantly concealed amusement. Boarding a small boat from a big frigate in even a moderate sea was no easy matter; probably every man on board had arrived headfirst at some time or other, and it was not in the tradition of the service, as understood in the *Indefatigable*, to laugh at a man who did his best without shirking.

'Are you taking charge of the brig?' asked the lieutenant.

'Yes, sir. The captain told me to take four of your men.'

'They had better be topmen, then,' said the lieutenant, casting his eyes aloft at the rigging of the brig. The fore-topsail yard was hanging precariously, and the jib halliard had slacked off so that the sail was flapping thunderously in the wind. 'Do you know these men, or shall I pick 'em for you?'

'I'd be obliged if you would, sir.'

The lieutenant shouted four names, and four men replied.

'Keep 'em away from drink and they'll be all right,' said the lieutenant. 'Watch the French crew. They'll recapture the ship and have you in a French gaol before you can say "Jack Robinson" if you don't.'

'Aye aye, sir,' said Hornblower.

The cutter surged alongside the brig, white water creaming between the two vessels. The tattooed sailor hastily concluded a bargain with another man on his thwart and pocketed a lump of tobacco – the men were leaving their possessions behind just like Hornblower – and sprang for the mainchains. Another man followed him, and they stood and waited while Hornblower with difficulty made his way forward along the plunging boat. He stood, balancing precariously, on the forward thwart. The main chains of the brig were far lower than the mizzen-chains of the *Indefatigable*, but this time he had to jump upwards. One of the seamen steadied him with an arm on his shoulder.

'Wait for it, sir,' he said. 'Get ready. Now jump, sir.'

Hornblower hurled himself, all arms and legs, like a leaping frog, at the mainchains. His hands reached the shrouds, but his knee slipped off, and the brig, rolling, lowered him thigh deep into the sea as the shrouds slipped through his hands. But the waiting seamen grabbed his wrists and hauled him on board, and two more seamen followed him. He led the way onto the deck.

The first sight to meet his eyes was a man seated on the hatch cover, his head thrown back, holding to his mouth a bottle, the bottom pointing straight up to the sky. He was one of a large group all sitting round the hatch cover; there were more bottles in evidence; one was passed by one man to another as he looked, and as he approached a roll of the ship brought an empty bottle rolling past his toes to clatter into the scuppers. Another of the group, with white hair blowing in the wind, rose to welcome him, and stood for a moment with waving arms and rolling eyes, bracing himself as though to say something of immense importance and seeking earnestly for the right words to use.

'Goddam English,' was what he finally said, and, having said it, he sat down with a bump on the hatch cover and from a seated position proceeded to lie down and compose himself to sleep with his head on his arms.

'They've made the best of their time, sir, by the Holy,' said the seaman at Hornblower's elbow.

'Wish we were as happy,' said another.

A case still a quarter full of bottles, each elaborately sealed, stood on the deck beside the hatch cover, and the seaman picked out a bottle to look at it curiously. Hornblower did not need to remember the lieutenant's warning; on his shore excursions with press gangs he had already had experience of the British seaman's tendency to drink. His boarding party would be as drunk as the Frenchmen in half an hour if he allowed it. A frightful mental picture of himself drifting in the Bay of Biscay with a disabled ship and a drunken crew rose in his mind and filled him with anxiety.

'Put that down,' he ordered.

The urgency of the situation made his seventeen-year-old voice crack like a fourteen-year-old's, and the seaman hesitated, holding the bottle in his hand.

'Put it down, d'ye hear?' said Hornblower, desperate with worry. This was his first independent command; conditions were absolutely novel, and excitement brought out all the passion of his mercurial temperament, while at the same time the more calculating part of his mind told him that if he were not obeyed now he never would be. His pistol was in his belt, and he put his hand on the butt, and it is conceivable that he would have drawn it and used it (if the priming had not got wet, he said to himself bitterly when he thought about the incident later on), but the seaman with one more glance at him put the bottle back into the case. The incident was closed, and it was time for the next step.

'Take these men forrard,' he said, giving the obvious order. 'Throw 'em into the forecastle.'

'Aye aye, sir.'

Most of the Frenchmen could still walk, but three were dragged by their collars, while the British herded the others before them.

'Come alongee,' said one of the seamen. 'Thisa waya.'

He evidently believed a Frenchman would understand him better if he spoke like that. The Frenchman who had greeted their arrival now awakened, and, suddenly realizing he was

42

being dragged forward, broke away and turned back to Hornblower.

'I officer,' he said, pointing to himself. 'I not go wit' zem.'

'Take him away!' said Hornblower. In his tense condition he could not stop to debate trifles.

He dragged the case of bottles down to the ship's side and pitched them overboard two at a time – obviously it was wine of some special vintage which the Frenchmen had decided to drink before the English could get their hands on it, but that weighed not at all with Hornblower, for a British seaman could get drunk on vintage claret as easily as upon service rum. The task was finished before the last of the Frenchmen disappeared into the forecastle, and Hornblower had time to look about him. The strong breeze blew confusingly round his ears, and the ceaseless thunder of the flapping jib made it hard to think as he looked at the ruin aloft. Every sail was flat aback, the brig was moving jerkily, gathering sternway for a space before her untended rudder threw her round to spill the wind and bring her up again like a jibbing horse. His mathematical mind had already had plenty of experience with a well-handled ship, with the delicate adjustment between after sails and headsails. Here the balance had been disturbed, and Hornblower was at work on the problem of forces acting on plane surfaces when his men came trooping back to him. One thing at least was certain, and that was that the precariously hanging foretopsail yard would tear itself free to do all sorts of unforeseeable damage if it were tossed about much more. This ship must be properly hove to, and Hornblower could guess how to set about it, and he formulated the order in his mind just in time to avoid any appearance of hesitation.

'Brace the after yards to larboard,' he said. 'Man the braces, men.'

They obeyed him, while he himself went gingerly to the wheel; he had served a few tricks as helmsman, learning his professional duties under Pellew's orders, but he did not feel happy about it. The spokes felt foreign to his fingers as he took hold; he spun the wheel experimentally but timidly. But it was easy. With the after yards braced round the brig rode more comfortably at once, and the spokes told their own story to his sensitive fingers as the ship became a thing of logical construction again. Hornblower's mind completed the solution of the problem of the effect of the rudder at the same time as his senses solved it empirically. The wheel could be safely lashed, he knew, in these conditions, and he slipped the becket over the spoke and stepped away from the wheel, with the *Marie Galante* riding comfortably and taking the seas on her starboard bow.

The seaman took his competence gratifyingly for granted, but Hornblower, looking at the tangle on the foremast, had not the remotest idea of how to deal with the next problem. He was not even sure about what was wrong. But the hands under his orders were seamen of vast experience, who must have dealt with similar emergencies a score of times. The first – indeed the only – thing to do was to delegate his responsibility.

'Who's the oldest seaman among you?' he demanded – his determination not to quaver made him curt.

'Matthews, sir,' said someone at length, indicating with his thumb the pigtailed and tattooed seaman upon whom he had fallen in the cutter.

'Very well, then. I'll rate you petty officer, Matthews. Get to work at once and clear that raffle away forrard. I'll be busy here aft.'

It was a nervous moment for Hornblower, but Matthews put his knuckles to his forehead.

'Aye aye, sir,' he said, quite as a matter of course.

'Get that jib in first, before it flogs itself to pieces,' said Hornblower, greatly emboldened.

'Aye aye, sir.'

'Carry on, then.'

The seaman turned to go forward, and Hornblower walked

aft. He took the telescope from its becket on the poop, and swept the horizon. There were a few sails in sight; the nearest ones he could recognize as prizes, which, with all sail set that they could carry, were heading for England as fast as they could go. Far away to windward he could see the *Indefatigable*'s topsails as she clawed after the rest of the convoy – she had already overhauled and captured all the slower and less weatherly vessels, so that each succeeding chase would be longer. Soon he would be alone on this wide sea, three hundred miles from England. Three hundred miles – two days with a fair wind; but how long if the wind turned foul?

He replaced the telescope; the men were already hard at work forward, so he went below and looked round the neat cabins of the officers; two single ones for the captain and the mate, presumably, and a double one for the bos'un and the cook or the carpenter. He found the lazarette, identifying it by the miscellaneous stores within it; the door was swinging to and fro with a bunch of keys dangling. The French captain, faced with the loss of all he possessed, had not even troubled to lock the door again after taking out the case of wine. Hornblower locked the door and put the keys in his pocket and felt suddenly lonely – his first experience of the loneliness of the man in command at sea. He went on deck again, and at sight of him Matthews hurried aft and knuckled his forehead.

'Beg pardon, sir, but we'll have to use the jeers to sling that yard again.'

'Very good.'

'We'll need more hands than we have, sir. Can I put some o' they Frenchies to work?'

'If you think you can. If any of them are sober enough.'

'I think I can, sir. Drunk or sober.'

'Very good.'

It was at this moment that Hornblower remembered with bitter self-reproach that the priming of his pistol was probably wet, and he had not scorn enough for himself at having put his trust in a pistol without re-priming after evolutions in a small boat. While Matthews went forward he dashed below again. There was a case of pistols which he remembered having seen in the captain's cabin, with a powder flask and bullet bag hanging beside it. He loaded both weapons and reprimed his own, and came on deck again with three pistols in his belt just as his men appeared from the forecastle herding half a dozen Frenchmen. He posed himself in the poop, straddling with his hands behind his back, trying to adopt an air of magnificent indifference and understanding. With the jeers taking the weight of yard and sail, an hour's hard work resulted in the yard being slung again and the sail reset.

When the work was advancing towards completion, Hornblower came to himself again to remember that in a few minutes he would have to set a course, and he dashed below again to set out the chart and the dividers and parallel rulers. From his pocket he extracted the crumpled scrap of paper with his position on it – he had thrust it in there so carelessly a little while back, at a time when the immediate problem before him was to transfer himself from the *Indefatigable* to the cutter. It made him unhappy to think how cavalierly he had treated that scrap of paper then; he began to feel that life in the Navy, although it seemed to move from one crisis to another, was really one continuous crisis, that even while dealing with one emergency it was necessary to be making plans to deal with the next. He bent over the chart, plotted his position, and laid off his course. It was a queer uncomfortable feeling to think that what had up to this moment been an academic exercise conducted under the reassuring supervision of Mr Soames was now something on which hinged his life and his reputation. He checked his working, decided on his course, and wrote it down on a scrap of paper for fear he should forget it.

So when the foretopsail yard was re-slung, and the prisoners herded back into the forecastle, and Matthews looked to him for further orders, he was ready.

'We'll square away,' he said. 'Matthews, send a man to the wheel.'

He himself gave a hand at the braces; the wind had moderated and he felt his men could handle the brig under her present sail.

'What course, sir?' asked the man at the wheel, and Hornblower dived into his pocket for his scrap of paper.

'Nor'-east by north,' he said, reading it out.

'Nor'-east by north, sir,' said the helmsman; and the *Marie Galante*, running free, set her course for England.

Night was closing in by now, and all round the circle of the horizon there was not a sail in sight. There must be plenty of ships just over the horizon, he knew, but that did not do much to ease his feeling of loneliness as darkness came on. There was so much to do, so much to bear in mind, and all the responsibility lay on his unaccustomed shoulders. The prisoners had to be battened down in the forecastle, a watch had to be set – there was even the trivial matter of hunting up flint and steel to light the binnacle lamp. A hand forward as a lookout, who could also keep an eye on the prisoners below; a hand aft at the wheel. Two hands snatching some sleep – knowing that to get in any sail would be an all-hands job – a hasty meal of water from the scuttle-butt and of biscuit from the cabin stores in the lazarette – a constant eye to be kept on the weather. Hornblower paced the deck in the darkness.

'Why don't you get some sleep, sir?' asked the man at the wheel.

'I will, later on, Hunter,' said Hornblower, trying not to allow his tone to reveal the fact that such a thing had never occurred to him.

He knew it was sensible advice, and he actually tried to follow it, retiring below to fling himself down on the captain's cot; but of course he could not sleep. When he heard the lookout bawling down the companionway to rouse the other two hands to relieve the watch (they were asleep in the next cabin to him) he could not prevent himself from getting up again and coming on deck to see that all was well. With Matthews in charge he felt he should not be anxious, and he drove himself below again, but he had hardly fallen onto the cot again when a new thought brought him to his feet again, his skin cold with anxiety, and a prodigious self-contempt vying with anxiety for first glance in his emotions. He rushed on deck and walked forward to where Matthews was squatting by the knightheads.

'Nothing has been done to see if the brig is taking in any water,' he said – he had hurriedly worked out the wording of that sentence during his walk forward, so as to cast no aspersion on Matthews and yet at the same time, for the sake of discipline, attributing no blame to himself.

'That's so, sir,' said Matthews.

'One of those shots fired by the *Indefatigable* hulled her,' went on Hornblower. 'What damage did it do?'

'I don't rightly know, sir,' said Matthews. 'I was in the cutter at the time.'

'We must look as soon as it's light,' said Hornblower.' And we'd better sound the well now.'

Those were brave words; during his rapid course in seamanship aboard the *Indefatigable* Hornblower had had a little instruction everywhere, working under the orders of every head of department in rotation. Once he had been with the carpenter when he sounded the well – whether he could find the well in this ship and sound it he did not know.

'Aye aye, sir,' said Matthews, without hesitation, and strolled aft to the pump. 'You'll need a light, sir. I'll get one.'

When he came back with the lantern he shone it on the coiled sounding line hanging beside the pump, so that Hornblower recognized it at once. He lifted it down, inserted the three-foot weighted rod into the aperture of the well, and then remembered in time to take it out again and make sure it was dry. Then he let it drop, paying out the line until he felt the rod strike the ship's bottom with a satisfactory thud. He hauled out the line again, and Matthews held the lantern as

Hornblower with some trepidation brought out the timber to examine it.

'Not a drop, sir!' said Matthews. 'Dry as yesterday's pannikin.'

Hornblower was agreeably surprised. Any ship he had ever heard of leaked to a certain extent; even in the well-found *Indefatigable* pumping had been necessary every day. He did not know whether this dryness was a remarkable phenomenon or a very remarkable one. He wanted to be both noncommittal and imperturbable.

'H'm,' was the comment he eventually produced. 'Very good, Matthews. Coil that line again.'

The knowledge that the *Marie Galante* was making no water at all might have encouraged him to sleep, if the wind had not chosen to veer steadily and strengthen itself somewhat soon after he retired again. It was Matthews who came down and pounded on his door with the unwelcome news.

'We can't keep the course you set much longer, sir,' concluded Matthews. 'And the wind's coming gusty-like.'

'Very good, I'll be up. Call all hands,' said Hornblower, with a testiness that might have been the result of a sudden awakening if it had not really disguised his inner quaverings.

With such a small crew he dared not run the slightest risk of being taken by surprise by the weather. Nothing could be done in a hurry, as he soon found. He had to take the wheel while his four hands laboured at reefing topsails and snugging the brig down; the task took half the night, and by the time it was finished it was quite plain that with the wind veering northerly the *Marie Galante* could not steer north-east by north any longer. Hornblower gave up the wheel and went below to the chart, but what he saw there only confirmed the pessimistic decision he had already reached by mental calculation. As close to the wind as they could lie on this tack they could not weather Ushant. Shorthanded as he was he did not dare continue in the hope that the wind might back; all his reading and all his instruction had warned him of the terrors of a lee shore. There was nothing for it but to go about; he returned to the deck with a heavy heart.

'All hands wear ship,' he said, trying to bellow the order in the manner of Mr Bolton, the third lieutenant of the *Indefatigable*.

They brought the brig safely round, and she took up her new course, close hauled on the starboard tack. Now she was heading away from the dangerous shores of France, without a doubt, but she was heading nearly as directly away from the friendly shores of England – gone was all hope of an easy two days' run to England; gone was any hope of sleep that night for Hornblower.

During the year before he joined the Navy Hornblower had attended classes given by a penniless French émigré in French, music, and dancing. Early enough the wretched émigré had found that Hornblower had no ear for music whatever, which made it almost impossible to teach him to dance, and so he had endeavoured to earn his fee by concentrating on French. A good deal of what he had taught Hornblower had found a permanent resting place in Hornblower's tenacious memory. He had never thought it would be of much use to him, but he discovered the contrary when the French captain at dawn insisted on an interview with him. The Frenchman had a little English, but it was a pleasant surprise to Hornblower to find that they actually could get along better in French, as soon as he could fight down his shyness sufficiently to produce the halting words.

The captain drank thirstily from the scuttlebut; his cheeks were of course unshaven and he wore a bleary look after twelve hours in a crowded forecastle, where he had been battened down three parts drunk.

'My men are hungry,' said the captain; he did not look hungry himself.

'Mine also,' said Hornblower. 'I also.'

It was natural when one spoke French to gesticulate, to

indicate his men with a wave of the hand and himself with a tap on the chest.

'I have a cook,' said the captain.

It took some time to arrange the terms of a truce. The Frenchmen were to be allowed on deck, the cook was to provide food for everyone on board, and while these amenities were permitted, until noon, the French would make no attempt to take the ship.

'Good,' said the captain at length; and when Hornblower had given the necessary orders permitting the release of the crew he shouted for the cook and entered into an urgent discussion regarding dinner. Soon smoke was issuing satisfactorily from the galley chimney.

Then the captain looked up at the grey sky, at the close reefed topsails, and glanced into the binnacle at the compass.

'A foul wind for England,' he remarked.

'Yes,' said Hornblower shortly. He did not want this Frenchman to guess at his trepidation and bitterness.

The captain seemed to be feeling the motion of the brig under his feet with attention.

'She rides a little heavily, does she not?' he said.

'Perhaps,' said Hornblower. He was not familiar with the *Marie Galante*, nor with ships at all, and he had no opinion on the subject, but he was not going to reveal his ignorance.

'Does she leak?' asked the captain.

'There is no water in her,' said Hornblower.

'Ah!' said the captain. 'But you would find none in the well. We are carrying a cargo of rice, you must remember.'

'Yes,' said Hornblower.

He found it very hard at that moment to remain outwardly unperturbed, as his mind grasped the implications of what was being said to him. Rice would absorb every drop of water taken in by the ship, so that no leak would be apparent on sounding the well – and yet every drop of water taken in would deprive her of that much buoyancy, all the same.

'One shot from your cursed frigate struck us in the hull,'

said the captain. 'Of course you have investigated the damage?'

'Of course,' said Hornblower, lying bravely.

But as soon as he could he had a private conversation with Matthews on the point, and Matthews instantly looked grave.

'Where did the shot hit her, sir?' he asked.

'Somewhere on the port side, forrard, I should judge.'

He and Matthews craned their necks over the ship's side.

'Can't see nothin', sir,' said Matthews. 'Lower me over the side in a bowline and I'll see what I can find, sir.'

Hornblower was about to agree and then changed his mind.

'I'll go over the side myself,' he said.

He could not analyse the motives which impelled him to say that. Partly he wanted to see things with his own eyes; partly he was influenced by the doctrine that he should never give an order he was not prepared to carry out himself – but mostly it must have been the desire to impose a penance on himself for his negligence.

Matthews and Carson put a bowline round him and lowered him over. He found himself dangling against the ship's side, with the sea bubbling just below him; as the ship pitched the sea came up to meet him, and he was wet to the waist in the first five seconds; and as the ship rolled he was alternately swung away from the side and bumped against it. The men with the line walked steadily aft, giving him the chance to examine the whole side of the brig above water, and there was not a shot hole to be seen. He said as much to Matthews when they hauled him on deck.

'Then it's below the waterline, sir,' said Matthews, saying just what was in Hornblower's mind. 'You're sure the shot hit her, sir?'

'Yes, I'm sure,' snapped Hornblower.

Lack of sleep and worry and a sense of guilt were all shortening his temper, and he had to speak sharply or break down in tears. But he had already decided on the next move –

he had made up his mind about that while they were hauling him up.

'We'll heave her to on the other tack and try again,' he said.

On the other tack the ship would incline over to the other side, and the shot-hole, if there was one, would not be so deeply submerged. Hornblower stood with the water dripping from his clothes as they wore the brig round; the wind was keen and cold, but he was shivering with expectancy rather than cold. The heeling of the brig laid him much more definitely against the side, and they lowered him until his legs were scraping over the marine growths which she carried there between wind and water. They then walked aft with him, dragging him along the side of the ship, and just abaft the foremast he found what he was seeking.

'Avast, there!' he yelled up to the deck, mastering the sick despair that he felt. The motion of the bowline along the ship ceased. 'Lower away! Another two feet!'

Now he was waist-deep in the water, and when the brig swayed the water closed briefly over his head, like a momentary death. Here it was, two feet below the waterline even with the brig hove to on this tack – a splintered, jagged hole, square rather than round, and a foot across. As the sea boiled round him Hornblower even fancied he could hear it bubbling into the ship, but that might be pure fancy.

He hailed the deck for them to haul him up again, and they stood eagerly listening for what he had to say.

'Two feet below the waterline, sir?' said Matthews. 'She was close hauled and heeling right over, of course, when we hit her. But her bows must have lifted just as we fired. And of course she's lower in the water now.'

That was the point. Whatever they did now, however much they heeled her, that hole would be under water. And on the other tack it would be far under water, with much additional pressure; yet on the present tack they were headed for France. And the more water they took in, the lower the brig would settle, and the greater would be the pressure forcing water in through the hole. Something must be done to plug the leak, and Hornblower's reading of the manuals of seamanship told him what it was.

'We must fother a sail and get it over that hole,' he announced. 'Call those Frenchmen over.'

To fother a sail was to make something like a vast hairy doormat out of it, by threading innumerable lengths of half-unravelled line through it. When this was done the sail would be lowered below the ship's bottom and placed against the hole. The inward pressure would then force the hairy mass so tightly against the hole that the entrance of water would be made at least much more difficult.

The Frenchmen were not quick to help in the task; it was no longer their ship, and they were heading for an English prison, so that even with their lives at stake they were somewhat apathetic. It took time to get out a new topgallant sail – Hornblower felt that the stouter the canvas the better – and to set a party to work cutting lengths of line, threading them through, and unravelling them. The French captain looked at them squatting on the deck all at work.

'Five years I spent in a prison hulk in Portsmouth during the last war,' he said. 'Five years.'

'Yes,' said Hornblower.

He might have felt sympathy, but he was not only preoccupied with his own problems but he was numb with cold. He not only had every intention if possible of escorting the French captain to England and to prison again but he also at that very moment intended to go below and appropriate some of his spare clothing.

Down below it seemed to Hornblower as if the noises all about him – the creaks and groans of a wooden ship at sea – were more pronounced than usual. The brig was riding easily enough hove-to, and yet the bulkheads down below were cracking and creaking as if the brig were racking herself to pieces in a storm. He dismissed the notion as a product of his over-stimulated imagination but by the time he had towelled himself into something like warmth and put on the captain's best suit it recurred to him; the brig was groaning as if in stress.

He came on deck again to see how the working party was progressing. He had hardly been on deck two minutes when one of the Frenchmen, reaching back for another length of line, stopped in his movement to stare at the deck. He picked at a deck seam, looked up and caught Hornblower's eye, and called to him. Hornblower made no pretence of understanding the words; the gestures explained themselves. The deck seam was opening a little; the pitch was bulging out of it. Hornblower looked at the phenomenon without understanding it – only a foot or two of the seam was open, and the rest of the deck seemed solid enough. No! Now that his attention was called to it, and he looked further, there were one or two other places in the deck where the pitch had risen in ridges from out of the seams. It was something beyond his limited experience, even beyond his extensive reading. But the French captain was at his side staring at the deck too.

'My God!' he said. 'The rice! The rice!'

The French word 'riz' that he used was unknown to Hornblower, but he stamped his foot on the deck and pointed down through it.

'The cargo!' he said in explanation. 'It – it grows bigger.'

Matthews was with them now, and without knowing a word of French he understood.

'Didn't I hear this brig was full of rice, sir?' he asked.

'Yes.'

'That's it, then. The water's got into it and it's swelling.'

So it would. Dry rice soaked in water would double or treble its volume. The cargo was swelling and bursting the seams of the ship open. Hornblower remembered the unnatural creaks and groans below. It was a black moment; he looked round at the unfriendly sea for inspiration and support, and found neither. Several seconds passed before he was ready to speak, and ready to maintain the dignity of a naval officer in face of difficulties.

'The sooner we get that sail over that hole the better, then,' he said. It was too much to be expected that his voice should sound quite natural. 'Hurry those Frenchmen up.'

He turned to pace the deck, so as to allow his feelings to subside and to set his thoughts running in an orderly fashion again, but the French captain was at his elbow, voluble as a Job's comforter.

'I said I thought the ship was riding heavily,' he said. 'She is lower in the water.'

'Go to the devil,' said Hornblower, in English – he could not think up the French for that phrase.

Even as he stood he felt a sudden sharp shock beneath his feet, as if someone had hit the deck underneath them with a mallet. The ship was springing apart bit by bit.

'Hurry with that sail!' he yelled, turning back to the working party, and then was angry with himself because the tone of his voice must have betrayed undignified agitation.

At last an area five feet square of the sail was fothered, lines were rove through the grommets, and the working party hurried forward to work the sail under the brig and drag it aft to the hole. Hornblower was taking off his clothes, not out of regard for the captain's property but so as to keep them dry for himself.

'I'll go over and see that it's in place,' he said. 'Matthews, get a bowline ready for me.'

Naked and wet, it seemed to him as if the wind blew clear through him; rubbing against the ship's side as she rolled he lost a good deal of skin, and the waves passing down the ship smacked at him with a boisterous lack of consideration. But he saw the fothered sail placed against the hole, and with intense satisfaction he saw the hairy mass suck into position, dimpling over the hole to form a deep hollow so that he could be sure that the hole was plugged solid. They hauled him up again when he hailed, and awaited his orders; he stood naked, stupid with cold and fatigue and lack of sleep, struggling to form his next decision.

'Lay her on the starboard tack,' he said at length.

If the brig were going to sink, it hardly mattered if it were one hundred or two hundred miles from the French coast; if she were to stay afloat he wanted to be well clear of that lee shore and the chance of recapture. The shot hole with its fothered sail would be deeper under water to increase the risk, but it seemed to be the best chance. The French captain saw them making preparations to wear the brig round, and turned upon Hornblower with voluble protests. With this wind they could make Bordeaux easily on the other tack. Hornblower was risking all their lives, he said. Into Hornblower's numb mind crept, uninvited, the translation of something he had previously wanted to say. He could use it now.

'Allez au diable,' he snapped, as he put the Frenchman's stout woollen shirt on over his head.

When his head emerged the Frenchman was still protesting volubly, so violently indeed that a new doubt came into Hornblower's mind. A word to Matthews sent him round the French prisoners to search for weapons. There was nothing to be found except the sailors' knives, but as a matter of precaution Hornblower had them all impounded, and when he had dressed he went to special trouble with his three pistols, drawing the charges from them and reloading and re-priming afresh. Three pistols in his belt looked piratical, as though he were still young enough to be playing imaginative games, but Hornblower felt in his bones that there might be a time when the Frenchmen might try to rise against their captors, and three pistols would not be too many against twelve desperate men who had makeshift weapons ready to hand, belaying pins and the like.

Matthews was awaiting him with a long face.

'Sir,' he said, 'begging your pardon, but I don't like the looks of it. Straight, I don't. I don't like the feel of her. She's settlin' down and she's opening up, I'm certain sure. Beg your pardon, sir, for saying so.'

Down below Hornblower had heard the fabric of the ship continuing to crack and complain; up here the deck seams were gaping more widely. There was a very likely explanation; the swelling of the rice must have forced open the ship's seams below water, so that plugging the shot-hole would have only eliminated what would be by now only a minor leak. Water must still be pouring in, the cargo still swelling, opening up the ship like an overblown flower. Ships were built to withstand blows from without, and there was nothing about their construction to resist an outward pressure. Wider and wider would gape the seams, and faster and faster the sea would gain access to the cargo.

'Look'e there, sir!' said Matthews suddenly.

In the broad light of day a small grey shape was hurrying along the weather scuppers; another one followed it and another after that. Rats! Something convulsive must be going on down below to bring them on deck in daytime, from out of their comfortable nests among the unlimited food of the cargo. The pressure must be enormous. Hornblower felt another small shock beneath his feet at that moment, as something further parted beneath them. But there was one more card to play, one last line of defence that he could think of.

'I'll jettison the cargo,' said Hornblower. He had never uttered that word in his life, but he had read it. 'Get the prisoners and we'll start.'

The battened-down hatch cover was domed upwards curiously and significantly; as the wedges were knocked out one plank tore loose at one end with a crash, pointing diagonally upwards, and as the working party lifted off the cover a brown form followed it upwards – a bag of rice, forced out by the underlying pressure until it jammed in the hatchway.

'Tail onto those tackles and sway it up,' said Hornblower.

Bag by bag the rice was hauled up from the hold; sometimes the bags split, allowing a torrent of rice to pour onto the deck, but that did not matter. Another section of the working party swept rice and bags to the lee side and into the ever-hungry sea. After the first three bags the difficulties increased, for the cargo was so tightly jammed below that it called for enormous force to tear each bag out of its position. Two men had to go down the hatchway to pry the bags loose and adjust the slings. There was a momentary hesitation on the part of the two Frenchmen to whom Hornblower pointed – the bags might not all be jammed and the hold of a tossing ship was a dangerous place wherein a roll might bury them alive – but Hornblower had no thought at that moment for other people's human fears. He scowled at the brief check and they hastened to lower themselves down the hatchway. The labour was enormous as it went on hour after hour; the men at the tackles were dripping with sweat and drooping with fatigue, but they had to relieve periodically the men below, for the bags had jammed themselves in tiers, pressed hard against the ship's bottom below and the deck beams above, and when the bags immediately below the hatchway had been swayed up the surrounding ones had to be pried loose, out of each tier. Then when a small clearance had been made in the neighbourhood of the hatchway, and they were getting deeper down into the hold, they made the inevitable discovery. The lower tiers of bags had been wetted, their contents had swelled, and the bags had burst. The lower half of the hold was packed solid with damp rice which could only be got out with shovels and a hoist. The still intact bags of the upper tiers, farther away from the hatchway, were still jammed tight, calling for much labour to free them and to manhandle them under the hatchway to be hoisted out.

Hornblower, facing the problem, was distracted by a touch on his elbow when Matthews came up to speak to him.

'It ain't no go, sir,' said Matthews. 'She's lower in the water an' settlin' fast.'

Hornblower walked to the ship's side with him and looked

over. There could be no doubt about it. He had been over the side himself and could remember the height of the waterline, and he had for a more exact guide the level of the fothered sail under the ship's bottom. The brig was a full six inches lower in the water – and this after fifty tons of rice at least had been hoisted out and flung over the side. The brig must be leaking like a basket, with water pouring in through the gaping seams to be sucked up immediately by the thirsty rice.

Hornblower's left hand was hurting him, and he looked down to discover that he was gripping the rail with it so tightly as to cause him pain, without knowing he was doing so. He released his grip and looked about him, at the afternoon sun, at the tossing sea. He did not want to give in and admit defeat. The French captain came up to him.

'This is folly,' he said. 'Madness, sir. My men are overcome by fatigue.'

Over by the hatchway, Hornblower saw, Hunter was driving the French seamen to their work with a rope's end, which he was using furiously. There was not much more work to be got out of the Frenchmen; and at that moment the *Marie Galante* rose heavily to a wave and wallowed down the further side. Even his inexperience could detect the sluggishness and ominous deadness of her movements. The brig had not much longer to float, and there was a good deal to do.

'I shall make preparations for abandoning the ship, Matthews,' he said.

He poked his chin upwards as he spoke; he would not allow either a Frenchman or a seaman to guess at his despair.

'Aye aye, sir,' said Matthews.

The *Marie Galante* carried a boat on chocks abaft the mainmast; at Matthews' summons the men abandoned their work on the cargo and hurried to the business of putting food and water in her.

'Beggin' your pardon, sir,' said Hunter aside to Hornblower, 'but you ought to see you have warm clothes, sir. I been in an open boat ten days once, sir.'

'Thank you, Hunter,' said Hornblower.

There was much to think of. Navigating instruments, charts, compass – would he be able to get a good observation with his sextant in a tossing little boat? Common prudence dictated that they should have all the food and water with them that the boat could carry; but – Hornblower eyed the wretched craft dubiously – seventeen men would fill it to over-flowing anyway. He would have to leave much to the judge-ment of the French captain and of Matthews.

The tackles were manned and the boat was swayed up from the chocks and lowered into the water in the tiny lee afforded on the lee quarter. The *Marie Galante* put her nose into a wave, refusing to rise to it; green water came over the star-board bow and poured aft along the deck before a sullen wallow on the part of the brig sent it into the scuppers. There was not much time to spare – a rending crash from below told that the cargo was still swelling and forcing the bulkheads. There was a panic among the Frenchmen, who began to tumble down into the boat with loud cries. The French cap-tain took one look at Hornblower and then followed them; two of the British seamen were already over the side fending off the boat.

'Go along,' said Hornblower to Matthews and Carson, who still lingered. He was the captain; it was his place to leave the ship last.

So waterlogged was the brig now that it was not at all difficult to step down into the boat from the deck; the British seamen were in the sternsheets and made room for him.

'Take the tiller, Matthews,' said Hornblower; he did not feel he was competent to handle that over-loaded boat. 'Shove off, there!'

The boat and the brig parted company; the *Marie Galante*, with her helm lashed, poked her nose into the wind and hung there. She had acquired a sudden list, with the starboard side scuppers nearly under water. Another wave broke over her deck, pouring up to the open hatchway. Now she righted herself, her deck nearly level with the sea, and then she sank, on an even keel, the water closing over her, her masts slowly disappearing. For an instant her sails even gleamed under the green water.

'She's gone,' said Matthews.

Hornblower watched the disappearance of his first command. The *Marie Galante* had been entrusted to him to bring into port, and he had failed, failed on his first independent mission. He looked very hard at the setting sun, hoping no one would notice the tears that were filling his eyes.

CHAPTER THREE

THE PENALTY OF FAILURE

DAYLIGHT crept over the tossing waters of the Bay of Biscay to reveal a small boat riding on its wide expanses. It was a very crowded boat; in the bows huddled the French crew of the sunken brig *Marie Galante*, amidships sat the captain and his mate, and in the sternsheets sat Midshipman Horatio Hornblower and the four English seamen who had once constituted the prize-crew of the brig. Hornblower was seasick, for his delicate stomach, having painfully accustomed itself to the motion of the *Indefatigable*, rebelled at the antics of the small boat as she pitched jerkily to her sea-anchor. He was cold and weary as well as seasick after his second night without sleep – he had been vomiting spasmodically all through the hours of darkness, and in the depression which seasickness brings he had thought gloomily about the loss of the *Marie Galante*. If he had only remembered earlier to plug that shot-hole! Excuses came to his mind only to be discarded. There had been so much to do, and so few men to do it with – the French crew to guard, the damage aloft to repair, the course to set. The absorbent qualities of the cargo of rice which the *Marie*

Galante carried had deceived him when he had remembered to sound the well. All this might be true, but the fact remained that he had lost his ship, his first command. In his own eyes there was no excuse for his failure.

The French crew had wakened with the dawn and were chattering like a nest of magpies; Matthews and Carson beside him were moving stiffly to ease their aching joints.

'Breakfast, sir?' said Matthews.

It was like the games Hornblower had played as a lonely little boy, when he had sat in the empty pig-trough and pretended he was cast away in an open boat. Then he had parcelled out the bit of bread or whatever it was which he had obtained from the kitchen into a dozen rations, counting them carefully, each one to last a day. But a small boy's eager appetite had made those days very short, not more than five minutes long; after standing up in the pig-trough and shading his eyes and looking round the horizon for the succour that he could not discover, he would sit down again, tell himself that the life of a castaway was hard, and then decide that another night had passed and that it was time to eat another ration from his dwindling supply. So here under Hornblower's eye the French captain and mate served out a biscuit of hard bread to each person in the boat, and filled the pannikin for each man in turn from the water breakers under the thwarts. But Hornblower when he sat in the pig-trough, despite his vivid imagination, never thought of this hideous seasickness, of the cold and the cramps, nor of how his skinny posterior would ache with its constant pressure against the hard timbers of the sternsheets; nor, in the sublime self-confidence of childhood, had he ever thought how heavy could be the burden of responsibility on the shoulders of a senior naval officer aged seventeen.

He dragged himself back from the memories of that recent childhood to face the present situation. The grey sky, as far as his inexperienced eye could tell, bore no presage of deterioration in the weather. He wetted his finger and held it up, looking in the boat's compass to gauge the direction of the wind.

'Backing westerly a little, sir,' said Matthews, who had been copying his movements.

'That's so,' agreed Hornblower, hurriedly going through in his mind his recent lessons in boxing the compass. His course to weather Ushant was nor'-east by north, he knew, and the boat close hauled would not lie closer than eight points off the wind – he had lain-to to the sea-anchor all night because the wind had been coming from too far north to enable him to steer for England. But now the wind had backed. Eight points from nor'-east by north was nor'-west by west, and the wind was even more westerly than that. Close hauled he could weather Ushant and even have a margin for contingencies, to keep him clear of the lee shore, which the seamanship books and his own common sense told him was so dangerous.

'We'll make sail, Matthews,' he said; his hand was still grasping the biscuit which his rebellious stomach refused to accept.

'Aye aye, sir.'

A shout to the Frenchmen crowded in the bows drew their attention; in the circumstances it hardly needed Hornblower's halting French to direct them to carry out the obvious task of getting in the sea-anchor. But it was not too easy, with the boat so crowded and hardly a foot of freeboard. The mast was already stepped, and the lug sail bent ready to hoist. Two Frenchmen, balancing precariously, tailed onto the halliard amd the sail rose up the mast.

'Hunter, take the sheet,' said Hornblower. 'Matthews, take the tiller. Keep her close hauled on the port tack.'

'Close hauled on the port tack, sir.'

The French captain had watched the proceedings with intense interest from his seat amidships. He had not understood the last, decisive order, but he grasped its meaning quickly enough when the boat came round and steadied on the port tack, heading for England. He stood up, spluttering angry protests.

'The wind is fair for Bordeaux,' he said, gesticulating with clenched fists. 'We could be there by to-morrow. Why do we go north?'

'We go to England,' said Hornblower.

'But – but – it will take us a week! A week even if the wind stays fair. This boat – it is too crowded. We cannot endure a storm. It is madness.'

Hornblower had guessed at the moment the captain stood up what he was going to say, and he hardly bothered to translate the expostulations to himself. He was too tired and too seasick to enter into an argument in a foreign language. He ignored the captain. Not for anything on earth would he turn the boat's head towards France. His naval career had only just begun, and even if it were to be blighted on account of the loss of the *Marie Galante* he had no intention of rotting for years in a French prison.

'Sir!' said the French captain.

The mate who shared the captain's thwart was protesting too, and now they turned to their crew behind them and told them what was going on. An angry movement stirred the crowd.

'Sir!' said the captain again. 'I insist that you head towards Bordeaux.'

He showed signs of advancing upon them; one of the crew behind him began to pull the boat-hook clear, and it would be a dangerous weapon. Hornblower pulled one of the pistols from his belt and pointed it at the captain, who, with the muzzle four feet from his breast, fell back before the gesture. Without taking his eyes off him Hornblower took a second pistol with his left hand.

'Take this, Matthews,' he said.

'Aye aye, sir,' said Matthews, obeying; and then, after a respectful pause, 'Beggin' your pardon, sir, but hadn't you better cock your pistol, sir?'

'Yes,' said Hornblower, exasperated at his own forgetfulness.

He drew the hammer back with a click, and the menacing sound made more acute still the French captain's sense of his own danger, with a cocked and loaded pistol pointed at his stomach in a heaving boat. He waved his hands desperately.

'Please,' he said, 'point it some other way, sir.'

He drew farther back, huddling against the men behind him.

'Hey, avast there, you,' shouted Matthews loudly – a French sailor was trying to let go the halliard unobserved.

'Shoot any man who looks dangerous, Matthews,' said Hornblower.

He was so intent on enforcing his will upon these men, so desperately anxious to retain his liberty, that his face was contracted into a beast-like scowl. No one looking at him could doubt his determination for a moment. He would allow no human life to come between him and his decisions. There was still a third pistol in his belt, and the Frenchmen could guess that if they tried a rush a quarter of them at least would meet their deaths before they overpowered the Englishmen, and the French captain knew he would be the first to die. His expressive hands, waving out from his sides – he could not take his eyes from the pistol – told his men to make no further resistance. Their murmurings died away, and the captain began to plead.

'Five years I was in an English prison during the last war,' he said. 'Let us reach an agreement. Let us go to France. When we reach the shore – anywhere you choose, sir – we will land and you can continue on your journey. Or we can all land, and I will use all my influence to have you and your men sent back to England under cartel, without exchange or ransom. I swear I will.'

'No,' said Hornblower.

England was far easier to reach from here than from the French Biscay coast; as for the other suggestion, Hornblower knew enough about the new government washed up by the revolution in France to be sure that they would never part with prisoners on the representation of a merchant captain. And trained seamen were scarce in France; it was his duty to keep these dozen from returning.

'No,' he said again, in reply to the captain's fresh protests.

'Shall I clout 'im on the jaw, sir?' asked Hunter, at Hornblower's side.

'No,' said Hornblower again; but the Frenchman saw the gesture and guessed at the meaning of the words, and subsided into sullen silence.

But he was roused again at the sight of Hornblower's pistol on his knee, still pointed at him. A sleepy finger might press that trigger.

'Sir,' he said, 'put that pistol away, I beg of you. It is dangerous.'

Hornblower's eye was cold and unsympathetic.

'Put it away, please. I will do nothing to interfere with your command of this boat. I promise you that.'

'Do you swear it?'

'I swear it.'

'And these others?'

The captain looked round at his crew with voluble explanations, and grudgingly they agreed.

'They swear it too.'

'Very well, then.'

Hornblower started to replace the pistol in his belt, and remembered to put it on half-cock in time to save himself from shooting himself in the stomach. Everyone in the boat relaxed into apathy. The boat was rising and swooping rhythmically now, a far more comfortable motion than when it had jerked to a sea-anchor, and Hornblower's stomach lost some of its resentment. He had been two nights without sleep. His head lowered on his chest, and then he leaned sideways against Hunter, and slept peacefully, while the boat, with the wind nearly abeam, headed steadily for England.

What woke him late in the day was when Matthews, cramped and weary, was compelled to surrender the tiller to Carson, and after that they kept watch and watch, a hand at the sheet and a hand at the tiller and the others trying to rest. Hornblower took his turn at the sheet, but he would not trust himself with the tiller, especially when night fell; he knew he had not the knack of keeping the boat on her course by the feel of the wind on his cheek and the tiller in his hand.

It was not until long after breakfast the next day – almost noon in fact – that they sighted the sail. It was a Frenchman who saw it first, and his excited cry roused them all. There were three square topsails coming up over the horizon on their weather bow, nearing them so rapidly on a converging course that each time the boat rose on a wave a considerably greater area of canvas was visible.

'What do you think she is, Matthews?' asked Hornblower, while the boat buzzed with the Frenchmen's excitement.

'I can't tell, sir, but I don't like the looks of her,' said Matthews doubtfully. 'She ought to have her t'gallants set in this breeze – and her courses too, an' she hasn't. An' I don't like the cut of her jib, sir. She – she might be a Frenchie to me, sir.'

Any ship travelling for peaceful purposes would naturally have all possible sail set. This ship had not. Hence she was engaged in some belligerent design, but there were more chances that she was British than that she was French, even in here in the Bay. Hornblower took a long look at her; a smallish vessel, although ship-rigged. Flush-decked, with a look of speed about her – her hull was visible at intervals now, with a line of gunports.

'She looks French all over to me, sir,' said Hunter. 'Privateer, seemly.'

'Stand by to jibe,' said Hornblower.

They brought the boat round before the wind, heading directly away from the ship. But in war as in the jungle, to fly is to invite pursuit and attack. The ship set courses and topgallants and came tearing down upon them, passed them at half a cable's length and then hove-to, having cut off their escape. The ship's rail was lined with a curious crowd – a large crew for a vessel that size. A hail came across the water to the boat, and the words were French. The English seamen subsided into curses, while the French captain cheerfully stood up and replied, and the French crew brought the boat alongside the ship.

A handsome young man in a plum-coloured coat with a lace stock greeted Hornblower when he stepped on the deck.

'Welcome, sir, to the *Pique*,' he said in French. 'I am Captain Neuville, of this privateer. And you are –?'

'Midshipman Hornblower, of His Britannic Majesty's ship *Indefatigable*,' growled Hornblower.

'You seem to be in evil humour,' said Neuville. 'Please do not be so distressed at the fortunes of war. You will be accommodated in this ship, until we return to port, with every comfort possible at sea. I beg of you to consider yourself quite at home. For instance, those pistols in your belt must discommode you more than a little. Permit me to relieve you of their weight.'

He took the pistols neatly from Hornblower's belt as he spoke, looked Hornblower keenly over, and then went on.

'That dirk that you wear at your side, sir. Would you oblige me by the loan of it? I assure you that I will return it to you when we part company. But while you are on board here I fear that your impetuous youth might lead you into some rash act while you are wearing a weapon which a credulous mind might believe to be lethal. A thousand thanks. And now might I show you the berth that is being prepared for you?'

With a courteous bow he led the way below. Two decks down, presumably at the level of a foot or two below the water line, was a wide bare 'tweendecks, dimly lighted and scantily ventilated by the hatchways.

'Our slave deck,' explained Neuville carelessly.

'Slave deck?' asked Hornblower.

'Yes. It is here that the slaves were confined during the middle passage.'

Much was clear to Hornblower at once. A slave ship could be readily converted into a privateer. She would already be armed with plenty of guns to defend herself against treacherous attacks while making her purchases in the African rivers; she was faster than the average merchant ship both because of the lack of need of hold space and because with a highly perishable cargo such as slaves speed was a desirable quality, and she was constructed to carry large numbers of men and the great quantities of food and water necessary to keep them supplied while at sea in search of prizes.

'Our market in San Domingo has been closed to us by recent events, of which you must have heard, sir,' went on Neuville, 'and so that the *Pique* could continue to return dividends to me I have converted her into a privateer. Moreover, seeing that the activities of the Committee of Public Safety at present make Paris a more unhealthy spot even than the West Coast of Africa, I decided to take command of my vessel myself. To say nothing of the fact that a certain resolution and hardihood are necessary to make a privateer a profitable investment.'

Neuville's face hardened for a moment into an expression of the grimmest determination, and then softened at once into its previous meaningless politeness.

'This door in this bulkhead,' he continued, 'leads to the quarters I have set aside for captured officers. Here, as you see, is your cot. Please make yourself at home here. Should this ship go into action – as I trust she will frequently do – the hatches above will be battened down. But except on those occasions you will of course be at liberty to move about the ship at your will. Yet I suppose I had better add that any hare-brained attempt on the part of prisoners to interfere with the working or wellbeing of this ship would be deeply resented by the crew. They serve on shares, you understand, and are risking their lives and their liberty. I would not be surprised if any rash person who endangered their dividends and freedom were dropped over the side into the sea.'

Hornblower forced himself to reply; he would not reveal that he was almost struck dumb by the calculating callousness of this last speech.

'I understand,' he said.

'Excellent! Now is there anything further you may need, sir?'

Hornblower looked round the bare quarters in which he was to suffer lonely confinement, lit by a dim glimmer of light from a swaying slush lamp.

'Could I have something to read?' he asked.

Neuville thought for a moment.

'I fear there are only professional books,' he said. 'But I can let you have Grandjean's *Principles of Navigation*, and Lebrun's *Handbook on Seamanship* and some similar volumes, if you think you can understand the French in which they are written.'

'I'll try,' said Hornblower.

Probably it was as well that Hornblower was provided with the materials for such strenuous mental exercise. The effort of reading French and of studying his profession at one and the same time kept his mind busy during the dreary days while the *Pique* cruised in search of prizes. Most of the time the Frenchmen ignored him – he had to force himself upon Neuville once to protest against the employment of his four British seamen on the menial work of pumping out the ship, but he had to retire worsted from the argument, if argument it could be called, when Neuville icily refused to discuss the question. Hornblower went back to his quarters with burning cheeks and red ears, and, as ever, when he was mentally disturbed, the thought of his guilt returned to him with new force.

If only he had plugged that shot-hole sooner! A clearer-headed officer, he told himself, would have done so. He had lost his ship, the *Indefatigable*'s precious prize, and there was no health in him. Sometimes he made himself review the situation calmly. Professionally, he might not – probably would not – suffer for his negligence. A midshipman with only four for a prize-crew, put on board a two-hundred-ton brig that had been subjected to considerable firing from a frigate's guns, would not be seriously blamed when she sank under him. But Hornblower knew at the same time that he was at least partly at fault. If it was ignorance – there was no excuse for ignorance. If he had allowed his multiple cares to distract him from the business of plugging the shot-hole immediately, that was incompetence, and there was no excuse for incompetence. When he thought along those lines he was overwhelmed by waves of despair and of self-contempt, and there was no one to comfort him. The day of his birthday, when he looked at himself at the vast age of eighteen, was the worst of all. Eighteen and a discredited prisoner in the hands of a French privateersman! His self-respect was at its lowest ebb.

The *Pique* was seeking her prey in the most frequented waters in the world, the approaches to the Channel, and there could be no more vivid demonstration of the vastness of the ocean than the fact that she cruised day after day without glimpsing a sail. She maintained a triangular course, reaching to the north-west, tacking to the south, running under easy sail north-easterly again, with lookouts at every masthead, with nothing to see but the tossing waste of water. Until the morning when a high-pitched yell from the foretopgallant masthead attracted the attention of everybody on deck, including Hornblower, standing lonely in the waist. Neuville, by the wheel, bellowed a question to the lookout, and Hornblower, thanks to his recent studies, could translate the answer. There was a sail visible to windward, and next moment the lookout reported that it had altered course and was running down towards them.

That meant a great deal. In wartime any merchant ship would be suspicious of strangers and would give them as wide a berth as possible; and especially when she was to windward and therefore far safer. Only someone prepared to fight or possessed of a perfectly morbid curiosity would abandon a windward position. A wild and unreasonable hope filled Hornblower's breast; a ship of war at sea – thanks to England's maritime mastery – would be far more probably English than French. And this was the cruising ground of the *Indefatigable*, his own ship, stationed there specially to fulfil the double function of looking out for French commerce-destroyers and intercepting French blockade-runners. A hundred miles from here she had put him and his prize crew on board the *Marie Galante*. It was a thousand to one, he exaggerated despairingly to himself, against any ship sighted being the *Indefatigable*. But – hope reasserted itself – the fact that she was coming down to investigate reduced the odds to ten to one at most. Less than ten to one.

He looked over at Neuville, trying to think his thoughts. The *Pique* was fast and handy, and there was a clear avenue of escape to leeward. The fact that the stranger had altered course towards them was a suspicious circumstance, but it was known that Indiamen, the richest prizes of all, had sometimes traded on the similarity of their appearance to that of ships of the line, and by showing a bold front had scared dangerous enemies away. That would be a temptation to a man eager to make a prize. At Neuville's orders all sail was set, ready for instant flight or pursuit, and, close-hauled, the *Pique* stood towards the stranger. It was not long before Hornblower, on the deck, caught a glimpse of a gleam of white, like a tiny grain of rice, far away on the horizon as the *Pique* lifted on a swell. Here came Matthews, red-faced and excited, running aft to Hornblower's side.

'That's the old *Indefatigable*, sir,' he said. 'I swear it!' He sprang onto the rail, holding on by the shrouds, and stared under his hand.

'Yes! There she is, sir! She's loosing her royals now, sir. We'll be back on board of her in time for grog!'

A French petty officer reached up and dragged Matthews by the seat of his trousers from his perch, and with a blow and a kick drove him forward again, while a moment later Neuville was shouting the orders that wore the ship round to head away directly from the *Indefatigable*. Neuville beckoned Hornblower over to his side.

'Your late ship, I understand, Mr Hornblower?'

'Yes.'

'What is her best point of sailing?'

Hornblower's eyes met Neuville's.

'Do not look so noble,' said Neuville, smiling with thin lips. 'I could undoubtedly induce you to give me the information. I know of ways. But it is unnecessary, fortunately for you. There is no ship on earth – especially none of His Britannic Majesty's clumsy frigates – that can outsail the *Pique* running before the wind. You will soon see that.'

He strolled to the taffrail and looked aft long and earnestly through his glass, but no more earnestly than did Hornblower with his naked eye.

'You see?' said Neuville, proffering the glass.

Hornblower took it, but more to catch a closer glimpse of his ship than to confirm his observations. He was homesick, desperately homesick, at that moment, for the *Indefatigable*. But there could be no denying that she was being left fast behind. Her topgallants were out of sight again now, and only her royals were visible.

'Two hours and we shall have run her mastheads under,' said Neuville, taking back the telescope and shutting it with a snap.

He left Hornblower standing sorrowful at the taffrail while he turned to berate the helmsman for not steering a steadier course; Hornblower heard the explosive words without listening to them, the wind blowing into his face and ruffling his hair over his ears, and the wake of the ship's passage boiling below him. So might Adam have looked back at Eden; Hornblower remembered the stuffy dark midshipmen's berth, the smells and the creakings, the bitter cold nights, turning out in response to the call for all hands, the weevilly bread and the wooden beef, and he yearned for them all, with the sick feeling of hopeless longing. Liberty was vanishing over the horizon. Yet it was not these personal feelings that drove him below in search of action. They may have quickened his wits, but it was a sense of duty which inspired him.

The slave-deck was deserted, as usual, with all hands at quarters. Beyond the bulkhead stood his cot with the books upon it and the slush lamp swaying above it. There was nothing there to give him any inspiration. There was another locked door in the after bulkhead. That opened into some kind of boatswain's store; twice he had seen it unlocked and paint and similar supplies brought out from it. Paint! That gave him an idea; he looked from the door up to the slush lamp and back again, and as he stepped forward he took his claspknife out of his pocket. But before very long he recoiled again, sneering at himself. The door was not panelled, but was made of two solid slabs of wood, with the cross-beams on the inside. There was the keyhole of the lock, but it presented no point of attack. It would take him hours and hours to cut through that door with his knife, at a time when minutes were precious.

His heart was beating feverishly – but no more feverishly than his mind was working – as he looked round again. He reached up to the lamp and shook it; nearly full. There was a moment when he stood hesitating, nerving himself, and then he threw himself into action. With a ruthless hand he tore the pages out of Grandjean's *Principes de la Navigation*, crumpling them up in small quantities into little loose balls which he laid at the foot of the door. He threw off his uniform coat and dragged his blue woollen jersey over his head; his long powerful fingers tore it across and plucked eagerly at it to unravel it. After starting some loose threads he would not waste more time on it, and dropped the garment onto the paper and looked round again. The mattress of the cot! It was stuffed with straw, by God! A slash of his knife tore open the ticking, and he scooped the stuff out by the armful; constant pressure had almost solidified it, but he shook it and handled it so that it bulked out far larger in a mass on the deck nearly up to his waist. That would give him the intense blaze he wanted. He stood still, compelling himself to think clearly and logically – it was impetuosity and lack of thought which had occasioned the loss of the *Marie Galante*, and now he had wasted time on his jersey. He worked out the successive steps to take. He made a long spill out of a page of the *Manuel de Matelotage*, and lighted it at the lamp. Then he poured out the grease – the lamp was hot and the grease liquid – over his balls of paper, over the deck, over the base of the door. A touch from his taper lighted one ball, the flame travelled quickly. He was committed now. He piled the straw upon the flames, and in a sudden access of insane strength he tore the cot from its fastenings, smashing it as he did so, and piled the fragments on the straw. Already the flames were racing through the straw. He dropped the lamp upon the pile grabbed his coat and walked out. He thought of closing the door, but decided against it – the more air the better. He wriggled into his coat and ran up the ladder.

On deck he forced himself to lounge nonchalantly against the rail, putting his shaking hands into his pockets. His excitement made him weak, nor was it lessened as he waited. Every minute before the fire could be discovered was important. A French officer said something to him with a triumphant laugh and pointed aft over the taffrail, presumably speaking about leaving the *Indefatigable* behind. Hornblower smiled bleakly at him; that was the first gesture that occurred to him, and then he thought that a smile was out of place, and he tried to assume a sullen scowl. The wind was blowing briskly, so that the *Pique* could only just carry all plain sail; Hornblower felt it on his cheeks, which were burning. Everyone on deck seemed unnaturally busy and preoccupied; Neuville was watching the helmsman with occasional glances aloft to see that every sail was doing its work; the men were at the guns, two hands and a petty officer heaving the log. God, how much longer would he have?

Look there! The coaming of the after hatchway appeared distorted, wavering in the shimmering air. Hot air must be coming up through it. And was that, or was it not, the ghost of a wreath of smoke? It was! In that moment the alarm was given. A loud cry, a rush of feet, an instant bustle, the loud beating of a drum, high-pitched shouts – 'Au feu! Au feu!'

The four elements of Aristotle, thought Hornblower insanely – earth, air, water, and fire – were the constant enemies of the seaman, but the lee shore, the gale, and the wave, were none of them as feared in wooden ships as fire. Timbers many years old and coated thick with paint burnt fiercely and readily. Sails and tarry rigging would burn like fireworks. And within the ship were tons and tons of gunpowder waiting its chance to blast the seamen into fragments. Hornblower watched the fire parties flinging themselves into their work, the pumps being dragged over the decks, the hoses rigged. Someone came racing aft with a message for Neuville, presumably to report the site of the fire. Neuville heard him, and darted a glance at Hornblower against the rail before he hurled orders back at the messenger. The smoke coming up through the after hatchway was dense now; at Neuville's orders the after guard flung themselves down the opening through the smoke. And there was more smoke, and more smoke; smoke caught up by the following wind and blown forward in wisps – smoke must be pouring out of the sides of the ship at the waterline.

Neuville took a stride towards Hornblower, his face working with rage, but a cry from the helmsman checked him. The helmsman, unable to take his hands from the wheel, pointed with his foot to the cabin skylight. There was a flickering of flame below it. A side pane fell in as they watched, and a rush of flame came through the opening. That store of paint, Hornblower calculated – he was calmer now, with a calm that

would astonish him later, when he came to look back on it –
must be immediately under the cabin, and blazing fiercely.
Neuville looked round him, at the sea and the sky, and put his
hands to his head in a furious gesture. For the first time in his
life Hornblower saw a man literally tearing his hair. But his
nerve held. A shout brought up another portable pump; four
men set to work on the handles, and the clank-clank, clank-
clank made an accompaniment that blended with the roar of
the fire. A thin jet of water was squirted down the gaping
skylight. More men formed a bucket chain, drawing water
from the sea and passing it from hand to hand to pour in the
skylight, but those buckets of water were less effective even
than the stream from the pumps. From below came the dull
thud of an explosion, and Hornblower caught his breath as he
expected the ship to be blown to pieces. But no further
explosion followed; either a gun had been set off by the
flames or a cask had burst violently in the heat. And then the
bucket line suddenly disintegrated; beneath the feet of one of
the men a seam had gaped in a broad red smile from which
came a rush of flame. Some officer had seized Neuville by the
arm and was arguing with him vehemently, and Hornblower
could see Neuville yield in despair. Hands went scurrying
aloft to get in the foretopsail and forecourse, and other hands
went to the main braces. Over went the wheel, and the *Pique*
came up into the wind.

The change was dramatic, although at first more apparent
than real; with the wind blowing in the opposite direction
the roar of the fire did not come so clearly to the ears of those
forward of it. But it was an immense gain, all the same; the
flames, which had started in the steerage in the farthest after-
part of the ship, no longer were blown forward, but were
turned back upon timber already half consumed. Yet the
after-part of the deck was fully alight; the helmsman was
driven from the wheel, and in a flash the flames took hold of
the driver and consumed it utterly – one moment the sail was
there, and the next there were only charred fragments hanging

from the gaff. But, head to wind, the other sails did not catch, and a mizzen-trysail hurriedly set kept the ship bows on.

It was then that Hornblower, looking forward, saw the *Indefatigable* again. She was tearing down towards them with all sail set; as the *Pique* lifted he could see the white bow wave foaming under her bowsprit. There was no question about surrender, for under the menace of that row of guns no ship of the *Pique*'s force, even if uninjured, could resist. A cable's length to windward the *Indefatigable* rounded-to, and she was hoisting out her boats before even she was fully round. Pellew had seen the smoke, and had deduced the reason for the *Pique*'s heaving to, and had made his preparations as he came up. Longboat and launch had each a pump in their bows where sometimes they carried a carronade; they dropped down to the stern of the *Pique* to cast their jets of water up into the flaming stern without more ado. Two gigs full of men ran straight aft to join in the battle with the flames, but Bolton, the third lieutenant, lingered for a moment as he caught Hornblower's eye.

'Good God, it's you!' he exclaimed. 'What are you doing here?'

Yet he did not stay for an answer. He picked out Neuville as the captain of the *Pique*, strode aft to receive his surrender, cast his eyes aloft to see that all was well there, and then took up the task of combating the fire. The flames were overcome in time, more because they had consumed everything within reach of them than for any other reason; the *Pique* was burnt from the taffrail forward for some feet of her length right to the water's edge, so that she presented a strange spectacle when viewed from the deck of the *Indefatigable*. Nevertheless, she was in no immediate danger; given even moderate good fortune and a little hard work she could be sailed to England to be repaired and sent to sea again.

But it was not her salvage that was important, but rather the fact that she was no longer in French hands, would no longer be available to prey on English commerce. That was the point that Sir Edward Pellew made in conversation with Hornblower, when the latter came on board to report himself. Hornblower had begun, at Pellew's order, by recounting what had happened to him from the time he had been sent as prize master on board the *Marie Galante*. As Hornblower had expected – perhaps as he had even feared – Pellew had passed lightly over the loss of the brig. She had been damaged by gunfire before surrendering, and no one now could establish whether the damage was small or great. Pellew did not give the matter a second thought. Hornblower had tried to save her and had been unsuccessful with his tiny crew – and at that moment the *Indefatigable* could not spare him a larger crew. He did not hold Hornblower culpable. Once again, it was more important that France should be deprived of the *Marie Galante*'s cargo than that England should benefit by it. The situation was exactly parallel to that of the salvaging of the *Pique*.

'It was lucky she caught fire like that,' commented Pellew, looking across to where the *Pique* lay, still hove-to with the boats clustering about her but with only the thinnest trail of smoke drifting from her stern. 'She was running clean away from us, and would have been out of sight in an hour. Have you any idea how it happened, Mr Hornblower?'

Hornblower was naturally expecting that question and was ready for it. Now was the time to answer truthfully and modestly, to receive the praise he deserved, a mention in the *Gazette*, perhaps even appointment as acting-lieutenant. But Pellew did not know the full details of the loss of the brig, and might make a false estimate of them even if he did.

'No, sir,' said Hornblower. 'I think it must have been spontaneous combustion in the paint-locker. I can't account for it otherwise.'

He alone knew of his remissness in plugging that shot-hole, he alone could decide on his punishment, and this was what he had chosen. This alone could re-establish him in his own eyes, and when the words were spoken he felt enormous relief, and not one single twinge of regret.

'It was fortunate, all the same,' mused Pellew.

CHAPTER FOUR

THE MAN WHO FELT QUEER

THIS time the wolf was prowling round outside the sheep-fold. H.M. frigate *Indefatigable* had chased the French corvette *Papillon* into the mouth of the Gironde, and was seeking a way of attacking her where she lay at anchor in the stream under the protection of the batteries at the mouth. Captain Pellew took his ship into shoal water as far as he dared, until in fact the batteries fired warning shots to make him keep his distance, and he stared long and keenly through his glass at the corvette. Then he shut his telescope and turned on his heel to give the order that worked the *Indefatigable* away from the dangerous lee shore – out of sight of land, in fact. His departure might lull the French into a sense of security which, he hoped, would prove unjustified. For he had no intention of leaving them undisturbed. If the corvette could be captured or sunk not only would she be unavailable for raids on British commerce, but also the French would be forced to increase their coastal defences at this point and lessen the effort that could be put out elsewhere. War is a matter of savage blow and counter blow, and even a forty-gun frigate could strike shrewd blows if shrewdly handled.

Midshipman Hornblower was walking the lee side of the quarterdeck, as became his lowly station as the junior officer of the watch, in the afternoon, when Midshipman Kennedy approached him. Kennedy took off his hat with a flourish and bowed low as his dancing master had once taught him, left foot advanced, hat down by the right knee. Hornblower entered into the spirit of the game, laid his hat against his stomach, and bent himself in the middle three times in quick succession. Thanks to his physical awkwardness he could parody ceremonial solemnity almost without trying.

'Most grave and reverend signor,' said Kennedy, 'I bear the compliments of Captain Sir Ed'ard Pellew, who humbly solicits Your Gravity's attendance at dinner at eight bells in the afternoon watch.'

'My respects to Sir Edward,' replied Hornblower, bowing to his knees at the mention of the name, 'and I shall condescend to make a brief appearance.'

'I am sure the captain will be both relieved and delighted,' said Kennedy. 'I will convey him my felicitations along with your most flattering acceptance.'

Both hats flourished with even greater elaboration than before, but at that moment both young men noticed Mr Bolton, the officer of the watch, looking at them from the windward side, and they hurriedly put their hats on and assumed attitudes more consonant with the dignity of officers holding their warrants from King George.

'What's in the captain's mind?' asked Hornblower.

Kennedy laid one finger alongside his nose.

'If I knew that I should rate a couple of epaulettes,' he said. 'Something's brewing, and I suppose one of these days we shall know what it is. Until then all that we little victims can do is to play unconscious of our doom. Meanwhile, be careful not to let the ship fall overboard.'

There was no sign of anything brewing while dinner was being eaten in the great cabin of the *Indefatigable*. Pellew was a courtly host at the head of the table. Conversation flowed freely and along indifferent channels among the senior officers present – the two lieutenants, Eccles and Chadd, and the sailing master, Soames. Hornblower and the other junior officer – Mallory, a midshipman of over two years' seniority – kept silent, as midshipmen should, thereby being able to devote their undivided attention to the food, so vastly superior to what was served in the midshipmen's berth.

'A glass of wine with you, Mr Hornblower,' said Pellew, raising his glass.

Hornblower tried to bow gracefully in his seat while raising his glass. He sipped cautiously, for he had early found that he had a weak head, and he disliked feeling drunk.

The table was cleared and there was a brief moment of expectancy as the company awaited Pellew's next move.

'Now, Mr Soames,' said Pellew, 'let us have that chart.'

It was a map of the mouth of the Gironde with the soundings; somebody had pencilled in the positions of the shore batteries.

'The *Papillon*,' said Sir Edward (he did not condescend to pronounce it French-fashion), 'lies just here. Mr Soames took the bearings.'

He indicated a pencilled cross on the chart, far up the channel.

'You gentlemen,' went on Pellew, 'are going in with the boats to fetch her out.'

So that was it. A cutting-out expedition.

'Mr Eccles will be in general command. I will ask him to tell you his plan.'

The grey-haired first lieutenant with the surprisingly young blue eyes looked round at the others.

'I shall have the launch,' he said, 'and Mr Soames the cutter. Mr Chadd and Mr Mallory will command the first and second gigs. And Mr Hornblower will command the jolly boat. Each of the boats except Mr Hornblower's will have a junior officer second in command.'

That would not be necessary for the jolly boat with its crew of seven. The launch and cutter would carry from thirty to forty men each, and the gigs twenty each; it was a large force that was being despatched – nearly half the ship's company.

'She's a ship of war,' explained Eccles, reading their

thoughts. 'No merchantman. Ten guns a side, and full of men.'

Nearer two hundred men than a hundred, certainly – plentiful opposition for a hundred and twenty British seamen.

'But we will be attacking her by night and taking her by surprise,' said Eccles, reading their thoughts again.

'Surprise,' put in Pellew, 'is more than half the battle, as you know, gentlemen – please pardon the interruption, Mr Eccles.'

'At the moment,' went on Eccles, 'we are out of sight of land. We are about to stand in again. We have never hung about this part of the coast, and the Frogs'll think we've gone for good. We'll make the land after nightfall, stand in as far as possible, and then the boats will go in. High water to-morrow morning is at four-fifty; dawn is at five-thirty. The attack will be delivered at four-thirty so that the watch below will have had time to get to sleep. The launch will attack on the starboard quarter, and the cutter on the larboard quarter. Mr Mallory's gig will attack on the larboard bow, and Mr Chadd's on the starboard bow. Mr Chadd will be responsible for cutting the corvette's cable as soon as he has mastered the forecastle, and the other boats' crews have at least reached the quarterdeck.'

Eccles looked round at the other three commanders of the large boats, and they nodded understanding. Then he went on.

'Mr Hornblower with the jolly boat will wait until the attack has gained a foothold on the deck. He will then board at the main chains, either to starboard or larboard as he sees fit, and he will at once ascend the main rigging, paying no attention to whatever fighting is going on on deck. He will see to it that the maintopsail is loosed and he will sheet it home on receipt of further orders. I myself, or Mr Soames in the event of my being killed or wounded, will send two hands to the wheel and will attend to steering the corvette as soon as she is under way. The tide will take us out, and the *Indefatigable* will be awaiting us just out of gunshot from the shore batteries.'

'Any comments, gentlemen?' asked Pellew.

That was the moment when Hornblower should have spoken up – the only moment when he could. Eccles' orders had set in motion sick feelings of apprehension in his stomach. Hornblower was no maintopman, and Hornblower knew it. He hated heights, and he hated going aloft. He knew he had none of the monkey-like agility and self-confidence of the good seaman. He was unsure of himself aloft in the dark even in the *Indefatigable*, and he was utterly appalled at the thought of going aloft in an entirely strange ship and finding his way among strange rigging. He felt himself quite unfitted for the duty assigned to him, and he should have raised a protest at once on account of his unfitness. But he let the opportunity pass, for he was overcome by the matter-of-fact way in which the other officers accepted the plan. He looked round at the unmoved faces; nobody was paying any attention to him, and he jibbed at making himself conspicuous. He swallowed; he even got as far as opening his mouth, but still no one looked at him, and his protest died stillborn.

'Very well, then, gentlemen,' said Pellew. 'I think you had better go into the details, Mr Eccles.'

Then it was too late. Eccles, with the chart before him, was pointing out the course to be taken through the shoals and mudbanks of the Gironde, and expatiating on the position of the shore batteries and on the influence of the lighthouse of Cordouan upon the distance to which the *Indefatigable* could approach in daylight. Hornblower listened, trying to concentrate despite his apprehensions. Eccles finished his remarks and Pellew closed the meeting.

'Since you all know your duties, gentlemen, I think you should start your preparations. The sun is about to set and you will find you have plenty to do.'

The boats crews had to be told off; it was necessary to see that the men were armed, and that the boats were provisioned in case of emergency. Every man had to be instructed in the duties expected of him. And Hornblower had to rehearse himself in ascending the main shrouds and laying out along the main topsail yard. He did it twice, forcing himself to make the difficult climb up the futtock shrouds, which, projecting outwards from the mainmast, made it necessary to climb several feet while hanging back downwards, locking fingers and toes into the ratlines. He could just manage it, moving slowly and carefully, although clumsily. He stood on the foot-rope and worked his way out to the yardarm – the footrope was attached along the yard so as to hang nearly four feet below it. The principle was to set his feet on the rope with his arms over the yard, then, holding the yard in his armpits, to shuffle sideways along the footrope to cast off the gaskets and loose the sail. Twice Hornblower made the whole journey, battling with the disquiet of his stomach at the thought of the hundred-foot drop below him. Finally, gulping with nervousness, he transferred his grip to the brace and forced himself to slide down it to the deck – that would be his best route when the time came to sheet the topsail home. It was a long perilous descent; Hornblower told himself – as indeed he had said to himself when he had first seen men go aloft – that similar feats in a circus at home would be received with 'ohs' and 'ahs' of appreciation. He was by no means satisfied with himself even when he reached the deck, and at the back of his mind was a vivid mental picture of his missing his hold when the time came for him to repeat the performance in the *Papillon*, and falling headlong to the deck – a second or two of frightful fear while rushing through the air, and then a shattering crash. And the success of the attack hinged on him, as much as on anyone – if the topsail were not promptly set to give the corvette steerage way she would run aground on one of the innumerable shoals in the river mouth to be igno-miniously recaptured, and half the crew of the *Indefatigable* would be dead or prisoners.

In the waist the jolly boat's crew was formed up for his

inspection. He saw to it that the oars were properly muffled, that each man had pistol and cutlass, and made sure that every pistol was at half cock so that there was no fear of a premature shot giving warning of the attack. He allocated duties to each man in the loosening of the top sail, laying stress on the possibility that casualties might necessitate unrehearsed changes in the scheme.

'I will mount the rigging first,' said Hornblower.

That had to be the case. He had to lead – it was expected of him. More than that; if he had given any other order it would have excited comment – and contempt.

'Jackson,' went on Hornblower, addressing the coxswain, 'you will quit the boat last and take command if I fall.'

'Aye aye, sir.'

It was usual to use the poetic expression 'fall' for 'die', and it was only after Hornblower had uttered the word that he thought about its horrible real meaning in the present circumstances.

'Is that all understood?' asked Hornblower harshly; it was his mental stress that made his voice grate so.

Everyone nodded except one man.

'Begging your pardon, sir,' said Hales, the young man who pulled stroke oar, 'I'm feeling a bit queer-like.'

Hales was a lightly built young fellow of swarthy countenance. He put his hand to his forehead with a vague gesture as he spoke.

'You're not the only one to feel queer,' snapped Hornblower.

The other men chuckled. The thought of running the gauntlet of the shore batteries, of boarding an armed corvette in the teeth of opposition, might well raise apprehension in the breast of a coward. Most of the men detailed for the expedition must have felt qualms to some extent.

'I don't mean that, sir,' said Hales indignantly. "Course I don't.'

But Hornblower and the others paid him no attention.

'You just keep your mouth shut,' growled Jackson. There could be nothing but contempt for a man who announced himself sick after being told off on a dangerous duty. Hornblower felt sympathy as well as contempt. He himself had been too much of a coward even to give voice to his apprehensions – too much afraid of what people would say about him.

'Dismiss,' said Hornblower. 'I'll pass the word for all of you when you are wanted.'

There were some hours yet to wait while the *Indefatigable* crept inshore, with the lead going steadily and Pellew himself attending to the course of the frigate. Hornblower, despite his nervousness and his miserable apprehensions, yet found time to appreciate the superb seamanship displayed as Pellew brought the big frigate in through these tricky waters on that dark night. His interest was so caught by the procedure that the little tremblings which had been assailing him ceased to manifest themselves; Hornblower was of the type that would continue to observe and to learn on his deathbed. By the time the *Indefatigable* had reached the point off the mouth of the river where it was desirable to launch the boats, Hornblower had learned a good deal about the practical application of the principles of coastwise navigation and a good deal about the organization of a cutting-out expedition – and by self analysis he had learned even more about the psychology of a raiding party before a raid.

He had mastered himself to all outside appearance by the time he went down into the jolly boat as she heaved on the inky-black water, and he gave the command to shove off in a quiet steady voice. Hornblower took the tiller – the feel of that solid bar of wood was reassuring, and it was old habit now to sit in the stern sheets with hand and elbow upon it, and the men began to pull slowly after the dark shapes of the four big boats; there was plenty of time, and the flowing tide would take them up the estuary. That was just as well, for on one side of them lay the batteries of St Dye, and inside the estuary on the other side was the fortress of Blaye; forty big guns trained to sweep the channel, and none of the five boats – certainly not the jolly boat – could withstand a single shot from one of them.

He kept his eyes attentively on the cutter ahead of him. Soames had the dreadful responsibility of taking the boats up the channel, while all he had to do was to follow in her wake – all, except to loose that maintopsail. Hornblower found himself shivering again.

Hales, the man who had said he felt queer, was pulling stroke oar; Hornblower could just see his dark form moving rhythmically back and forward at each slow stroke. After a single glance Hornblower paid him no more attention, and was staring after the cutter when a sudden commotion brought his mind back into the boat. Someone had missed his stroke; someone had thrown all six oars into confusion as a result. There was even a slight clatter.

'Mind what you're doing, blast you, Hales,' whispered Jackson, the coxswain, with desperate urgency.

For answer there was a sudden cry from Hales, loud but fortunately not too loud, and Hales pitched forward against Hornblower's and Jackson's legs, kicking and writhing.

'The bastard's having a fit,' growled Jackson.

The kicking and writhing went on. Across the water through the darkness came a sharp scornful whisper.

'Mr Hornblower,' said the voice – it was Eccles putting a world of exasperation into his *sotto voce* question – 'cannot you keep your men quiet?'

Eccles had brought the launch round almost alongside the jolly boat to say this to him, and the desperate need for silence was dramatically demonstrated by the absence of any of the usual blasphemy; Hornblower could picture the cutting reprimand that would be administered to him to-morrow publicly on the quarterdeck. He opened his mouth to make an explanation, but he fortunately realized that raiders in open boats did not make explanations when under the guns of the fortress of Blaye.

'Aye aye, sir,' was all he whispered back, and the launch continued on its mission of shepherding the flotilla in the tracks of the cutter.

'Take his oar, Jackson,' he whispered furiously to the coxswain, and he stooped and with his own hands dragged the writhing figure towards him and out of Jackson's way.

'You might try pouring water on 'im, sir,' suggested Jackson hoarsely, as he moved to the afterthwart. 'There's the baler 'andy.'

Seawater was the seaman's cure for every ill, his panacea; seeing how often sailors had not merely wet jackets but wet bedding as well they should never have a day's illness. But Hornblower let the sick man lie. His struggles were coming to an end, and Hornblower wished to make no noise with the baler. The lives of more than a hundred men depended on silence. Now that they were well into the actual estuary they were within easy reach of cannon shot from the shore – and a single cannon shot would rouse the crew of the *Papillon*, ready to man the bulwarks to beat off the attack, ready to drop cannon balls into the boats alongside, ready to shatter approaching boats with a tempest of grape.

Silently the boats glided up the estuary; Soames in the cutter was setting a slow pace, with only an occasional stroke at the oars to maintain steerage way. Presumably he knew very well what he was doing; the channel he had selected was an obscure one between mudbanks, impracticable for anything except small boats, and he had a twenty-foot pole with him with which to take the soundings – quicker and much more silent than using the lead. Minutes were passing fast, and yet the night was still utterly dark, with no hint of approaching dawn. Strain his eyes as he would Hornblower could not be sure that he could see the flat shores on either side of him. It would call for sharp eyes on the land to detect the little boats being carried up by the tide.

Hales at his feet stirred and then stirred again. His hand, feeling round in the darkness, found Hornblower's ankle and apparently examined it with curiosity. He muttered something, the words dragging out into a moan.

'Shut up!' whispered Hornblower, trying, like the saint of old, to make a tongue of his whole body, that he might express the urgency of the occasion without making a sound audible at any distance. Hales set his elbow on Hornblower's knee and levered himself up into a sitting position, and then levered himself further until he was standing, swaying with bent knees and supporting himself against Hornblower.

'Sit down, damn you!' whispered Hornblower, shaking with fury and anxiety.

'Where's Mary?' asked Hales in a conversational tone.

'Shut up!'

'Mary!' said Hales, lurching against him. 'Mary!'

Each successive word was louder. Hornblower felt instinctively that Hales would soon be speaking in a loud voice, that he might even soon be shouting. Old recollections of conversations with his doctor father stirred at the back of his mind; he remembered that persons emerging from epileptic fits were not responsible for their actions, and might be, and often were, dangerous.

'Mary!' said Hales again.

Victory and the lives of a hundred men depended on silencing Hales, and silencing him instantly. Hornblower thought of the pistol in his belt, and of using the butt, but there was another weapon more conveniently to his hand. He unshipped the tiller, a three-foot bar of solid oak, and he swung it with all the venom and fury of despair. The tiller crashed down on Hales' head, and Hales, an unuttered word cut short in his throat, fell silent in the bottom of the boat. There was no sound from the boat's crew, save for something like a sigh from Jackson, whether approving or disapproving Hornblower neither knew nor cared. He had done his duty, and he was certain of it. He had struck down a helpless idiot; most probably he had killed him, but the surprise upon which the success of the expedition depended had not been imperilled. He reshipped the tiller and resumed the silent task of keeping in the wake of the gigs.

Far away ahead – in the darkness it was impossible to estimate the distance – there was a nucleus of greater darkness, close on the surface of the black water. It might be the corvette. A dozen more silent strokes, and Hornblower was sure of it. Soames had done a magnificent job of pilotage, leading the boats straight to that objective. The cutter and launch were diverging now from the two gigs. The four boats were separating in readiness to launch their simultaneous converging attack.

'Easy!' whispered Hornblower, and the jolly boat's crew ceased to pull.

Hornblower had his orders. He had to wait until the attack had gained a foothold on the deck. His hand clenched convulsively on the tiller; the excitement of dealing with Hales had driven the thought of having to ascend strange rigging in the darkness clear out of his head, and now it recurred with redoubled urgency. Hornblower was afraid.

Although he could see the corvette, the boats had vanished from his sight, had passed out of his field of vision. The corvette rode to her anchor, her spars just visible against the night sky – that was where he had to climb! She seemed to tower up hugely. Close by the corvette he saw a splash in the dark water – the boats were closing in fast and someone's stroke had been a little careless. At the same moment came a shout from the corvette's deck, and when the shout was repeated it was echoed a hundred fold from the boats rushing alongside. The yelling was lusty and prolonged, of set purpose. A sleeping enemy would be bewildered by the din, and the progress of the shouting would tell each boat's crew of the extent of the success of the others. The British seamen were yelling like madmen. A flash and a bang from the corvette's deck told of the firing of the first shot; soon pistols were popping and muskets banging from several points of the deck.

'Give way!' said Hornblower. He uttered the order as if it had been torn from him by the rack.

The jolly boat moved forward, while Hornblower fought down his feelings and tried to make out what was going on on board. He could see no reason for choosing either side of the corvette in preference to the other, and the larboard side was the nearer, and so he steered the boat to the larboard main chains. So interested was he in what he was doing that he only remembered in the nick of time to give the order, 'In oars.' He put the tiller over and the boat swirled round and the bowman hooked on. From the deck just above came a noise exactly like a tinker hammering on a cooking-pot – Hornblower noted the curious noise as he stood up in the stern sheets. He felt the cutlass at his side and the pistol in his belt, and then he sprang for the chains. With a mad leap he reached them and hauled himself up. The shrouds came into his hands, his feet found the ratlines beneath them, and he began to climb. As his head cleared the bulwark and he could see the deck the flash of a pistol shot illuminated the scene momentarily, fixing the struggle on the deck in a static moment, like a picture. Before and below him a British seaman was fighting a furious cutlass duel with a French officer, and he realized with vague astonishment that the kettle-mending noise he had heard was the sound of cutlass against cutlass – that clash of steel against steel that poets wrote about. So much for romance.

The realization carried him far up the shrouds. At his elbow he felt the futtock shrouds and he transferred himself to them, hanging back downward with his toes hooked into the ratlines and his hands clinging like death. That only lasted for two or three desperate seconds, and then he hauled himself onto the topmast shrouds and began the final ascent, his lungs bursting with the effort. Here was the topsail yard, and Hornblower flung himself across it and felt with his feet for the footrope. Merciful God! There was no footrope – his feet searching in the darkness met only unresisting air. A hundred feet above the deck he hung, squirming and kicking like a baby held up at arm's length in its father's hands. There was no footrope; it may have been with this very situation in mind that the Frenchmen had removed it. There was no footrope, so that he could not make his way out to the yardarm. Yet the gaskets must be cast off and the sail loosed – everything depended on that. Hornblower had seen daredevil seamen run out along the yards standing upright, as though walking a tightrope. That was the only way to reach the yardarm now.

For a moment he could not breathe as his weak flesh revolted against the thought of walking along that yard above the black abyss. This was fear, the fear that stripped a man of his manhood, turning his bowels to water and his limbs to paper. Yet his furiously active mind continued to work. He had been resolute enough in dealing with Hales. Where he personally was not involved he had been brave enough; he had not hesitated to strike down the wretched epileptic with all the strength of his arm. That was the poor sort of courage he was capable of displaying. In the simple vulgar matter of physical bravery he was utterly wanting. This was cowardice, the sort of thing that men spoke about behind their hands to other men. He could not bear the thought of that in himself – it was worse (awful though the alternative might be) than the thought of falling through the night to the deck. With a gasp he brought his knee up onto the yard, heaving himself up until he stood upright. He felt the rounded, canvas-covered timber under his feet, and his instincts told him not to dally there for a moment.

'Come on, men!' he yelled, and he dashed out along the yard.

It was twenty feet to the yardarm, and he covered the distance in a few frantic strides. Utterly reckless by now, he put his hands down on the yard, clasped it, and laid his body across it again, his hands seeking the gaskets. A thump on the yard told him that Oldroyd, who had been detailed to come after him, had followed him out along the yard – he had six feet less to go. There could be no doubt that the other members of the jolly boat's crew were on the yard, and that Clough had led the way to the starboard yardarm. It was obvious from the rapidity with which the sail came loose. Here was the brace beside him. Without any thought of danger now, for he was delirious with excitement and triumph, he grasped it with both hands and jerked himself off the yard. His waving legs found the rope and twined about it, and he let himself slide down it.

Fool that he was! Would he never learn sense and prudence? Would he never remember that vigilance and precaution must never be relaxed? He had allowed himself to slide so fast that the rope seared his hands, and when he tried to tighten his grip so as to slow down his progress it caused him such agony that he had to relax it again and slide on down with the rope stripping the skin from his hands as though peeling off a glove. His feet reached the deck and he momentarily forgot the pain as he looked round him.

There was the faintest grey light beginning to show now, and there were no sounds of battle. It had been a well-worked surprise – a hundred men flung suddenly on the deck of the corvette had swept away the anchor watch and mastered the vessel in a single rush before the watch below could come up to offer any resistance. Chadd's stentorian voice came pealing from the forecastle.

'Cable's cut, sir!'

Then Eccles bellowed from aft.

'Mr Hornblower!'

'Sir!' yelled Hornblower.

'Man the halliards!'

A rush of men came to help – not only his own boat's crew but every man of initiative and spirit. Halliards, sheets and braces; the sail was trimmed round and was drawing full in the light southerly air, and the *Papillon* swung round to go down with the first of the ebb. Dawn was coming up fast, with a trifle of mist on the surface of the water.

Over the starboard quarter came a sullen bellowing roar, and then the misty air was torn by a series of infernal screams, supernaturally loud. The first cannon balls Hornblower ever heard were passing him by.

'Mr Chadd! Set the headsails! Loose the foretops'l. Get aloft, some of you, and set the mizzen tops'l.'

From the port bow came another salvo – Blaye was firing at them from one side, St Dye from the other, now they could guess what had happened on board the *Papillon*. But the corvette was moving fast with wind and tide, and it would be no easy matter to cripple her in the half light. It had been a very near-run thing; a few seconds' delay could have been fatal. Only one shot from the next salvo passed within hearing, and its passage was marked by a loud snap overhead.

'Mr Mallory, get that forestay spliced!'

'Aye aye, sir!'

It was light enough to look round the deck now; he could see Eccles at the break of the poop, directing the handling of the corvette, and Soames beside the wheel conning her down the channel. Two groups of red-coated marines, with bayonets fixed, stood guard over the hatchways. There were four or five men lying on the deck in curiously abandoned attitudes. Dead men; Hornblower could look at them with the callousness of youth. But there was a wounded man, too, crouched groaning over his shattered thigh – Hornblower could not look at him as disinterestedly, and he was glad, maybe only for his own sake, when at that moment a seaman asked for and received permission from Mallory to leave his duties and attend to him.

'Stand by to go about!' shouted Eccles from the poop; the corvette had reached the tip of the middle ground shoal and was about to make the turn that would carry her into the open sea.

The men came running to the braces, and Hornblower tailed on along with them. But the first contact with the harsh rope gave him such pain that he almost cried out. His hands were like raw meat, and fresh-killed at that, for blood was running from them. Now that his attention was called to them they smarted unbearably.

The headsail sheets came over, and the corvette went handily about.

'There's the old *Indy*!' shouted somebody.

The *Indefatigable* was plainly visible now, lying-to just out of shot from the shore batteries, ready to rendezvous with her prize. Somebody cheered, and the cheering was taken up by everyone, even while the last shots from St Dye, fired at extreme range, pitched sullenly into the water alongside. Hornblower had gingerly extracted his handkerchief from his pocket and was trying to wrap it round his hand.

'Can I help you with that, sir?' asked Jackson.

Jackson shook his head as he looked at the raw surface.

'You was careless, sir. You ought to 'a gone down 'and over 'and,' he said, when Hornblower explained to him how the injury had been caused. 'Very careless, you was, beggin' your pardon for saying so, sir. But you young gennelmen often is. You don't 'ave no thought for your necks, nor your 'ides, sir.'

Hornblower looked up at the maintopsail yard high above his head, and remembered how he had walked along that slender stick of timber out to the yardarm in the dark. At the recollection of it, even here with the solid deck under his feet, he shuddered a little.

'Sorry, sir. Didn't mean to 'urt you,' said Jackson, tying the knot. 'There, that's done, as good as I can do it, sir.'

'Thank you, Jackson,' said Hornblower.

'We got to report the jolly boat as lost, sir,' went on Jackson.

'Lost?'

'She ain't towing alongside, sir. You see, we didn't leave no boatkeeper in 'er. Wells, 'e was to be boatkeeper, you remember, sir. But I sent 'im up the rigging a'head o' me, seeing that 'Ales couldn't go. We wasn't too many for the job.

So the jolly boat must 'a come adrift, sir, when the ship went about.'

'What about Hales, then?' asked Hornblower.

"E was still in the boat, sir.'

Hornblower looked back up the estuary of the Gironde. Somewhere up there the jolly boat was drifting about, and lying in it was Hales, probably dead, possibly alive. In either case the French would find him, surely enough, but a cold wave of regret extinguished the warm feeling of triumph in Hornblower's bosom when he thought about Hales back there. If it had not been for Hales he would never have nerved himself (so at least he thought) to run out to the maintopsail yardarm; he would at this moment be ruined and branded as a coward instead of basking in the satisfaction of having capably done his duty.

Jackson saw the bleak look in his face.

'Don't you take on so, sir,' he said. 'They won't 'old the loss of the jolly boat agin you, not the captain and Mr Eccles, they won't.'

'I wasn't thinking about the jolly boat,' said Hornblower. 'I was thinking about Hales.'

'Oh, 'im?' said Jackson. 'Don't you fret about 'im, sir. 'E wouldn't never 'ave made no seaman, not no 'ow.'

CHAPTER FIVE

THE MAN WHO SAW GOD

WINTER had come to the Bay of Biscay. With the passing of the Equinox the gales began to increase in violence, adding infinitely to the labours and dangers of the British Navy watching over the coast of France; easterly gales, bitter cold, which the storm-tossed ships had to endure as best they could, when the spray froze on the rigging and the labouring hulls leaked like baskets; westerly gales, when the ships had to claw their way to safety from a lee shore and make a risky compromise between gaining sufficient sea-room and maintaining a position from which they could pounce on any French vessel venturing out of harbour. The storm-tossed ships, we speak about. But those ships were full of storm-tossed men, who week by week and month by month had to endure the continual cold and the continual wet, the salt provisions, the endless toil, the boredom and misery of life in the blockading fleet. Even in the frigates, the eyes and claws of the blockaders, boredom had to be endured, the boredom of long periods with the hatches battened down, with the deck seams above dripping water on the men below, long nights and short days, broken sleep and yet not enough to do.

Even in the *Indefatigable* there was a feeling of restlessness in the air, and even a mere midshipman like Hornblower could be aware of it as he was looking over the men of his division before the captain's regular weekly inspection.

'What's the matter with your face, Styles?' he asked.

'Boils, sir. Awful bad.'

On Styles' cheeks and lips there were half a dozen dabs of sticking plaster.

'Have you done anything about them?'

'Surgeon's mate, sir, 'e give me plaister for 'em, an' 'e says they'll soon come right, sir.'

'Very well.'

Now was there, or was there not, something strained about the expressions on the faces of the men on either side of Styles? Did they look like men smiling secretly to themselves? Laughing up their sleeves? Hornblower did not want to be an object of derision; it was bad for discipline – and it was worse for discipline if the men shared some secret unknown to their officers. He glanced sharply along the line again. Styles was standing like a block of wood, with no expression at all on his swarthy face; the black ringlets over his ears were properly combed, and no fault could be found with him. But Hornblower sensed that the recent conversation was a source of amusement to the rest of his division, and he did not like it.

After divisions he tackled Mr Low the surgeon, in the gunroom.

'Boils?' said Low. 'Of course the men have boils. Salt pork and split peas for nine weeks on end – what d'you expect but boils? Boils – gurry sores – blains – all the plagues of Egypt.'

'On their faces?'

'That's one locality for boils. You'll find out others from your own personal experience.'

'Does your mate attend to them?' persisted Hornblower.

'Of course.'

'What's he like?'

'Muggridge?'

'Is that his name?'

'He's a good surgeon's mate. Get him to compound a black draught for you and you'll see. In fact, I'd prescribe one for you – you seem in a mighty bad temper, young man.'

Mr Low finished his glass of rum and pounded on the table for the steward. Hornblower realized that he was lucky to have found Low sober enough to give him even this much information, and turned away to go aloft so as to brood over the question in the solitude of the mizzen-top. This was his new station in action; when the men were not at their quarters a man might find a little blessed solitude there – something hard to find in the crowded *Indefatigable*. Bundled up in his peajacket, Hornblower sat in the mizzen-top; over his head the mizzen-topmast drew erratic circles against the grey sky; beside him the topmast shrouds sang their high-pitched note in the blustering gale, and below him the life of the ship went on as she rolled and pitched, standing to the northward under close reefed topsails. At eight bells she would wear to the southward again on her incessant patrol. Until that time Hornblower was free to meditate on the boils on Styles' face and the covert grins on the faces of the other men of the division.

Two hands appeared on the stout wooden barricade surrounding the top, and as Hornblower looked up with annoyance at having his meditations interrupted a head appeared above them. It was Finch, another man in Hornblower's division, who also had his station in action here in the mizzentop. He was a frail little man with wispy hair and pale blue eyes and a foolish smile, which lit up his face when, after betraying some disappointment at finding the mizzen-top already occupied, he recognized Hornblower.

'Beg pardon, sir,' he said. 'I didn't know as how you was up here.'

Finch was hanging on uncomfortably, back downwards, in the act of transferring himself from the futtock shrouds to the top, and each roll threatened to shake him loose.

'Oh come here if you want to,' said Hornblower, cursing himself for his soft heartedness. A taut officer, he felt, would have told Finch to go back whence he came and not bother him.

'Thank 'ee, sir. Thank 'ee,' said Finch, bringing his leg over the barricade and allowing the ship's roll to drop him into the top.

He crouched down to peer under the foot of the mizzen-topsail forward to the mainmast head, and then turned back to smile disarmingly at Hornblower like a child caught in moderate mischief. Hornblower knew that Finch was a little weak in the head – the all embracing press swept up idiots and landsmen to help man the fleet – although he was a trained seaman who could hand, reef and steer. That smile betrayed him.

'It's better up here than down below, sir,' said Finch, apologetically.

'You're right,' said Hornblower, with a disinterested intonation which would discourage conversation.

He turned away to ignore Finch, settled his back again

comfortably, and allowed the steady swing of the top to mesmerize him into dreamy thought that might deal with his problem. Yet it was not easy, for Finch was as restless almost as a squirrel in a cage, peering forward, changing his position, and so continually breaking in on Hornblower's train of thought, wasting the minutes of his precious half-hour of freedom.

'What the devil's the matter with you, Finch?' he rasped at last, patience quite exhausted.

'The Devil, sir?' said Finch. 'It isn't the Devil. He's not up here, begging your pardon, sir.'

That weak mysterious grin again, like a mischievous child. A great depth of secrets lay in those strange blue eyes. Finch peered under the topsail again; it was a gesture like a baby's playing peep-bo.

'There!' said Finch. 'I saw him that time, sir. God's come back to the maintop, sir.'

'God?'

'Aye indeed, sir. Sometimes He's in the maintop. More often than not, sir. I saw Him that time, with His beard all a-blowing in the wind. 'Tis only from here that you can see Him, sir.'

What could be said to a man with that sort of delusion? Hornblower racked his brains for an answer, and found none. Finch seemed to have forgotten his presence, and was playing peep-bo again under the foot of the mizzen-topsail.

'There He is!' said Finch to himself. 'There He is again! God's in the maintop, and the Devil's in the cable tier.'

'Very appropriate,' said Hornblower cynically, but to himself. He had no thought of laughing at Finch's delusions.

'The Devil's in the cable tier during the dog watches,' said Finch again to no one at all. 'God stays in the maintop for ever.'

'A curious timetable,' was Hornblower's *sotto voce* comment.

From down on the deck below came the first strokes of eight bells, and at the same moment the pipes of the bosun's mates began to twitter, and the bellow of Waldron the bos'un made itself heard.

'Turn out the watch below! All hands wear ship! All hands! All hands! You, master-at-arms, take the name of the last man up the hatchway. All hands!'

The interval of peace, short as it was, and broken by Finch's disturbing presence, was at an end. Hornblower dived over the barricade and gripped the futtock shrouds; not for him was the easy descent through the lubber's hole, not when the first lieutenant might see him and reprimand him for unseamanlike behaviour. Finch waited for him to quit the top, but even with this length start Hornblower was easily outpaced in the descent to the deck, for Finch, like the skilled seaman he was, ran down the shrouds as lightly as a monkey. Then the thought of Finch's curious illusions was temporarily submerged in the business of laying the ship on her new course.

But later in the day Hornblower's mind reverted inevitably to the odd things Finch had been saying. There could be no doubt that Finch firmly believed he saw what he said he saw. Both his words and his expression made that certain. He had spoken about God's beard – it was a pity that he had not spared a few words to describe the Devil in the cable tier. Horns, cloven hoof, and pitchfork? Hornblower wondered. And why was the Devil only loose in the cable tier during the dog watches? Strange that he should keep to a timetable. Hornblower caught his breath as the sudden thought came to him that perhaps there might be some worldly explanation. The Devil might well be loose in the cable tier in a metaphorical fashion during the dog watches. Devil's work might be going on there. Hornblower had to decide on what was his duty; and he had to decide further on what was expedient. He could report his suspicions to Eccles, the first lieutenant; but after a year of service Hornblower was under no illusions about what might happen to a junior midshipman who worried a first lieutenant with unfounded suspicions. It would be better to see for himself first, as far as that went. But he did not know what he would find – if he should find anything at all – and he did not know how he should deal with it if he found anything. Much worse than that, he did not know if he would be able to deal with it in officer-like fashion. He could make a fool of himself. He might mishandle whatever situation he found, and bring down obloquy and derision upon his head, and he might imperil the discipline of the ship – weaken the slender thread of allegiance that bound officers and men together, the discipline which kept three hundred men at the bidding of their captain suffering untold hardship without demur; which made them ready to face death at the word of command. When eight bells told the end of the afternoon watch and the beginning of the first dog watch it was with trepidation that Hornblower went below to put a candle in a lantern and make his way forward to the cable tier.

It was dark down here, stuffy, odorous; and as the ship heaved and rolled he found himself stumbling over the various obstacles that impeded his progress. Yet forward there was a faint light, a murmur of voices. Hornblower choked down his fear that perhaps mutiny was being planned. He put his hand over the horn window of the lantern, so as to obscure its light, and crept forward. Two lanterns swung from the low deck-beams, and crouching under them were a score or more of men – more than that, even – and the buzz of their talk came loudly but indistinguishably to Hornblower's ears. Then the buzz increased to a roar, and someone in the centre of the circle rose suddenly to as near his full height as the deck-beams allowed. He was shaking himself violently from side to side for no apparent reason; his face was away from Hornblower, who saw with a gasp that his hands were tied behind him. The men roared again, like spectators at a prize-fight, and the man with his hands tied swung round so that Hornblower could see his face. It was Styles, the man who suffered from boils; Hornblower knew him at once. But that was not what made the most impression on Hornblower.

Clinging to the man's face, weird in the shifting meagre light, was a grey writhing shape, and it was to shake this off that Styles was flinging himself about so violently. It was a rat; Hornblower's stomach turned over with horror.

With a wild jerk of his head Styles broke the grip of the rat's teeth and flung the creature down, and then instantly plunged down on his knees, with his hands still bound behind him, to pursue it with his own teeth.

'Time!' roared a voice at that moment – the voice of Partridge, bosun's mate. Hornblower had been roused by it often enough to recognize it at once.

'Five dead,' said another voice. 'Pay all bets of evens or better.'

Hornblower plunged forward. Part of the cable had been coiled down to make a rat pit ten feet across in which knelt Styles with dead and living rats about his knees. Partridge squatted beside the ring with a sandglass – used for timing the casting of the log – in front of him.

'Six dead,' protested someone. 'That 'un's dead.'

'No, he ain't.'

''Is back's broken. 'E's a dead 'un.'

''E ain't a dead 'un,' said Partridge.

The man who had protested looked up at that moment and caught sight of Hornblower, and his words died away unspoken; at his silence the others followed his glance and stiffened into rigidity, and Hornblower stepped forward. He was still wondering what he should do; he was still fighting down the nausea excited by the horrible things he had seen. Desperately he mastered his horror, and, thinking fast, took his stand on discipline.

'Who's in charge here?' he demanded.

He ran his eye round the circle. Petty officers and second-class warrant officers, mainly; bosun's mates, carpenter's mates. Muggridge, the surgeon's mate – his presence explained much. But his own position was not easy. A midshipman of scant service depended for his authority on board largely on the force of his own personality. He was only a warrant officer himself; when all was said and done a midshipman was not nearly as important to the ship's economy – and was far more easily replaced – than, say, Washburn, the cooper's mate over there, who knew all about the making and storage of the ship's water barrels.

'Who's in charge here?' he demanded again, and once more received no direct reply.

'We ain't on watch,' said a voice in the background.

Hornblower by now had mastered his horror; his indignation still flared within him, but he could appear outwardly calm.

'No, you're not on watch,' he said coldly. 'You're gambling.'

Muggridge took up the defence at that.

'Gambling, Mr Hornblower?' he said. 'That's a very serious charge. Just a gentlemanly competition. You'll find it hard to sub – substantiate any charges of gambling.'

Muggridge had been drinking, quite obviously, following perhaps the example of the head of his department. There was always brandy to be got in the medical stores. A surge of wrath made Hornblower tremble; the effort necessary to keep himself standing stock still was almost too much for him. But the rise in internal pressure brought him inspiration.

'Mr Muggridge,' he said icily, 'I advise you not to say too much. There are other charges possible, Mr Muggridge. A member of His Majesty's forces can be charged with rendering himself unfit for service, Mr Muggridge. And similarly there might be charges of aiding and abetting which might include *you*. I should consult the Articles of War if I were you, Mr Muggridge. The punishment for such an offence is flogging round the fleet I believe.'

Hornblower pointed to Styles, with the blood streaming from his bitten face, and gave more force to his argument by the gesture. He had met the men's arguments with a more effective one along the same lines; they had taken up a legalistic defence and he had legalistically beaten it down.

He had the upper hand now and could give vent to his moral indignation.

'I could bring charges against every one of you,' he roared. 'You could be court martialled – disrated – flogged – every man Jack of you. By God, one more look like that from you, Partridge, and I'll do it. You'd all be in irons five minutes after I spoke to Mr Eccles. I'll have no more of these filthy games. Let those rats loose, there you, Oldroyd, and you, Lewis. Styles, get your face plastered up again. You, Partridge, take these men and coil this cable down properly again before Mr Waldron sees it. I'll keep my eye on all of you in future. The next hint I have of misbehaviour and you'll all be at the gratings. I've said it, and by God I mean it!'

Hornblower was surprised both at his own volubility and at his self possession. He had not known himself capable of carrying off matters with such a high hand. He sought about in his mind for a final salvo with which to make his retirement dignified, and it came to him as he turned away so that he turned back to deliver it.

'After this I want to see you in the dog watches skylarking on deck, not skulking in the cable tiers like a lot of Frenchmen.'

That was the sort of speech to be expected of a pompous old captain, not a junior midshipman, but it served to give dignity to his retirement. There was a feverish buzz of voices as he left the group. Hornblower went up on deck, under the cheerless grey sky dark with premature night, to walk the deck to keep himself warm while the *Indefatigable* slashed her way to windward in the teeth of a roaring westerly, the spray flying in sheets over her bows, the straining seams leaking and her fabric groaning; the end of a day like all the preceding ones and the predecessor probably of innumerable more.

Yet the days passed, and with them came at last a break in the monotony. In the sombre dawn a hoarse bellow from the lookout turned every eye to windward, to where a dull blotch on the horizon marked the presence of a ship. The watch came running to the braces as the *Indefatigable* was laid as close to the wind as she would lie. Captain Pellew came on deck with a peajacket over his nightshirt, his wigless head comical in a pink nightcap; he trained his glass on the strange sail – a dozen glasses were pointing in that direction. Hornblower, looking through the glass reserved for the junior officer of the watch saw the grey rectangle split into three, saw the three grow narrow, and then broaden again to coalesce into a single rectangle again.

'She's gone about,' said Pellew. 'Hands 'bout ship!'

Round came the *Indefatigable* on the other tack; the watch raced aloft to shake out a reef from the topsails while from the deck the officers looked up at the straining canvas to calculate the chances of the gale which howled round their ears splitting the sails or carrying away a spar. The *Indefatigable* lay over until it was hard to keep one's footing on the streaming deck; everyone without immediate duties clung to the weather rail and peered at the other ship.

'Fore- and maintopmasts exactly equal,' said Lieutenant Bolton to Hornblower, his telescope to his eye. 'Topsails white as milady's fingers. She's a Frenchie all right.'

The sails of British ships were darkened with long service in all weathers; when a French ship escaped from harbour to run the blockade her spotless unweathered canvas disclosed her nationality without real need to take into consideration less obvious technical characteristics.

'We're weathering on her,' said Hornblower; his eye was aching with staring through the glass, and his arms even were weary with holding the telescope to his eye, but in the excitement of the chase he could not relax.

'Not as much as I'd like,' growled Bolton.

'Hands to the mainbrace!' roared Pellew at that moment.

It was a matter of the most vital concern to trim the sails so as to lie as close as possible to the wind; a hundred yards gained to windward would count as much as a mile gained in a stern chase. Pellew was looking up at the sails, back at the fleeting wake, across at the French ship, gauging the strength of the wind, estimating the strain on the rigging, doing everything that a lifetime of experience could suggest to close the gap between the two ships. Pellew's next order sent all hands to run out the guns on the weather side; that would in part counteract the heel and give the *Indefatigable* more grip upon the water.

'Now we're walking up to her,' said Bolton with grudging optimism.

'Beat to quarters!' shouted Pellew.

The ship had been expecting that order. The roar of the marine bandsmen's drums echoed through the ship; the pipes twittered as the bosun's mates repeated the order, and the men ran in disciplined fashion to their duties. Hornblower, jumping for the weather mizzen shrouds, saw the eager grins on half a dozen faces – battle and the imminent possibility of death were a welcome change from the eternal monotony of the blockade. Up in the mizzen-top he looked over his men. They were uncovering the locks of their muskets and looking to the priming; satisfied with their readiness for action Hornblower turned his attention to the swivel gun. He took the tarpaulin from the breech and the tompion from the muzzle, cast off the lashings which secured it, and saw that the swivel moved freely in the socket and the trunnions freely in the crotch. A jerk of the lanyard showed him that the lock was sparkling well and there was no need for a new flint. Finch came climbing into the top with the canvas belt over his shoulder containing the charges for the gun; the bags of musket balls lay handy in a garland fixed to the barricade. Finch rammed home a cartridge down the short muzzle; Hornblower had ready a bag of balls to ram down onto it. Then he took a priming-quill and forced it down the touchhole, feeling sensitively to make sure the sharp point pierced the thin serge bag of the cartridge. Priming-quill and flintlock were necessary up here in the top, where no slow match or port-fire could be used with the danger of fire so great and where fire would be so difficult to control in the sails and the rigging. Yet musketry and swivel-gun fire from the tops were an important tactical consideration. With the ships laid yard-arm to yardarm Hornblower's men could clear the hostile quarterdeck where centred the brains and control of the enemy.

'Stop that, Finch!' said Hornblower irritably; turning, he had caught sight of him peering up at the maintop and at this moment of tension Finch's delusions annoyed him.

'Beg your pardon, sir,' said Finch, resuming his duties.

But a moment later Hornblower heard Finch whispering to himself.

'Mr Bracegirdle's there,' whispered Finch, 'an' Oldroyd's there, an' all those others. But *He's* there too, so He is.'

'Hands wear ship!' came the shouted order from the deck below.

The old *Indefatigable* was spinning round on her heel, the yards groaning as the braces swung them round. The French ship had made a bold attempt to rake her enemy as she clawed up to her, but Pellew's prompt handling defeated the plan. Now the ships were broadside to broadside, running free before the wind at long cannon shot.

'Just look at 'im!' roared Douglas, one of the musket men in the top. 'Twenty guns a side. Looks brave enough, doesn't he?'

Standing beside Douglas Hornblower could look down on the Frenchman's deck, her guns run out with the guns' crews clustering round them, officers in white breeches and blue coats walking up and down, the spray flying from her bows as she drove headlong before the wind.

'She'll look braver still when we take her into Plymouth Sound,' said the seaman on the far side of Hornblower.

The *Indefatigable* was slightly the faster ship; an occasional touch of starboard helm was working her in closer to the enemy, into decisive range, without allowing the Frenchman to headreach upon her. Hornblower was impressed by the silence on both sides; he had always understood that the French were likely to open fire at long range and to squander ineffectively the first carefully loaded broadside.

'When's he goin' to fire?' asked Douglas, echoing Hornblower's thoughts.

'In his own good time,' piped Finch.

The gap of tossing water between the two ships was growing narrower. Hornblower swung the swivel gun round and looked along the sights. He could aim well enough at the Frenchman's quarter-deck, but it was much too long a range for a bag of musket balls – in any case he dared not open fire until Pellew gave permission.

'Them's the men for us!' said Douglas, pointing to the Frenchman's mizzen-top.

It looked as if there were soldiers up there, judging by the blue uniforms and the crossbelts; the French often eked out their scanty crews of trained seamen by shipping soldiers; in the British Navy the marines were never employed aloft. The French soldiers saw the gesture and shook their fists, and a young officer among them drew his sword and brandished it over his head. With the ships parallel to each other like this the French mizzen-top would be Hornblower's particular objective should he decide on trying to silence the firing there instead of sweeping the quarter-deck. He gazed curiously at the men it was his duty to kill. So interested was he that the bang of a cannon took him by surprise; before he could look down the rest of the Frenchman's broadside had gone off in straggling fashion, and a moment later the *Indefatigable* lurched as all her guns went off together. The wind blew the smoke forward, so that in the mizzen-top they were not troubled by it at all. Hornblower's glance showed him dead men flung about on the *Indefatigable*'s deck, dead men falling on the Frenchman's deck. Still the range was too great – very long musket shot, his eye told him.

'They're shootin' at us, sir,' said Herbert.

'Let 'em,' said Hornblower.

No musket fired from a heaving masthead at that range could possibly score a hit; that was obvious – so obvious that even Hornblower, madly excited as he was, could not help but be aware of it, and his certainty was apparent in his tone. It was interesting to see how the two calm words steadied the men. Down below the guns were roaring away continuously, and the ships were nearing each other fast.

'Open fire now, men!' said Hornblower. 'Finch!'

He stared down the short length of the swivel gun. In the coarse V of the notch on the muzzle he could see the Frenchman's wheel, the two quartermasters standing behind it, the two officers beside it. He jerked the lanyard. A tenth of a second's delay, and then the gun roared out. He was conscious, before the smoke whirled round him, of the firing quill, blown from the touchhole, flying past his temple. Finch was already sponging out the gun. The musket balls must have spread badly; only one of the helmsmen was down and someone else was already running to take his place. At that moment the whole top lurched frightfully; Hornblower felt it but he could not explain it. There was too much happening at once. The solid timbers under his feet jarred him as he stood – perhaps a shot had hit the mizzen-mast. Finch was ramming in the cartridge; something struck the breech of the gun a heavy blow and left a bright splash of metal there – a musket bullet from the Frenchman's mizzen-top. Hornblower tried to keep his head; he took out another sharpened quill and coaxed it down into the touchhole. It had to be done purposefully and yet gently; a quill broken off in the touchhole was likely to be a maddening nuisance. He felt the point of the quill pierce the cartridge; Finch rammed home the wad on top of the musket balls. A bullet struck the barricade beside him as Hornblower trained the gun down, but he gave it no thought. Surely the top was swaying more even than the heavy sea justified? No matter. He had a clear shot at the enemy's quarterdeck. He tugged at the lanyard. He saw men fall. He actually saw the spokes of the wheel spin round as it was left untended. Then the two ships came together with a shattering crash and his world dissolved into chaos compared with which what had gone before was orderly.

The mast was falling. The top swung round in a dizzy arc so that only his fortunate grip on the swivel saved him from being flung out like a stone from a sling. It wheeled round. With the shrouds on one side shot away and two cannon balls in its heart the mast tottered and rolled. Then the tug of the mizzen-stays inclined it forward, the tug of the other shrouds inclined it to starboard, and the wind in the mizzen-topsail took charge when the back stays parted. The mast crashed forward; the topmast caught against the mainyard and the whole structure hung there before it could dissolve into its constituent parts. The severed butt-end of the mast must be resting on the deck for the moment; mast and topmast were still united at the cap and the trestle-trees into one continuous length, although why the topmast had not snapped at the cap was hard to say. With the lower end of the mast resting precariously on the deck and the topmast resting against the mainyard, Hornblower and Finch still had a chance of life, but the ship's motion, another shot from the Frenchman, or the parting of the over-strained material could all end that chance. The mast could slip outwards, the topmast could break, the butt-end of the mast could slip along the deck – they had to save themselves if they could before any one of these imminent events occurred. The maintopmast and everything above it was involved in the general ruin. It too had fallen and was dangling, sails spars and ropes in one frightful tangle. The mizzen-topsail had torn itself free. Hornblower's eyes met Finch's; Finch and he were clinging to the swivel gun, and there was no one else in the steeply inclined top.

The starboard side mizzen-topmast shrouds still survived; they, as well as the topmast, were resting across the mainyard, strained taut as fiddle strings, the mainyard tightening them just as the bridge tightens the strings of a fiddle. But along those shrouds lay the only way to safety – a sloping path from the peril of the top to the comparative safety of the mainyard.

The mast began to slip, to roll, out towards the end of the yard. Even if the mainyard held, the mizzen-mast would soon fall into the sea alongside. All about them were thunderous noises – spars smashing, ropes parting; the guns were still bellowing and everyone below seemed to be yelling and screaming.

The top lurched again, frightfully. Two of the shrouds parted with the strain, with a noise clearly audible through the other din, and as they parted the mast twisted with a jerk, swinging further round the mizzen-top, the swivel gun, and the two wretched beings who clung to it. Finch's staring blue eyes rolled with the movement of the top. Later Hornblower knew that the whole period of the fall of the mast was no longer than a few seconds, but at this time it seemed as if he had at least long minutes in which to think. Like Finch's, his eyes stared round him, saw the chance of safety.

'The mainyard!' he screamed.

Finch's face bore its foolish smile. Although instinct or training kept him gripping the swivel gun he seemingly had no fear, no desire to gain the safety of the mainyard.

'Finch, you fool!' yelled Hornblower.

He locked a desperate knee round the swivel so as to free a hand with which to gesticulate, but still Finch made no move.

'Jump, damn you!' raved Hornblower. 'The shrouds – the yard. Jump!'

Finch only smiled.

'Jump and get to the maintop! Oh, Christ –!' Inspiration came in that frightful moment. 'The maintop! God's there, Finch! Go along to God, quick!'

Those words penetrated into Finch's addled brain. He nodded with sublime unworldliness. Then he let go of the swivel and seemed to launch himself into the air like a frog. His body fell across the mizzen-topmast shrouds and he began to scramble along them. The mast rolled again, so that when Hornblower launched himself at the shrouds it was a longer jump. Only his shoulders reached the outermost shroud. He swung off, clung, nearly lost his grip, but regained it as a counterlurch of the leaning mast came to his assistance. Then he was scrambling along the shrouds, mad with panic. Here was the precious mainyard, and he threw himself across it, grappling its welcome solidity with his body, his feet feeling for the footrope. He was safe and steady on the yard just as the outward roll of the *Indefatigable* gave the balancing spars their final impetus, and the mizzen-topmast parted company from the broken mizzen-mast and the whole wreck fell down into the sea alongside. Hornblower shuffled along the yard, whither Finch had preceded him, to be received with rapture in the maintop by Midshipman Bracegirdle. Bracegirdle was not God, but as Hornblower leaned across the breastwork of the maintop he thought to himself that if he had not spoken about God being in the maintop Finch would never have made that leap.

'Thought we'd lost you,' said Bracegirdle, helping him in and thumping him on the back. 'Midshipman Hornblower, our flying angel.'

Finch was in the top, too, smiling his fool's smile and surrounded by the crew of the top. Everything seemed mad and exhilarating. It was a shock to remember that they were in the midst of a battle, and yet the firing had ceased, and even the yelling had almost died away. He staggered to the side of the top – strange how difficult it was to walk – and looked over. Bracegirdle came with him. Foreshortened by the height he could make out a crowd of figures on the Frenchman's deck. Those check shirts must surely be worn by British sailors. Surely that was Eccles, the *Indefatigable*'s first lieutenant on the quarterdeck with a speaking trumpet.

'What has happened?' he asked Bracegirdle, bewildered.

'What has happened?' Bracegirdle stared for a moment before he understood. 'We carried her by boarding. Eccles and the boarders were over the ship's side the moment we touched. Why, man, didn't you see?'

'No, I didn't see it,' said Hornblower. He forced himself to joke. 'Other matters demanded my attention at that moment.'

He remembered how the mizzen-top had lurched and swung, and he felt suddenly sick. But he did not want Brace-girdle to see it.

'I must go on deck and report,' he said.

The descent of the main shrouds was a slow, ticklish business, for neither his hands nor his feet seemed to wish to go where he tried to place them. Even when he reached the deck he still felt insecure. Bolton was on the quarterdeck supervising the clearing away of the wreck of the mizzen-mast. He gave a start of surprise as Hornblower approached.

'I thought you were overside with Davy Jones,' he said. He glanced aloft. 'You reached the mainyard in time?'

'Yes, sir.'

'Excellent. I think you're born to be hanged, Hornblower.' Bolton turned away to bellow at the men. ''Vast heaving, there! Clynes, get down into the chains with that tackle! Steady, now, or you'll lose it.'

He watched the labours of the men for some moments before he turned back to Hornblower.

'No more trouble with the men for a couple of months,' he said. 'We'll work 'em 'til they drop, refitting. Prize crew will leave us shorthanded, to say nothing of our butcher's bill. It'll be a long time before they want something new. It'll be a long time for you, too, I fancy, Hornblower.'

'Yes, sir,' said Hornblower.

CHAPTER SIX

THE FROGS AND THE LOBSTERS

'THEY'RE coming,' said Midshipman Kennedy.

Midshipman Hornblower's unmusical ear caught the raucous sounds of a military band, and soon, with a gleam of scarlet and white and gold, the head of the column came round the corner. The hot sunshine was reflected from the brass instruments; behind them the regimental colour flapped from its staff, borne proudly by an ensign with the colour guard round him. Two mounted officers rode behind the colour, and after them came the long red serpent of the half-battalion, the fixed bayonets flashing in the sun, while all the children of Plymouth, still not sated with military pomp, ran along with them.

The sailors standing ready on the quay looked at the soldiers marching up curiously, with something of pity and something of contempt mingled with their curiosity. The rigid drill, the heavy clothing, the iron discipline, the dull routine of the soldier were in sharp contrast with the far more flexible conditions in which the sailor lived. The sailors watched as the band ended with a flourish, and one of the mounted officers wheeled his horse to face the column. A shouted order turned every man to face the quayside, the movements being made so exactly together that five hundred boot-heels made a single sound. A huge sergeant-major, his sash gleaming on his chest, and the silver mounting of his cane winking in the sun, dressed the already perfect line. A third order brought down every musket-butt to earth.

'Unfix – bayonets!' roared the mounted officer, uttering the first words Hornblower had understood.

Hornblower positively goggled at the ensuing formalities, as the fuglemen strode their three paces forward, all exactly to time like marionettes worked by the same strings, turned their heads to look down the line, and gave the time for detaching the bayonets, for sheathing them, and for returning the muskets to the men's sides. The fuglemen fell back into their places, exactly to time again as far as Hornblower could see, but not exactly enough apparently, as the sergeant-major bellowed his discontent and brought the fuglemen out and sent them back again.

'I'd like to see him laying aloft on a stormy night,' muttered Kennedy. 'D'ye think he could take the maintops'l earring?'

'These lobsters!' said Midshipman Bracegirdle.

The scarlet lines stood rigid, all five companies, the sergeants with their halberds indicating the intervals – from halberd to halberd the line of faces dipped down and then up again, with the men exactly sized off, the tallest men at the flanks and the shortest men in the centre of each company. Not a finger moved, not an eyebrow twitched. Down every back hung rigidly a powdered pigtail.

The mounted officer trotted down the line to where the naval party waited, and Lieutenant Bolton, in command, stepped forward with his hand to his hat rim.

'My men are ready to embark, sir,' said the army officer. 'The baggage will be here immediately.'

'Aye aye, major,' said Bolton – the army title and the navy reply in strange contrast.

'It would be better to address me as "My lord"' said the major.

'Aye aye, sir – my lord,' replied Bolton, caught quite off his balance.

His Lordship, the Earl of Edrington, major commanding this wing of the 43rd Foot, was a heavily built young man in his early twenties. He was a fine soldierly figure in his well-fitting uniform, and mounted on a magnificent charger, but he seemed a little young for his present responsible command. But the practice of the purchase of commissions was liable to put very young men in high command, and the Army seemed satisfied with the system.

'The French auxiliaries have their orders to report here,' went on Lord Edrington. 'I suppose arrangements have been made for their transport as well?'

'Yes, my lord.'

'Not one of the beggars can speak English, as far as I can make out. Have you got an officer to interpret?'

'Yes, sir. Mr Hornblower!'

'Sir!'

'You will attend to the embarkation of the French troops.'

'Aye aye, sir.'

More military music – Hornblower's tone-deaf ear distinguished it as making a thinner noise than the British infantry band – heralded the arrival of the Frenchmen farther down the quay by a side road, and Hornblower hastened there. This was the Royal, Christian, and Catholic French Army, or a detachment of it at least – a battalion of the force raised by the émigré French nobles to fight against the Revolution. There was the white flag with the golden lilies at the head of the column, and a group of mounted officers to whom Hornblower touched his hat. One of them acknowledged his salute.

'The Marquis of Pouzauges, Brigadier General in the service of His Most Christian Majesty Louis XVII' said this individual in French by way of introduction. He wore a glittering white uniform with a blue ribbon across it.

Stumbling over the French words, Hornblower introduced himself as an aspirant of his Britannic Majesty's Marine, deputed to arrange the embarkation of the French troops.

'Very good,' said Pouzauges. 'We are ready.'

Hornblower looked down the French column. The men were standing in all attitudes, gazing about them. They were all well enough dressed, in blue uniforms which Hornblower guessed had been supplied by the British government, but the white crossbelts were already dirty, the metalwork tarnished, the arms dull. Yet doubtless they could fight.

'Those are the transports allotted to your men, sir,' said

Hornblower, pointing. 'The *Sophia* will take three hundred, and the *Dumbarton* – that one over there – will take two hundred and fifty. Here at the quay are the lighters to ferry the men out.'

'Give the orders, M. de Moncoutant,' said Pouzauges to one of the officers beside him.

The hired baggage carts had now come creaking up along the column, piled high with the men's kits, and the column broke into chattering swarms as the men hunted up their possessions. It was some time before the men were reassembled, each with his own kit-bag; and then there arose the question of detailing a fatigue party to deal with the regimental baggage, and the men who were given the task yielded up their bags with obvious reluctance to their comrades, clearly in despair of ever seeing any of the contents again. Hornblower was still giving out information.

'All horses must go to the *Sophia*,' he said. 'She has accommodation for six chargers. The regimental baggage –'

He broke off short, for his eye had been caught by a singular jumble of apparatus lying in one of the carts.

'What is that, if you please?' he asked, curiosity overpowering him.

'That, sir,' said Pouzauges, 'is a guillotine.'

'A guillotine?'

Hornblower had read much lately about this instrument. The Red Revolutionaries had set one up in Paris and kept it hard at work. The King of France, Louis XVI himself, had died under it. He did not expect to find one in the train of a counter-revolutionary army.

'Yes,' said Pouzauges, 'we take it with us to France. It is in my mind to give those anarchists a taste of their own medicine.'

Hornblower did not have to make reply, fortunately, as a bellow from Bolton interrupted the conversation.

'What the hell's all this delay for, Mr Hornblower? D'you want us to miss the tide?'

It was of course typical of life in any service that Hornblower should be reprimanded for the time wasted by the inefficiency of the French arrangements – that was the sort of thing he had already come to expect, and he had already learned that it was better to submit silently to reprimand than to offer excuses. He addressed himself again to the task of getting the French aboard their transports. It was a weary midshipman who at last reported himself to Bolton with his tally sheets and the news that the last Frenchman and horse and pieces of baggage were safely aboard, and he was greeted with the order to get his things together quickly and transfer them and himself to the *Sophia*, where his services as interpreter were still needed.

The convoy dropped quickly down Plymouth Sound, rounded the Eddystone, and headed down channel, with H.M.S. *Indefatigable* flying her distinguishing pennant, the two gun-brigs which had been ordered to assist in convoying the expedition, and the four transports – a small enough force, it seemed to Hornblower, with which to attempt the overthrow of the French republic. There were only eleven hundred infantry; the half battalion of the 43rd and the weak battalion of Frenchmen (if they could be called that, seeing that many of them were soldiers of fortune of all nations) and although Hornblower had enough sense not to try to judge the Frenchmen as they lay in rows in the dark and stinking 'tweendecks in the agonies of seasickness he was puzzled that anyone could expect results from such a small force. His historical reading had told him of many small raids, in many wars, launched against the shores of France, and although he knew that they had once been described by an opposition statesman as 'breaking windows with guineas' he had been inclined to approve of them in principle, as bringing about a dissipation of the French strength – until now, when he found himself part of such an expedition.

So it was with relief that he heard from Pouzauges that the troops he had seen did not constitute the whole of the force to be employed – were indeed only a minor fraction of it. A little pale with seasickness, but manfully combating it, Pouzauges laid out a map on the cabin table and explained the plan.

'The Christian Army,' explained Pouzauges, 'will land here, at Quiberon. They sailed from Portsmouth – these English names are hard to pronounce – the day before we left Plymouth. There are five thousand men under the Baron de Charette. They will march on Vannes and Rennes.'

'And what is your regiment to do?' asked Hornblower.

Pouzauges pointed to the map again.

'Here is the town of Muzillac,' he said. 'Twenty leagues from Quiberon. Here the main road from the south crosses the river Marais, where the tide ceases to flow. It is only a little river, as you see, but its banks are marshy, and the road passes it not only by a bridge but by a long causeway. The rebel armies are to the south, and on their northward march must come by Muzillac. We shall be there. We shall destroy the bridge and defend the crossing, delaying the rebels long enough to enable M. de Charette to raise all Brittany. He will soon have twenty thousand men in arms, the rebels will come back to their allegiance, and we shall march on Paris to restore His Most Christian Majesty to the throne.'

So that was the plan. Hornblower was infected with the Frenchmen's enthusiasm. Certainly the road passed within ten miles of the coast, and there, in the broad estuary of the Vilaine, it should be possible to land a small force and seize Muzillac. There should be no difficulty about defending a causeway such as Pouzauges described for a day or two against even a large force. That would afford Charette every chance.

'My friend M. de Moncoutant here,' went on Pouzauges, 'is Lord of Muzillac. The people there will welcome him.'

'Most of them will,' said Moncoutant, his grey eyes narrowing. 'Some will be sorry to see me. But I shall be glad of the encounter.'

Western France, the Vendée and Brittany, had long been in a turmoil, and the population there, under the leadership of the nobility, had risen in arms more than once against the Paris government. But every rebellion had ended in defeat; the Royalist force now being convoyed to France was composed of the fragments of the defeated armies – a final cast of the dice, and a desperate one. Regarded in that light, the plan did not seem so sound.

It was a grey morning – a morning of grey sky and grey rocks – when the convoy rounded Belle Ile and stood in towards the estuary of the Vilaine river. Far to the northward were to be seen white topsails in Quiberon Bay – Hornblower, from the deck of the *Sophia*, saw signals pass back and forth from the *Indefatigable* as she reported her arrival to the senior officer of the main expedition there. It was a proof of the mobility and ubiquity of naval power that it could take advantage of the configuration of the land so that two blows could be struck almost in sight of each other from the sea yet separated by forty miles of roads on land. Hornblower raked the forbidding shore with his glass, reread the orders for the captain of the *Sophia*, and stared again at the shore. He could distinguish the narrow mouth of the Marais river and the strip of mud where the troops were to land. The lead was going in the chains as the *Sophia* crept towards her allotted anchorage, and the ship was rolling uneasily; these waters, sheltered though they were, were a Bedlam of conflicting currents that could make a choppy sea even in a calm. Then the anchor cable rumbled out through the hawsehole and the *Sophia* swung to the current, while the crew set to work hoisting out the boats.

'France, dear beautiful France,' said Pouzauges at Hornblower's side.

A hail came over the water from the *Indefatigable*.

'Mr Hornblower!'

'Sir!' yelled Hornblower back through the captain's megaphone.

'You will go on shore with the French troops and stay with them until you receive further orders.'

'Aye aye, sir.'

So that was the way in which he was to set foot on foreign soil for the first time in his life.

Pouzauges' men were now pouring up from below; it was a slow and exasperating business getting them down the ship's side into the waiting boats. Hornblower wondered idly regarding what was happening on shore at this moment – without doubt mounted messengers were galloping north and south with the news of the arrival of the expedition, and soon the French Revolutionary generals would be parading their men and marching them hurriedly towards this place; it was well that the important strategic point that had to be seized was less than ten miles inland. He turned back to his duties; as soon as the men were ashore he would have to see that the baggage and reserve ammunition were landed, as well as the horses, now standing miserably in improvised stalls forward of the mainmast.

The first boats had left the ship's side; Hornblower watched the men stagger up the shore through mud and water, the French on the left and the red-coated British infantry on the right. There were some fishermen's cottages in sight up the beach, and Hornblower saw advance parties go forward to seize them; at least the landing had been effected without a single shot being fired. He came on shore with the ammunition, to find Bolton in charge of the beach.

'Get those ammunition boxes well above high-water mark,' said Bolton. 'We can't send 'em forward until the Lobsters have found us some carts for 'em. And we'll need horses for those guns too.'

At that moment Bolton's working party was engaged in manhandling two six-pounder guns in field carriages up the beach; they were to be manned by seamen and drawn by horses commandeered by the landing party, for it was in the old tradition that a British expeditionary force should always be thrown on shore dependent for military necessities on the countryside. Pouzauges and his staff were waiting impatiently for their chargers, and mounted them the moment they had been coaxed out of the boats onto the beach.

'Forward for France!' shouted Pouzauges, drawing his sword and raising the hilt to his lips.

Moncoutant and the others clattered forward to head the advancing infantry, while Pouzauges lingered to exchange a few words with Lord Edrington. The British infantry was drawn up in a rigid scarlet line; farther inland occasional red dots marked where the light company had been thrown forward as pickets. Hornblower could not hear the conversation, but he noticed that Bolton was drawn into it, and finally Bolton called him over.

'You must go forward with the Frogs, Hornblower,' he said.

'I'll give you a horse,' added Edrington. 'Take that one – the roan. I've got to have someone I can trust along with them. Keep your eye on them and let me know the moment they get up to any monkey tricks – God knows what they'll do next.'

'Here's the rest of your stores coming ashore,' said Bolton. 'I'll send 'em up as soon as you send some carts back to me. What the hell's *that*?'

'That's a portable guillotine, sir,' said Hornblower. 'Part of the French baggage.'

All three turned and looked at Pouzauges, sitting his horse impatiently during this conversation, which he did not understand. He knew what they were referring to, all the same.

'That's the first thing to be sent to Muzillac,' he said to Hornblower. 'Will you have the goodness to tell these gentlemen so?'

Hornblower translated.

'I'll send the guns and a load of ammunition first,' said Bolton. 'But I'll see he gets it soon. Now off you go.'

Hornblower dubiously approached the roan horse. All he knew about riding he had learned in farmyards, but he got his foot up into the stirrup and climbed in the saddle, grabbing nervously at the reins as the animal started to move off. It seemed as far down to the ground from there as it did from the maintopgallant yard. Pouzauges wheeled his horse about and started up the beach, and the roan followed its example, with Hornblower hanging on desperately, spattered by the mud thrown up by the French horse's heels.

From the fishing hamlet a muddy lane, bordered by green turf banks, led inland, and Pouzauges trotted smartly along it, Hornblower jolting behind him. They covered three or four miles before they overtook the rear of the French infantry, marching rapidly through the mud, and Pouzauges pulled his horse to a walk. When the column climbed a slight undulation they could see the white banner far ahead. Over the banks Hornblower could see rocky fields; out on the left there was a small farmhouse of grey stone. A blue-uniformed soldier was leading away a white horse pulling a cart, while two or three more soldiers were holding back the farmer's frantic wife. So the expeditionary force had secured some of its necessary transport. In another field a soldier was prodding a cow along with his bayonet – Hornblower could not imagine with what motive. Twice he heard distant musket shots to which no one seemed to pay any attention. Then, coming down the road, they encountered two soldiers leading bony horses towards the beach; the jests hurled at them by the marching column had set the men's faces in broad grins. But a little way farther on Hornblower saw a plough standing lonely in a little field, and a grey bundle lying near it. The bundle was a dead man.

Over on their right was the marshy river valley, and it was not long before Hornblower could see, far ahead, the bridge and the causeway which they had been sent to seize. The lane they were following came down a slight incline into the town, passing between a few grey cottages before emerging into the highroad along which there lay the town. There was a grey stone church, there was a building that could easily be identified as an inn and postinghouse with soldiers swarming round it, a slight broadening of the high-road, with an avenue of trees, which Hornblower assumed must be the central square of the town. A few faces peered from upper windows, but otherwise the houses were shut and there were no civilians to be seen except two women hastily shuttering their shops. Pouzauges reined up his horse in the square and began issuing orders. Already the horses were being led out of the posthouse, and groups of men were bustling to and fro on seemingly urgent errands. In obedience to Pouzauges one officer called his men together – he had to expostulate and gesticulate before he succeeded – and started towards the bridge. Another party started along the highway in the opposite direction to guard against the possible surprise attack from there. A crowd of men squatted in the square devouring the bread that was brought out from one of the shops after its door had been beaten in, and two or three times civilians were dragged up to Pouzauges and at his orders were hurried away again to the town jail. The seizure of the town of Muzillac was complete.

Pouzauges seemed to think so, too, after an interval, for with a glance at Hornblower he turned his horse and trotted towards the causeway. The town ended before the road entered the marshes, and in a bit of waste ground beside the road the party sent out in this direction had already lighted a fire, and the men were gathered round it, toasting on their bayonets chunks of meat cut from a cow whose half-flayed corpse lay beside the fire. Farther on, where the causeway became the bridge over the river, a sentry sat sunning himself, with his musket leaning against the parapet of the bridge at his back. Everything was peaceful enough. Pouzauges trotted as far as the crown of the bridge, with Hornblower beside him, and looked over the country on the farther side. There was no sign of any enemy, and when they returned there was a mounted red-coated soldier waiting for them – Lord Edrington.

'I've come to see for myself,' he said. 'The position looks strong enough in all conscience here. Once you have the guns posted you should be able to hold this bridge until you can blow up the arch. But there's a ford, passable at low water, half a mile lower down. That is where I shall station myself – if we lose the ford they can turn the whole position and cut us off from the shore. Tell this gentleman – what's his name? – what I said.'

Hornblower translated as well as he could, and stood by as interpreter while the two commanders pointed here and there and settled their respective duties.

'That's settled, then,' said Edrington at length. 'Don't forget, Mr Hornblower, that I must be kept informed of every development.'

He nodded to them and wheeled his horse and trotted off. As he left a cart approached from the direction of Muzillac, while behind it a loud clanking heralded the arrival of the two six-pounders, each drawn painfully by a couple of horses led by seamen. Sitting upon the front of the cart was Midshipman Bracegirdle, who saluted Hornblower with a broad grin.

'From quarterdeck to dung cart is no more than a step,' he announced, swinging himself down. 'From midshipman to captain of artillery.'

He looked along the causeway and then around him.

'Put the guns over there and they'll sweep the whole length,' suggested Hornblower.

'Exactly,' said Bracegirdle.

Under his orders the guns were wheeled off the road and pointed along the causeway, and the dung cart was unloaded of its contents, a tarpaulin spread on the ground, the gunpowder cartridges laid on it and covered with another tarpaulin. The shot and the bags of grape were piled beside the guns, the seamen working with a will under the stimulus of their novel surroundings.

'Poverty brings strange bedfellows,' said Bracegirdle. 'And wars strange duties. Have you ever blown up a bridge?'

'Never,' said Hornblower.

'Neither have I. Come, and let us do it. May I offer you a place in my carriage?'

Hornblower climbed up into the cart with Bracegirdle, and two seamen led the plodding horse along the causeway to the bridge. There they halted and looked down at the muddy water – running swiftly with the ebb – craning their heads over the parapet to look at the solid stone construction.

'It is the keystone of the arch which we should blow out,' said Bracegirdle.

That was the proverbial recipe for the destruction of a bridge, but as Hornblower looked from the bridge to Bracegirdle and back again the idea did not seem easy to execute. Gunpowder exploded upwards and had to be held in on all sides – how was that to be done under the arch of the bridge?

'What about the pier?' he asked tentatively.

'We can but look and see,' said Bracegirdle, and turned to the seaman by the cart. 'Hannay, bring a rope.'

They fastened the rope to the parapet and slid down it to a precarious foothold on the slippery ledge round the base of the pier, the river gurgling at their feet.

'That seems to be the solution,' said Bracegirdle, crouching almost double under the arch.

Time slipped by fast as they made their preparations; a working party had to be brought from the guard of the bridge, picks and crowbars had to be found or extemporized, and some of the huge blocks with which the pier was built had to be picked out at the shoulder of the arch. Two kegs of gunpowder, lowered gingerly from above, had to be thrust into the holes so formed, a length of slow match put in at each bunghole and led to the exterior, while the kegs were tamped into their caves with all the stones and earth that could be crammed into them. It was almost twilight under the arch when the work was finished, the working party made laboriously to climb the rope up to the bridge and Bracegirdle and Hornblower left to look at each other again.

'I'll fire the fuses,' said Bracegirdle. 'You go next, sir.'

It was not a matter for much argument. Bracegirdle was under orders to destroy the bridge, and Hornblower addressed himself to climbing up the rope while Bracegirdle took his tinderbox from his pocket. Once on the roadway of the bridge Hornblower sent away the cart and waited. It was only two or three minutes before Bracegirdle appeared, frantically climbing the rope and hurling himself over the parapet.

'Run!' was all that was said.

Together they scurried down the bridge and halted breathless to crouch by the abutment of the causeway. Then came a dull explosion, a tremor of the earth under their feet, and a cloud of smoke.

'Let's come and see,' said Bracegirdle.

They retraced their steps towards where the bridge was still shrouded in smoke and dust.

'Only partly –' began Bracegirdle as they neared the scene and the dust cleared away.

And at that moment there was a second explosion which made them stagger as they stood. A lump of the roadbed hit the parapet beside them and burst like a shell, spattering them with fragments. There was a rumble and a clatter as the arch subsided into the river.

'That must have been the second keg going off,' said Bracegirdle, wiping his face. 'We should have remembered the fuses were likely to be of different lengths. Two promising careers might have ended suddenly if we had been any nearer.'

'At any rate, the bridge is gone,' said Hornblower.

'All's well that ends well,' said Bracegirdle.

Seventy pounds of gunpowder had done their work. The bridge was cut clear across, leaving a ragged gap several feet wide, beyond which the roadway reached out towards the gap from the farther pier as a witness to the toughness of the mortar. Beneath their feet as they peered over they could see the river bed almost choked with lumps of stone.

'We'll need no more than an anchor watch to-night,' said Bracegirdle.

Hornblower looked round to where the roan horse was tethered; he was tempted to return to Muzillac on foot, leading the animal, but shame forbade. He climbed with an effort into the saddle and headed the animal back up the road; ahead of him the sky was beginning to turn red with the approach of sunset.

He entered the main street of the town and rounded the slight bend to the central square, to see something that made him, without his own volition, tug at his reins and halt his horse. The square was full of people, townsfolk and soldiers, and in the centre of the square a tall narrow rectangle reached upwards towards the sky with a glittering blade at its upper end. The blade fell with a reverberating thump, and the little group of men round the base of the rectangle dragged something to one side and added it to the heap already there. The portable guillotine was at work.

Hornblower sat sick and horrified – this was worse than any flogging at the gratings. He was about to urge his horse forward when a strange sound caught his ear. A man was singing, loud and clear, and out from a building at the side of the square emerged a little procession. In front walked a big man with dark curly hair, wearing a white shirt and dark breeches. At either side and behind him walked soldiers. It was this man who was singing; the tune meant nothing to Hornblower, but he could hear the words distinctly – it was one of the verses of the French revolutionary song, echoes of which had penetrated even across the Channel.

'Oh, sacred love of the Fatherland . . .' sang the man in the white shirt; and when the civilians in the square heard what he was singing, there was a rustle among them and they dropped to the knees, their heads bowed and their hands crossed upon their breasts.

The executioners were winding the blade up again, and the man in the white shirt followed its rise with his eyes while he still sang without a tremor in his voice. The blade reached the top, and the singing ceased at last as the executioners fell on the man with the white shirt and led him to the guillotine. Then the blade fell with another echoing crash.

It seemed that this was to be the last execution, for the soldiers began to push the civilians back towards their homes, and Hornblower urged his horse forward through the dissolving crowd. He was nearly thrown from his saddle when the animal plunged sideways, snorting furiously – it had scented the horrid heap that lay beside the guillotine. At the side of the square was a house with a balcony, and Hornblower looked up at it in time to see Pouzauges still standing there, wearing his white uniform and blue ribbon, his staff about him and his hands on the rail. There were sentries at the door, and to one of them Hornblower handed over his horse as he entered; Pouzauges was just descending the stairs.

'Good evening, sir,' said Pouzauges with perfect courtesy. 'I am glad you have found your way to headquarters. I trust it was without trouble? We are about to dine and will enjoy your company. You have your horse, I suppose? M. de Villers here will give orders for it to be looked after, I am sure.'

It was all hard to believe. It was hard to believe that this polished gentleman had ordered the butchery that had just ended; it was hard to believe that the elegant young men with whom he sat at dinner were staking their lives on the overthrow of a barbarous but lusty young republic. But it was equally hard to believe, when he climbed into a four-poster bed that night, that he, Midshipman Horatio Hornblower, was in imminent deadly peril himself.

Outside in the street women wailed as the headless corpses, the harvest of the executions, were carried away, and he thought he would never sleep, but youth and fatigue had their way, and he slept for most of the night, although he awoke with the feeling that he had just been fighting off a nightmare. Everything was strange to him in the darkness, and it was several moments before he could account for the strangeness. He was in a bed and not – as he had spent the preceding three hundred nights – in a hammock; and the bed was steady as a rock instead of swaying about with the lively motion of a frigate. The stuffiness about him was the stuffiness of bed curtains, and not the stuffiness of the midshipmen's berth with its compound smell of stale humanity and stale bilgewater. He was on shore, in a house, in a bed, and everything about him was dead quiet, unnaturally so to a man accustomed to the noises of a wooden ship at sea.

Of course; he was in a house in the town of Muzillac in Brittany. He was sleeping in the headquarters of Brigadier General the Marquis de Pouzauges, commanding the French troops who constituted part of this expedition, which was itself part of a larger force invading Revolutionary France in the royalist cause. Hornblower felt a quickening of the pulse, a faint sick feeling of insecurity, as he realized afresh that he was now in France, ten miles from the sea and the *Indefatigable* with only a rabble of Frenchmen – half of them mercenaries only nominally Frenchmen at that – around him to preserve him from death or captivity. He regretted his knowledge of French – if he had had none he would not be here, and good fortune might even have put him among the British half-battalion of the 43rd guarding the ford a mile away.

It was partly the thought of the British troops which roused him out of bed. It was his duty to see that liaison was kept up with them, and the situation might have changed while he slept. He drew aside the bed curtains and stepped down to the floor; as his legs took the weight of his body they protested furiously – all the riding he had done yesterday had left every muscle and joint aching so that he could hardly walk. But he hobbled in the darkness over to the window, found the latch of the shutters, and pushed them open. A three-quarter moon was shining down into the empty street of the town, and looking down he could see the three-cornered hat of the sentry posted outside, and the bayonet reflecting the moonlight. Returning from the window, he found his coat and his shoes and put them on, belted his cutlass about him, and then he crept downstairs as quietly as he could. In the room off the entrance hall a tallow dip guttered on the table, and beside it a French sergeant slept with his head on his arms, lightly, for he raised his head as Hornblower paused in the doorway. On the floor of the room the rest of the guard off duty were snoring stertorously, huddled together like pigs in a sty, their muskets stacked against the wall.

Hornblower nodded to the sergeant, opened the front door and stepped out into the street. His lungs expanded gratefully as he breathed in the clean night air – morning air, rather, for there to the east the sky was assuming a lighter tinge – and the sentry, catching sight of the British naval officer, came clumsily to attention. In the square there still stood the gaunt harsh framework of the guillotine reaching up to the moonlit sky, and round it the black patch of the blood of its victims. Hornblower wondered who they were, who it could have been that the Royalists should seize and kill at such short notice, and he decided that they must have been petty officials of the Revolutionary government – the mayor and the customs officer and so on – if they were not merely men against whom the émigrés had cherished grudges since the days of the Revolution itself. It was a savage, merciless world, and at the moment he was very much alone in it, lonely, depressed, and unhappy.

He was distracted from these thoughts by the sergeant of the guard emerging from the door with a file of men; the sentry in the street was relieved, and the party went on round the house to relieve the others. Then across the street he saw four drummers appear from another house, with a sergeant commanding them. They formed into a line, their drumsticks poised high before their faces, and then at a word from the sergeant, the eight drumsticks fell together with a crash, and the drummers proceeded to march slowly along the street beating out a jerky exhilarating rhythm. At the first corner they stopped, and the drums rolled long and menacingly, and then they marched on again, beating out the previous rhythm. They were beating to arms, calling the men to their duties from their billets, and Hornblower, tone-deaf but highly sensitive to rhythm, thought it was fine music, real music. He turned back to headquarters with his depression fallen away from him. The sergeant of the guard came marching back with the relieved sentries; the first of the awakened soldiers were beginning to appear sleepily in the streets, and then, with a clatter of hoofs, a mounted messenger came riding up to headquarters, and the day was begun.

A pale young French officer read the note which the messenger brought, and politely handed it to Hornblower to read; he had to puzzle over it for a space – he was not accustomed to hand-written French – but its meaning became clear to him at length. It implied no new development; the main expeditionary force, landed yesterday at Quiberon, would move forward this morning on Vannes and Rennes while the subsidiary force to which Hornblower was attached must maintain its position at Muzillac, guarding its flank. The Marquis de Pouzauges, immaculate in his white uniform and blue ribbon, appeared at that moment, read the note without comment, and turned to Hornblower with a polite invitation to breakfast.

They went back to the big kitchen with its copper cooking pans glittering on the walls, and a silent woman brought them coffee and bread. She might be a patriotic Frenchwoman and an enthusiastic counter-revolutionary, but she showed no signs of it. Her feelings, of course, might easily have been influenced by the fact that this horde of men had taken over her house and were eating her food and sleeping in her rooms without payment. Maybe some of the horses and wagons seized for the use of the army were hers too – and maybe some of the people who had died under the guillotine last night were her friends. But she brought coffee, and the staff, standing about in the big kitchen with their spurs clinking, began

to breakfast. Hornblower took his cup and a piece of bread –
for four months before this his only bread had been ship's
biscuit – and sipped at the stuff. He was not sure if he liked
it; he had only tasted coffee three or four times before. But the
second time he raised his cup to his lips he did not sip; before
he could do so, the distant boom of a cannon made him lower
his cup and stand stock still. The cannon shot was repeated,
and again, and then it was echoed by a sharper, nearer note –
Midshipman Bracegirdle's six-pounders on the causeway.

In the kitchen there was instant stir and bustle. Somebody
knocked a cup over and sent a river of black liquid swirling
across the table. Somebody else managed to catch his spurs
together so that he stumbled into somebody else's arms.
Everyone seemed to be speaking at once. Hornblower was as
excited as the rest of them; he wanted to rush out and see
what was happening, but he thought at that moment of the
disciplined calm which he had seen in H.M.S. *Indefatigable* as
she went into action. He was not of this breed of Frenchmen,
and to prove it he made himself put his cup to his lips again
and drink calmly. Already most of the staff had dashed out of
the kitchen shouting for their horses. It would take time to
saddle up; he met Pouzauges' eye as the latter strode up and
down the kitchen, and drained his cup – a trifle too hot for
comfort, but he felt it was a good gesture. There was bread to
eat, and he made himself bite and chew and swallow, although
he had no appetite; if he was to be in the field all day, he could
not tell when he would get his next meal, and so he crammed
a half loaf into his pocket.

The horses were being brought into the yard and saddled;
the excitement had infected them, and they plunged and
sidled about amid the curses of the officers. Pouzauges leapt
up into his saddle and clattered away with the rest of the staff
behind him, leaving behind only a single soldier holding
Hornblower's roan. That was as it had better be – Hornblower knew that he would not keep his seat for half a
minute if the horse took it into his head to plunge or rear. He

walked slowly out to the animal, which was calmer now when the groom petted him, and climbed with infinite slowness and precaution into the saddle. With a pull at the bit he checked the brute's exuberance and walked it sedately into the street and towards the bridge in the wake of the galloping staff. It was better to make sure of arriving by keeping his horse down to a walk than to gallop and be thrown. The guns were still booming and he could see the puffs of smoke from Bracegirdle's six-pounders. On his left, the sun was rising in a clear sky.

At the bridge the situation seemed obvious enough. Where the arch had been blown up a few skirmishers on either side were firing at each other across the gap, and at the far end of the causeway, across the Marais, a cloud of smoke revealed the presence of a hostile battery firing slowly and at extreme range. Beside the causeway on this side were Bracegirdle's two six-pounders, almost perfectly covered by a dip in the ground. Bracegirdle, with his cutlass belted round him, was standing between the guns which his party of seamen were working, and he waved his hand lightheartedly at Hornblower when he caught sight of him. A dark column of infantry appeared on the distant causeway. Bang – bang went Bracegirdle's guns. Hornblower's horse plunged at the noise, distracting him, but when he had time to look again, the column had disappeared. Then suddenly the causeway parapet near him flew into splinters; something hit the roadbed beside his horse's feet a tremendous blow and passed on with a roar – that was the closest so far in his life that a cannon shot had missed him. He lost a stirrup during the resultant struggle with his horse, and deemed it wiser, as soon as he regained moderate control, to dismount and lead the animal off the causeway towards the guns. Bracegirdle met him with a grin.

'No chance of their crossing here,' he said. 'At least, not if the Frogs stick to their work, and it looks as if they're willing to. The gap's within grapeshot range, they'll never bridge it. Can't think what they're burning powder for.'

'Testing our strength, I suppose,' said Hornblower, with an air of infinite military wisdom.

He would have been shaking with excitement if he had allowed his body to take charge. He did not know if he were being stiltedly unnatural, but even if he were that was better than to display excitement. There was something strangely pleasant, in a nightmare fashion, in standing here posing as a hardened veteran with cannon balls howling overhead; Bracegirdle seemed happy and smiling and quite master of himself, and Hornblower looked sharply at him, wondering if this were as much a pose as his own. He could not tell.

'Here they come again,' said Bracegirdle. 'Oh, only skirmishers.'

A few scattered men were running out along the causeway to the bridge. At long musket range they fell to the ground and began spasmodic firing; already there were some dead men lying over there and the skirmishers took cover behind the corpses. On this side of the gap the skirmishers, better sheltered, fired back at them.

'They haven't a chance, here at any rate,' said Bracegirdle. 'And look there.'

The main body of the Royalist force, summoned from the town, was marching up along the road. While they watched it, a cannon shot from the other side struck the head of the column and ploughed into it – Hornblower saw dead men flung this way and that, and the column wavered. Pouzauges came riding up and yelled orders, and the column, leaving its dead and wounded on the road, changed direction and took shelter in the marshy fields beside the causeway.

With nearly all the Royalist force assembled, it seemed indeed as if it would be utterly impossible for the Revolutionaries to force a crossing here.

'I'd better report on this to the Lobsters,' said Hornblower.

'There was firing down that way at dawn,' agreed Bracegirdle.

Skirting the wide marsh here ran a narrow path through

the lush grass, leading to the ford which the 43rd were guarding. Hornblower led his horse onto the path before he mounted; he felt he would be more sure in that way of persuading the horse to take that direction. It was not long before he saw a dab of scarlet on the river bank – pickets thrown out from the main body to watch against any unlikely attempt to cross the marshes and stream round the British flank. Then he saw the cottage that indicated the site of the ford; in the field beside it was a wide patch of scarlet indicating where the main body was waiting for developments. At this point the marsh narrowed where a ridge of slightly higher ground approached the water; a company of redcoats was drawn up here with Lord Edrington on horseback beside them. Hornblower rode up and made his report, somewhat jerkily as his horse moved restlessly under him.

'No serious attack, you say?' asked Edrington.

'No sign of one when I left, sir.'

'Indeed?' Edrington stared across the river. 'And here it's the same story. No attempt to cross the ford in force. Why should they show their hand and then not attack?'

'I thought they were burning powder unnecessarily, sir,' said Hornblower.

'They're not fools,' snapped Edrington, with another penetrating look across the river. 'At any rate, there's no harm in assuming they are not.'

He turned his horse and cantered back to the main body and gave an order to a captain, who scrambled to his feet to receive it. The captain bellowed an order, and his company stood up and fell into line, rigid and motionless. Two further orders turned them to the right and marched them off in file, every man in step, every musket sloped at the same angle. Edrington watched them go.

'No harm in having a flank guard,' he said.

The sound of a cannon across the water recalled them to the river; on the other side of the marsh a column of troops could be seen marching rapidly along the bank.

'That's the same column coming back, sir,' said the company commander. 'That or another just like it.'

'Marching about and firing random shots,' said Edrington. 'Mr Hornblower, have the émigré troops any flank guard out towards Quiberon?'

'Towards Quiberon, sir?' said Hornblower, taken aback.

'Damn it, can't you hear a plain question? Is there, or is there not?'

'I don't know, sir,' confessed Hornblower miserably.

There were five thousand émigré troops at Quiberon, and it seemed quite unnecessary to keep a guard out in that direction.

'Then present my compliments to the French émigré general, and suggest he posts a strong detachment up the road, if he has not done so.'

'Aye aye, sir.'

Hornblower turned his horse's head back up the path towards the bridge. The sun was shining strongly now over the deserted fields. He could still hear the occasional thud of a cannon shot, but overhead a lark was singing in the blue sky. Then as he headed up the last low ridge towards Muzillac and the bridge he heard a sudden irregular outburst of firing; he fancied he heard screams and shouts, and what he saw as he topped the rise, made him snatch at his reins and drag his horse to a halt. The fields before him were covered with fugitives in blue uniforms with white crossbelts, all running madly towards him. In among the fugitives were galloping horsemen, whirling sabres that flashed in the sunshine. Farther out to the left a whole column of horsemen were trotting fast across the fields, and farther back the sun glittered on lines of bayonets moving rapidly from the high road towards the sea.

There could be no doubt of what had happened; during those sick seconds when he sat and stared, Hornblower realized the truth; the Revolutionaries had pushed in a force between Quiberon and Muzillac, and, keeping the émigrés occupied by demonstrations from across the river, had rushed down and brought off a complete surprise by this attack from an unexpected quarter. Heaven only knew what had happened at Quiberon – but this was no time to think about that. Hornblower dragged his horse's head round and kicked his heels into the brute's sides, urging him frantically back up the path towards the British. He bounced and rolled in his saddle, clinging on madly, consumed with fear lest he lose his seat and be captured by the pursuing French.

At the clatter of hoofs every eye turned towards him when he reached the British post. Edrington was there, standing with his horse's bridle over his arm.

'The French!' yelled Hornblower hoarsely, pointing back. 'They're coming!'

'I expected nothing else,' said Edrington.

He shouted an order before he put his foot in the stirrup to mount. The main body of the 43rd was standing in line by the time he was in the saddle. His adjutant went galloping off to recall the company from the water's edge.

'The French are in force, horse, foot, and guns, I suppose?' asked Edrington.

'Horse and foot at least, sir,' gasped Hornblower, trying to keep his head clear. 'I saw no guns.'

'And the émigrés are running like rabbits?'

'Yes, sir.'

'Here come the first of them.'

Over the nearest ridge a few blue uniforms made their appearance, their wearers still running while stumbling with fatigue.

'I suppose we must cover their retreat, although they're not worth saving,' said Edrington. 'Look there!'

The company he had sent out as a flank guard was in sight on the crest of a slight slope: it was formed into a tiny square, red against the green, and as they watched they saw a mob of horsemen flood up the hill towards it and break into an eddy around it.

'Just as well I had them posted there,' remarked Edrington calmly. 'Ah, here comes Mayne's company.'

The force from the ford came marching up. Harsh orders were shouted. Two companies wheeled round while the sergeant-major with his sabre and his silver-headed cane regulated the pace and the alignment as if the men were on the barrack square.

'I would suggest you stay by me, Mr Hornblower,' said Edrington.

He moved his horse up into the interval between the two columns, and Hornblower followed him dumbly. Another order, and the force began to march steadily across the valley, the sergeants calling the step and the sergeant-major watching the intervals. All round them now were fleeing émigré soldiers, most of them in the last stages of exhaustion – Hornblower noticed more than one of them fall down on the ground gasping and incapable of further movement. And then over the low slope to the right appeared a line of plumes, a line of sabres – a regiment of cavalry trotting rapidly forward. Hornblower saw the sabres lifted, saw the horses break into a gallop, heard the yells of the charging men. The redcoats around him halted; another shouted order, another slow, deliberate movement, and the half-battalion was in a square with the mounted officers in the centre and the colours waving over their heads. The charging horsemen were less than a hundred yards away. Some officer with a deep voice began giving orders, intoning them as if at some solemn ceremony. The first order brought the muskets from the men's shoulders, and the second was answered by a simultaneous click of opened priming pans. The third order brought the muskets to the present along one face of the square.

'Too high!' said the sergeant-major. 'Lower, there, number seven.'

The charging horsemen were only thirty yards away; Hornblower saw the leading men, their cloaks flying from their shoulders, leaning along their horses' necks with their sabre pointed forward at the full stretch of their arms.

'Fire!' said the deep voice.

In reply came a single sharp explosion as every musket went off at once. The smoke swirled round the square and disappeared. Where Hornblower had been looking, there were now a score of horses and men on the ground, some struggling in agony, some lying still. The cavalry regiment split like a torrent encountering a rock and hurtled harmlessly past the other faces of the square.

'Well enough,' said Edrington.

The deep voice was intoning again; like marionettes all on the same string the company that had fired now reloaded, every man biting out his bullet at the same instant, every man ramming home his charge, every man spitting his bullet into his musket barrel with the same instantaneous inclination of the head. Edrington looked keenly at the cavalry collecting together in a disorderly mob down the valley.

'The 43rd will advance!' he ordered.

With solemn ritual the square opened up again into two columns and continued its interrupted march. The detached company came marching up to join them from out of a ring of dead men and horses. Someone raised a cheer.

'Silence in the ranks!' bellowed the sergeant-major. 'Sergeant, take that man's name.'

But Hornblower noticed how the sergeant-major was eyeing keenly the distance between the columns; it had to be maintained exactly so that a company wheeling back filled it to make the square.

'Here they come again,' said Edrington.

The cavalry were forming for a new charge, but the square was ready for them. Now the horses were blown and the men were less enthusiastic. It was not a solid wall of horses that came down on them, but isolated groups, rushing first at one face and then at another, and pulling up or swerving aside as they reached the line of bayonets. The attacks were too feeble to meet with company volleys; at the word of command sections here and there gave fire to the more determined groups. Hornblower saw one man – an officer, judging by his gold lace – rein up before the bayonets and pull out a pistol. Before he could discharge it, half a dozen muskets went off together; the officer's face became a horrible bloody mask, and he and his horse fell together to the ground. Then all at once the cavalry wheeled off, like starlings over a field, and the march could be resumed.

'No discipline about these Frogs, not on either side,' said Edrington.

The march was headed for the sea, for the blessed shelter of the *Indefatigable*, but it seemed to Hornblower as if the pace was intolerably slow. The men were marching at the parade step, with agonizing deliberation, while all round them and far ahead of them the fugitive émigrés poured in a broad stream towards safety. Looking back, Hornblower saw the fields full of marching columns – hurrying swarms, rather – of Revolutionary infantry in hot pursuit of them.

'Once let men run, and you can't do anything else with them,' commented Edrington, following Hornblower's gaze.

Shouts and shots over to the flank caught their attention. Trotting over the fields, leaping wildly at the bumps, came a cart drawn by a lean horse. Someone in a seaman's frock and trousers was holding the reins; other seamen were visible over the sides firing muskets at the horsemen hovering about them. It was Bracegirdle with his dung cart; he might have lost his guns but he had saved his men. The pursuers dropped away as the cart neared the columns; Bracegirdle, standing up in the cart, caught sight of Hornblower on his horse and waved to him excitedly.

'Boadicea and her chariot!' he yelled.

'I'll thank you, sir!' shouted Edrington with lungs of brass, 'to go on and prepare for our embarkation.'

'Aye aye, sir!'

The lean horse trotted on with the cart lurching after it and the grinning seamen clinging on to the sides. At the flank appeared a swarm of infantry, a mad, gesticulating crowd, half running to cut off the 43rd's retreat. Edrington swept his glance round the fields.

'The 43rd will form line!' he shouted.

Like some ponderous machine, well oiled, the half battalion fronted towards the swarm; the columns became lines, each man moving into his position like bricks laid on a wall.

'The 43rd will advance!'

The scarlet line swept forward, slowly, inexorably. The swarm hastened to meet it, officers to the front waving their swords and calling on their men to follow.

'Make ready!'

Every musket came down together; the priming pans clicked.

'Present!'

Up came the muskets, and the swarm hesitated before that fearful menace. Individuals tried to get back into the crowd to cover themselves from the volley with the bodies of their comrades.

'Fire!'

A crashing volley; Hornblower, looking over the heads of the British infantry from his point of vantage on horseback, saw the whole face of the swarm go down in swathes. Still the red line moved forward, at each deliberate step a shouted order brought a machine-like response as the men reloaded; five hundred mouths spat in five hundred bullets, five hundred right arms raised five hundred ramrods at once. When the muskets came to the present the red line was at the swathe of dead and wounded, for the swarm had withdrawn before the advance, and shrank back still further at the threat of the volley. The volley was fired; the advance went on. Another volley; another advance. Now the swarm was shredding away. Now men were running from it. Now every man had turned tail and fled from that frightful musketry.

The hillside was as black with fugitives as it had been when the émigrés were fleeing.

'Halt!'

The advance ceased; the line became a double column, and the retreat began again.

'Very creditable,' remarked Edrington.

Hornblower's horse was trying jerkily to pick its way over a carpet of dead and wounded, and he was so busy keeping his seat, and his brain was in such a whirl, that he did not immediately realize that they had topped the last rise, so that before them lay the glittering waters of the estuary. The strip of muddy beach was packed solid with émigrés. There were the ships riding at anchor, and there, blessed sight, were the boats swarming towards the shore. It was high time, for already the boldest of the Revolutionary infantry were hovering round the columns, taking long shots into them. Here and there a man fell.

'Close up!' snapped the sergeants, and the files marched on stolidly, leaving the wounded and dead behind them.

The adjutant's horse suddenly snorted and plunged, and then fell first to its knees, and, kicking, to its side, while the freckle-faced adjutant freed his feet from the stirrups and flung himself out of the saddle just in time to escape being pinned underneath.

'Are you hit, Stanley?' asked Edrington.

'No, my lord. All safe and sound,' said the adjutant, brushing at his scarlet coat.

'You won't have to foot it far,' said Edrington. 'No need to throw out skirmishers to drive those fellows off. This is where we must make our stand.'

He looked about him, at the fishermen's cottages above the beach, the panic-stricken émigrés at the water's edge, and the masses of Revolutionary infantry coming up in pursuit, leaving small enough time for preparation. Some of the redcoats poured into the cottages, appearing a moment later at the windows; it was fortunate that the fishing hamlet guarded one flank of the gap down to the beach while the other was guarded by a steep and inaccessible headland on whose summit a small block of redcoats established themselves. In the gap between the two points the remaining four companies formed a long line just sheltered by the crest of the beach.

The boats of the squadron were already loading with émigrés among the small breakers below. Hornblower heard the crack of a single pistol-shot; he could guess that some officer down there was enforcing his orders in the only possible way to prevent the fear-driven men from pouring into the boats and swamping them. As if in answer came the roar of cannon on the other side. A battery of artillery had unlimbered just out of musket range and was firing at the British position, while all about it gathered the massed battalions of the Revolutionary infantry. The cannon balls howled close overhead.

'Let them fire away,' said Edrington. 'The longer the better.'

The artillery could do little harm to the British in the fold of ground that protected them, and the Revolutionary commander must have realized that as well as the necessity for wasting no time. Over there the drums began to roll – a noise of indescribable menace – and then the columns surged forward. So close were they already that Hornblower could see the features of the officers in the lead, waving their hats and swords.

'43rd, make ready!' said Edrington, and the priming pans clicked as one. 'Seven paces forward – march!'

One – two – three – seven paces, painstakingly taken, took the line to the little crest.

'Present! Fire!'

A volley nothing could withstand. The columns halted, swayed, received another smashing volley, and another, and fell back in ruin.

'Excellent!' said Edrington.

The battery boomed again; a file of two redcoat soldiers was tossed back like dolls, to lie in a horrible bloody mass close beside Hornblower's horse's feet.

'Close up!' said a sergeant, and the men on either side had filled the gap.

'43rd, seven paces back – march!'

The line was below the crest again, as the redcoated marionettes withdrew in steady time. Hornblower could not remember later whether it was twice or three times more that the Revolutionary masses came on again, each time to be dashed back by that disciplined musketry. But the sun was nearly setting in the ocean behind him when he looked back to see the beach almost cleared and Bracegirdle plodding up to them to report.

'I can spare one company now,' said Edrington in reply but not taking his eyes off the French masses. 'After they are on board, have every boat ready and waiting.'

One company filed off; another attack was beaten back – after the preceding failures it was not pressed home with anything like the dash and fire of the earlier ones. Now the battery was turning its attention to the headland on the flank, and sending its balls among the redcoats there, while a battalion of French moved over to the attack at that point.

'That gives us time,' said Edrington. 'Captain Griffin, you can march the men off. Colour party, remain here.'

Down the beach went the centre companies to the waiting boats, while the colours still waved to mark their old position, visible over the crest to the French. The company in the cottages came out, formed up, and marched down as well. Edrington trotted across to the foot of the little headland; he watched the French forming for the attack and the infantry wading out to the boats.

'Now, grenadiers!' he yelled suddenly. 'Run for it! Colour party!'

Down the steep seaward face of the headland came the last company, running, sliding, and stumbling. A musket, clumsily handled, went off unexpectedly. The last man came down the slope as the colour party reached the water's edge and began to climb into a boat with its precious burden. A wild yell went up from the French, and their whole mass came rushing towards the evacuated position.

'Now, sir,' said Edrington, turning his horse seawards.

Hornblower fell from his saddle as his horse splashed into the shallows. He let go of the reins and plunged out, waist deep, shoulder deep, to where the longboat lay on its oars with its four-pounder gun in its bows and Bracegirdle beside it to haul him in. He looked up in time to see a curious incident; Edrington had reached the *Indefatigable*'s gig, still holding his horse's reins. With the French pouring down the beach towards them, he turned and took a musket from the nearest soldier, pressed the muzzle to the horse's head, and fired. The horse fell in its death agony in the shallows; only Hornblower's roan remained as prize to the Revolutionaries.

'Back water!' said Bracegirdle, and the longboat backed away from the beach; Hornblower lay in the eyes of the boat feeling as if he had not the strength to move a limb, and the beach was covered with shouting, gesticulating Frenchmen, lit redly by the sunset.

'One moment,' said Bracegirdle, reaching for the lanyard of the four-pounder, and tugging at it smartly.

The gun roared out in Hornblower's ear, and the charge cut a swathe of destruction on the beach.

'That was canister,' said Bracegirdle. 'Eighty-four balls. Easy, port! Give way, starboard!'

The longboat turned, away from the beach and towards the welcoming ships. Hornblower looked back at the darkening coast of France. This was the end of an incident; his country's attempt to overturn the Revolution had met with a bloody repulse. Newspapers in Paris would exult; the *Gazette* in London would give the incident five cold lines. Clairvoyant, Hornblower could foresee that in a year's time the world would hardly remember the incident. In twenty years it would be entirely forgotten. Yet those headless corpses up there in Muzillac; those shattered redcoats; those Frenchmen caught in the four-pounder's blast of canister – they were all as dead as if it had been a day in which history had been changed. And he was just as weary. And in his pocket there was still the bread he had put there that morning and forgotten all about.

CHAPTER SEVEN

THE SPANISH GALLEYS

THE old *Indefatigable* was lying at anchor in the Bay of Cadiz at the time when Spain made peace with France. Hornblower happened to be midshipman of the watch, and it was he who called the attention of Lieutenant Chadd to the approach of the eight-oared pinnace, with the red and yellow of Spain dropping at the stern. Chadd's glass made out the gleam of gold on epaulette and cocked hat, and bellowed the order for sideboys and marine guard to give the traditional honours to a captain in an allied service. Pellew, hurriedly warned, was at the gangway to meet his visitor, and it was at the gangway that the entire interview took place. The Spaniard, making a low bow with his hat across his stomach, offered a sealed envelope to the Englishman.

'Here, Mr Hornblower,' said Pellew, holding the letter unopened, 'speak French to this fellow. Ask him to come below for a glass of wine.'

But the Spaniard, with a further bow, declined the refreshment, and, with another bow, requested that Pellew open the letter immediately. Pellew broke the seal and read the contents, struggling with the French which he could read to a small extent although he could not speak it at all. He handed it to Hornblower.

'This means the Dagoes have made peace, doesn't it?'

Hornblower struggled through twelve lines of compliments addressed by His Excellency the Duke of Belchite (Grandee of the First Class, with eighteen other titles ending with Captain-General of Andalusia) to the Most Gallant Ship-Captain Sir Edward Pellew, Knight of the Bath. The second paragraph was short and contained only a brief intimation of peace. The third paragraph was as long as the first, and repeated its phraseology almost word for word in a ponderous farewell.

'That's all, sir,' said Hornblower.

But the Spanish captain had a verbal message with which to supplement the written one.

'Please tell your captain,' he said, in his lisping Spanish-French, 'that now as a neutral power, Spain must enforce her rights. You have already been at anchor here for twenty-four hours. Six hours from now' – the Spaniard took a gold watch from his pocket and glanced at it – 'if you are within range of the batteries at Puntales there they will be given orders to fire on you.'

Hornblower could only translate the brutal message without any attempt at softening it, and Pellew listened, white with anger despite his tan.

'Tell him –' he began, and then mastered his rage. 'Damme if I'll let him see he has made me angry.'

He put his hat across his stomach and bowed in as faithful an imitation of the Spaniard's courtliness as he could manage, before he turned to Hornblower.

'Tell him I have received his message with pleasure. Tell him I much regret that circumstances are separating him from me, and that I hope I shall always enjoy his personal friendship whatever the relations between our countries. Tell him – oh, you can tell him the sort of thing I want said, can't you, Hornblower? Let's see him over the side with dignity. Sideboys! Bosun's mates! Drummers!'

Hornblower poured out compliments to the best of his ability, and at every phrase the two captains exchanged bows, the Spaniard withdrawing a pace at each bow and Pellew following him up, not to be outdone in courtesy. The drums beat a ruffle, the marines presented arms, the pipes shrilled and twittered until the Spaniard's head had descended to the level of the maindeck, when Pellew stiffened up, clapped his hat on his head, and swung round on his first lieutenant.

'Mr Eccles, I want to be under way within the hour, if you please.'

Then he stamped down below to regain his equanimity in private.

Hands were aloft loosing sail ready to sheet home, while the clank of the capstan told how other men were heaving the cable short, and Hornblower was standing on the port-side gangway with Mr Wales the carpenter, looking over at the white houses of one of the most beautiful cities in Europe.

'I've been ashore there twice,' said Wales. 'The wine's good – vino, they calls it – if you happens to like that kind o' muck. But don't you ever try that brandy, Mr Hornblower. Poison, it is, rank poison. Hello! We're going to have an escort, I see.'

Two long sharp prows had emerged from the inner bay, and were pointing towards the *Indefatigable*. Hornblower could not restrain himself from giving a cry of surprise as he followed Wales' gaze. The vessels approaching were galleys; along each side of them the oars were lifting and falling rhythmically, catching the sunlight as they feathered. The effect, as a hundred oars swung like one, was perfectly beautiful. Hornblower remembered a line in a Latin poet which he had translated as a schoolboy, and recalled his surprise when he discovered that to a Roman the 'white wings' of a ship of war were her oars. Now the simile was plain; even a gull in flight, which Hornblower had always looked upon until now as displaying the perfection of motion, was not more beautiful than those galleys. They lay low in the water, immensely long for their beam. Neither the sails nor the lateen yards were set on the low raking masts. The bows blazed with gilding, while the waters of the bay foamed round them as they headed into the teeth of the gentle breeze with the Spanish red and gold streaming aft from the masthead. Up – forward – down – went the oars with unchanging rhythm, the blades not varying an inch in their distance apart during the whole of the stroke. From the bows of each two long guns looked straight forward in the direction the galleys pointed.

'Twenty-four pounders,' said Wales. 'If they catch you in a calm, they'll knock you to pieces. Lie off on your quarter where you can't bring a gun to bear and rake you till you strike. An' then God help you – better a Turkish prison than a Spanish one.'

In a line-ahead that might have been drawn with a ruler and measured with a chain the galleys passed close along the port side of the *Indefatigable* and went ahead of her. As they passed the roll of the drum and the call of the pipes summoned the crew of the *Indefatigable* to attention out of compliment to the flag and the commission pendant going by, while the galleys' officers returned the salute.

'It don't seem right, somehow,' muttered Wales under his breath, 'to salute 'em like they was a frigate.'

Level with the *Indefatigable*'s bowsprit the leader backed her starboard side oars, and spun like a top, despite her length and narrow beam, across the frigate's bows. The gentle wind blew straight to the frigate from the galley, and then from her consort as the latter followed; and a foul stench came back on the air and assailed Hornblower's nostrils, and not Hornblower's alone, clearly, for it brought forth cries of disgust from all the men on deck.

'They all stink like that,' explained Wales. 'Four men to the oar an' fifty oars. Two hundred galley slaves, that is. All chained to their benches. When you goes aboard one of them as a slave you're chained to your bench, an' you're never unchained until they drop you overside. Sometimes when the hands aren't busy they'll hose out the bilge, but that doesn't happen often, bein' Dagoes an' not many of 'em.'

Hornblower as always sought exact information.

'How many, Mr Wales?'

'Thirty, mebbe. Enough to hand the sails if they're making a passage. Or to man the guns – they strike the yards and sails, like now, before they goes into action, Mr Hornblower,' said Wales, pontifical as usual, and with that slight emphasis on the 'Mister' inevitable when a warrant officer of sixty with no hope of further promotion addressed a warrant officer of eighteen (his nominal equal in rank) who might some day be an admiral. 'So you see how it is. With no more than thirty of a crew an' two hundred slaves they daren't let 'em loose, not ever.'

The galleys had turned again, and were now passing down the *Indefatigable*'s starboard side. The beat of the oars had slowed very noticeably, and Hornblower had ample time to observe the vessels closely, the low forecastle and high poop with the gangway connecting them along the whole length of the galley; upon that gangway walked a man with a whip. The rowers were invisible below the bulwarks, the oars being worked through holes in the sides closed, as far as Hornblower could see, with sheets of leather round the oar-looms to keep out the sea. On the poop stood two men at the tiller and a small group of officers, their gold lace flashing in the sunshine. Save for the gold lace and the twenty-four-pounder bow chasers Hornblower was looking at exactly the same sort of vessel as the ancients used to fight their battles. Polybius and Thucydides wrote about galleys almost identical with these – for that matter it was not much more than two hundred years since the galleys had fought their last great battle at Lepanto against the Turks. But those battles had been fought with hundreds of galleys a side.

'How many do they have in commission now?' asked Hornblower.

'A dozen, mebbe – not that I knows for sure, o' course. Carthagena's their usual station, beyond the Gut.'

Wales, as Hornblower understood, meant by this through

the Strait of Gibraltar in the Mediterranean.

'Too frail for the Atlantic,' Hornblower commented.

It was easy to deduce the reasons for the survival of this small number – the innate conservatism of the Spaniards would account for it to a large extent. Then there was the point that condemnation to the galleys was one way of disposing of criminals. And when all was said and done a galley might still be useful in a calm – merchant ships becalmed while trying to pass the Strait of Gibraltar might be snapped up by galleys pushing out from Cadiz or Carthagena. And at the very lowest estimate there might be some employment for galleys to tow vessels in and out of harbour with the wind unfavourable.

'Mr Hornblower!' said Eccles. 'My respects to the captain, and we're ready to get under way.'

Hornblower dived below with his message.

'My compliments to Mr Eccles,' said Pellew, looking up from his desk, 'and I'll be on deck immediately.'

There was just enough of a southerly breeze to enable the *Indefatigable* to weather the point in safety. With her anchor catted she braced round her yards and began to steal seaward; in the disciplined stillness which prevailed the sound of the ripple of water under her cutwater was clearly to be heard – a musical note which told nothing, in its innocence, of the savagery and danger of the world of the sea into which she was entering. Creeping along under her topsails the *Indefatigable* made no more than three knots, and the galleys came surging past her again, oars beating their fastest rhythm, as if the galleys were boasting of their independence of the elements. Their gilt flashed in the sun as they overtook to windward, and once again their foul stench offended the nostrils of the men of the *Indefatigable*.

'I'd be obliged if they'd keep to leeward of us,' muttered Pellew, watching them through his glass. 'But I suppose that's not Spanish courtesy. Mr Cutler!'

'Sir!' said the gunner.

'You may commence the salute.'

'Aye aye, sir.'

The forward carronade on the lee side roared out the first of its compliments, and the fort of Puntales began its reply. The sound of the salute rolled round the beautiful bay; nation was speaking to nation in all courtesy.

'The next time we hear those guns they'll be shotted, I fancy,' said Pellew, gazing across at Puntales and the flag of Spain flying above it.

Indeed, the tide of war was turning against England. Nation after nation had retired from the contest against France, some worsted by arms, and some by the diplomacy of the vigorous young republic. To any thinking mind it was obvious that once the step from war to neutrality had been taken, the next step would be easy, from neutrality to war on the other side. Hornblower could foresee, close at hand, a time when all Europe would be arrayed in hostility to England, when she would be battling for her life against the rejuvenescent power of France and the malignity of the whole world.

'Set sail, please, Mr Eccles,' said Pellew.

Two hundred trained pairs of legs raced aloft; two hundred trained pairs of arms let loose the canvas, and the *Indefatigable* doubled her speed, heeling slightly to the gentle breeze. Now she was meeting the long Atlantic swell. So were the galleys; as the *Indefatigable* overtook them, Hornblower could see the leader put her nose into a long roller so that a cloud of spray broke over her forecastle. That was asking too much of such frail craft. Back went one bank of oars; forward went the other. The galleys rolled hideously for a moment in the trough of the sea before they completed their turn and headed back for the safe waters of Cadiz Bay. Someone forward in the *Indefatigable* began to boo, and the cry was instantly taken up through the ship. A storm of boos and whistles and catcalls pursued the galleys, the men momentarily quite out of hand while Pellew spluttered with rage on the quarterdeck and the petty officers strove in vain to take the names of the offenders. It was an ominous farewell to Spain.

Ominous indeed. It was not long before Captain Pellew gave the news to the ship that Spain had completed her change-over; with the treasure convoy safely in she had declared war against England; the revolutionary republic had won the alliance of the most decayed monarchy in Europe. British resources were now stretched to the utmost; there was another thousand miles of coast to watch, another fleet to blockade, another horde of privateers to guard against, and far fewer harbours in which to take refuge and from which to draw the fresh water and the meagre stores which enabled the hard-worked crews to remain at sea. It was then that friendship had to be cultivated with the half savage Barbary States, and the insolence of the Deys and the Sultans had to be tolerated so that North Africa could provide the skinny bullocks and the barley grain to feed the British garrisons in the Mediterranean – all of them beleagured on land – and the ships which kept open the way to them. Oran, Tetuan, Algiers wallowed in unwontedly honest prosperity with the influx of British gold.

It was a day of glassy calm in the Straits of Gibraltar. The sea was like a silver shield, the sky like a bowl of sapphire, with the mountains of Africa on the one hand, the mountains of Spain on the other as dark serrations on the horizon. It was not a comfortable situation for the *Indefatigable*, but that was not because of the blazing sun which softened the pitch in the deck seams. There is almost always a slight current setting inwards into the Mediterranean from the Atlantic, and the prevailing winds blow in the same direction. In a calm like this it was not unusual for a ship to be carried far through the Straits, past the Rock of Gibraltar, and then to have to beat for days and even weeks to make Gibraltar Bay. So that Pellew was not unnaturally anxious about his convoy of grain ships from Oran. Gibraltar had to be revictualled – Spain had already marched an army up for the siege – and he dared not risk being carried past his destination. His orders to his reluctant convoy had been enforced by flag and gun signals, for no short-handed merchant ship relished the prospect of the labour Pellew wished to be executed. The *Indefatigable* no less than her convoy had lowered boats, and the helpless ships were now all in tow. That was backbreaking, exhausting labour, the men at the oars tugging and straining, dragging the oar blades through the water, while the towlines tightened and bucked with superhuman perversity and the ships sheered freakishly from side to side. It was less than a mile an hour, that the ships made in this fashion, at the cost of the complete exhaustion of the boats' crews, but at least it postponed the time when the Gibraltar current would carry them to leeward, and similarly gave more chance for the longed-for southerly wind – two hours of a southerly wind was all they wished for – to waft them up to the Mole.

Down in the *Indefatigable*'s longboat and cutter the men tugging at their oars were so stupefied with their toil that they did not hear the commotion in the ship. They were just tugging and straining, under the pitiless sky, living through their two hours' spell of misery, but they were roused by the voice of the captain himself, hailing them from the forecastle.

'Mr Bolton! Mr Chadd! Cast off there, if you please. You'd better come and arm your men at once. Here come our friends from Cadiz.'

Back on the quarterdeck, Pellew looked through his glass at the hazy horizon; he could make out from here by now what had first been reported from the masthead.

'They're heading straight for us,' he said.

The two galleys were on their way from Cadiz; presumably a fast horseman from the lookout point at Tarifa had brought them the news of this golden opportunity, of the flat calm and the scattered and helpless convoy. This was the moment for galleys to justify their continued existence. They could capture and at least burn, although they could not hope to carry off, the unfortunate merchant ships, while the *Indefatigable* lay helpless hardly out of cannon's range. Pellew looked round at the two merchant ships and the three brigs; one of them was within half a mile of him and might be covered by his gunfire, but the others – a mile and a half, two miles away – had no such protection.

'Pistols and cutlasses, my lads!' he said to the men pouring up from overside. 'Clap onto that stay tackle now. Smartly with that carronade, Mr Cutler!'

The *Indefatigable* had been in too many expeditions where minutes counted to waste any time over these preparations. The boats' crews seized their arms, the six-pounder carronades were lowered into the bows of the cutter and longboat, and soon the boats, crowded with armed men, and provisioned against sudden emergency, were pulling away to meet the galleys.

'What the devil d'you think you're doing, Mr Hornblower?'

Pellew had just caught sight of Hornblower in the act of swinging out of the jolly boat which was his special charge. He wondered what his midshipman thought he could achieve against a war-galley with a twelve-foot boat and a crew of six.

'We can pull to one of the convoy and reinforce the crew, sir,' said Hornblower.

'Oh, very well then, carry on. I'll trust to your good sense, even though that's a broken reed.'

'Good on you, sir!' said Jackson ecstatically, as the jolly boat shoved off from the frigate. 'Good on you! No one else wouldn't never have thought of that.'

Jackson, the coxswain of the jolly boat, obviously thought that Hornblower had no intention of carrying out his suggestion to reinforce the crew of one of the merchant ships.

'Those stinking Dagoes,' said stroke oar, between his teeth.

Hornblower was conscious of the presence in his crew of the same feeling of violent hostility toward the Spanish galleys as he felt within himself. In a fleeting moment of analysis, he attributed it to the circumstances in which they had first made the galleys' acquaintance, as well as to the stench which the galleys trailed after them. He had never known this feeling of personal hatred before; when previously he had fought it had been as a servant of the King, not out of personal animosity. Yet here he was gripping the tiller under the scorching sky and leaning forward in his eagerness to be at actual grips with his enemy.

The longboat and cutter had a long start of them, and even though they were manned by crews who had already served a spell at the oars they were skimming over the water at such a speed that the jolly boat with all the advantage of the glassy-smooth water only slowly caught up to them. Overside the sea was of the bluest, deepest blue until the oar blades churned it white. Ahead of them the vessels of the convoy lay scattered where the sudden calm had caught them, and just beyond them Hornblower caught sight of the flash of oar blades as the galleys came sweeping down on their prey. Longboat and cutter were diverging in an endeavour to cover as many vessels as possible, and the gig was still far astern. There would hardly be time to board a ship even if Hornblower should wish to. He put the tiller over to incline his course after the cutter; one of the galleys at that moment abruptly made its appearance in the gap between two of the merchant ships. Hornblower saw the cutter swing round to point her six-pounder carronade at the advancing bows.

'Pull, you men! Pull!' he shrieked mad with excitement.

He could not imagine what was going to happen, but he wanted to be in the fray. That six-pounder popgun was grossly inaccurate at any range longer than musket shot. It would serve to hurl a mass of grape into a crowd of men, but its ball would have small effect on the strengthened bows of a war galley.

'Pull!' shrieked Hornblower again. He was nearly up to them, wide on the cutter's quarter.

The carronade boomed out. Hornblower thought he saw the splinters fly from the galley's bow, but the shot had no more effect on deterring her than a peashooter could stop a charging bull. The galley turned a little, getting exactly into line, and then her oars' beat quickened. She was coming down to ram, like the Greeks at Salamis.

'Pull!' shrieked Hornblower.

Instinctively, he gave the tiller a touch to take the jolly boat out into a flanking position.

'Easy!'

The jolly boat's oars stilled, as their way carried them past the cutter. Hornblower could see Soames standing up in the sternsheets looking at the death which was cleaving the blue water towards him. Bow to bow the cutter might have stood a chance, but too late the cutter tried to evade the blow altogether. Hornblower saw her turn, presenting her vulnerable side to the galley's stem. That was all he could see, for the next moment the galley herself hid from him the final act of the tragedy. The jolly boat's starboard side oars only just cleared the galley's starboard oars as she swept by. Hornblower heard a shriek and a crash, saw the galley's forward motion almost cease at the collision. He was mad with the lust of fighting, quite insane, and his mind was working with the rapidity of insanity.

'Give way, port!' he yelled, and the jolly boat swung round under the galley's stern. 'Give way all!'

The jolly boat leaped after the galley like a terrier after a bull.

'Grapple them, damn you, Jackson!'

Jackson shouted an oath in reply, as he leaped forward, seemingly hurdling the men at the oars without breaking their stroke. In the bows Jackson seized the boat's grapnel on its long line and flung it hard and true. It caught somewhere in the elaborate gilt rail on the galley's quarter. Jackson hauled on the line, the oars tugged madly in the effort to carry the jolly boat up to the galley's stern. At that moment Hornblower saw it, the sight which would long haunt his dreams – up from under the galley's stern came the shattered forepart of the cutter, still with men clinging to it who had survived the long passage under the whole length of the galley which had overrun them. There were straining faces, empurpled faces, faces already relaxing in death. But in a moment it was past and gone, and Hornblower felt the jerk transmitted through the line to the jolly boat as the galley leaped forward.

'I can't hold her!' shouted Jackson.

'Take a turn round the cleat, you fool!'

The galley was towing the jolly boat now, dragging her along at the end of a twenty-foot line close on her quarter, just clear of the arc of her rudder. The white water bubbled all around her, her bows were cocked up with the strain. It was a mad moment, as though they had harpooned a whale. Some one came running aft on the Spaniard's poop, knife in hand to cut the line.

'Shoot him, Jackson!' shrieked Hornblower again.

Jackson's pistol cracked, and the Spaniard fell to the deck out of sight – a good shot. Despite his fighting madness, despite the turmoil of rushing water and glaring sun, Hornblower tried to think out his next move. Inclination and common sense alike told him that the best plan was to close with the enemy despite the odds.

'Pull up to them, there!' he shouted – everyone in the boat was shouting and yelling. The men in the bows of the jolly boat faced forward and took the grapnel line and began to haul in on it, but the speed of the boat through the water made any progress difficult, and after a yard or so had been gained the difficulty became insurmountable, for the grapnel was caught in the poop rail ten or eleven feet above water, and the angle of pull became progressively steeper as the jolly boat neared the stern of the galley. The boat's bow cocked higher out of the water than ever.

'Belay!' said Hornblower, and then, his voice rising again, 'Out pistols, lads!'

A row of four or five swarthy faces had appeared at the

stern of the galley. Muskets were pointing into the jolly boat, and there was a brief but furious exchange of shots. One man fell groaning into the bottom of the jolly boat, but the row of faces disappeared. Standing up precariously in the swaying sternsheets, Hornblower could still see nothing of the galley's poop deck save for the tops of two heads, belonging, it was clear, to the men at the tiller.

'Reload,' he said to his men, remembering by a miracle to give the order. The ramrods went down the pistol barrels.

'Do that carefully if you ever want to see Pompey again,' said Hornblower.

He was shaking with excitement and mad with the fury of fighting, and it was the automatic, drilled part of him which was giving these level-headed orders. His higher faculties were quite negatived by his lust for blood. He was seeing things through a pink mist – that was how he remembered it when he looked back upon it later. There was a sudden crash of glass. Someone had thrust a musket barrel through the big stern window of the galley's after cabin. Luckily having thrust it through he had to recover himself to take aim. An irregular volley of pistols almost coincided with the report of the musket. Where the Spaniard's bullet went no one knew; but the Spaniard fell back from the window.

'By God! That's our way!' screamed Hornblower, and then, steadying himself, 'Reload.'

As the bullets were being spat into the barrels he stood up. His unused pistols were still in his belt; his cutlass was at his side.

'Come aft, here,' he said to stroke oar; the jolly boat would stand no more weight in the bows than she had already. 'And you, too.'

Hornblower poised himself on the thwarts, eyeing the grapnel line and the cabin window.

'Bring 'em after me one at a time, Jackson,' he said.

Then he braced himself and flung himself at the grapnel line. His feet grazed the water as the line sagged, but using all his clumsy strength his arms carried him upwards. Here was the shattered window at his side; he swung up his feet, kicked out a big remaining piece of the pane, and then shot his feet through and then the rest of himself. He came down on the deck of the cabin with a thud; it was dark in here compared with the blinding sun outside. As he got to his feet, he trod on something which gave out a cry of pain – the wounded Spaniard, evidently – and the hand with which he drew his cutlass was sticky with blood. Spanish blood. Rising, he hit his head a thunderous crash on the deck-beams above, for the little cabin was very low, hardly more than five feet, and so severe was the blow that his senses almost left him. But before him was the cabin door and he reeled out through it, cutlass in hand. Over his head he heard a stamping of feet, and shots were fired behind him and above him – a further exchange, he presumed, between the jolly boat and the galley's stern rail. The cabin door opened into a low half-deck, and Hornblower reeled along it out into the sunshine again. He was on the tiny strip of maindeck at the break of the poop. Before him stretched the narrow gangway between the two sets of rowers; he could look down at these latter – two seas of bearded faces, mops of hair and lean sunburned bodies, swinging rhythmically back and forward to the beat of the oars.

That was all the impression he could form of them at the moment. At the far end of the gangway at the break of the forecastle stood the overseer with his whip; he was shouting words in rhythmic succession to the slaves – Spanish numbers, perhaps, to give them the time. There were three or four men on the forecastle; below them the half-doors through the forecastle bulkhead were hooked open, through which Hornblower could see the two big guns illuminated by the light through the port holes out of which they were run almost at the water level. The guns' crews were standing by the guns, but numerically they were far fewer than two twenty-four pounders would demand. Hornblower remembered Wales' estimate of no more than thirty for a galley's crew. The men of one gun at least had been called aft to defend the poop against the jolly boat's attack.

A step behind him made him leap with anxiety and he swung round with his cutlass ready to meet Jackson stumbling out of the half deck, cutlass in hand.

'Nigh on cracked my nut,' said Jackson.

He was speaking thickly like a drunken man, and his words were chorused by further shots fired from the poop at the level of the top of their heads.

'Oldroyd's comin' next,' said Jackson. 'Franklin's dead.'

On either side of them a companion ladder mounted to the poop deck. It seemed logical, mathematical, that they should each go up one but Hornblower thought better of it.

'Come along,' he said, and headed for the starboard ladder, and, with Oldroyd putting in an appearance at that moment, he yelled to him to follow.

The handropes of the ladder were of twisted red and yellow cord – he even could notice that as he rushed up the ladder, pistol in hand and cutlass in the other. After the first step, his eye was above deck level. There were more than a dozen men crowded on the tiny poop, but two were lying dead, and one was groaning with his back to the rail, and two stood by the tiller. The others were looking over the rail at the jolly boat. Hornblower was still insane with fighting madness. He must have leaped up the final two or three steps with a bound like a stag's, and he was screaming like a maniac as he flung himself at the Spaniards. His pistol went off apparently without his willing it, but the face of the man a yard away dissolved into bloody ruin, and Hornblower dropped the weapon and snatched the second, his thumb going to the hammer as he whirled his cutlass down with a crash on the sword which the next Spaniard raised as a feeble guard. He struck and struck and struck with a lunatic's strength. Here was Jackson beside him shouting hoarsely and striking out right and left.

'Kill 'em! Kill 'em!' shouted Jackson.

Hornblower saw Jackson's cutlass flash down on the head of the defenceless man at the tiller. Then out of the tail of his eye he saw another sword threaten him as he battered with his cutlass at the man before him, but his pistol saved him as he fired automatically again. Another pistol went off beside him – Oldroyd's, he supposed – and then the fight on the poop was over. By what miracle of ineptitude the Spaniards had allowed the attack to take them by surprise Hornblower never could discover. Perhaps they were ignorant of the wounding of the man in the cabin, and had relied on him to defend that route; perhaps it had never occurred to them that three men could be so utterly desperate as to attack a dozen; perhaps they never realized that three men had made the perilous passage of the grapnel line; perhaps – most probably – in the mad excitement of it all, they simply lost their heads, for five minutes could hardly have elapsed altogether from the time the jolly boat hooked on until the poop was cleared. Two or three Spaniards ran down the companion to the maindeck, and forward along the gangway between the rows of slaves. One was caught against the rail and made a gesture of surrender, but Jackson's hand was already at his throat. Jackson was a man of immense physical strength; he bent the Spaniard back over the rail, farther and farther, and then caught him by the thigh with his other hand and heaved him over. He fell with a shriek before Hornblower could interpose. The poop deck was covered with writhing men, like the bottom of a boat filled with flapping fish. One man was getting to his knees when Jackson and Oldroyd seized him. They swung him up to toss him over the rail.

'Stop that!' said Hornblower, and quite callously they dropped him again with a crash on the bloody planks.

Jackson and Oldroyd were like drunken men, unsteady on their feet, glazed of eye and stertorous of breath; Hornblower was just coming out of his insane fit. He stepped forward to the break of the poop, wiping the sweat out of his eyes while trying to wipe away the red mist that tinged his vision. Forward by the forecastle were gathered the rest of the Spaniards, a large group of them; as Hornblower came forward, one of them fired a musket at him but the ball went wide. Down below him the rowers were still swinging rhythmically, forward and back, forward and back, the hairy heads and the naked bodies moving in time to the oars; in time to the voice of the overseer, too, for the latter was still standing on the gangway (the rest of the Spaniards were clustered behind him) calling the time – 'Seis, siete, ocho.'

'Stop!' bellowed Hornblower.

He walked to the starboard side to be in full view of the starboard side rowers. He held up his hand and bellowed again. A hairy face or two was raised, but the oars still swung.

'Uno, doce, tres,' said the overseer.

Jackson appeared at Hornblower's elbow, and levelled a pistol to shoot the nearest rower.

'Oh, belay that!' said Hornblower testily. He knew he was sick of killings now. 'Find my pistols and reload them.'

He stood at the top of the companion like a man in a dream – in a nightmare. The galley slaves went on swinging and pulling; his dozen enemies were still clustered at the break of the forecastle thirty yards away; behind him the wounded Spaniards groaned away their lives. Another appeal to the rowers was as much ignored as the preceding ones. Oldroyd must have had the clearest head or have recovered himself quickest.

'I'll haul down his colours, sir, shall I?' he said.

Hornblower woke from his dream. On a staff above the taffrail fluttered the yellow and red.

'Yes, haul 'em down at once,' he said.

Now his mind was clear, and now his horizon was no longer bounded by the narrow limits of the galley. He looked about him, over the blue, blue sea. There were the merchant ships; over there lay the *Indefatigable*. Behind him boiled the white wake of the galley – a curved wake. Not until that moment did he realize that he was in control of the tiller, and that for the last three minutes, the galley had been cutting over the blue seas unsteered.

'Take the tiller, Oldroyd,' he ordered.

Was that a galley disappearing into the hazy distance? It must be, and far in its wake was the longboat. And there, on the port bow, was the gig, resting on her oars – Hornblower could see little figures standing waving in bow and stern, and it dawned upon him that this was in acknowledgement of the hauling down of the Spanish colours. Another musket banged off forward, and the rail close at his hip was struck a tremendous blow which sent gilded splinters flying in the sunlight. But he had all his wits about him again, and he ran back over the dying men; at the after end of the poop he was out of sight of the gangway and safe from shot. He could still see the gig on the port bow.

'Starboard your helm, Oldroyd.'

The galley turned slowly – her narrow length made her unhandy if the rudder were not assisted by the oars – but soon the bow was about to obscure the gig.

'Midships!'

Amazing that there, leaping in the white water that boiled under the galley's stern, was the jolly boat with one live man and two dead men still aboard.

'Where are the others, Bromley?' yelled Jackson.

Bromley pointed overside. They had been shot from the taffrail at the moment that Hornblower and the others were preparing to attack the poop.

'Why in hell don't you come aboard?'

Bromley took hold of his left arm with his right; the limb was clearly useless. There was no reinforcement to be obtained here, and yet full possession must be taken of the galley. Otherwise it was even conceivable that they would be carried off to Algeciras; even if they were masters of the rudder the man who controlled the oars dictated the course of the ship if he willed. There was only one course left to try.

Now that his fighting madness had ebbed away, Hornblower was in a sombre mood. He did not care what happened to him; hope and fear had alike deserted him, along with his previous exalted condition. It might be resignation that possessed him now. His mind, still calculating, told him that with only one thing left to do to achieve victory he must attempt it, and the flat, dead condition of his spirits enabled him to carry the attempt through like an automaton, unwavering and emotionless. He walked forward to the poop rail again; the Spaniards were still clustered at the far end of the gangway, with the overseer still giving the time to the oars. They looked up at him as he stood there. With the utmost care and attention he sheathed his cutlass, which he had held in his hand up to that moment. He noticed the blood on his coat and on his hands as he did so. Slowly he settled the sheathed weapon at his side.

'My pistols, Jackson,' he said.

Jackson handed him the pistols and with the same callous care he thrust them into his belt. He turned back to Oldroyd, the Spaniards watching every movement fascinated.

'Stay by the tiller, Oldroyd. Jackson, follow me. Do nothing without my orders.'

With the sun pouring down on his face, he strode down the companion ladder, walked to the gangway, and approached the Spaniards along it. On either side of him the hairy heads and naked bodies of the galley slaves still swung with the oars. He neared the Spaniards; swords and muskets and pistols were handled nervously, but every eye was on his face. Behind him Jackson coughed. Two yards only from the group, Hornblower halted and swept them with his glance. Then, with a gesture, he indicated the whole of the group except the overseer; and then pointed to the forecastle.

'Get forrard, all of you,' he said.

They stood staring at him, although they must have understood the gesture.

'Get forrard,' said Hornblower with a wave of his hand and a tap of his foot on the gangway.

There was only one man who seemed likely to demur actively, and Hornblower had it in mind to snatch a pistol from his belt and shoot him on the spot. But the pistol might misfire, the shot might arouse the Spaniards out of their fascinated dream. He stared the man down.

'Get forrard, I say.'

They began to move, they began to shamble off. Hornblower watched them go. Now his emotions were returning to him, and his heart was thumping madly in his chest so that it was hard to control himself. Yet he must not be precipitate. He had to wait until the others were well clear before he could address himself to the overseer.

'Stop those men,' he said.

He glared into the overseer's eyes while pointing to the oarsmen; the overseer's lips moved, but he made no sound.

'Stop them,' said Hornblower, and this time he put his hand to the butt of his pistol.

That sufficed. The overseer raised his voice in a high-pitched order, and the oars instantly ceased. Strange what sudden stillness possessed the ship with the cessation of the grinding of the oars in the tholes. Now it was easy to hear the bubbling of the water round the galley as her way carried her forward. Hornblower turned back to hail Oldroyd.

'Oldroyd! Where away's the gig?'

'Close on the starboard bow, sir!'

'How close?'

'Two cable's lengths, sir. She's pulling for us now.'

'Steer for her while you've steerage way.'

'Aye aye, sir.'

How long would it take the gig under oars to cover a quarter of a mile? Hornblower feared anticlimax, feared a sudden revulsion of feeling among the Spaniards at this late moment. Mere waiting might occasion it, and he must not stand merely idle. He could still hear the motion of the galley through the water, and he turned to Jackson.

'This ship carries her way well, Jackson, doesn't she?' he

said, and he made himself laugh as he spoke, as if everything in the world was a matter of sublime certainty.

'Aye, sir, I suppose she does, sir,' said the startled Jackson; he was fidgeting nervously with his pistols.

'And look at the man there,' went on Hornblower, pointing to a galley slave. 'Did you ever see such a beard in your life?'

'N-no, sir.'

'Speak to me, you fool. Talk naturally.'

'I – I dunno what to say, sir.'

'You've no sense, damn you, Jackson. See the welt on that fellow's shoulder? He must have caught it from the overseer's whip not so long ago.'

'Mebbe you're right, sir.'

Hornblower was repressing his impatience and was about to make another speech when he heard a rasping thump alongside and a moment later the gig's crew was pouring over the bulwarks. The relief was inexpressible. Hornblower was about to relax completely when he remembered appearances. He stiffened himself up.

'Glad to see you aboard, sir,' he said, as Lieutenant Chadd swung his legs over and dropped to the maindeck at the break of the forecastle.

'Glad to see *you*,' said Chadd, looking about him curiously.

'These men forrard are prisoners, sir,' said Hornblower. 'It might be well to secure them. I think that is all that remains to be done.'

Now he could not relax; it seemed to him as if he must remain strained and tense for ever. Strained and yet stupid, even when he heard the cheers of the hands in the *Indefatigable* as the galley came alongside her. Stupid and dull, making a stumbling report to Captain Pellew, forcing himself to remember to commend the bravery of Jackson and Oldroyd in the highest terms.

'The Admiral will be pleased,' said Pellew, looking at Hornblower keenly.

'I'm glad, sir,' Hornblower heard himself say.

'Now that we've lost poor Soames,' went on Pellew, 'we shall need another watch-keeping officer. I have it in mind to give you an order as acting-lieutenant.'

'Thank you, sir,' said Hornblower, still stupid.

Soames had been a grey-haired officer of vast experience. He had sailed the seven seas, he had fought in a score of actions. But, faced with a new situation, he had not had the quickness of thought to keep his boat from under the ram of the galley. Soames was dead, and acting-lieutenant Hornblower would take his place. Fighting madness, sheer insanity, had won him this promise of promotion. Hornblower had never realized the black depths of lunacy into which he could sink. Like Soames, like all the rest of the crew of the *Indefatigable*, he had allowed himself to be carried away by his blind hatred for the galleys, and only good fortune had allowed him to live through it. That was something worth remembering.

CHAPTER EIGHT

THE EXAMINATION FOR LIEUTENANT

H.M.S. *Indefatigable* was gliding into Gibraltar Bay, with Acting-Lieutenant Horatio Hornblower stiff and self-conscious on the quarterdeck beside Captain Pellew. He kept his telescope trained over toward Algeciras; it was a strange situation, this, that major naval bases of two hostile powers should be no more than six miles apart, and while approaching the harbour it was as well to keep close watch on Algeciras, for there was always the possibility that a squadron of Spaniards might push out suddenly to pounce on an unwary frigate coming in.

'Eight ships – nine ships with their yards crossed, sir,' reported Hornblower.

'Thank you,' answered Pellew. 'Hands 'bout ship.'

The *Indefatigable* tacked and headed in toward the Mole. Gibraltar harbour was, as usual, crowded with shipping, for the whole naval effort of England in the Mediterranean was perforce based here. Pellew clewed up his topsails and put his helm over. Then the cable roared out and the *Indefatigable* swung at anchor.

'Call away my gig,' ordered Pellew.

Pellew favoured dark blue and white as the colour scheme for his boat and its crew – dark blue shirts and white trousers for the men, with white hats with blue ribbons. The boat was of dark blue picked out with white, the oars had white looms and blue blades. The general effect was very smart indeed as the drive of the oars sent the gig skimming over the water to carry Pellew to pay his respects to the port admiral. It was not long after his return that a messenger came scurrying up to Hornblower.

'Captain's compliments, sir, and he'd like to see you in his cabin.'

'Examine your conscience well,' grinned Midshipman Bracegirdle. 'What crimes have you committed?'

'I wish I knew,' said Hornblower, quite genuinely.

It is always a nervous moment going in to see the captain in reply to his summons. Hornblower swallowed as he approached the cabin door, and he had to brace himself a little to knock and enter. But there was nothing to be alarmed about; Pellew looked up with a smile from his desk.

'Ah, Mr Hornblower, I hope you will consider this good news. There will be an examination for lieutenant to-morrow, in the *Santa Barbara* there. You are ready to take it, I hope?'

Hornblower was about to say 'I suppose so, sir,' but checked himself.

'Yes, sir,' he said – Pellew hated slipshod answers.

'Very well, then. You report there at three P.M. with your certificates and journals.'

'Aye aye, sir.'

That was a very brief conversation for such an important

subject. Hornblower had Pellew's order as acting-lieutenant for two months now. To-morrow he would take his examination. If he should pass the admiral would confirm the order next day, and Hornblower would be a lieutenant with two month's seniority already. But if he should fail! That would mean he had been found unfit for lieutenant's rank. He would revert to midshipman, the two months' seniority would be lost, and it would be six months at least before he could try again. Eight months' seniority was a matter of enormous importance. It would affect all his subsequent career.

'Tell Mr Bolton you have my permission to leave the ship to-morrow, and you may use one of the ship's boats.'

'Thank you, sir.'

'Good luck, Hornblower.'

During the next twenty-four hours Hornblower had not merely to try to read all through Norie's *Epitome of Navigation* again, and Clarke's *Complete Handbook of Seamanship*, but he had to see that his number one uniform was spick and span. It cost his spirit ration to prevail on the warrant cook to allow the gunroom attendant to heat a flatiron in the galley and iron out his neck handkerchief. Bracegirdle lent him a clean shirt, but there was a feverish moment when it was discovered that the gunroom's supply of shoe blacking had dried to a chip. Two midshipmen had to work it soft with lard, and the resultant compound, when applied to Hornblower's buckled shoes, was stubbornly resistant to taking a polish; only much labour with the gunroom's moulting shoebrush and then with a soft cloth brought those shoes up to a condition of brightness worthy of an examination for lieutenant. And as for the cocked hat – the life of a cocked hat in the midshipman's berth is hard, and some of the dents could not be entirely eliminated.

'Take it off as soon as you can and keep it under your arm,' advised Bracegirdle. 'Maybe they won't see you come up the ship's side.'

Everybody turned out to see Hornblower leave the ship, with his sword and his white breeches and his buckled shoes, his bundle of journals under his arm and his certificates of sobriety and good conduct in his pocket. The winter afternoon was already far advanced as he was rowed over to the *Santa Barbara* and went up the ship's side to report himself to the officer of the watch.

The *Santa Barbara* was a prison hulk, one of the prizes captured in Rodney's action off Cadiz in 1780 and kept rotting at her moorings, mastless, ever since, a storeship in time of peace and a prison in time of war. Redcoated soldiers, muskets loaded and bayonets fixed, guarded the gangways; on forecastle and quarterdeck were carronades, trained inboard and depressed to sweep the waist, wherein a few prisoners took the air, ragged and unhappy. As Hornblower came up the side he caught a whiff of the stench within, where two thousand prisoners were confined. Hornblower reported himself to the officer of the watch as come on board, and for what purpose.

'Whoever would have guessed it?' said the officer of the watch – an elderly lieutenant with white hair hanging down to his shoulders – running his eye over Hornblower's immaculate uniform and the portfolio under his arm. 'Fifteen of your kind have already come on board, and – Holy Gemini, see there!'

Quite a flotilla of small craft was closing in on the *Santa Barbara*. Each boat held at least one cocked-hatted and white-breeched midshipman, and some held four or five.

'Every courtesy young gentleman in the Mediterranean Fleet is ambitious for an epaulet,' said the lieutenant. 'Just wait until the examining board sees how many there are of you! I wouldn't be in your shoes, young shaver, for something. Go aft, there, and wait in the portside cabin.'

It was already uncomfortably full; when Hornblower entered, fifteen pairs of eyes measured him up. There were officers of all ages from eighteen to forty, all in their number one's, all nervous – one or two of them had Norie's *Epitome* open on their laps and were anxiously reading passages about which they were doubtful. One little group was passing a bottle from hand to hand, presumably in an effort to keep up their courage. But no sooner had Hornblower entered than a stream of newcomers followed him. The cabin began to fill, and soon it was tightly packed. Half the forty men present found seats on the deck, and the others were forced to stand.

'Forty years back,' said a loud voice somewhere, 'my grandad marched with Clive to revenge the Black Hole of Calcutta. If he could but have witnessed the fate of his posterity!'

'Have a drink,' said another voice, 'and to hell with care.'

'Forty of us,' commented a tall, thin, clerkly officer, counting heads. 'How many of us will they pass, do you think? Five?'

'To hell with care,' repeated the bibulous voice in the corner, and lifted itself in song. 'Begone, dull care; I prithee be gone from me –'

'Cheese it, you fool!' rasped another voice. 'Hark to that!'

The air was filled with the long-drawn twittering of the pipes of the bos'n's mates, and someone on deck was shouting an order.

'A captain coming on board,' remarked someone.

An officer had his eye at the crack of the door. 'It's Dreadnought Foster,' he reported.

'He's a tail twister if ever there was one,' said a fat young officer, seated comfortably with his back to the bulkhead.

Again the pipes twittered.

'Harvey, of the dockyard,' reported the lookout.

The third captain followed immediately. 'It's Black Charlie Hammond,' said the lookout. 'Looking as if he'd lost a guinea and found sixpence.'

'Black Charlie?' exclaimed someone, scrambling to his feet in haste and pushing to the door. 'Let's see! So it is! Then here is one young gentleman who will not stay for an answer. I know too well what that answer would be. "Six months more at sea, sir, and damn your eyes for your impertinence in presenting yourself for examination in your present state of ignorance." Black Charlie won't ever forget that I lost his pet poodle overside from the cutter in Port-o'-Spain when he was first of the *Pegasus*. Good-bye, gentlemen. Give my regards to the examining board.'

With that he was gone, and they saw him explaining himself to the officer of the watch and hailing a shore boat to take him back to his ship. 'One fewer of us, at least,' said the clerkly officer. 'What is it, my man?'

'The board's compliments, sir,' said the marine messenger, 'an' will the first young gentleman please to come along?'

There was a momentary hesitation; no one was anxious to be the first victim.

'The one nearest the door,' said an elderly master's mate. 'Will you volunteer, sir?'

'I'll be the Daniel,' said the erstwhile lookout desperately. 'Remember me in your prayers.'

He pulled his coat smooth, twitched at his neckcloth, and was gone, the remainder waiting in gloomy silence, relieved only by the glug-glug of the bottle as the bibulous midshipman took another swig. A full ten minutes passed before the candidate for promotion returned, making a brave effort to smile.

'Six months more at sea?' asked someone.

'No,' was the unexpected answer. 'Three! ... I was told to send the next man. It had better be you.'

'But what did they ask you?'

'They began by asking me to define a rhumb line. ... But don't keep them waiting, I advise you.' Some thirty officers had their textbooks open on the instant to reread about rhumb lines.

'You were there ten minutes,' said the clerkly officer, looking at his watch. 'Forty of us, ten minutes each – why, it'll be midnight before they reach the last of us. They'll never do it.'

'They'll be hungry,' said someone.

'Hungry for our blood,' said another.

'Perhaps they'll try us in batches,' suggested a third, 'like the French tribunals.'

Listening to them, Hornblower was reminded of French aristocrats jesting at the foot of the scaffold. Candidates departed and candidates returned, some gloomy, some smiling. The cabin was already far less crowded; Hornblower was able to secure sufficient deck space to seat himself, and he stretched out his legs with a nonchalant sigh of relief, and he no sooner emitted the sigh than he realized that it was a stage effect which he had put on for his own benefit. He was as nervous as he could be. The winter night was falling, and some good Samaritan on board sent in a couple of purser's dips to give a feeble illumination to the darkening cabin.

'They are passing one in three,' said the clerkly officer, making ready for his turn. 'May I be the third.'

Hornblower got to his feet again when he left; it would be his turn next. He stepped out under the halfdeck into the dark night and breathed the chill fresh air. A gentle breeze was blowing from the southward, cooled, presumably, by the snow-clad Atlas Mountains of Africa across the strait. There was neither moon nor stars. Here came the clerkly officer back again.

'Hurry,' he said. 'They're impatient.'

Hornblower made his way past the sentry to the after cabin; it was brightly lit, so that he blinked as he entered, and stumbled over some obstruction. And it was only then that he remembered that he had not straightened his neckcloth and seen to it that his sword hung correctly at his side. He went on blinking in his nervousness at the three grim faces across the table.

'Well, sir?' said a stern voice. 'Report yourself. We have no time to waste.'

'H-Hornblower, sir. H-Horatio H-Hornblower. M-Midshipman – I mean Acting-Lieutenant, H.M.S. *Indefatigable*.'

'Your certificates, please,' said the right-hand face.

Hornblower handed them over, and as he waited for them to be examined, the left-hand face suddenly spoke. 'You are close-hauled on the port tack, Mr Hornblower, beating up channel with a nor-easterly wind blowing hard, with Dover bearing north two miles. Is that clear?'

'Yes, sir.'

'Now the wind veers four points and takes you flat aback. What do you do, sir? What do you do?'

Hornblower's mind, if it was thinking about anything at all at that moment, was thinking about rhumb lines; this question took him as much aback as the situation it envisaged. His mouth opened and shut, but there was no word he could say.

'By now you're dismasted,' said the middle face – a swarthy face; Hornblower was making the deduction that it must belong to Black Charlie Hammond. He could think about that even if he could not force his mind to think at all about his examination.

'Dismasted,' said the left-hand face, with a smile like Nero enjoying a Christian's death agony. 'With Dover cliffs under your lee. You are in serious trouble, Mr – ah – Hornblower.'

Serious indeed. Hornblower's mouth opened and shut again. His dulled mind heard, without paying special attention to it, the thud of a cannon shot somewhere not too far off. The board passed no remark on it either, but a moment later there came a series of further cannon shots which brought the three captains to their feet. Unceremoniously they rushed out of the cabin, sweeping out of the way the sentry at the door. Hornblower followed them; they arrived in the waist just in time to see a rocket soar up into the night sky and burst in a shower of red stars. It was the general alarm; over the water of the anchorage they could hear the drums rolling as all the ships present beat to quarters. On the portside gangway the remainder of the candidates were clustered, speaking excitedly.

'See there!' said a voice.

Across half a mile of dark water a yellow light grew until

the ship there was wrapped in flame. She had every sail set and was heading straight into the crowded anchorage.

'Fire ships!'

'Officer of the watch! Call my gig!' bellowed Foster.

A line of fire ships was running before the wind, straight at the crowd of anchored ships. The *Santa Barbara* was full of the wildest bustle as the seamen and marines came pouring on deck, and as captains and candidates shouted for boats to take them back to their ships. A line of orange flame lit up the water, followed at once by the roar of a broadside; some ship was firing her guns in the endeavour to sink a fire ship. Let one of those blazing hulls make contact with one of the anchored ships, even for a few seconds, and the fire would be transmitted to the dry, painted timber, to the tarred cordage, to the inflammable sails, so that nothing would put it out. To men in highly combustible ships filled with explosives fire was the deadliest and most dreaded peril of the sea.

'You shore boat, there!' bellowed Hammond suddenly. 'You shore boat! Come alongside! Come alongside, blast you!'

His eye had been quick to sight the pair-oar rowing by.

'Come alongside or I'll fire into you!' supplemented Foster. 'Sentry, there, make ready to give them a shot!'

At the threat the wherry turned and glided towards the mizzen chains.

'Here you are, gentlemen,' said Hammond.

The three captains rushed to the mizzen chains and flung themselves down into the boat. Hornblower was at their heels. He knew there was small enough chance of a junior officer getting a boat to take him back to his ship, to which it was his bounden duty to go as soon as possible. After the captains had reached their destinations he could use this boat to reach the *Indefatigable*. He threw himself off into the stern-sheets as she pushed off, knocking the breath out of Captain Harvey, his sword scabbard clattering on the gunwale. But

the three captains accepted his uninvited presence there
without comment.

'Pull for the *Dreadnought*,' said Foster.

'Dammit, I'm the senior!' said Hammond. 'Pull for
Calypso.'

'*Calypso* it is,' said Harvey. He had his hand on the tiller,
heading the boat across the dark water.

'Pull! Oh, pull!' said Foster, in agony. There can be no
mental torture like that of a captain whose ship is in peril and
he not on board.

'There's one of them,' said Harvey.

Just ahead, a small brig was bearing down on them under
topsails; they could see the glow of the fire, and as they
watched the fire suddenly burst into roaring fury, wrapping
the whole vessel in flames in a moment, like a set piece in a
fireworks display. Flames spouted out of the holes in her sides
and roared up through her hatchways. The very water around
her glowed vivid red. They saw her halt in her career and
begin to swing slowly around.

'She's across *Santa Barbara*'s cable,' said Foster.

'She's nearly clear,' added Hammond. 'God help 'em on
board there. She'll be alongside her in a minute.'

Hornblower thought of two thousand Spanish and French
prisoners battened down below decks in the hulk.

'With a man at her wheel she could be steered clear,' said
Foster. 'We ought to do it!'

Then things happened rapidly. Harvey put the tiller over.
'Pull away!' he roared at the boatmen.

The latter displayed an easily understood reluctance to row
up to that fiery hull.

'Pull!' said Harvey.

He whipped out his sword from its scabbard, and the blade
reflected the red fire as he thrust it menacingly at the stroke
oar's throat. With a kind of sob, stroke tugged at his oar and
the boat leaped forward.

'Lay us under her counter,' said Foster. 'I'll jump for it.'

At last Hornblower found his tongue. 'Let me go, sir. I'll handle her.'

'Come with me, if you like,' replied Foster. 'It may need two of us.'

His nickname of Dreadnought Foster may have had its origin in the name of his ship, but it was appropriate enough in all circumstances. Harvey swung the boat under the fire ship's stern; she was before the wind again now, and just gathering way, just heading down upon the *Santa Barbara*.

For a moment Hornblower was the nearest man in the boat to the brig and there was no time to be lost. He stood up on the thwart and jumped; his hands gripped something, and with a kick and a struggle he dragged his ungainly body up onto the deck. With the brig before the wind, the flames were blown forward; right aft here it was merely frightfully hot, but Hornblower's ears were filled with the roar of the flames and the crackling and banging of the burning wood. He stepped forward to the wheel and seized the spokes, the wheel was lashed with a loop of line, and as he cast this off and took hold of the wheel again he could feel the rudder below him bite into the water. He flung his weight on the spoke and spun the wheel over. The brig was about to collide with the *Santa Barbara*, starboard bow to starboard bow, and the flames lit an anxious gesticulating crowd on the *Santa Barbara*'s forecastle.

'Hard over!' roared Foster's voice in Hornblower's ear.

'Hard over it is!' said Hornblower, and the brig answered her wheel at that moment, and her bow turned away, avoiding the collision.

An immense fountain of flame poured out from the hatchway abaft the mainmast, setting mast and rigging ablaze, and at the same time a flaw of wind blew a wave of flame aft. Some instinct made Hornblower while holding the wheel with one hand snatch out his neckcloth with the other and bury his face in it. The flame whirled round him and was gone again. But the distractions had been dangerous; the brig had continued to turn under full helm, and now her stern was swinging in to bump against the *Santa Barbara*'s bow. Hornblower desperately spun the wheel over the other way. The flames had driven Foster aft to the taffrail, but now he returned.

'Hard-a-lee!'

The brig was already responding. Her starboard quarter bumped the *Santa Barbara* in the waist, and then bumped clear.

'Midships!' shouted Foster.

At a distance of only two or three yards the fire ship passed on down the *Santa Barbara*'s side; an anxious group ran along her gangways keeping up with her as she did so. On the quarterdeck another group stood by with a spar to boom the fire ship off; Hornblower saw them out of the tail of his eye as they went by. Now they were clear.

'There's the *Dauntless* on the port bow,' said Foster. 'Keep her clear.'

'Aye, aye, sir.'

The din of the fire was tremendous; it could hardly be believed that on this little area of deck it was still possible to breathe and live. Hornblower felt the appalling heat on his hands and face. Both masts were immense pyramids of flame.

'Starboard a point,' said Foster. 'We'll lay her aground on the shoal by the Neutral Ground.'

'Starboard a point,' responded Hornblower.

He was being borne along on a wave of the highest exaltation; the roar of the fire was intoxicating, and he knew not a moment's fear. Then the whole deck only a yard or two forward of the wheel opened up in flame. Fire spouted out of the gaping seams and the heat was utterly unbearable, and the fire moved rapidly aft as the seams gaped progressively backward.

Hornblower felt for the loopline to lash the wheel, but before he could do so the wheel spun idly under his hand, presumably as the tiller ropes below him were burned away, and at the same time the deck under his feet heaved and warped in the fire. He staggered back to the taffrail. Foster was there.

'Tiller ropes burned away, sir,' reported Hornblower.

Flames roared up beside them. His coat sleeve was smouldering.

'Jump!' said Foster.

Hornblower felt Foster shoving him – everything was insane. He heaved himself over, gasped with fright as he hung in the air, and then felt the breath knocked out of his body as he hit the water. The water closed over him, and he knew panic as he struggled back to the surface. It was cold – the Mediterranean in December is cold. For the moment the air in his clothes supported him, despite the weight of the sword at his side, but he could see nothing in the darkness, with his eyes still dazzled by the roaring flames. Somebody splashed beside him.

'They were following us in the boat to take us off,' said Foster's voice. 'Can you swim?'

'Yes, sir. Not very well.'

'That might describe me,' said Foster; and then he lifted his voice to hail, 'Ahoy! Ahoy! Hammond! Harvey! Ahoy!'

He tried to raise himself as well as his voice, fell back with a splash, and splashed and splashed again, the water flowing into his mouth cutting short something he tried to say. Hornblower, beating the water with increasing feebleness, could still spare a thought – such were the vagaries of his wayward mind – for the interesting fact that even captains of much seniority were only mortal men after all. He tried to unbuckle his sword belt, failed, and sank deep with the effort, only just succeeding in struggling back to the surface. He gasped for breath, but in another attempt he managed to draw his sword half out of its scabbard, and as he struggled it slid out the rest of the way by its own weight; yet he was not conscious of any noticeable relief.

It was then that he heard the splashing and grinding of oars and loud voices, and he saw the dark shape of the approaching boat, and he uttered a spluttering cry. In a second or two the boat was up to them, and he was clutching the gunwale in panic.

They were lifting Foster in over the stern, and Hornblower knew he must keep still and make no effort to climb in, but it called for all his resolution to make himself hang quietly onto the side of the boat and wait his turn. He was interested in this overmastering fear, while he despised himself for it. It called for a conscious and serious effort of willpower to make his hands alternately release their death-like grip on the gunwale, so that the men in the boat could pass him round to the stern. Then they dragged him in and he fell face downward in the bottom of the boat, on the verge of fainting. Then somebody spoke in the boat, and Hornblower felt a cold shiver pass over his skin, and his feeble muscles tensed themselves, for the words spoken were Spanish – at any rate an unknown tongue, and Spanish presumably.

Somebody else answered in the same language. Hornblower tried to struggle up, and a restraining hand was laid on his shoulder. He rolled over, and with his eyes now accustomed to the darkness, he could see the three swarthy faces with the long black moustaches. These men were not Gibraltarians. On the instant he could guess who they were – the crew of one of the fire ships who had steered their craft in past the Mole, set fire to it, and made their escape in the boat. Foster was sitting doubled up, in the bottom of the boat, and now he lifted his face from his knees and stared round him.

'Who are these fellows?' he asked feebly – his struggle in the water had left him as weak as Hornblower.

'Spanish fire ship's crew, I fancy, sir,' said Hornblower. 'We're prisoners.'

'Are we indeed!'

The knowledge galvanized him into activity just as it had Hornblower. He tried to get to his feet, and the Spaniard at the tiller thrust him down with a hand on his shoulder. Foster tried to put his hand away, and raised his voice in a feeble cry, but the man at the tiller was standing no nonsense. He brought out, in a lightning gesture, a knife from his belt. The light from the fire ship, burning itself harmlessly out on the shoal in the distance, ran redly along the blade, and Foster ceased to struggle. Men might call him Dreadnought Foster, but he could recognize the need for discretion.

'How are we heading?' he asked Hornblower, sufficiently quietly not to irritate their captors.

'North, sir. Maybe they're going to land on the Neutral Ground and make for the Line.'

'That's their best chance,' agreed Foster.

He turned his neck uncomfortably to look back up the harbour.

'Two other ships burning themselves out up there,' he said. 'There were three fire ships came in, I fancy.'

'I saw three, sir.'

'Then there's no damage done. But a bold endeavour. Whoever would have credited the Dons with making such an attempt?'

'They have learned about fire ships from us, perhaps, sir,' suggested Hornblower.

'We may have "nursed the pinion that impelled the steel," you think?'

'It is possible, sir.'

Foster was a cool enough customer, quoting poetry and discussing the naval situation while being carried off into captivity by a Spaniard who guarded him with a drawn knife. Cool might be a too accurate adjective; Hornblower was shivering in his wet clothes as the chill night air blew over him, and he felt weak and feeble after all the excitement and exertions of the day.

'Boat ahoy!' came a hail across the water; there was a dark nucleus in the night over there. The Spaniard in the stern-sheets instantly dragged the tiller over, heading the boat directly away from it, while the two at the oars redoubled their exertions.

'Guard boat –' said Foster, but cut his explanation short at a further threat from the knife.

Of course there would be a boat rowing guard at this northern end of the anchorage; they might have thought of it.

'Boat ahoy!' came the hail again. 'Lay on your oars or I'll fire into you!'

The Spaniard made no reply, and a second later came the flash and report of a musket shot. They heard nothing of the bullet, but the shot would put the fleet – towards which they were heading again – on the alert. But the Spaniards were going to play the game out to the end. They rowed doggedly on.

'Boat ahoy!'

This was another hail, from a boat right ahead of them. The Spaniards at the oars ceased their efforts in dismay, but a roar from the steersman set them instantly to work again. Hornblower could see the new boat almost directly ahead of them, and heard another hail from it as it rested on its oars. The Spaniard at the tiller shouted an order, and the stroke oar backed water and the boat turned sharply; another order, and both rowers tugged ahead again and the boat surged forward to ram. Should they succeed in overturning the intercepting boat they might make their escape even now, while the pursuing boat stopped to pick up their friends.

Everything happened at once, with everyone shouting at the full pitch of his lungs, seemingly. There was the crash of the collision, both boats heeling wildly as the bow of the Spanish boat rode up over the British boat but failed to overturn it. Someone fired a pistol, and the next moment the pursuing guard boat came dashing alongside, its crew leaping madly aboard them. Somebody flung himself on top of Hornblower, crushing the breath out of him and threatening to keep it out permanently with a hand on his throat. Hornblower heard Foster bellowing in protest, and a moment later his assailant released him, so that he could hear the midshipman of the guard boat apologizing for this rough treatment of a post captain of the Royal Navy. Someone unmasked the guard boat's lantern, and by its light Foster revealed himself, bedraggled and battered. The light shone on their sullen prisoners.

'Boats ahoy!' came another hail, and yet another boat emerged from the darkness and pulled towards them.

'Cap'n Hammond, I believe!' hailed Foster, with an ominous rasp in his voice.

'Thank God!' they heard Hammond say, and the boat pulled into the faint circle of light.

'But no thanks to you,' said Foster bitterly.

'After your fire ship cleared the *Santa Barbara* a puff of wind took you on faster than we could keep up with you,' explained Harvey.

'We followed as fast as we could get these rock scorpions to row,' added Hammond.

'And yet it called for Spaniards to save us from drowning,' sneered Foster. The memory of his struggle in the water rankled, apparently. 'I thought I could rely on two brother captains.'

'What are you implying, sir?' snapped Hammond.

'I make no implications, but others may read implications into a simple statement of fact.'

'I consider that an offensive remark, sir,' said Harvey, 'addressed to me equally with Captain Hammond.'

'I congratulate you on your perspicacity, sir,' replied Foster.

'I understand,' said Harvey. 'This is not a discussion we can pursue with these men present. I shall send a friend to wait on you.'

'He will be welcome.'

'Then I wish you a very good night, sir.'

'And I, too, sir,' said Hammond. 'Give way there.'

The boat pulled out of the circle of light, leaving an

audience open-mouthed at this strange freak of human behaviour, that a man saved first from death and then from captivity should wantonly thrust himself into peril again. Foster looked after the boat for some seconds before speaking; perhaps he was already regretting his rather hysterical outburst.

'I shall have much to do before morning,' he said, more to himself than to anyone near him, and then addressed himself to the midshipman of the guard boat, 'You, sir, will take charge of these prisoners and convey me to my ship.'

'Aye aye, sir.'

'Is there anyone here who can speak their lingo? I would have it explained to them that I shall send them back to Cartagena under cartel, free without exchange. They saved our lives, and that is the least we can do in return.' The final explanatory sentence was addressed to Hornblower.

'I think that is just, sir.'

'And you, my fire-breathing friend. May I offer you my thanks? You did well. Should I live beyond to-morrow, I shall see that authority is informed of your actions.'

'Thank you, sir.' A question trembled on Hornblower's lips. It called for a little resolution to thrust it out, 'And my examination, sir? My certificate?'

Foster shook his head. 'That particular examining board will never reassemble, I fancy. You must wait your opportunity to go before another one.'

'Aye aye, sir,' said Hornblower, with despondency apparent in his tone.

'Now lookee here, Mr Hornblower,' said Foster, turning upon him. 'To the best of my recollection, you were flat aback, about to lose your spars and with Dover cliffs under your lee. In one more minute you would have been failed – it was the warning gun that saved you. Is not that so?'

'I suppose it is, sir.'

'Then be thankful for small mercies. And even more thankful for big ones.'

CHAPTER NINE

NOAH'S ARK

ACTING-LIEUTENANT HORNBLOWER sat in the stern-sheets of the longboat beside Mr Tapling of the diplomatic service, with his feet among bags of gold. About him rose the steep shores of the Gulf of Oran, and ahead of him lay the city, white in the sunshine, like a mass of blocks of marble dumped by a careless hand upon the hillsides where they rose from the water. The oar blades, as the boat's crew pulled away rhyth-mically over the gentle swell, were biting into the clearest emerald green, and it was only a moment since they had left behind the bluest the Mediterranean could show.

'A pretty sight from here,' said Tapling, gazing at the town they were approaching, 'but closer inspection will show that the eye is deceived. And as for the nose! The stinks of the true believers have to be smelt to be believed. Lay her alongside the jetty there, Mr Hornblower, beyond those xebecs.'

'Aye aye, sir,' said the coxswain, when Hornblower gave the order.

'There's a sentry on the waterfront battery here,' com-mented Tapling, looking about him keenly, 'not more than half asleep, either. And notice the two guns in the two castles. Thirty-two pounders, without a doubt. Stone shot piled in readiness. A stone shot flying into fragments on impact effects damage out of proportion to its size. And the walls seem sound enough. To seize Oran by a *coup de main* would not be easy, I am afraid. If His Nibs the Bey should choose to cut our throats and keep our gold it would be long before we were avenged, Mr Hornblower.'

'I don't think I should find any satisfaction in being avenged in any case, sir,' said Hornblower.

'There's some truth in that. But doubtless His Nibs will spare us this time. The goose lays golden eggs – a boatload of gold every month must make a dazzling prospect for a pirate Bey in these days of convoys.'

'Way 'nough,' called the coxswain. 'Oars!'

The longboat came gliding alongside the jetty and hooked on neatly. A few seated figures in the shade turned eyes at least, and in some cases even their heads as well, to look at the British boat's crew. A number of swarthy Moors appeared on the decks of the xebecs and gazed down at them, and one or two shouted remarks to them.

'No doubt they are describing the ancestry of the infidels,' said Tapling. 'Sticks and stones may break my bones, but names can never hurt me, especially when I do not understand them. Where's our man?'

He shaded his eyes to look along the waterfront.

'No one in sight, sir, that looks like a Christian,' said Hornblower.

'Our man's no Christian,' said Tapling. 'White, but no Christian. White by courtesy at that – French-Arab-Levantine mixture. His Britannic Majesty's Consul at Oran *pro tem.*, and a Mussulman from expediency. Though there are very serious disadvantages about being a true believer. Who would want four wives at any time, especially when he pays for the doubtful privilege by abstaining from wine?'

Tapling stepped up onto the jetty and Hornblower followed him. The gentle swell that rolled up the Gulf broke soothingly below them, and the blinding heat of the noonday sun was reflected up into their faces from the stone blocks on which they stood. Far down the Gulf lay the two anchored ships – the storeship and H.M.S. *Indefatigable* – lovely on the blue and silver surface.

'And yet I would rather see Drury Lane on a Saturday night,' said Tapling.

He turned back to look at the city wall, which guarded the place from seaborne attack. A narrow gate, flanked by bastions, opened onto the waterfront. Sentries in red caftans were visible on the summit. In the deep shadow of the gate something was moving, but it was hard with eyes dazzled by the sun to see what it was. Then it emerged from the shadow as a little group coming towards them – a half-naked Negro leading a donkey, and on the back of the donkey, seated sideways far back towards the root of the tail, a vast figure in a blue robe.

'Shall we meet His Britannic Majesty's Consul halfway?' asked Tapling. 'No. Let him come to us.'

The Negro halted the donkey, and the man on the donkey's back slid to the ground and came towards them – a mountainous man, waddling straddle-legged in his robe, his huge clay-coloured face topped by a white turban. A scanty black moustache and beard sprouted from his lip and chin.

'Your servant, Mr Duras,' said Tapling. 'And may I present Acting-Lieutenant Horatio Hornblower, of the frigate *Indefatigable*?'

Mr Duras nodded his perspiring head.

'Have you brought the money?' he asked, in guttural French; it took Hornblower a moment or two to adjust his mind to the language and his ear to Duras' intonation.

'Seven thousand golden guineas,' replied Tapling, in reasonably good French.

'Good,' said Duras, with a trace of relief. 'Is it in the boat?'

'It is in the boat, and it stays in the boat at present,' answered Tapling. 'Do you remember the conditions agreed upon? Four hundred fat cattle, fifteen hundred fanegas of barley grain. When I see those in the lighters, and the lighters alongside the ships down the bay, then I hand over the money. Have you the stores ready?'

'Soon.'

'As I expected. How long?'

'Soon – very soon.'

Tapling made a grimace of resignation.

'Then we shall return to the ships. To-morrow, perhaps, or the day after, we shall come back with the gold.'

Alarm appeared on Duras' sweating face.

'No, do not do that,' he said, hastily. 'You do not know His Highness the Bey. He is changeable. If he knows the gold is here he will give orders for the cattle to be brought. Take the gold away, and he will not stir. And – and – he will be angry with me.'

'Ira principis mors est,' said Tapling, and in response to Duras' blank look obliged by a translation. 'The wrath of the prince means death. Is not that so?'

'Yes,' said Duras, and he in turn said something in an unknown language, and stabbed at the air with his fingers in a peculiar gesture; and then translated, 'May it not happen.'

'Certainly we hope it may not happen,' agreed Tapling with disarming cordiality. 'The bowstring, the hook, even the bastinado are all unpleasant. It might be better if you went to the Bey and prevailed upon him to give the necessary orders for the grain and the cattle. Or we shall leave at nightfall.'

Tapling glanced up at the sun to lay stress on the time limit.

'I shall go,' said Duras, spreading his hands in a deprecatory gesture. 'I shall go. But I beg of you, do not depart. Perhaps His Highness is busy in his harem. Then no one may disturb him. But I shall try. The grain is here ready – it lies in the Kasbah there. It is only the cattle that have to be brought in. Please be patient. I implore you. His Highness is not accustomed to commerce, as you know, sir. Still less is he accustomed to commerce after the fashion of the Franks.'

Duras wiped his streaming face with a corner of his robe.

'Pardon me,' he said, 'I do not feel well. But I shall go to His Highness. I shall go. Please wait for me.'

'Until sunset,' said Tapling implacably.

Duras called to his Negro attendant, who had been crouching huddled up under the donkey's belly to take advantage of the shade it cast. With an effort Duras hoisted his ponderous weight onto the donkey's hind quarters. He wiped his face again and looked at them with a trace of bewilderment.

'Wait for me,' were the last words he said as the donkey was led away back into the city gate.

'He is afraid of the Bey,' said Tapling watching him go. 'I would rather face twenty Beys than Admiral Sir John Jervis in a tantrum. What will he do when he hears about this further delay, with the Fleet on short rations already? He'll have my guts for a necktie.'

'One cannot expect punctuality of these people,' said Hornblower with the easy philosophy of the man who does not bear the responsibility. But he thought of the British Navy, without friends, without allies, maintaining desperately the blockade of a hostile Europe, in face of superior numbers, storms, disease, and now famine.

'Look at that!' said Tapling pointing suddenly.

It was a big grey rat which had made its appearance in the dry storm gutter that crossed the waterfront here. Regardless of the bright sunshine it sat up and looked round at the world; even when Tapling stamped his foot it showed no great signs of alarm. When he stamped a second time it slowly turned to hide itself again in the drain, missed its footing so that it lay writhing for a moment at the mouth of the drain, and then regained its feet and disappeared into the darkness.

'An old rat, I suppose,' said Tapling meditatively. 'Senile, possibly. Even blind, it may be.'

Hornblower cared nothing about rats, senile or otherwise. He took a step or two back in the direction of the longboat and the civilian officer conformed to his movements.

'Rig that mains'l so that it gives us some shade, Maxwell,' said Hornblower. 'We're here for the rest of the day.'

'A great comfort,' said Tapling, seating himself on a stone bollard beside the boat, 'to be here in a heathen port. No need to worry in case any men run off. No need to worry about liquor. Only about bullocks and barley. And how to get a spark on this tinder.'

He blew through the pipe that he took from his pocket, preparatory to filling it. The boat was shaded by the mainsail now, and the hands sat in the bows yarning in low tones, while the others made themselves as comfortable as possible in the sternsheets; the boat rolled peacefully in the tiny swell, the rhythmic sound as the fendoffs creaked between her gunwale and the jetty having a soothing effect while city and port dozed in the blazing afternoon heat. Yet it was not easy for a young man of Hornblower's active temperament to endure prolonged inaction. He climbed up on the jetty to stretch his legs, and paced up and down; a Moor in a white gown and turban came staggering in the sunshine along the waterfront. His gait was unsteady, and he walked with his legs well apart to provide a firmer base for his swaying body.

'What was it you said, sir, about liquor being abhorred by the Moslems?' said Hornblower to Tapling down in the sternsheets.

'Not necessarily abhorred,' replied Tapling, guardedly. 'But anathematized, illegal, unlawful, and hard to obtain.'

'Someone here has contrived to obtain some, sir,' said Hornblower.

'Let me see,' said Tapling, scrambling up; the hands, bored with waiting and interested as ever in liquor, landed from the bows to stare as well.

'That looks like a man who has taken drink,' agreed Tapling.

'Three sheets in the wind, sir,' said Maxwell, as the Moor staggered.

'And taken all aback,' supplemented Tapling, as the Moor swerved wildly to one side in a semicircle.

At the end of the semicircle he fell with a crash on his face; his brown legs emerged from the robe a couple of times and were drawn in again, and he lay passive, his head on his arms, his turban fallen on the ground to reveal his shaven skull with a tassel of hair on the crown.

'Totally dismasted,' said Hornblower.

'And hard aground,' said Tapling.

But the Moor now lay oblivious of everything.

'And here's Duras,' said Hornblower.

Out through the gate came the massive figure on the little donkey; another donkey bearing another portly figure followed, each donkey being led by a Negro slave, and after them came a dozen swarthy individuals whose muskets, and whose pretence at uniform, indicated that they were soldiers.

'The Treasurer of His Highness,' said Duras, by way of introduction when he and the other had dismounted. 'Come to fetch the gold.'

The portly Moor looked loftily upon them; Duras was still streaming with sweat in the hot sun.

'The gold is there,' said Tapling, pointing. 'In the stern-sheets of the longboat. You will have a closer view of it when we have a closer view of the stores we are to buy.'

Duras translated this speech into Arabic. There was a rapid interchange of sentences, before the Treasurer apparently yielded. He turned and waved his arms back to the gate in what was evidently a prearranged signal. A dreary procession immediately emerged – a long line of men, all of them almost naked, white, black, and mulatto, each man staggering along under the burden of a sack of grain. Overseers with sticks walked with them.

'The money,' said Duras, as a result of something said by the Treasurer.

A word from Tapling set the hands to work lifting the heavy bags of gold onto the quay.

'With the corn on the jetty I will put the gold there too,' said Tapling to Hornblower. 'Keep your eye on it while I look at some of those sacks.'

Tapling walked over to the slave gang. Here and there he opened a sack, looked into it, and inspected handfuls of the golden barley grain; other sacks he felt from the outside.

'No hope of looking over every sack in a hundred ton of barley,' he remarked, strolling back again to Hornblower. 'Much of it is sand, I expect. But that is the way of the heathen. The price is adjusted accordingly. Very well, Effendi.'

At a sign from Duras, and under the urgings of the over-seers, the slaves burst into activity, trotting up to the quayside and dropping their sacks into the lighter which lay there. The first dozen men were organized into a working party to distribute the cargo evenly into the bottom of the lighter, while the others trotted off, their bodies gleaming with sweat, to fetch fresh loads. At the same time a couple of swarthy herdsmen came out through the gate driving a small herd of cattle.

'Scrubby little creatures,' said Tapling, looking them over critically, 'but that was allowed for in the price, too.'

'The gold,' said Duras.

In reply Tapling opened one of the bags at his feet, filled his hand with golden guineas, and let them cascade through his fingers into the bag again.

'Five hundred guineas there,' he said. 'Fourteen bags, as you see. They will be yours when the lighters are loaded and unmoored.'

Duras wiped his face with a weary gesture. His knees seemed to be weak, and he leaned upon the patient donkey that stood behind him.

The cattle were being driven down a gangway into another lighter, and a second herd had now appeared and was waiting.

'Things move faster than you feared,' said Hornblower.

'See how they drive the poor wretches,' replied Tapling sententiously. 'See! Things move fast when you have no concern for human flesh and blood.'

A coloured slave had fallen to the ground under his burden. He lay there disregarding the blows rained on him by the sticks of the overseers. There was a small movement of his legs. Someone dragged him out of the way at last and the sacks continued to be carried to the lighter. The other lighter was filling fast with cattle, packed into a tight, bellowing mass in which no movement was possible.

'His Nibs is actually keeping his word,' marvelled Tapling. 'I'd 'a settled for the half, if I had been asked beforehand.'

One of the herdsmen on the quay had sat down with his face in his hands; now he fell over limply on his side.

'Sir –' began Hornblower to Tapling, and the two men looked at each other with the same awful thought occurring to them at the same moment.

Duras began to say something; with one hand on the withers of the donkey and the other gesticulating in the air it seemed that he was making something of a speech, but there was no sense in the words he was roaring out in a hoarse voice. His face was swollen beyond its customary fatness and his expression was widely distorted, while his cheeks were so suffused with blood as to look dark under his tan. Duras quitted his hold of the donkey and began to reel about in half circles, under the eyes of Moors and Englishmen. His voice died away to a whisper, his legs gave way under him, and he fell to his hands and knees and then to his face.

'That's the plague!' said Tapling. 'The Black Death! I saw it in Smyrna in '96.'

He and the other Englishmen had shrunk back on the one side, the soldiers and the Treasurer on the other, leaving the palpitating body lying in the clear space between them.

'The plague, by St Peter!' squealed one of the young sailors. He would have headed a rush to the longboat.

'Stand still, there!' roared Hornblower, scared of the plague but with the habits of discipline so deeply engrained in him by now that he checked the panic automatically.

'I was a fool not to have thought of it before,' said Tapling. 'That dying rat – that fellow over there who we thought was drunk. I should have known!'

The soldier who appeared to be the sergeant in command of the Treasurer's escort was in explosive conversation with the chief of the overseers of the slaves, both of them staring and pointing at the dying Duras; the Treasurer himself was clutching his robe about him and looking down at the wretched man at his feet in fascinated horror.

'Well, sir,' said Hornblower to Tapling, 'what do we do?'

Hornblower was of the temperament that demands immediate action in face of a crisis.

'Do?' replied Tapling with a bitter smile. 'We stay here and rot.'

'Stay *here*?'

'The fleet will never have us back. Not until we have served three weeks of quarantine. Three weeks after the last case has occurred. Here in Oran.'

'Nonsense!' said Hornblower, with all the respect due to his senior startled out of him. 'No one would order that.'

'Would they not? Have you ever seen an epidemic in a fleet?'

Hornblower had not, but he had heard enough about them – fleets where nine out of ten had died of putrid fevers. Crowded ships with twenty-two inches of hammock space per man were ideal breeding places for epidemics. He realized that no captain, no admiral, would run that risk for the sake of a longboat's crew of twenty men.

The two xebecs against the jetty had suddenly cast off, and were working their way out of the harbour under sweeps.

'The plague can only have struck to-day,' mused Hornblower, the habit of deduction strong in him despite his sick fear.

The cattle herders were abandoning their work, giving a wide berth to that one of their number who was lying on the quay. Up at the town gate it appeared that the guard was employed in driving people back into the town – apparently the rumour of plague had spread sufficiently therein to cause a panic, while the guard had just received orders not to allow the population to stream out into the surrounding country. There would be frightful things happening in the town soon. The Treasurer was climbing on his donkey; the crowd of grain-carrying slaves was melting away as the overseers fled.

'I must report this to the ship,' said Hornblower; Tapling, as a civilian diplomatic officer, held no authority over him. The whole responsibility was Hornblower's. The longboat and the longboat's crew were Hornblower's command, entrusted to him by Captain Pellew whose authority derived from the King.

Amazing how the panic was spreading. The Treasurer was gone; Duras' Negro slave had ridden off on his late master's donkey; the soldiers had hastened off in a single group. The waterfront was deserted now except for the dead and dying; along the waterfront, presumably, at the foot of the wall, lay the way to the open country which all desired to seek. The Englishmen were standing alone, with the bags of gold at their feet.

'Plague spreads through the air,' said Tapling. 'Even the rats die of it. We have been here for hours. We were near enough to – that –' he nodded at the dying Duras – 'to speak to him, to catch his breath. Which of us will be the first?'

'We'll see when the time comes,' said Hornblower. It was his contrary nature to be sanguine in the face of depression; besides, he did not want the men to hear what Tapling was saying.

'And there's the fleet!' said Tapling bitterly. 'This lot' – he nodded at the deserted lighters, one almost full of cattle, the other almost full of grain sacks – 'this lot would be a Godsend. The men are on two-thirds rations.'

'Damn it, we can do something about it,' said Hornblower. 'Maxwell, put the gold back in the boat, and get that awning in.'

The officer of the watch in H.M.S. *Indefatigable* saw the ship's longboat returning from the town. A slight breeze had swung the frigate and the *Caroline* (the transport brig) to their anchors, and the longboat, instead of running alongside, came up under the *Indefatigable*'s stern to leeward.

'Mr Christie!' hailed Hornblower, standing up in the bows of the longboat.

The officer of the watch came aft to the taffrail.

'What is it?' he demanded, puzzled.

'I must speak to the Captain.'

'Then come on board and speak to him. What the devil –?'

'Please ask the Captain if I may speak to him.'

Pellew appeared at the after-cabin window; he could hardly have helped hearing the bellowed conversation.

'Yes, Mr Hornblower?'

Hornblower told him the news.

'Keep to loo'ard, Mr Hornblower.'

'Yes, sir. But the stores –'

'What about them?'

Hornblower outlined the situation and made his request.

'It's not very regular,' mused Pellew. 'Besides –'

He did not want to shout aloud his thoughts that perhaps everyone in the longboat would soon be dead of plague.

'We'll be all right, sir. It's a week's rations for the squadron.'

That was the point, the vital matter. Pellew had to balance the possible loss of a transport brig against the possible gain of supplies, immeasurably more important, which would enable the squadron to maintain its watch over the outlet to the Mediterranean. Looked at in that light Hornblower's suggestion had added force.

'Oh, very well, Mr Hornblower. By the time you bring the stores out I'll have the crew transferred. I appoint you to the command of the *Caroline*.'

'Thank you, sir.'

'Mr Tapling will continue as passenger with you.'

'Very good, sir.'

So when the crew of the longboat, toiling and sweating at the sweeps, brought the two lighters down the bay, they found the *Caroline* swinging deserted at her anchors, while a dozen curious telescopes from the *Indefatigable* watched the proceedings. Hornblower went up the brig's side with half a dozen hands.

'She's like a blooming Noah's Ark, sir,' said Maxwell.

The comparison was apt; the *Caroline* was flush-decked, and the whole available deck area was divided by partitions into stalls for the cattle, while to enable the ship to be worked light gangways had been laid over the stalls into a practically continuous upper deck.

'An' all the animiles, sir,' said another seaman.

'But Noah's animals walked in two by two,' said Hornblower. 'We're not so lucky. And we've got to get the grain on board first. Get those hatches unbattened.'

In ordinary conditions a working party of two or three hundred men from the *Indefatigable* would have made short work of getting in the cargo from the lighters, but now it had to be done by the longboat's complement of eighteen. Luckily Pellew had had the forethought and kindness to have the ballast struck out of the holds, or they would have had to do that weary job first.

'Tail on to those tackles, men,' said Hornblower.

Pellew saw the first bundle of grain sacks rise slowly into the air from the lighter, and swung over and down the *Caroline*'s hatchway.

'He'll be all right,' he decided. 'Man the capstan and get under way, if you please, Mr Bolton.'

Hornblower, directing the work on the tackles, heard Pellew's voice come to him through the speaking trumpet.

'Good luck, Mr Hornblower. Report in three weeks at Gibraltar.'

'Very good, sir. Thank you, sir.'

Hornblower turned back to find a seaman at his elbow knuckling his forehead.

'Beg pardon, sir. But can you hear those cattle bellerin', sir? 'Tis mortal hot, an' 'tis water they want, sir.'

'Hell,' said Hornblower.

He would never get the cattle on board before nightfall. He left a small party at work transferring cargo, and with the rest of the men he began to extemporize a method of watering the unfortunate cattle in the lighter. Half *Caroline*'s hold space was filled with water barrels and fodder, but it was an awkward business getting water down to the lighter with pump and hose, and the poor brutes down there surged about uncontrollably at the prospect of water. Hornblower saw the lighter heel and almost capsize; one of his men – luckily one who could swim – went hastily overboard from the lighter to avoid being crushed to death.

'Hell,' said Hornblower again, and that was by no means the last time.

Without any skilled advice he was having to learn the business of managing livestock at sea; each moment brought its lessons. A naval officer on active service indeed found himself engaged on strange duties. It was well after dark before Hornblower called a halt to the labours of his men, and it was before dawn that he roused them up to work again. It was still early in the morning that the last of the grain sacks was stowed away and Hornblower had to face the operation of swaying up the cattle from the lighter. After their night down there, with little water and less food, they were in no mood to be trifled with, but it was easier at first while they were crowded together. A bellyband was slipped round the nearest, the tackle hooked on, and the animal was swayed up, lowered to the deck through an opening in the gangways, and herded into one of the stalls with ease. The seamen, shouting and waving their shirts, thought it was great fun, but they were not sure when the next one, released from its bellyband, went on the rampage and chased them about the deck, threatening death with its horns, until it wandered into its stall where the bar could be promptly dropped to shut it in. Hornblower, looking at the sun rising rapidly in the east, did not think it fun at all.

And the emptier the lighter became, the more room the cattle had to rush about in it; to capture each one so as to put a bellyband on it was a desperate adventure. Nor were those half-wild bullocks soothed by the sight of their companions being successively hauled bellowing into the air over their heads. Before the day was half done Hornblower's men were as weary as if they had fought a battle, and there was not one of them who would not gladly have quitted this novel employment in exchange for some normal seaman's duty like going aloft to reef topsails on a stormy night. As soon as Hornblower had the notion of dividing the interior of the lighter up into sections with barricades of stout spars the work became easier, but it took time, and before it was done the cattle had already suffered a couple of casualties – weaker members of the herd crushed underfoot in the course of the wild rushes about the lighter.

And there was a distraction when a boat came out from the shore, with swarthy Moors at the oars and the Treasurer in the stern. Hornblower left Tapling to negotiate – apparently the Bey at least had not been so frightened of the plague as to forget to ask for his money. All Hornblower insisted upon was that the boat should keep well to leeward, and the money was floated off to it headed up in an empty rum-puncheon. Night found not more than half the cattle in the stalls on board, with Hornblower worrying about feeding and watering them, and snatching at hints diplomatically won from those members of his crew who had had bucolic experience. But the earliest dawn saw him driving his men to work again, and deriving a momentary satisfaction from the sight of Tapling having to leap for his life to the gangway out of reach of a maddened bullock which was charging about the deck and refusing to enter a stall. And by the time the last animal was safely packed in Hornblower was faced with another problem – that of dealing with what one of the men elegantly termed 'mucking out'. Fodder – water – mucking out; that deck-load of cattle seemed to promise enough work in itself to keep his eighteen men busy, without any thought of the needs of handling the ship.

But there were advantages about the men being kept busy, as Hornblower grimly decided; there had not been a single mention of plague since the work began. The anchorage where the *Caroline* lay was exposed to north-easterly winds, and it was necessary that he should take her out to sea before such a wind should blow. He mustered his men to divide them into watches; he was the only navigator, so that he had to appoint the coxswain and the under-coxswain, Jordan, as officers of the watch. Someone volunteered as cook, and Hornblower, running his eye over his assembled company, appointed Tapling as cook's mate. Tapling opened his mouth to protest, but there was that in Hornblower's expression which cut the protest short. There was no bos'n, no carpenter – no surgeon either, as Hornblower pointed out to himself gloomily. But on the other hand if the need for a doctor should arise it would, he hoped, be mercifully brief.

'Port watch, loose the jibs and main tops'l,' ordered Hornblower. 'Starboard watch, man the capstan.'

So began that voyage of H.M. transport brig *Caroline* which became legendary (thanks to the highly coloured accounts retailed by the crew during innumerable dog-watches in later commissions) throughout the King's navy. The *Caroline* spent her three weeks of quarantine in homeless wanderings about the western Mediterranean. It was necessary that she should keep close up to the Straits, for fear lest the westerlies and the prevailing inward set of the current should take her out of reach of Gibraltar when the time came, so she beat about between the coasts of Spain and Africa trailing behind her a growing farmyard stench. The *Caroline* was a worn-out ship; with any sort of sea running she leaked like a sieve; and there were always hands at work on the pumps, either pumping her out or pumping sea water on to her deck to clean it or pumping up fresh water for the cattle.

Her top hamper made her almost unmanageable in a fresh breeze; her deck seams leaked, of course, when she worked, allowing a constant drip of unspeakable filth down below. The one consolation was in the supply of fresh meat – a commodity some of Hornblower's men had not tasted for three months. Hornblower recklessly sacrificed a bullock a day, for in that Mediterranean climate meat could not be kept sweet. So his men feasted on steaks and fresh tongues; there were plenty of men on board who had never in their whole lives before eaten a beef steak.

But fresh water was the trouble – it was a greater anxiety to Hornblower than even it was to the average ship's captain, for the cattle were always thirsty; twice Hornblower had to land a raiding party at dawn on the coast of Spain, seize a fishing village, and fill his water casks in the local stream.

It was a dangerous adventure, and the second landing revealed the danger, for while the *Caroline* was trying to claw off the land again a Spanish guarda-costa lugger came gliding round the point with all sail set. Maxwell saw her first, but Hornblower saw her before he could report her presence.

'Very well, Maxwell,' said Hornblower, trying to sound composed.

He turned his glass upon her. She was no more than three miles off, a trifle to windward, and the *Caroline* was embayed, cut off by the land from all chance of escape. The lugger could go three feet to her two, while the *Caroline*'s clumsy superstructure prevented her from lying nearer than eight points to the wind. As Hornblower gazed, the accumulated irritation of the past seventeen days boiled over. He was furious with fate for having thrust this ridiculous mission on him. He hated the *Caroline* and her clumsiness and her stinks and her cargo. He raged against the destiny which had caught him in this hopeless position.

'Hell!' said Hornblower, actually stamping his feet on the upper gangway in his anger. 'Hell *and* damnation!'

He was dancing with rage, he observed with some curiosity. But with his fighting madness at the boil there was no chance of his yielding without a struggle, and his mental convulsions resulted in his producing a scheme for action. How many men of a crew did a Spanish guarda-costa carry? Twenty? That would be an outside figure – those luggers were only intended to act against petty smugglers. And with surprise on his side there was still a chance, despite the four eight-pounders that the lugger carried.

'Pistols and cutlasses, men,' he said. 'Jordan, choose two men and show yourselves up here. But the rest of you keep under cover. Hide yourselves. Yes, Mr Tapling, you may serve with us. See that you are armed.'

No one would expect resistance from a laden cattle transport; the Spaniards would expect to find on board a crew of a dozen at most, and not a disciplined force of twenty. The problem lay in luring the lugger within reach.

'Full and by,' called Hornblower down to the helmsman below. 'Be ready to jump, men. Maxwell, if a man shows himself before my order shoot him with your own hand. You hear me? That's an order, and you disobey me at your peril.'

'Aye aye, sir,' said Maxwell.

The lugger was romping up towards them; even in that light air there was a white wave under her sharp bows. Hornblower glanced up to make sure that the *Caroline* was displaying no colours. That made his plan legal under the laws of war. The report of a gun and a puff of smoke came from the lugger as she fired across the *Caroline*'s bows.

'I'm going to heave to, Jordan,' said Hornblower. 'Main tops'l braces. Helm-a-lee.'

The *Caroline* came to the wind and lay there wallowing, a surrendered and helpless ship apparently, if ever there was one.

'Not a sound, men,' said Hornblower.

The cattle bellowed mournfully. Here came the lugger, her crew plainly visible now. Hornblower could see an officer clinging to the main shrouds ready to board, but no one else seemed to have a care in the world. Everyone seemed to be looking up at the clumsy superstructure and laughing at the farmyard noises issuing from it.

'Wait, men, wait,' said Hornblower.

The lugger was coming alongside when Hornblower suddenly realized, with a hot flood of blood under his skin, that he himself was unarmed. He had told his men to take pistols and cutlasses; he had advised Tapling to arm himself, and yet he had clean forgotten about his own need for weapons. But it was too late now to try to remedy that. Someone in the lugger hailed in Spanish, and Hornblower spread his hands in a show of incomprehension. Now they were alongside.

'Come on, men!' shouted Hornblower.

He ran across the superstructure and with a gulp he flung himself across the gap at the officer in the shrouds. He gulped again as he went through the air; he fell with all his weight on the unfortunate man, clasped him round the shoulders, and fell with him to the deck. There were shouts and yells behind him as the *Caroline* spewed up her crew into the lugger. A rush of feet, a clatter and a clash. Hornblower got to his feet empty-handed. Maxwell was just striking down a man with his cutlass. Tapling was heading a rush forward into the bows, waving a cutlass and yelling like a madman. Then it was all over; the astonished Spaniards were unable to lift a hand in their own defence.

So it came about that on the twenty-second day of her quarantine the *Caroline* came into Gibraltar Bay with a captured guarda-costa lugger under her lee. A thick barn-yard stench trailed with her, too, but at least, when Hornblower went on board the *Indefatigable* to make his report, he had a suitable reply ready for Mr Midshipman Bracegirdle.

'Hullo, Noah, how are Shem and Ham?' asked Mr Bracegirdle.

'Shem and Ham have taken a prize,' said Hornblower. 'I regret that Mr Bracegirdle can't say the same.'

But the Chief Commissary of the squadron, when Hornblower reported to him, had a comment to which even Hornblower was unable to make a reply.

'Do you mean to tell me, Mr Hornblower,' said the Chief Commissary, 'that you allowed your men to eat fresh beef? A bullock a day for your eighteen men? There must have been plenty of ship's provisions on board. That was wanton extravagance, Mr Hornblower, I'm surprised at you.'

CHAPTER TEN

THE DUCHESS AND THE DEVIL

ACTING-LIEUTENANT HORNBLOWER was bringing the sloop *Le Rêve*, prize of H.M.S. *Indefatigable*, to anchor in Gibraltar Bay. He was nervous; if anyone had asked him if he thought that all the telescopes in the Mediterranean Fleet were trained upon him he would have laughed at the fantastic suggestion, but he felt as if they were. Nobody ever gauged more cautiously the strength of the gentle following breeze, or estimated more anxiously the distances between the big anchored ships of the line, or calculated more carefully the space *Le Rêve* would need to swing at her anchor. Jackson, his petty officer, was standing forward awaiting the order to take in the jib, and he acted quickly at Hornblower's hail.

'Helm-a-lee,' said Hornblower next, and *Le Rêve* rounded into the wind. 'Brail up!'

Le Rêve crept forward, her momentum diminishing as the wind took her way off her.

'Let go!'

The cable growled a protest as the anchor took it out through the hawsehole – that welcome splash of the anchor, telling of the journey's end. Hornblower watched carefully while *Le Rêve* took up on her cable, and then relaxed a little. He had brought the prize safely in. The commodore – Captain Sir Edward Pellew of H.M.S. *Indefatigable* – had clearly not yet returned, so that it was Hornblower's duty to report to the port admiral.

'Get the boat hoisted out,' he ordered, and then, remembering his humanitarian duty, 'and you can let the prisoners up on deck.'

They had been battened down below for the last forty-eight hours, because the fear of a recapture was the nightmare of every prizemaster. But here in the Bay with the

Mediterranean fleet all round that danger was at an end. Two hands at the oars of the gig sent her skimming over the water, and in ten minutes Hornblower was reporting his arrival to the admiral.

'You say she shows a fair turn of speed?' said the latter, looking over at the prize.

'Yes, sir. And she's handy enough,' said Hornblower.

'I'll purchase her into the service. Never enough despatch vessels,' mused the Admiral.

Even with that hint it was a pleasant surprise to Hornblower when he received heavily sealed official orders and, opening them, read that 'you are hereby requested and required' to take H.M. sloop *Le Rêve* under his command and to proceed 'with the utmost expedition' to Plymouth as soon as the despatches destined for England should be put in his charge. It was an independent command; it was a chance o seeing England again (it was three years since Hornblower had last set foot on the English shore) and it was a high professional compliment. But there was another letter, delivered at the same moment, which Hornblower read with less elation.

'Their Excellencies, Major-General Sir Hew and Lady Dalrymple, request the pleasure of Acting-Lieutenant Horatio Hornblower's company at dinner to-day, at three o'clock, at Government House.'

It might be a pleasure to dine with the Governor of Gibraltar and his lady, but it was only a mixed pleasure at best for an acting-lieutenant with a single sea chest, faced with the need to dress himself suitably for such a function. Yet it was hardly possible for a young man to walk up to Government House from the landing slip without a thrill of excitement, especially as his friend Mr Midshipman Bracegirdle, who came from a wealthy family and had a handsome allowance, had lent him a pair of the finest white stockings of China silk – Bracegirdle's calves were plump, and Hornblower's were skinny, but that difficulty had been artistically circumvented. Two small pads of oakum, some strips of sticking plaster from the surgeon's stores, and Hornblower now had a couple of legs of which no one need be ashamed. He could put his left leg forward to make his bow without any fear of wrinkles in his stockings, and sublimely conscious, as Brace-girdle said, of a leg of which any gentleman would be proud.

At Government House the usual polished and languid aide-de-camp took charge of Hornblower and led him forward. He made his bow to Sir Hew, a red-faced and fussy old gentleman, and to Lady Dalrymple, a red-faced and fussy old lady.

'Mr Hornblower,' said the latter, 'I must present you – Your Grace, this is Mr Hornblower, the new captain of *Le Rêve*. Her Grace the Duchess of Wharfedale.'

A duchess, no less! Hornblower poked forward his padded leg, pointed his toe, laid his hand on his heart and bowed with all the depth the tightness of his breeches allowed – he had still been growing when he bought them on joining the *Indefatigable*. Bold blue eyes, and a once beautiful middle-aged face.

'So this 'ere's the feller in question?' said the duchess. 'Matilda, my dear, are you going to hentrust me to a hinfant in harms?'

The startling vulgarity of the accent took Hornblower's breath away. He had been ready for almost anything except that a superbly dressed duchess should speak in the accent of Seven Dials. He raised his eyes to stare, while forgetting to straighten himself up, standing with his chin poked forward and his hand still on his heart.

'You look like a gander on a green,' said the duchess. 'I hexpects you to 'iss hany moment.'

She stuck her own chin out and swung from side to side with her hands on her knees in a perfect imitation of a bel-ligerent goose, apparently with so close a resemblance to Hornblower as well as to excite a roar of laughter from the other guests. Hornblower stood in blushing confusion.

'Don't be 'ard on the young feller,' said the duchess, coming to his defence and patting him on the shoulder. "'E's on'y young, an' thet's nothink to be ashamed of. Somethink to be prard of, for thet matter, to be trusted with a ship at thet hage.'

It was lucky that the announcement of dinner came to save Hornblower from the further confusion into which this kindly remark had thrown him. Hornblower naturally found himself with the riff-raff, the ragtag and bobtail of the middle of the table along with the other junior officers – Sir Hew sat at one end with the duchess, while Lady Dalrymple sat with a commodore at the other. Moreover, there were not nearly as many women as men; that was only to be expected, as Gibraltar was, technically at least, a beleaguered fortress. So Hornblower had no woman on either side of him; at his right sat the young aid-de-camp who had first taken him in charge.

'Your health, Your Grace,' said the commodore, looking down the length of the table and raising his glass.

'Thank'ee,' replied the duchess. 'Just in time to save my life. I was wonderin' 'oo'd come to my rescue.'

She raised her brimming glass to her lips and when she put it down again it was empty.

'A jolly boon companion you are going to have,' said the aide-de-camp to Hornblower.

'How is she going to be my companion?' asked Hornblower, quite bewildered.

The aide-de-camp looked at him pityingly.

'So you have not been informed?' he asked. 'As always, the man most concerned is the last to know. When you sail with your despatches to-morrow you will have the honour of bearing Her Grace with you to England.'

'God bless my soul,' said Hornblower.

'Let's hope He does,' said the aide-de-camp piously, nosing his wine. 'Poor stuff this sweet Malaga is. Old Hare bought a job lot in '95, and every governor since then seems to think it's his duty to use it up.'

'But who *is* she?' asked Hornblower.

'Her Grace the Duchess of Wharfedale,' replied the aide-de-camp. 'Did you not hear Lady Dalrymple's introduction?'

'But she doesn't talk like a duchess,' protested Hornblower.

'No. The old duke was in his dotage when he married her. She was an innkeeper's widow, so her friends say. You can imagine, if you like, what her enemies say.'

'But what is she doing here?' went on Hornblower.

'She is on her way back to England. She was at Florence when the French marched in, I understand. She reached Leghorn, and bribed a coaster to bring her here. She asked Sir Hew to find her a passage, and Sir Hew asked the Admiral – Sir Hew would ask anyone for anything on behalf of a duchess, even one said by her friends to be an innkeeper's widow.

'I see,' said Hornblower.

There was a burst of merriment from the head of the table, and the duchess was prodding the governor's scarlet-coated ribs with the handle of her knife, as if to make sure he saw the joke.

'Maybe you will not lack for mirth on your homeward voyage,' said the aide-de-camp.

Just then a smoking sirloin of beef was put down in front of Hornblower, and all his other worries vanished before the necessity of carving it and remembering his manners. He took the carving knife and fork gingerly in his hands and glanced round at the company.

'May I help you to some of this beef, Your Grace? Madam? Sir? Well done or underdone, sir? A little of the brown fat?'

In the hot room the sweat ran down his face as he wrestled with the joint; he was fortunate that most of the guests desired helpings from the other removes so that he had little carving to do. He put a couple of haggled slices on his own plate as the simplest way of concealing the worst results of his own handiwork.

'Beef from Tetuan,' sniffed the aide-de-camp. 'Tough and stringy.'

That was all very well for a governor's aide-de-camp – he

could not guess how delicious was this food to a young naval officer fresh from beating about at sea in an over-crowded frigate. Even the thought of having to act as host to a duchess could not entirely spoil Hornblower's appetite. And the final dishes, the meringues and macaroons, the custards and the fruits, were ecstasy for a young man whose last pudding had been currant duff last Sunday.

'Those sweet things spoil a man's palate,' said the aide-de-camp – much Hornblower cared.

They were drinking formal toasts now. Hornblower stood for the King and the royal family, and raised his glass for the duchess.

'And now for the enemy,' said Sir Hew, 'may their treasure galleons try to cross the Atlantic.'

'A supplement to that, Sir Hew,' said the commodore at the other end, 'may the Dons make up their minds to leave Cadiz.'

There was a growl almost like wild animals from round the table. Most of the naval officers present were from Jervis' Mediterranean squadron which had beaten about in the Atlantic for the past several months hoping to catch the Spaniards should they come out. Jervis had to detach his ships to Gibraltar two at a time to replenish their stores, and these officers were from the two ships of the line present at the moment in Gibraltar.

'Johnny Jervis would say amen to that,' said Sir Hew. 'A bumper to the Dons then, gentlemen, and may they come out from Cadiz.'

The ladies left them then, gathered together by Lady Dalrymple, and as soon as it was decently possible Hornblower made his excuses and slipped away, determined not to be heavy with wine the night before he sailed in independent command.

Maybe the prospect of the coming on board of the duchess was a useful counter-irritant, and saved Hornblower from worrying too much about his first command. He was up before dawn – before even the brief Mediterranean twilight had begun – to see that his precious ship was in condition to face the sea, and the enemies who swarmed upon the sea. He had four popgun four-pounders to deal with those enemies, which meant that he was safe from no one; his was the weakest vessel at sea, for the smallest trading brig carried a more powerful armament. So that like all weak creatures his only safety lay in flight – Hornblower looked aloft in the half-light, where the sails would be set on which so much might depend. He went over the watch bill with his two watch-keeping officers, Midshipman Hunter and Master's Mate Winyatt, to make sure that every man of his crew of eleven knew his duty. Then all that remained was to put on his smartest seagoing uniform, try to eat breakfast, and wait for the duchess.

She came early, fortunately; Their Excellencies had had to rise at a most unpleasant hour to see her off. Mr Hunter reported the approach of the governor's launch with suppressed excitement.

'Thank you, Mr Hunter,' said Hornblower coldly – that was what the service demanded, even though not so many weeks before they had been playing follow-my-leader through the *Indefatigable*'s rigging together.

The launch swirled alongside, and two neatly dressed seamen hooked on the ladder. *Le Rêve* had such a small freeboard that boarding her presented no problem even for ladies. The governor stepped on board to the twittering of the only two pipes *Le Rêve* could muster, and Lady Dalrymple followed him. Then came the duchess, and the duchess's companion; the latter was a younger woman, as beautiful as the duchess must once have been. A couple of aides-de-camp followed, and by that time the minute deck of *Le Rêve* was positively crowded, so that there was no room left to bring up the duchess's baggage.

'Let us show you your quarters, Your Grace,' said the governor.

Lady Dalrymple squawked her sympathy at sight of the minute cabin, which the two cots almost filled, and everyone's head, inevitably, bumped against the deck-beam above.

'We shall live through it,' said the duchess stoically, 'an' that's more than many a man makin' a little trip to Tyburn could say.'

One of the aides-de-camp produced a last minute packet of despatches and demanded Hornblower's signature on the receipt; the last farewells were said, and Sir Hew and Lady Dalrymple went down the side again to the twittering of the pipes.

'Man the windlass!' bellowed Hornblower the moment the launch's crew bent to their oars.

A few seconds' lusty work brought *Le Rêve* up to her anchor.

'Anchor's aweigh, sir,' reported Winyatt.

'Jib halliards!' shouted Hornblower. 'Mains'l halliards!'

Le Rêve came round before the wind as her sails were set and her rudder took a grip on the water. Everyone was so busy catting the anchor and setting sail that it was Hornblower himself who dipped his colours in salute as *Le Rêve* crept out beyond the mole before the gentle south-easter, and dipped her nose to the first of the big Atlantic rollers coming in through the Gut. Through the skylight beside him he heard a clatter and a wail, as something fell in the cabin with that first roll, but he could spare no attention for the woman below. He had the glass to his eye now, training it first on Algeciras and then upon Tarifa – some well-manned privateer or ship of war might easily dash out to snap up such a defenceless prey as *Le Rêve*. He could not relax while the forenoon watch wore on. They rounded Cape Marroqui and he set a course for St Vincent, and then the mountains of Southern Spain began to sink below the horizon. Cape Trafalgar was just visible on the starboard bow when at last he shut the telescope and began to wonder about dinner; it was pleasant to be captain of his own ship and to be able to order dinner when he chose. His aching legs told him he had been on his feet too long – eleven continuous hours; if the future brought him many independent commands he would wear himself out by this sort of behaviour.

Down below he relaxed gratefully on the locker, and sent the cook to knock at the duchess's cabin door to ask with his compliments if all was well; he heard the duchess's sharp voice saying that they needed nothing, not even dinner. Hornblower philosophically shrugged his shoulders and ate his dinner with a young man's appetite. He went on deck again as night closed in upon them; Winyatt had the watch.

'It's coming up thick, sir,' he said.

So it was. The sun was invisible on the horizon, engulfed in watery mist. It was the price he had to pay for a fair wind, he knew; in the winter months in these latitudes there was always likely to be fog where the cool land breeze reached the Atlantic.

'It'll be thicker still by morning,' he said gloomily, and revised his night orders, setting a course due west instead of west by north as he originally intended. He wanted to make certain of keeping clear of Cape St Vincent in the event of fog.

That was one of those minute trifles which may affect a man's whole after life – Hornblower had plenty of time later to reflect on what might have happened had he not ordered that alteration of course. During the night he was often on deck, peering through the increasing mist, but at the time when the crisis came he was down below snatching a little sleep. What woke him was a seaman shaking his shoulder violently.

'Please, sir. Please, sir. Mr Hunter sent me. Please, sir, won't you come on deck, he says, sir.'

'I'll come,' said Hornblower, blinking himself awake and rolling out of his cot.

The faintest beginnings of dawn were imparting some slight luminosity to the mist which was close about them. *Le Rêve* was lurching over an ugly sea with barely enough wind behind her to give her steerage way. Hunter was standing with his back to the wheel in an attitude of tense anxiety.

'Listen!' he said, as Hornblower appeared.

He half-whispered the word, and in his excitement he omitted the 'sir' which was due to his captain – and in his excitement Hornblower did not notice the omission. Hornblower listened. He heard the shipboard noises he could expect – the clattering of the blocks as *Le Rêve* lurched, the sound of the sea at her bows. Then he heard other shipboard noises. There were other blocks clattering; the sea was breaking beneath other bows.

'There's a ship close alongside,' said Hornblower.

'Yes, sir,' said Hunter. 'And after I sent below for you I heard an order given. And it was in Spanish – some foreign tongue, anyway.'

The tenseness of fear was all about the little ship like the fog.

'Call all hands. Quietly,' said Hornblower.

But as he gave the order he wondered if it would be any use. He could send his men to their stations, he could man and load his four-pounders, but if that ship out there in the fog was of any force greater than a merchant ship he was in deadly peril. Then he tried to comfort himself – perhaps the ship was some fat Spanish galleon bulging with treasure, and were he to board her boldly she would become his prize and make him rich for life.

'A 'appy Valentine's day to you,' said a voice beside him, and he nearly jumped out of his skin with surprise. He had actually forgotten the presence of the duchess on board.

'Stop that row!' he whispered furiously at her, and she pulled up abruptly in astonishment. She was bundled up in a cloak and hood against the damp air, and no further detail could be seen of her in the darkness and fog.

'May I hask –' she began.

'Shut up!' whispered Hornblower.

A harsh voice could be heard through the fog, other voices repeating the order, whistles being blown, much noise and bustle.

'That's Spanish, sir, isn't it?' whispered Hunter.

'Spanish for certain. Calling the watch. Listen!'

The two double-strokes of a ship's bell came to them across the water. Four bells in the morning watch. And instantly from all round them a dozen other bells could be heard, as if echoing the first.

'We're in the middle of a fleet, by God!' whispered Hunter.

'Big ships, too, sir,' supplemented Winyatt who had joined them with the calling of all hands. 'I could hear half a dozen different pipes when they called the watch.'

'The Dons are out, then,' said Hunter.

And the course I set has taken us into the midst of them, thought Hornblower bitterly. The coincidence was maddening, heartbreaking. But he forbore to waste breath over it. He even suppressed the frantic gibe that rose to his lips at the memory of Sir Hew's toast about the Spaniards coming out from Cadiz.

'They're setting more sail,' was what he said. 'Dagos snug down at night, just like some fat Indiaman. They only set their t'gallants at daybreak.'

All round them through the fog could be heard the whine of sheaves in blocks, the stamp-and-go of the men at the halliards, the sound of ropes thrown on decks, the chatter of a myriad voices.

'They make enough noise about it, blast 'em,' said Hunter.

The tension under which he laboured was apparent as he stood straining to peer through the mist.

'Please God they're on a different course to us,' said Winyatt, more sensibly. 'Then we'll soon be through 'em.'

'Not likely,' said Hornblower.

Le Rêve was running almost directly before what little wind there was; if the Spaniards were beating against it or had it on their beam they would be crossing her course at a considerable angle, so that the volume of sound from the nearest ship would have diminished or increased considerably in this time, and there was no indication of that whatever. It was far more likely that *Le Rêve* had overhauled the Spanish fleet under its nightly short canvas and had sailed forward into the middle of it. It was a problem what to do next in that case, to shorten sail, or to heave to, and let the Spaniards get ahead of them again, or to clap on sail to pass through. But the passage of the minutes brought clear proof that fleet and sloop were on practically the same course, as otherwise they could hardly fail to pass some ship close. As long as the mist held they were safest as they were.

But that was hardly to be expected with the coming of day.

'Can't we alter course, sir?' asked Winyatt.

'Wait,' said Hornblower.

In the faint growing light he had seen shreds of denser mist blowing past them – a clear indication that they could not hope for continuous fog. At that moment they ran out of a fog bank into a clear patch of water.

'There she is, by God!' said Hunter.

Both officers and seamen began to move about in sudden panic.

'Stand still, damn you!' rasped Hornblower, his nervous tension releasing itself in the fierce monosyllables.

Less than a cable's length away a three-decked ship of the line was standing along parallel to them on their starboard side. Ahead and on the port side could be seen the outlines, still shadowy, of other battleships. Nothing could save them if they drew attention to themselves; all that could be done was to keep going as if they had as much right there as the ships of the line. It was possible that in the happy-go-lucky Spanish navy the officer of the watch over there did not know that no sloop like *Le Rêve* was attached to the fleet – or even possibly by a miracle there *might* be one. *Le Rêve* was French built and French rigged, after all. Side by side *Le Rêve* and the battleship sailed over the lumpy sea. They were within point-blank range of fifty big guns, when one well-aimed shot would sink them. Hunter was uttering filthy curses under his breath, but discipline had asserted itself; a telescope over there on the Spaniard's deck would not discover any suspicious bustle on board the sloop. Another shred of fog drifted past them, and then they were deep in a fresh fog bank.

'Thank God!' said Hunter, indifferent to the contrast between this present piety and his preceding blasphemy.

'Hands wear ship,' said Hornblower. 'Lay her on the port tack.'

There was no need to tell the hands to do it quietly; they were as well aware of their danger as anyone. *Le Rêve* silently rounded-to, the sheets were hauled in and coiled down without a sound; and the sloop, as close to the wind as she would lie, heeled to the small wind, meeting the lumpy waves with her port bow.

'We'll be crossing their course now,' said Hornblower.

'Please God it'll be under their sterns and not their bows,' said Winyatt.

There was the duchess still in her cloak and hood, standing right aft as much out of the way as possible.

'Don't you think Your Grace had better go below?' asked Hornblower, making use by a great effort of the formal form of address.

'Oh, no, *please*,' said the duchess. 'I couldn't bear it.' Hornblower shrugged his shoulders, and promptly forgot the duchess's presence again as a new anxiety struck him. He dived below and came up again with the two big sealed envelopes of despatches. He took a belaying pin from the rail and began very carefully to tie the envelopes to the pin with a bit of line.

'Please,' said the duchess, 'please, Mr Hornblower, tell me what you are doing?'

'I want to make sure these will sink when I throw them overboard if we're captured,' said Hornblower grimly.

'Then they'll be lost for good?'

'Better that than that the Spaniards should read 'em,' said Hornblower with all the patience he could muster.

'I could look after them for you,' said the duchess. 'Indeed I could.'

Hornblower looked keenly at her.

'No,' he said, 'they might search your baggage. Probably they would.'

'Baggage!' said the duchess. 'As if I'd put them in my baggage! I'll put them next my skin – they won't search *me* in any case. They'll never find 'em, not if I put 'em up my petticoats.'

There was a brutal realism about those words that staggered Hornblower a little, but which also brought him to admit to himself that there was something in what the duchess was saying.

'If they capture us,' said the duchess, '– I pray they won't, but if they do – they'll never keep me prisoner. You know that. They'll send me to Lisbon or put me aboard a King's ship as soon as they can. Then the despatches will be delivered eventually. Late, but better late than never.'

'That's so,' mused Hornblower.

'I'll guard them like my life,' said the duchess. 'I swear I'll never part from them. I'll tell no one I have them, not until I hand them to a King's officer.'

She met Hornblower's eyes with transparent honesty in her expression.

'Fog's thinning, sir,' said Winyatt.

'Quick!' said the duchess.

There was no time for further debate. Hornblower slipped the envelopes from their binding of rope and handed them over to her, and replaced the belaying pin in the rail.

'These damned French fashions,' said the duchess. 'I was right when I said I'd put these letters up my petticoats. There's no room in my bosom.'

Certainly the upper part of her gown was not at all capacious; the waist was close up under the armpits and the rest of the dress hung down from there quite straight in utter defiance of anatomy.

'Give me a yard of that rope, quick!' said the duchess.

Winyatt cut her a length of the line with his knife and handed it to her. Already she was hauling at her petticoats; the appalled Hornblower saw a gleam of white thigh above her stocking tops before he tore his glance away. The fog was certainly thinning.

'You can look at me now,' said the duchess; but her petticoats only just fell in time as Hornblower looked round again. 'They're inside my shift, next my skin as I promised. With these Directory fashions no one wears stays any more. So I tied the rope round my waist outside my shift. One envelope is flat against my chest and the other against my back. Would you suspect anything?'

She turned round for Hornblower's inspection.

'No, nothing shows,' he said. 'I must thank Your Grace.'

'There is a certain thickening,' said the duchess, 'but it does not matter what the Spaniards suspect as long as they do not suspect the truth.'

Momentary cessation of the need for action brought some embarrassment to Hornblower. To discuss with a woman her shift and stays – or the absence of them – was a strange thing to do.

A watery sun, still nearly level, was breaking through the mist and shining in his eyes. The mainsail cast a watery shadow on the deck. With every second the sun was growing brighter.

'Here it comes,' said Hunter.

The horizon ahead expanded rapidly, from a few yards to a hundred, from a hundred yards to half a mile. The sea was covered with ships. No less than six were in plain sight, four ships of the line and two big frigates, with the red-and-gold of Spain at their mastheads, and, what marked them even more obviously as Spaniards, huge wooden crosses hanging at their peaks.

'Wear ship again, Mr Hunter,' said Hornblower. 'Back into the fog.'

That was the one chance of safety. Those ships running down towards them were bound to ask questions, and they could not hope to avoid them all. *Le Rêve* spun around on her heel, but the fog-bank from which she had emerged was already attenuated, sucked up by the thirsty sun. They could see a drifting stretch of it ahead, but it was lazily rolling away from them at the same time as it was dwindling. The heavy sound of a cannon shot reached their ears, and close on their starboard quarter a ball threw up a fountain of water before plunging into the side of a wave just ahead. Hornblower looked round just in time to see the last of the puff of smoke from the bows of the frigate astern pursuing them.

'Starboard two points,' he said to the helmsman, trying to gauge at one and the same moment the frigate's course, the direction of the wind, the bearing of the other ships, and that of the thin last nucleus of that wisp of fog.

'Starboard two points,' said the helmsman.

'Fore and main sheets!' said Hunter.

Another shot, far astern this time but laid true for line; Hornblower suddenly remembered the duchess.

'You must go below, Your Grace,' he said curtly.

'Oh, no, no, no!' burst out the duchess with angry vehemence. 'Please let me stay here. I can't go below to where that seasick maid of mine lies hoping to die. Not in that stinking box of a cabin.'

There would be no safety in that cabin, Hornblower reflected – *Le Rêve*'s scantlings were too fragile to keep out any shot at all. Down below the water line in the hold the women might be safe, but they would have to lie flat on top of beef barrels.

'Sail ahead!' screamed the lookout.

The mist there was parting and the outline of a ship of the line was emerging from it, less than a mile away and on almost the same course as *Le Rêve*'s. Thud – thud from the frigate astern. Those gunshots by now would have warned the whole Spanish fleet that something unusual was happening. The battleship ahead would know that the little sloop was being pursued. A ball tore through the air close by, with its usual terrifying noise. The ship ahead was awaiting their coming; Hornblower saw her topsails slowly turning.

'Hands to the sheets!' said Hornblower. 'Mr Hunter, jibe her over.'

Le Rêve came round again, heading for the lessening gap on the port side. The frigate astern turned to intercept. More jets of smoke from her bows. With an appalling noise a shot passed within a few feet of Hornblower, so that the wind of it made him stagger. There was a hole in the mainsail.

'Your Grace,' said Hornblower, 'those aren't warning shots –'

It was the ship of the line which fired them, having succeeded in clearing away and manning some of her upper-deck guns. It was as if the end of the world had come. One shot hit *Le Rêve*'s hull, and they felt the deck heave under their feet as a result as if the little ship were disintegrating. But the mast was hit at the same moment, stays and shrouds parting, splinters raining all round. Mast, sails, boom, gaff and all went from above them over the side to windward. The wreckage dragged in the sea and turned the helpless wreck round with the last of her way. The little group aft stood momentarily dazed.

'Anybody hurt?' asked Hornblower, recovering himself.

'On'y a scratch, sir,' said one voice.

It seemed a miracle that no one was killed.

'Carpenter's mate, sound the well,' said Hornblower and then, recollecting himself, 'No, damn it. Belay that order. If the Dons can save the ship, let 'em try.'

Already the ship of the line whose salvo had done the damage was filling her topsails again and bearing away from them, while the frigate which had pursued them was running down on them fast. A wailing figure came scrambling out of the afterhatch way. It was the duchess's maid, so mad with terror that her seasickness was forgotten. The duchess put a protective arm round her and tried to comfort her.

'Your Grace had better look to your baggage,' said Hornblower. 'No doubt you'll be leaving us shortly for other quarters with the Dons. I hope you will be more comfortable.'

He was trying desperately hard to speak in a matter-of-fact way, as if nothing out of the ordinary were happening, as if he were not soon to be a prisoner of the Spaniards; but the duchess saw the working of the usually firm mouth, and marked how the hands were tight clenched.

'How can I tell you how sorry I am about this?' asked the duchess, her voice soft with pity.

'That makes it the harder for me to bear,' said Hornblower, and he even forced a smile.

The Spanish frigate was just rounding-to, a cable's length to windward.

'Please, sir,' said Hunter.

'Well?'

'We can fight, sir. You give the word. Cold shot to drop in the boats when they try to board. We could beat 'em off once, perhaps.'

Hornblower's tortured misery nearly made him snap out 'Don't be a fool', but he checked himself. He contented himself with pointing to the frigate. Twenty guns were glaring at them at far less than point-blank range. The very boat the frigate was hoisting out would be manned by at least twice as many men as *Le Rêve* carried – she was no bigger than many a pleasure yacht. It was not odds of ten to one, or a hundred to one, but odds of ten thousand to one.

'I understand, sir,' said Hunter.

Now the Spanish frigate's boat was in the water, about to shove off.

'A private word with you, please, Mr Hornblower,' said the duchess suddenly.

Hunter and Winyatt heard what she said, and withdrew out of earshot.

'Yes, Your Grace?' said Hornblower.

The duchess stood there, still with her arm round her weeping maid, looking straight at him.

'I'm no more of a duchess than you are,' she said.

'Good God!' said Hornblower. 'Who – who are you, then?'

'Kitty Cobham.'

The name meant a little to Hornblower, but only a little.

'You're too young for that name to have any memories for you, Mr Hornblower, I see. It's five years since last I trod the boards.'

That was it. Kitty Cobham the actress.

'I can't tell it all now,' said the duchess – the Spanish boat was dancing over the waves towards them. 'But when the French marched into Florence that was only the last of my misfortunes. I was penniless when I escaped from them. Who would lift a finger for a onetime actress – one who had been betrayed and deserted? What was I to do? But a duchess – that was another story. Old Dalrymple at Gibraltar could not do enough for the Duchess of Wharfedale.'

'Why did you choose that title?' asked Hornblower in spite of himself.

'I knew of her,' said the duchess with a shrug of the shoulders. 'I knew her to be what I played her as. That was why I chose her – I always played character parts better than straight comedy. And not nearly so tedious in a long role.'

'But my despatches!' said Hornblower in a sudden panic of realization. 'Give them back, quick.'

'If you wish me to,' said the duchess. 'But I can still be the duchess when the Spaniards come. They will still set me free as speedily as they can. I'll guard those despatches better than my life – I swear it, I swear it! In less than a month I'll deliver them, if you trust me.'

Hornblower looked at the pleading eyes. She might be a spy, ingeniously trying to preserve the despatches from being thrown overboard before the Spaniards took possession. But no spy could have hoped that *Le Rêve* would run into the midst of the Spanish fleet.

'I made use of the bottle, I know,' said the Duchess. 'I drank. Yes, I did. But I stayed sober in Gibraltar, didn't I? And I won't touch a drop, not a drop, until I'm in England. I'll swear that, too. Please, sir – please. I beg of you. Let me do what I can for my country.'

It was a strange decision for a man of nineteen to have to make – one who had never exchanged a word with an actress in his life before. A harsh voice overside told him that the Spanish boat was about to hook on.

'Keep them, then,' said Hornblower. 'Deliver them when you can.'

He had not taken his eyes from her face. He was looking for a gleam of triumph in her expression. Had he seen anything of the sort he would have torn the despatches from her body at that moment. But all he saw was the natural look of pleasure, and it was then that he made up his mind to trust her – not before.

'Oh, thank you, sir,' said the duchess.

The Spanish boat had hooked on now, and a Spanish lieutenant was awkwardly trying to climb aboard. He arrived on the deck on his hands and knees, and Hornblower stepped over to receive him as he got to his feet. Captor and captive exchange bows. Hornblower could not understand what the Spaniard said, but obviously they were formal sentences that he was using. The Spaniard caught sight of the two women aft and halted in surprise; Hornblower hastily made the presentation in what he hoped was Spanish.

'Señor el tenente Espanol,' he said. 'Señora la Duquesa de Wharfedale.'

The title clearly had its effect; the lieutenant bowed profoundly, and his bow was received with the most lofty aloofness by the duchess. Hornblower could be sure the despatches were safe. That was some alleviation of the misery of standing here on the deck of his water-logged little ship, a prisoner of the Spaniards. As he waited he heard, from far to leeward, roll upon roll of thunder coming up against the wind. No thunder could endure that long. What he could hear must be the broadsides of ships in action – of fleets in action. Somewhere over there by Cape St Vincent the British fleet must have caught the Spaniards at last. Fiercer and fiercer sounded the roll of the artillery. There was excitement among the Spaniards who had scrambled on to the deck of *Le Rêve*, while Hornblower stood bareheaded waiting to be taken into captivity.

Captivity was a dreadful thing. Once the numbness had worn off Hornblower came to realize what a dreadful thing it was. Not even the news of the dreadful battering which the Spanish navy had received at St Vincent could relieve the misery and despair of being a prisoner. It was not the physical conditions – ten square feet of floor space per man in an empty sail loft at Ferrol along with other captive warrant officers – for they were no worse than what a junior officer often had to put up with at sea. It was the loss of freedom, the fact of being a captive, that was so dreadful.

There were four months of it before the first letter came through to Hornblower; the Spanish government, inefficient in all ways, had the worst postal system in Europe. But here was the letter, addressed and re-addressed, now safely in his hands after he had practically snatched it from a stupid Spanish non-commissioned officer who had been puzzling over the strange name. Hornblower did not know the handwriting, and when he broke the seal and opened the letter the salutation made him think for a moment that he had opened someone else's letter.

'Darling Boy,' it began. Now who on earth would call him that? He read on in a dream.

'Darling Boy,

I hope it will give you happiness to hear that what you gave me has reached its destination. They told me, when I delivered it, that you are a prisoner, and my heart bleeds for you. And they told me too that they were pleased with you for what you had done. And one of those admirals is a shareholder in Drury Lane. Whoever would have thought of such a thing? But he smiled at me, and I smiled at him. I did not know he was a shareholder then, and I only smiled out of the kindness of my heart. And all that I told him about my dangers and perils with my precious burden were only histrionic exercises, I am afraid. Yet he believed me, and so struck was he by my smile and my adventures, that he demanded a part for me from Sherry, and behold, now I am playing second lead, usually a tragic mother, and receiving the acclaim of the groundlings. There are compensations in growing old, which I am discovering too. And I have not tasted wine since I saw you last, nor shall I ever again. As one more reward, my admiral promised me that he would forward this letter to you in the next cartel – an expression which no doubt means more to you than to me. I only hope that it reaches you in good time and brings you comfort in your affliction.

I pray nightly for you.

> Ever your devoted friend,
> Katharine Cobham.'

Comfort in his affliction? A little, perhaps. There was some comfort in knowing that the despatches had been delivered; there was some comfort in a second-hand report that Their Lordships were pleased with him. There was comfort even in knowing that the duchess was re-established on the stage. But the sum total was nothing compared with his misery.

Here was a guard come to bring him to the commandant, and beside the commandant was the Irish renegade who served as interpreter. There were further papers on the commandant's desk – it looked as if the same cartel which had brought in Kitty Cobham's note had brought in letters for the commandant.

'Good afternoon, sir,' said the commandant, always polite, offering a chair.

'Good afternoon, sir, and many thanks,' said Hornblower. He was learning Spanish slowly and painfully.

'You have been promoted,' said the Irishman in English.

'W-what?' said Hornblower.

'Promoted,' said the Irishman. 'Here is the letter – "The Spanish authorities are informed that on account of his meritorious service the acting-commission of Mr Horatio Hornblower, midshipman and acting-lieutenant, has been confirmed. Their Lordships of the Admiralty express their confidence that Mr Horatio Hornblower will be admitted immediately to the privileges of commissioned rank." There you are, young man.'

'My felicitations, sir,' said the commandant.

'Many thanks, sir,' said Hornblower.

The commandant was a kindly old gentleman with a pleasant smile for the awkward young man. He went on to say more, but Hornblower's Spanish was not equal to the technicalities he used, and Hornblower in despair looked at the interpreter.

'Now that you are a commissioned officer,' said the latter, 'you will be transferred to the quarters for captured officers.'

'Thank you,' said Hornblower.

'You will receive the half pay of your rank.'

'Thank you.'

'And your parole will be accepted. You will be at liberty to visit in the town and the neighbourhood for two hours each day on giving your parole.'

'Thank you,' said Hornblower.

Perhaps, during the long months which followed, it was some mitigation of his unhappiness that for two hours each day his parole gave him freedom; freedom to wander in the streets of the little town, to have a cup of chocolate or a glass of wine – providing he had any money – making polite and laborious conversation with Spanish soldiers or sailors or civilians. But it was better to spend his two hours wandering over the goat paths of the headland in the wind and the sun, in the companionship of the sea, which might alleviate the sick misery of captivity. There was slightly better food, slightly better quarters. And there was the knowledge that now he was a lieutenant, that he held the King's commission, that if ever, ever, the war should end and he should be set free he could starve on half pay – for with the end of the war there would be no employment for junior lieutenants. But he had earned his promotion. He had gained the approval of authority, that was something to think about on his solitary walks.

There came a day of south-westerly gales, with the wind shrieking in from across the Atlantic. Across three thousand miles of water it came, building up its strength unimpeded on its way, and heaping up the sea into racing mountain ridges which came crashing in upon the Spanish coast in thunder and spray. Hornblower stood on the headland above Ferrol harbour, holding his worn greatcoat about him as he leaned forward into the wind to keep his footing. So powerful was the wind that it was difficult to breathe while facing it. If he turned his back he could breathe more easily, but then the wind blew his wild hair forward over his eyes, almost inverted his greatcoat over his head, and furthermore forced him into little tottering steps down the slope towards Ferrol, whither he had no wish to return at present. For two hours he was alone and free, and those two hours were precious. He could breathe the Atlantic air, he could walk, he could do as he liked during that time. He could stare out to sea; it was not unusual to catch sight, from the headland, of some British ship of war which might be working slowly along the coast in the hope of snapping up a coasting vessel while keeping a watchful eye upon the Spanish naval activity. When such a ship went by during Hornblower's two hours of freedom, he would stand and gaze at it, as a man dying of thirst might gaze at a bucket of water held beyond his reach; he would note all the little details, the cut of the topsails and the style of the paint, while misery wrung his bowels. For this was the end of his second year as a prisoner of war. For twenty-two months, for twenty-two hours every day, he had been under lock and key, herded with five other junior lieutenants in a single room in the fortress of Ferrol. And to-day the wind roared by him, shouting in its outrageous freedom. He was facing into the wind; before him lay Corunna, its white houses resembling pieces of sugar scattered over the the slopes. Between him and Corunna was all the open space of Corunna Bay, flogged white by the wind, and on his left hand was the narrow entrance to Ferrol Bay. On his right was the open Atlantic; from the foot of the low cliffs there the long wicked reef of the Dientes del Diablo – the Devil's Teeth – ran out to the northward, square across the path of the racing rollers driven by the wind. At half-minute intervals the rollers would crash against the reef with an impact that shook even the solid headland on which Hornblower stood, and each roller dissolved into spray which was instantly whirled away by the wind to reveal again the long black tusks of the rocks.

Hornblower was not alone on the headland; a few yards away from him a Spanish militia artilleryman on lookout duty gazed with watery eyes through a telescope with which he continually swept the seaward horizon. When at war with England it was necessary to be vigilant; a fleet might suddenly appear over the horizon, to land a little army to capture Ferrol, and burn the dockyard installations and the ships. No hope of that to-day, thought Hornblower – there could be no landing of troops on that raging lee shore.

But all the same the sentry was undoubtedly staring very fixedly through his telescope right to windward; the sentry wiped his streaming eyes with his coat sleeve and stared again. Hornblower peered in the same direction, unable to see what it was that had attracted the sentry's attention. The sentry muttered something to himself, and then turned and ran clumsily down to the little stone guardhouse where sheltered the rest of the militia detachment stationed there to man the guns of the battery on the headland. He returned with the sergeant of the guard, who took the telescope and peered out to windward in the direction pointed out by the sentry. The two of them jabbered in their barbarous Gallego dialect; in two years of steady application Hornblower had mastered Galician as well as Castilian, but in that howling gale he could not intercept a word. Then finally, just as the sergeant nodded in agreement, Hornblower saw with his naked eyes what they were discussing. A pale grey square on the horizon above the grey sea – a ship's topsail. She must be running before the gale making for the shelter of Corunna or Ferrol.

It was a rash thing for a ship to do, because it would be no easy matter for her to round-to into Corunna Bay and anchor, and it would be even harder for her to hit off the narrow entrance to the Ferrol inlet. A cautious captain would claw out to sea and heave-to with a generous amount of sea room until the wind moderated. These Spanish captains, said Hornblower to himself, with a shrug of his shoulders; but naturally they would always wish to make harbour as quickly as possible when the Royal Navy was sweeping the seas. But the sergeant and the sentry were more excited than the appearance of a single ship would seem to justify. Hornblower could contain himself no longer, and edged up to the chattering pair, mentally framing his sentences in the unfamiliar tongue.

'Please, gentlemen,' he said, and then started again, shouting against the wind. 'Please, gentlemen, what is it that you see?'

The sergeant gave him a glance, and then, reaching some undiscoverable decision, handed over the telescope – Hornblower could hardly restrain himself from snatching it from his hands. With the telescope to his eye he could see far better; he could see a ship-rigged vessel, under close-reefed topsails (and that was much more sail than it was wise to carry) hurtling wildly towards them. And then a moment later he saw the other square of grey. Another topsail. Another ship. The foretopmast was noticeably shorter than the maintopmast, and not only that, but the whole effect was familiar – she was a British ship of war, a British frigate, plunging along in hot pursuit of the other, which seemed most likely to be a

Spanish privateer. It was a close chase; it would be a very near thing, whether the Spaniard would reach the protection of the shore batteries before the frigate overhauled her. He lowered the telescope to rest his eye, and instantly the sergeant snatched it from him. He had been watching the Englishman's face, and Hornblower's expression had told him what he wanted to know. Those two ships out there were behaving in such a way as to justify his rousing his officer and giving the alarm. Sergeant and sentry went running back to the guardhouse, and in a few moments the artillerymen were pouring out to man the batteries on the verge of the cliff. Soon enough came a mounted officer urging his horse up the path; a single glance through the telescope sufficed for him. He went clattering down to the battery and the next moment the boom of a gun from there alerted the rest of the defences. The flag of Spain rose up the flagstaff beside the battery, and Hornblower saw an answering flag rise up the flagstaff on San Anton where another battery guarded Corunna Bay. All the guns of the harbour defences were now manned, and there would be no mercy shown to any English ship that came in range.

Pursuer and pursued had covered quite half the distance already towards Corunna. They were hull-up over the horizon now to Hornblower on the headland, who could see them plunging madly over the grey sea – Hornblower momentarily expected to see them carry away their topmasts or their sails blow from the bolt-ropes. The frigate was half a mile astern still, and she would have to be much closer than that to have any hope of hitting with her guns in that sea. Here came the commandant and his staff, clattering on horseback up the path to see the climax of the drama; the commandant caught sight of Hornblower and doffed his hat with Spanish courtesy, while Hornblower, hatless, tried to bow with equal courtesy. Hornblower walked over to him with an urgent request – he had to lay his hand on the Spaniard's saddlebow and shout up into his face to be understood.

'My parole expires in ten minutes, sir,' he yelled. 'May I please extend it? May I please stay?'

'Yes, stay, señor,' said the commandant generously.

Hornblower watched the chase, and at the same time observed closely the preparations for defence. He had given his parole, but no part of the gentlemanly code prevented him from taking note of all he could see. One day he might be free, and one day it might be useful to know all about the defences of Ferrol. Everyone else of the large group on the headland was watching, the chase, and excitement rose higher as the ships came racing nearer. The English captain was keeping a hundred yards or more to seaward of the Spaniard, but he was quite unable to overhaul her – in fact it seemed to Hornblower as if the Spaniard was actually increasing his lead. But the English frigate being to seaward meant that escape in that direction was cut off. Any turn away from the land would reduce the Spaniard's lead to a negligible distance. If he did not get into Corunna Bay or Ferrol Inlet he was doomed.

Now he was level with the Corunna headland, and it was time to put his helm hard over and turn into the bay and hope that his anchors would hold in the lee of the headland. But with a wind of that violence hurtling against cliffs and headlands strange things can happen. A flaw of wind coming out of the bay must have caught her aback as she tried to round-to. Hornblower saw her stagger, saw her heel as the back-lash died away and the gale caught her again. She was laid over almost on her beam-ends and as she righted herself Hornblower saw a momentary gap open up in her maintopsail. It was momentary because from the time the gap appeared the life of the topsail was momentary; the gap appeared and at once the sail vanished, blown into ribbons as soon as its continuity was impaired. With the loss of its balancing pressure the ship became unmanageable; the gale pressing against the foretopsail swung her round again before the wind like a weathervane. If there had been time to spare to set a fragment

of sail farther aft she would have been saved, but in those
enclosed waters there was no time to spare. At one moment
she was about to round the Corunna headland; at the next
she had lost the opportunity for ever.

There was still the chance that she might fetch the opening
to the Ferrol inlet; the wind was nearly fair for her to do that
– nearly. Hornblower on the Ferrol headland was thinking
along with the Spanish captain down there on the heaving
deck. He saw him try to steady the ship so as to head for the
narrow entrance, notorious among seamen for its difficulty.
He saw him get her on her course, and for a few seconds as
she flew across the mouth of the bay it seemed as if the
Spaniard would succeed, against all probability, in exactly
hitting off the entrance to the inlet. Then the backlash hit her
again. Had she been quick on the helm she might still have
been safe, but with her sail pressure so outbalanced she was
bound to be slow in her response to her rudder. The shrieking
wind blew her bows round, and it was instantly obvious, too,
that she was doomed, but the Spanish captain played the
game out to the last. He would not pile his ship up against
the foot of the low cliffs. He put his helm hard over; with the
aid of the wind rebounding from the cliffs he made a gallant
attempt to clear the Ferrol headland altogether and give himself a chance to claw out to sea.

A gallant attempt, but doomed to failure as soon as begun;
he actually cleared the headland, but the wind blew his bows
round again, and, bows first, the ship plunged right at the
long jagged line of the Devil's Teeth. Hornblower, the commandant, and everyone, hurried across the headland to look
down at the final act of the tragedy. With tremendous speed,
driving straight before the wind, she raced at the reef. A
roller picked her up as she neared it and seemed to increase
her speed. Then she struck, and vanished from sight for a
second as the roller burst into spray all about her. When the
spray cleared she lay there transformed. Her three masts had
all gone with the shock, and it was only a black hulk which

emerged from the white foam. Her speed and the roller behind her had carried her almost over the reef – doubtless tearing her bottom out – and she hung by her stern, which stood out clear of the water, while her bows were just submerged in the comparatively still water in the lee of the reef.

There were men still alive on her. Hornblower could see them crouching for shelter under the break of her poop. Another Atlantic roller came surging up, and exploded on the Devil's Teeth, wrapping the wreck round with spray. But yet she emerged again, black against the creaming foam. She had cleared the reef sufficiently far to find shelter for most of her length in the lee of the thing that had destroyed her. Hornblower could see those living creatures crouching on her deck. They had a little longer to live – they might live five minutes, perhaps, if they were lucky. Five hours if they were not.

All round him the Spaniards were shouting maledictions. Women were weeping; some of the men were shaking their fists with rage at the British frigate, which, well satisfied with the destruction of her victim, had rounded-to in time and was now clawing out to sea again under storm canvas. It was horrible to see those poor devils down there die. If some larger wave than usual, bursting on the reef, did not lift the stern of the wreck clear so that she sank, she would still break up for the survivors to be whirled away with the fragments. And, if it took a long time for her to break up, the wretched men sheltering there would not be able to endure the constant beating of the cold spray upon them. Something should be done to save them, but no boat could round the headland and weather the Devil's Teeth to reach the wreck. That was so obvious as not to call for a second thought. But ... Hornblower's thoughts began to race as he started to work on the alternatives. The commandant on his horse was speaking vehemently to a Spanish naval officer, clearly on the same subject, and the naval officer was spreading his hands and saying that any attempt would be hopeless. And yet ... For two years Hornblower had been a prisoner; all his pent-up restlessness was seeking an outlet, and after two years of the misery of confinement he did not care whether he lived or died. He went up to the commandant and broke into the argument.

'Sir,' he said, 'let me try to save them. Perhaps from the little bay there. ... Perhaps some of the fishermen would come with me.'

The commandant looked at the officer and the officer shrugged his shoulders.

'What do you suggest, sir?' asked the commandant of Hornblower.

'We might carry a boat across the headland from the dock-yard,' said Hornblower, struggling to word his ideas in Spanish, 'but we must be quick – quick!'

He pointed to the wreck, and force was added to his words by the sight of a roller bursting over the Devil's Teeth.

'How would you carry a boat?' asked the commandant.

To shout his plan in English against that wind would have been a strain; to do so in Spanish was beyond him.

'I can show you at the dockyard, sir,' he yelled. 'I cannot explain. But we must hurry!'

'You want to go to the dockyard, then?'

'Yes – oh, yes.'

'Mount behind me, sir,' said the commandant.

Awkwardly Hornblower scrambled up to a seat astride the horse's haunches and clutched at the commandant's belt. He bumped frightfully as the animal wheeled round and trotted down the slope. All the idlers of the town and garrison ran beside them.

The dockyard at Ferrol was almost a phantom organiza-tion, withered away like a tree deprived of its roots, thanks to the British blockade. Situated as it was at the most distant corner of Spain, connected with the interior by only the roughest of roads, it relied on receiving its supplies by sea, and any such reliance was likely with British cruisers off the coast to be disappointed. The last visit of Spanish ships of war had stripped the place of almost all its stores, and many of the dockyard hands had been pressed as seamen at the same time. But all that Hornblower needed was there, as he knew, thanks to his careful observation. He slid off the horse's hindquarters – miraculously avoiding an instinctive kick from the irritated animal – and collected his thoughts. He pointed to a low dray – a mere platform on wheels – which was used for carrying beef barrels and brandy kegs to the pier.

'Horses,' he said, and a dozen willing hands set to work harnessing a team.

Beside the jetty floated half a dozen boats. There was tackle and shears, all the apparatus necessary for swinging heavy weights about. To put slings under a boat and swing her up was the work of only a minute or two. These Spaniards might be dilatory and lazy as a rule, but inspire them with the need for instant action, catch their enthusiasm, present them with a novel plan, and they would work like madmen – and some of them were skilled workmen, too. Oars, mast and sail (not that they would need the sail), rudder, tiller and balers were all present. A group came running from a store shed with chocks for the boat, and the moment these were set up on the dray the dray was backed under the tackle and the boat lowered on to them.

'Empty barrels,' said Hornblower. 'Little ones – so.'

A swarthy Galician fisherman grasped his intention at once, and amplified Hornblower's halting sentences with voluble explanation. A dozen empty water breakers, with their bungs driven well home, were brought, and the swarthy fisherman climbed on the dray and began to lash them under the thwarts. Properly secured, they would keep the boat afloat even were she filled to the gunwale with water.

'I want six men,' shouted Hornblower, standing on the dray and looking round at the crowd. 'Six fishermen who know little boats.'

The swarthy fisherman lashing the breakers in the boat looked up from his task.

'I know whom we need, sir,' he said.

He shouted a string of names, and half a dozen men came forward; burly, weather-beaten fellows, with the self-reliant look in their faces of men used to meeting difficulties. It was apparent that the swarthy Galician was their captain.

'Let us go, then,' said Hornblower, but the Galician checked him.

Hornblower did not hear what he said, but some of the crowd nodded, turned away, and came hastening back staggering under a breaker of fresh water and a box that must contain biscuit. Hornblower was cross with himself for forgetting the possibility of their being blown out to sea. And the commandant, still sitting his horse and watching these preparations with a keen eye, took note of these stores too.

'Remember, sir, that I have your parole,' he said.

'You have my parole, sir,' said Hornblower – for a few blessed moments he had actually forgotten that he was a prisoner.

The stores were safely put away into the sternsheets and the fishing-boat captain caught Hornblower's eye and got a nod from him.

'Let us go,' he roared to the crowd.

The iron-shod hoofs clashed on the cobbles and the dray lurched forward, with men leading the horses, men swarming alongside, and Hornblower and the captain riding on the dray like triumphing generals in a procession. They went through the dockyard gate, along the level main street of the little town, and turned up a steep lane which climbed the ridge constituting the backbone of the headland. The enthusiasm of the crowd was still lively; when the horses slowed as they breasted the slope a hundred men pushed at the back, strained at the sides, tugged at the traces to run the dray up the hillside. At the crest the lane became a track, but the dray still lurched and rumbled along. From the track diverged an even worse track, winding its way sideways down the slope through arbutus and myrtle towards the sandy cove which Hornblower had first had in mind – on fine days he had seen fishermen working a seine net on that beach, and he himself had taken note of it as a suitable place for a landing party should the Royal Navy ever plan a descent against Ferrol.

The wind was blowing as wildly as ever; it shrieked round Hornblower's ears. The sea as it came in view was chaotic with wave-crests, and then as they turned a shoulder of the slope they could see the line of the Devil's Teeth running out from the shore up there to windward, and still hanging precariously from their jagged fangs was the wreck, black against the seething foam. Somebody raised a shout at the sight, everybody heaved at the dray, so that the horses actually broke into a trot and the dray leaped and bounced over the obstructions in its way.

'Slowly,' roared Hornblower. 'Slowly!'

If they were to break an axle or smash a wheel at this moment the attempt would end in ludicrous failure. The commandant on his horse enforced Hornblower's cries with loud orders of his own, and restrained the reckless enthusiasm of his people. More sedately the dray went on down the trail to the edge of the sandy beach. The wind picked up even the damp sand and flung it stinging into their faces, but only small waves broke here, for the beach was in a recess in the shoreline, the south-westerly wind was blowing a trifle off shore here, and up to windward the Devil's Teeth broke the force of the rollers as they raced along in a direction nearly parallel to the shoreline. The wheels plunged into the sand and the horses stopped at the water's edge. A score of willing hands unharnessed them and a hundred willing arms thrust the dray out into the water – all these things were easy with such vast manpower available. As the first wave broke over the floor of the dray the crew scrambled up and stood ready. There were rocks here, but mighty heaves by the militiamen and the dockyard workers waist-deep in water forced the dray over them. The boat almost floated off its chocks, and the crew forced it clear and scrambled aboard, the wind beginning to swing her immediately. They grabbed for their oars and put their backs into half a dozen fierce strokes which brought her under command; the Galician captain had already laid a steering oar in the notch in the stern, with no attempt at shipping rudder and tiller. As he braced himself to steer he glanced at Hornblower, who tacitly left the job to him.

Hornblower, bent against the wind, was standing in the sternsheets planning a route through the rocks which would lead them to the wreck. The shore and the friendly beach were gone now, incredibly far away, and the boat was struggling out through a welter of water with the wind howling round her. In those jumbled waves her motion was senseless and she lurched in every direction successively. It was well that the boatmen were used to rowing in broken water so that their oars kept the boat under way, giving the captain the means by which, tugging fiercely at the steering oar, he could guide her through that maniacal confusion. Hornblower, planning his course, was able to guide the captain by his gestures, so that the captain could devote all the necessary attention to keeping the boat from being suddenly capsized by an unexpected wave. The wind howled, and the boat heaved and pitched as she met each lumpy wave, but yard by yard they were struggling up to the wreck. If there was any order in the waves at all, they were swinging round the outer end of the Devil's Teeth, so that the boat had to be carefully steered, turning to meet the waves with her bows and then turning back to gain precarious yards against the wind. Hornblower spared a glance for the men at the oars; at every second they were exerting their utmost strength. There could never be a moment's respite – tug and strain, tug and strain, until Hornblower wondered how human hearts and sinews could endure it.

But they were edging up towards the wreck. Hornblower, when the wind and spray allowed, could see the whole extent of her canted deck now. He could see human figures cowering under the break of the poop. He saw somebody there wave an arm to him. Next moment his attention was called away when a jagged monster suddenly leaped out of the sea twenty yards ahead. For a second he could not imagine what it was, and then it leaped clear again and he recognized it – the butt end of a broken mast. The mast was still anchored to the ship by a single surviving shroud attached to the upper end of the mast and to the ship, and the mast, drifting down to leeward, was jerking and leaping on the waves as though some sea god below the surface was threatening them with his wrath. Hornblower called the steersman's attention to the menace and received a nod in return; the steersman's shouted 'Nombre de Dios' was whirled away in the wind. They kept clear of the mast, and as they pulled up along it Hornblower could form a clearer notion of the speed of their progress now that he had a stationary object to help his judgement. He could see the painful inches gained at each frantic tug on the oars, and could see how the boat stopped dead or even went astern when the wilder gusts hit her, the oar blades pulling ineffectively through the water. Every inch of gain was only won at the cost of an infinity of labour.

Now they were past the mast, close to the submerged bows of the ship, and close enough to the Devil's Teeth to be deluged with spray as each wave burst on the farther side of the reef. There were inches of water washing back and forth in the bottom of the boat, but there was neither time nor opportunity to bale it out. This was the trickiest part of the whole effort, to get close enough alongside the wreck to be able to take off the survivors without stoving in the boat; there were wicked fangs of rock all about the after end of the wreck, while forward, although the forecastle was above the surface at times the forward part of the waist was submerged. But the ship was canted a little over to port, towards them, which made the approach easier. When the water was at its lowest level, immediately before the next roller broke on the reef, Hornblower, standing up and craning his neck, could see no rocks beside the wreck in the middle part of the waist where the deck came down to water level. It was easy to direct the steersman towards that particular point, and then, as the boat moved in, to wave his arms and demand the attention of the little group under the break of the poop, and to point to the spot to which they were approaching. A wave burst upon the reef, broken over the stern of the wreck, and filled the boat almost full. She swung back and forth in the eddies, but the kegs kept her afloat and quick handling of the steering oar and lusty rowing kept her from being dashed against either the wreck or the rocks.

'Now!' shouted Hornblower – it did not matter that he spoke English at this decisive moment. The boat surged forward, while the survivors, releasing themselves from the lashings which had held them in their shelter, came slithering down the deck towards them. It was a little of a shock to see there were but four of them – twenty or thirty men must have been swept overboard when the ship hit the reef. The bows of the boat moved towards the wreck. At a shouted order from the steersman the oars fell still. One survivor braced himself and flung himself into the bows. A stroke of the oars, a tug at the steering oar, and the boat nosed forward again, and another survivor plunged into the boat. Then Hornblower, who had been watching the sea, saw the next breaker rear up over the reef. At his warning shout the boat backed away to safety – comparative safety – while the remaining survivors went scrambling back up the deck to the shelter of the poop. The wave burst and roared, the foam hissed and the spray rattled, and then they crept up to the wreck again. The third survivor poised himself for his leap, mistimed it, and fell into the sea, and no one ever saw him again. He was gone, sunk like a stone, crippled as he was with cold and exhaustion, but there was no time to spare for lamentation. The fourth survivor was waiting his chance and jumped at once, landing safely in the bows.

'Any more?' shouted Hornblower, and receiving a shake of the head in reply; they had saved three lives at the risk of eight.

'Let us go,' said Hornblower, but the steersman needed no telling.

Already he had allowed the wind to drift the boat away from the wreck, away from the rocks – away from the shore. An occasional strong pull at the oars sufficed to keep her bows to wind and wave. Hornblower looked down at the fainting survivors lying in the bottom of the boat with the water washing over them. He bent down and shook them into consciousness; he picked up the balers and forced them into their numb hands. They must keep active or die. It was astounding to find darkness closing about them, and it was urgent that they should decide on their next move immediately. The men at the oars were in no shape for any prolonged further rowing; if they tried to return to the sandy cove whence they had started they might be overtaken both by night and by exhaustion while still among the treacherous rocks off the shore there. Hornblower sat down beside the Galician captain, who laconically gave his views while vigilantly observing the waves racing down upon them.

'It's growing dark,' said the captain, glancing round the sky. 'Rocks. The men are tired.'

'We had better not go back,' said Hornblower.

'No.'

'Then we must get out to sea.'

Years of duty on blockade, of beating about off a lee shore, had ingrained into Hornblower the necessity for seeking sea-room.

'Yes,' said the captain, and he added something which Hornblower, thanks to the wind and his unfamiliarity with the language, was unable to catch. The captain roared the expression again, and accompanied his words with a vivid bit of pantomime with the one hand he could spare from the steering oar.

'A sea anchor,' decided Hornblower to himself. 'Quite right.'

He looked back at the vanishing shore, and gauged the direction of the wind. It seemed to be backing a little southerly; the coast here trended away from them. They could ride to a sea anchor through the hours of darkness and run no risk of being cast ashore as long as these conditions persisted.

'Good,' said Hornblower aloud.

He imitated the other's bit of pantomime and the captain gave him a glance of approval. At a bellow from him the two men forward took in their oars and set to work at constructing a sea anchor – merely a pair of oars attached to a long painter paid out over the bows. With this gale blowing the pressure of the wind on the boat set up enough drag on the float to keep their bows to the sea. Hornblower watched as the sea anchor began to take hold of the water.

'Good,' he said again.

'Good,' said the captain, taking in his steering oar.

Hornblower realized only now that he had been long exposed to a winter gale while wet to the skin. He was numb with cold, and he was shivering uncontrollably. At his feet one of the three survivors of the wreck was lying helpless; the other two had succeeded in baling out most of the water and as a result of their exertions were conscious and alert. The men who had been rowing sat drooping with weariness on their thwarts. The Galician captain was already down in the bottom of the boat lifting the helpless man in his arms. It was a common impulse of them all to huddle down into the bottom of the boat, beneath the thwarts, away from that shrieking wind.

So the night came down on them. Hornblower found himself welcoming the contact of other human bodies; he felt an arm round him and he put his arm round someone else. Around them a little water still surged about on the floorboards; above them the wind still shrieked and howled. The boat stood first on her head and then on her tail as the waves passed under them, and at the moment of climbing each crest she gave a shuddering jerk as she snubbed herself to the sea anchor. Every few seconds a new spat of spray whirled into the boat upon their shrinking bodies; it did not seem long before the accumulation of spray in the bottom of the boat made it necessary for them to disentangle themselves, and set about, groping in the darkness, the task of baling the water out again. Then they could huddle down again under the thwarts.

It was when they pulled themselves together for the third baling that in the middle of his nightmare of cold and exhaustion Hornblower was conscious that the body across which his arm lay was unnaturally stiff; the man the captain had been trying to revive had died as he lay there between the captain and Hornblower. The captain dragged the body away into the sternsheets in the darkness, and the night went on, cold wind and cold spray, jerk, pitch, and roll, sit up and bale and cower down and shudder. It was hideous torment; Hornblower could not trust himself to believe his eyes when he saw the first signs that the darkness was lessening. And then the grey dawn came gradually over the grey sea, and they were free to wonder what to do next. But as the light increased the problem was solved for them, for one of the fishermen, raising himself up in the boat, gave a hoarse cry, and pointed to the northern horizon, and there, almost hull-up, was a ship, hove-to under storm canvas. The captain took one glance at her – his eyesight must have been marvellous – and identified her.

'The English frigate,' he said.

She must have made nearly the same amount of leeway hove-to as the boat did riding to her sea anchor.

'Signal to her,' said Hornblower, and no one raised any objections.

The only white object available was Hornblower's shirt, and he took it off, shuddering in the cold, and they tied it to an oar and raised the oar in the maststep. The captain saw

Hornblower putting on his dripping coat over his bare ribs and in a single movement peeled off his thick blue jersey and offered it to him.

'Thank you, no,' protested Hornblower, but the captain insisted; with a wide grin he pointed to the stiffened corpse lying in the sternsheets and announced he would replace the jersey with the dead man's clothing.

The argument was interrupted by a further cry from one of the fishermen. The frigate was coming to the wind; with treble-reefed fore and maintopsails she was heading for them under the impulse of the lessening gale. Hornblower saw her running down on them; a glance in the other direction showed him the Galician mountains, faint on the southern horizon – warmth, freedom and friendship on the one hand; solitude and captivity on the other. Under the lee of the frigate the boat bobbed and heaved fantastically; many inquisitive faces looked down on them. They were cold and cramped; the frigate dropped a boat and a couple of nimble seamen scrambled on board. A line was flung from the frigate, a whip lowered a breeches ring into the boat, and the English seamen helped the Spaniards one by one into the breeches and held them steady as they were swung up to the frigate's deck.

'I go last,' said Hornblower when they turned to him. 'I am a King's officer.'

'Good Lor' lumme,' said the seamen.

'Send the body up, too,' said Hornblower. 'It can be given decent burial.'

The stiff corpse was grotesque as it swayed through the air. The Galician captain tried to dispute with Hornblower the honour of going last, but Hornblower would not be argued with. Then finally the seamen helped him put his legs into the breeches, and secured him with a line round his waist. Up he soared, swaying dizzily with the roll of the ship; then they drew him in to the deck, lowering and shortening, until half a dozen strong arms took his weight and laid him gently on the deck.

'There you are, my hearty, safe and sound,' said a bearded seaman.

'I am a King's officer,' said Hornblower. 'Where's the officer of the watch?'

Wearing marvellous dry clothing, Hornblower found himself soon drinking hot rum-and-water in the cabin of Captain George Crome, of His Majesty's frigate *Syrtis*. Crome was a thin pale man with a depressed expression, but Hornblower knew of him as a first-rate officer.

'These Galicians make good seamen,' said Crome. 'I can't press them. But perhaps a few will volunteer sooner than go to a prison hulk.'

'Sir,' said Hornblower, and hesitated. It is ill for a junior lieutenant to argue with a post captain.

'Well?'

'Those men came to sea to save life. They are not liable to capture.'

Crome's cold grey eyes became actively frosty – Hornblower was right about it being ill for a junior lieutenant to argue with a post captain.

'Are you telling me my duty, sir?' he asked.

'Good heavens no, sir,' said Hornblower hastily. 'It's a long time since I read the Admiralty Instructions and I expect my memory's at fault.'

'Admiralty Instructions, eh?' said Crome, in a slightly different tone of voice.

'I expect I'm wrong, sir,' said Hornblower, 'but I seem to remember the same instruction applied to the other two – the survivors.'

Even a post captain could only contravene Admiralty Instructions at his peril.

'I'll consider it,' said Crome.

'I had the dead man sent on board, sir,' went on Hornblower, 'in the hope that perhaps you might give him proper burial. Those Galicians risked their lives to save him, sir, and I expect they'd be gratified.'

'A Popish burial? I'll give orders to give 'em a free hand.'

'Thank you, sir,' said Hornblower.

'And now as regards yourself. You say you hold a commission as lieutenant. You can do duty in this ship until we meet the admiral again. Then he can decide. I haven't heard of the *Indefatigable* paying off, and legally you may still be borne on her books.'

And that was when the devil came to tempt Hornblower, as he took another sip of hot rum-and-water. The joy of being in a King's ship again was so keen as to be almost painful. To taste salt beef and biscuit again, and never again to taste beans and garbanzos. To have a ship's deck under his feet, to talk English. To be free – to be free! There was precious little chance of ever falling again into Spanish hands. Hornblower remembered with agonizing clarity the flat depression of captivity. All he had to do was not to say a word. He had only to keep silence for a day or two. But the devil did not tempt him long, only until he had taken his next sip of rum-and-water. Then he thrust the devil behind him and met Crome's eyes again.

'I'm sorry, sir,' he said.

'What for?'

'I am here on parole. I gave my word before I left the beach.'

'You did? That alters the case. You were within your rights, of course.'

The giving of parole by captive British officers was so usual as to excite no comment.

'It was in the usual form, I suppose?' went on Crome. 'That you would make no attempt to escape?'

'Yes, sir.'

'Then what do you decide as a result?'

Of course Crome could not attempt to influence a gentleman's decision on a matter as personal as a parole.

'I must go back, sir,' said Hornblower, 'at the first opportunity.'

He felt the sway of the ship, he looked round the homely cabin, and his heart was breaking.

'You can at least dine and sleep on board to-night,' said Crome. 'I'll not venture inshore again until the wind moderates. I'll send you to Corunna under a flag of truce when I can. And I'll see what the Instructions say about those prisoners.'

It was a sunny morning when the sentry at Fort San Anton, in the harbour of Corunna, called his officer's attention to the fact that the British cruiser off the headland had hove-to out of gunshot and was lowering a boat. The sentry's responsibility ended there, and he could watch idly as his officer observed that the cutter, running smartly in under sail, was flying a white flag. She hove-to within musket shot, and it was a mild surprise to the sentry when in reply to the officer's hail someone rose up in the boat and replied in unmistakable Gallego dialect. Summoned alongside the landing slip, the cutter put ashore ten men and then headed out again to the frigate. Nine men were laughing and shouting; the tenth, the youngest, walked with a fixed expression on his face with never a sign of emotion – his expression did not change even when the others, with obvious affection, put their arms round his shoulders. No one ever troubled to explain to the sentry who the imperturbable young man was, and he was not very interested. After he had seen the group shipped off across Corunna Bay towards Ferrol he quite forgot the incident.

It was almost spring when a Spanish militia officer came into the barracks which served as a prison for officers in Ferrol.

'Señor Hornblower?' he asked – at least Hornblower, in the corner, knew that was what he was trying to say. He was used to the way Spaniards mutilated his name.

'Yes?' he said, rising.

'Would you please come with me? The commandant has sent me for you, sir.'

The commandant was all smiles. He held a despatch in his hands.

'This, sir,' he said, waving it at Hornblower, 'is a personal order. It is countersigned by the Duke of Fuentesauco, Minister of Marine, but it is signed by the First Minister, Prince of the Peace and Duke of Alcudia.'

'Yes, sir,' said Hornblower.

He should have begun to hope at that moment, but there comes a time in a prisoner's life when he ceases to hope. He was more interested, even, in that strange title of Prince of the Peace which was now beginning to be heard in Spain.

'It says: "We, Carlos Leonardo Luis Manuel de Godoy y Boegas, First Minister of His Most Catholic Majesty, Prince of the Peace, Duke of Alcudia and Grandee of the First Class, Count of Alcudia, Knight of the Most Sacred Order of the Golden Fleece, Knight of the Holy Order of Santiago, Knight of the Most Distinguished Order of Calatrava, Captain General of His Most Catholic Majesty's forces by Land and Sea, Colonel General of the Guardia de Corps, Admiral of the Two Oceans, General of the cavalry, of the infantry, and of the artillery" – in any event, sir, it is an order to me to take immediate steps to set you at liberty. I am to restore you under flag of truce to your fellow countrymen, in recognition of "your courage and self-sacrifice in saving life at the peril of your own".'

'Thank you, sir,' said Hornblower.

MORE ABOUT PENGUINS
AND PELICANS

Penguinews, which appears every month, contains details of all the new books issued by Penguins as they are published. From time to time it is supplemented by *Penguins in Print*, which is our complete list of almost 5,000 titles.

A specimen copy of *Penguinews* will be sent to you free on request. Please write to Dept EP, Penguin Books Ltd, Harmondsworth, Middlesex, for your copy.

In the U.S.A.: For a complete list of books available from Penguins in the United States write to Dept CS, Penguin Books, 625 Madison Avenue, New York, New York 10022.

In Canada: For a complete list of books available from Penguins in Canada write to Penguin Books Canada Ltd, 2801 John Street, Markham, Ontario L3R 1B4.